THE BIOGRAPH GIRL

WILLIAM J. MANN

Kensington Books

http://www.kensingtonbooks.com

KENSINGTON BOOKS are published by

Kensington Publishing Corp.
850 Third Avenue
New York, NY 10022

ISBN 1-57566-666-9

First Hardcover Printing: June 2000
First Trade Paperback Printing: June 2001
10 9 8 7 6 5 4 3 2 1

Printed in the United States of America

*For my mother and my father,
who bought me a typewriter
when I was nine.*

December 28, 1938

"Go on," Lester said. "Get out before anyone sees you."

He kissed the dead girl on her forehead. She was so lovely, lying there on that metal slab. So slight, so young, with the same pale skin as I had, the same platinum blonde hair.

"Go on," Lester said again and pulled the sheet up to cover her face.

"But if they ask to see the body—"

"They won't." He wouldn't look at me. I remember how much that hurt. He just kept staring down at her. "They'll believe it's you."

And she could have been—twenty years before, when I was as young, when I had been as filled with promise. I reached down and touched her hand through the sheet. She was still warm.

"Molly," I said. That was all.

Lester opened the door to the hall. Suddenly there was a symphony of sound—tinny and sharp, bouncing off the linoleum floors and tiled walls, as if the hospital had just reawakened into frantic life. Everywhere around us there was a rush of activity—the ringing of bells, the grinding of gurney wheels, the flapping of white medical smocks.

"*Go,* Florence," Lester said, angry now, finally turning to face me. "This was *your* wish, after all. Not mine."

I looked at him, at his big, round, frozen eyes. I gripped my purse tightly, pulling it up so that it covered my mouth and chin. He was right. This was my wish, my decision.

My chance.

The moment he declared me dead, I would be free.

There were reporters in the waiting area off the hall.

Reporters. With *cameras.* So they had come after all. I wouldn't have imagined it. I turned to ask Lester what I should do, but he was gone, out another door. There was just Molly. Molly, growing cold.

I tried to calm my breathing. I stood there against the doorjamb for some time steadying myself. I continued to hold my purse close to my breast, as a mother might a child on a lifeboat. There were four of them out there: a woman in cat's-eye glasses and three bored-looking men wearing fedoras and smoking cigarettes. They all looked up when a nurse in a starched white uniform approached them, preparing to read from a clipboard.

This was my chance to escape, while they were distracted. I took a long, deep breath and stepped into the hallway.

The nurse began her recitation. "Florence Lawrence died at 3:10 P.M. this afternoon. Dr. Lester Slocum applied a stomach pump but to no avail."

I made my way forward, praying they would not notice me. *Don't be silly, Flo. You're just some dyed-blond middle-aged floozie to them. They're not going to recognize you.*

But I stayed to the far wall just the same, my breath loud and arduous to my ears, as if the soundtrack on a motion picture had been amplified for effect. I kept my eyes averted from them and their cameras, looking at the wall as I passed. Taped there were paper cutouts of Christmas trees made by the little ones in the children's ward. One read:

PEACE AND LOVE TO ALL THE WORLD

"The cause of death," the nurse was saying as I passed, "was ingestion of ant paste."

"Ant paste?" one man asked, his lips pulled back in revulsion.

"It's got arsenic in it," the woman with the cat's-eye glasses said matter-of-factly over her shoulder.

The man behind her made a short whistle. "What a way to go."

I felt terribly weak then, as if my knees would no longer support me, as if my legs would fail and I'd fall right there in front of them. *Walk, Florence,* I commanded myself, but it was my mother's voice now—or Mr. Griffith's. Or maybe even Harry's. *They won't know you. They haven't known you for twenty years.*

But one man did look over as I passed. His camera was slung low at his side, its big, round lamp asleep. I looked away from him, trying to hide my fear—as well as the stains of vomit and blood on my blouse. I sensed his eyes on me, his sudden interest—*felt* rather than saw him turn and point me out to the others. I clutched my purse even more fiercely to my heart as I hurried for the door. I dared not turn around, not even to see if he followed, if he'd raised his camera to flash—that horrible glare that had often left me blinded for days. I dared not turn around to see them, to see if the woman in the cat's-eye glasses now began the chase, pen and notebook in hand. I felt the old terror collect at the back of my throat—or was it simply the bile once more? I pushed forward, out the emergency room door and into the dimming sunlight, and began to run. They were in pursuit again, and this time I was determined not to be caught.

"Harry! Dear God, Harry, help me!"

A man claws my face. I feel a sharp sting of pain and shriek out. "Harry!" I scream. "Harry!"

But I can't see him. He's lost somewhere within the crush of people. We're on the track at Union Station in St. Louis—except all I can see are people pushing at me, encircling me. There are hands, hands, hands everywhere. They pull at my dress, yank at my arms. I feel the buttons on my coat pop off one by one, torn by fingers that I cannot see. A dozen flashbulbs burst at once—the horrible sound of cameras snapping like reptiles. I recoil from the light, my eyes burning. The acrid smoke of the magnesium flares fills my nostrils.

A woman is suddenly in front of me, grinning hideously in my face, her eyes shiny and wild.

"It's her!" she shouts. "It's The Biograph Girl!*"*

She snatches the hat from my head and holds it aloft like a prize.

The crowd surges once again and I feel myself going under. I begin to scream. I truly believe it is the moment of my death.

But they hadn't followed. I ran for three blocks past the hospital, ran like a crazy woman, ran as if I were Carole Lombard or Claudette Colbert in one of those madcap screwball comedies so popular then. I ran until I was finally stopped from crossing the street by a line of traffic, buses belching smoke and big black automobiles bleating their horns. I turned around, out of breath, and saw no one behind me. No one had followed.

No one.

I stumbled to a bench and sat, laughing at myself.

"Oh, Flo, you're not in St. Louis anymore," I whispered aloud. "It's been a long, long time since St. Louis. You can walk right by them now and they don't even know you. No one's going to chase you down anymore."

There was relief in that, of course, relief that I'd not been seen, that I'd gotten away, that my plan had worked—but there was also the odd, misplaced disappointment that I'd felt too often before.

My plan had worked because *no one remembered.*

Oh, some editor over at the *Herald* or *The Hollywood Reporter* apparently had. He'd recollected the name Florence Lawrence—recalled that she'd been The Biograph Girl, the world's first movie star, who once received six thousand letters in a single week. He'd remembered, if dimly—and sent down his reporters to get the scoop, yet another Hollywood scandal they could splash across their pages:

FORGOTTEN STAR TAKES OWN LIFE
BY DRINKING ANT POISON

Good for page ten or so.

But the reporters themselves didn't remember. I imagined they found the assignment tedious. Those men had looked so bored. And their readers—maybe a handful would recall those long-ago days before the movies had learned to talk, before Technicolor had splashed gaudy primary hues all over the silver screen, before movie theaters themselves were turned into palaces fit for desert sheiks, before features had dared to progress beyond ten or eleven minutes. Maybe a handful. But most people wouldn't know the name Florence Lawrence or care.

Page ten, if I was lucky.

Even if I *was* the one who'd started all of this—all of this foolishness with the reporters and the cameras and the flashing bulbs. I was the *first,* the very first in a long, long line of movie stars—in another time, another world. Now how different everything had become, and yet how much the same. On the lot at Metro the previous week, I had heard poor Garbo wailing about how the photographers had followed her almost to the studio gates, how she couldn't feel safe, not even at home. And yet I didn't dare approach her, didn't dare attempt any consolation—for who was *I* to her? Who was I—except the one who had started it all?

As if you have any right to sit there feeling sorry for yourself, Florence.

Mother's voice again. Definitely Mother's this time.

What of that poor creature on the hospital slab, the girl Lester will say is you, the girl who will be buried out beside me in Hollywood Memorial Cemetery, the place I had planned for you?

Oh, I hadn't forgotten her. Molly. Dear sweet little Molly. I took a long breath and closed my eyes. I imagined she was fully cold by now. I didn't feel much guilt, just a vague sadness—a *wistfulness,* really, more than anything else. She'd been a girl *meant* to die young. I predicted it the first day I met her. *This one will never grow old, wasted, worn.*

Molly had trusted me. Maybe even come to love me. Her own mother hadn't cared a whit for her—and I *did* care about Molly. No matter what Lester might think now. I *did* care about her. Very much.

But she was dead. Dead like Harlow, like La Marr, like Mabel Normand—like Peg Entwistle, the girl who'd jumped from the Hollywood sign. I knew what I'd done, and I'd have to live with it all the rest of my life. But I had no choice, none really—it was the chance I'd been waiting for. It was the only way.

And Molly was just a girl. A girl among hundreds.

I couldn't change what happened. And *wouldn't* have either, I supposed, hard as that sounds. Molly had given me a rare gift. For with Molly dead, so was Florence Lawrence—finally, at long last. That girl few remembered, the one who took her own life because she was old and forgotten and couldn't find work anymore. I believe I cried a little, sitting on that bench in the middle of the evening rush hour—tears for a girl even *I* could barely recall now, tears for how pathetically she'd ended her life.

Ant paste? What a way to go.

I sat and watched the world go past me: businessmen on their way home from work, children with their yapping little dogs on leashes, actresses from the extra ranks done up in mascara and rouge stepping off the bus and heading back wearily to their flats along La Cienega Boulevard. I watched them and marveled at the never-ending rhythm of the world, the dizziness that stops for no one.

Then I stood and entered the flow. Where I was headed, I had no clue—but I began to walk. I couldn't stay here. Eventually, *someone* would spot me, *someone* would know me: Marian, perhaps, or one of the other waxworks Metro kept on the payroll, like dear old King or Flossie Turner. I had to get out of Hollywood—not even go back to collect my things. Only my purse—that was all I could take with me. I tightened my grip on its patent leather hide.

The sun was low in the sky as I walked up La Cienega, then down Santa Monica. I remember so vividly the pinkness of the clouds, the reddening of the sky over the hills. I must have walked ten miles that way, clutching my purse in front of me so tightly that my fingers began to ache. It contained the trinkets of my old life: a few faded photographs of Mother, of Ducks, of Mr. Griffith and Linda, of Harry. I had exactly four dollars and sixty-seven cents to my name.

When I finally looked around and saw where I had traveled, night had come, and I was on the shore highway. I remember the bite to the air, the chilly slap of the sea against my face, and the sudden, delirious urge to laugh—to double over into laughter, in fact, to dance a merry jig on the macadam. But instead, alone on the road, smelling the salt of the sea, I began to *whistle*. Just what tune I no longer recall, but it hardly matters. I just went on whistling—never once turning around, walking onward as if I had a destination, an appointment, somewhere to go. I had nowhere, of course—a terrifying reality, but I indulged in no fear, not then, just the giddiness of being in the world without a home, without a purpose, without a name.

Fifty-Nine Years Later

"God," Anita says, "it's like something out of *Dark Shadows*."

Richard just nods in agreement. The place does look like some Gothic mansion, all brownstone and ivy and enormous stained glass windows of saints and dragons. Ancient oaks loom over its three stories, shading much of the manor from the late-morning sunlight.

"I half expect to see a sign saying, 'I'd turn back if I were you,' and an animatronic owl hooting in the trees," Richard jokes to Anita.

They approach like a couple of wary explorers. At the start of the walk leading up to the front door stands a slab of marble with ST. MARY'S HOME lettered in Old English script.

"*You* ring the bell when we get there," Richard insists.

"Why do *I* have to?" Anita asks.

"He's your uncle."

"Yeah, but it's *your* story."

Richard smirks over at her. He's unnerved by the quiet. Just the faint rustle of leaves from the trees above, the occasional shrill call of some mysterious bird. It's a whole other world away from the noisy streets of Manhattan, where leaves don't rustle and the only sounds of birds come from dirty pigeons on the roof.

"They know we're coming, right?" Richard asks for the third time.

"I've *told* you. Sister Jean does. I didn't speak to Uncle Stan. He doesn't get out of bed much anymore, remember?"

"But his memory is okay, right?" Richard stops walking and faces Anita. "I mean, he *is* ninety-four. I hope we didn't come all the way up here to Buffalo to this creepy old place just to find out he's lost in the upper stratosphere somewhere."

"Richard, do you think I would have wasted an entire Saturday if I didn't think this was going to be worthwhile? I'll have you know that I'm missing out on a very big audition today so I could bring you here."

"For what?" He smirks again. "They looking for more dancers for *Grease?*"

"No, they're looking for a girl for *All My Children* to play a street-walker who gets murdered. The auditions continue tomorrow, so I'm going over. I'd be *perfect.*"

Richard laughs. "Neet, you're gonna get typecast. Didn't you do that same bit on *Miami Vice?*"

She grins back at him. "That was ten years ago and I was *seventeen.* And I'll take whatever work I can get." She tosses her long blond hair in the way Richard adores. It's so Farrah. So Susan Lucci. Anita *should* be a star, he thinks. She's drop-dead gorgeous, has a great figure, and is a pretty good actress to boot—that is, when she gets the chance to show what she can do.

If only Ben weren't so goddamned determined to stay in New York and avoid L.A. *That's* where Anita could make it as an actress, become the star she should be.

"So trust me," Anita's saying. "Uncle Stan is sharp as a tack. Mother said so."

"You know, you should just move to L.A. on your own," Richard tells her.

"Where'd *that* come from?"

"I was just watching you, admiring your star quality," he says.

"I couldn't leave Ben," she replies simply. "He needs me."

Goddamn Ben. There's so much about him that drives Richard buggy. Always has been—ever since they were both teenagers back in Chicopee sharing the same room. Mom would call them down to dinner and Ben would arrive shirtless, smelling of boy sweat and motor oil. "I can't eat next to *that,*" Richard would gripe.

Mom would just shake her head and say, "No one would ever believe you were twins—and identical ones at that," before ordering Ben back upstairs to wash his hands and put on a shirt.

"So when's the last time you saw Uncle Stan?" Richard asks.

"Oh, a *long* time ago. I was just a kid—back in the seventies some-time. He was living with my Aunt Trinka then. She's not the easiest woman to deal with, so Mother and I didn't visit Uncle Stan very often. But Mother saw him just about five months ago—after he'd come here—and she said he was just as bright and sassy as she'd always re-membered him."

Richard sighs. "I hope so." He looks up at the imposing entrance—huge polished oak double doors with stained glass insets of Mary rising to heaven. "Well, let's go bring the broomstick back to the Emerald City."

They climb the gently rising steps and approach the front doors. Anita rings the bell. Inside a deep, mournful chime echoes across marble. They both instinctively pull back.

"If Lurch answers the door, I'm out of here," Richard whispers.

"Stop," Anita hisses. "These are *nuns*. You gotta be polite."

There's no sound, no movement from within.

"Maybe we should just go in?" Richard suggests.

"Mother said ring the bell."

"Then ring it again. Maybe no one heard it."

"How could anyone not hear *that?*"

"Just ring it again."

She does. The same deep reverberation from within. They wait. Richard swallows.

"Maybe they're—" Anita starts. But then the door begins to open slowly, revealing first the sparkle of an overhead chandelier and then a tiny, brown-spotted hand.

A little nun looks up at them, her face an old apple. She's in full black habit with only a wimple of white around her face. "Yes?" she asks.

"*Hel*—lo," Anita says, and Richard recognizes her actressy voice, the one that sounds so congenial and professional, as if she were a door-to-door saleswoman pitching rosary beads. "We're here to see Stanley Soboleski."

"Oh, yes," the old nun says. "Sister Jean told me he was having visitors."

She pulls open the door with noticeable difficulty. Richard observes, with his reporter's eye, that she has a limp: one leg is longer than the other, fitted with a higher black shoe. She closes the door behind them. "I'm Sister Augustine," she says cheerfully.

"I'm Anita Murawski," Anita says. "And this is Richard Sheehan. He's . . . my brother-in-law."

Sister Augustine keeps her eyes on Anita, as if she were studying her. Richard's busy looking around, taking in the vastness of the room. It's a large foyer, with a parquetry floor and a cathedral ceiling open through to the second-floor landing. A great curving staircase, with marble steps and polished oak banister, ascends from the middle of the room. In the center hangs an ornate chandelier of gold gilt, dripping with crystals. On this floor, several plush chairs are arranged around an antique Heppelwhite desk, on which rests a Bible. A simple wooden crucifix hangs on the wall, facing a somber portrait of the Pope.

"Nice place you got here." Richard smiles.

"Oh, thank you," Sister Augustine says. "I've been here for fifty years. I remember the day the Bishop first blessed the place."

"*Fifty years,*" Richard repeats. For a moment he considers interviewing *her.*

"Please," she says, gesturing with her bony hand toward the chairs. "Have a seat. I'll tell Sister Jean you're here."

"Thank you," Anita says. They watch as Sister Augustine hobbles down the hallway and disappears around the bend.

"Brother-in-law," Richard whispers. "*That's* expanding the definition of family. Not sure the Catholic hierarchy would approve."

Anita smirks. "You're my live-in boyfriend's brother. Makes sense to me."

"Perfect sense. Except the 'in-law' part is kind of a contradiction in terms."

They hear the clack of shoes coming down the hall. From the gait it's obvious this newcomer is no relic like Sister Augustine. Richard and Anita look up to see a tall, pretty woman with short reddish-blond hair and a scattering of light freckles across her cheeks. She's young—early to mid-thirties, probably—and dressed in a conservative plaid skirt and white blouse. A simple silver crucifix hangs from around her neck.

"Ms. Murawski?" she says. "I'm Sister Jean."

The women shake hands. "This is Richard Sheehan," Anita says, pointing over at Richard.

Sister Jean takes his hand and smiles warmly. "The brother-in-law, Sister Augustine said," she remarks. "So are you related to Stanley as well?"

"No," Richard says with a grin. "I'm—from the other side of the family."

Sister Jean nods. "Well, shall we go upstairs? Stanley has been so excited about your visit. He says you're going to interview him."

"Yes," Anita says. "Well, Richard is."

They begin to climb the marble staircase. "You're a writer, Mr. Sheehan?" Sister Jean asks as they go.

"Yep," Richard responds, tapping his tape recorder in his jacket pocket. "At least, that's what I call myself."

"Who do you write for?"

"Anyone who'll pay me." He laughs. "This particular piece is for the *Times* Sunday magazine."

"And the subject . . . ?"

"I'm writing about the very old. How it feels to live so long. What living does to a person, decade after decade after decade."

They reach the top of the stairs. Sister Jean pauses at the landing. "Did you see the article in *National Geographic* a few months ago about those old Russian women? They were like a hundred and forty or something astounding like that, and they said they attributed it all to cold air."

Richard smiles. Sister Jean seems warm, quite real, and natural—nothing like the harpies he remembers from St. Thomas à Becket Academy back in Chicopee. "That's not what my piece is going to be about," he tells her. "I want to write about the *experience* of living, of being one person one year and another twenty years later—how we change, how we grow, and, I suppose, how we stay the same. How we adapt to a world that often changes faster than we do."

"Mighty big topics," Sister Jean says.

"Well, these people have lived through so much," Richard says. "I'm thirty-four, and sometimes I can't remember what life was like pre-ATM machines and computers. I've never written on a typewriter. But these people were around before *automobiles*—before Social Security!"

Jean laughs. "I often wonder myself how people got by without voice mail and answering machines. I imagine we'll be saying the same thing about E-mail soon enough."

"In my line of work, I say it already."

Jean cocks her head at him. "So your wife must be Stanley's niece as well?"

"Oh, I'm not married," Richard says, moving his eyes over to look at Anita. She bites her lip.

Sister Jean is looking at him. "Then you must—"

"Be gay," Richard finishes with a little smile. He loves doing that, just to see people's reactions.

The nun seems only momentarily taken aback. "That wasn't what I was going to suggest," she says. "I was going to say then you must be the brother of Ms. Murawski's husband."

"My twin brother is Anita's boyfriend," Richard explains. "Hence the brother-in-law."

Richard senses something cool about Sister Jean. He usually trusts his instincts. They've served him well tracking down stories and saved his ass a couple times. He figures she can accept their rather unorthodox set of relationships.

"Well," Sister Jean says, grinning, "if your boyfriend is Mr. Sheehan's twin, Ms. Murawski, he must be very good-looking and charming."

"Oh, don't say that in front of Richard," Anita laughs. "He already knows he's cute. *Too* well."

"Actually, Sister," Richard says in a conspiratorial whisper, "you'd never know Ben and I were twins. See, *I* comb my hair and clean my nails."

"Don't start," Anita warns. "Ben's just a little—well, less *precise* about his appearance."

They resume walking, heading down a wide corridor. Richard looks into the rooms as they pass. He makes out withered bare feet with hardened toenails protruding off the ends of beds. In the doorway of one room an old woman sits in a wheelchair with a purple velvet ribbon in her hair. Her face comes alive for a second when she sees them approach, but then it fades again, and she resumes the circular motion of her hands on the tray in front of her.

Richard notices Anita shiver. He slips his arm around her waist as they walk.

"I understand you're an actress," Sister Jean says to Anita.

"Yes."

"Might I have seen you somewhere?"

"Commercials mostly. I've done some off Broadway. Well, off-*off*-Broadway."

"And don't forget *Miami Vice*," Richard says.

"Oh, you, hush," Anita tells him.

"Actually, Sister," Richard says, "Anita and my partner, Rex, who's also an actor, have both appeared in my brother's movies. Ben's a filmmaker."

"How fascinating," Sister Jean says. She stops walking abruptly. "Well, here we are," she announces.

They peer into Uncle Stan's room. Sister Jean steps aside so that Anita can go first. She enters a bit timidly, knocking gently on the opened door and whispering, "Uncle Stan?" They all step quietly inside.

The first thing Richard notices is not the old man asleep in the bed, but the picture hanging on the opposite wall. It's a faded old theater poster, featuring a raven-haired woman in a pink-plumed hat. A large water stain has dried across the bottom. Richard can make out the words:

THE MAJESTIC THEATER, INDIANAPOLIS

And below that is a list of all the theater's acts, headed up by somebody named Gaby Dubois. Maybe she's the woman with the pink plumes. Richard walks up to the poster, which is framed and safeguarded behind a pane of glass. Rex would love this, he thinks. Rex is a big old movie and theater freak. He does a one-man show playing all the Barrymores, from Maurice down to Drew.

Anita has approached Uncle Stan's bed. "I hate to wake him," she says. "He seems so peaceful."

The thin white sheet has been drawn up to his waist. He wears a red-and-white-checked flannel nightshirt. His head is tipped back, and his mouth is open, a toothless black hole, but he doesn't snore. For an old man, he still has a considerable amount of hair, shockingly white against his pillow. His face is lined deeply; his Adam's apple is prominent in his scrawny neck.

"Uncle Stan?" Anita whispers.

He doesn't move, not so much as the flutter of an eyelid. "You know," Anita says, looking up at Sister Jean, "I can't imagine he'll recognize me after all these years."

"Oh, he was quite aware of you when we spoke this morning," the nun says. "He told me that you were his favorite sister's granddaughter and that you were a famous actress."

Anita smiles, turning back to the man in the bed. "Uncle Stan?"

Richard glances at the theater poster again. The eyes of the lady with the plumes are the kind that appear to follow you around the room. He feels a chill. He looks back at the old man in the bed.

"Uncle Stan?" Anita says, a little louder now.

"Stanley, your niece is here," Sister Jean announces in an official voice.

Richard peers in closely. "Uh," he says. "I don't think he's breathing."

Anita has placed her hand on Uncle Stan's shoulder. She pulls it back quickly. "Oh, my God," she gasps.

Sister Jean moves quickly to grip the old man's pulse. She appears to count in her head. She drops his wrist and then leans in fiercely in front of his face. *"Stanley!"*

"Oh, my God," Anita repeats, stepping backward, bumping into Richard.

Sister Jean presses a buzzer beside the bed.

"Is he . . . ?" Anita asks.

"Katie!" Sister Jean barks suddenly, stepping back to call out the door. "Sister Kate!"

"It's okay, Neet," Richard says, putting his arm around Anita.

A gray-haired nun in a black veil and a floral-print dress appears in the doorway. "Give me the stethoscope," Sister Jean orders. Sister Kate unhooks it from around her waist and hands it over. Sister Jean plugs the stethoscope into her ears and slips it up under the old man's shirt. She listens.

Anita's eyes are wide. "Is he . . . ?"

Sister Jean's face relaxes into resignation. She makes the Sign of the Cross. She unplugs the stethoscope and lets it dangle in front of her. "Miss Murawski, I am very sorry."

"He's *dead*," Anita says in stunned disbelief.

"I am truly, truly sorry," Sister Jean repeats, and her eyes mist over. "He was alert and talking this morning, so excited about your visit."

"He's dead," Anita says, turning to Richard, as if he hadn't heard. He can't help but smile. "Sorry, babe," he says and laughs a little. Then a little more.

Anita does, too. "Oh, my God," she says, laughing. "We drove for six hours—"

Richard starts laughing so hard he drops into the chair behind him. "Four hundred miles!"

Anita covers her mouth and looks over at Sister Jean, who appears bewildered by their laughter. "You must think we're terrible," she says. "It's just that—well, I hardly knew him—and, well, Richard kept thinking this was going to be a waste of time and I kept telling him, no, Uncle Stan was sharp as a—" She bubbles over into laughter again.

"Go on, Katie," Sister Jean tells the other nun. "I'll take it from here."

Richard's laughing silently in the chair. Anita giggles a little as she looks down at Uncle Stan. "Well, rest in peace, you sweet old man."

"He really was, you know," Sister Jean says. "I've only been here a little more than a year, but he was one of the dearest men at St. Mary's."

Anita gently strokes his spotted gray hand. "He's still warm," she says tenderly. She looks up at Sister Jean. "I suppose you'll need to call a doctor or something to pronounce him dead."

"Actually, I can do that. I'm a nurse-practitioner—part of the reason they wanted me as administrator here." She winks over at them. "Kind of a jill-of-all-trades, you know. But I will need to call his next of kin— his daughter, Mrs. Gawlak. She must be . . . your mother's aunt, yes?"

"That's right," Anita says. "My aunt Trinka." She makes a sour face.

"I'm sure she'll want to come up," Sister Jean says. "She's not far away—just up in Niagara Falls. Maybe you'd want to wait for her."

"No, Sister. Frankly I wouldn't. Aunt Trinka has never approved of my—lifestyle, shall we say. Looks down on actresses."

Sister Jean smiles. "I think we've all got an aunt Trinka somewhere."

They've moved away from the bed and are now standing near the door. "But you know what?" Anita says. "I imagine you must have a chapel here. Maybe I *should* go say a prayer or something—and you can tell Aunt Trinka I did at least that, okay?"

Sister Jean nods. "I'll be sure to tell her what a devoted niece you were."

"Thanks, Sister."

Sister Jean calls again to Sister Kate and asks her to take Anita to the chapel. Anita starts to follow, then turns back to Richard. "Sorry for the wasted trip," she says with a crooked little smile.

"Hey," he says, "people die."

Anita suddenly looks as if she's going to cry. She disappears around the corner after Sister Kate.

There's a moment of awkward silence. Then Richard says with a sigh, "Ninety-four. Guess that's not too bad, huh?"

Sister Jean smiles. "Oh, we've got older folks than him."

Richard looks at her, an idea suddenly striking him. "Sister, I wonder, since we've come all the way here—" He pauses, clumsy in his request. "I wonder—are there any others at St. Mary's who are very old—ninety or over—whose memories are still sharp? Who might be willing to talk with me?"

He watches as the nun's eyes move past him, over his shoulder. Her gaze seems to come to rest on the old theater poster on the wall. Her face betrays nothing for a moment, and Richard fears he may have offended her, may have encroached upon the safe environment she's devoted herself to ensuring the old folks. But then she smiles and returns her gaze to Richard's face.

"I tell you what, Mr. Sheehan. I need to call Mr. Soboleski's daughter, and I've got to get someone to attend to him, dress him up nice and all that. And then there's a ton of paperwork and—well, I may not have a chance to take you around to meet everyone. But I can—" She pauses, seeming to consider something. "I *can* leave you with someone who'll probably have everything you're looking for and then some."

Richard grins.

"Mr. Sheehan," Sister Jean tells him, "let me introduce you to Flo."

One Hundred Years Earlier

So. Where to begin?

The stage, I think. That's where it all started for me. Everything. The stage was my kindergarten. My earliest memories are all lit with footlights shining up into my eyes. Not much of a childhood, some have judged. But I tell those blue-nosed busybodies I regret *nothing* in my life—so long as I enjoyed doing it at the time.

And I *loved* performing on the stage—or, more accurately, I loved the applause. That's the rub of it, you know, the heart of all my troubles in my life. My love of the applause. But I've come to learn—and you should remember this if you want to understand everything else—that if you want a place in the sun you've got to expect a few blisters on your face.

So it's not surprising that walking along the coast highway I thought less of Molly and the events of the past day than about that old theater—oh, where was it? Indianapolis, I think—the night I saw my first moving pictures, back before the century had turned.

Between the steady crash of waves, I could hear the incessant clatter of dancers' shoes as they scurried up the wooden steps to the stage. Strange, isn't it, that with a life as colorful as mine it would be *sound* that first comes to my mind. You'd think it would be images, hues, textures I'd remember first: the faded red of the velvet curtain or the pink plumes of Gaby's hat. But instead what always comes first is the barking of trained seals, the tinkling of old pianos, the applause of the audience. Above all, *that's* what I remembered that night standing on the beach: the thunder of the crowd, the hoots of appreciation, the whistles, the whoops. The *applause.*

I was hidden in a fold of musty-smelling curtain, its edges frayed, its gold fringe loose and straggly. Like my hair.

"Florence," Mother scolded. "Come here immediately."

The dancers on stage had started their act. The piano player's shaky tenor struggled to rise above the *tap-tap-tap* of the girls' shoes. "Wait— till—the sun shines—Nellie—"

"Honestly," my mother said, pulling me roughly from the curtain by my arm towards her, "why can't you take better care of yourself?" She thrust a comb into my hair.

"She looks fine, Lotta," Ducks told her. "The crowd will love her, as they always do."

My mother scoffed at him. Ducks was forever getting in the way, telling her how to raise me. My earliest memories are of him, not of my mother, who was off touring with a company only a few months after I was born. The very first thing I ever remember is Ducks's harmonica, the sound of it, tinny and repetitious, filtering into my bedroom late at night. That and the smell of his cigar. Whenever I'd call out, he'd come in, puffing away, reassuring me that someone was indeed outside that door.

Ducks. Henry Ambrose Duxworthy, from the little town of Romney Marsh, in County Kent, England. He used to tell me stories of hillsides covered with sheep, of the great white cliffs of Dover, of the music halls of London, where he'd gotten his start. There had been some nasty business with a boy—he never quite explained what—but he stowed away in the steerage of a great ocean liner and arrived in New York penniless and without a friend. Oh, Ducks loved a good story, but I had no reason to doubt him about this. On the London stage, he'd been a master juggler, and he found work in the burlesque theaters of New York. Later, he hooked up with a traveling troupe of acrobats and played all over North America. He was young, agile, and carefree, and at fifty-five—the age he was now—he still possessed a youth's merry twinkle and love of mischief.

That's why I doted on him, and he on me. "One lies and the other swears by it," Mother would chide after she'd discover one—or both— of us had eaten all the pudding but denied the deed to her face. And yet Mother depended on Ducks—had ever since they'd hooked up on the road and he'd joined her company as leading man. He was there to secure our bookings, to rustle up an audience when necessary, to tuck me into my makeshift bed in a gypsy wagon as we rattled over the desolate roads between shows.

He was a round, balding man with an enormous mustache. The picture I carried of him for years showed him in his usual slouch hat and bow tie, his trusty old side-by-side shotgun at his belt—to protect us from the bandits and thieves that prowled the backroads then. Ducks was our defender, yet I could never imagine him firing a shot. He was such a marshmallow, always taking the young, handsome juveniles in our company under his wing, buying them new hats and frock coats, spoiling them with sweetmeats until they left him for someone else in another company and broke his heart. That was the story of Ducks's life. Over and over again.

I loved Ducks like no one else. He was everything to me: father, brother, companion, friend, nurse. If not for him, I might have been merely a girl, terrified and frail, the way they grew them in those days. Ducks taught me about chance, about risk, about love. I remember how he fell so hard one time for one of our juvenile actors, a strapping lad from Missouri with wavy hair and violet eyes who let Ducks buy him new clothes and a pocket watch and tickets to see Lillian Russell—and slugged him in the kisser when he attempted just to hold his hand.

"Why did you even *try?*" Mother had scolded, placing a slab of raw beef on Ducks's swollen lip. "Why take that chance without being *sure?*"

He'd looked over at me to answer. "If love is worth pursuing," he said, and I've never forgotten it, "you've got to risk a few fat lips and bloody noses here and there."

Ducks was always first in my heart. Not that I didn't love my mother. Quite the contrary. I *adored* her. There was no one more enchanting than Mother. She was a beautiful, glamorous figure with giant hats and great big eyes outlined with thick black mascara. If Ducks's harmonica is my earliest memory, my mother's face hovering over my crib—enormous and beautiful—is the next.

She was an imperious woman, a woman whose steely determination to succeed shone from her black Irish eyes, whose fierce insistence on independence left Ducks to do the coddling and nurturing of her daughter. From the time I was very young, my image of my mother was one of supreme struggle and sacrifice. She had suffered grandly in her life, as grandly as any of the roles she had played on the stage—that was obvious. But it would be left for me to gather clues about just what her suffering was all about. Mother would never share a word of insight about her past—our past—with me.

During our run at the Majestic Theater in Indianapolis, I was six years old. Six, seven, eight—somewhere around there. Already I'd been on the stage for several years, on the road with Mother and Ducks much of that time. I remember little of Hamilton, the town where I was born, at the point of Lake Ontario. Mother provided only the most superficial of details and then only her version of events. But she delighted in telling the story, time and again, of how I won the children's amateur talent contest in Hamilton. "That child has more talent in her little pinky than most gals got in their entire body," the theater manager had told my mother, and she believed him.

"I'm taking Flo on the road," she announced to Ducks. "She can sing and dance like no other child her age. She'll be a hit in between acts of our plays."

We left Canada in a horse-drawn calash, one of those old-style carriages with two wheels and a collapsible top. I remember sitting between Ducks and Mother, watching the flies on the shiny brown butts of the horses, their tails flicking this way and that. We passed the cabinet-making shop, where I knew the strange old man I called "Father" lived. My brother Norman stood out in front—all cowlick and freckles—and waved to us with such a sad look on his little face.

"We'll send for you," Mother called out cheerily to him.

But we never did.

She pulled the comb through my hair, snapping a snarl. I made a little sound of pain as my hair was yanked away from my scalp.

"Hush now," Mother reprimanded me. "Don't start crying or I'll give you something to *really* cry about."

My eyes found Ducks's. He stuck out his bottom lip in a silent symbol of support.

"There," Mother said finally. "Now you look like the little lady they've all come to see."

"Is *zat* who zey've come for?" Mademoiselle Gaby Dubois sauntered by in her plumes and feathers. I looked up at her in awe. A pink fluff drifted from her large hat and landed on my sleeve. I could not take my eyes from it.

She laughed. My mother seemed suitably embarrassed. "My, my," Gaby asked the stagehands around us in her lilting French accent, "did you know zey've all come to see Baby Flo? Well, zen, I might as well go home."

They joshed her, flattered her, begged her not to leave—precisely what she wanted them to do. She had a way with men. Ducks always said that Gaby's voice sounded as if it were covered with confectionery sugar. It was low and breathy, but Mother called it all an act.

"She's from Mackinac City, Michigan," she'd tell anyone who'd listen. "She's never been to Paris any more than I have, so don't let her fool you."

Ducks picked me up and sat me on his lap. Onstage, the dancers were finishing their act. Mother was watching them with disdain. "Don't mind your mother, Florrie," Ducks told me, stroking my hair. "She's just high-strung because all them important birds are gonna be in the audience tonight."

I'd seen them. No, they hadn't come to see me. They hadn't even come for Gaby. They'd come to see the *Vitascope*, that strange machine the stagehands had lugged up the stairs and propped in the balcony. We'd heard the hype, of course, seen the bills posted along the fences and theater walls. But I couldn't imagine what in God's heaven it was.

I touched Ducks's bushy mustache and found a flake of food there. I brushed it off. "Why does everyone want to see the Vitascoper?" I asked him petulantly.

He smiled. "The Vitascope, Florrie. Mr. Edison made it. It makes real pretty pictures. You'll see."

I sniffed. "It might be that they came to see the Vitascoper, but it'll be *Baby Flo* they remember."

It's strange how one remembers things. The flake of food in Ducks's mustache, the pink fluff from Gaby's hat. Maybe it's because that night turned out to be so memorable. I remember that gig at the Majestic Theater better than any of the others on that tour, as if it were yesterday. I remember the cramped little room we were given, a cold-water, one-room flat with no toilet over a dry goods store. It was like so many of the rooms we stayed in as we made our way from city to city, from Chicago to Little Rock to Fort Bend to Cincinnati. Ducks and Mother slept in the bed; I was given a mattress on the floor. I remember how cold it got in our little room at night and the musty blankets Mother piled on top of me. It was during the fall, I think, getting near on to Thanksgiving, because I remember Ducks buying a turkey and tying it up in the hall, planning to kill it later that week. Poor creature. I remember it gobbling all night, leaving droppings everywhere. I recall how people came and went, in and out of that small flat, and all they talked about was the Vitascope.

"I never imagined we'd be sharing billing with a *machine*," Mother had harrumphed.

I knew, even then, how much Mother despised playing the tanks. How much she hated these little theaters out in the sticks, how superior she felt to the lowbrow performers around us: the gin-swilling chorus girls, the pratfall comedians, the Michigan-born Gaby Dubois.

"Your mother is a great actress, one of the greatest of all time," Ducks would often remind me. I believed him. I had no reason not to. Mother's stage name was Charlotte Lawrence, and she was the head of the Lawrence Dramatic Company, one of the most respected companies in Canada—or so Ducks assured me. But when the company folded—temporarily, Mother insisted—it was Baby Flo who became the family's chief breadwinner.

I had quite the following, too. I could whistle, you see, whistle like a man, and I was just a little girl. They loved novelty acts in those days, especially ones with adorable little moppets with oversize ribbons in their hair. I played the part superbly, even if—like most of us child performers—I thought the whole sugary-sweet routine was a toxic farce. Backstage, after a particularly cloying song about the little match girl or some such trifle, I'd mock vomit into a bucket. But I learned to smile pretty and bat my eyelashes whenever in view of the audience or the press.

In Akron, there was a big story in the local paper. A large picture of me with my giant hair ribbons and crooked smile.

BABY FLO, THE CHILD WONDER WHISTLER

She can whistle prettier than a songbird, the paper wrote.

That night, they lined up around the block to see me. I peered out the side door to see them. "You see, Flo?" Ducks had said. "All for you."

"They're *daft,*" I said in awe of their stupidity.

But if my silly little songs and whistles made them applaud—so be it. I'd give them what they paid to see.

Afterward, when we tried to exit by the theater's back door, a throng of little girls crushed around the old brownstone steps. "May we see her?" they cried. "May we see Baby Flo?"

My heart was in my throat. Ducks held me up over his head and the little girls all clapped. One threw me a bouquet of daisies tied with a bright pink ribbon. "Doesn't she have beautiful hair?" Ducks asked them. "Have you ever seen such beautiful hair?"

"You're going to be a big, big star," Mother had promised me many times since then. "You and I will be the most famous mother and daughter in the theater!"

But not here, not at the Majestic Theater in Indianapolis, Indiana, the tenth theater we'd been to this season, traipsing all through the American Midwest, here in this dingy, musty place that couldn't seem to rid itself of the smell of skunk—one had crawled under the stage and died six months earlier. Here the bill included a number of folks with whom we'd worked before: Gaby Dubois. Huber and Cohen, the Mystifying Mesmerists. Frank McGinty, the one-legged acrobat.

Poor old Mr. McGinty didn't speak or sing or tell jokes—he just got up there and swung from his wires and hopped through his hoops. I always felt terribly bad for him. He worked so hard, always dripping with sweat when he came off the stage, and nobody seemed to notice. He had the first slot in the program, and that was the worst. People were still filing into their rows during the first slot, taking off their coats, switching seats with the person next to them. But the Great McGinty never complained. He'd always finish to a scattering of applause and then hobble down the wooden steps leading from the stage to our waiting area. He never said a word to us, just covered his sweaty face with a damp cloth and disappeared into the dressing room.

I peered out into the audience from between the old dusty curtains. Men with high silk hats had entered and were taking their seats. They seemed somber and serious, not at all impressed by the dancers on the stage. These were the *important birds* Ducks had said were coming. My eyes sought out the strange machine sitting in the second balcony. *That* was what they had come to see. Not me. Not the Great McGinty. Not Gaby.

The Vitascope.

I didn't care about any old machine, I decided. I'd make them applaud for *me. I'd be the reason they'd be glad they came.* I wanted to be as big a star as Gaby. I cared little for Mother's grand dreams of great roles, great acting. I wanted to be adored as Gaby was adored, whistled at and cheered by the men in the front seats. I pressed the delicate pink fluff to my lips. I wanted to *be* Gaby Dubois.

The dancers had finished. They clattered back down the steps. The piano was playing fast and furious, the stagehand switching the card on the easel to read:

BABY FLO
THE CHILD WONDER WHISTLER

The crowd ignited into applause. I stood for a moment relishing it until Mother pushed me forward. I tossed my blond curls as I danced out onto the stage. I wished I could see the men in the tall hats. Were they smiling? Did I manage to break the stone of their faces? Or did they still sit there in the dark, waiting only for that silly machine, the machine Ducks had promised would make pretty pictures on the wall?

My dance ended. I approached the footlights and positioned myself close to the edge of the stage. As practiced, I looked up innocently into the crowd. I could only see the outlines of people, my eyes caught in the glare of the gas lamps. I scanned the crowd, finding the cluster of tall hats. Then I lifted my eyes upward to the balconies, where I knew the poor children sat, where indeed I sat with Mother on days we were not performing. "Sing to the balconies," Mother always urged. "If the balconies can hear you, everyone can."

In the center of the second balcony squatted the strange contraption that Mr. Edison had made. I wouldn't look at it. I opened my mouth to sing, projecting my voice as far as I could, as far as my six-year-old lungs could muster, to the farthest seat in the topmost balcony. This one was my showstopper—an old Scottish tune Ducks had taught me, one he'd sung as a boy on the music hall stages of London during the Crimean War. It was a man's song, which made my singing it even more of a novelty, a paean to a bonny lass—the kind of goo I'd barf up later to the delight of the stagehands backstage. But here, in the footlights, I was heartbreakingly earnest.

The piano player began the first chords. *"For bonny Annie Laurie, I will lay me doon and dee,"* I sang, substituting the Scots for "down" and "die." *"Her brow, it is a snowdrift, her neck is like a swan . . . ."*

I turned my eyes. There was Mother, as always, in the wings, mouthing the words along with me.

"Her face it is a fairy, that the sun shone on—"

Now Ducks began his accompaniment with his harmonica in place of the song's usual bagpipes. Some in the audience were singing along with me. *"Then glory is serene . . . and bonny Annie Laurie . . . I will lay me doon and dee, I will lay me doon and . . . dee!"*

There was no time for applause. Ducks had taught me to take a deep breath quickly after finishing the song and launch immediately into the whistled version. This is what they came to hear—loud and shrill. Men hooted as I whistled; little girls clapped their hands. And when I'd finished, I wasn't ready to leave—not yet—not when I had them just where I wanted them. I quickly broke into another tune—I don't remember what now, something light and sentimental I'm sure, maybe the one about the little boy being put off the train as he tries to get back to his dying mother. Or else the slightly naughty one about sweet, sweet Mary Jean and all the good times she's seen. *That* one would always—as they used to say—bring the house down.

How they cheered. I curtsied left, right, and center. Still they cheered. I saw even the men in the high silk hats stand and applaud. I imagined that the hoots came from them, that I had won their hearts, that they might even forget about the silly old machine they'd come to see. I winked at the audience, a little trick that no one had taught me, that I'd started doing on my own. Those closest to the stage called out to me, "That's the girl, Flo!" I lingered in the applause a trifle too long, as I often did; the stagehand had already changed name cards to announce the Mystifying Mesmerists. Mother looked cross, motioning for me to get off the stage. I obeyed, reluctantly.

"Never overstay your welcome, Florence," she told me, shaking her finger at me as I scurried down the steps. "If there's one rule you should never, ever forget, it's that. Never overstay your welcome."

It was time for the Vitascope. "Come along, Florrie," Ducks said. "They're letting us sit out in the audience to watch."

This was a special treat. Usually the performers were kept securely behind the curtain at all times. But tonight even Gaby slipped into a seat in back. I sat between Mother and Ducks.

It's funny how unprepared we are for the moments that influence our lives. I may have been young, but I considered myself wiser than most, certainly more clever than the children who flocked around the stage entrance to throw me daisies. I was only six—or seven or eight or maybe nine—but I had already seen a great deal, already been to more places than many people visit in their entire lives. I'd seen a man collapse on stage and die. I'd seen Ducks go off with a sailor and close the door behind them, barring my entrance—but I already knew what they did behind that closed door. I'd seen Mother naked with a man in her bed, and her silent mouthings of ecstasy left more of an impression on me than her frantic attempts to cover her breasts when she caught me standing wide-eyed in the doorway.

I was wise to the world. But sitting there that night at the old Majestic Theater in Indianapolis, I was thoroughly unprepared for what I was about to experience.

The lights dimmed. My eyes did not adjust right away. The theater became as black as a night without a moon, and I felt Ducks's warm hand take mine in case I became frightened. Suddenly a strange whirring sound came from above and behind, like the spinning of a fan or the flapping of wings. I had not noticed the white sheet that had been hung down from the rafters once Gaby had finished her dance. Now it flickered with a bright silver light, and the whirring sound increased.

Then, all at once, the figure of a woman flashed forth upon the sheet—but it wasn't just a pretty picture, as Ducks had promised. The woman was *moving*, whirling through the twists and spins of a serpentine dance. "That's Annabelle!" proclaimed Ducks, and there was a gasp and murmur from the crowd, a ripple of startled appreciation. The woman danced and kicked as if suspended there in the darkness, her filmy dress rising and falling and floating every which way. Then, without warning, she was gone, and the theater went dark again.

Such applause I have never heard. Not for me, not for Gaby, not for any of us who danced or sang or whistled upon the stage. Many in the audience stood, prompting Ducks to shout, "Down in front!" For no sooner had the applause begun than another picture appeared on the sheet, a street scene this time, with tall buildings and throngs of people.

"Herald Square," Mother breathed in awe.

"Have you been there, Mother?" I asked. "Where is it?"

"New York," she said, enraptured, her eyes not moving from the image.

This was followed by another dancing girl and then a boat upon the sea, with waves so rough and high that many in the front seats shouted that they'd get wet. I watched in studied wonder, confounded at how I could be seeing such things. How could those women dance in the air? How could waves be captured and thrown onto a sheet?

Another spell of darkness, another burst of applause. Then two large faces—a man with a mustache and a portly woman—appeared in front of us. "Who are they?" I asked. Their faces were so large I could see the man wink and the woman's dimples as she turned.

"That's May Irwin and John Rice," Ducks said, a sense of wonderment in his voice. "It's from the play—"

Something seemed to occur to him all at once. "Florrie," he commanded. "Cover your eyes."

I did as I was told, just as I heard Mother shriek. I couldn't help myself. I raised my index finger like the blade of a scissors and saw the man on the screen reach over and kiss the woman. In enormous detail. Repeated over and over and over again. The audience howled its approval.

Mother stole a glance at me. "Florence!" she reprimanded me. I closed my fingers.

Finally, there was a prolonged darkness. The audience began cheering, assuming the show was over. But instead, one last image flickered upon the sheet: a train. It moved along at a brisk pace from some distance away. I was fascinated. It seemed as if the train were coming closer to us, as if it really lurked there behind the sheet, in the dark shadows of the stage. A sudden, horrifying stillness descended over the audience. I pushed back in my seat. The train *was* there, surging forward on unseen tracks. Although the only sound was the whirring above, I could hear its engine, its bellowing horn, its clatter on the tracks. I could smell the smoke, taste the ash of the burning coal. I'd ridden many trains, watched still more. And this one was bearing right down upon us!

The audience screamed. People stood. A few ran into the aisles. Mother grabbed me, attempted to shield me with her body. The train barreled down and was about to come crashing into all our laps—

And suddenly the lights came back on and the whirring noise ceased. There was stunned silence for several seconds, then anxious, embarrassed laughter. Ducks said, "Well, I'll be an old fool." Mother wiped her brow.

"The train, Ducks," I asked him breathlessly. "Where did it go?"

He hoisted me up on his shoulders as the crowd stood and cheered, stamping their feet. The important men who'd come to see Edison's latest marvel threw their high silk hats into the air. "*That's* where the train went." Ducks laughed, turning around and pointing up at the strange black machine on the second balcony. "It went back inside the Vitascope!"

I stared up into the cold black eye of the projector. Such a strange-looking thing, nothing anyone would recognize today. Lots of wires, as I recall—an odd shape, like a sewing machine. But it transfixed me. I sat there on Ducks's shoulders, the cheers of the crowd ringing in my ears, and wished with all my might that I, too, might someday go inside the Vitascope.

The Present

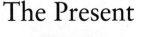

Her first instinct was not to trust him, this handsome journalist, and usually she trusts her instincts. Ever since her experience in Hartford, Sister Jean found reporters to be shifty and unreliable, out for their own ends, willing to play sincere for the sake of a story.

But she likes him. Maybe because he wasn't afraid to be himself in front of her. People sometimes tend to be edgy around nuns. She can't abide that.

Of course, Richard Sheehan also looks an awful lot like Victor, and *that* could be the reason she melted: the same dark eyes, the same straight black hair thinning just a little along the hairline, the same sweep of wide shoulders across a strong back. It was just a year last week since Victor died. Jean sees him almost every day—in the eyes of strangers like Richard Sheehan.

"Who is Flo?" Richard is asking her now.

Jean smiles. "Come along. I'll introduce you."

She figures that Flo will know for sure whether or not Richard can be trusted. Flo can smell a schemer from the next town before he even turns his wiles on her. "That's because I've been one myself," she's told Jean. "Among other things."

It was as if after living all this time Flo had learned how to really *see*: right through the skin, behind the eyes, into the soul.

"You've been wounded," she told Jean the day they met, Jean's first day at St. Mary's.

Wounded. It had been just weeks since the terrible events in Hartford. Flo had seen the pain in Jean's eyes—the only one who had.

"I may have a few scars," Jean admitted, "but they've healed."

"If a wound leaves a scar," Flo told her, "that's not being fully healed."

Jean had nodded; she'd felt the same way many times. Flo and she were friends from that point on.

In those difficult first months, Jean would sometimes wake late at night and not remember where she was. The transition had happened so fast. She'd sit up in bed and try to make out her surroundings or comprehend the stillness. Where were the sirens, the sounds of traffic? Jean would get up and wander through the corridors as the wind whistled in the eaves of the old manor. She'd check with the sisters on night duty, look in on sleeping residents.

Flo was always awake during these times. "Come in," she'd say. "Sit down and we'll talk away the night." So they would, about everything. Church teaching, soap operas, modern technology, whiskey versus gin, the meaning of family. "You come on down here whenever you like," Flo told her. "I hardly ever sleep."

Jean walks now with Richard down the corridor, past more rooms with old women sitting blank eyed in their chairs. One sings about the old gray mare who ain't what she used to be. There's a sudden whiff of urine, a passing cloud of disinfectant. Then they turn into a large common room, where the light is so bright Jean notices Richard blinking his eyes several times in an effort to get used to it.

"This is what we call our day room," Jean tells him.

The room is a cacophony of color. Pink and purple artificial leather chairs are scattered throughout. Half a dozen residents mill about wearing bright clothes: green stretch pants or blowsy blue robes. Each wall in the room is adorned with theater posters like the one in Stanley Soboleski's room, their faded reds and golds preserved under glass. Jean smiles to herself when she sees Richard's surprise at the room after the starkness of the corridor and the somber elegance of the foyer. There's a crucifix here, as there is in every room, but the walls here are painted a vital yellow instead of the drab off-white present everywhere else. And it's not the austere visage of the Pope that stares down at them from the walls of the day room, but the faces of tightrope walkers, grinning clowns, and actresses with thick black contours around their eyes.

"Well," Richard Sheehan says, his lips stretching into a broad smile, "it's not your father's Catholic rest home."

"Flo was the decorator," Jean explains.

"Really?"

"Yes. She and I went on a brightening campaign right after I first got here, bringing color back to most of the rooms."

"How old *is* she?" Richard asks.

"She'll be a hundred and seven in a few months," Jean tells him, proud as a stage mother.

"A hundred and seven!" Richard looks as if he's hit the jackpot.

"More and more people are living past the century mark these days, Mr. Sheehan," Jean says. "It's really not so surprising anymore. They're the fastest-growing segment of the population, believe it or not."

"Where is she?" Richard asks.

"Right here," comes a voice. Jean turns. Flo has spotted them from across the room and overheard their conversation. She's wearing a flowing paisley caftan; her white hair is pulled back in an enormous red satin bow. There's a small hump to her back, one of the few significant signs of her advanced age. Otherwise, she could pass for eighty. She's barefoot, with her toenails painted hot pink, and she's smoking a cigarette from a long black holder. She's just finished passing out boxes of Girl Scout cookies to the other people in the room.

"Flo," says Jean. "I want you to meet someone."

"You allow smoking in here?" Richard asks.

Jean just smiles. "This is our designated smoking section. Flo insisted she wasn't going to give up *all* earthly vices when she came to live here. I learned rather quickly after I arrived that some rules were made to be broken."

Flo has moved closer to them. She walks slowly, with a little hunch, but there's a steadiness that belies her age. She eyes Richard cagily.

"Who is this young man?" she asks Jean.

Her voice is worn by years of too much smoke and laughter, but it's a good voice: deep and throaty, honest and real. She lifts the cigarette to her lips in a dramatic gesture, inhaling for punctuation. Jean suppresses a smile. Flo likes to perform for new faces. Her hand is knotty and discolored in places, but her nails are painted hot pink like her toes, and she wears a large gold medallion ring on her forefinger.

"Flo, this is Richard Sheehan. He's a writer."

Flo's eyes regard him with even greater suspicion. "A writer? I didn't think we liked writers, Jeannie."

"I think you'll like what he's writing about."

"I'd be terribly grateful if you'd just give me a few minutes of your time," Richard says.

Flo turns to the old folks eating their Girl Scout cookies. "Henrietta, come here, dear," she calls. A chubby woman wearing a blue-and-red polka-dot dress hurries over as best she can. "Collect the money when you pass out the boxes," Flo tells her. "Remember: no bucks, no box."

"Yes, Flo," Henrietta says, turning back to scold an old man who is attempting to pilfer a box from the pile on the table.

"What happened to the honor system?" Jean asks. "I thought we agreed people could just leave their money on the table."

Flo raises an eyebrow. "We got screwed last time," she says. "Somebody in this wing didn't put in his fair share."

"You're selling *Girl Scout cookies?*" Richard asks.

Flo smirks. "He's a bright boy, Jeannie. Can't keep anything from these reporters."

Richard's eyes twinkle. "Just wondering if you'd made the girls' version of Eagle Scout yet," he says, returning Flo's smirk.

Oh, boy, Jean thinks. *He's attempting to spar with Flo.*

"No, not yet," Flo says, her eyes taking hold of Richard's and not letting go. "But I have *made it* with a few Eagle Scouts in my day, however."

Richard looks suitably chastised—or amused.

"Flo's in charge of selling the cookies in this wing," Jean explains. "It's for the daughter of our cook."

Flo sighs. "Gertie's a sweetheart of a woman, except she can't cook worth beans." She smiles. "No, I take that back. Beans, she can cook." She returns her attention to Richard. "So who the hell d'ya write for?"

"*The New York Times,*" he tells her.

"Weeeell," Flo says, leaning back and grinning wide, revealing perfectly aligned false teeth. "Aren't *we* big-time?" She takes a long drag on her cigarette, then exhales the smoke over her shoulder, away from the man's face. "Never could figure out what was so special about being a writer. It's just putting one word after another."

Jean smiles. Flo's giving him the grand treatment. The tough-old-broad routine. The young nun supposes she should really make this easier on Mr. Sheehan, but Flo's just so much fun to watch in action. Why deny her a little pleasure?

"Sit down," Flo commands. Richard looks around, takes a seat on a pink chair. "So what're you writing about?"

He seems prepared for the question. "About life. As seen by those who've lived the longest. What living does to someone. How they see the world after—"

"How old are you?"

"Me?"

"You see me talking to anyone else?"

He smiles up at his inquisitor. "I'm thirty-four," he tells her.

"Where were you born?"

"Massachusetts."

"Your parents still living?"

"Just my mother."

"And how old is she?"

"Sixty-one."

"Where in Massachusetts?" Jean interjects.

Flo cuts her off. "Jeannie, *I'm* conducting this interview if you please."

"Sorry, Flo."

"Actually," Richard says, "I thought *I* was—"

"Not until I find out about *you.*" Flo folds her arms across her chest. "What else have you written?"

"Magazine articles mostly. I used to be on staff at the *Times* until I went freelance a few years ago. Oh, and I've tried my hand at a couple of screenplays."

"*Screenplays.* Not films. So I take it they're unproduced."

He smiles sheepishly. "That's correct."

"They used to call them scenarios in my day. They any good?"

"I think so."

"So why haven't they been made?"

"Too much sex, I guess," Richard says, and he winks at her.

For a second, Flo looks surprised. Surprised that he'd say such a thing in front of an old lady and a nun. Then she laughs. Puts her hands on her hips, leans back, and laughs. Jean smiles right along with her. She knows now that Flo will like Richard Sheehan as much as she's sure he's already begun liking her.

"Too much sex?" Flo guffaws. "I didn't think that was possible these days."

Richard watches the ancient creature in front of him. Her every gesture, her every expression is exaggerated, as if she were performing on a stage. Her mouth is painted scarlet over and above her upper lip to create a beestung look—the look popular nearly a century ago. Her agility is as smooth as a sixty-year-old's, her wit as spunky as a teenager's. He is, in a word, entranced.

She's taken the seat opposite him. Her gaze remains locked to his. She smooths out her caftan across her knees, sitting on the edge of her chair like a coquette. She even bats her eyelashes—her real lashes still, Richard observes, long and thick—and places her hand over her heart.

"Do you have movie connections, Mr. Sheehan?" she asks.

"Well, my brother is a filmmaker."

"Really? And what films has he made?"

"Oh, just some shorts. Independent stuff. One got him some attention, but that was almost ten years ago. It was on the nuclear-arms race. It was about this family who survives a nuclear-bomb attack, or at least, they *think* they do—"

"A family?" asks Sister Jean. "Not *One Chance, One World?*"

Richard nods. "Yes. That's the one. You know it?"

"A wonderful film," the young nun says, and for the first time, Richard sees some genuine surprise and admiration in her face. "I was involved in the peace movement then. We showed that film many times."

"Yeah. Ben made it while he was at NYU Film School. He's never really been able to match its success."

"Who was the star?" Flo asks.

Richard smiles. "The bomb."

"No picture's worth your nickel without a star," Flo says, raising her chin just a bit.

"Well, Ben has used his girlfriend—Anita—in a number of pictures since then," Richard says. "She's the woman I came up here with."

Sister Jean leans in toward Flo. "Stanley Soboleski's niece."

"Oh." Flo draws on her cigarette, then lets out the smoke. "Heard he went over to the other side today."

"Flo," Sister Jean says incredulously. "How *do* you find out things?"

"Just keep your ear to the ground, right, Mr. Reporter?" She winks at Richard.

"That's right," he says.

"Ear to the ground *and* to the wall," Flo says. She squints her eyes over at Richard. "Let's see. You married? No. You're a homosexual."

Richard laughs out loud. He feels his face redden. For all his militancy, for all of the ACT UP demos he's participated in, he feels suddenly exposed and embarrassed, as if Flo had just guessed the brand of his underwear.

"Flo," Sister Jean scolds mildly.

"Aren't I right?" the old woman asks.

"Yes," Richard admits. "Yes, you're right."

"See, Jean? They admit it these days. You can talk about it openly now." She grins. "Anita Loos was one of the first to observe it. 'Men no longer prefer blondes,' she said. 'Nowadays gentlemen more and more prefer gentlemen.'" Flo chuckles. "And it's about time, I say. Never could understand why it was such a big dark secret. Spent most of my life with homosexuals."

"Well, I keep no secrets," Richard assures her.

Flo smiles shrewdly at him. "Come now, Mr. Sheehan. We *all* keep one or two."

He smiles. "Might I ask *you* a few questions now?"

"A few," Flo says.

"Are you really a hundred and six?"

"No, I'm actually twenty-seven. I've just lived hard."

He laughs.

"Let's just say I'm not as young as my teeth or as old as my tongue," she tells him.

"Flo will be a hundred and seven next January," Jean explains.

"And your health? You seem amazingly spry."

"Spry?" Flo wrinkles up her face. "I hate that word."

"Flo's in excellent health," Sister Jean says. "Some arthritis, and she had some eye problems last year—"

"Cataracts," Flo tells him. "But I got them removed."

"Overall, she's one of our healthiest residents," Sister Jean says, looking over at Flo. "It just so happens that she's also our oldest."

"Amazing," Richard says.

"We think so," Sister Jean agrees.

"What do you attribute it to?" Richard asks.

"Who the hell knows?" Flo takes another long puff on her cigarette. "Been smoking these damn things for over eighty years. And I've never been known to go soft on the Scotch—not until I moved here anyway. Guess God's just forgotten I'm down here."

She is extraordinary, Richard thinks. His excitement seems to catch him by the throat. "And—and—well, where were you born?" he asks as dozens of other thoughts crowd into his mind.

"Canada."

"And what did you do? When did you—" He stops, realizing the enormity of the life sitting next to him. Where does he possibly begin?

"Flo was an actress, too, like Ms. Murawski," Sister Jean interjects.

"These *posters,*" Richard says, looking up at the faces on the walls.

"Most are from revues I appeared in," Flo says, a little less saucy now, more humble. "What was I to do with them? Sister Jean insisted we hang them."

"Not standard issue for a Catholic rest home, I assume," Richard says.

"No," Sister Jean admits. "But I got the board to agree. Flo had them all down in storage. The residents love them. We've even put them in some rooms. Mr. Soboleski—"

"Yes," Richard says. "Gaby Dubois."

"Ah," Flo says, waving her cigarette dismissively. "She was a big phony. Pretended to be French and oh so elegant. Not so elegant when they dragged her body out of the Hudson River, where she'd fallen, stinking drunk. Everybody found out *then* she'd been just a butcher's daughter from Michigan."

"What about this guy over here?" Richard points at a poster opposite them.

Flo claps her hands. "Oh, the Great McGinty! How he chased the ladies! Even on one leg!" She laughs. "What a performer. He'd string a wire across the stage and walk along it on his one leg. He'd have the audience on the edge of their seats. I'd watch from the wings, terrified each time that he'd fall. But he never did. Falling just once would've meant he was through. You couldn't fall and get back up again. You'd get pelted with tomatoes and chased off the stage."

"This is it," Richard says, sitting forward in his chair, his face lighting up. "This is the kind of stuff I'm looking for. Do I have your permission to tape record this?"

"Richard!" It's Anita, walking into the room, clearly annoyed. "Where have you been?"

"I thought you were still in the chapel," he tells her.

"One Hail Mary doesn't take very long," she says.

"I'm doing an interview," Richard explains.

Anita eyes Sister Jean and Flo. "Look, I don't mean to interrupt, but I don't want to be here when Aunt Trinka arrives."

"But—" Richard looks over at Flo. To leave now could be disaster. Old people had a way of kicking the bucket without much warning. Look at Uncle Stan.

"So you're the actress," Flo observes, sizing Anita up.

Anita looks surprised. "Yes, I am."

"Good bone structure to the face," Flo says. "See?" She lifts her chin, turning her profile to Anita. "It's the nose that defines your face. Nose and cheekbones. You ever have any work done?"

Anita seems taken aback. "No," she says, and Richard knows she's lying.

Flo sniffs. "Me neither. Sex appeal is fifty percent what you've got and fifty percent what you can *convince* 'em you've got." She winks at Anita. "You've done films?"

Sister Jean explains, "Flo was an actress, too."

"Really?" Anita says, warming a bit, sitting on the arm of Richard's chair. "Well, I've done some independent short films directed by my boyfriend."

"And she's done a lot of TV," Richard offers.

"But I prefer film," Anita adds quickly, a little haughtily. "TV cameras seem to add ten pounds to me."

Flo makes a face at her. "Then make it a point never to eat TV cameras."

They laugh, especially Anita. "How about you?" she asks. "Did you work on the stage or in the movies?"

Flo's eyelids flutter just a little. She hesitates, Richard notices. But she smiles quickly. "Go look at the poster behind me," she says coyly.

Anita obeys. She walks up to a large painted image of a little girl. The child stands on a stage in a white gingham dress and with an enormous white bow in her blond hair. "'Baby Flo,'" Anita reads, "'the Child Wonder Whistler.'"

"The Child Wonder Whistler?" Richard repeats, grinning, looking over at Flo.

"They came from *everywhere* to hear me," Flo says. "In the sticks, they'd arrive in their farm overalls and straw hats. In the cities, they'd line up for five or six blocks. All to hear a little girl put her lips together and blow." She chuckles. "I was doing it long before that chicky Lauren Bacall came along."

Sister Jean reaches over and touches Flo's hand. "Why don't you do a song for them?" she suggests.

Flo arches a stenciled eyebrow. "I'm a bit tired from hawking those Girl Scout cookies all morning," she protests.

"Please," Richard says.

Flo laughs. That's all the coaxing she needs, what Richard assumes she's been angling for. Slowly she pulls her pink lips together, her face creasing in a thousand directions. She purses her mouth as if for a kiss, raising her chin into the air. She closes her eyes. Then, from her old throat, with seemingly the greatest of ease, comes the melodious sound of a nightingale.

She whistles. Just what tune Richard can't tell—one of those old, forgotten ditties they used to sing a century ago. Anita settles down next to Richard. She can't help but smile.

Flo finishes with a flourish, whistling like a bird calling its mate just as the sun peeks over the horizon. When she opens her eyes she's looking directly at Richard, a little girl again awaiting the applause of the audience. Richard complies. "Bravo!" he cries.

The old woman smiles contentedly. She's not going anywhere, Richard realizes. She's not going to die unexpectedly. She might even outlive *him*.

He leans forward closer to her. "May I schedule a formal interview with you for later this week, Miss—Miss—?"

"It's Bridgewood," Sister Jean says. "Florence Bridgewood."

"Yes," Flo says. She holds Richard's gaze. She seems as captivated by him as he is of her. "Yes, Mr. Sheehan. You may schedule an interview."

December 29, 1938

Yes, yes—the girl on the hospital slab. I suppose it's only natural that you would be curious about her. But I don't know what you want me to say about her. What do you want me to admit? She was just a girl. A girl among the thousands who used to descend like pigeons every week on Hollywood. Who probably still do. Girls with high hopes and ridiculous dreams, girls who wanted to be stars. I remember once saying to Flossie Turner, as we watched them stream through the gate at Metro, that if all those sweet young things were laid end to end, I wouldn't be the least bit surprised.

Right from the start, Molly reminded me of myself, and of Linda, too—from the very first day I came across her in the wardrobe closet at Metro, her pale blue eyes puffy from lack of sleep. Her skin was so white and so thin you could see the crosshatch of blue veins beneath it. Just like Linda. Soft, translucent.

She was holding a costume of Garbo's up in front of her, like a little girl playing dress up. I asked her her name.

"Molly," she'd told me.

Molly. Just a girl. Among thousands. I took her back to my little cottage, offered her a glass of beer and a cigarette. "No, thank you," she had said. "I don't drink and I don't smoke."

Now she was dead. I took in a long, cold breath, sitting there on the beach. The sun was coming up; the sky was turning pink. A flock of gulls landed on the sand in front of me, each one in turn stretching its wings.

Oh, Lester. What have we done?

But nothing really. Nothing. "I'd like to repay you, Flo, for all your kindnesses," Molly had said once.

You have, my dear. More than you'll ever know.

Suddenly I was backlit by a rosy glow, the way Mr. Griffith had pioneered the use of movie lighting. I noticed the long shadow I now cast across the sand.

Had I really been up all night? I supposed I had, but I couldn't be sure. There were chunks of time I couldn't remember, and after a while, the darkness obliterated all sense of time, despite the occasional glare of a passing car's headlights. How long I'd been sitting on the beach I didn't know, but the arrival of the sun signaled it was a new day—the first day of my new life.

I stood with some difficulty. My calves ached. I trudged up through the sand back to the road. I still had no idea where I was going. I just clutched my purse ahead of me and resumed my walk.

How far had I come? Hollywood seemed far away, yet how far could it really be? I tried to think of nothing except the sound of the waves against the sand. When thoughts tried to intrude, the sound of the constant surf chased them away, like those little birds that scamper across the beach, running from the onrushing waves each time, never learning.

But I couldn't entirely banish thoughts of Molly—and they became jumbled in my mind with thoughts of Linda.

Linda's voice: "I'm not sure you want to be an actress at all."

How the idea had startled me. What an absurd remark. I told her so.

"I'm not so sure, Flo." The sun had filled Linda's white hair. "I think you just want the applause."

We were in San Francisco, on a hill overlooking the old town, before the earthquake and the fire destroyed it forever. I was fourteen, fifteen—somewhere in there. The Lawrence Dramatic Company had been on a west coast tour—oh, how excited we were! Mother was in her glory. We received good notices for our costume melodrama, *The Winds of Pompeii*—less for our performances than for our papier-mâché volcano that spewed real smoke. But we didn't mind. We were performing. That was all that mattered.

"You don't know what you say," I responded haughtily to Linda. "I was *born* to be an actress. Just ask Mother."

Headlights startled me, wrenching me back to the ambiguous present. I found myself awash in a light incongruous to the dawn. I recoiled. The warmth of the automobile that slowed down next to me felt improper, too familiar, like a hand on my leg on a barstool.

"Hey, lady, need a lift?"

In the glare of the headlights, I couldn't see the speaker's face, but his voice revealed his gender.

"It's still pretty dark out there," he was saying. He sounded young, innocent. Even kind. "Wouldn't want you to get run down."

I considered his words, the first spoken to me since I'd been declared dead. I glimpsed the whites of his eyes over the steering wheel. The car was large, expensive. A Franklin, most likely—a newer version of the one I used to drive.

I hadn't answered him. "Where you headed?" he asked at last.

"San Francisco," I told him plainly. I surprised myself as much as him.

The man laughed. "You're *walking* to San Francisco? Lady, you're nuts. Get in the car. I can take you as far as Santa Barbara."

We never got that far.

"You okay?" he asked me after we'd gone a little way.

"Yes," I told him. "I'm okay."

He seemed unconvinced. He made a sound—a sigh—then returned his gaze to the road. In the backseat were gaily wrapped boxes. Christmas gifts, I imagined. On the floor at my feet were three empty beer bottles that clinked together as we drove. He didn't seem drunk, but I could smell alcohol on his breath. I'd gotten very familiar with the scent. Charles, and Bolton, too, had tried to hide their drinking from me, but I'd always been able to tell. I swore I could smell even *vodka* on their breath.

Still, I wouldn't have minded a nip of something myself just then. Sitting there, I had a sudden memory: Mary Pickford, age sixteen, aghast as she watched me knock back a shot of whiskey and light a cigarette nearly in the same gesture. Remembering her reaction, I couldn't help but smile.

The driver seemed to notice. He looked over out of the corner of his eye. I kept one hand hovering over my chest, playing idly with the buttons of my blouse. It was still dark, but I didn't want him to ask about the stains. Certainly I need not worry that he might recognize me. He hadn't even been *born* when The Biograph Girl was all the rage.

I stared straight ahead at the swath of light cut by the car's headlights on the road before us. Eventually he switched them off. The day was still hazy with the purple of dawn, but the sun was strong enough now to see by. I thought of nothing except getting to where I was going, for now I had a destination. *I was going to San Francisco.*

The road passed by under our wheels.

"Did you have a good Christmas?" The driver's voice snapped the stillness.

I looked over at him, not comprehending the question at first. "I was working," I finally said.

"Oh, going home now to celebrate?" He smiled. The sun revealed I was right: He *was* young. Maybe no more than twenty. "Your family live in San Francisco?"

"No," I said. "My family's all gone."

He seemed eager to chat. "What kind of work do you do that keeps you busy on Christmas?"

I would need to become used to questions, I reasoned. I'd have to become comfortable with providing answers. New answers. So I told him, "Odd jobs," not really lying. "Been out of work. You know, with times being so hard."

"They're getting better," he said with all the cocky optimism of a child. "Mark my words. Good times are just around the corner. You married?"

"Divorced," I told him.

"Ah," he said. He was young—and he was new to Hollywood. There was a strange quirk to his voice—I'd heard it before, years ago, playing the tanks all around the country. Midwest. No. Minnesota—that's what it was.

Not many divorcées in Minnesota, I thought. *And the ones who were —*

"I could get you some work," he said, deeper voiced suddenly, and he looked over at me full face for the first time.

I didn't respond.

"I'm an agent. For the movies." He grinned. He still had freckles across the bridge of his nose. "Ever do any movie work?"

I laughed. "Oh, hasn't everyone out here at one time or another?"

"Well, don't give up. Do you know how many years Jean Harlow had to work as an extra before she caught on?"

I looked over at him. It was no longer dark enough that he could claim not to see the lines around my eyes, my fallen chin. "Harlow did it the right way," I told him. "She died while she was still on top, still young and still loved."

"Well, I represent a young lady who's going to be the next Harlow," he told me. "She's young. She's beautiful. She's very talented."

I laughed again, shaking my head. "For heaven's sakes, just marry her and hop on the next train back to Duluth."

He had slowed down. He turned to me. "Do you take me for a child?" he asked, making no effort to disguise his contempt.

"All men are children," I said, this time exposing my own scorn. I turned away, considering the conversation over.

But when he rolled the car to a stop and I turned to look at him, I could see he wouldn't allow me to have the last word.

I'd been raped before. Twice, actually—if husbands can be counted as rapists, as I believe they can. I knew what portents led up to it. I recognized once more the change in the air, the sudden dampness, the precipitate cold. Part of me wanted simply to bear it, to pretend even to like it, just so we could get on, so he would take me at least part of the way to San Francisco. I already knew the terror, the pain of the act, the sting and the shame of the aftermath. I could bear it again if I had to, even in the state I was in, and still come out alive.

Yet I was free finally, free from all that. I had walked away from the hospital and no one had stopped me. I was charting a new life, starting over. Molly had given me a tremendous gift. To submit to this man would have degraded her sacrifice.

So I fought back.

Men don't like to be laughed at. Especially young men—especially drunk young men whose prim and pure girlfriends from places like Duluth, Minnesota, never allow them more than a good-night kiss. Especially spoiled, privileged young men in their fathers' cars, who watch with mounting indignation as an older woman—careworn, divorced, one they can tell has "been around"—laughs at them. I remember thinking these thoughts, realizing these truths, as I looked over at him, his eyes hard, his gold pocket watch glittering in the morning sun.

"You're awfully pretty to be wandering alone on the highway," he said to me, his voice lower and deeper than before.

"No, I'm not," I said. "I used to be pretty. I'm not anymore."

He laughed. "I like mature women," he said. "Do you like younger men? Maybe I could convince you to forget about San Francisco."

He lit up a cigarette, then asked if I wanted one. I accepted, wary of him, using the opportunity for delay. We smoked in silence for a while, the surf still pounding below us. My right hand casually found the door handle and rested there. Few cars passed us on the road.

He took one last long drag on his cigarette before rolling down his window and tossing the stub out onto the street. I felt the sudden smite of cold air against my face.

"Whaddya say, honey?" he asked very low and significantly.

I looked down to see he had unfastened his pants. I said nothing, made no movement. I continued to puff my cigarette calmly, feeling his hand creep under my dress, around the curve of my thigh, between my legs. He moved closer to me, dropping his face to my neck. I felt the slithery warmth of his tongue.

That was when I lowered the lit cigarette into his ear.

He screamed. I unlatched the door, jumped down out of the car, and ran into the sandy scrub, somehow maintaining the presence of mind to keep clutching my purse. He pursued me. Crazily, in broad daylight, he *pursued* me. His pride had been wounded, and I would pay. It was the same old story. Charles, Bolton—how many others? I don't think I expected to get away. But I *ran*. Even then, in the moment, I took some degree of satisfaction in the fact that I didn't stay there, that I *ran*— through the sand, losing my shoes, tearing my dress, cutting myself against the sharp bare fingers of bushes. Yet somehow I managed to hang on to my purse, still gripped close to my heart, as if it had become a part of me.

The man finally caught me by my waist, toppling me over face first into the sand. I felt warm blood in my nose.

"You fucking ugly bitch," he growled over me and tore my panties down. He clamped his hand, reeking of tobacco, over my mouth. I struggled and kicked, but he was younger, stronger, more desperate than I was. I felt his hot fingers enter me, opening me up.

No, I told myself. *No longer. This cannot happen to me now in this life.* Not anymore.

Somehow I managed to work my hand under him and grip his scrotum in my palm. I twisted it with all my strength. He screamed like a cat whose tail has been caught by the rocker, like a dog run down in the road. He stood, then fell backward and curled into a fetal ball.

I found my feet and stood over him, looking down.

"You bitch!" he cursed. "You fucking *biiiiitch!*"

My eyes must have been wild. I bore down on him, one of the ancient Furies unleashed.

"Did you think you could just *do* this to me?" I seethed at him, bending now over his writhing form, my face not more than a foot away from his. "That I would *let* you?"

My voice sounded shrill, hard, alien to my ears. It was the voice of an old woman, some harpy, some witch—my mother's voice even. I was shouting, using the discovered breath of my new life, the lungs I had fought so hard to win. "You pathetic little man! I say no! Do you hear me? *I say no!*"

I must have terrified him with my sudden ferocity. He cowered, crawling away from me in the sand. When he was about two yards off, he finally stood, struggling to hitch up his pants. I remember such little details about him revealed by that powerful morning sun: the way his cowlick stood up in back, the diagonal yellow-and-red pattern of his tie, the pearl clasp that held it to his shirt. The way he turned and ran back to his car, terrified of the crazy woman he'd picked up along the road.

I found my shoes. And his gold pocket watch, too, shimmering in the sand. I picked it up, examined it, confirmed that it was still ticking, and dropped it into my purse. My knees were scraped, my nose was bleeding, and I had started to smell, since it had been more than a day since I had bathed. But as I put on my shoes, I could barely suppress a giggle.

So I'll walk to San Francisco if I have to.

At least now, I knew where I was going.

The Present

Unlike his brother, Benjamin Cartwright Sheehan doesn't care that he's losing his hair. All right, so he *does* care—cares a lot—but he's damned if he's going to turn it into some big tragedy the way Richard has, some drama of epic proportions. No Minoxidil for him, no hair-thickening gels. Ben just lets it grow long and ties it back in a short ponytail.

"Why don't you just buzz it all off?" Richard's boyfriend Rex suggests. They're spending the day together while Richard and Anita are in Buffalo. "That's what all the guys who are losing their hair are doing these days."

Ben scoffs. "All the *gay* guys, you mean."

"Bruce Willis," Rex offers. *"He* wasn't gay last I checked."

"It just doesn't matter to me the way it matters to you and Richard," Ben tells him.

"It doesn't matter to me," Rex says, running a hand through his own dirty-blond locks, still thick enough for now—but for how long, Ben wonders, how long?

"You're just twenty-six," Ben says. "You've got hair to spare. Wait a few years."

He looks at his watch. They're going to be late if they don't leave soon. He opens his closet, running his fingers across the shirts hanging there, trying to choose the right one.

"I think Richard looks very sexy with a receding hairline," Rex says, "especially now that he wears his hair really cropped."

Rex and Richard have been together for almost six years now. Ben has to acknowledge that his early predictions were wrong, that the union is apparently durable. Rex isn't that much younger than Anita, but Ben had loved teasing his brother that he was robbing the cradle. Sexy Rexy—as all their friends inevitably called him—was, after all, not just young but a porn actor. Or an *erotic artiste,* as Rex chose to style himself back then.

But Rex has turned out to be a pretty solid guy—despite his love for Alanis Morrisette and his habit of wearing too short electric blue hot pants. He puts up with Richard's arrogance and sarcasm in ways Ben has never been able to manage. Ben likes Rex. He's used him in a couple of his short films as a way of helping him move beyond his porn image. Now Rex has put together a one-man show about the Barrymores called *Broadway Royals*. Rex plays, sometimes all at once, every Barrymore who ever trod a stage or mugged a camera, from alcoholic Jack to feisty little Drew. When the show ran for a week at the Actors' Playhouse last year, all agreed he was best as the queenly Ethel.

Of course, Ben hadn't been able to make any of the performances, not even the Sunday matinee. It had been crunch time over at the ad agency where he worked, with Ben splicing boring travelogue videos together late into the night, every night. Finally he just told Anita to go to the show without him. He feels bad about that, and he has promised as soon as Rex does the show again, he'll be there for opening night—wherever it is. Rex, of course, never held it against him; Rex doesn't hold grudges. But Richard, the grudge*meister*, certainly has—just as he's held *everything* against Ben these last thirty years.

"No, not that one," Rex tells him now as Ben withdraws a plaid shirt.

"Why not?"

"It's dull. You have such pretty blue eyes. Wear something to set them off."

Ben smirks. "We're just going to see my agent. It's not like I'm babe hunting."

"Is he still officially your agent?"

Ben shrugs. "Well, neither of us has fired the other. I just haven't been able to get him rocked for anything since *One Chance*."

"What do you need him for anyway?" Rex is looking at himself in the full-length mirror on the wall. Ben notices the boy wonder seems to be getting a little paunch. "I don't have an agent. If this idea is really as good as you say it is, why not just make it yourself like you have your other films and try to get it distributed on your own?"

"Because Xerxes *knows* people." He replaces the dull shirt in the closet and fishes around for something else. "And you gotta *know* people to get anywhere."

That's why none of his films since *One Chance, One World* have been distributed outside of New York. Ben's convinced that if Xerxes had gotten behind them they'd have been hits on the festival circuit, the way *One Chance* had been. Without Xerxes, Ben just didn't know the right people. Xerxes was based in New York, but he was affiliated with

William Fucking *Morris,* for God's sake, and flitted between the left and right coasts as often as most people crossed Fifth Avenue.

Ben remembers a time when Xerxes returned his calls. That was when Ben had been touted as a new young breakthrough, when *One Chance, One World* was the talk of the circuit. Xerxes took Ben with him to lunches with New Line execs. He invited Ben to parties at his posh house in Greenwich, where he'd stand eating herring on a cracker between Danny DeVito and Jessica Lange. Once Xerxes had even introduced him to Jane Campion, but Ben had been too dry mouthed to make conversation.

Now the invites no longer arrive in the mail. The lunches have ceased. It's increasingly rare for Xerxes to return Ben's calls. Today's appointment was secured nearly three weeks ago.

"Things are constantly changing in the industry," Ben tells Rex, turning to look at him. "That's why I need an agent—why I need Xerxes. I'm not going to make a film funded by what's left over from my ad agency paycheck again."

Ben sighs. He turns back to his closet, riffles through the shirts hanging there. Some he's had since he was a teenager. He settles on a shirt Anita bought him for Christmas last year, a solid baby blue oxford.

"Much better," Richard agrees.

"You sound like my mother," Ben sighs.

"No one can sound like your mother," Rex tells him.

Ain't it the truth? How often Mom finds her way into the unlikeliest of moments. "Benjamin Cartwright," she's saying now. Ben's just a gangly teenager, and she's sitting in front of the television eating Drake's Coffeecake Juniors. "If you don't start taking care of yourself, no girl's ever gonna want to go out with you."

He peels off his T-shirt, slips on the oxford. "Anita likes me just the way I am," he tells Rex, buttoning the shirt.

"That's good," he says with a smile, "'cuz there's always Richard to reference."

"Richard's just a gay clone," Ben says. It's true: Richard started pumping iron five years ago, filling out his string bean Sheehan body quickly and with apparently very little effort. Richard looks good—Ben gives him that. His transformation had actually been a bit eerie to watch. They've got the same dimples, the same freckles on the shoulders, the same receding hairline. But when Ben looks at Richard he sees what he would look like cleaned up and beefed out: big rounded pectorals, chiseled abs, carefully contoured biceps and triceps. And styled hair, moisturized skin, and Versace shirts.

"Come on. We're going to be late if we're going to go uptown and then back," Rex says, looking at *his* watch now. "Remember we're meeting Richard and Anita at seven."

"They'll never be back by then. They went all the fuck way up to Buffalo."

"I told them we'd meet them at Big Cup at seven and decide about dinner."

"Well, it won't take me long with Xerxes." Ben pulls on his sneakers—worn, dirty—and laces them up. "I just want to present this new idea to him in person."

"And you're not going to tell me what it is?"

"You can hear it when I tell him." He stands. "Ready, Sexy Rexy?"

"You know I hate it when you call me that," he says.

"Make you a deal. If Xerxes likes this idea, I'll never call you that again."

If Xerxes likes this idea.

Ben likes to tell people he's an award-winning filmmaker. And he *is*, damn it. He *is*. His twenty-minute film, *One Chance, One World,* took second place in the very prestigious National Student Film Festival in 1989. So what if that was nearly a decade ago? He's made others—little, no-budget shorts that never really got seen, but he's *still* a filmmaker, damn it. Hey—Emily Dickinson never got *anything* published until after her death. Did that make her not a writer?

But she was busy, that little voice—Mom's?—says inside Ben's head. She was forever scribbling something down as she looked out that damn window of hers in Amherst. Meanwhile Ben hasn't worked on a film in almost a year.

He used to say he was determined to direct a major motion picture by the time he was thirty. When that milestone passed, he decided it hadn't been realistic, and has settled on forty instead. Now when he tells people his goal and lets on that he's just thirty-four, he can bask in their assurances that he still has plenty of time.

He had this great idea last summer. Rex would play a boy right off the bus from Arkansas, stepping wide-eyed into Times Square in New York, and Anita would play the prostitute who suckers him and then promptly falls for his innocence. But Xerxes—when Ben had finally been let in to pitch it to him—said it had been done, a million times, and there was no way he could get him any financing for it. "You'll have to raise the cash yourself, Benny Boy," he told him. "But if you believe in it, do it. Then we'll see what we can do."

Like so many of his ideas, however, this one evaporated in the late-night humidity of his cramped apartment in Hell's Kitchen during the dog days of August. He worked a goddamn nine-to-five job, after all, editing commercial videotape at Penn's Advertising Agency, and when he got home at night, he was tired. Damn tired.

"You know, I'm not some rich kid with a trust fund who can spend all day shooting and scrap whatever footage he doesn't want," Ben has bitched regularly to Anita. "I know plenty of those guys. I went to school with them. Annoying rich kids with pretension dribbling like snot out of their noses. They don't have to hold down a fucking goddamn boring full-time job just so they can pay the rent and buy groceries. They might cry poor, but Daddy's money will take care of them in a pinch."

Of course, it was *Ben's* daddy's money that had enabled him to go to NYU—but it only existed because Daddy had dropped dead, and his life insurance had been earmarked for Ben's and Richard's college education. Oh, had Mom ever squawked about *that:* "I can't *touch* the goddamn account. Can't even put on a new roof. It's all for you to waltz off to school with."

And Mom could never understand why he chose film school—could never see what possible benefits would come out of that. Making movies wasn't a *real* job to her. Not like journalism, the field Richard chose. Even after *One Chance, One World* came out and gotten some impressive media attention, Mom had just said, "I don't know, Benjamin. Maybe next time Richard can help you with the dialogue. He's the writer, after all."

Ah, what did Mom know? To her, Richard could do no wrong. That's because he's always indulged her. Watching those silly four o'clock movies with her back when they were in high school. And now—he was *killing* her, for God's sake! The last time they were all up in Chicopee with her, Richard brought her a goddamn *coconut creme pie* and she'd eaten practically *the whole thing* in fourteen-and-a-half-minutes. (Ben knows; he timed her.) "Let her be," Richard tells him. "Let her have some pleasures in life."

Yet Ben can't forget the taunts of his classmates: "Ben, son of Orca." Somehow the slurs were never directed at Richard. Mom would sit for hours on the overstuffed brown corduroy couch in the years after Dad died, the shades drawn, the living room dark and dusty. She said she liked it dark so she could see the television better. She'd always been addicted to the tube: she'd named her sons Benjamin Cartwright—after Lorne Greene on *Bonanza*—and Richard Kimble—after David Janssen on *The Fugitive.* And together they were Richard Benjamin, Mom's all-time favorite actor. (Of course, Benjamin became Ben, but Richard has stubbornly refused to be called Rich or Rick or—"heaven forbid," he's sniffed—*Dick*.)

Mom and Richard have always had this bond that excluded Ben. It was bad enough before Dad died, but afterward, Ben often felt outside, as if he had no one, no family. Mom and Richard would sit there together in the living room eating Devil Dogs and watching the soaps, crying over poor Nola on *The Guiding Light,* who finally got her comeuppance from that handsome Kelly Nelson but who was, down deep, just a scared little girl trying to find her way. That's what Mom would blather about at the dinner table. "Ah, you guys are full of shit," Ben would tell them on his way out to his afternoon paper route. Mom would snap that he should watch his mouth, that she didn't like boys who swore.

He'd been Dad's boy. He took some solace in that. It was a queer situation. Mom and Dad hadn't exactly had the most loving marriage. Way before Dad got sick, he started sleeping in the den, and he and Mom often went days seeming not to notice the other. Mom and Richard would be curled up on the couch watching soap operas, and Ben and Dad would be rebuilding an Oldsmobile in the garage. That was just the way it was in their house: two factions, two families, sharing little else than a toilet and a pot roast dinner on Sunday. When Dad died, Ben was like an expatriate, a man without a country. Mom and Richard still had each other; Ben felt he had no one.

Thank God for Dad's life insurance, Ben thinks. Without it, he and Richard would still be trapped back in Chicopee, watching their mother get fatter and fatter like a creature out of the mind of Lewis Carroll. *Thank God Dad got us out of there.*

Who'd have thought old Francis Xavier Sheehan would have had such foresight? Working in the rubber factory, he was determined that his boys would never have to follow in his grimy footsteps. His insurance policies—and numerous student loans—allowed the two working-class Sheehan boys of Chicopee, Massachusetts, to graduate from the Columbia journalism program and the New York University Film School.

But what good does a degree from NYU do you when you still have to make a living? "If I was in L.A., it'd be easier," Ben has said to friends when they ask how his film career is progressing.

"Then let's go," Anita has pleaded. "Let's move to Hollywood."

"Not yet, sweetheart," he's insisted. "Not until I can save up more cash, get a couple more pictures under my belt. You want to arrive in L.A. a *somebody.*"

He remembers the six months he spent in Los Angeles as a nobody.

Everyone back in New York had thought *One Chance, One World*—a quasidocumentary short about the nuclear arms race—would be Ben's ticket to fame. It won him second place in the National Student Film Festival, and that *did* entitle him to a six-month scholarship on various Hollywood lots. But bright young whiz kids are as plentiful as raw footage in Tinseltown—and most had far better connections than Ben. The first-place winner was given the rush—and was today a hotshot director for Disney—but Ben, as befit second place, was barely acknowledged. He usually stood at parties near the food so when no one was talking to him he could pretend to be one of the caterers.

Sure, he got what the festival organizers had promised: a seat in some planning sessions, perfunctory introductions to a handful of movers and shakers. He watched some pros at work: John Sayles making *Eight Men Out*, Wes Craven cutting *The Serpent and the Rainbow*. Then George Lucas's people had expressed possible interest in backing a full-length feature of *One Chance, One World*. There were a couple of heady meetings back and forth for a few days; this was when Xerxes signed Ben on as a client. "You're gonna be famous, kid," Xerxes promised him, and that was exactly what he wrote back home to Mom. Maybe, *finally,* Mom might acknowledge his potential the way she always had Richard's. He was going to be the kind of filmmaker he'd dreamed of becoming ever since he was a kid and would lie awake at night, annoying the shit out of Richard, reading interviews in *Cineaste* with Lindsay Anderson and Martin Scorsese.

But then, suddenly, the world shifted on its axis. The Berlin Wall came down and the Soviet Union went belly up. Lucas stopped returning Xerxes's calls. No one was interested in a picture on an arms race that wasn't racing anymore.

Ben has tried to come up with other ideas ever since. He and Anita got together after he'd placed an ad looking for an actress to play Queen Elizabeth I in a comic short he was sure would win all sorts of accolades. After auditioning her, he didn't think she was a very good actress—an opinion that's never wavered for him—but he *was* entranced by her bouncy walk, her incandescent smile, and her perky little tits. He'd always been a sucker for a pretty girl. Too many times he'd gotten distracted from his work by his latest love: a bankteller with green eyes, a Brazilian dancer, a waitress with a beauty mark like Cindy Crawford's, the barely legal intern at the ad agency. As many might have predicted, and many certainly did, the film on Queen Elizabeth only got as far as ordering the ruffles for the gowns. Ben blamed it on script problems with a collaborator, but in truth, he had lost the passion for the project—his perennial dilemma—and found it instead with Anita in bed.

*　　*　　*

"Ah, so I got *something* out of it anyway," Ben murmurs to himself.

"What's that?" Rex asks.

"Oh, nothing."

They're riding the subway up to Xerxes's office on the Upper West Side. Rex goes back to reading *Entertainment Weekly.* Ben studies his hands and reassures himself that *this time* he's hit solid gold. *This time* there would be no wasted months planning outlines he'd later crumple up and toss into the trash, no footage shot that he'd later scrap. "You need something more personal, more original," Xerxes has told him year after year. "Something like you did with *One Chance.*"

In that, he'd focused on a family: the father a raving hawk, the mother a bleeding-heart lib who gets caught up in the peace movement. The arms race is seen through their eyes, Reagan and Andropov and Dr. Helen Caldicott are heard through their ears. When—in the film's last five minutes—Ben created a montage of nuclear war, viewers saw the end of the world through the eyes of this family they'd come to identify with.

"Something like that," Xerxes had urged. "This is the era of *People* magazine, of *Hard Copy.* Give me a *person.* Make this *real.*"

Real. What the fuck did that mean? Oh, Ben imagines they'd all claim *Richard's* screenplay had been "real." Richard had written a screenplay a couple years ago about the AIDS epidemic based on a friend of his who had died, who'd suffered a lot and wasted down to nothing. He offered it to Ben. "Whaddya think, Ben? Think the Sheehan boys can work together?"

"AIDS is too big for me to tackle," Ben had said after reading Richard's script. "I'm not the director for it."

Richard had looked hurt. "You mean you don't like it?"

"It's just not for me," Ben had insisted.

And it wasn't, Ben thinks again now, as the subway lurches and screeches and the lights momentarily go out. He and Rex have never discussed Richard's screenplay. *Too touchy,* Ben thinks. Rex is HIV-positive, and Richard had written it during a time when Rex had been pretty sick. As therapy, Ben assumes.

But, hey, he thinks, *I can't be expected to be my brother's therapist. I just didn't like the script.*

He's sitting across from an old Chinese woman, who, when the lights come back on, is staring at him. Ben averts his eyes.

It wasn't for me, he thinks again. *It just wasn't.*

"I don't like diseases," he told Anita after he'd turned Richard down.

"I know," she answered, taking his hand.

His father had died of cancer, wasting away in front of all of them in that little house on the dead-end street in Chicopee. Mom had been no help at all—retreating into herself and her boxes of Hostess Cupcakes and Devil Dogs. Richard had railed against the injustice of it all, demanding that the doctors do more—but it had been *Ben* who had cleaned the bedpan and wiped his father's mouth when he couldn't keep his food down anymore. It had been *Ben* who'd been with him when he died.

I don't like diseases.

And damn Richard for thinking he could make it in Ben's world. Movies were *his* territory; did Ben try to write for *Vanity Fair?*

Okay, so maybe Richard's screenplay wasn't bad. It was . . . okay. It did have a lot going for it, and when Ben admits that to himself, he feels a little guilty about turning his brother down. *Maybe we could have done something together. Maybe even gotten past some of the shit that's been between us for so long . . . .*

"Give me something *personal,*" Xerxes had insisted.

The old Chinese woman is still staring at him.

"Okay," Ben says. "Just hear me out."

Xerxes Stavropoulous is leaning back in his chair, his feet up on his desk, his hands laced behind his curly black-haired head. Ben is standing in front of the desk like a stand-up comic trying out a new bit. Rex is sitting straight-backed in a chair against the wall, legs crossed, hands folded in his lap.

"I'm listening," Xerxes says.

"Marge Schott," Ben tells him.

"Marge who?"

"Marge Schott. The owner of the Cincinnati Reds. The one who made all those racist remarks and acts like a man."

He can't see Rex's reaction. He doesn't want to turn around to find out.

Xerxes leans forward, placing his hands in front of him on the glass top of his desk. "I know who Marge Schott is," he says.

"So I was thinking of doing kind of an up-close-and-personal look at her—maybe she'd even talk to me. You know, make her *real.* Show how racism affects baseball. You know, a whole look inside the culture of sports."

Xerxes is silent. Ben turns around to Rex, who just gives him a wan smile.

"Well, what do you guys think?"

"Well, I don't know, Ben," Xerxes says, stroking his short-cropped goatee. "I mean, isn't she kind of old news?"

"No, no. Well, sure, she hasn't made any headlines lately, but she's still the owner, and apparently she was never really sorry for what she said."

"She *does* look like a man," Rex says. "Is she a dyke?"

"I don't think so," Ben says, gesturing at him as if he's just made a pertinent point. "But that could be part of it. Why we'd even think such a thing. A whole exploration of gender and what we expect women and men to be. She swears and makes racist comments like any male owner."

Xerxes is quiet. He leans back in his chair, pulls out a box of cigars. He opens the lid, offers one to Ben, who shakes his head. "You mind?" he asks Rex.

"Actually, yes," Rex says, crossing his legs and placing his hands over his upturned knee. "Secondhand smoke, you know."

Xerxes sighs, says nothing, just puts the cigars away. "Benny Boy," he says at last. "You're still pulling out these die-hard liberal ideas, aren't you? You're a hippie out of his time."

He isn't really. Back in film school, he'd been a passionate leftie, but now he just wants to find something that will work. And what was wrong with that?

"I believe in the film's premise," Ben tells him.

"If you believe in it, then do it." Xerxes reaches over instinctively for a cigar to punctuate his pronouncement, but seems to remember Rex's objection and stops himself. "Do it, show me the finished product, and we'll see what we can do then."

"You don't think you can help me get any financing—"

"Look, Ben. I'm here to help you sell a finished product—"

"No, you're here to help me get my career going again."

Those were Anita's words. After all, she'd said, speaking from experience, what good was an agent who didn't push you? Who didn't *believe* in you?

Xerxes stands up. He fumbles for a pink hard candy in a dish on his desk. He unwraps it, pops it into his mouth. "I'm sorry if the Schott idea doesn't get me hard. Maybe I'm being shortsighted. But I just can't see anybody I know coming up with cash for it."

He comes around to the front of his desk. He leans against it, crossing his arms over his chest and looking at Ben. "Benny, let's face it. You've been flitting from one idea to the next for more than a year. You've got to pick an idea, stick with it, and do it."

"I've done that, and nothing I've done has gotten you hard."

"Keep trying."

"But I can't do something of quality without money."

Xerxes moves closer to him. Ben can smell the watermelon candy in his mouth. "The money will come when the idea comes from here." He taps Ben's chest.

He thinks this is the same old pattern, Ben realizes. *He thinks this idea will evaporate, too. That I'll forget about it in a few months. But I won't. This time it's the real thing.*

Then why hasn't he even told Anita about it? "Oh, Ben, let's just go to L.A.," she'd said just last night. "It'll be easier there."

You're holding her back, you know. It's Mom's voice. Or Richard's. Anita *should* be in L.A., where maybe she could make it on television or in the movies. The only reason she stays in New York is because of Ben.

He's well aware of her sacrifice. But he was also convinced that Anita's talent was minuscule. *So we should move to L.A. so she can get walk-ons on* The Nanny?

Anita knew the score. Moving to Hollywood guaranteed nothing. She'd been there before, given it her best shot. She was born up near Buffalo, but at age ten her divorced mother had taken her out to Hollywood, scandalizing their conservative Catholic relatives. Mrs. Murawski was determined her pretty little girl would make them both rich. Anita acted in a slew of commercials in the early 80s, most of which she still has on videotape: Prell shampoo, Burger King, Children's Tylenol. At eleven, she was one of the original Toys " Я " Us kids. At thirteen, she did a walk-on on *The Cosby Show.* At fourteen, she won her biggest part ever: a murdered teenaged streetwalker on *Miami Vice.*

She'd come back to New York only temporarily. Her father lived in Brooklyn. He had gotten sick—cancer, just like Ben's dad—and she wanted to be nearby in his last months. She did some acting off-off-Broadway, and answered Ben's ad for his abortive Elizabethan comedy. Their fathers' cancer had been a bond, although neither talked about it much. They moved in together. When her father finally died, Ben accompanied Anita to the funeral. He met all her clan. "When do you plan on getting married?" her mother's prune-faced aunt Trinka had asked. "We don't," Ben had answered honestly. Only later did he think maybe Anita had thought otherwise.

He expected she'd leave then, return with her mother to the west coast. But Mrs. Murawski was tired of the studio game; she told Anita she was on her own. Anita kept making vague plans to return, but she never left. It's been more than seven years now.

They've settled into a kind of mindless routine that neither talks much about, not even when Ben's old roving eye starts up again and

Anita discovers lipstick on his collar. She bore his indiscretion nobly, as if she were playing in a television movie, saying only, as she scrubbed the collar with Wisk, "Did you have to be so cliched?"

Ben will tell friends that, sure, they'd have it easier if they moved to L.A. "But who wants to *live* there?" he quickly adds. "What is L.A. anyway but smog, imported palm trees, and ex–East Coasters missing the snow at Christmastime?" Richard just griped that his brother was simply too scared to try.

Last week, Anita had dragged Ben to the Unitarian-Universalist church. A lot of actors and artsy folk go there on Sunday mornings, finding the Unitarians' free-and-easy approach to spirituality a refreshing change from the rigid religions of their childhood. No Jesus stuff or heavy incense or talk of sin, the kind of church Ben remembered all too well from back in Chicopee.

This day, the minister's words spoke to Ben in a way he hadn't expected. She told the parable of the Sufi trickster, Nasrudin, who was riding the train to the city. He'd lost his connecting ticket, and he'd become frantic, looking everywhere for it: under the seat cushions, in the seat pocket in front of him, in the aisle. Finally he leaned over to the man seated in front of him. "Sir," he asked, "have you seen a ticket up there? I may have dropped it. I have looked everywhere."

The man in front of him told him that there was no ticket there. "But," he asked, "have you looked in the front pocket of your jacket? People often place their tickets there—and never think to look in the most obvious place!"

Nasrudin merely scowled. "My good sir, don't you think I know that? But, sir, if I *do* look in my front pocket and the ticket isn't there, then I will have lost *all* hope."

But Ben won't give up hope this time, not even after he realizes that Xerxes has given him the brush-off. Again. He'd just have to find some way of raising the dough on his own.

Like holding up this goddamn gay cafe at gunpoint.

"Well, you were right," Rex says, looking at his watch. "They're late."

"Buffalo's a long way away," Ben says grumpily.

They both sip their lattes in silence for a few minutes. Rex still hasn't said anything about the Marge Schott idea since they left Xerxes's office. He's reading *H/X*, a gay newspaper with lots of pictures of buffed-up men without shirts, and Ben wonders if he's trying to avoid talking about it. The cafe is very bright—Ben prefers his coffeehouses, like his coffee, dark—and it's filled with shaved-headed muscle boys. There's only one woman in the entire room, a Gen-Xer with short green hair and eyebrow rings. Ben assumes she's a lesbian. He can't wait for Anita to get there.

"I'm thinking of calling it *Hard Ball,*" Ben says, referring to his film idea.

Rex laughs. "I think I made a picture by that name back in my porno days."

"You can't copyright titles." He's determined to get Rex's approval. "I want to intercut it with actual footage of Schott with actors as ballplayers and fans. They can react to what she says. That way I can get a dialogue about racism and gender and the sports culture going." Rex's eyes betray no reaction one way or another. "You see? It can be *personal.* It can be *real.*"

Ben pushes away at the doubt that nags at him like a pesty fly. *This is timely, this is relevant,* he tells himself. *This is sexy. This will get me noticed.*

You're just lucky you got a brother like Richard, Benjamin.

Mom again.

Richard's got a good head on his shoulders. You listen to him.

"So whaddya think, Rex? What do you think Richard will—"

But it's too late. He sees Rex's eyes move toward the door and the smile that spreads across his face. "Here they are," he says, waving to catch the attention of Anita and Richard.

Richard. He's here. No more holding it back from him. Ben would know soon enough what his brother thought of his idea.

Why should that matter so? What was it about his goddamn twin brother? Ben might resent Richard, but he also crazily wanted his approval. Back in high school, Ben would secretly glow if Richard, who always got the better grades, said something—*anything*—about one of Ben's oral reports. "That was interesting," Richard once said after Ben had made a presentation on auto racing. He'd beamed all day.

When Richard, who had more friends, would occasionally invite Ben along on some outing, it always made Ben feel good. Not that he often went—he had his paper route every afternoon or else he just preferred to hang back and not try to keep up with the banter among Richard's groupies—but he was always so grateful to be asked. It made him angry—*furious*—when he'd think about it later on, how much he craved Richard's approval, how thankful he was for scraps.

Richard was a goddamn golden boy. There's no explaining golden boys; they just appear, and they go through life with the world at their feet. Richard had a steady string of pretty girlfriends—Ben had none—

even if he later claimed to have known all along that he was gay. He was voted Most Handsome in their senior class—a slap at Ben if there ever was one, given that they were identical twins.

There's always been this dividing line between them, as real as the line of chalk Richard had drawn down the center of their bedroom one day when they were ten. "That's your side of the room, and this is mine," he'd announced. Ben had just shrugged and called him an asshole. Today he thinks it a might fine idea indeed. *You stay on your side, and I'll stay on mine.*

Ben watches his brother make his way through the crush of muscle boys. They all seem to know him, call out his name. He waves, blows a few kisses.

Anita's behind him. "Do we have a story for you!" she sings.

"You're late," Ben says, giving her a quick kiss. She sits down next to him.

Richard follows, sliding in next to Rex and nuzzling him behind the ear. "It's good to be back, Nooker," he says. Ben makes a face: *Nooker* is what Richard calls Rex, and they won't ever reveal what it means. "What a drive all the way back from Buffalo."

"So how was Uncle Stan?" Rex asks.

Anita looks over at him with tired eyes. "Uncle Stan is dead," she says. Then both she and Richard start laughing.

"Dead?" Rex repeats. "You mean you got all the way up there and—"

"And the old guy was history," Richard finishes, standing back up. "What do you want, Neet? I'll go up to the counter."

"A mochacinno," she says. Richard nods, heading off to place their order.

"So what a waste of time, huh?" Rex asks.

"Not exactly," she says.

Ben senses something in her tone. "What do you mean, not exactly?" he asks.

She grins over at him. "We have an idea for you, sweetheart."

Ben pulls back just a little. "What do you mean, an idea for me?"

"Now don't go getting all defensive," she says.

"Ben's got his own idea," Rex tells her. "We went to see Xerxes today."

She looks at Ben. He can see a little hurt in her eyes. "Why didn't you tell me?"

"It's just that—well, it's still taking shape."

Richard's returned with Anita's mochacinno and his own cup of coffee, dark black. Anita thanks him, takes a sip. Ben watches her intently.

"Did you tell him?" Richard asks.

"No," Anita says.

Ben ignores whatever's on their minds. "So you didn't see Uncle Stan at all?"

"Just his body," Anita says quietly. "And I even said a prayer. I told the nun in charge to tell Aunt Trinka, who was on her way up."

"Oh, God. Did you see her?"

"No," Anita says. "We made it out just in time." The week after *One Chance, One World* got written up in the *Times*, Aunt Trinka's only comment was: "Too many pinko films already."

"Excuse me," a man says, bending down at their table. They all look up at him. "Are you two . . . brothers?"

It's a good-looking muscle boy in a white-rib tank. He hovers over their table with a quizzical expression on his face. Ben notices Richard spark right up. What was it about gay men that made them always on the ready?

"Twins," Richard says, and Ben detects his brother's chest swelling out.

"*No*," says the muscle boy in disbelief, looking back and forth between them—but mostly at Richard. He balances an enormous cup of coffee in his palm. "Both gay?"

"Ben hasn't come out yet," Rex interjects, and they all laugh—Richard and the muscle boy especially, eyes still locked—in that annoying way gay guys laugh together.

"Oh, no, not my Benny," Anita chimes in, grabbing his arm and pulling him in for a kiss. "He's one of the last of the original straight men."

"Yeah, like Abbott for Costello," Richard jokes.

Ben just grins.

"Nature versus nurture," the muscle boy says, shrugging as he moves on.

As if he even knows what that means, Ben thinks. *Ditz head.*

"What is it with gay guys these days?" Ben asks. "Do you all have to have seventeen-inch biceps to be admitted into the club?"

"No," Richard says, deadpan. "I think they'll let you in with sixteen." He winks. "Let's see," he says, raising Ben's arm.

"Cut it out," Ben snaps, pulling his arm back. "Why don't you go follow muscle head over there and deconstruct Judy Garland films?"

Rex laughs. "Hey, Ben," he says, "speaking of Judy, I've got a great idea. *Seriously.* What about doing something on a star who died mysteriously? People like that kind of thing. Hollywood scandal and intrigue. Like Marilyn."

"She's been done to death," Richard says. "Excuse the pun."

"Then Jean Harlow," Rex says. "Or, I know—Thelma Todd."

"Who's she?" Anita asks.

Rex's eyes glow. He leans across the table toward Ben. "Thelma Todd would be *perfect*. She was killed by gangsters back in the thirties. Gorgeous blonde. Funny, too. You could get clips from her films—"

"Rex," Ben says, exhausted, "how timely is that? Who'd care about some old forgotten film star?"

He shrugs. "I would." He gets campy, swishing an invisible cigarette between his fingers as if he were Bette Davis. "*Lots* of us remember Thelma Todd. *Lots* of us!"

"Well, that's the gist of the idea we had," Anita says. "Will you at least hear us out, Ben?"

He sighs. "Go ahead."

"It'd be a documentary on *life*." Anita sounds like Richard. "On *living*. On what living does to a person. About all the different lives we lead in the course of one long life."

"I'm not sure I follow," Ben says.

"I like it," Rex offers. Ben shoots him a look.

"Just listen, Ben. We found the perfect subject. We met her today at St. Mary's. She's one hundred and *six*. Sharp as anything. *Sharper*. She's wild. She's hot. She's—"

"A former actress," Richard tells Rex, looking over at his lover.

"Really? From what?"

"Vaudeville, I guess," Anita says. "We didn't get all the details. But she started telling us some stories about her days on the stage, about one-legged acrobats and singers—she's so sharp, so spunky. She whistled for us!"

"Whistled?" Rex asks.

"Yeah, that's what she did as a little girl on the stage." Richard laughs. "It was amazing. What did they call her again?"

"The Baby Whistler or something," Anita says. "Anyway, her name is Florence Bridgewood, and she's perfect, Ben. Just *perfect*."

She looks at him. He doesn't respond. He just looks back at her. "Thanks, hon," he says at last. "But I'm sticking with Marge Schott."

"Marge Schott?" Anita asks.

"Marge Schott?" Richard repeats.

Ben sighs, picks up his coffee cup, sees that it's empty, then puts it down. "Look, I'm sure your old actress is a fascinating old lady, but I want to make a *splash* here. This isn't my first film. I need a major follow-up to *One Chance*—I have to go high profile. Something that's going to get *noticed*."

Anita sighs, sounding like the air rushing from a deflated tire.

"I appreciate the suggestion, though," Ben says. "I really do. It's a good idea for an article. But not a documentary. Marge Schott—now *there's* a topic. Her name's been in all the papers. I mean, who the hell is Florence Bridgewood?"

"That's what *I'm* wondering," Rex says quietly. Ben looks over at him. He seems lost in thought. "What did you say they called her on the stage?"

"The Baby Whistler," Anita says.

"No, no," Richard says. "That's not it. Baby Flo—that's what they called her."

"Baby Flo," Rex repeats as if trying it out in his mind. "The Child Wonder Whistler."

"Yeah," Richard says, looking over at him. "That's *it*. How'd you know?"

"Have you heard of her?" Anita asks.

"I've seen the name," Rex says, thinking. Then he seems to remember where and laughs. "But, no, it can't be her. Can't be the one I'm thinking of."

"Why not?" Anita asks.

"Because Baby Flo, the Child Wonder Whistler, has been dead for more than fifty years." He grins. "She grew up to be the world's first movie star, and she killed herself after her career faded. She took poison, I think. Ant paste or something like that."

"That's horrible," Anita says, recoiling. "Well, this woman was very much alive."

"What was her last name again?" Rex asks.

"Bridgewood."

"Florence Bridgewood," Rex says more to himself than anyone else. "I'll look her up when I get home later. I'll report back what I find out."

"Well, tell *her*," Ben says, pointing to Anita. "Because I want to be clear with you all. This isn't my story."

Richard smirks. "We heard you, Ben. Loud and clear."

New Year's Day, 1939

She was my first friend in my new life. Her name was Doris, and I thought she was beautiful.

"Jeepers" was her first word to me. I looked up into great saucers for eyes, deep brown like the coffee she poured for me. "You sure look like you've been through the wringer."

I imagined I did indeed look that way. For the briefest of seconds, I averted my eyes. Might she recognize me? *Don't be silly, Flo,* I told myself. *She's not going to recognize you. She's far too young.*

"You all right, honey?" she asked, leaning in toward me.

I was sitting on a stool in the roadside diner where she worked. I can still smell the strong coffee brewing on the stove, the wafting cinnamon of fresh-baked doughnuts.

I glanced up at the mirror behind the counter. The left side of my face was sunburned. My nose was crusty with blood. My hair was windswept. My dress was torn—I'd pinned it together with a safety pin I'd miraculously found in my purse—and dirty with sand. My calves and shins were scraped.

"Yes," I told her. "I'm all right."

And I was. Really, I was. Sitting there, drinking coffee, still alive—that *proved* I was all right. I'd followed the road along the coast, always heading north. I accepted no more rides, just kept walking. I stopped to rest only when my legs felt as if they'd burn off, and I ate only at night, from trash cans that stood behind people's houses. Once a man spotted me and shooed me away from his back porch as if I were some stray cat. I slept on the beach, shivering, covering myself with an old tarp that had once wrapped somebody's boat. I urinated under piers; I drank water from an old rusty faucet. None of it caused me to ponder; I felt no irony in who I had been and what I had become. I had stopped thinking. I processed none of it, not once feeling even slightly afraid or sorry for myself. How many days passed I wasn't sure. Not until the morning I stumbled into Doris's diner did I finally lift my eyes up from the ground and take a good look at where I was.

The clock on the wall read ten o'clock. There was no one else in the diner but me.

"I've given you some extra toast," Doris said, setting a plate of scrambled eggs and bacon in front of me. "Looks like you could use it."

I smiled up at her in gratitude.

"Too much partyin' last night, huh?" she asked, clearly curious about this strange old creature that sat before her. She leaned on the counter with her elbows, staring at me.

I wasn't sure what she meant, so I just smiled at her again.

"I knew I'd get a few stragglers from the party over at the Rotarians' club," she said, narrowing her eyes. "When I opened at five, there was already a line. Folks so hungover they could drink six cups of black coffee and still stagger out of here. Nobody since then, though. Everybody's sleeping it off. Me, I just went to bed at nine-thirty. Why bother waiting up till twelve? What's the big deal with midnight anyway? It's just another day."

"So," I said, realizing it for the first time, "it's . . . New Year's Day."

She looked at me in puzzlement. "Gosh, I guess you *did* have a *real* swell time last night."

I laughed, just a little. "It's my birthday," I said. Just a week ago I had dreaded this day—but now that it was here, it made me feel giddy. Alive.

She raised her coffee cup in salute. "A New Year's baby, huh?"

"Mother always said I waited until one minute after midnight." I smiled.

"Well, I won't even ask you how old you are, so don't worry about that."

I observed her. Thirty, maybe. But with *years* added around her eyes. She might have been as old as I was if you just looked at her eyes.

"All that matters is I've crossed the line of forty," I told her. "That's the line in the sand for women. Before that, you can rely on Max Factor. After forty, you're responsible for your own face."

"Well, you've got a good face," she told me. She startled me with her assessment. I managed a small smile.

"So you had *double* reason to celebrate last night," she went on. "Well, good for you. Me, I just went to bed." Yes, her eyes revealed how tired she was. "Besides, I had to get up early and come in here. Where'd you blow in from?"

Her eyes. So dark. She might have been Mexican.

"Hollywood," I told her.

She smiled queerly at me. "That's a long drive from here."

"No," I said, weakly lifting a forkful of eggs to my mouth. "I walked."

"*Walked?*" She backed away from me. "Honey, Hollywood's almost a hundred miles away."

"Yes, I know," I said quietly. "I'm going to San Francisco."

"San Francisco?" She ran her hands over her black hair, whch was wrapped in a white hair net. "Lady, you can't walk to San Francisco."

"No," I agreed. I snapped open my purse, which sat beside me on the counter. I took out the gold pocket watch. "I aim to pawn this to buy a bus ticket."

She squinted at it. "Is it real gold?"

"I'm not sure," I admitted, "but I imagine it is."

"How long have you been walking?"

"A few days."

"A few days." She sighed, shaking her head. "And your birthday, too. Why don't you go to the little girls' room and wash up? There are some clean towels on the shelf over the sink. I'll keep your breakfast hot."

I did as she suggested. The water felt good against my face. I combed my hair roughly with my fingers, peering hard into the mirror. I tried to sear my memory with my appearance, to remember always what I looked like in that moment.

It worked. I have never forgotten that face.

"My name's Doris," she told me when I came out and took my seat again at the counter. She had refilled my coffee cup. She poured herself some more too, and came around to sit on the stool beside me. I finished my breakfast. Nothing has ever tasted better, before or since. Not the sumptuous feasts Mr. Laemmle wooed me with. Not the elaborate dinners prepared by Charles's cook or the elegant banquets on the *S.S. Olympic*. This was by far my greatest feast: slightly runny, very yellow scrambled eggs and four crispy strips of salty bacon.

"I'm Flo," I told her.

When I first sat down, when my mind first began to think again, I had decided I needed a new name. I had even started rolling over a few of them in my mind—but when Doris told me her name, I responded without thinking, telling her the truth. I had many last names to choose from, but I'd always been Flo.

"Well, Flo," Doris said, peering close again, "I think you're going to need a little more than what you'll get from hocking that pocket watch."

"It's a start," I told her.

She grinned. Dark eyes, olive skin. Her nails were painted scarlet and chipped; she wore no lipstick. Her ears were pierced with small gold studs. She chewed gum.

"You runnin' from somebody? Don't have to tell me if you are. I've seen a lot of desperate folks come through here. Husbands that can't find jobs who've taken off and left the little lady and kiddies behind. Times are tough." Doris stood, cleared away my plate. I wiped my mouth with a napkin. "And gals like you," she said, looking back at me from the sink, "always running from somebody who did 'em wrong."

"No one did me wrong," I said, again without thinking.

Doris folded her arms across her chest. Her forearms were covered with soft dark hair. "Well, no matter. But like I said, you're gonna need more than what you can get for that watch."

I nodded. "Do you know where I could sell it?"

"Yeah. There's a fella coming around in a bit. Hang around until then."

She moved off to take the order of two newcomers: a man and a woman, presumably married, well dressed, who had stepped inside the diner to the cheery ring of the bell over the door. They were laughing, sparkling even—celebrating the first day of the new year. I watched them for a bit, the easy way they touched each other, the comfortable silence that settled over them after Doris had moved away. There was no need for extraneous conversation. He helped her off with her coat. She wore her hair the way Ginger Rogers did, curled up on top and long in the back. They sat in a booth, both on one side.

I sipped my coffee. I stared back at my reflection in the mirror. I'd gotten some of the blood off, and my hair looked a trifle better. But my dress was still dirty and soiled. The stains of blood and vomit were now covered by a gritty film of sand.

At the end of the counter were some old newspapers, folded and slipped between the big black cash register and the glass doughnut case. I reached over and pulled one out, opening it in front of me. *The Los Angeles Examiner.* It was dated December 29.

I was just trying to wile away the time, waiting for the man Doris said might buy the pocket watch. I don't think I expected to see what I did there in the newspaper.

FIRST GREAT FEMININE FILM STAR A SUICIDE

Front page.
I'd made the front page.
The headline continued:

FLORENCE LAWRENCE ENDS LIFE WITH POISON IN HOLLYWOOD HOME AFTER LONG CAREER

And there was my face, staring up at me from the counter, perfectly framed in an iris. I pulled the paper closer. It wouldn't do for Doris to recognize me. But I didn't look like that—not anymore. The caption read:

THE BIOGRAPH GIRL—IN HER DAYS OF GLORY

I'd made the front page.
"Oh, dear God," I said, and the words seemed to blur together as I tried to read.

> *Impoverished and dogged by ill health, Florence Lawrence,*
> *first great feminine star of the films, drank ant poison and ended*
> *her life in her West Hollywood home yesterday. Miss Lawrence*
> *had collapsed when an ambulance arrived before her home at 532*
> *Westbourne Drive and took her to Beverly Hills Receiving*
> *Hospital.*
> *There Dr. Lester Slocum applied a stomach pump and*
> *antidotes to no avail. Miss Lawrence died an hour later, at*
> *3:10 P.M.*

"Oh, dear, oh, dear, oh—" I couldn't go on reading.
Doris's voice: "Honey, are you all right?"
But it was as if she were miles away. I covered my face with my hands.
"Oh, dear God," I cried. "Molly!"
I passed out, falling hard from the stool to the floor.

"Flo! Flo!"
In the swirling darkness, it was my mother calling to me. We were in St. Louis, and she was snapping a horrible vial of ammonia under my nose. It was only a matter of seconds that I was out, but in that time, I became utterly convinced I was back in St. Louis on the platform of Union Station, and Mother was there, and Harry, too—

But this wasn't my mother. This was Doris, and it was the scent of coffee that awakened me—coffee and something else even more pleasant. Doris's perfume.

"Get her some water," Doris was instructing the well-dressed man, who stood over me with his wife, staring down with startled looks on their faces. It took him a second to obey her command, but then he moved off with a sudden burst of energy.

"Here," Doris said, when the man had returned with a glass. "Drink this, honey."

She was cradling my head in the crook of her arm, supporting my back with her strong hand. I tasted the water. It was cool and clear, and it revived me immediately.

"I'm fine," I insisted, attempting to stand up.

"You're going to sit over here," Doris told me, helping me over to a booth. I slid in along the blue leather seat. I tried to sit up straight, but found I needed to rest my head against the back. My skin was warm and clammy.

"Flo, I'm going to call a doctor," Doris whispered to me.

"No," I said. "No doctor. I'll be fine."

She looked at me with those great dark eyes. "Sister, you need some rest, a good bath, and maybe a doctor's attention."

"I need to get to San Francisco," I said.

She just shook her head. "What's there? Why can't it wait?"

The man and his wife were eager to get out of there. He coughed behind Doris to get her attention. "How much do we owe?" he asked.

She hurried over to the cash register and took their money. They departed as quickly as they could. I heard the engine of their car start, the crunching of gravel as they backed out of the lot and found the road again. Doris returned and sat across from me in the booth.

"You in trouble with the law?"

I considered the question. I averted her gaze. "No," I answered finally. "I don't believe I am."

She looked at me intently. "What are you running from then?"

"Just myself." I met her eyes, then smiled.

She smiled too. "Guess I can understand. Did some running of my own a while back." She shook a cigarette out of a pack she held in her front pocket. She offered me one, which I gladly accepted. She put both between her lips and lit them with one match, handing mine to me across the table. I inhaled, the delicious taste of tar and smoke reviving me even more than the water.

We smoked in silence for a few minutes. "Who's Molly?" she asked.

"Just a girl," I said.

She nodded. We were quiet a few more minutes. "You sure you don't need to see a doctor?" she asked.

"Not sure," I said, exhaling smoke in rings the way Ducks had taught me. "But for now, I don't want a doctor. I've got my reasons."

"You've got to get out of those clothes," Doris said. "Looks like you got sick all over your blouse."

I stubbed the cigarette out in an ashtray.

"Can you walk?" she asked.

"I think so." My feet and calves ached, but I stood up, gathered my balance and followed Doris into the back room. There, she gave me a new blouse and brassiere, a fresh pair of panties and a different dress. There was a small tub, and she drew some water for me to bathe in. She took my torn underwear, stained with dried brown blood, held them in her hand and looked at them, then tossed them into the trash.

"How much will you give her for it?"

When I came back into the diner, Doris was leaning across the counter toward a rotund man with a cigar clenched between his teeth. The man was turning the pocket watch over in his plump pink hands.

"Don't try to con her, Winnie," Doris told him. "I'll know if you do."

He grinned, turning to me. "Are you our mystery lady?"

"There's no mystery to me," I told him, sitting down beside him on the next stool. "Not any more than most women."

He was young. Late twenties, I presumed. Quite fat, maybe three hundred pounds. He seemed to perch precariously on his stool. He smoked a foul-smelling cigar and wore a bright red necktie and a wrinkled, peach-colored suit. His broad-brimmed hat sat on the counter beside his sandwich. He was dangling the watch in front of his face, squinting at it.

"Five dollars," he said finally.

"Winnie, give the damn thing back to me," Doris said.

He looked hurt. "All right. Seven."

"Make it ten and you have a deal," I said. Doris looked over at me, a little surprised, then turned her gaze back at him.

He sniffed, plopping the watch down on the counter, and reached for his wallet inside his coat. He produced a ten dollar bill and handed it to me.

"Just a minute," Doris said, snatching the bill and holding it up to the light. She narrowed her eyes at it. Apparently satisfied, she handed it over to me.

"Thank you," I said.

"So," the man said, raising a corner of his ham and cheese sandwich to his mouth, "what's your name?"

"I told you," Doris said. "That's Flo."

"Flo what?" he asked, chewing.

For a second, I was frightened. Did he recognize me? My hair was combed now, my face washed, the caked blood scraped out of my nostrils. "Flo Bridgewood," I said at last, choosing the least traceable of my names.

"Bridgewood," he repeated. "Not from around here?"

"Originally from Canada," I told him. It wasn't necessary to lie, not when there were so many truths to pick from.

"Well, Miss Bridgewood, allow me to introduce myself. I am Winston Pichel, and my good friend Doris here tells me you are heading to San Francisco."

"That's right."

"Well, perhaps I can save you bus fare, my good lady. I am heading there myself."

"Thank you, but I think I'll purchase my own ticket."

Doris refilled my cup with coffee. She winked at me in sisterly camaraderie, then moved out into the kitchen through the swinging doors, leaving us alone.

"Well," Winston Pichel shrugged, raising his own cup to his lips, pinky extended, "have it your way." He set his cup back down, patted his mouth precisely with his napkin. He lit another cigar and looked over at me. "I called you 'Miss' earlier. Should that have been 'Mrs.?'"

"Doesn't matter. I'm divorced."

"Ah," he said, eyes lighting up. "A divorcée."

I studied him. "And are *you* married, Mr. Pichel? No, I don't imagine you are." I smiled. "You're a homosexual."

He looked stunned. Remembering the look on his face, the pallor that suddenly washed over his complexion, I don't think he was upset so much by my guessing the truth, but rather by the way I'd snatched control of the conversation right from under his cigar.

"You needn't worry," I told him, still smiling. "I've nothing against homosexuals. Been around them most of my life, in fact. Your secret, such as it is, is safe with me."

He seemed to gather his wits. "My dear lady, I am highly offended—"

I laughed. "Don't be. If you choose, forget I said a word. Tell me all about your wife back in Toledo, the one whose picture you no doubt carry in your wallet, and I'll believe you if you want me to. Tell me how much you miss her since you spend so much time on the road, selling whatever it is that you sell, eating your dinners in lonely roadside diners such as this, even on New Year's Day." I leaned in closer to him and whispered, "What would you say if I told you I'd seen Clark Gable in his skivvies?"

"I'd say you were mad." He took a long puff on his cigar in an almost defiant gesture.

"On second thought, Mr. Pichel," I said, smiling again, "maybe I *will* take you up on your offer for a ride. Can always use this ten spot for cigarettes and coffee."

He was looking deeply into my eyes. "Who *are* you, Florence Bridgewood?"

I laughed. "That, my friend, is what I'm aiming to find out."

"You plan on making it on your own in San Francisco?"

"Looks as if she's been making it on her own for some time," Doris said, coming back out from the kitchen and lighting another cigarette for me.

I inhaled it deeply, then let out the smoke and looked Winnie in the eyes. "I've still got everything I had twenty years ago," I told him, then grinned over at Doris. "Just a little lower—that's all."

Doris laughed. "I like you, Flo. Too bad I'm not going with you."

What keeps her here? What keeps so many people rooted to the spot?

She was my first friend in my new life. I never saw her again after that day, but she was the one who made everything that came after possible. *I like you, Flo,* she'd said.

When I went to pay her for my breakfast with the few dollars I had in my purse, she held up her hand. "Consider it a birthday gift, honey. I remember my own running days all too well."

Outside Winston Pichel was revving up his shiny red convertible. "Ready, Mystery Lady?"

"As I'll ever be," I said. He reached across the seat to hold open the door for me. I slipped in beside him. "When I was a girl," I told him, "we were always on the road. We had a motto. 'Look ahead a little, and gamble a lot.'"

He grinned at me.

I held my purse securely in my lap. "Drive on, Mr. Pichel," I told him. "Drive on."

The Present

"If you see a McDonald's, stop," Richard says, looking up from the papers on his lap.

"Uh, hel-*lo*, Mr. Bodybuilder. Fat and cholesterol check," Anita says. She's driving Richard's car, a '94 Saab Turbo convertible, top up, because it had looked like rain when they set out. Richard had asked her to drive because he wanted a chance to read over all the materials Rex had found for him. He's been absorbed by them ever since they left the city at six A.M., but now suddenly he's lifted his face from his lap and become interested in food.

"Oh, please, *tell* me about it," Rex says from the backseat. "Honey, really—*McDonald's?* You won't even let me make fish sticks for supper anymore. Used to be your favorite. Mrs. Paul's, baked beans, and Tater Tots."

Richard grins. "That was what Mom used to make Ben and me every Friday." He pats his stomach, flat as a plain in Iowa. "But beauty *does* require sacrifice."

"So *McDonald's?*" Anita asks. "What're you gonna eat? Just the sesame-seed bun?"

"I'm just *really* hungry," Richard laments. "I'd eat an Egg McMuffin at this point. We should've stopped before we left the city."

"I just want to make sure we get to Buffalo early enough," Anita says. "This interview could go on for a while. I don't want to drive back when it's dark."

"I'll drive, I'll drive," Richard promises. "Where are we now?"

Rex is playing navigator. He hauls up the Allstate Motor Club Road Atlas, crinkling its pages as he seeks out their place. "Heading into Elmira," he says.

Anita nods. "Okay. We can stop for a quick bite there."

Outside, the gray asphalt of the metro area has given way to soft golden hills and miles of orange maple trees stretching into the horizon.

The threat of rain is gone. It's a screamingly beautiful autumn day, the scents of burning leaves and apples and fresh-cut hay in the air.

"You finding anything in those photocopies I made for you, hon?" Rex asks, leaning over the seat to rest his chin on Richard's shoulder.

"Hard to say, Nooker," Richard tells him. "I mean, it *can't* be. But still . . ."

Ever since they'd told him about Flo, Rex had had a hunch he'd heard of her. "Baby Flo, the Child Wonder Whistler," he'd mused out loud, leafing through the tattered old movie books he'd had since he was a kid. They were stacked in two bookcases and piled high along the walls in his and Richard's second bedroom, a room Richard had converted into a writing space. "Let me see, Baby Flo, Baby Flo . . ." Rex had said, researching.

"It can't be the same person," he'd said after about an hour as he handed Richard three books with pages marked. "But read for yourself."

Sitting on Richard's lap now were several photocopied pages. The first one read:

FLORENCE LAWRENCE. Born 1890, Hamilton, Ontario, Canada. The first performer to have her name revealed to the public, making her the world's first movie star in 1910. Began career on stage in vaudeville and touring companies as a child, being billed as Baby Flo, the Child Wonder Whistler. She worked for Edison, Vitagraph, and finally Biograph under D.W. GRIFFITH, where she obtained international fame as "The Biograph Girl." Lured by CARL LAEMMLE to his independent film company, IMP, in 1910, she began being billed under her real name, thus launching the STAR SYSTEM. Her career declined in the midteens. Forgotten by the industry she had helped to create, she was put on the payroll at MGM as an act of charity. She killed herself by swallowing ant paste in 1938.

All of the entries on Florence Lawrence read the same, with just scraps of information on who this woman was. "It *can't* be the same person," Richard echoes now.

"No way," Anita agrees.

"It's pretty weird, though," Rex says, leaning over the seat, hands folded under his chin. "You gotta admit that."

"It's *definitely* weird," Anita says.

"I mean, everything fits. The Child Wonder Whistler. The age. That she was born in Canada."

"Maybe she knew her," Richard says. "Maybe there's—some connection."

"Maybe she didn't really die," Anita offers, switching on the radio. Sheryl Crow warbles about all she wants to do is have some fun. "Maybe it's been a mistake all these years."

"You've been watching too many soap operas," Richard scolds. "Or acting in them."

Anita pouts. "I didn't get the part," she tells them.

"On *All My Children?* Aw, Neet," Rex commiserates.

Richard smirks. "Hey, don't feel so bad. Maybe you can play Marge Schott."

Anita glares over at him. "Can you *believe* he really wants to do that?" That's all the excuse she needs to go off on Ben. "I mean, *really*. He's had some lame ideas in the past, but *this* one—" She sighs as if she's not sure whether she should continue, but decides to plow on. "It's getting hard, guys. It's getting really hard."

"What are you going to do?" Richard asks.

"I don't know." Her voice has dropped and her lips have pursed; Richard detects the little sad lines that creep in around her eyes. They make her look old. She looks old whenever she talks about Ben these days.

"I love him," she's saying. "I'll never stop. But he just can't seem to get it together. If he were happy just editing those video commercials over at the ad agency, I wouldn't care if he *never* made another film. But he's *not* happy. Not content. And it's hard to wake up to that, day after day after day."

"My brother has *never* been content," Richard says. "But he's never had the wherewithal to do anything about it either."

"Who knows?" Rex sighs. "Maybe we'll all be sitting with egg on our faces a year from now when he accepts the Academy Award for best documentary for *Hard Ball*."

Richard scoffs. Sheryl Crow sings about the sun coming up over Santa Monica Boulevard.

"Hey, there's a Mickey D's," Richard calls out. "Pull off and let's eat."

He gripes about all the grease, of course, but scarfs down his hash browns in about two bites. He doesn't talk much, doesn't hear Anita going on and on about how unhappy Ben is, how goddamn stubborn he is. He doesn't need to hear—he knows it all already. Instead, he keeps studying the photocopies.

Florence Lawrence. Florence Bridgewood.

They pile back into the Saab and continue on. It's such pretty country, the hills now fall away into sharp-cut gorges. It's about as far away from the hardscrabble terrain of Hollywood that one could get. What would an old movie actress be doing out here? The very idea is absurd.

It doesn't matter. Richard doesn't need her to be anything other than what she is: a great old lady with a sharp mind and wit. It'll be a fantastic interview. What are the paths taken over a long life? How does one start from one place and end up in another? What happens in between? What gets left behind?

But still, if there's a connection . . .

They arrive in Buffalo a little before noon. "There it is," Anita says, coming round the bend. St. Mary's looms through the trees. The day has darkened again; rainclouds obscure the sun.

"It looks like something out of *Dark Shadows,*" Rex says in a hushed voice.

"Tell us about it," Richard agrees, grinning.

They park the Saab in the lot. There are five cars already there: four big black shiny Buicks—and one aquamarine Bel-Air, circa 1957. Convertible.

"Wonder who owns *that?*" Anita asks.

"Probably Flo," Richard quips.

From the backseat, Anita gathers the bouquet of black-eyed Susans they've brought for Flo. "Well," she chirps, "let's go get her."

They make their way up the walk and climb the front steps. Once more the great bell reverberates inside the walls. Again old Sister Augustine opens the door and welcomes them. "Oh, Flo's got *bows* in her hair just for you." She smiles, her ancient face crinkling in a thousand directions when she smiles.

"Geez," Rex gushes to Richard, looking around at the chandelier and marble floor and gold-gilt banister. "What *is* this? Buckingham Palace?"

"At least the Church is putting the collection plate to good use for a change," Richard whispers. They follow Sister Augustine up the stairs.

Sister Jean is standing in front of the day room to greet them. Richard thinks she looks particularly bright and pretty today: a yellow blouse and a blue wraparound skirt, her cheeks flushed high and her face free of makeup. "Good morning, Ms. Murawski," she says, shaking Anita's hand. "And how are you, Mr. Sheehan?"

"Great, just great, Sister," Richard says. "This is my lover, Rex Rousseau."

Sister Jean turns and clasps Rex's hand warmly, meeting his gaze. "Wonderful to meet you, Mr. Rousseau," says Sister Jean. "Welcome to St. Mary's."

* * *

Jean notes the sudden awkwardness in the young man's eyes. She's seen it before. At St. Vincent's, before she came here, many of the homeless were men with AIDS or women who turned tricks for a living. "What must a nun think of *me?*" one man had asked, averting his eyes, needle tracks scarring his arms.

"I'm not sure," Jean had replied. "I know that *I* think you're all right. And so does God."

"Good to meet you, too, Sister," says Rex Rousseau. *Could that possibly be his real name?* Jean thinks it sounds like the stage name for a porn star. He smiles at her with all the hesitancy of a young boy in front of his fourth grade teacher. She's seen *that* look before, too. All these grown people with intimidating memories of Catholic school.

"Is Flo here yet?" Richard asks.

"Oh, yes," Jean says. "With bells on." She gestures for them to enter the day room.

"Wow," says Rex. "What a difference." He looks around at the bright colors of the walls, the exotic theater posters with their lions and clowns and magicians and one-legged acrobats.

"It was Flo's idea," Jean tells him. "She got the board to agree that the color scheme in here was not to be messed with."

"And you went along with her," Richard says, laughing.

"You better believe it. I knew what was good for me."

"You know, Sister," Richard tells her, "if the nuns back at St. Thomas à Becket Academy had been as cool as you, I would've had a much better time in grade school. I tried to redecorate the chapel once in *Partridge Family* psychedelia and was told I was a heretic."

"So was Jesus." Jean winks at him. "People forget that. And I'm sure He would've loved *The Partridge Family.*"

They all laugh.

She loved dispelling the stereotype of the uptight nun. She hadn't even gone to Catholic school. She was a public school kid in the little mill town of Putnam, Connecticut, in the hills of the industrial northeast. In those days, she'd had nary a thought about nuns or priests or even Jesus, despite her nominal Catholicism. That is, until her junior year in high school, when her life suddenly changed.

That was the year of Jean's Great Transformation. She had shocked her parents by telling them she wanted to enter the convent. They weren't particularly religious; her mother, in fact, had cried for days after her announcement. Her father had been born a Presbyterian and had never bothered to officially convert, despite the fact that he attended midnight Mass every Christmas Eve with Jean and her mother. That was the extent of their churchgoing. Jean was sent to catechism class when she was a girl, and she'd been confirmed, but there was never much talk about God or the Pope or sin in her house.

They were decent, hardworking folk, but Jean remembers few expressions of love from her parents. The first fifteen years of her life now seemed to her to have been one long stretch of careful neutrality. Watching television shows like *Family Affair* or *The Brady Bunch* had made Jean feel oddly alien, as if *family* were a concept she couldn't quite grasp.

Then came the day when her world was broken open wide by a four-foot-seven-inch nun. She had come to speak to Jean's social studies class. Her name was Anne Drew—Sister Anne Drew. At first, Jean had thought she meant "Andrew"—the way nuns used to take men's names. "No, no," Sister Anne had laughed. "I don't go in for all that sexist stuff."

She wore no veil, and the day she came to their class, she was wearing work boots and khakis. "I apologize for not getting a little more dressed," she told the students, "but I've just come from an emergency. A family in inner-city Hartford was burned out of their house last night—it was probably arson—and we were there trying to pick through the rubble to find the little girl's doll."

Jean was captivated by her. She listened intently to Anne Drew's description of her work with the poor. She ran a homeless shelter in Hartford. This was back in the early 70s before the problem was made even worse under Reagan. She lived on her own, in a small apartment partially paid for by the order. Anne was maybe forty then, a little older than Jean is now. She was short—at fifteen, Jean was already taller than she was—with close-cropped, prematurely gray hair framing an unlined, youthful face.

Anne Drew had stood in front of the class and asked for volunteers. Jean's hand was the first to go up. When her classmates all faded away after one or two visits to the shelter, Jean continued trekking on down to Hartford. She cooked soup—always without beef stock, because Anne was a vegetarian—and served it in large plastic bowls to the drug addicts and hookers who came to their doors.

"It's who *Jesus* walked among," Jean argued to her parents when they became concerned about her activities, about her twice-weekly visits to the shelter and the occasional overnight stay on the weekends. When Jean announced she wanted to leave Putnam and enroll in a Catholic convent school run by the Sisters of Mercy in upstate New York, her mother had wailed, "We'll never have grandchildren!" But eventually her parents came around, and Jean—barely seventeen—went off to become a nun.

Her studies were an inspiration. The order paid for her training as a nurse, as well as providing a spiritual base she'd never found at home. She discovered God in her deepest thoughts and in the faces of the people she worked with. The sisters were ecstatic to have her. Their ranks were diminishing; it was rare that a young girl, on her own initiative, chose to enter the convent. They became her family, awed by her youthful idealism to make a difference. As part of her novitiate, she accompanied Anne and some other sisters to Central America, helping the poor and displaced in El Salvador, even venturing into Nicaragua.

"You inspire us all," one old nun in her eighties told Jean upon her return. During her whole time in novitiate, Jean never once met a sister who was cross or cruel. She couldn't understand reactions like the one she'd seen in Richard Sheehan or so many others.

At least—not then. Later, she came to understand better how rigid even the most compassionate people can become.

Even someone as sainted to her as Anne Drew.

"There she is," Richard says, pointing across the room.

Jean blinks back to the present. Flo's seated against the far wall in a large orange pseudoleather armchair. She's smoking, of course, gripping that long cigarette holder with fingers capped with her signature scarlet. She's wearing a bright green silk dress, and her pure white hair is tied up in large bows of green velvet. Her lips are a shocking shade of violet.

"Well, if it isn't my entourage," she says in that raspy, ancient rattle of hers, grinning widely, opening her arms as if to embrace them.

"Hello, Flo," Richard says warmly. "I *can* call you Flo, can't I?"

"You can call me anything you like except late for dinner," she tells him. They all laugh.

Anita presents her with the flowers. Flo receives them gratefully, her eyes growing wide. She cradles them in her lap.

There's an opened box of Samoas on the table near her chair. Flo gestures to it. "Have a cookie," she offers. "Because of me, Gertie's daughter took first place."

"Hey, congratulations," Richard says, helping himself to one. He gently presses Rex forward. "Flo, this is Rex Rousseau," he says.

Rex steps forward and bows his head quickly. "Pleased to meet you, Miss Bridgewood," he says.

"Rex Rousseau?" she quizzes. "You must be an actor, too, with a handle like that."

"I am," Rex says, and Jean smiles to note he's blushing.

"What kind of parts do you play?" Flo asks.

"Well, I've done a few things, here and there—"

Richard nudges him with his elbow. "You're not gonna tell her about *Dennis Does Dallas?*"

Rex gives him an angry look, but Flo doesn't miss the reference. "Blue movies, eh?" she says. "I knew a few of those kind in my day."

Rex sighs. "I'm through with that. I'm doing a one-man show on the Barrymores that's received some good notices."

"Which Barrymores?"

"All of them."

"You play *all* of them?" Flo blinks. "Even Ethel?"

Rex smiles. "Especially Ethel."

Flo nods. "I think I'm beginning to get the drift here. Such a sharp dresser, too. Come here closer and let me see your necktie."

Rex steps forward. Flo reaches out with her gnarled hand and inspects the satin fabric between her fingers. She looks up at him, round blue eyes and furrowed brow. "You married?" she asks abruptly.

"Flo—" Jean warns.

Richard grins. "Yes, actually, Flo, he is"—he pauses—"to me."

She sniffs. "That's what I thought. I mean, if you're playing Ethel Barrymore, you *must* be a pansy." She lets go of Richard's tie.

Jean looks over at Richard and Rex to see if they're offended. They're clearly not. "Pansy" isn't a pejorative for Flo; it's merely a descriptive, what they used to say back in the days of gas lamps and streetcars.

"And you, missy," Flo says to Anita. "Did you get that part?"

Anita shakes her head. "No. Guess I was too late." She smirks. "Or too old."

"I'd argue with you and tell you that you're still a chick, 'cause you are," Flo says, "but I know how those casting agents think. Twenty-four, out the door."

They all laugh again.

"So how d'ya want to begin?" Flo asks.

Jean smiles. She hasn't seen Flo so revved up since the talent show she'd organized last winter. She'd spent weeks on it, interviewing residents and lining up all the acts. Anybody who still had it together sang a little song or did a little dance. Flo, of course, whistled and brought the day room down with cheers.

"Well," Richard is saying, "I was thinking we'd just have a conversation. With your permission, I'll set up my tape recorder."

"Let me see that thing."

He hands it to her. She narrows her eyes and studies it, turning it over in her hands. "So small. I've never seen anything like it."

"Oh, it works," Richard assures her. She hands it back to him and he switches it on. "Do I have your permission to tape record this interview?" he asks.

"Yes, you most certainly do," she replies.

He smiles, hitting the STOP button and then REWIND. The tape hums for a second, then clicks. He hits PLAY.

"Do I have your permission to tape record this interview?"

"Yes, you most certainly do."

Rex laughs. "What do you think of that?" he asks. "Hearing your voice?"

Flo eyes him. "Young man, I'm not so much a relic I've never been tape-recorded before."

Jean sees Rex blush again. *Oh, poor man,* she thinks. *Don't tangle with Flo.*

"Still," Flo muses, "with a rasp like that, I'd never have made it in talking pictures."

They laugh. Jean notices a look pass between the three visitors.

"Well, let's just start at the beginning and see where we go," Richard suggests, setting the tape recorder on the table in front of Flo. They all take seats in a semicircle around her.

Jean watches Flo carefully. The old woman has put out her cigarette and folded her hands in her lap. She seems pleased by the attention, but still on her guard, like an owl perched on a branch.

"You said you were born in Canada," Richard says. "What town?"

"Hamilton," Flo replies.

Jean notices another look pass around from Richard to Anita to Rex.

"Hamilton," Richard repeats. "What was Hamilton like a century ago?"

"Not sure I know. We left when I was still quite young. We lived in many places—here in Buffalo for a while, then out west. My mother was an actress, you see, and we were on the road a great deal. She was one of the best of her time."

"What was her name?"

"Charlotte Dunn." Jean detects just the slightest pause between the first and last names.

"Was that her stage name?" Richard asks.

"No, that was her real—you know, back in those days, names were changed so easily and often. It was so different then. I remember once, when we were playing in San Francisco—" She pauses, looking around at the group. "Have any of you ever been to San Francisco?"

They all had. "Well," Flo sniffs, "you don't remember it before the earthquake. I don't imagine many do anymore. How sad. How very, very sad indeed."

And so she goes on to describe San Francisco before the great cata-clysm: the charming, pastel-colored houses, the tinkling streetcars, the hills and winding streets and palm trees and everywhere the magnificent views of ocean, sky, and land. And then she describes New York at the turn of the century, and Philadelphia, and Chicago . . . .

Jean observes the skill with which Flo deflects any question that pries too much into the particulars of her long life. She's always done that, ever since Jean has known her. She'll talk about her days on the stage, but never about specific shows, precise years. It was always a colorful panorama of places and names and lively anecdotes—about the smoke-spewing papier-mâché volcano she'd once made, about the old actor who'd dropped dead on the stage while playing King Lear, about the fires she'd escaped—barely with her life . . . .

But try to pin her down, as Richard—as skilled a journalist as he might be—was trying to do, and you'd get nowhere. Flo would wax nostalgical for Lillian Russell or Eddie Foy, but ask if she'd ever worked with them, and she'd just smile enigmatically. Jean had learned to leave her with her memories. It was enough that she shared what she did.

And yet she admits to herself that she *had* hoped Flo would be a little more straightforward with Richard Sheehan. She's long been curious to know just how many of Flo's stories were true, to find out just who this woman is—or was. "A former vaudeville actress," her predecessor at St. Mary's, old Sister Michael, had told her when she retired. And that's still about all Jean knew.

Oh, Flo had admitted to being married—twice, Jean thought, because she'd used different names. Harry was one. Harry she spoke of occasionally, with some fondness. The other might have been Carl. Or Charles. There were no children, at least none that Jean knew about. There had been a brother, Jean thought—but wasn't sure. In Flo's records, next to the line marked family, there was one word: *None.*

"I don't count family by blood," Flo had once told her.

"Oh, no?" Jean asked. "How do you count it?"

"By time spent together. By sharing the chores. By taking drives. By being there."

Jean had looked over at her. The glow in Flo's eyes had made Jean feel honored to be in the same room with her, with this ancient noble lady. Flo was one of the wise old women Anne Drew had told her she'd meet as she went out into the world. "Old women are the wisest creatures on earth," Anne had told her. "Except maybe for old cats."

Flo certainly had a feline edge to her, Jean thought. A sly, knowing sense about her every move, her every word. Jean *adored* her. Had from the moment she first arrived at St. Mary's when Flo was one of the first to greet her. "Ah, a baby chick," Flo had said derisively, apprising her appearance. "But then again," she reconsidered, "maybe we *could* use a little hot young blood around here."

In those trying first months, it had been Flo who sustained Jean. Among all the residents and staff, it was only Flo who won Jean's trust. With Flo, she sought refuge on those cold February nights when the wind whistled through the eaves of the great old house and the snow piled up outside. Jean had been very blue last winter: Victor had died, and the memories of St. Vincent's were crashing in around her. That had been her life's work, what she had always wanted to do, why she'd entered religious life. Making a difference, helping the sick and the hungry and the destitute. Sometimes now she walked down the great staircase of St. Mary's and felt physically sickened by the opulence, the glittery chandelier and stately marble. They had sent her here to *punish* her, to *imprison* her, to keep her safely away from her temptations. At such times, when she felt down and heavy in her heart, sometimes even prayer wasn't enough. She'd make a pot of tea and sit with Flo, listening to the old wise woman tell her tales.

As she was now.

"But you *were* Baby Flo, the Child Wonder Whistler," Richard persists.

"I was," Flo says with a smile.

He smiles in return. "You know what's interesting, Flo? I've found a record of *another* child actress who was also known by that name." He withdraws the photocopies from his inside jacket pocket.

Flo's eyes are suddenly on alert. "That's not possible," she says. "I was the only one."

"Well, it says here—and I'm wondering if you know something about this—" Richard lifts the paper to read. Jean sees Flo's fingers lace together in her lap. "There was an actress by the name of Florence Lawrence. Did you know her?"

A beat. "Of course," Flo says. "Everyone knew her."

"Well, when she was a child, she was also known as Baby Flo, the Child Wonder Whistler. Later, she became known all over the world as The Biograph Girl, the very first movie star."

There's no reaction from Flo.

Richard continues, although there's the slightest quaver now to his voice. "And, Flo, the strangest thing is—well, she was also from Hamilton and"—he laughs nervously—"if she were alive today, she'd be one hundred and six."

A sudden, awkward silence descends over the group. Jean looks over at Flo. She sits there impassively, hands clasped in her lap. The others are all intently looking at her. Anita Murawski is literally sitting at the edge of her seat. Jean feels suddenly alarmed, as if she's made some horrible mistake letting these people in, as if they've just sprung something terrible on Flo that she didn't want to hear.

Or remember.

"Flo," she asks, "are you all—"

"She killed herself," Flo says finally, not flinching from their stare.

"Yes," Richard says. "That's what it says here. In 1938."

Flo narrows her eyes, then smiles coyly. "But why are we talking about her? I thought you were here to interview me."

"I am," Richard says. He tries to smile but he's uncomfortable. "I have to ask you, Flo. By whatever logic—by whatever means—are you The Biograph Girl?"

She meets his gaze and smiles—almost in relief, Jean thinks, as if he's asked her the one question she can answer directly.

"No, Mr. Sheehan," she says. "I'm *not* The Biograph Girl."

The rest of the interview goes as it had before: Flo speaking about life in the past, how things have changed, how much she has seen, how she learned to drive a car, what it was like to live through two world wars, how she felt watching a man walk on the moon—all wonderful and fascinating insights and experiences.

But precious little about herself.

Richard respected the line she so firmly drew in the sand. But when they said good-bye, there was still something in all of their eyes as they shook Flo's hand and thanked her.

"Mr. Sheehan," Jean asks now, as they walk out of the day room.

"Yes?" he says.

"There isn't something I should know, is there? I don't want anything upsetting Flo. I mean, the woman who killed herself—might she have been a relation of Flo's?"

He shrugs. "Your guess is as good as mine." He withdraws the photocopies from his jacket and hands them to her. "Here. I've got the originals at home. See for yourself. An amazing coincidence."

"Is that all it is?"

He smiles. "What else could it be?"

But Jean knows he doesn't believe it. Not for an instant.

She looks over at Flo, now busying herself picking up coffee cups from the tables in the day room. *Who is she really?* Jean thinks. She's never really known, and she suspects no one else at St. Mary's over the years has known either. *Who is this wise old woman she's come to rely on, to trust, to love? Who is Florence Bridgewood?*

August 1904

Names, names, names. You get confused by all the names. I don't wonder. I've lived a long life. There are a lot of names.

Linda? Yes, that's one of the names I've mentioned. But I can't really tell you about Linda until I've told you first about San Francisco. It's still the most beautiful place on earth, you know, with the possible exception of the island of Santorini in the Aegean Sea. But back before the earthquake—oh, then San Francisco was an enchanted village on a hill. I don't imagine there are many who remember it from that time—how could there be? Sad. How very sad. It was like a fairy tale kingdom—it really was. A charming village out of a storybook—that's the only way I can describe it.

And if you know anything about me yet, you know I don't go in for sugarcoated reveries or drippy nostalgic hyperbole. Get out the barf bucket again when I hear that kind of stuff! So I really mean it when I say that San Francisco before the great earthquake was *magical*. The little colorful houses, the cobblestone streets, the astounding tableau of hill and sky and sea—

"I never want to leave," I told Ducks the day we arrived, turning in place to see the panorama around me.

"Some folks never do," he said.

You have to *see* it in your mind. Really *see* it. Only then can I tell you about Linda.

It's a summer day. Linda and I are on the crest of a hill overlooking the Mission district. The sky is defiantly blue and the sun is directly overhead and warm. It's one of those quintessential San Francisco summers, with none of the mugginess of New York. Whenever I think of that day—or any of those days I spent with Linda in the Golden City—I think of brightness and warmth and hillsides of wildflowers.

Now it's true I'm not one to go on much about sunshine and daffodils. I admit that, when I first saw Linda, I thought she was just a silly little filly. All lace and fluff. And maybe she was. But that day, I'm telling you—I've never *known* a day so warm or bright or filled with fragrance.

So there.

I can see her still, weaving daisies through her hair.

"Tell me, Flo," she said. "Suppose they let you play Juliet. Suppose you could be the leading actress of any company in the country—but the audience was forbidden to ever applaud. Would you still want to be an actress then?"

"It's too silly a scenario for me to even consider," I replied.

Mother had hired Linda to play the ingenue part in *The Winds of Pompeii*. I had wanted the role, but Mother had forbidden it, telling me I was still too young.

"But I'm *fourteen!*" I protested. Or fifteen, sixteen—somewhere there.

Oh, I was prepared to hate Linda. She came in off the dusty street carrying a basket of oranges, her blond hair blowing in the breeze. Her hair was even blonder than mine, white almost, nearly invisible from a distance in the bright sun. "Well, if it ain't Rebecca of Sunnybrook Farm," I sneered to Ducks.

"Her name's Linda Arvidson," he told me.

"Bet she doesn't even smoke cigarettes."

I was right. No cigarettes, no beer, no obscenities passed her lips. Her first gesture was to offer me an orange. "Why aren't *you* playing the ingenue?" she asked. "You're certainly pretty enough."

"My mother's the company manager," I explained, finding myself accepting her gift.

"I would think that would entitle you to all *sorts* of perks," she said.

I shook my head. "I'm not ready, she says."

Linda smiled. "I imagine you'll only be ready once *she's* ready to share the spotlight."

It wasn't the last time Linda would speak the truth so plainly. Mother wasn't aging well. Her face was deeply lined, and the rough brown skin of too many days in the sun could no longer be lightened or softened by any of the expensive creams she bought. I'd find her sitting alone on the back steps of the theaters we played, just sitting there, staring up at the moon. Sometimes Ducks would be behind her playing his harmonica, and I loved to sit there and fall asleep to the sound. Sometimes I'd forget where we were—in five months we'd played eleven cities, from Albany to Detroit to Chicago to Little Rock. Sometimes none of us spoke, except on stage, for days.

Oh, Mother. All those years together, and I hardly knew you. During our brief sojourn in Buffalo with my grandmother, I'd come to discern that Mother had once been persona non grata to her family for choosing a life on the stage. But hard as that must have been, it wasn't enough to account for the grand sadness that seemed to envelop her at all times, the sense of great tragedy that trailed her like a shadow.

As I reached young womanhood, my mother's air of melancholy only seemed to deepen with the lines on her careworn face. The impossible grandeur that she tried to impart was less able to conceal her weariness. She now carried a brass-handled cane with a pearl stud at the top. Her moonlit vigils on the back porches of theaters became regular occurrences.

It was one such night when I found her sitting out back, the crickets chirping rhythmically, her cane in her hands. She called me over to her, breaking her usual silence.

"Florence," Mother said. "I've gotten a letter from your brother Norman. He asked about you."

My brother. He was still living in Buffalo with my grandmother. He'd hated me when Mother and I had come back. I suppose he resented me, thinking I'd stolen Mother away.

"He wouldn't care if I were alive or dead," I said to Mother.

"That's not true, Florence." Her voice was queer. Soft, vague. "You're his baby sister. He'd take care of you if—"

"If *what*, Mother?"

She tapped her cane impatiently on the steps. "Oh, Florence. I don't know *what* is best. These theaters we're playing—these half-empty houses. What's the point anymore? All my dreams—it's too late, Florence, too late."

For her, maybe. But not for me.

"You said I would be *famous*, Mother. All my life you promised me that! I still believe in the dream! Don't you?"

She looked at me with such empty eyes. She didn't believe it. I could see that. She was tired, old. She had barnstormed through North America for nearly thirty years, and still she was playing on run-down stages to half-filled houses. She no longer believed—in herself or in any of the rest of us.

We carried Mother's depression with us like a heavy trunk of extra props. Ducks tried to cheer her up, spicing her rum and playing silly songs on his harmonica. But by the time we reached the end of our tour, we all shared her weariness.

Then an amazing bolt of luck hit us. Ducks was sitting there on the back steps of an old theater in Chicago, puffing his cigar late one night. He seemed mesmerized by the rings of smoke that billowed one after another up into the air. "Florrie," he said at last. "Run inside and fetch me that funnel from our prop trunk."

I did as he asked. When I returned he placed the funnel—a large old tin thing—over his face, the narrow end pointed up at the sky.

I laughed. "Ducks, whatever are you doing?"

He didn't answer. He just kept puffing away on his cigar. The smoke escaped from the funnel as if from a chimney.

"Eureka!" he exclaimed. "I've got a brilliant idea."

The next morning, our hands were slathered in plaster and papier-mâché. We molded the gunk around the metal hoop structure of an old antebellum costume skirt. Mother spied us and asked us just what we thought we were doing.

"This is what our drama needs, Lotta. How can we tell the story of Pompeii without a volcano?"

"We are serious actors," she sniffed. "We need no gimmicks."

Ducks chuckled. "I think we need something, pet. Filling half a house means the other half is empty."

There was an agent in town. I can't recall his name, but he was big in those days. One of those high-hatted men in waistcoat and pipe who consorted with people like Ziegfeld and Daly. What made him especially important was that he had connections in San Francisco, the heart of the West Coast theater. East Coast celebrity did not carry much weight in the west. Mother knew this; we never attempted to venture much past the Mississippi. But Ducks, inspired by his cigar, had other ideas.

I helped him lift the heavy plaster pyramid into a wagon. We filled another wagon with old rags. We each pulled one down the street, causing passersby to stop and stare. But Ducks paid them no mind, so excited was he by his brainstorm. We knew we could never get an appointment to see this Mr. Important Agent, but we found out where he was staying, and set up camp in front of his hotel. After piling the rags underneath our volcano, we set fire to them, prompting a policeman to walk over and threaten us.

"Just watch, Officer," Ducks pleaded. "We won't let them burn for long."

By constantly batting out the flames, we caused great clouds of smoke to puff from the hole we'd made in top. "Voila!" Ducks exclaimed. "The volcano of Pompeii!"

"Well, I'll be damned," said the policeman.

We drew quite the crowd, all of whom oohed and ahhed over such a marvel. We kept up our routine, lighting the rags, stamping out the flames, causing the rags to smolder and the volcano to puff.

And just as Ducks figured, soon the agent came out from the hotel, intending to hail a cab.

"Come see *The Winds of Pompeii*," Ducks barked as if to the throng in general but really for the agent's ears alone. "The season's most sensational theatrical experience. See a real live volcano erupt upon the stage."

I shall never forget seeing the agent stop and turn, glance in our direction. I studied his face carefully, watched all of his movements. He looked at the smoky contraption in our rusty old wagon, then around at the crowd that had gathered. I remember watching him remove first one white glove, then the other, folding them both into his right palm. Then he strode toward us, and I knew our fortunes had changed.

Thanks to Ducks. Always thanks to Ducks. The agent hired us for a West Coast run after our assiduous assurances that of course our volcano was safe, that there was no threat of fire. That was the ever present worry for theaters in those days, and in truth, we had no idea whether or not we'd burn the house down. We were fortunate; we never burned anything more than an old curtain once in Sacramento, for which he had to pay twelve dollars and forty cents. But that old volcano did us far, far more good than harm.

It brought me to Linda.

We were booked into the Grand Opera House on Mission Street. In those days, Mission, near Third, was called South-of-the-Slot—not the best of places for a young lady to walk alone, Mother told me. Pawn shops and saloons, and a scattering of dingy nickelodeons. But in the midst of it all, languishing in lonesome splendor, was the old opera house, and I found it staggeringly beautiful. The extravagantly tiled floors and lavish red curtain still recalled the theater's glory days when Henry Irving and Ellen Terry themselves had trod the boards. To be sure, there had been bigger companies and more stellar names there, but the Lawrence Dramatic Company brought the first-ever erupting volcano to the opera house, and that was something in itself.

But the manager still treated us with contempt. Mother tried introducing the company, but all he cared to see was the volcano. "*Sir,*" Mother said, "I'll have you know the Lawrence Dramatic Company is an *esteemed* company throughout—"

"Listen, old woman. If you didn't have that fire-breathing contraption, you'd never have been invited out to make the trip."

He was a barrel-chested souse with hair growing out of his nose. He got real close to Mother's face when he talked. She didn't dignify his rudeness. She simply withdrew her lace handkerchief from her sleeve, wiped her face, and said demurely as she turned away, "Sir, it is impolite to spit when you speak." We all covered our mouths to hide our laughter.

I played the part of a child, on stage for no more than ten minutes. Behind the curtain, I passed out helmets to the actors playing soldiers and occasionally would help the prop boy fan the smoldering ashes to create the volcano's smoke. But mostly I'd watch Linda. She was the kind of actress I wanted to be, poised and beautiful, ethereal even—and when she came out for her curtain call, the audience always got to its feet.

"We've *got* to make good here," I told Linda. "If we fail in San Francisco, word of it will make its way through theatrical circles like shit through a sewer."

"Oh, Flo," she said. "How you talk."

But I could tell I charmed her. She had never quite met a girl like me. Or me one like her, I suppose. I didn't have a lot of contact with girls my age, and I felt rather puffed up by her attention. When she asked if I wanted to climb the hill behind the theater to get a better look at the city, I made it into a race. I won, of course; she came up huffing and puffing with her basket of oranges like the little nelly she was.

"What do you want more than anything, Flo?" she asked me, catching her breath and settling down on the grassy hill.

"To be a great actress," I answered, assuming she'd challenge me.

But she didn't. She just began picking her flowers. "Look," she said at last, pointing. "Between those two hills. Can you see it?"

Yes, I could. The water. The Pacific Ocean. Green against the blue sky. Oh, what a magnificent city it was. Never before had I been able to see so far. Its vast sweep overwhelmed me. Up each hill and around every corner, I was continuously discovering a new vista of sun and sky and ocean and mountain—all there in one staggering view.

"I'll talk to your mother," Linda said, peeling an orange now and handing me a wedge, "if you really think you still want to play the ingenue."

"But you must come with us," I said. "When we go back east, you must come." I bit into my orange. It was sweet and tart at the same time, and I pulled the pulp through my teeth.

"You know I can't, Flo. Not yet. My family is here. But I will follow. I promise."

"Oh, you must, you *must*—if you want to be an actress. New York is where you have *got* to be. Have you read about all the new theaters springing up? All along Broadway, from Thirty-fourth up to Forty-sixth Street. Dozens of them. They say the lights—"

Linda looked over at me with enormous blue eyes. "Are like the walk into heaven," she finished.

How beautiful she looked in the sun. "Why are *you* an actress?" I asked her suddenly. "You say *I* don't really want it. That all *I* want is the applause. Why are *you* an actress?"

She laughed. "Oh, what an enormous question, Flo. I'm not quite sure I know the answer." She paused. "But I know it's not the applause."

The hillside around us blazed with yellow flowers that day—in my mind they're daffodils, but it was likely too late in the season for daffodils. Or maybe not. Maybe there were *dozens* of daffodils reflecting the golden light of the noonday sun. Daffodils and buttercups and sunflowers as dazzling as Linda's sun-soaked hair, her bright yellow dress, her happy laugh. Sunflowers. Yes, I'm sure there were sunflowers. And calla lilies. Everywhere.

"There's nothing quite like it," she said finally, looking over at me with those pale blue eyes that were nearly translucent, her knees bent and pulled up to her chest, her arms crossed over them and her face resting on her hands. "I only feel truly alive when I'm on the stage."

This made me pause. I couldn't say the same. I had a flash of memory then—of riding a horse in Buffalo, saddling him up and mounting him like a boy, galloping faster and faster through the meadow with the air filling up my lungs until I thought they might burst. I'd felt alive then, gloriously alive. The stage was thrilling, the applause intoxicating—but I had many moments of life beyond the footlights.

Moments, in fact, like this one.

"Did you know I used to whistle for the audience when I was very young?" I asked Linda suddenly.

"Whistle!"

"Yes," I said. "Whistle and dance and sing. Sometimes Mother would have to come out onto the stage and escort me off, because I wouldn't want to leave."

She laughed, draping her arm around my shoulder. "My first experience on the stage was a dramatic recital at Sherman and Clay Hall on Sutter Street," she told me. "A friend and I performed Shakespeare and scenes from the Greek tragedies. We sold all our tickets, and it was quite the success."

"I think you'll be very famous," I said, watching every gesture she made. The way she flung back her hair, the idle way she plucked a blade of grass and drew it across her face.

"It's more than the applause, Flo. It's the *magic* of it all. The *illusion*. What things we get to make up! What histories we get to create for ourselves!" She smiled over at me. "We aren't only this," she said, pulling at the pink skin on the back of her hand. "We can be so much more."

It's true Molly reminded me of Linda. Molly once said a very similar thing to me. "I was only a girl from Iowa before I came here. Now I can be so much more."

She was blond like Linda—but more like me really when I think of it. Molly didn't have the aura that seemed to always hover around Linda's being, like overexposed film. Molly wasn't nearly so celestial. She was very human. Just a little bit of ant paste and she was gone.

Linda, in contrast, lived into her sixties. I remember seeing the notice in *Variety*. I clipped it out, kept it in my Bible for decades until it turned yellow and began to crumble.

Linda Arvidson, actress.

Then I threw it away.

It was our last day in San Francisco. My heart was weighted down as if a brick were tied to it. I told Linda to come to meet me in front of the theater. I had a surprise for her.

"Hop in," I shouted.

There, parked in the street and gleaming in the sun, was a newfangled automobilly.

"Flo!" Linda exclaimed.

Automobillies were suddenly the rage, scaring the horses and kicking up dust all over the city. I'd won over the crabby Mr. Todsol, the theater manager, and he'd agreed to let me drive his.

I turned the crank. It made a horrible noise.

"Oh, Flo!" Linda laughed, clapping her hands to her face. "Have you ever taken one of these things?"

"Sure I have," I told her. Well, only once: Mr. Todsol had given me a brief lesson. But I was an expert horsewoman. Certainly maneuvering a machine couldn't be as difficult as breaking in a mare.

It was a two-cylinder Ford Model A, all shiny brass and copper. It held a leather seat that could fit two snugly and a steering wheel mounted in the center on a long angled post. There was no roof to the contraption; if you got caught in a sudden downpour, you'd get drenched.

"Here," I said to Linda. "Put this on."

From the seat of the car, I withdrew a long, tightly belted leather overcoat that kept off the grime. She held it up, smiled timidly, and slipped it on. "And these, too," I said, handing her an elegant pair of fringed foot muffs Mr. Todsol had bought for his wife. They'd ward off the wind that whistled up through the floorboards. Later, I remember owning a pair that could be filled with hot water before a long journey. Oh, the things we did in those early years of automobiling!

We took our seats. I unlocked the brake. And off we went, whizzing down Mission and then up a steep, winding road.

"Oh, *do* be careful, Flo," Linda shouted, holding on to her hat.

I felt a surge of passion rise from my gut and force its way through my lips. *"Yippee!"* I cried as we careened down the other side of the hill, honking at plodding horse-pulled wagons, arousing so much sand and dirt that we both began wheezing and coughing.

"Take it easy," Linda cried, laughing even as tears streamed down both her cheeks.

I waved to passersby. Linda shouted that I should keep my eyes on the road. It felt so magnificent to be behind the wheel. So powerful. So giddy. I let out another long whoop. *"Hooray!"* I shouted as the wind took my hat.

We skidded back to a stop in front of the theater. "There," I said, turning to her. "How alive do you feel *now?*"

Our eyes held in girlish wonder. Suddenly she leaned over and kissed me square on the lips. A quick, sweet kiss—the only kiss we ever shared.

A kiss that has lingered for a lifetime.

Linda told Mother she wouldn't be performing that night, our last in San Francisco.

"What do you mean? How *dare* you quit now?" Mother screamed.

"I can't go on. My throat is sore."

I looked at her. What could she mean? Just hours before, she'd laughed and sung as we drove over the hills. But she insisted.

"Where can I find an ingenue for one night?" Mother lamented.

"Behind you," Linda said.

Mother didn't even need to turn around. I saw her back stiffen, her shoulders square. "Absolutely not," she said.

Ducks added in his two cents. "Well, Lotta, Florrie does know all the lines, all the action."

"*No,*" Mother snarled and stormed off in a huff. Ducks followed her. Linda slipped out the back door, but I hovered near the curtain. From the stillness behind, I heard Mother continue to refuse.

"Now, Lotta, be reasonable," Ducks cajoled.

I heard something crash. She had thrown something. "She's not *ready,* I tell you!"

"You always said she'd be the greatest actress in the world some-day!" Ducks shouted back at her. "You've been priming her since she was three!"

"Yes, someday!" she snapped. "Not *now!*"

I stood in a fold of the curtain, the rope of the pull in my hands. Their voices echoed through the cavernous old theater—the very place where Caruso would sing a couple of years from then, just as the earthquake struck.

"Lotta, you have no other choice. We have no other girl. Flo knows all the lines, all the bits of business—"

"She's not ready! She's *not!*"

"It's not *she* who's unready, Lotta." Ducks's voice was low and hard now. "I think it's *you* who are not yet ready, unwilling to acknowledge your daughter is a *woman*—a young, beautiful woman who will steal some of your applause and pull the spotlight from your own careworn face!"

Mother was quiet. Then I heard a horrible sound like none before. Mother was crying. In all my life, I'd never known her to cry. I pulled the curtain rope to my mouth and bit hard.

"Oh, Ducks," she said, "the years go so fast—faster for a woman, don't you think?"

Ducks made a small laugh. I could hear him pat his belly. "Perchance you're right, Lotta. We of the male species can get away with far more. A protruding gut, a shiny pate covered by poorly woven wigs. What a sight most leading men are! And yet still we go on."

"Oh, Ducks, it's not just that. It's all of this—this vagabond life. My own mother called it sinful, and who am I to argue that she was wrong? Who am *I?*"

There was a heavy silence. I sensed that their eyes spoke to each other in ways words could not. I heard her move away then and approach the stage. I tensed in the curtains, terrified that she'd apprehend me there. But she stopped.

"Ducks," she said, and I heard her skirts swish as she turned. "When I married Bridgewood, do you remember what I said?"

"I'll never forget," he said. "You told me, 'I am going to leave the stage and live the way life's supposed to be.' It nearly broke my heart watching you go."

"I *believed* that," Mother said. "It's what my mother always wanted for me. The stage—what kind of life is that? What legacy am I giving to my daughter? My *baby?* A night here, a week there, in one-room flats, at the mercy of gin-soaked theater managers—what kind of life is that?"

"The life I want," I said, surprising myself, emerging from my hiding place. I stood there unblinking, staring at them.

Mother just looked at me. "Oh, Florrie," she said at last, a rare instance of her calling me anything other than Florence. I thought she might cry again. Or embrace me. But she didn't. She simply looked at me and then looked away.

"More than anything I want to be an actress, Mother," I said.

She sighed. "And so you will." Her brow was creased; her lips were tight. She looked over at Ducks, who nodded at her in support. She looked back at me. "Will Linda's costumes fit you?"

"Oh, Mother, thank you!"

"Ducks, print up a new bill replacing Linda's name with Florence's," Mother instructed. She paused. "She'll be . . . Florence Lawrence, of course."

"Florence Lawrence?" I asked. "It sounds . . . peculiar."

Mother arched an eyebrow at me. "This is the Lawrence Dramatic Company, and I'm Mrs. Lawrence, and you're my daughter. So you'll be Florence Lawrence."

That was the night she came into being. Florence Lawrence. The night I became the creature the world would eventually come to know as The Biograph Girl. Come to know—and forget.

Florence Lawrence made her debut on the stage of the Grand Opera House in the magical city of old San Francisco—in a theater that no longer exists, in a city that has long since crumbled into dust and blown away with the breeze.

But I've never forgotten that night. I remember the long white dress I wore, pinned hastily in back, my hair braided with leaves. I remember gesturing with my arms to the audience, throwing my voice as far as it could go, all the way up to the balconies, the wonderful, delirious echo it made through the old hall.

And the applause. Oh, how I remember the applause. The lights came up and the audience stood. Hats were tossed in the air. There were whistles and hoots and the stamping of feet. So what if they cheered more for that puffy old papier-mâché volcano than they did for me? I was still there, in the spotlight, taking my curtsy. And in the front row beamed Linda, standing and cheering. When the lights came up, I could see her eyes were only on me.

The Present

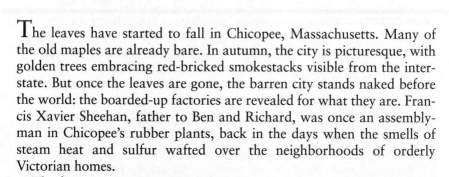

The leaves have started to fall in Chicopee, Massachusetts. Many of the old maples are already bare. In autumn, the city is picturesque, with golden trees embracing red-bricked smokestacks visible from the interstate. But once the leaves are gone, the barren city stands naked before the world: the boarded-up factories are revealed for what they are. Francis Xavier Sheehan, father to Ben and Richard, was once an assemblyman in Chicopee's rubber plants, back in the days when the smells of steam heat and sulfur wafted over the neighborhoods of orderly Victorian homes.

The factories are vacant now, but Ben remembers those odors, sharp and tart, mingling with the slightly kinder fragrances of kielbasa and sauerkraut coming from the houses up and down Grand Avenue. He can see Grand now, up ahead. This is where he and his friends would play stickball in between the rumbling trucks that used the street as a shortcut to the factories. They were a bunch of rowdy youths, smoking and cursing, for whom Ben imagines just two fates: jail or the U.S. Army. Mostly Irish and Polish kids back then, in the late 60s, the days of the moon walk and *Laugh-In* and riots on the UMass campus. Now most of Chicopee is Puerto Rican. Kowalski's Super is now Ortiz Deli.

A sudden boom overhead. Anita arches her neck to look out the car window. "Jesus," she says as a great shadow passes over the car.

"Westover Air Force Base," Ben tells her. "Growing up here, you get used to it."

"I'd be afraid to walk out on the street with those monstrosities flying overhead." She shivers. "That thing looked like the Batplane."

Ben laughs. Three blocks ahead, he can see his mother's street. He just can't bring himself to say *his* street anymore, not after so many years living along the cracked concrete avenues of New York. But this *was* his neighborhood—his and Richard's. Grand Avenue was Ben's paper route, in fact—the Caseys and the Piatrowskis and the Driscolls and the Adamczyks and the Fletchners—an unbroken sequence of green lawns, gray driveways, Virgin Marys, and mailboxes with names stenciled in gold.

Ben delivered the afternoon daily, his burlap sack slung over his shoulder, heavy with papers. It took him exactly one hour and fifteen minutes if he didn't encounter an unruly dog. Meanwhile, Richard would be home watching the soaps with Mom, the shades drawn in the living room. Often, when Ben got back, they'd have eaten dinner already, early at four o'clock, sitting in front of the TV.

"Ben," Anita had asked him last night, "tell me again why we're going to see your mother."

They had just crawled into bed. She was wearing her black teddy, the one Ben had bought for her as a first-year anniversary present. Usually she wore a T-shirt and panties to bed, cold cream on her face; by wearing the teddy, she was signaling she wanted to have sex. But Ben was far too tired to comply. He'd worked ten hours over at the ad agency, splicing together video clips of a family on a cruise ship off the coast of Norway for a travelogue. And he'd been up late the night before typing up a synopsis of the Marge Schott idea to send over to Xerxes.

"We're going because I haven't been home in a while," Ben answered Anita, closing his eyes, trying to pretend he hadn't noticed the teddy.

She curled up beside him. He could feel her warm breasts resting against his shoulder. Once that might have sent him over the edge; tired or not, he'd have risen to the occasion.

"I'd rather we just stayed home," she purred into his ear. "What do you say? We could sleep in late."

"Maybe Sunday."

"I have an audition on Sunday."

"Oh, well, then."

He heard her sigh. "Oh, Ben," she said and rolled over to her side of the bed.

He felt shitty doing this to her. But he just didn't have it in him these days to make love to her. Part of him wished that Anita *would* go off and move to L.A. He knew that was what she wanted to do. He'd miss her, of course, but there would be a certain relief, a certain lifting of responsibility. *Go*, he thought sometimes when he'd wake earlier than she did. He'd lie there, head in his arm, watching her sleep. *Go before you waste any more time.*

He knows he's holding her back. Just why she stays, he cannot fathom. Looking over at her last night in bed and looking over at her now in the car, Ben can still see the pretty girl he'd fallen in love with, the woman with whom he'd expected to spend his life. But now . . . ?

I don't deserve her, he thinks. *I've held her back too long. Mom is right. I'm nothing but a—*

"Your mother has the wierdest ideas," Anita says suddenly, startling Ben. He looks over at her. "I mean, I just hope she doesn't start going on about how *sick* she is."

They've just turned right onto Ben's childhood street. Anita sighs. "I mean, I'm always *this* close to saying, 'Well, if you'd *drop* a hundred pounds—'"

"*Don't,*" Ben snaps. "I *mean* it, Anita. Don't say that."

She's right, of course. All of Mom's health problems—from her asthma to her arthritis to her high blood pressure—were exacerbated by her weight. Yet in twenty years—ever since Mom had started packing on the pounds after Dad died—Ben has never once mentioned her weight to her. It's as if she was as trim as she used to be—the pretty, smiling mother staring out at him from photos in his scrapbook, her twin three-year-old sons on each knee, her husband standing stoically behind her.

Not that he indulges her the way Richard does, bringing her boxes of Little Debbies as treats. He'll confront Richard, telling him he's killing her, but he never says a word to his mother. She just goes on eating whatever Richard brings her, patting his face with her big chubby mitt of a hand.

"Well," Ben says now, taking in a long breath, "here we are."

The house looks the same as it always has: a small ranch at the end of a dead-end street in a neighborhood of ranch houses that all look exactly alike. Over the garage hangs the rusty rim of a basketball hoop; the netting is long since gone. Under the large picture window in the living room, the facade of pink brick is slightly cracked and worn. The rest of the house is sided in beige aluminum; one wooden shutter is missing from an unused bedroom window. That was Ben's and Richard's room. He notices with a small smile that on the window is the remnant of an old Tot Finder decal stuck on by Mom when he and Richard were five. In case the house ever went up in smoke, she wanted the firefighters to know who to rescue first.

The morning is bright. There are songbirds chirping in the trees. Mom's in the doorway. The *whole* doorway. She opens the screen door.

"Well, I was starting to get worried," she calls out to them.

"Hello, Mrs. Sheehan," Anita says, approaching her. They kiss.

"Hi, Mom," Ben says.

She gives him her cheek. He kisses it. "Is that your car?" she asks. "Did you finally buy one? What kind is that?"

"No, it's a rental," Ben says.

"It's a Geo," Anita says.

"A Geo? Never heard of it. You're father used to swear by Oldsmobiles. Well, don't buy a car if it's going to be that small."

They all enter the house.

Right away Ben is once again struck by the smell. Mom's house always smells the same: *bacon.* She might not have cooked bacon in *weeks,* but somehow the smell permeates everything: the emerald green shag rug, the brown corduroy sofa, the long dark green curtains in the living room, which are, as always, drawn. On the wall, Ben's and Richard's high school pictures hang over the television set. They both wear absurdly wide ties and lapels, and their hair is identically parted in the middle—except Richard's is neater. And his tie isn't askew.

"When you called yesterday to say you were coming, I thought maybe you had an announcement or something," Mom says, waddling in front of them into the kitchen. She's got an Entenmann's apple strudel cake set out on a plate for them. "Here," she says, "sit down and cut yourself a piece. Benny, you want milk?"

He smiles. "Sure."

"Anita, you'll have coffee? I've made some."

"Thanks, Mrs. Sheehan."

They sit down, but don't yet slice into the cake. Ben's mother opens the refrigerator, pours a glass of milk for her son. She's about five two with completely gray hair. Her elbows disappear into her arms. She wears a polka-dotted dress Ben knows she made herself—she makes most of her clothes now—just a tent with sleeve holes and buttons up the front. On her feet she wears flip-flops.

"So," she says, "have you seen Richard?"

"I see him all the time, Mom," Ben says.

"That's good." She pours two cups of coffee.

That's good. Ben knows what she means. So long as he stays in touch with Richard, he'll be all right. *Richard* will look out for him. *Richard* has all the answers.

Well, where was Richard when Dad was sick? Where was the perfect son when Dad needed him? For that matter, where were you, *Mom?*

"I've boxed up some of your father's old clothes," Mom is telling him as if sensing where Ben's thoughts were drifting. Being in the house, looking down the hallway toward Dad's old room, always brought those days into sharp relief for him again. "You want to take them? Or should I call Goodwill?"

"Oh, no, I'll take them," Ben says.

"They're a little musty."

"You know, those styles are back in now," Anita says helpfully.

No one responds.

Dad's clothes. Ben remembers a red-and-blue-checked shirt. He wonders if that was in the box. And his robe. White terry cloth. Dad always wore his robe in bed.

He died in that robe.

"Rosemary! Benny! Somebody!"

Ben would bound down the hall to find Dad struggling to get out of bed, but tipping precariously off the side. He couldn't walk toward the end, and he would shit himself two, three times a day. The sheets and his terry cloth robe were regularly soiled with what looked to Ben like coffee—with the same consistency, too. There was hardly any odor. Once he got used to it, it really wasn't so horrible changing his father's sheets, wiping his father's ass.

"You're a good boy, Benny," his father would rasp. "A good boy. Just remember to always do your best, never cheat, and work your hardest."

"Jesus, Dad, that's a tall order," Ben would say, managing a grin as he snapped his father's diaper around his waist.

Ben was fourteen. Mom would be on the couch in the living room, sometimes in tears, unable to face what her husband had become. In time, she didn't even stir when he called, fiercely intent on her afternoon soaps or reruns of *Bewitched* or *Bonanza*. They had a visiting nurse for a while, but Ben took to skipping school to stay home with Dad. "He's needed at home," Mom told the principal when he called. "I can't do it alone. And besides, I'd rather have Ben miss classes than Richard."

Ben would sit at his father's side as he struggled to eat, jabbing himself with the fork. Finally, without words, Ben just took the fork and gently began to feed his father. Dad just looked at him with his big, round, sunken eyeballs and gratefully accepted his son's ministrations.

It was Ben who rubbed A & D into Dad's raw butt and legs. It was Ben who placed the cold press on Dad's head when he cried that the pain there had grown too intense. It was Ben who was with him at the end.

"He's gone," Ben had said simply to Mom and Richard on Thanksgiving morning when each got up in turn, groggy eyed and disbelieving, several hours later.

"Oh, Lord!" Mom cries now almost spilling Ben's milk as she tries to carry it and the cups of coffee at the same time. Anita leaps up and helps her. They settle the glass and cups on the table. Mom sighes, out of breath, and then passes out paper plates and plastic forks.

"Whatsa matter?" she asks. "Don't you want any cake? Dig in."

Ben cuts three slices of the strudel, careful to make sure each is exactly the same size. "Don't be stingy." Mom laughs. She sits down and takes a bite. "Good, huh?"

"Mmm," agrees Anita.

"I talked with Richard last night," Mom tells them, food in her mouth. "He said he knew you were coming but not what you were going to tell me."

A plane taking off from Westover rocks the house for a brief second. They wait for the noise to subside, as they've become accustomed to doing, barely noticing they're doing it, and then continue.

"Mom, we're not here to tell you anything," Ben says. "Can't we just come for a visit?"

"All the way from New York?"

"Well, we hadn't been up in a while," Anita says.

Mom tilts her head. Her eyes are small, her lips pink. Ben notices she put on a little lipstick this morning. Well, that's *something,* at least. "Benny," she says, "just come out and ask for it. You know I don't like playing games."

"Mom—"

"Richard told me something about this new movie you're planning." She's finished her cake. "And I'm afraid to say I don't have any money to give you. I just don't."

"Mom, I didn't come looking for financial backing. Is that what Richard said?"

"No, no, don't go blaming Richard." She shrugs. "I just thought it was odd you coming up like this out of the blue."

"Mom, Richard and Rex come up often," Ben says. "I just wanted to come and see you—that's all."

"Well, Richard has a car," she says, sipping her coffee. "What kind is it again?"

Ben feels his throat tighten. "It's a Saab, Mom."

"Can't believe what it costs him to keep it garaged in the city." She shrugs. "But I guess he's making good money writing for all them magazines. I was worried when he left his full-time job at the *Times* to go freelance, but I guess he was right. He seems to be doing just f—"

"Richard's got a good head on his shoulders. Right, Mom?"

Anita looks over at Ben. She makes a face in support. He closes his eyes and swallows his cake with a long sip of milk. *Damn it!* It always happens. He sits here with his mother drinking a glass of milk, getting a goddamn milk mustache on his upper lip, hearing her talk about Richard—and he's a kid again.

"You know, Ben," Mom had said at this very table, right before Ben and Richard went off to college, "I'm going to leave the house to you. Just you."

He had looked up at her. She was sitting right where she is now—but she was sixty, seventy pounds lighter and her hair still had flashes of red and gold. They were eating cake, too, just as they are now. Ben remembers being touched by his mother's words. As if she were sharing a secret with him, something special between them. It wasn't often that they shared anything, just the two of them, the way she and Richard would watch TV together and eat sweets.

"Just me?" Ben had asked. "Not Richard, too?"

She shook her head. "Just you, Ben."

"You're not sick or anything, Mom, are you?"

She sighed. "Not any more than usual. I just want to make plans—that's all. Who knows if I'll make it through your college years. I know I'm not long for this world. And I just wanted to make sure you were taken care of."

"But what about Richard?"

"Oh," she said, and she had smiled—Ben would never forget that smile. "Richard can take care of himself."

And I can't. Ben finishes the last of his cake. *So I get this run-down old house in the Chicopee Falls projects. That's taking care of me. That's all I need.*

What was even worse, Ben thought, was that she certainly had told Richard, too, and Ben could imagine what she had said. "You understand, darling. Ben will need a place to live or at least the money he can get from selling the place. You, of course, darling, will be living in some fabulous Fifth Avenue penthouse by then."

"More?" she asks, interrupting Ben's conceit.

"No, thanks." Ben pushes the paper plate away from him.

"Well," Anita says. "Ben *has* come up with a new movie idea. That much is true."

"And what, may I ask, is it about?"

Ben looks over at his mother. "Mom, have you heard of Marge Schott?"

"Marge who?"

"Marge Schott. She's the owner of the Cincinnati Reds."

"I don't follow football."

"Baseball, Mom. Anyway, she's—"

"Benny, how can you make a movie about somebody nobody's ever heard of?"

He sighs. "Mother, you can't judge what people have heard of by your own lack of awareness."

She makes a face. "You want more cake?" she asks Anita, turning her back to Ben.

"No, thank you, Mrs. Sheehan."

"You gonna play this Marge lady?" she asks.

Anita grins. "No, I don't think so."

Mom picks up their three paper plates and takes them to the sink, wiping them off with a sponge and setting them in the drainer to dry. "Well, Richard told me he gave you another idea but you didn't like it," she says, her back to them.

Damn Richard. "It wasn't right for me," Ben says irritably.

"What did *you* think, Anita? Did *you* like Richard's idea?"

Ben feels the anger surge up, as if he's about to puke out his cake. He can't hold it back anymore. "Oh, I'm sure Richard told you Anita liked the idea, too. What *else* did he tell you? That it was about an old movie star? Maybe the two of you used to watch her on the four o'clock movie?"

"I'd never heard of her." Mom shrugs. "My favorite is Paula Prentiss—you know: Richard Benjamin's wife."

"Well, Paula Prentiss wasn't even *born* when this old broad was on the screen." Ben gets up and goes over to the back door. Outside, he can see the railroad track, now all grown over with maple saplings and goldenrod. When he was a boy the freight train still occasionally rumbled through those trees, carrying coal and rubber to the factories and plants, its whistle long and mournful in the distance.

"Talk about making a movie about somebody no one's ever heard of," he says, too defensively for his own liking. "I mean, at least *Marge Schott* has made the evening news. Who ever heard of Florence Lawrence? And besides, it's not even her."

"Sounds as if *something* strange is going on, to hear Richard tell it," Mom says.

Ben's going to bite his brother's head off when he next sees him for sharing all this with Mom. But it's too late to stop Anita: She's off and running her mouth.

"I'll say," she's babbling. Mom sits back down at the table to listen. "I went with Richard and Rex up to see her. She's a real trip, Mrs. Sheehan. You'd never believe it. She's a hundred and six and is as spry as a—well, a sixty-year-old!"

Mom makes a small smile. "I imagine she gets around better than I do."

Anita laughs awkwardly. "Well, she's—she's just amazing—that's all. And her memory—oh, God, she was telling us about the organ grinders on the streets of New York at the turn of the century and the boys hawking papers on the street and about World War I and the Great Depression—"

Ben's leaning against the sink, watching them, his arms folded in front of his chest. "An old lady's memories do not a movie make," he says.

"I know, sweetheart." Anita tries to contain herself, but can't. "It's just that, well, she's a *mystery*—that's all. She was known as Baby Flo, the Child Wonder Whistler, and she was born in Hamilton, Ontario—"

"Just like this Florence Lawrence actress who killed herself," Mom says. Richard's filled her in well.

"But she says she's not her. And how could she be, really? I mean, all the papers reported that Florence Lawrence *died*. There had to have been a body—an autopsy. She couldn't just have walked away!"

"Maybe it's her sister," Mom says, leaning over and touching Anita's hand. "Maybe she had a twin."

"You know, I've *thought* of that," Anita says.

"Oh, come on. The evil-twin theory?" Ben scoffs.

"Well, anyway," Anita continues, "Richard's doing this article for the *Times* and he's doing some more research. He's determined to get to the bottom of it."

Something twists down inside Ben's gut. Not anger anymore really— although it does make him nuts to realize he's starting to get caught up in this story himself. That's what's got hold of him: that old scent of a story. He's a filmmaker—he recognizes good material. Maybe not the old lady, but Anita's enthusiasm. Richard's determination. The mystery of it all . . .

No, it's not timely, he scolds himself. *Not like Marge Schott. Who the hell is Florence Bridgewood anyway?*

"I remember once, Benny," Mom is saying, "when you were maybe ten or eleven, you took your father's old Super-8-millimeter camera out to see Aunt Bridget at the nursing home. Do you remember?"

He does, but he doesn't say so.

"Well, you got her talking. Remember? She hardly ever spoke. Oh, she was like ninety or something," Mom tells Anita, reaching over and touching her hand again. "We'd go out to visit her and she'd just sit there. My grandmother's sister. From the old country. A bitter old lady. *Hated* being there in the home. But then Benny came out with his camera and started asking her questions. What was it, Benny, a school project?"

"Yeah," he admits.

"Well, he ran out of film! She just kept going on and on. She had actually met—which President was it, Benny?"

"Teddy Roosevelt."

"She talked a blue streak! It was fascinating. Told stories none of us ever knew before. About growing up in County Cork, taking the boat over here, Ellis Island, all that kind of stuff. And do you know what? She died a week later. We still have that film somewhere down in the basement. What did you get on the project, Benny? An A plus or something, right?"

"It was just an A, Mom," he says, sitting back down at the table.

"Well, all this just reminded me of that." She shrugs. "You want some more cake?"

The sun slants through the tall windows of the Chelsea town house Richard and Rex share, spilling across the high-gloss wood floors. Ever since they bought the place six months ago, they've been constantly remodeling, knocking down walls, adding glass brick and Art Deco tiles. "Sure wish Billy Haines were still alive," Rex had mused, trying to explain to the young pierced and purple-haired decorator the classic Metro-Goldwyn-Mayer look he wanted.

It's a lazy late Sunday morning, and they're still in bed, mugs of hazelnut coffee steaming on their side tables. The *New York Times* is spread out in its various sections across the white down comforter. They usually get up around nine on Sunday mornings, make coffee, get the paper, and crawl back into bed.

But this morning, Richard's engrossed not so much in the Arts and Leisure or Travel sections—his two favorites—but instead in a pile of photocopies he got yesterday at the Library for the Performing Arts at Lincoln Center.

"Just look," he says to Rex, who glances over at the papers in Richard's hand. "*Movie Mirror,* 1921. 'The Return of Florence Lawrence.' She's making a comeback. And it says here that she spent a chunk of her childhood in Buffalo. Another clue."

"Yeah, our Flo said she spent time there, too."

"Precisely."

Rex lifts a sheet from the pile. It's Florence Lawrence's obituary from the *Los Angeles Examiner.* He reads out loud: "'First Great Feminine Film Star a Suicide.'" He looks over at Richard. "What do they mean, 'feminine film star?' Were all the other ones really butch?"

"It just means first female star," Richard says. "According to this, a guy named King Baggott was the first male star."

"King Faggot?" Rex laughs. "What's up with these names, huh?"

"Read the obituary," Richard says. "She left a note."

Rex looks again at the paper in his hand. "'A note lying on the table was addressed to "Bob," a studio employee, who shared Miss Lawrence's home.'" He looks up at Richard. "Well, well."

"Just read."

"'The note read: "Good-bye, my darlings. You've all been swell guys. Everything is yours. Lovingly, Florence."'"

Rex puts down the paper and looks up into Richard's eyes.

"Curiouser and curiouser, huh?" Richard asks. "How could she leave a note, drink poison, get pronounced dead, and turn up at St. Mary's Home in Buffalo sixty years later?"

Rex nods, then looks back down at the paper and continues reading. "'The final act in Florence Lawrence's life developed when she hammered at the door of her nearest neighbor, screaming, "For God's sake, get a doctor!" When an ambulance arrived before her home at 532 Westbourne Drive, she had collapsed and was taken to Beverly Hills Receiving Hospital.

"'There Dr. Lester Slocum applied a stomach pump and antidotes to no avail. Miss Lawrence died an hour later, at 3:10 P.M.'"

They exchange googy-eyed looks. Rex gives a brief *Twilight Zone* "doo-doo-doo-doo, doo-doo-doo-doo" before resuming reading.

"'Deputy Sheriffs Harry Zahn and K.W. Cook found Miss Lawrence's tiny, flat-roofed home of peach-colored stucco unswept and disheveled, testifying to her upset state of mind. On a stand beside the actress's bed officers found an almost emptied bottle of ant poison and a partly filled bottle containing cough syrup. A glass standing beside them still contained drops that were a mixture of the fluids.

"'The deputies reasoned that Miss Lawrence mixed and drank her poisoned cocktail and lay on the bed to die, but had changed her mind and attempted to summon help—too late.'"

They're quiet for a minute. "Oh, I *love* it," Rex finally says. "'*Poisoned cocktail.*' So 1930s melodramatic." He thinks for a minute. "Come to think of it, I made a film by that name, too. *Poisoned Cock Tail.*"

Richard playfully slaps him with the front section of the *Times*.

"It doesn't figure," he says after Rex stops laughing. "If they had been able to save her, there wouldn't have been a body to pronounce dead." He's talking more to himself than to Rex. "It *can't* be the same person. We're being absurd."

"And look here, look at the subhead," Rex points out:

FIRE ACCIDENT CUT SHORT CAREER

"It says she got burned saving some guy from a studio fire. Left scars on her face. But there were no scars on the old lady."

"No, there weren't," Richard says, considering it. "But read what else the article says." He points to a spot in the story and reads: "'Burns had left scars on her face not readily visible to the eye, but marked to the camera—' That's why Florence Lawrence's career ended. She was never able to recover her place at the box office after 1915."

"Oh, aging actresses will find *anything* to rationalize declining box office," Rex says. "How can scars not be visible to the eye but show up to the camera? That doesn't make any sense."

"Not a lot of what we're thinking *does*," Richard admits.

Rex yawns, stretches. "Hate to break it to you, sugarplum, but we've got to start getting up. I've got the decorators coming in at noon." He sits up, swinging his legs off the bed.

"Oh, not *today*, Nooker. It's *Sunday*. What are they going to be doing?"

"The island in the kitchen. Those funky tiles we picked out, remember?"

"How could I forget?" Richard collects the papers on the bed and sets them on the floor. "And how much is that costing us again?"

"Oh, don't be such a sourpuss."

Rex stands, wrapping his green satin robe around his body. Richard catches a glimpse of him in the full-length mirror that stands near their closet. He's put on a little weight since starting the new drug cocktails, making him a little soft around the waist, a far cry from the taut little perennial bottom boy of his half dozen porn films. Rex had made them when he first came to New York eight years ago, when his name was still Ralph Russo, the proverbial starving actor right off the bus from Harrisburg, Pennsylvania. Richard's seen the videos: low-budget, kinky, with Rex strung up to the ceiling in leather restraints and taking whatever abuse his leather-clad masters chose to dish out. "Oh, they were all such *queens*," Rex has told him. "They'd dress up in their butch leather and chains and bark orders at me when the cameras were rolling, but afterward, they'd open their mouths and sequined purses would fall out."

Richard finds nothing erotic about the videos. After all, that's his little *Nooker* hanging upside down from the ceiling. It's hard to eroticize the scene when Rex is out in the kitchen asking him if he wants Franco-American spaghetti with his fish sticks. But mostly, Richard suspects, why he finds the videos difficult to watch is he keeps wondering if the scene being played is the one in which Rex got infected, even though the sex on the screen always appeared to be safe. "There were times," Rex admits today, "we said to hell with the condom."

Four years ago, Rex nearly died. Pneumocystis. It had taken over quite suddenly, despite the Bactrim and AZT—or maybe, as Rex came to think, *because* of them. He just kept getting worse, wasting down to about ninety pounds, coughing up blood and going yellow right before Richard's eyes. They'd spent two years trying to prepare themselves for this possibility, but there's no way to prepare for such a thing—not really.

Richard seemed frozen, unable to act. There was a sense of unreality to it: how could Rex—his cute, silly, far younger and far less cynical boyfriend—have this disease while Richard remained negative? What kind of sense did that make? Ben and Anita did what they could, as did legions of their other friends. But all Richard could do was stand and stare, clenching and unclenching his fists, as the home health aides—and later, after Rex was admitted, the nurses in the hospital—administered his meds and turned him over every few hours so he wouldn't get bedsores.

It's like Dad all over again, Richard thought. *And I was helpless then, too. Unable to do my part, pull my weight. I just stood on the sidelines then, too, leaving everything to Ben.*

He'd loved his father, and he supposed Dad had loved him, too, although it was always Ben he spent time with, Ben he built motors with in the garage or shot baskets with in the driveway. Richard had tried to find common ground between them—they both loved pistachio ice cream and *M*A*S*H*—but such things only went so far. With Mom, he could talk about anything, tell her about his hopes and ambitions, and she always cheered him on. Dad was more reserved, uttering just a couple of syllables a day, it seemed. That suited Ben okay, because he never spoke much either. They'd be out in the garage working for hours, never saying a word. Richard had to content himself with his father's clap on the back after nailing down straight A's.

Was he proud of me? Richard was never entirely sure. *Did he suspect I was queer? Is that why he preferred Ben, because Ben was a real boy? Real boys don't sit inside with their mothers watching* The Guiding Light *and Loretta Young movies.*

If Dad hadn't died, Richard thinks now, *if he had lived, and seen what I've done, the house I live in, the car I drive . . .*

But he did die—and Richard never had the chance to say anything, let alone good-bye.

He doesn't like to remember how he recoiled from changing Dad's diapers, or how, a decade later, he saw the process repeat itself with Rex. He couldn't bring himself to hold Rex's head when he puked up blood. *I don't deserve him,* Richard thought about both Dad and Rex and occasionally still does. *I don't deserve him to get well.*

Rex had been his first boyfriend to last more than a few months, and now the Fates were snatching him away. If the Sheehan brothers were notoriously dissimilar in most things, they shared one trait in common: They each spent their lives going through lovers at least as fast as they went through razor blades. Once Ben got to college, he made up for lost time in high school by screwing every girl who said yes. Richard, meanwhile, was heading into the Village on a near nightly basis, cruising the Saint and the piers. That he managed to avoid the virus even with all that is something he still thanks God for every night.

But I didn't avoid it, not really, he thinks. Not when Rex is positive. Sometimes, in the weeks when Rex was the sickest, Richard would think back to his days as a single man and damn the irony. Of all the men he'd loved, the one he'd picked to last wouldn't.

"You've got to find *something*," Richard had begged Rex's doctors. They'd been together just two years at that point, but Richard couldn't imagine life without Rex. Just as, once before, he couldn't imagine life without Dad.

That was when he started writing the screenplay. He'd seen other friends die—what gay man in New York in the early 90s hadn't?—and he'd hoped the writing might help him find a way to handle Rex's impending death. He'd be down writing in the living room while Anita and Rex's mom changed his linens. He wasn't proud of it, but it was the only way he'd been able to cope.

"He can't die," Richard had said, glassy eyed, to Ben and Anita after a particularly savage episode with Rex. In a single night, twenty pounds of flesh had seemed to melt away through night sweats. "He can't die. There's so much I still want to do with him."

What's amazing is, he didn't. Unlike Dad, there was salvation for Rex. His worst illness had struck just as the new drug cocktails became available. They'd never heard of these protease inhibitors, so none of them reacted with much optimism. Yet within days, Rex was sitting up in bed. In just a few weeks, he'd put back all of the weight he'd lost. In three months, he was back at work, writing the first draft of *Broadway Royals.*

They hardly ever talk about that whole time anymore, except when Richard jams the refrigerator too full and Nooker can't find his Norrvir. "I'm taking my pills," he insists to his friends, "but I'm not going to become one."

Their lives have settled into a quiet assumption of survival. "Guess you're stuck with me," Rex has joked to Richard.

Now, watching Rex as he fusses around the apartment, picking up their dirty clothes so he won't have to be embarrassed in front of the decorators, Richard still can't imagine living without him. He also can't imagine going through that kind of sickness again. *Could I have done it? Could I have really been there for Rex the way Ben was there for Dad had he not gotten better?*

Four years later, and the memory of Rex wasting away in that hospital bed hasn't left him. *They say it can be hiding in the brain. In the marrow. Don't let that be the case. Please let it be gone. Please.*

It's been six years now. They'd met not cute but rather ordinary: at a mutual friend's dinner party, talking about the don't-ask-don't-tell policy. The party got a little dreary, so Richard made eyes at Rex and Rex made eyes back. Both assumed it would be just another quickie, a pleasant Friday night into Saturday morning, and when it was done, they'd shake hands and write down their numbers and that would be that. But Rex had ended up cooking breakfast, and over scrambled eggs and potato pancakes, they'd shared mutual Catholic school horror stories and their love for Myrna Loy. All at once, to work off their breakfast, they decided to go Rollerblading through Central Park, and then, famished by midafternoon, they'd gone for Indian food, prompting a trip to the gym and finally a night out dancing at the Roxy. It went like that the entire weekend, and they came back for more Monday night and Tuesday. By Wednesday, they'd used the "L" word for the first time. Within five weeks, they were living together.

Ben and Anita had predicted they wouldn't last. They'd joshed that Richard was robbing the cradle. Sure, there's eight years difference between Rex and Richard, but Richard doesn't feel it. At least, not usually. Oh, all right, so Nooker has odd taste in music—whiny slacker girls— and he wears old 70s fashions—the kind of silky, shiny, pointy-collared shirts Richard wore to high school—as a sign of being hip. But he's given Richard a sense of *home* that he's never had before.

Never. When Richard was quitting his full-time reporter job and going freelance, it was Rex who provided the emotional support he needed to take that leap. "Sweetheart, you move with the flow," Rex told him. "You know when the time's right. I know you can do it. And if you can't, well, then we'll figure that out as it comes."

Sure, he seems flighty—never missing an episode of Ricki Lake or getting in a tizzy trying to decide which wallpaper was best for the upstairs bathroom—but there's a solidness to Rex that belies his image. Rex had been the one to hold his own family together after his father went bankrupt back in Harrisburg. He still sends money home from his acting gigs, and he's the one his mother still calls when she's had a fight with any of her other kids. "You're my *rock*," she says to him as he stands there in his fuzzy slippers and frilly apron, licking cake batter from the electric mixer beaters.

He's Richard's rock, too. Oh, sure, Richard pays ninety percent of their household expenses—not a lot of income from Rex's gigs these days—but there's no question of Rex's contribution. Rex just seems to have this sixth sense whenever Richard comes home foul mooded and depressed. He instinctively knows how to stroke the infamous Sheehan ego. "Great letters on the Internet about that piece you did for *Vanity Fair,*" he'll say when he senses Richard's feeling down about not selling his screenplay. "Here, I printed them out for you."

"Rex is a *saint* for putting up with you," Ben has said many times, and for once, Richard agrees that his brother is right.

Richard knows he's ego driven. Arrogant, some have called him. All those sweaty mornings pumping up at the gym—he doesn't do it for his fucking health. It matters a great deal to him to see heads turn as he walks down the street—to get the looks that say: *You are fine. You are hot. You did* good.

There was only one boyfriend before Rex that Richard ever felt strongly about, and he's smart enough to know why. The guy's name was Scott, a drop-dead gorgeous, cleft-chinned blond model who'd once made the cover of *Men's Health.* They dated for just three months, and Richard loved walking into bars with Scott, loved watching his friends' reactions when he introduced them. Scott made him look even *better.* And when Scott broke up with him—the only boyfriend *ever* to break up with him—Richard had been crushed for weeks.

That wasn't love, he tells himself now. *That was just part of the game. The challenge. The dream to have it all.*

"Richard will go *far*—as far as he wants," Mom would say at the dinner table. "Won't you, Richard?"

Dad, of course, never said a word. Richard would look over at him during Mom's effusive praise but he'd just sit there, eating his cube steak with A-1 sauce without ever looking up. After dinner he'd motion to Ben and they'd go out to the driveway and shoot some hoops. Richard would hear the *thump, thump, thump* of the ball as he sat at the table, now cleared of dinner plates, working on his school project. He'd carefully cut out pictures from magazines, pasting them onto construction paper, neatly writing the captions under them.

"Ben's just like your father," Mom would sigh, standing over Richard's shoulder, complimenting him on how beautifully he printed. "Your father has said he'll fix the roof, but does he ever? I've been waiting for a color TV set for *years*. And now Ben's turning out just like him. He won't start his project until the night before it's due. But *you,* Richard—*you'll* show them."

Goddamn Ben, Richard thinks, throwing his legs off the side of the bed and standing up—finally responding to Rex's threats that he get up now or he'd come in and *pull* him out of bed. *Goddamn Ben. Squandering Dad's money. Dad worked hard to leave us that money—*

surprised us all. And now Ben's squandered the education Dad got for him, fulfilling all of Mom's predictions. He's proving to be the loser she always said he'd be.

"Sure, I work hard," Richard says, defending himself to no one in particular, but everyone just the same. He pulls on a pair of boxer briefs, admiring his body in the mirror. He flexes. "I'll be damned if I'm gonna let it all go to waste."

So how come you haven't gotten a book published yet? How come none of your screenplays have sold?

That's his own voice. He's been hearing it a lot these days, especially as Rex's renovations have become increasingly expensive. Richard likes to live as big as he can—driving that goddamn Saab that the bank has threatened to repossess *twice,* buying this amazing apartment in Chelsea and weighting himself down with an absurd mortgage for the next thirty years. He gave up job security because he realized his job at the *Times* was dead-end, that too many people were in front of him in line, that he would never write a great novel or blockbuster movie that way. Going freelance was his only option if he wanted to take that next step. But it sure made paying the bills a constant struggle.

"Goddamn Ben," he whispers, and he thinks about the screenplay he'd written while Rex was sick. It was hard, wrenching stuff—but funny, too. Funny and sweet, so Rex had thought. Ben was a fool to pass it up. *We could've* both *made it big with that,* Richard thinks.

"I don't like diseases," Ben had said. *And I do?* Richard had thought. What a crock that excuse was. Ben was just too fucking stubborn to let Richard in. Mom's right: If Ben didn't accept Richard's help, he'd get nowhere fast. His lack of movement these past few years simply confirms that assessment. If Ben had agreed and they'd done that film together, Richard is convinced they'd have had a hit on their hands by now.

"Both of us, you idiot," Richard says to the mirror. "Both of us."

"Who are you talking to, honey?"

Rex is standing behind him with some envelopes in his hand.

Richard looks at him and smiles. Just the sight of Rex calms him down. "You know, Nooker," he says, "one of these days I'm gonna do something *big.*"

Rex smiles. "You can do it today. You can move the tiles up from the foyer. They weigh a *ton.*" He kisses Richard lightly on the cheek. "Sorry. I forgot to give you the mail yesterday."

"Oh, yeah, right," Richard says. "You just didn't want me freaking out about all the bills."

He takes the envelopes from Rex. There are certainly bills aplenty. The wallpaper. The new furniture. The recessed lighting. The electrician.

"Hey." Richard's about to put the bills on the bedside table when he notices a long, legal-size envelope among them. *State of California, Department of Health Services, Vital Statistics.* "Hey," he says again, his adrenaline suddenly pumping. "It's *here.*"

Rex squints his eyes to see. "What's here?"

Richard looks at him brightly. "This is *Florence Lawrence's death certificate,*" he says.

He tears open the envelope. A pink photocopied document falls out, framed in a blue filigreed pattern. Richard picks it up off the floor: *Standard Certificate of Death.*

"Okay, let's see," he says, reading the handwriting that's filled in the particulars. "'Full name: Florence Lawrence. Residence: West Hollywood, California.'"

"Hey," Rex laughs, "old Flo was a WeHo girl."

Richard skims down the list, itemizing. "'Female. Caucasian. Divorced. If married, widowed, or divorced, name of husband or wife: Henry Bolton.'" He looks over at Rex. "Who was he? Some actor or somebody?"

Rex shakes his head. "Never heard of him." He peers around at the certificate. "Oh, look—suicide. And there *was* an autopsy."

"Yeah," Richard says quietly. "There *was* an autopsy."

Rex goes on reading: "'Date of birth, January 1, 1890.' Hey, the old girl was born on New Year's Day."

Richard nods. "'Birthplace: Hamilton.' Just like—" He pauses. He sees the name on the next line and feels as if a cold invisible hand has just touched him on the shoulder. The top of his head goes numb.

"Rex, look," he says softly.

"What? Where?"

Richard points. He speaks slowly, reading the words. "'Father's name: Charles Bridgewood.'"

"Bridgewood," Rex repeats, whispering.

"Bridgewood," Richard says again.

December 1906

My grandmother once said that Bridgewood was no kind of name. I'll never forget it. She was standing out at her backyard fence, on a miserably hot summer night, talking with her neighbor, a wrinkled old pear of a woman, Mrs. O'Shaugnessy. They were all Irish on Grandmother's street. Grandmama herself had been born in County Cork—a prim, white-haired lady in her perennial black widow's dress. It was the first night of the great Pan-American Exposition, as I recall—we could see the lights from the fair glowing over the trees. Mrs. O'Shaugnessy was asking Grandmama what our name was—Mother's and mine and my brother Norman's. We'd just recently arrived in Buffalo to live for a while, in my grandmother's house, in the town where my mother had been born. I was nine, ten—somewhere around there. The Year of the Fair.

And Grandmama told Mrs. O'Shaugnessy our name was *Bridgewood*. I remember the old lady made a face and asked what kind of name was that.

Grandmama responded, "It's no kind of name."

She didn't know I was hiding under the back porch. I'd gone there to escape my brother, who resented my presence and was constantly tormenting me. I hated him. I despised *everything* about Buffalo, in fact—especially Grandmama, who could make Mother cry with her hard words. Grandmama had held a grudge against Mother for years. Mother had married an Englishman, hadn't she? And all the Irish hated the English. And Mother was an *actress,* living a sinful, heathen life. When she had gotten married, Mother had tried to give up the stage, but Grandmama didn't see it that way. Hadn't she met her husband while she'd been performing? Hadn't he been one of those men who came to watch her dance? Hadn't he come *every night* to see her? He was an old man, some *thirty years* her senior—as old as her own father. Grandmama had called Bridgewood the devil himself.

It's no kind of name.

So I didn't mind very much when I gave it up and became Florence Lawrence. Not at first. Later, I came to mind very much. But then I was happy to shed anything that reminded me of that bitter-faced old man who lived over his cabinet shop in Hamilton. I barely knew my father. Occasionally, on Sundays, before we left Canada, my mother would take me to his shop, where he always sat, frowning and hunched over a piece of wood, carving it with his knife. I'd just stand there, mute and unmoving, watching him. His shop smelled of sawdust and pine, of stains and paint. I remember my footsteps in the wood dust on the floor.

I never asked why we didn't live with him. It just seemed natural that we didn't. It was Ducks, after all, who took me to the market on his shoulders. It was Ducks who the other children assumed to be my father. But I knew he wasn't. I always understood the truth. My father was a frightening old man who never smiled, who rarely spoke to me. He had flaking, wrinkled skin, white hair and horrible, horrible hands—scarred and spotted, with his left ring finger cut off at the knuckle. I would stand there in his shop and look up at him, never speaking, as he whittled away with his knife. A plain-faced woman always lurked somewhere in the background, making his food—my half sister, as I'd learn later, from my father's first marriage, to a "respectable" woman—but she rarely spoke either. She just looked at me as if I were some urchin wandered in from the street.

A few years after we left, my father killed himself. Oh, that's not what the papers said. That's not what Mother told me. But he did. Shut all his windows and lay in front of his coal stove. He was seventy-two years old. My brother found him there five days later. Cold and hard. I hated to think about it. As a girl I'd put my hands to my ears and scrunch up my face whenever Norman tried to taunt me with the fact. *My father killed himself.* Grandmother said suicides burned the longest in hell.

Even longer than murderers.

My mother was a proud woman. *Lawrence* was her idea, her creation, pulled out of the air. I can see her now, her great eyes widening, her gray hair swept up, her high lace collar too tight on her throat.

"You will not defame the name of Lawrence by appearing in the flickers," she's warning, adamantly opposed to the idea of earning some extra money by working in moving pictures. But her fears were groundless: In those chaotic early years, no one was billed in the movies. Sometimes there wasn't even a title—just scenes running together up on the screen in those dusty, cramped nickelodeons.

We were living in New York, in a tiny two-room flat with a shared bath on the third floor of a brownstone tenement on West Fiftieth Street. We paid eighteen dollars a month. Ducks and his current companion, a young man named Jimmie, lived one floor up.

Jimmie had been a dancer, but was too plump to have much of a career. He was more pretty than handsome, with absurdly long eyelashes and big red pouty lips. Ducks enjoyed spoiling him, as he did all his beaus. He'd spend all his hard-earned cash on sweetmeats and candied apples for Jimmie, and when Jimmie complained that Ducks's snoring kept him awake at night, poor old Ducks would hobble downstairs and sleep on our floor.

How I remember Mother in that little place, boiling water on the stove, dropping in eggs she'd bought on the street and carried up in her apron. On Christmas Eve that year, we bought a small evergreen tree from a vendor on the street. Ducks dragged it up the three flights of stairs, its needles scattering everywhere. We popped corn over the fire and Jimmie strung it along a silk thread Mother had found in her sewing box. That was the extent of the tree's decoration. But it smelled so lovely—bringing a little bit of the forest into the city, a sharp sting of pine.

Times were hard. Work was very difficult to come by. But we knew if we were to make it on the stage, we had to be in New York. Broadway was in its thrilling infancy then. The Belasco was the first, but the west forties were filled with theaters, their great white lights turning night into day. That season I remember Blanche Ring and Vernon Castle in *About Town* and Lew Fields's and May Irwin's names up in electric bulbs on the marquees.

Linda and I wrote constantly back and forth. I told her all about the lights of Broadway, about saving my money so I could see Clara Palmer in *The Blue Moon*. I couldn't wait for Linda to be here with me. That Christmas she sent me a pair of mittens. "It must already be snowing there," she wrote. "I've never seen snow."

It did indeed snow a great deal that winter. When I think back it's *always* snowing that first season in New York. Cold, wet, blowing snow. I wore the mittens conspicuously. "They're from *Linda,*" I told Ducks.

"Honestly," Mother sniffed. "You act as if she were a beau."

We were heading out to another casting call. Mother had turned her entire ambition to me, determined that, if we couldn't be the most famous mother and daughter in the theater, I'd still be the most famous actress on my own. She accompanied me on every audition, traipsing up Broadway and down to the Village, sharing my disappointment each time another girl was chosen. How old was I? Fifteen? Sixteen? Somewhere around there. I was taller than Mother, but hardly. Neither of us stood much more than five feet. I was pretty, if I do say so myself. Blond, as Mother had been before her hair went gray. Trim, small waist, round breasts.

"You're as pretty as any of them up there with their names in lights," Mother said every day. It was her grit and drive that pushed me; she had more energy than girls half her age.

Which served her well. New York was a hard, fast place. The sidewalks and streets were always burdened with people, pushing and elbowing their way past anyone who dared to dawdle. Laborers carrying vegetable and fruit crates from long, rattling wagons. Hawkers with their stinking wooden pallets of fish covered with ice. Street urchins and dirty-faced little pickpockets crouched over steam vents on cold nights. Turn a corner and you'd suddenly be accosted by an onrushing pack of olive-skinned young men—Italians or Greeks or Jews—chattering away in their incomprehensible tongues. We'd turn another corner only to be assaulted by a squawking gaggle of hens, feathers flying, as some vendor shooed them along in front of him.

And then there were the *cars*. Suddenly the streets were *filled* with them, their shiny metal glinting in the sun, their horns bleating like sheep, their proud drivers lording over the slowpoke horses and wagons that continued to trudge by, as if from another time. They'd come careening down Broadway and screeching around the square, scaring the horses and prompting bets to be laid down in saloons on which pedestrian or horse cart would be run over next.

Through it all, every day, went Mother. Of course, I'd accompany her, but it was Mother who led the way, Mother who had the nerve to dodge the automobiles and push through the chickens and the crowds. She'd pick up the *Dramatic Mirror* and pull out her map. "Today we head over to Broadway," she'd say or, "Down to the Village we go." We'd trudge into the marble lobby and ride the squeaking iron elevator cage up to the producer's office. Somehow Mother always managed to weasel me up to the front of the line or else bang on a frosted-glass door she'd been forbidden to enter. *"Here's* your girl," she'd say to the fat men in shirtsleeves and vests, cigars clenched arrogantly between their lips. She'd take my hand and urge me up in front of them. "Have a good look at your next star, gentlemen, for here she is."

They usually called me very pretty. But despite Mother's best efforts, I landed no work on the stage. She began taking in laundry in our small apartment and sold off her jewelry and pearl-studded cane to buy food and pay the rent. Ducks did what he could to help, but he was now supporting Jimmie, whose demands were not only increasingly extravagant but also more frequent.

I didn't love New York the way I had loved San Francisco. There were too many people, and the buildings were far too close together. There were no views, no panoramas of land, sea, and sky as there were in my fabled Golden City. The gutters were filled with mud and horse piss, and the early morning stench that rose to our windows was often unbearable.

Still, there was an excitement I couldn't deny. New York had a brash charm unique in itself, a color and character all its own. On the corners, boys in knickers hawked newspapers. Some were wide-eyed and friendly; others chewed tobacco and spat it rudely on the street when you passed. Girls, many younger than I, with painted mouths and cheeks sold hot roasted ears of corn down by the piers. Organ grinders cranked out tinkly little tunes while their spider monkeys danced on their leashes, dropping little turds all in a row. Vendors with horse-drawn wagons sold flavored gum drops and sugar-roasted peanuts for a nickel a bag. Sometimes, without any of us making an issue of it, such goodies stood in for dinner.

I remember the first time I walked across the bridge that connects the island of Manhattan with Brooklyn. I'd seen it all lit up at night like an electric carnival, and I marveled at the great ships that passed beneath it. Its sheer size seemed unreal, like some strange optical illusion, so Ducks and I decided to go the distance and walk its span of sixteen hundred feet. We looked down at the steamboats and up at the rattling trains that passed overhead. We felt terribly small. The giant skeleton of iron and steel trembled under our feet. Behind us the city of millions was slowly popping into electric life against the gray-and-purple twilight.

If only Linda were here to see. I held her latest letter in my coat pocket. In it, she told me she had gotten married. Her new husband was a playwright. They were coming to New York to sell his play to Mr. Belasco.

That thought sustained me. *Linda would be in New York soon.* Every day I waited for the telegram announcing her arrival in the city.

Oh, it was all romantic tomfoolery—I knew that even then, but there aren't many things in life more potent than that. Even for a girl as cynical as I'd already become, the fragrance of fresh oranges could still transport me across time and space.

"Well," Mother sniffed, "maybe her husband can at least get you some work with Belasco."

"Maybe he can get *all* of us work," I suggested.

"Well, in the meantime," Ducks said, pouring us all some beer, "I've taken a job at Vitagraph out in Flatbush for a few days. They needed someone who could ride a horse."

"Oh, Ducks," Mother said, frowning. "The *flickers?*"

"Five dollars a day, Lotta."

"Oh, Mother, I can ride a horse." I looked at her wide-eyed and willing. I thought of the Vitascope, how thrilling it had been to watch pictures dance on the screen. "What do you say, Mother?"

I remember the wind whistling outside our window. A five-cent baker's pie was warming in the oven, the smell of cinnamon and apples filling the room. Mother had traded her services for the pie; the baker's freshly laundered socks and undershirts were strung across our kitchen. Outside in the snow on the window ledge a bottle of beer chilled for dinner. That and egg soup were our holiday meal.

It was Christmas Day.

I've never been good with dates, but I know that my first day in front of a moving picture camera was December 28, 1906, and at the end of the day, I found a dead man.

Cold and blue. Almost black. Hanging from a tree in Bronx Park. No one knew how long he'd been hanging there. I watched the men cut him down. We never learned who he was or why he'd taken his own life.

December 28. I used to mark the anniversary every year on my calendar. Sometimes we'd all have a toast—in those years when there were still people to toast with—Mother or Harry or Pop Lubin or Charles and I. The last time I raised a glass to the memory of that date was the night before I walked away from all of it. Lester had brought over a bottle of champagne, a sweet gesture, the kind of thing Lester was always doing. Bob was there, and Marian.

And Molly, too, of course. Standing right there next to me with the platinum growing out of her hair in streaks.

"Here's to a new life in pictures!" Lester exclaimed. The cork popped, hitting the ceiling. "Here's to the return of The Biograph Girl!"

The movies. I had no idea that cold and bitter morning when we set out for the Edison studios in the Bronx how much they'd shape my life. All of our lives. To appear in one seemed demeaning to Mother, who still carried with her delusions of grandeur on the stage. But when I first saw myself up there on the screen, twenty feet tall, what I saw was so startling, so astounding, that I couldn't look at anyone else in the picture.

I wore the mittens Linda had sent and wrapped my scarf completely around my head, leaving just little slits for my eyes. It wouldn't do for my face to be all purple from cold when we got there.

"There's not enough sun," Mother kept griping. She was only reluctantly going anyway. "They'll never be able to photograph us."

Back then, you see, moving pictures could only be shot when there was sunlight. Arc lamps were still some years in the future. But the Edison crew was game. They assured us they'd get in as much footage as they could whenever the sun peeked out from the clouds.

"Over here, Miss Lawrence," the assistant director, Mr. McCutcheon, called. "Here's your noble steed."

The horse whinnied at me. He was agitated, lifting his front legs and shaking his head. "Can you calm him?" the assistant director asked.

I looked into the animal's eyes. They were black and wild. "I'll do what I can," I promised.

Mother was introducing herself to the other players, acting like some grande dame of the theater. They were from Buffalo Bill Cody's Wild West Show. The picture was called *Daniel Boone, or Pioneer Days in America*. I was to play one of the Boone girls; Mother had been assigned the part of Mrs. Boone.

I mounted the horse. I pressed my legs firmly around him the way a man would, stroking his neck, whispering soothing words into his high, active ears. He was a fine horse, with a strong back and good withers. He was just excited—maybe from being penned up too long, maybe from the bitter cold, maybe from the snapping bonfire where we warmed our hands and faces between scenes.

The director was Mr. Edwin Porter, who was quite famous, I learned—the director of *The Great Train Robbery*, the biggest hit of all time. He was perched on a small incline and shouted his direction through a megaphone. The camera—a big, heavy clumsy box mounted on a large tripod—stood off to his left.

"All right, Miss Lawrence," Mr. Porter boomed at me. "Now it's your turn. Ride in toward the camera, but for heaven's sake, don't knock it over."

I gave the horse a kick. He whinnied and began to buck. I attempted to steady him, knowing that if I failed to do so I might never be hired by Mr. Porter again. I'd told him I was an expert rider. And I was. I had learned when I was just a girl, and I had ridden through all those frontier towns we played out west. I couldn't understand why this horse wasn't cooperating. I'd always been able to soothe a horse before. He raised his front legs, snorting furiously. "Come on, boy," I said, reaching around to stroke the side of his face. "Come on."

He lurched. I gave a kick again, but he reared up, spat, and bounded off in the wrong direction, away from the scene. The camera would get only a look at the horse's ass—and me bouncing off its back like some pampered city girl.

"Whoa, boy!" I called. "Whoa!"

I heard Mr. Porter cry out after us. I pulled on the reins, bringing the animal to a halt. "Please, boy," I said. "Come on, boy. Let's go."

I felt the animal tremble. Poor thing. He was terrified. But of what?

Why do you want to be an actress, Flo?

Linda's voice.

Is it just the applause?

Why was I thinking of Linda all of a sudden? What was I doing on top of this terrified horse?

It was cold and a light snowy mist had begun to fall. I just sat there still on the horse, continuing to whisper reassurances into his ear. "It'll be all right, boy," I promised him. "We'll do our bit and then we'll go home."

Finally I was able to turn him around. We trotted back toward the camera. "Have him under control now, girl?" Mr. Porter called.

"I think so," I said, but in truth I had no idea.

"All right, then. We'll give you another shot."

This time the horse did as I bid him. We galloped toward the camera, clearing it by about a foot. Mr. Porter called, "Perfect!"

That's when someone yelled, "Fire!" The bonfire had gotten loose, igniting a series of small grass fires. I dismounted, thanked my horse, and allowed him to be led away from the flames, which were spooking him even more now. I took a seat on a log at some distance watching the men hoot and holler as they stamped out the flames.

From my coat, I withdrew a tablet of paper, borrowed pen and ink from Mr. McCutcheon, and wrote:

Dear Linda,
I am making a moving picture today. What a curious experience it has been. The sun has gone behind a cloud and a fire has broken out. We may need to begin again tomorrow.

I looked up. Above me stood a man from the Wild West Show. He was playing an Indian in the film; his face was painted with black smudges. He offered me a cigarette. "Might as well warm your lungs," he said.

I smiled up at him. He lit the cigarette for me and handed it down. I took in a long, delicious drag.

"Some trick riding there," he said, smiling a crooked grin.

I raised my eyes. He was handsome, with dyed black hair and steel gray eyes. Older than I was. Maybe thirty. "Thanks," I said, taking his comment as a compliment.

He sat down next to me on the log. "You're mighty purty, Miz Boone," he whispered in my ear.

He smelled of gin. My first instinct was to pull away, but I didn't. He seemed to be friendly with Mr. McCutcheon and the others; it wouldn't do to offend them. In the old days, of course, when Mother was the boss, none of our actors would have dared sit so close to me. Mother would've had them tossed out—but first I'd have landed my own fist on their jaw. I'd always taken care of myself. In Buffalo, I'd rassled it up with Norman many a time when his teasing got too severe. I may have been just a girl, but I got my licks in.

Now, however, I felt my face flush as the actor nuzzled my hair with his nose. I stiffened. "Just keepin' warm," he said with his lopsided grin. When he asked me if I wanted another cigarette, I declined.

He was handsome—I couldn't deny that. His proximity made me uncomfortable, but I admit there was a tangle of feelings wrapped up in that discomfort. There was something warm and thrilling to his nearness, too—warm and a little heady. I could smell gin and tobacco but also sweat and . . . something else. Mother and her actors had all treated me like a child. When this man kissed my ear, I wasn't sure how I felt. I finally just stood and headed off into the trees.

It was too late to do any more filming. It was getting dark, and I was cold and damp. In my head, I was composing the rest of my letter to Linda. I planned to tell her:

> It is a queer thing, making movies. Nothing at all like acting on the stage. Strange men, calamity after calamity—and no applause.

That's when I bumped into the body dangling from the tree.

A man. Dead. Hanging.

I screamed.

My Indian-painted friend rushed up behind me. "Miz Boone," he ordered, "cover your eyes."

But I couldn't. I just stood there and screamed. The dead man's eyes were open and black. His neck was broken at a horrible angle. He wore a waistcoat and vest. A pocket watch had come loose and now swayed lifelessly at his side. His black eyes faced me, but his body was turned toward the woods.

He'd killed himself.

Like my father.

Mr. Porter and the others were gathering around. Mother was suddenly behind me. "Florence, come away with me," she said.

But I broke free of her. I turned to my new friend. "May I have another cigarette please?" I asked. Mother watched me warily.

He lit it for me. I thanked him, inhaling the smoke, holding my gaze with his. He took off his coat, draped it around my shoulders. "There," he said. "Don't you fret over no hanged man."

Mother turned and walked away.

My friend and I moved off, too, just as I heard them cut the dead man down.

We went to a tavern in the Village. There were dozens of them in those days—seedy little places with bartenders who wore eye patches and patrons who spat on the floor. My friend was staying at the boardinghouse above. I drank several whiskeys and smoked perhaps a dozen cigarettes. At one point, a little drunk and very tired, I turned to my friend and said, "Do you know that suicides burn even longer in hell than murderers?"

He put his arm around me and kissed me with his hot, smoky breath. "Don't you let that trouble your dreams, Miz Boone," he said, his tongue traveling from my mouth down my neck and forcing its way under my high-buttoned collar.

I don't remember agreeing to go upstairs with him. But I'm sure I must have. I went up willingly—I'm quite certain of that—and smoked some more cigarettes and drank some more whiskey. When he reached over with his big hand—I remember how dirty it was with grime caked into his pores, oil defining his fingernails—I didn't protest. I let him touch my throat, cup my breasts, slip his fingers through the laces of my bodice.

But I *did* say no, finally, when he began to unbutton my blouse.

"Stop," I told him. I tried to push his hands away. "No, please. No more."

But I was too weak, too drunk. And after all, he *had* bought me all those whiskeys and given me all those cigarettes. He *had* comforted me when I found the dead man.

"You're so purty, Miz Boone," he kept saying over and over, and finally I just turned my face from his and allowed his weight to collapse upon me.

I hated it. Later, when I thought about it, I felt shame, revulsion. But while it happened, I simply hated the *feel* of it, the roughness of his hands and his sandpapery face, the hot pain that sliced up through me. I cried all during it, and afterward I bled all over the sheets.

He laughed at me, called me a child. He told me to get up, get dressed, get out of his room. I was bleeding quite a bit. I felt queasy and confused from the whiskey and cigarettes. There was a burning sensation inside me that wouldn't go away. I pulled on my shoes and stumbled down the stairs.

Outside, with a tickle of fresh snowfall on my face, I tried to take hold of myself. I thought of Linda. Soon she would be in New York. Soon she would be with me, and we could become famous actresses together.

I got lost finding my way home. I wandered through the Village, not sure which way was uptown. It began to snow furiously. I could barely see through the near solid blanket of blowing white that seemed to drop down from the sky. I huddled in a doorway for a time, drunk and disoriented, trying to remember my name.

"I'm Florence Lawrence now," I kept saying over and over again. "I'm *Florence Lawrence*."

Florence Bridgewood could have found her way home. I'm sure of that. Even if Bridgewood was no kind of name, Florence Bridgewood still could have found her way home.

But Florence Lawrence—*she* just fell down, drunk and bleeding in the snow. She just lay there shivering—almost until daybreak—until a policeman happened upon her and took pity and then took her home.

The Present

"Flo, you know Mr. Sheehan is coming back today," Sister Jean says.

Flo sits opposite a mirror in her room. A nurse's aide is behind her, tying her long, wispy white hair with a bright red bow. Over Flo's bed—a hospital bed that stands in sharp contrast to the maplewood bureau and soft upholstered sitting chairs also in the room—hangs a poster of a little girl, a woman, and a man with a walrus mustache. The poster reads:

BABY FLO, THE CHILD WONDER WHISTLER
WITH CHARLOTTE LAWRENCE AND HENRY
DUXWORTHY

The man is playing a harmonica. The golden-haired little girl stands with her arms outstretched, as if to embrace the audience.

"Flo, did you hear me?"

She turns and smiles. "Yes, Jeannie, I know Mr. Sheehan is coming today," she says.

Jean watches her intently. Has for the last couple of days. She's read the material Richard left with her. So many similarities between the two women. But it was impossible. There was *no way* Flo could be this Florence Lawrence person. No way in the world.

"No way in the *world*," Jean could hear Anne Drew telling her, many times, about so many things, "doesn't mean there's no way in heaven."

Anne had believed in miracles. She never accepted the literal truth. "Don't look to numbers or facts for the truth," she'd taught Jean. "Look to the heart." Which was why it was so hard for Jean when Anne failed, at the very end, to look into her own heart.

"We take care of our own," old Sister William had told her the day Jean learned she was being reassigned from St. Vincent's to St. Mary's. "Believe me, Jean. This will be the best thing for you."

Jean grinned ironically. "Delivering me from temptation, Sister?"

Sister William was from the old school. Still in a black veil and high black lace shoes. But Jean had always found her to be warm and understanding. "It's Anne's recommendation," Sister William admitted. "St. Mary's needs someone like you."

"St. *Vincent's* needs me," Jean pleaded. "Don't send me away."

"You've been devoted to the community of St. Vincent's, Jean. I can't deny that." Sister William took in a long breath. "But in light of what's happened . . ."

Devoted to the community of St. Vincent's. Of *course* she was devoted to them. They were her *family,* those crack addicts and homeless wanderers, those streetwalkers with AIDS, those motherless children. *They were why I became a nun.*

She's been devoted to the residents of St. Mary's, too, as best as she's been able. But it's been different. Many of these folks had been wealthy Catholic fund-raisers and organizers in their day; dear as many of them are, Jean's never felt they needed her—not in the way the people at St. Vincent's needed her.

Only with Flo has there been a connection beyond the superficial. With Flo she felt a sense of kinship. Neither really fit in at St. Mary's. Neither truly belonged. Flo would never have come to a place like this if she hadn't, finally, been forced by physical limitations to do so—and even then, she'd lived on her own a lot longer than most folks her age. Both she and Jean had unconventional tastes, unorthodox senses of humor. Sister Michael, Jean's predecessor, would never have encouraged Flo's theatrical redecoration of the place. She and Flo had fought tooth and nail over Flo's smoking. Jean—although a strict nonsmoker herself—is far more indulgent.

There's a spiritual connection, too. Flo was only a nominal Catholic—"There's some Irish in me" is all she's told Jean—but they share some very similar views on God. "Oh, He's not some crucifix on a wall," Flo has said to Jean, who wholeheartedly agreed. Flo summed up Jean's beliefs in her usual straightforward way: "God's in the eyes of people I love and who have loved me. God's in the soft caress of a young man in the Temple of Dionysus."

That last part hadn't made complete sense to Jean—one more of the mysteries surrounding Flo Bridgewood—but she understood the old woman's gist. "God's our family," Jean said to her.

"And family," Flo reiterated, "isn't counted by blood."

They were all gone, her family, Flo told Jean the first day they met. "I saw them all go," she said, her eyes faraway, "and I'm still here."

It was the same for Jean. Her parents were dead. Anne was dead. And

Victor, too. There was no one. Even the other Sisters felt distant. After what had happened, they saw her through different eyes, and their treatment of her was still painful. The family they'd shared seemed part of an irretrievable past.

But with Flo, Jean had found *home* again. They shared thoughts of God and love and loss late into the night. Flo made her laugh as no one else ever had, teaching her the peculiar brand of folk wisdom that seemed Flo's own. She'd learned a lot with all those years under her belt. "If at first you don't succeed, Jeannie, sure—try, try again," she said. "Then quit. No use being a damn fool about it." Their laughter would echo through the quiet corridors at two A.M.

Flo was her family now—and part of her feared she had failed to protect her. What had Richard Sheehan discovered? *We take care of our own.* Yes, yes—that's what she has to do. She needs to take care of her own.

She sits down next to Flo. The nurse's aide combs the old woman's hair back. "She sure is a pretty one, isn't she, Sister Jean?" the aide asks.

"She sure is," Jean answers. "You think you're pretty, Flo?"

Flo just smiles at herself in the mirror.

She's somewhere else today, Jean thinks. *In her own world, her own space, among her own secrets and truths.*

What truths did Flo keep? *We all have them,* Jean thinks. Surprising, startling little truths that observers would never suspect. In smaller minds, such truths might diminish respect for a person; in others, they simply enlarge the canvas of the person's life. When they'd cleaned out Stanley Soboleski's trunks in the storage area, they'd found dozens of frayed women's brassieres and panties, vintage 1940—and faded yellow photographs of Mr. Soboleski wearing them. His poor daughter—Anita had called her Aunt Trinka, Jean thought—had nearly collapsed on the floor in embarrassment. Jean suspected that she had known her father's secret truth all these years, but never thought it would rise up and grab her as it did. And in front of a roomful of nuns.

Jean respected people's truths. Their secrets. She'd learned that little piece of wisdom on her own. Anne taught her many things, but not that particular bit. Anne could never find it in her heart to see Jean's truth, and that sorrow would forever stay with Jean, the memory of that rejection. But what had happened with Victor would always—*always*—feel right in her heart. So that's where Jean kept it. Always there. Her truth.

She studies Flo now as she faces the mirror. In the material Richard had left, there was an old photograph of Florence Lawrence. A pretty girl in profile, with a prominent nose and strong jaw. Was there a resemblance? Possibly—and yet . . .

"Mr. Sheehan hopes to be finished today so he can write his article," Jean tells Flo gently. She smiles. "You like him well enough, don't you?"

"Oh, yes." Flo taps the aide's hand resting on her shoulder. "Very nice, Cassie. That'll be all."

"Beautiful as ever, Miss Flo," the aide says, winking as she leaves.

Flo turns in her seat. She cocks her head at Jean. "Do *you* like him?"

"I do." Jean *does* like Richard Sheehan. She has almost from the start—but she's worried now. Worried about what he may have opened up. "I just noticed that you seemed—well—a little cagey the other day, Flo."

The two women hold each other's gaze. Flo finally turns away, smirking. "Why, Jeannie, whatever do you mean?"

"Flo, you know I've never pried."

"No, you never have."

"I haven't thought it my business." She hesitates. "But you're my *family*, Flo. I want to do what's right for you."

Flo stands with some difficulty. Then she straightens up, walking confidently to her bureau. She unscrews her lipstick and carries it back to the mirror, then sits down and shakily applies the bright red color to her lips, going above the line to create her own 1920s look.

"What do you mean, cagey?" she asks, looking at Jean through the mirror. "Did you think I wasn't being fair to the poor man?"

"Flo, you tell him just what you want. Nothing more. And if you don't want to see him again, that'll be the end of it."

Flo appraises herself, pursing her lips. She seems to be considering something. "No, I'll see him." She looks at Jean through the mirror again. "I *want* to see him."

"All right then, Flo."

She closes her eyes and takes a deep breath. "Jeannie, do you remember that woman? What was her name again? Her mother was here, died a few years back—"

"You mean Clare Blake?"

"Yes." Flo smoothes out her silk flower-patterned dress neatly across her lap. "Clare Blake. Remember how she was doing that oral-history project? She'd gone back to school, to the community college over in Buffalo, and she was interviewing all us old-timers like we were aliens crash-landed from outer space."

"I remember." Clare Blake had had none of Richard Sheehan's charm and had shown none of his respect. Jean remembers Clare shouting at the folks gathered in the day room, "I'll talk really loud so you all can hear me." Old Mr. Soboleski—bless his soul—kept turning down his hearing aid so that eventually he silenced the patronizing woman altogether. "Tell me your stories," Clare Blake had yelled at them. "Tell me everything you remember."

Flo twinkles. "Would you say I was cagey with Clare Blake?"

"I'd say you were *brilliant* with her." Jean grins. Flo had begun telling a story—whether it was true or not, Jean didn't know—about seeing President William McKinley at the Pan-American Exposition just moments before he was assassinated. Clare Blake's eyes had widened and she'd begun squealing, "Oh, this is good. This is perfect. I'll get an A!" But then suddenly Flo had stopped, staring blank eyed at the woman. "Go *on!*" Clare Blake had insisted. "Go on! You were waiting in line and *then—*"

"I don't know what you're talking about," Flo had said dreamily. "Who are you?"

Poor Clare Blake had gone away with about twenty minutes of unfinished stories.

"You were brilliant," Jean says again.

"I have my reasons for everything I do," Flo says, patting Jean's leg.

"Flo," Jean asks, reaching over and taking Flo's old spotted hands in her own, "I need to ask you. Did you tell Richard the whole truth? Did you answer him—honestly—each time?"

Flo studies her. She reaches up and gently caresses Jean's face. "Of course, Jeannie," she says. "Have you ever known me to lie?"

No, Jean thinks. But she fooled Clare Blake. She could be quite clever working around the truth when she wanted to.

"You tell Richard to come see me in my room this time," Flo says. "I want to show him my posters here. Tell him—tell him I'm ready for anything he wants to ask me."

Richard's driving this time. Rex is up front next to him. Anita and Ben are in the back seat.

"How was Mom?" Richard asks, lifting an eye to the rearview mirror.

"I'm sure she's already called and filled you in on *every* detail of our visit," Ben says. Anita's dozing against his shoulder. He doesn't know *why* he agreed to come with them to see this old dame.

Yes, you know why, Ben, Mom's voice says in his head. *You're thinking it's not such a bad idea anymore.*

Rex is still studying Florence Lawrence's death certificate. "Ben," he says, over his shoulder, "Richard also dug up an old biographical article on Florence Lawrence. Guess where she lived and went to school as a girl?"

"You got me."

"Buffalo."

"Well, you're a regular Sherlock, aren't you, Richard?"

"It wasn't so hard to find out this stuff," Richard tells him.

Anita picked her head up. "Buffalo? You mean Florence Lawrence has a connection to Buffalo and her real last name was Bridgewood? Oh, this is just getting *too* weird now."

Ben looks out the window at the passing trees. Buffalo's still a long way off. He's going to have to put up with Richard's smug sleuthing all the way there.

"I'll admit you're on to something that may turn out to be interesting," he says. "Beyond that, I'm not certain of anything. What are you going to do anyway? Shove those papers in the old lady's face and say, 'Gotcha!'?"

"I'm just going to ask her about it," Richard says. "If she still claims no connection, then I'll ask Sister Jean if I can see her records—"

"Supposing she doesn't *want* to be found out?" Anita asks. "I mean, if she *is* The Biograph Girl and all that. Or her sister. Or whatever. Supposing she doesn't *want* to be reminded of it? I mean, it *was* an awfully long time ago."

No one says a word. The only sound is the steady rush of the road under the Saab's wheels.

Ben laughs, breaking the silence. "Well, honey, that's the press for ya. Always barging right in even when they're not invited."

"Hey, you're going ahead with that Marge Schott idea even though *she* said she wouldn't cooperate with you," Richard says.

"I never planned on doing it *with* her," Ben tells him. "Actually, I don't even *want* her involvement. It's not even really *about* her. It's about race and gender and cultural attitudes."

Yet even as he says the words, Ben knows the rush of passion he'd felt just a few days ago has subsided. The thrill in his blood is gone; the fire in his belly is beginning to smolder.

He hates that. How many times has it happened?

Why not try Richard's idea? His mother's goddamn voice again. *Richard thinks it could make a good movie. Maybe Anita and Rex can star in it. You know, Benny, you ought to do something for poor Rex. Who knows how long he's gonna be around? He might even go before me. Poor Richard. But he'll meet someone else, I'm sure. Of course he will, a successful, handsome writer like he is. You know, Benny, why don't you cut your hair short like Richard does? That ponytail just makes you look like a hippy. You're losing your hair pretty fast, you know. I think faster than Richard.*

Ben rolls down his window for some air.

"Hey, I'm cold," Anita says.

"Ah, shit," Ben says and rolls the window back up.

"Hey," Ben says, stepping out of the car and looking up at St. Mary's through the trees. "It looks like something out of—"

"We know," Richard says. *"Dark Shadows."*

"I was going to say it looks like Manderly."

Rex laughs, affecting a mock British accent. "'Last night, I dreamed I went to Manderly again. . . .'"

Richard grins. He watches Ben, who doesn't crack a smile. They make their way up the walk. It's getting to be familiar territory for Richard now. Again he notices the aquamarine Bel-Air parked among the black sedans.

Sister Jean meets them at the door this time. She eyes Ben. "Each time, you get a little larger," she tells the group.

"I hope it's okay, Sister," Richard says. "This is my brother, Ben Sheehan."

Sister Jean's face glows. She reaches out to shake Ben's hand. "Oh, *yes,*" she gushes. "The director of *One Chance, One World.*"

Richard can see Ben's face flush, how surprised he is by the recognition. "That's right," he says awkwardly.

"A wonderful, *wonderful* film," Sister Jean says. "So inspiring. *Thank* you."

"Thank *you,*" Ben says, a little embarrassed, but eminently pleased, too, Richard can tell—and he can't help but be a little moved by his brother's reaction.

They head upstairs to Flo's room. She's sitting in an armchair next to her bed. She seems asleep, but her eyes open as soon as she hears them enter. Richard spies the poster on the wall: CHARLOTTE LAW-RENCE. In the *Movie Mirror* article, Florence Lawrence's mother's name was given as *Lotta.* Could it be a nickname for Charlotte?

"Hello, Richard," Flo says.

He shakes her hand warmly. Anita offers her another bouquet, this time daisies, which Flo takes and inhales deeply, clasping it to her bosom. Sister Jean then takes the flowers and slips them into a vase near Flo's bed.

It's a hospital bed, Richard notices. There's some kind of monitor off to one side, and a guardrail in the down position. It reminds him that despite her agility, despite her sharpness, Flo is still a very, very old woman.

One hundred and six.

The same age as—

"This is my boyfriend Ben," Anita is telling Flo.

"Oh, you must be the movie director," Flo says, shaking Ben's hand. He seems pleased again. "Yes," he says. "Yes, I am."

Sister Jean is standing behind him, her face lit up like a teenage fan. "What are you working on now?" she asks.

He hesitates. "Uh—well, it's still coming together," he says.

"Jeannie," Flo scolds. "You never ask a filmmaker what he's working on. Trade secrets, you know."

Richard smiles. He wonders how many trade secrets Flo is keeping herself.

"Hello, Sexy Rexy," Flo calls. "How are you today?"

"I *swear* I didn't tell her to say that," Ben says, laughing. Richard can tell his brother is already enjoying Flo, that despite his protestations he's pleased as punch he came.

Rex bends and kisses Flo's outstretched hand. "Flo can call me anything she likes—except late for dinner." She laughs out loud that he remembered her quip.

Supposing she doesn't want to be found out? Supposing she doesn't want to be reminded of all that?

Richard stiffens. *You're a journalist,* he tells himself. *You smell a story. You need to pursue it.*

No matter what.

You know, Nooker, one of these days I'm gonna do something big.

"And you?" Flo asks Anita. "Any work yet?"

"A shampoo commercial—that's all."

"It's a pity," Flo says, looking at Jean. "Look how pretty she is. But you should be out in California. Isn't that still the case, that you have to go to Hollywood to make movies?"

Anita smiles tightly. Richard watches to see if she looks at Ben. She doesn't. "Yes, Flo," she says. "That's still the case."

Richard sits down opposite Flo and takes out his tape recorder. "Did *you* ever work in Hollywood, Flo?"

She smiles. The rest of them all take seats: Ben and Anita in chairs, Sister Jean on the bed, Rex on the floor.

"I was there for a spell, yes," Flo tells them.

"I thought you were just a stage actress," Richard says.

"Why did you think that?" she asks. "These posters?"

"That's how you described yourself."

She smiles weakly, as if letting down a guard. "Well, the stage was my first love. One never forgets one's first love, I suppose."

"You obviously haven't," Richard says warmly.

"Is that turned on?" she asks, indicating the tape recorder.

"Yes," Richard tells her.

Flo moves her eyes over to Ben. "Mr. Sheehan," Flo tells him, "if you're going to make movies, you have to go west. Colonel Selig did it first, back in oh-seven, I believe. Then along went the Christie brothers and Dave Nestor, although Mr. Griffith didn't go out for another couple of years. We were dependent on the sun back then, you see. We could work outside all year round in California. Couldn't do that in New York."

"We?" Richard asks.

Flo smiles. "I made my first moving picture in December of 1906, out in Bronx Park in New York."

Richard hesitates. He notices Flo's eyes are on him, as if challenging him. *1906.* That was when Florence Lawrence made her first film, Richard remembers. There had been a filmography attached to one of the articles. *Daniel Boone,* he thinks—for the Edison company.

Which had its studio out in the Bronx.

He slowly reaches into his jacket and pulls out the death certificate. He hands it to Flo. She takes it, looks down at it. "My glasses, Jean," she says.

Sister Jean fetches Flo's eyeglasses from the table beside her bed. They're thick and old—light blue frames with tiny faux pearls in the corners. Flo puts them on gingerly, then looks down again at the certificate in her hands. She's quiet. She seems to be fascinated by the document, reading every line.

"It's Florence Lawrence's death certificate," Richard tells her quietly. "You see, it says *Bridgewood* was her real name."

"Oh, Richard," Sister Jean says disapprovingly, suddenly clucking over them like an old maid schoolmarm. "Flo, if this disturbs you, you don't have to—"

Flo doesn't look up. She keeps reading. "I see what it is, Richard," she says, "and, no, it doesn't disturb me, Jean." She puts it down and takes off her glasses. "At least, not much."

"I'm sorry if I—" Richard begins.

"No, don't be," Flo tells him. She takes a long breath and looks past them. Or *through* them—at something very far away, something none of them can see. "It's just strange—that's all. After all this time. To see what they wrote."

There's a heaviness to the room that feels physical to Richard. As if the force of gravity has suddenly been cranked up a hundred times, and all of them are weighted down under the burden. He watches Flo with unblinking eyes: how she draws her lips together and folds the certificate into threes along its creases. He sees Anita and Ben leaning forward in their chairs, senses Rex and Sister Jean now standing over his shoulder.

"Flo," Richard says, breaking the silence, "are you—is that—"

She looks up at him with astonishingly clear blue eyes.

"Are you the woman described in that record?"

"Yes," she says, very softly.

"But you said no last time. You told us you weren't. Why, Flo? And how is it possible that—"

She smiles, leaning in toward Richard and staring directly into his eyes, making sure she speaks directly over the tape recorder. "Last time," she tells him, "you asked me, 'Are you The Biograph Girl?' That's exactly how you put it. *'Are you The Biograph Girl?'* And I told you no—because I'm *not*. Heaven *knows* I'm not. I'm not even Florence Lawrence, not anymore. Haven't been for a long, long time." She pauses. "But many years ago, in another life, I was."

She looks over at the rest of them and then back at Richard. "Once, a long time ago, I was indeed The Biograph Girl."

Autumn 1908

It means "Living Picture." I always liked that about the name Biograph. *Living Picture.* For that's what we made: pictures that *lived*. Pictures of life. And I was the Living Picture Girl—the Girl of Life.

The envelope came addressed simply:

The Biograph Girl, New York

Just that, nothing else, and still it found me.

"Here's another haul," Harry called, dumping the contents of a burlap sack on the table.

Letters spilled in front of me. The red smudges of postmarks heralded places even *I* had never been—towns with names like Black Sequoia and Prince Rupert and East Moscow. I ran my hands through them, marveling over their number.

They were all for *me*.

"Read this one, Flo," Harry said.

I took the letter from his hand. "'Dear Mrs. Jones,'" I read and laughed out loud. "Mrs. Jones" was the name of my character in the Biograph films. How sweet, how innocent were those early days. The public assumed I really *was* "Mrs. Jones," that I really *was* married to John Compson, who played my husband in the films. We weren't acting out stories to them—we were really *living*. Living Pictures, after all. It was as if some magic camera had caught us as we went about our days, and the whole world watched what we did. In those fresh, giddy, early days, some people honestly and truly *believed that.*

Dear Mrs. Jones,
You are the most talented actress on the motion picture screen. You speak more with your eyes in one reel of film than Sarah Bernhardt does in an entire play with words.

Sincerely,
Mr. Thomas Hearn
Little Rock, Arkansas

"Arkansas!" Dorothy West, another actress, exclaimed. "Where *haven't* the flickers gone!"

Such fame as mine had never been known. You need to understand that if you are to understand everything else. In the matter of just a few years, moving pictures had become staggeringly popular. There were nickelodeons *everywhere*—hundreds in New York City alone. "Electric vaudeville," they were sometimes called. Enterprising men by the thousands converted dry goods stores into movie theaters, buying their chairs from funeral parlors and their film at five cents per foot. All of the big moguls started that way—Zukor and Fox and Mr. Mayer. Their fame and fortune began with their little nickel theaters—and *I* was their first star.

Nothing—*nothing*—like this had ever existed before. Stage stars were known only to those who could afford to see their plays. Singers were only known by their sheet music and reputation; there were no records yet, no radio. The movies offered amusement to the masses. Thousands of new immigrants were pouring into the country every month, and few could afford legitimate theater prices. Many didn't speak English. The movies were their only option. We spoke a universal language: no words back then, not even subtitles. Just music and pantomime and the delirium of the collective imagination.

"Read this one," Harry told me, and I read it aloud:

To The Biograph Girl,
If ever I meet you, I will take you in my arms and carry you away. You will be mine and mine only—forever.

Signed,
Mr. Gilbert T. Rook
Bangor, Maine

* * *

I shivered. Harry just laughed, his big old booming laugh. "Well," he said, puffing out his chest in that absurd way he had, "Mr. Rook will have to come through *me* first."

Everyone laughed. But I'd had enough reading for one day.

I'd been with Biograph four months. That was all it took. Four short months. The letters began arriving at the studio on East Fourteenth Street my third week there. Mr. Griffith said nothing, just handed me the letters. First two or three. Then a stack tied with twine. Then the burlap sacks piled up outside the studio doors.

The trade papers noticed me, too. *The Biograph Girl,* read one editorial, *is the spirit of youth itself.* Another, clipped out and pasted into my scrapbook for so many years: *There is something about The Biograph Girl that makes everyone love her.*

Oh, yes, those were heady, delirious days.

I came to Biograph because of Harry. I suppose it's time I told you about him. Harry's the only man I ever really truly loved, though I think I came to realize that only later, after the bad times had receded. When Harry and I were alone, out on our farm, he could be so kind. I remember how he'd cut down the Christmas tree and haul it into the house, huffing and puffing, and how he'd struggle to make it straight in the stand. He'd drop his big bear arm around my shoulders and beam up at his handiwork, his eyes moist. "You're my greatest gift, Florrie," he'd say, his voice choked with sincere emotion. "I need nothing more."

Except—he did. We all did. It was Harry who brought me to my fame. Harry—with his warm round eyes and shy smile, his soft Southern drawl, his obsessive devotion to me and my career. He couldn't have known how it all would end, what it would do to me, to him, to us.

I'd been working at the Vitagraph studios out in Flatbush, sewing costumes and mending canvas in addition to acting. Mr. J. Stuart Blackton paid me fifteen dollars a week. Mother and Ducks found work there, too, but the leading lady was another Florence: Florence Turner, whom everyone called Flossie.

In those days, spies lurked everywhere. Rivalries among the fledgling studios was fierce. Patent litigation hung like the sword of Damocles over all our heads. It was a rascally business; Thomas Edison threatened to shut us all down for infringement on his patents. In the midst of this, a quiet, aristocratic Southern gentleman named David Wark Griffith had been named artistic director over at Biograph. He wanted to improve the quality of moving pictures, he said, lift them out of the flickers category and make them the equal of the legitimate theater. So he set about assembling a stock company of the best actors he could find.

Enter Harry Solter into the life of Florence Lawrence.

I was a girl wise to the world but innocent of love—of love returned, that is. Having not heard from Linda in months, I was lonely and downcast when Harry first appeared in front of me. I felt friendless and alone, and Mother never failed to remind me how disgraceful it was to be working in pictures. "The longer we stay here," she would say, "the more likely this will remain our lot."

"Excuse me, Miss Lawrence?"

I looked up and I saw him. Dear Harry—standing in front of me on the steps of the Flatbush studio, a bouquet of slightly wilted chrysanthemums in his hand. I was struck by how tall he was, more than six feet, with me barely five two. He wasn't what one might call handsome, with a craggy face and ungainly ears, but he was sturdy and solid, with enormous shoulders and a prominent jaw, and the deepest, bluest, most intense eyes I'd ever seen.

"Those aren't for me, are they?" I asked, gesturing to the flowers.

He nodded. "I've been hoping to talk with you."

Such lovely puppy dog eyes. How polite Harry was. Chivalrous, even. Sweet.

And yet how many men had seemed that way at first? In the past six months I'd made two dozen pictures with at least as many actors. I'd even been on the road for a short spell, appearing in a burlesque farce, *The Seminary Girls*. I was no longer the young innocent who could be had for a few cigarettes, a couple of whiskeys, and some comforting words.

"Well, thank you, Mr. Solter, but let's get to the point quickly, shall we?" I didn't yet accept his flowers.

He flushed. "Well, Miss Lawrence—well, you see, I've been working over at Biograph and—the director there would like to talk with you."

I grabbed him by the wrist and quickly pulled him over to a corner. "What are you trying to do?" I whispered. "Get me fired?"

"You've not signed any contract with Vitagraph, have you?" He was still proffering those damned mums.

"No," I said.

"Well, Mr. Griffith said he'd pay you *twenty-five dollars,* and you won't have to do any sewing or mending—just acting. He wants you to be the leading lady of Biograph's new stock company."

I was stunned. *Twenty-five dollars? Leading lady?* "I don't understand—"

"He's seen you in several pictures. He's been very impressed."

"He wants . . . *me?*" I asked.

Harry nodded. I took the chrysanthemums then, without ever removing my eyes from Harry's face. How kind, how gentle he was. He made a little shy smile and shifted his feet.

That's how I try to remember Harry. That's how I *do* remember him, most of the time. The other Harry—the one who came later—I try not to remember him at all.

I fell in love with him. Oh, that's so clear to me now. How Harry came to fill that place inside me that felt so bereft.

"Mother," I'd said just days before. "I do believe Linda is dead."

She scoffed. "She's just embarrassed because that *great and important* husband she was bragging about probably amounted to nothing. I'm sure Belasco turned him away at the door."

"I haven't heard from her in *nine months,*" I said, turning to Ducks.

He made a sympathetic face. He was getting old now, pure white hair and sunken eyes. "Don't lose hope, Florrie," he said, and his old hand reached out for mine.

I took it. "My last letter came back unforwarded. They must have left San Francisco. They were coming *here.* But if she *were* in New York, she would have contacted me."

Mother sniffed. "She always put on too many airs for me."

"They weren't airs, Mother," I snapped. "She just wanted to be a true actress. She was an *artist.*"

But it terrified me that I was already using the past tense in talking about her. I'd hoped that with my sudden, daunting fame as The Biograph Girl, I'd hear from her, that she'd see me up there on the screen and contact me.

But she never did.

It was easier to believe Linda was dead than merely gone.

"Here you go, Miss Lawrence."

He had borrowed a car to take me over to Biograph, a shiny convertible. I could see how proud he was that he drove an automobile and not a wagon.

"Here," he insisted. "Let me help you in."

I grinned at him. "Might I drive, Mr. Solter? I've had experience."

His face flushed. "Oh, that wouldn't do, Miss Lawrence. A gentleman should never allow a lady to drive a car."

"Oh," I said, unable to hide my amusement. "I see."

He opened the passenger-side door for me. I gathered my skirts and stepped up into the car. He smiled at me; I smiled back. "Are you in?" he asked.

How polite he was. Solicitous. No man had ever been quite so solicitous toward me before, with the exception of Ducks.

Harry closed the door gently. Then he stood straight, cleared his throat, and flattened his lapels. He proceeded to the front of the car to turn the crank. He glanced over at me, giving me a little nod before bending down to his task.

The crank made a terrible grinding sound. The car did not start.

He stood up, nodded at me again, his face red, and tried once more. The same horrible sound.

"Mr. Solter?" I asked.

"Don't worry yourself, my good lady. I'm sure it's just a minor adjustment. I can lift the hood and—"

"But, Mr. Solter," I suggested, careful not to sound too condescending, "I think the problem is simply that you're turning the crank the wrong way."

He just looked at me. Then he laughed. "Miss Lawrence, I assure you—"

I let myself out of the car and hurried around to the front. "See?" I said, turning the crank myself in the correct direction. The car began to rumble. "I've driven these plenty of times."

He managed a tight smile. He thanked me, then insisted on helping me back into the car, opening the door for me and closing it once again after my skirts were safely inside. Then he walked around the front and settled himself behind the wheel.

"I'll go slow," he promised. "I'm sure you don't want the wind to ruin your hair."

"Heaven forbid," I said.

Poor Harry. Poor, darling, sweet Harry. He drove slowly because that was the only way he could drive. He was terrified behind the wheel. I saw the big beads of sweat run down the side of his face and drop off onto his high starched collar. I later learned the car was Mr. Griffith's, and he'd lent it to Harry to make an impression on me. And it did—or rather, Harry did. Oh, the wild driving I could have shown him in that car. But in some odd way, I felt content to settle back in the seat and let Harry worry about the wheel. I felt content and comfortable and secure.

Oh, Harry, when I think of how it all ended—who could have predicted it? No one, not then. Not in those first few days, when all his stumblings and bumblings made me smile and laugh and fall head over anklets in love with him. He was gentle, unassuming, yet so earnest it made me want to cry. The drops of sweat beading off his chin cinched it. No man had ever tried so hard to take care of me—no one since Ducks. It didn't matter that I needed no taking care of—not then anyway. What mattered was that he wanted to.

Harry was more than ten years my senior, the son of Southern share-croppers. He'd left home at the tender age of seven to follow the circus. He'd ridden elephants and tamed lions; he'd barked in front of the bearded lady's tent. He'd acted in Shakespeare on the West Coast and performed blackface in New York. He'd ridden in gaily colored wagons with Gypsies. There wasn't much Harry hadn't done.

He was like a boy, really, but when he laughed, he would shake the room. A big man, tall and thick, but gentle, too. Like the docile bears he'd performed with in the circus, with hands to match. I remember his hands so well: twisted knuckles, crooked thumbs, the way his palms would sweat when they were holding mine. He was constantly breaking our grip to wipe his hands on his pants and apologize. I'd just laugh at him. When he took my little hand in his big bear paw, it would disappear completely.

Yes, I fell in love with Harry Solter. We might have made a family someday, a real family, he and I and our little—

But enough. It didn't happen. Instead I became a movie star.

Harry stopped the car in front of the now famous old brownstone at Number 11 East Fourteenth Street. I remember looking up at the big oak door with the frosted glass, the number 11 painted on in gold leaf. Harry helped me out of the car and then hurried to open the door for me as a proper Southern gentleman should. Inside the brownstone, I liked what I saw. I stepped across the marble foyer to discover a company just taking form, a magic just beginning to coalesce.

You see, I had no idea, not then, of the importance of what Mr. Griffith was doing, no clue that his muttered conversations with his cameramen and lighting assistants would intrude upon the established perception of art, forcing a place among the masters for the upstart discipline we called *film*.

Yet I suppose I *should* have suspected something more was afoot than moviemaking as usual. Mr. Ranous, the director at Vitagraph, had never aimed a spotlight at me in the dark and told his cameraman to keep cranking. Prevailing wisdom insisted that only full, bright, overhead light would do. Mr. Griffith's pictures with their chiaroscuro lighting unnerved some in Biograph's front offices, but the trade papers pronounced them magnificent.

And the close-up—Mr. Griffith didn't invent it, but he used it more often and more cleverly than most, a development we actresses applauded wholeheartedly. He had a way with us. He was never crude, never uttered a profanity in front of his actresses. He complimented us, coddled us even. He was Southern, like Harry. They both treated me as if I were some fragile piece of ancient ceramic, as if I might break if they dropped me, as if the harsh sunlight up on the roof might wilt my "delicate womanhood," as Mr. Griffith called it. Yes, they were always trying to protect me. I could never quite figure out from what.

Later, to both my amusement and chagrin, I learned that Mr. Griffith had, in reality, meant Florence *Turner* when he sent Harry on his errand to Vitagraph. It had been Flossie *Turner* who had so impressed him. But by then, it didn't matter, for I'd proven my worth to him. By then I'd shown him it wasn't just fancy lighting and camerawork that brought people into the theaters. Good old-fashioned star power—such as we had on the stage—could do it, too.

I think I took Mr. Griffith by complete surprise when I'd mount a horse easily, hiking my skirts and riding it like a man. On our outdoor shooting days, Mr. Griffith never seemed to know quite what to make of me. "You have a boy in your soul, Miss Lawrence," he said. I took it as a compliment; I'm not sure he meant it as such.

But he brought something out in me I hadn't known was there. Once, when I was playing a part that called for me to be terrified by an intruder, I was prepared to use all the stock-in-trade mannerisms Mother had taught me for expressing terror on the stage: wide eyes, hands in my hair. But Mr. Griffith had other ideas.

"We don't have to play to the balconies, Miss Lawrence," he told me. "The camera sees much more intimately."

"Then how shall I do it?" I asked.

"Have you ever been *really* terrified, Miss Lawrence?" he asked. "I mean terrified beyond any words to describe your fear?"

Once. When I was a girl. Back in Buffalo, at the great world's fair. But that's a story for another time. I can't bear it right now.

"Yes," I told him plainly. "I have."

"And what did you do? How did you react?"

"I laughed."

Mr. Griffith smiled. "Do it," he instructed.

I wish I could remember the name of that picture. There were so many. But it worked—as he knew it would. My terror bubbled over into madness. I remember how terrified I was, watching myself up on the screen later. I knew it was a photoplay. I knew it was *me* up there, acting out a part. But I sat in terror nonetheless.

We made close to seventy pictures together, David Wark Griffith and

I. Mostly one reelers, with the occasional "select picture" running to two. Within a few short months, it was clear that we had the most popular pictures on the market, far surpassing anything else. And I—The Biograph Girl—was the most popular player.

In the *world*.

Now even Bernhardt herself was considering making pictures. Ellen Terry had done a series of films; Maurice Costello had signed up over at Vitagraph. Stage stars were slowly climbing down off their pedestals, and moving picture theaters were becoming huge, glamorous palaces. Much of the credit went to D.W. Griffith and the humble studio he lorded over at Number 11 East Fourteenth Street.

"And much of the credit for *his* success," Harry often reminded me, "is due to you."

The Girl and the Outlaw. The Stolen Jewels, with Harry as my leading man. *The Barbarian Ingomar. The Romance of a Jewess. The Feud and the Turkey. Those Awful Hats. The Salvation Army Lass. The Drunkard's Reformation.* Even Shakespeare: *The Taming of the Shrew.* Harry played Petruchio to my Katherine. And of course, the Mr. and Mrs. Jones pictures.

Who recalls such pictures today? Such queer titles, no? But ninety-odd years ago, they were the biggest moneymakers of the era, the movies everyone was flocking to see—and The Biograph Girl was the star of them all.

"Mr. Griffith," I announced one morning, having carefully considered the situation with Harry and Mother the night before. "I would like a raise to thirty-five dollars a week."

He looked at me as if dumbstruck. He blinked a few times. I had been working for him just a few months.

But Harry had urged me. "You're Mrs. *Jones.* He knows that. He knows how the public waits in line for blocks every time a new Jones picture is released. Go ahead and tell him what you want. You'll get it."

"Oh, Florence," Mother had countered, elbowing her way past Harry, to whom she was growing increasingly resentful. "Don't rock the boat. Mr. Griffith might get angry."

But the sacks of letters spurred me on. "Harry's right, Mother. I can get what I want. I'm *The Biograph Girl.*"

Such was precisely the reason Mr. Griffith and the other bosses feared our star power, why they kept our names carefully locked away in the studio files. When I presented him with my demand, all he could do was sigh and shrug. "All right, Miss Lawrence," he said. "I'll talk to the bookkeeper."

And when I demanded my own dressing table, apart from the others, I got that, too.

* * *

A brisk autumn morning. I tied on my bonnet, gathered my skirts, and stepped outside into the glorious day, heading down to Fourteenth Street. My heart was singing. I walked with an utter belief in the future, a self-assuredness and tenacity I've never quite known before or since. My stride was quick and confident through the crowded streets to the Sixth Avenue "L."

Along the way, I acknowledged the warm, surprised expressions I encountered. "Excuse me, madam," one courteous lady said, stopping me in my stride. "But aren't you *The Biograph Girl?*"

"Yes," I said, shaking her hand, kissing her three little children all in a row. I signed a scrap of paper for them:

Warmest wishes from The Biograph Girl.

How simple it was in those first months. How sustaining was the unconsidered assumption that it would last.

But on the subway that day, something happened. I caught the eye of a man whose incessant stare frightened me. He never looked away, just stared at me with black eyes through thick, dirty glasses, stroking his unkempt black beard. Even when I stepped off the train, he glared at me through the window.

His face stayed with me all day. At lunch I thought I saw him behind the chestnut vendor's cart. *You're being absurd, Flo,* I told myself. But Dorothy West and the other girls had all seen men like him themselves. *I will take you in my arms and carry you away.*

Later that night, walking home, I heard the steady *clack-clack* of footsteps behind me. I turned around three times, and no one was ever there. Just shadows, long and obscene against the brick pavement. *You're being foolish,* I scolded myself.

Yet did Lillian Russell take the "L" to the theater? Did *she* walk home unescorted? Of course not—and I was at least as famous as she was, even if no one knew my real name.

Sometimes there would be three or four bright-eyed youths gathered around the doors of Number 11. I'd always try to be gracious, but occasionally one of them would become a bit too aggressive. Once a young woman grabbed my hand and twisted my arm trying to get my attention. I was more startled than hurt; she never even apologized.

Inside, however, all was safe. I ran into Harry's arms. "Florrie, you're trembling," he said, wrapping me in his musky warmth.

I felt comforted the way Ducks had once comforted me, as we made our way through the hordes of little children crushing around the theater door. They were all clamoring for me, for a ribbon from my hair, for a touch of my dress. Ducks would carry me, shield me from their little grasping hands. It was now happening all over again. The more my fame grew, the more I felt like Baby Flo again. I buried my face deep within Harry's chest and waited for my heart to stop thudding in my ears. This was why I loved him. This is why I came to believe I could not live without him.

But I wouldn't have changed things. Oh, no. I wouldn't have put the brakes on fame, no sirree. I was far too caught up in the magic, the very real magic that was being conjured behind the doors of Number 11. Oh, the joy I felt in that place, the symbiosis of talent, the thrill of creation. The "nursery of genius" it's been called, and that was what it was. Here was where the movies were born.

All of those who worked there—they're all gone now. Mr. Griffith and Dorothy West. Billy Bitzer, the cameraman. My darling John Compson and dear little Adele de Garde. Nothing's left, not even the structure itself. Number 11 is now just the stuff of dreams—appropriate, perhaps, for dreams were what we made.

I was happy, perhaps fully for the first time in my life.

Harry and I kept our budding romance as secret as we could, meeting in broom closets for a quick little kiss, passing daisy petals back and forth between us during scenes.

We'd sneak off at lunchtime and order wonderful steamed cheese sandwiches at a little diner near the studio. But were never able to finish because the butterflies had yet to give up our bellies. We'd just gaze into each other's eyes across the table and suddenly burst into laughter—two children having the ride of their lives, with no reason to think it would ever end. Sometimes we'd take the subway uptown, pulling our broadbrimmed hats far down our faces so as not to be recognized. When someone would begin to look too long or to point, we'd burst into laughter and jump off at the next stop, thrilled to make the escape.

On Lexington Avenue, Harry bought me hats and scarves and magnificent satin ribbons for my hair. It was so *delectable*, so *intoxicating* to be treated so well—so much like a *girl*, for the first time in my life. At times, it seemed I was playing a joke on him, maybe even being a little bit unfair—as if one day I'd just have to tell him with the truth: I wasn't a little filly who could be charmed by flowers and ribbons. I really didn't need a man to open the door for me. But I was having such a marvelous time playing the part, watching him do all these lovely, silly things, that I couldn't bear to burst the bubble, not yet.

It all changed the day Linda showed up.

I recognized her standing beside Mr. Griffith, listening intently as he pointed up to the camera and then around at the scenery.

My heart began to race. It was *Linda*—after so long—*here,* in the studio.

"Linda?" I said, approaching. "Linda Arvidson?"

She didn't seem surprised to see me. She glanced briefly up at Mr. Griffith, then over at me. "Hello, Flo," she said and clasped my hand.

"Miss Lawrence, I see you're acquainted with Miss Arvidson." Mr. Griffith raised his sharp chin. "She's to join our company."

I looked at her with wide eyes. "How long have you been in New York?" I asked. "Why did you never contact me?"

"I'm sorry, Flo. It's . . . rather a long story."

Her words stung. That was all she said. As if nothing else was needed. She returned her attention to Mr. Griffith. He escorted her around the studio, his arm draped about her shoulder. I felt my back stiffen, my neck lengthen.

Harry came up behind me. "Flo," he whispered. "She's his wife."

"His—?"

Harry put his finger to his lips. "It's a secret, Flo. Mr. Griffith doesn't want anyone to know because he doesn't want to be charged with favoritism. He trusted me with the truth, and I'm trusting you."

I looked back over at them. Linda was laughing, gazing up at Mr. Griffith with undisguised adoration in her eyes.

So *Mr. Griffith* was the husband of whom she had written. The talented, ambitious playwright determined to conquer Broadway. So she'd been here *all along,* holed up in their apartment probably, listening to her husband's stories of the studio, hearing all about his work, all about—me—

The sun was coming in through the tall dusty windows of the studio. It fell upon her, reflecting off her golden skin and near-white hair—just as it had on that hillside in San Francisco. How infused with light she had been on that day, too, a day of sun and daisies and buttercups and Linda's laughter.

She spied me watching her. Eventually she broke free from Mr. Griffith—from *her husband*—and approached me, taking me by the arm and leading me down the steps to the dank basement.

"I'm sorry this had to come as such a surprise," she said.

"You said his name was Larry."

"It was the name David was using then on the stage. Lawrence Griffith. David Wark Griffith is much more noble sounding, don't you think?"

I didn't answer. I just looked at her, trying to find something in her face that I recognized. "You've been in New York for *months,*" I finally said. "Every day I've been waiting to hear from you."

She took my hand. I looked into her blue eyes. They were still pale and translucent, but they weren't the same. "Oh, Flo, forgive me," she was saying. "I *couldn't* contact you. To do so might have given away David's and my secret. Once he told me the name of his new leading lady, I knew I would have to wait before I saw you. Oh, Flo, you're so wonderful on the screen—just as you were that night in San Francisco in your mother's company."

I smiled weakly.

"I'm sure you have a great future ahead of you," Linda said. "Oh, my dear, we *all* do! David truly *believes* in motion pictures. He believes he can make art as well as any producer on the stage. You believe it, too, don't you, Flo?"

"Yes," I told her.

"He's a brilliant man, don't you think?" Linda gazed off toward the stairs with an insipid glint. "David Wark Griffith. It will be a name to contend with. As big as Belasco."

"I wanted to show you around New York," I said simply.

"Oh, Flo." She put her arm around me. She didn't smell the way she had in San Francisco, the way I remembered. Then she'd smelled of oranges and daffodils. Now she smelled of perfume—heavy, sweet, *expensive* perfume, no doubt bought by her adoring husband with the profits I'd made for him.

"Oh, Flo," she repeated as if I were a child, "I've *seen* New York. I think David and I scoured every last block of this town, first looking for a place to live, then trying to find work. *Now,* of course," she said, her voice rising merrily, "we're taken out to *all* the finest restaurants by Mr. Kennedy and the other Biograph bigwigs."

She leaned in close to me. "You mustn't *ever* give away our secret now, will you? Only a very few people know. You *do* promise, don't you?"

I gave my word.

"David is planning some big things, Flo." Linda still held my hand but she was gazing over at the stairs again. "Already the trade papers are calling him the movies' first true artist."

"You're going to act with us now?"

She smiled. "Yes, Flo. He wants me to play in *Enoch Arden*. He says

I'd be perfect, that no one else—" She stopped, looking at me. "Well, I'm sure *you'd* be wonderful, Flo, but David has so many other pictures planned for you."

I didn't say anything. She went on and on, gushing about "David's" big future, about "David's" grand vision, about what "David" said she'd bring to *Enoch Arden,* about all the other roles he wanted her to play. . . .

Then suddenly she embraced and kissed me. "Oh, it's *so* good to see you again, Flo."

I pulled back from the thickness of her perfume. "I've got to go home now, Linda," I said.

"All right. Good night, Flo," she said, kissing me again.

We climbed the stairs. Linda moved off in another direction. I passed by Mr. Griffith. He was standing there stiffly, watching me.

"Your secret is safe with me," I told him. I paused, then added deliberately, *"David."*

It was the first time I'd ever called him that. He swallowed, his big Adam's apple bobbing up and down quickly in his long neck.

Harry escorted me home. I was steely in the cab, as if an iron bar had been inserted up my spine. "I thought *I* was Biograph's leading lady," I said.

"Well, sure, you are, Flo," he said.

We got out of the cab. I looked up at Harry with a hard expression. The sun was setting. The sky between the buildings was a spill of reds and golds and deep purples. There was a sting to the air, an early winter bite. "And for how long?" I asked him. "Now that the director's *wife* has joined the company?"

Harry was silent as we resumed walking. The only sound was our shoes against the brick sidewalk. At last he said, "You're the only one the public would accept as Mrs. Jones."

"That's right," I said, and I shiver now remembering the hardness in my voice. "*I am The Biograph Girl.* And Mr. and Mrs. Griffith *both* had best not forget that."

Harry and I made love for the first time that night. Mother had already fallen asleep, and we found ourselves drinking too much.

"Florrie," Harry protested. "That's enough for you."

I began to cry. He stood up and came over to where I sat, stooping beside me to take my hands.

"Don't worry, Florrie," he said. "You'll always be The Biograph Girl. Linda can't change that."

I didn't fully understand my tears. But I wasn't crying for The Biograph Girl.

"Once, years ago," I told Harry, "Linda asked me what I wanted more than anything."

"And what did you tell her?"

"To be a great actress."

"And you are. The greatest. And as the movies get bigger, so will you."

I let him slide into the chair next to me. There wasn't much room for the both of us, but he wedged himself in beside me. I felt ridiculous and weak, unable to move, crushed by his massive frame. But it was easier to let him embrace me than to push free.

Maybe this was all right then. Here, in Harry's arms, I didn't have to think about questions like the one Linda had asked me. Seeing her again had just brought all that back. Maybe it was all right just to be a girl.

Harry began to kiss me. I didn't stop him. We had to be very quiet for fear of awaking Mother. It was quick. I felt no real passion, but no pain either. The nicest part was afterward when I could fall asleep with his raspy breath next to me. I could block out all else and think only of that. *Harry will take care of me. The way Mr. Griffith takes care of Linda.*

The next morning, of course, he insisted he marry me. I agreed. I knew how angry it would make Mother, but I didn't care. "It's *time* I was married," I reasoned aloud to myself. How old was I then? Eighteen? Nineteen? Around there, I suppose. We ran off that very evening and found a justice of the peace who hitched us up with very few questions. His wife stood in as our witness.

Mother, as expected, was apoplectic. "How *could* you?" she screamed. "What ever *possessed* you? He's going *nowhere*, Florence. *Nowhere!* What a *pointless* match! What have you *shackled* yourself to?"

I was packing my clothes, preparing to move into Harry's much smaller apartment in the Village. "Mother," I said calmly, folding a blouse into my suitcase, "just because *you* didn't marry for love is no reason *I* shouldn't."

Her face grew stony. "Who's to say I *didn't* marry for love? And who's to say you *have?*"

"Come now, Mother. You never loved old Bridgewood. You just married him because you felt like a whore on the stage."

I've never forgotten the look of hatred on my mother's face at that moment. It was as if I were a stranger. She should have slapped me, and I half expected she might—but she didn't. Not even to slap me did my mother touch me.

"I loved him," she said softly. "Why do you think he did what he did?"

So it was true. It had been no accident with the stove. *He killed him-*

self. I saw Mother's eyes suddenly well with tears. She didn't cry, though—of course not. She bit back the tears as usual and hardened her stare. Finally I dropped my eyes, realizing there were parts of my mother's pain that I'd never know.

"Go," she said. "Go to your *husband*."

She spit the final word.

I'd never really been separated from my mother before. Walking out that door that night was the most agonizing step I'd ever taken, like ripping away a piece of my own flesh. But I wouldn't let her see my struggle, just as she had hidden hers from me. We barely even said good-bye.

That night, lying in Harry's arms in Harry's bed, all I could do was cry. "Come on, Florrie," he tried to reassure me. He tried to make love to me. "Come on, Florrie. I'll take care of you now."

"No," I ordered, but he persisted, his fingers moving inside me, forcing their way into me—until I sat up and shrieked, "No, Harry. Please, no!" He rolled over without saying a word. But I couldn't sleep with him there, his hot man smell choking the room, his bestial snoring. I ordered him away. For the first night of our marriage, I made my husband sleep on the couch.

But it didn't matter. He loved me anyway. He brought me little gifts of pinecones and ribbon, of poinsettias and holly. He'd sit across from me at the table with his big adoring eyes, watching me open the letters addressed to The Biograph Girl, thrilled over each and every one, so proud of my fame.

"Here's another offer of marriage," I said. "He says he's a millionaire from Detroit."

Harry made a wan smile. "S'pose you could've done better than me, huh, Flo?"

I just laughed. I picked up another letter from the pile. It looked to be addressed by a child. The postmark was Mount Pleasant, Michigan.

I opened it. The short note was written in pencil, in a child's very best penmanship:

> *When my teacher asked who I loved most in this world, I said Jesus. But who I really meant to say was The Biograph Girl.*
>
> *Lester H. Slocum*

"How darling," I said as I pressed the letter to my lips for a kiss.

The Present

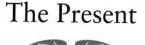

They're all silent. Stunned.

It's Ben who speaks first. "So it's true," he says. "You really *are* . . . her."

Flo smiles wearily. "I *was* her," she corrects him.

Sister Jean has tears in her eyes. She's sitting on the edge of Flo's bed, just staring at the old woman. Richard's writing furiously in his reporter's notepad, as he has been all through Flo's stories. He's changed the cassette in the tape recorder twice.

"It's unbelievable," Anita says.

Rex whispers, *"You actually worked with D. W. Griffith."*

"If I'd have stayed with him," Flo says, "maybe I'd have become as big as Mary Pickford."

"You were *bigger* than Pickford," Rex says.

"Then. Not later." Flo sighs. "But we want different things as we go through life, as we change."

"There was supposedly a fire, Flo," Richard says, finally adding his own observations. "A fire that ended Florence Lawrence's career. The article mentioned scars."

She pulls back a little—a trifle defensive, Richard thinks. "There *was* a fire," she says, as if he'd doubted it. "I saved Matt Moore. Carried him down the stairs, and he was no small man."

"But I don't see any scars," Richard tells her, studying her face.

She smiles. "You don't have to see the scars for them to be there."

Their eyes hold. He hadn't expected her to admit to all this. He'd expected weeks of research, investigative reporting. Even now, he's not sure he can simply take her at face value. She could be some crank, some publicity hound who thinks *why not?* Why *not* be Florence Lawrence if they think I am? But at *a hundred and six?* And knowing all those details? The ring of truth is there—scars or no scars, autopsy or no autopsy. Richard's learned how to recognize it.

"So I *can* print this?" he asks. "I *can* reveal who you are?"

She looks over at Sister Jean. "What do you think, Jeannie?"

"It's up to you, Flo."

She looks back over at Richard. "It was all such a long time ago," she says. "Who would care now?"

"Oh, but people *will* care, Flo," Rex interjects breathlessly. "That's why it's so *important* to tell your story. You're a link to *history*. Film is an *art* now. You might not have realized it at the time, but what you were doing with Griffith—my *God,* Flo, this is like finding buried treasure—like—like—finding a collaborator of *Mozart* or *Beethoven* still alive, like finding one of Manet's students who could describe the origins of modern art. You owe it to *history* to tell your story, Flo!"

"No, you don't, Flo," Sister Jean says, stepping forward, standing between Flo and the rest. "You don't owe anything to anyone except yourself." She looks back over at the group. "We don't have to go any farther than right here."

Flo says quietly, "He's right, Jeannie. I never realized how important it was until it was gone."

Anita gets up from her chair, kneels before Flo and takes her hand. "This will make you famous all over again," she says in awe.

Flo looks down at her. She says nothing.

"But *how,* Flo?" Richard says at last. *"How* did you do it?"

"What do you mean?"

"How—and *why*—did people think you had—you had *died?"*

She sighs. "There was just a mix-up at the hospital," she tells him.

"That's all?" he asks. "A mix-up?"

"That's all."

"But *someone* died," he persists. "*Someone* was autopsied. *Someone* was buried and listed as you."

Sister Jean walks up behind Flo, places her hands on the old woman's shoulders. "You know, Flo, maybe you shouldn't say anything else," she says. "Maybe we should talk privately before you go any farther."

Flo reaches behind her and pats Jean's hands. "It's all right, Jeannie. There's nothing much to tell. They made a mistake. Simple as that. And I decided to jump at the chance, to get the hell out of there, start over. Don't you see? It gave me the chance to go back to being just Florence Bridgewood. I walked away, left everything behind—took nothing that would link me to who I once was."

"But still, I don't get how you could just—"

She smiles. "It's been *such* a long time, my friends. So very long. And really, the most interesting part came later, after all that, when I was able to get away from *her.*"

"From who?" Ben asks.

She grins cagily. "Florence Lawrence."

"But, Flo," Richard says, pushing. "Why would they think this other woman was you? Were you at the hospital for something else? Were you sick?"

"No, no, I wasn't sick," she says.

"Then how did the mix-up happen?"

She drops her eyes. "I'm not sure I know. Really, Richard, what's far more interesting is what came afterward. Don't you want to know about my life in San Francisco? That's where I was headed."

"Did she *look* like you, this other woman?" Richard interrupts. "Did she have a similar name?"

"She was just a girl." Flo's voice trails off. She closes her eyes, seeming to fade out right in front of them. Her energy drops like the mercury on a cold day.

"You knew her?" Richard asks.

"Flo," Sister Jean says, clearly anxious now. "I think we should take a break."

"Did you *know* her, Flo?" Richard persists. "Were you at the hospital?"

"*Mr.* Sheehan," Sister Jean demands, raising her voice. "I think you can appreciate that Flo is tired. I'm going to have to ask all of you to leave. At once."

They stand—Richard last, and reluctantly. As he passes by Flo, she takes his hand. "She was just a girl," she tells him quietly, her big, round blue eyes looking up at him.

"Could she be making it all up?" Anita asks. "*Pretending* to be Florence Lawrence so she can get some attention?"

"Oh, come off it. She's *it,*" Ben says. "She's the real McCoy."

"*You've* had quite the sudden turnaround," Richard says.

They're in a room off Sister Jean's office, seated around a large oak conference table. A portrait of the Pope hangs opposite a theater poster of the Great McGinty.

Ben shrugs. "It's those stories—about Biograph—about the early days. How could she make those up? And what would be the point? She's a hundred and six."

"I must say, for once I agree with you, brother," Richard says.

Rex is still mesmerized. "She worked with *Mary Pickford,*" he's gushing. "She worked with . . . Lionel *Barrymore!*" He looks around at the group. "She could tell me if I'm on the mark in my show!"

Richard ignores him. "But the girl—the girl they buried as Florence Lawrence. There was a death certificate. There was an autopsy. There had to be *collusion* in this."

"Richard!" Anita gasps. "Are you thinking she could have done something . . . criminal?"

"Well, I have to consider the possibility," he says. "She *knew* her. That much is obvious. She *knew* this girl. But why the hospital would think she was Florence Lawrence is beyond me."

"Oh, let it go, Richard," Ben says. "In those days nothing was computerized, nothing was as ironclad as it is today. Hospitals make mistakes. And she admits she took advantage of their mistake. That's the only 'criminal' thing she did."

"But come *on*, Ben. Why would they think it was Florence Lawrence in the first place?" Richard is pretty heated. He looks around the table. "Come on, you guys. We've read the obituary notices. It's all pretty clear what happened. She took the poison, then freaked out, banging on her neighbors' doors. The ambulance came and took her to the hospital. The doctor tried to save her, but failed. Everyone knew it was Florence Lawrence. She left a goddamn *note*, for crying out loud. She said, 'Sorry, guys, but this is the only way. Good-bye.' Or something like that. So how could a mix-up happen? Something doesn't fit here."

Ben shrugs. "Okay. Maybe she took the poison, but they pumped her clean. Then she walked out, and somebody accidentally switched the charts."

"But who did they autopsy then?" Richard asks. "Who did they bury? Wouldn't *somebody* have missed this girl? Why didn't her family ever say, 'Hey, that's our daughter?' Or sister? Or whoever?"

"Because *she was just a girl*," Anita says quietly.

"Yeah. Just a girl." Richard sighs. He looks around at them. "Flo's not telling us something. And until I find out all of it, I can't go any farther with this story."

Though it kills him.

He can feel the warm blood in his face, the tingling in his fingers. At Columbia, he'd had a journalism professor named Reynaud Beylarian. Old Professor Beylarian had been a reporter back in the 30s and 40s for the Hearst syndicate. He told Richard that when a reporter just *happens on* a story—not a story he's been assigned to or has been researching for months, but just a story he stumbles on—nothing in the world was more fulfilling. "Not sex, not brandy, not a good Cuban cigar," Professor Beylarian had said. "There is nothing quite as sublime—as intoxicating—as that."

In his mind, Richard's bursting in on Mady Crenshaw, his editor, telling her that she *has* to stop whatever she's doing, that she *has* to listen to what he's found. He indulges in a moment of giddy fantasy: being interviewed on *Entertainment Tonight,* writing a bestselling book, winning the Pulitzer Prize. *Careful, Richard,* he tries to caution himself. *There's so much you don't know. You can't run off half-assed with guesswork and unanswered questions.*

But for the moment, he finds caution impossible. In his head, he's already writing his lead:

> *Like the raising of the* Titanic, *like some archaeological excavation of ancient Rome, Florence Lawrence—the world's first movie star—has come back from the dead.*

Well, Ben is thinking, *maybe Richard isn't going to move ahead on this story, but there's no reason for me to delay.*

He grins, hoping the others won't notice. *You need something personal,* Xerxes had said. *Something timely. Something for* Hard Copy *and* People *magazine.*

He should've brought his camera. He needs to get Flo on video, talking about the past. About the movies. About D.W. Griffith and all the rest. It's brilliant. It's got everything: art, mystery, romance. The cult of celebrity and the pursuit of the press. It's perfect, perfect, *perfect.*

And if something criminal turns up—well, he can't imagine anything will. That sweet old lady didn't do anything criminal.

But if she did . . .

"Give me something personal," Xerxes had said.

I'll deal with whatever comes. I don't want to hurt Flo. But Richard's right about one thing: We got to tell the truth.

Whatever secrets that old lady held could just make his movie all the more interesting.

Sister Jean looks over at Flo.

"Is there anything I should know?" she asks. "About that girl, about your . . . *former life?*"

Flo is visibly tired. "Will you help me onto the bed, Jeannie?"

Jean takes Flo's hands and assists her as she stands. She steadies her on her feet and they look each other directly in the eyes. Jean can read nothing there. She guides her as she takes the few steps across the floor. She cranks the lowering mechanism on the bed and helps Flo lean back and lie down.

The old woman sighs, staring up at the ceiling. "No, Jeannie," she says finally. "There's nothing you need to know."

"They're going to have more questions, Flo. Do you want to answer them?"

"Richard's a good man," she says. "I trust him. Don't you?"

"He's a reporter," Jean says. "They're a breed apart."

She knows of what she speaks. In Hartford, at St. Vincent's, Jean had trusted a reporter. A white bank executive had been murdered as she walked to her car one night; the police were on the hunt for a homeless black man. Racial tensions were high in the city. Jean was aware of the crime, but had not given much thought to the sad-eyed, quiet man who'd shown up at the shelter that same evening. A week went by; the man spoke little, yet was unfailingly polite. When a local journalist spotted him and prepared to tip off the police, Jean had pleaded for restraint in the coverage. "Go easy," she begged. "For the sake of the rest of the people here."

"Sure, sure," the reporter had promised. But his eyes seemed to pulsate with excitement in their sockets. The next day there was a front-page story with a photo of the shelter and its glassy-eyed—but innocent—residents. St. Vincent's was accused of harboring criminals.

The bad publicity was just six months prior to Jean's eventual dismissal. While not directly connected, it couldn't have endeared her to the diocese.

She looks down now at the frail old woman in the bed. "I think we should wait before you say anything else," Jean tells her. "In fact, I think we should talk with a lawyer."

Flo's tired blue eyes find hers. "A lawyer?"

Jean caresses Flo's forehead with the back of her hand. "Flo, who was the girl they thought was you?"

Flo's quiet. She closes her eyes. "Her name was Molly."

"You knew her?"

"I knew her."

"How?"

Jean sees tears. Quiet, almost invisible tears leaking from under Flo's eyelids. Tears nearly a century old.

"That's all right, Flo," Jean whispers, taking her hands in her own. "No more for today. Don't worry about a thing. I'm here. I'll take care of you."

* * *

What have I done? Why did I allow these people in to question Flo?

It had seemed so innocent at first. Even Flo had thought it a game. Up until just an hour ago, it was all just an interesting, quirky little story.

How quickly things change. How easily we can find ourselves trapped by other people's agendas.

She opens the door to the conference room. All four of them turn their eager faces to look at her.

"I'm sorry," Jean says, shutting the door behind her. "Flo's too tired to go on. If she wants to talk further, I'll let you know."

"Sister," Richard says. "I want to do right by Flo. I've come to care about her very much. I want to treat her honorably and fairly."

"If you want to be honorable, Mr. Sheehan," Jean tells him, "I suggest you erase those tapes and shred your notes."

He blinks at her.

Jean stands over him, defiant. "I understand your arguments that Flo represents an important piece of history, that she was part of a significant movement in the development of an art form. But she's also a very old woman who enjoys her life here tremendously and I don't want anything to affect that. She's frail, vulnerable."

"I'd hardly call her frail," Richard says.

Jean seethes. Could they really be that oblivious? "That's because she's *here,*" she snaps. "Oh, she's *loved* putting on a grand old show for you. The tough-old-broad routine, I call it. But she's *one hundred and six.* She has to be helped in and out of bed. She can't walk up stairs. She can't bear a shower anymore because the water hurts her skin. She can't step into a bathtub, so we have to sponge bathe her. Sometimes she gets so tired she falls asleep in the middle of a sentence. Why do you think she had to come here to live at St. Mary's? Because she *couldn't take care of herself* all alone anymore." Jean sighs, her voice cracking ever so slightly. "Tough as she is."

She sits down at the table with them. They're all quiet. She looks around at each of them. "Flo's lived a long, long life and deserves to have her last years peaceful and free of intrusion."

Richard smiles kindly. "I agree, Sister. But with all respect, I'm not going to destroy my tapes."

She sighs. "I didn't think you would," she says.

He places his hands on the papers in front of him. "The first thing, Sister," he says, "is to confirm what she says is true. I mean, the evidence that exists seems incontrovertible that Florence Lawrence is *dead.* I need proof that what Flo says is true. I'm a *reporter,* after all."

Sister Jean looks at him. At his eyes, so ferocious now, at the steeliness of his jaw. "I'm well aware you're a reporter, Richard," she says.

"May I see her records?"

"No," she says plainly.

"Then how can I prove—"

Jean smiles. "That's not my concern."

Richard smiles back at her. "You're stonewalling, aren't you, Sister?"

She shrugs.

"You're afraid of what might turn up. About the girl. The one they autopsied and buried as Florence Lawrence."

"*If* Flo's being truthful," she says, going eyeball to eyeball with him. "You said it yourself, Richard. How can we prove she is who she says she is? You're right. The evidence seems irrefutable. I've read the articles. Florence Lawrence is *dead*. Dead and buried. Why should we believe Flo Bridgewood? Sure, she might say that Florence Lawrence didn't die—but who's she? Just some very, very old lady in a rest home in Buffalo. You, on the other hand, have a signed document from the Los Angeles county coroner."

"But it's *her*," Ben says quietly.

They turn to look at him.

"I *believed* her, Sister," he says. "Didn't you?"

Jean sees his eyes. The same color, the same shape as Richard's. But the fierceness isn't there. The determination. They're gentle eyes, the way Flo had described Harry's. She thinks of how moved she was by Ben's film, by his vision of peace.

"I'm not sure, Ben," she says, more gently, more honestly now. "I'm just not sure."

"What about these posters?" Rex asks suddenly. "Of Baby Flo and Lotta Lawrence? If she *isn't* Florence Lawrence, why would she have them?"

"Actually, Nooker, they might prove just the opposite," Richard says, sitting back down now, giving up for the moment on persuading Sister Jean. "She says she just walked off, left everything behind. She wouldn't have carted these around with her if she didn't want to be known. How could she end up with all this stuff?"

"Well, then, there you have it," Jean says, turning her glare back at him. "This all must be a mix-up somehow."

"Of course, someone *could* have saved them for her," Richard says.

"Maybe she's just an obsessed fan of Florence Lawrence's," Anita offers.

"Come off it, sweetheart," Ben says, annoyed. "This isn't a soap opera." He turns back to Sister Jean. "Flo's telling the *truth*, Sister. That's *The Biograph Girl* up there."

He has such beautiful eyes, Jean thinks. *Eyes like Victor's.*

Ben's the only one of the group she trusts. The others have their own agendas. Especially his brother Richard.

I won't let them take Flo away from me, Jean's thinking. *I don't care who she is. Or what she's done. She's my* family. *I have no one else.*

Ben's eyes are still focused on her. They seem to read her mind, understand her fear. Jean remembers the first time she saw his film *One Chance, One World.* It was during a peace rally in Hartford, and she and Anne Drew had both been deeply moved. "If only more people could see this film," Jean had said.

What a difference a decade makes. Then, her anger had been easier to direct. Nuclear proliferation. Welfare cuts. Reagan. James Waat. Ed Meese. Al Haig. A consortium of evil old white men—although, as the other nuns pointed out, at least they were pro-life. Jean just scoffed at that idea. "I would hardly call men who slash programs for the poor and build weapons of mass destruction *pro-life*," she argued.

The bad guys wore suits and ties. The good guys wore dungarees and tiny gold crosses around their necks. It was so much easier then.

She could pinpoint with some accuracy the day it all became more difficult. One year and five months ago, to be exact, when Jean was still director of St. Vincent de Paul's. It was a bright, golden spring morning, and Anne Drew—sick and near death—had walked into Jean's room and discovered Victor in her bed.

Oh, the screaming that had ensued—the wailing.

Dishes smashed. Chairs overturned.

Who would have thought a dying woman had so much strength?

"How could you just break your vows so *cavalierly?*" Anne had cried.

The cancer had progressed to the point where she was thin and wasted; the chemo treatments had left her nearly bald. A horrible wig sat on her head. It slipped, hanging off to the side, as Anne threw her tirade.

"Anne," Jean had pleaded over and over again after Victor had hurriedly dressed and slunk out the back stairs. "I didn't break them cavalierly."

"Didn't that promise *mean* anything to you? A promise made before God?"

Jean stood directly in front of her, eyes locked. "Anne, Anne," she said, "of *course* my vows meant *everything* to me. That's why I'm asking you to give me at least that much. That what I did might have been wrong, but it wasn't cavalier. It wasn't *easy*."

Oh, no, it was hardly easy. It was the most difficult thing Jean had ever done. She sits here now and looks over at the eyes of the man sitting next to her. So clear. So filled with truth.

Or, at least, she hoped so. She's looked for that clarity, that honesty in the eyes of many men in her life, but found it only rarely. Not even her own father had had it. Only a few missionary priests, the ones who worked with the poor in Central America—and Victor. *Victor's* eyes had been the most true she had ever seen. Eyes more like a woman's than a man's.

In his gaze, all of her seemingly ironclad dogma lost its relevance. It was a child's gaze. The gaze of the Christ child, she told herself. Anne Drew would call that a rationalization for what she had done. Maybe it was. Maybe what she did *was* a sin.

But it wasn't easy. Oh, no, not easy at all. It wasn't impulsive. It was carefully considered and carefully acted upon. Of course, that only made it worse to Anne. Jean had hoped it would help her understand. But it only made it worse.

"I love you," Victor had said in his sweet Latino cadence to Jean after they had made love, his big brown eyes full of her.

"And I you, Victor," she'd replied.

At first, when his cracked lips touched hers, she had felt nothing—no stir, no flush. His rough hands had caressed her own, and she watched as if removed somehow, as if seated up near the ceiling, observing, not participating. It was only when he began to cry—small, quirky sobs that made him shake as if he had the hiccups—that she began to feel some passion. She took his face between her hands and kissed him tenderly. She eased him back gently onto the bed, and he had entered her—the first and only time a man had ever done so.

"Then you *planned* it?" Anne Drew asked—broken now, exhausted, sitting opposite her on the couch, her face like a skull.

"Yes," Jean admitted. "I planned it. Would you have me surrender my vows without even a consideration?"

That afternoon, she had bought a package of condoms. How strange an experience that was. How terrifying. She hadn't been able to look at the cashier in the pharmacy, a pimply girl with wire-framed glasses. When Victor had slipped off his denim shorts and Jean felt his hardness against her thigh, she reached over to the night table and handed him a foil-wrapped condom. He seemed surprised. But he accepted it.

"Give me at least the fact that I didn't break my vows lightly, that I *thought* about it, about *all* of the implications, *all* of the consequences over and over and over again," Jean said.

"And *still* went ahead with it."

Jean stiffened. "Yes. And still went ahead with it."

Victor had been homeless off and on since he was fifteen. He was twenty-five when Jean met him. Yet the cruelties of life hadn't soured him. He wasn't like the others at St. Vincent's: hard eyed and blunt, worn raw from their years on the street. He was a man, big and strong, muscular like Richard Sheehan—but a boy, too, soft, gentle, finding pleasure in the stacks of comic books left behind at the shelter. He would laugh uproariously during a game of Twister. He delighted in watching the girls play double Dutch jump rope out on the sidewalk, clapping and whistling when they were done.

He'd arrived at St. Vincent's about six months after Jean had taken over from Anne Drew. Despite a mastectomy, Anne had been told the cancer had recurred. It had spread throughout her body. Jean found herself not only taking over at St. Vincent's, but becoming Anne's chief caregiver as well.

"What would I do without you, Jeannie?" Anne would ask each time Jean showed up at the old Victorian house they shared, paid for by the order, a jar of chicken soup and *The Hartford Courant* in her hands. She'd sit by Anne's bedside until the other woman had finished her soup. She'd read to her, comb her hair, help her wash her face when she was too weak to make the walk to the bathroom.

"Anne," Jean had said that terrible golden spring morning. The sun had filled the room. Outside the buds on the trees had burst into lush green life. "What are you doing out of bed?"

Jean was fully dressed by then, sitting on the edge of her bed, tying her shoes. But Victor lay behind her, his brown nakedness covered only by a thin white sheet. Anne had said nothing, just turned on her heel and walked—with supreme difficulty—back down the stairs. Only then did the screaming start.

Jean has never known why Anne came upstairs that morning. She hadn't been upstairs in *months*. She was too weak. They had been very quiet, she and Victor. Anne couldn't *possibly* have heard them. They had come through the back door the night before. Victor waited meekly on the couch while Jean first checked on Anne. Her friend was sound asleep; Jean kissed her lightly on the forehead and pulled up her sheet. Then, her heart high in her ears, she led Victor upstairs.

He'd been a junkie. She would've bought the condoms even if he hadn't been. The fact that his records indicated sero-negativity for HIV wasn't enough to assuage her concerns for safety. She had thought through *everything* before saying yes—all of the risks, all of the eventualities. It was only after months of his gentle caressing of her hair, his entreating protestations of love, that she had decided to go ahead.

She knew, of course, there was a chance they'd be discovered. And if that happened, she was prepared to accept whatever sanctions were doled out.

"I have no regrets," she told Anne simply. She had loved Victor almost from the day he first arrived at St. Vincent's. She saw Jesus in his eyes, in the way he talked, in the way he moved his hands. She would hold him, night after night, as he cried in cold terror, wanting the drugs, *needing* them, begging her for them.

"We'll get through this, Victor," she promised. "We'll get through to the other side."

She prayed for guidance, of course, and the answer she seemed to get—over and over—was to trust her own heart. *That's all we can rely on, in the end,* Anne herself had told her so many times.

She tried to dissuade herself nonetheless. *Oh, Jean, it's only your hormones, raging against the approach of middle age, fearful of never being satisfied before it's too late. You can't go ahead with this. This is breaking too many boundaries. Your heart is* wrong.

But she could never convince herself of that.

The heart is never wrong.

Her particular affection for Victor was noticed by the other residents. That was unavoidable, she assumed. But it wasn't until afterward that she learned the extent of their talk.

"I didn't want to believe the stories!" Anne cried. She stood from the couch, but had to steady herself against a chair to keep from falling. "I said it *couldn't* be true."

"It *wasn't*," Jean told her. "Not until last night."

"And all along I thought you were sincere," Anne said bitterly.

"Anne! How have I been insincere?"

"Pretending to care about me."

"Of *course* I care about you! My, God, Anne!"

"Don't speak of God to me," Anne spit at her. "Don't speak to me at all—ever again!"

She ordered her out of the house. The next day Anne Drew—her dearest Anne Drew, her mentor, her guardian, the woman who had done more than anyone else to shape her life, her vision, and her work—reported her to their superior and to the board of St. Vincent de Paul's.

She was jealous, Jean came to realize. She was *jealous* of Victor. It wasn't the vows. It was that somehow Jean's love for Victor threatened her love for Anne. Sister Anne Drew had always seemed so wise to

Jean—far more wise than Jean ever hoped she might become. But Jean realized then that even the wisest people can sometimes fail to grasp the simplest truths.

Within a month Jean had been transferred to St. Mary's—an assignment she would never have pursued. She was dumped into the lap of luxury with wealthy old white people and a gaggle of retired nuns—even the help were *years* older than Jean. No temptations here. St. Vincent's was turned over to a group of sisters with no experience. It broke Jean's heart, but she took her punishment—for she had acknowledged all along that listening to her heart might come with consequences.

One month after Jean left, Victor died of an overdose. They'd never had a chance to say good-bye. The day of his funeral, Anne died as well—in a hospital bed and not at home as she had wanted. She died in the middle of the day, while the staff was busy with lunch, with no one around her. She had steadfastly refused to permit any visits from Jean.

In the end, Jean firmly believes, it wasn't the cancer that killed her. It was her heart.

So she had no one left. No one except Flo.

And she wasn't going to lose her too.

"What are you going to do?" she asks Richard, stopping him as the group files out to leave.

"Dig in," he said. "Start researching to see what I can discover."

"You'll try to prove it on your own, you mean."

He sighs. "Sister, I don't want to hurt Flo. But I can't just walk away from this story."

They don't say anything more. She nods good-bye to Anita and Rex, who follow Richard out the door.

"Sister," Ben Sheehan says.

She looks at him and smiles. He *does* have Victor's eyes, even if they're blue. "Yes, Ben?"

"I want you to know something," he tells her. "I will do everything in my power to protect Flo. No matter what Richard turns up. I mean that."

She clasps his hand. She feels her instincts about him validated. "Thank you," she says emotionally.

He smiles. "There are ways of Flo telling her story on her own terms, you know," he says. "We don't need reporters."

She nods, although she's not quite sure she understands.

"I'll do what I can," he promises.

She thanks him again. Then they're all gone.

* * *

She trusts me, Ben thinks. *That's good because she doesn't trust Richard anymore.*

"I hate to admit it, hon, but you were right," Ben whispers to Anita, slipping his arm around her waist as they walk back to the car. "This is perfect. This is *it!*"

"You're going to do it? Make a movie about Flo?"

"Keep quiet," he says. "I don't want Richard or Rex to hear." They're ahead, unlocking the car. "Richard's screwed up his chances for getting back in, being so hard-assed and all. But I think I got the Big Nun to trust me."

"What about the unanswered questions?"

"We'll get to them," Ben says.

"Well, Richard should write the screenplay. He's doing the research."

"All in good time, sweetheart. I'm not letting my brother determine how we go forward here." Richard, with all his superior airs. Richard, with all Mom's gilded promise.

"You just listen to Richard, Benjamin," Mom's saying. "He'll show you the way."

Only once had he cracked, showed Mom the pain he felt when she said things like that. "I can find my own way, Mother," he insisted. "Can't you ever give me any credit?"

She laughed—*laughed,* as if he'd told her some hilarious joke and she'd just gotten the punchline. "Oh, Benny," she said, full of mirth, "you can hardly find your way around the block."

Ben stops. Anita looks up at him. "This is going to be *my* show from here on in," he vows. "Richard would just antagonize Sister Jean further. We'll do it *my* way. Or else it's not going to get done."

Anita just keeps looking at him.

Ben laughs. "This is *it,* babe. What we've been waiting for. This is going to be *big.*"

Summer 1935

*F*lo.
Wake up, Flo.
Molly?
Flo, wake up.
Molly? Is that you? I can't see you.
Here, Flo. Here I am.
Oh, Molly. It's been so long. You used to come to me more often. I haven't seen you in so long. Oh, but you're still so pretty. Just like you looked that day. Oh, Molly, I've thought about you every day since. Every single day.

And now they've been *asking* about you. Wanting to know if I knew you. But how could I tell them? I haven't, you know. I haven't told them a word. I know how hurtful that would be for you. I've never told, Molly.

Never.

They wouldn't understand anyway. They didn't know you. How lovely you were. How guileless. They never knew the fidelity in your eyes, the conviction. How strong your faith—in the world, in yourself.

In me.

"When I was ten years old," Molly told me, the very first day I met her, "my father locked me in the outhouse for three days."

She sat on the edge of my bed, her feet barely touching the floor. She shivered in her yellow gingham dress. I sat beside her, wrapping my arms around her slight frame as she told her story.

"My sisters taunted me through the little moon-faced opening all three days. '*Molly-Olly on the tolly,*' they'd chant. My mother was too drunk to notice I was gone. *Three days* I was in there. Three whole days. And it was August, Flo. *Hot.* Hazy-air kind of hot. Hot-bug-chirpin' kind of hot. Oh, boy, and the outhouse stank like the dickens. Sometimes I had to push my nose and mouth down through the dirt under the wood of the back wall just to get a breath.

"When Papa finally let me out, I remember rubbing my eyes because the sun was so bright and I'd been in the dark for three days. He gave me an ice cream cone—blackberry walnut, I remember. Oh, boy, did it ever taste good. Papa told me he loved me, and I promised him from then on I'd be the best girl in the world."

"But what had you done, Molly?" I asked, her tiny hands clasped in mine.

"I'd said a bad thing." She rested her head on my shoulder. "I'd said, '*Bloody balls.*' Even now, saying it to you, I feel filthy, like I got tar on my tongue."

Poor girl. I reached up to stroke her long, silky hair.

"Papa would say it when he was shoeing the horses and he'd hammer his thumb by mistake. '*Bloody balls!*' he'd shout, and we'd all run into the barn. 'Bloody balls! Bloody balls!' So when Mama fell on me that day, stone drunk, as we were carrying eggs back into the house, I said it. There were smashed eggs everywhere. Mama was facedown in the yolk and the mud. '*Bloody balls!*' I shouted as loud as I could. And so I spent three days in the outhouse. I've never said it again—not till now."

I felt her tears on my neck.

"Bloody balls," she said again, quiet this time.

She was just a girl from Red Oak, Iowa—a teenager when I first met her. She was standing in the wardrobe closet imagining she was a star, holding up one of Garbo's gowns from *Anna Karenina* in front of her, bowing to herself in the mirror. I'd only been on the lot myself for a week. She was, as they say, fresh off the bus.

How she got the job at Metro wasn't hard to discern. Lots of girls landed places on the lot by sleeping with studio underlings. It wasn't anything they needed to be ashamed of, since so many did it. I, of course, hadn't needed to rely on such shenanigans. I doubt, first of all, that any of those underlings would have been interested in a swap with me. I was there, instead, on the good graces of Mr. Louis B. Mayer, who remembered The Biograph Girl in her days of glory and took pity on her current destitution.

But Molly had had no glory days. She *was,* however, pretty and soft, and not above getting her way through the only means she knew.

"I ran away from home when I was fourteen," she told me, sitting there amid the costumes of so many dreams. "I had no money. I wanted to be a dancer. There was a theater in Omaha that hired me. I danced in the chorus. And did other things, too."

I could well imagine. How many men had there been? Enough certainly to make her an expert on getting ahead. But not too many to dim her sincerity, her absolute ingenuousness. Despite everything, Molly was still an innocent, a babe.

Oh, yes, she enchanted me. True, she looked like Linda, so blond and pale, with such translucent eyes. But she reminded me of myself, too—or rather, of the Florence Lawrence who existed in those early, hopeful, hungry days before St. Louis. The girl who lived for the applause. Molly didn't have the smarts or the resiliency of Florence Bridgewood, but she had the grace and the charm—and the *ambition*—of The Biograph Girl.

"How did you end up out here?" I asked her.

She smiled. "All roads lead to Hollywood, I guess. I saved up for train fare from Omaha to Dallas, then joined a company that was heading west. Thirteen cities in nine weeks. I learned how to dance very quickly."

"I know the life," I told her.

"One of the dancers was working at Warner. He introduced me around, and I ended up here. You know."

Oh, I did.

"Flo," she told me, suddenly filled with a glow so bright I'd swear I could see an aura around her. "I want to be a *huge* star. It's all I've wanted ever since I was a little girl. I'd sneak off the farm and walk the seven miles into town. There was a little theater there—the Lyric. They had plaster angels out front and the most beautiful red velvet curtain inside. It was like nothing else in Red Oak, which was so gray and so flat—nothing red about it and not so many oaks. I'd run off to the Lyric as often as I could. Chancing a whipping from Papa was worth it to see Gloria Swanson or Leatrice Joy or—Garbo."

She pressed her face into the satin brocade of Garbo's gown. She was too young to remember me on the screen. She hadn't even been *born* at the time of the fire. I reached over and stroked her hair. How I loved to do that. So soft. So blond, as mine had been.

"And your family?" I asked. "They must wonder what's become of you."

She looked up at me. "They're probably glad I'm gone. Papa said I was too much of a dreamer for them. A changeling child. Left on their doorstep. Not one of theirs."

No, not one of theirs. Not possible. Such a sweet child.

Sweet—sweet like—oh, how did the words go?

Her face it is a fairy, that the sun shone on—
For bonny Annie Laurie . . .

"I'm going to be a big star, Flo," she promised me that day, interrupting my reveries. "A big, big star. You'll see."

There were so many girls like Molly. You saw them everywhere. Walking onto the lot, in herds like skittish deer. Fresh-scrubbed faces and checkered blouses, well-turned calves and high-heeled shoes. All wanting a piece of that elusive glory we'd unknowingly begotten, like medieval alchemists, in that little studio at Number 11 East Fourteenth Street. All of that seemed so long ago now. A world none of them knew.

I'd sit there and watch them stream through the gates. Some had appointments, but many more were empty-handed and absurdly sanguine. None of us from the old days spoke of them. We just watched them come in, all big eyes and tremulous smiles. I once saw a young girl approach Flossie Turner and ask her where she could sign up to be in the movies. Dear old Flossie had just embraced her. Reached out and wrapped her arms tightly around her, hugging the slight, pitiful bird to her breast.

Later, I'd say to Flossie that if all those sweet young things were laid end to end—oh, but I've told you that already, haven't I?

In my first weeks on the MGM lot, I'd sometimes get lost in its vastness. This was during the height of the studio's "golden era," remember—a time when whole lives were spent behind its walls. In truth, it was indeed a small city, self-contained and self-sufficient, with its own security force, fire department, grocery store, and pharmacy. Four thousand people worked behind those enormous Corinthian columns running along Washington Boulevard. There were acres of sound stages: rows and rows of them, befitting the description "film factory." The stars' dressing rooms—often as elaborately designed as their homes—lined the property. Cutting through the center was the gargantuan pool with its wind-whipping devices used to create the illusion of the sea.

Oh, and the back lot—the sets of Old Heidelberg still stood from *The Student Prince,* and the dingy waterfronts from *Anna Christie* still evoked O'Neill. I'd watch as Johnny Weissmuller swung across the Tarzan river on a vine. Occasionally I'd wander down an avenue of brownstone facades, thinking I was back on Fifth Avenue in New York. But I'd turn a corner and find myself in nineteenth-century London or the Wild West or ancient Babylon. I'd knock on the plaster and get a hollow sound: This was the make-believe truth we'd invented.

That first day, I was nearly run over by a property man.

"Out of the way, out of the way," he had yelled.

"Excuse me, sir," I chided, "but you don't need to be so rude."

"Ah, shut up, lady and move yer ass," he barked. *"Garbo's* coming through."

I pulled into the shadows, and there she was. Almost gliding on the air as she passed down the stairs. She was surrounded by an entourage of hairdressers and costume people, all chattering like chipmunks, but *she* was silent. She breezed by in a filmy white gown that lifted in the air as she walked.

She looked so sad. Garbo. I read once where Clare Boothe Luce called her a deer trapped in a woman's body living resentfully in the Hollywood zoo.

I was a star like her once, I thought. No, no—not like her. None of this had existed in my time. No wind-whipped pools, no streets of plaster, no dressing rooms the size of haciendas. But the magic—the dreams—*these* were in place from the beginning. *These* I still recognized—these, and the strange melancholy I'd seen in Garbo's eyes.

I had just divorced Bolton. Oh, his story isn't important—suffice to say that I hated him for what he'd done to me. Once again, I had hoped marriage—my third, you know—might give me the escape I so desperately desired. But it hadn't. It only made things worse. There was nothing to do after the divorce but reclaim my name—or rather, *her* name—Florence Lawrence—and come back to the studios.

People have called Mr. Mayer a tyrant, a miser, a hypocrite, a lech— and maybe it's true. I've heard the stories. But he was good to me, and I was grateful. Without his offer of employment, appearing in the backgrounds of scenes or among the crowds, I would have been living on the street. Or reduced to selling cosmetics from a wagon, the way poor Karl Dane sold hot dogs outside the studio gates.

"Thanks, Karl," I said, taking the steaming dog in the slightly stale bun from his hand.

Once he'd been a popular comic star, the big Swedish blockhead in countless pictures. Now I handed him my dime and he accepted it without ever once making eye contact with me.

I sat down on the curb and began to eat my lunch. It was maybe my third or fourth day at the studio. I still knew precious few people outside of the other waxworks—my old IMP costar, King Baggott, and Flossie Turner, once the queen of Vitagraph, had also been taken in by Mr. Mayer's charity.

But today I ate not in the commissary with them, but alone, out at the curb. I spied a young man sitting not three feet from me. He smiled. I even imagined he might be flirting. He was very handsome, with black hair and blue eyes and a dimple in his chin. He reminded me of Charles—the way he'd looked before he'd gotten mean.

But this man was so *young*. He couldn't be flirting with *me*. Still, I smiled back, just in case.

"Say," he called over to me, "where'd you get that relish?"

I brightened. "There's a condiments table over to the side of the wagon," I told him. "Ask Karl."

The young man stood, nodded to me, and went off to find his relish. That might have been the end of it, but I was suddenly charged with the desire not to let him go. "What's your name?" I asked him when he'd sat back down.

"Bob Cole," he said. "And yours."

"I'm Flo."

"Well, hiya, Flo." He wiped his hand on his dungarees and edged over closer to me. We shook hands. "Pleased to meet ya. You new here?"

"Mr. Mayer just hired me." I tossed my hair back, the way that once delighted Harry so, that made him enthuse about how beautiful I was. "It's pretty swell getting a salary every week, with times being so tough everywhere else."

"I'll say." Bob finished his dog in two bites. "Finally I saved up enough to move out of my parents' house to a place of my own."

"Oh, I'd just *love* to have a place of my own again," I told him. Just for a second did the images of my old homes pass before me—Charles's house in the hills, my beloved farm out in New Jersey. "I'm living in a boardinghouse right now."

"Well, you're in luck," Bob said. "The place I just took, over in West Hollywood, has a cottage and a converted garage. I need somebody to help with the rent. You could have the cottage. It's actually pretty nice. I wouldn't mind."

"My," I said, laughing. "You certainly waste no time."

"I just believe in going for the moment," he said. "I can take you over there this afternoon if you'd like to see it."

"I'd like that very much." I smiled prettily. "Maybe we might even have dinner."

He blushed, just a little. "Sorry, ma'am," he said. "But I've got plans— one of the new script girls." He winked at me. "You understand."

I hesitated for just a second, then winked back at him. "Of course," I said.

Men. Those creatures with two legs and eight hands. Why did I still bother after all this time? I understood completely.

"What's your last name?" Bob asked suddenly.

"Lawrence," I told him. "Florence Lawrence."

He paused. "I've heard of you," he said. "I'd never forget a name like that."

I smiled. "I made movies a long time ago. But you're too young, Bob. You couldn't remember that."

He nodded, seeming to agree. "Well, both my parents have worked in the films since Colonel Selig first came out here in oh-seven. They were cutters, you know. They knew *everyone*. I imagine they must have mentioned your name to me. Because I'll tell you—it sure would be hard to forget a name like Florence Lawrence."

No, not so hard.

"I was the biggest star in the *world*," I told Molly. "I got letters from *everywhere*—from Kansas and Tennessee and Italy and Spain."

"Oh, Flo, how *exciting* that must have been!"

I took her hand. She made me feel young. That was what was so precious about her. She made me feel like a *girl*. We were walking down Hollywood Boulevard. The Chinese Theater was just ahead on our right. A Mae West picture was opening tonight and the crowds were beginning to gather. Otto K. Oleson was aiming his crisscrossing spotlights at the purple sky.

"Exciting," I said. "Yes, it was exciting. But we had no idea. None!"

"No idea of what?" Molly asked.

"Of what we were doing, of what it was all leading up to." I looked over at her. Molly's eyes reflected the lights of the sky. They were filled with adoration. How absurd. How deliciously, intoxicatingly absurd. No one had looked at me in that way in a very long time.

We reached the theater. Curious bystanders gathered to await the limousines that would soon arrive. Some were pointing down at Norma Talmadge's footsteps in the cement. Molly broke free of my grip and stooped down to place her hand into the imprint of Gloria Swanson's palm.

"Look," she said, beaming up at me. "It fits!"

"Come on along, Molly," I said as the crowd filed in around us, "before we can't get out of here."

"But Mr. Griffith, Flo," she said, trailing along behind me. "*He* knew. He believed moving pictures had a future, didn't he?"

"Yes," I told her. "He believed."

"Might things have been different if you had stayed with him?" she asked.

"What do you mean, *different?*"

"I don't know, Flo. Just that, well, maybe you might have—"

"*Might haves* are silly to think of," I said, ending the conversation. I wanted to get out of there. Too many people now. The first limousine had arrived. Constance Bennett, I think. The cameras had begun to pop. The mob was starting to shout, to push. One man elbowed me hard in the ribs.

"Come on, Molly," I said, grabbing her hand again. "Let's go."

Once we were safely across the street I began breathing easier, the reassuring fragrance of orange blossoms in my lungs.

Molly had a falling out with the girls in her house. I never knew all the details, didn't care to, but it was something about the boyfriend of one of them. I imagine Molly slept with him. That was her way. He was an assistant casting director at Metro.

"Thanks for letting me stay here, Flo," Molly said.

I'd set the cottage up as brightly as I could, with yellow polka-dot curtains on the windows, a bright red-and-white-checked tablecloth, and a braided rug on the floor of the living room. I'd turned Bob's cramped, dark little place into home.

I looked over at her. She was wearing scarlet lipstick. No other makeup. With her pale face, she looked like one of those dolls you try to win at a carnival.

"It'll be a little cramped," I told her, "but we'll make do." I poured two glasses of iced tea. I knew Molly didn't drink beer. The ice cubes popped a little as the tea flowed over them. Molly accepted one and drank gratefully.

It was a terribly hot day in August. Hot-bug kind of hot, I imagine Molly would have said. The cicadas were singing loudly in the palm trees. Bob was out back pushing his rusty old lawn mower, the tangy odor of cut grass everywhere. He'd taken off his shirt. The sweat ran down his back in shiny rivulets.

Molly bent over to peer out the small kitchen window. "He sure is swell lookin'," she said. Her small suitcase was set down at her feet. "What's his name?"

"That's Bob," I told her.

She licked her lips. "Sure is sweet," she said, apparently about the iced tea. "Thanks again, Flo."

I smiled. I'd been glad to offer her a room. Otherwise she would have ended up on the street. I knew that feeling. She had been so thankful she'd thrown her thin little arms around my neck and kissed me. Smack dab on the lips. Left a slash of red that took hours to wash off.

"Well, let me get you set up in here," I said, picking up her suitcase and carrying it into my little sewing room. I took a pillow out of the closet. "There's just a cot, but it should be comfortable enough."

Molly stood in the doorway looking at the little room. "Oh, it's wonderful, Flo. Thank you so much."

"It'll be nice to have the company," I told her.

"Someday, Flo, when I'm a big star, as big as Jean Harlow, I'll buy you a grand house on Sunset Boulevard." She took another sip of her iced tea. "I promise."

"I'll hold you to it," I said.

"Flo," Molly asked, setting her glass down and popping open her suitcase on the cot, "where did the stars live when you were big?"

A beat. "We were still in New York then," I told her, not looking up as I arranged the pillow on the cot. "Not many had come out west yet."

"I can't *imagine* making pictures in New York," Molly said, lifting out a lacy white slip from her suitcase and hanging it in the closet. "So cold and dreary."

"That's why we came out here."

Outside, Bob passed by the window, pushing the mower. Molly bent down to peer out again at him. I folded my arms across my chest. "I'll introduce you when he's finished," I told her.

"Oh, I'm not interested in dating him or anything like that, Flo," Molly said. "I just think he's cute. You said he knows Douglas Shearer?"

"Oh, yes," I said. "Quite well."

I wasn't surprised Molly remembered that little tidbit about Bob. He worked in the recorded-sound division at MGM, where Douglas Shearer was in charge—so he'd met Norma, too, who was Douglas's sister. He was even on a nodding friendly basis with Mr. Thalberg. Sometimes he'd wangle an invitation to some soiree or another, and he'd come home dazzled, talking of Crawford and Gable and Bob Montgomery and Myrna Loy. "Harlow was there," he told me breathlessly one night, "in a silver lamé dress so tight they must have *sewed* her into it."

I picked up Molly's empty glass. There were lipstick stains on the rim. She was looking out the window again, trying to ascertain where Bob had disappeared to.

"He's putting the mower away, I imagine," I said to her.

She looked up at me, a little embarrassed. "Oh, Flo, I was just looking at the view." She smiled. "So tell me. What do I need to know? Any house rules?"

She went back to unpacking her suitcase, lifting each item and care-fully shaking out the wrinkles. A silk blouse. A plaid skirt. Another slip, black this time. She hung each carefully in the closet.

"Well," I began, "a few." I heard Bob come through the screen door into the kitchen. I turned and saw him shirtless and sweating, opening the icebox and taking out the pitcher of iced tea. He poured himself a glass and drank it all in several gulps, without pausing for breath. Then he turned to go back outside.

"*First* thing," I said, more to him than Molly. "Make sure you put whatever you take out of the icebox back in."

Bob looked back and smiled sheepishly at me. "Sorry, Flo," he said, replacing the pitcher in the icebox.

I gestured with my head. "Bob, come on in and meet Molly. She'll be staying here for a spell."

He wiped his brow with the back of his hand. He smelled pungently of grass and sweat. He took a few steps toward me and peered into the little room. He grinned.

"How do you?" he asked, all flashy white teeth and sinewy, soiled torso.

They shook hands. I saw the look pass between them. I knew then and there it would be just a matter of days before they slept with each other. I supposed I'd known it from the moment I'd offered Molly a place to stay. *They'll sleep together. She and Bob.*

And what was the harm in it anyway? They were *children,* I told my-self. That's what children *do.* Affairs don't need any pretext; they start with a look and end with breakfast. Or at least a sip of water from a rusty old canteen. That's what the dark-eyed island boy had offered me so many years before. You see, I was a child once, too, as fueled by the passion of youth as they were. Passion and youth went hand in hand. True, I had never slept with as many men as Molly, but that didn't mean I was dispossessed of passion. Far from it. Florence Bridgewood had been as passionate as they came.

In the moments when I was alone with Molly, when we'd laugh like schoolgirls or hold hands in the night, I could imagine I was still as young and as pretty as I had been that day with Linda on that hill in old San Francisco or that I had discovered my soul again in the way I had with my dark-eyed lover. The rest of the time—when I was alone, when I'd sit on the curb smiling ridiculously at strangers—my imagination wasn't nearly as yielding or as generous.

"Pleased to meet you, I'm *sure,*" Molly said to Bob in return. I saw the subtle puckering of her too red lips.

"*Secondly,*" I said sharply, my voice breaking the space between them. "The trash goes out on Tuesday, and the iceman comes on Thursday."

Neither paid any attention.

I turned to leave. Bob was helping Molly place her now empty suitcase on the top shelf in the closet. "Oh, and Molly," I said, turning back just once, "don't leave food sitting out. We've got a problem with ants."

I loved her. I truly did. I'd walk into her room late at night as she slept and just stare down at her, listening to her breathe.

"Annie Laurie," I'd whisper in the dark.

Bonny Annie Laurie . . .

Certainly we bore a resemblance to each other. The same height, the same coloring. One time a very attractive young man on the lot asked if we were mother and daughter. "No." Molly had laughed. "She's my *sister!*" She got a big kick out of that.

I *did* love her. You need to believe that. Loved her as I might have my own daughter, had I been given the chance. And she loved me. She'd cry in my arms and I'd comfort her when she awoke from the nightmares that tore through her sleep on a near nightly basis. I'd come rushing into her little room and wrap my arms around her shaking form, assuring her that Papa wasn't going to strike her, that Mama wasn't really dead, that Mama was only sleeping.

Sleeping off a long drunk, I imagined.

"I'll show them," she'd say after I'd dried her tears and she had composed herself. "I'll show all of them back in Red Oak. I'll become a big, big star and they'll wish they'd loved me better. Oh, how they'll wish that!"

She truly believed it. She truly believed her dreams were attainable. But then, all of those who flocked down on Hollywood like so many simpering doves believed their dreams. Poor little girl. Yes, there were times I'd get angry with her. Found myself at my wit's end with her innocence—with her beauty, her youth. But I *loved* her. You must never doubt that I loved her, or you'll understand nothing of what came later.

"Flo," she asked, the red glow of dawn glinting off her eyes, "when you were big, did you get many fan letters?"

I looked over at her. Her head was cocked to one side as she paused in lacing up her blouse. The sun was just coming up, a reddish glow at the windowsill. We were dressing for an early call at the studio.

"You silly girl," I said, turning away, unable to bear looking at her any longer. "Of course I did. They came in big sacks to the studio every day."

She slithered her legs into a pair of hose. "Mr. Mayer was one of your fans, wasn't he?"

"Yes," I said slowly, repeating the story I'd told her several times before. "Mr. Mayer showed all of my pictures in his nickelodeon back in Haverhill, Massachusetts. He has great affection for all us old-timers. That's why he's given us all work."

"Well, I'm glad to hear that Mr. Mayer is so kind," Molly said. "I hope someday when *I'm* old, after *I'm* done with being a big star, somebody will give *me* work, too."

She meant no disrespect. That was the rub: Molly was *never* discourteous. Not to me, not to anyone. She played no games. She never gossiped about the other girls at the studio. Instead, she *complimented* them on their hair and clothes. Such a thing was *unheard* of, you understand. She never tore anyone down to build herself up. There was just no malice to Molly. *None.* I never saw her be cruel. Cruelty requires an ounce of bitterness, and there was nothing bitter about Molly. Nothing at all, despite everything.

Yes, that was the rub.

Because I *could* be cruel. I'm not proud of the fact, but I could. And Molly sometimes made me angry.

I'm glad to hear Mr. Mayer is so kind.

"I don't accept charity," I snapped at her. "Never have, never will." I sucked in my gut, lacing up my girdle as tight as I could make it. "I *work* for my pay. The only way I've ever gotten by is through my own sheer will and determination. I've never asked for favors and never *given* any either."

The last was a dig. I'm not sure she got it. "I'm sorry, Flo," she said in a small voice. "I didn't mean to make you mad."

"Well, you did. Now forget it."

She stood in front of the full-length mirror. How pretty she was. I could see myself behind her. It was my mother looking back at me: Mother at the end of her time on the stage, hard faced and brown, stubbornly resisting her daughter's emergence into the spotlight.

We took the streetcar down to Culver City. The guard at the gate recognized us, waved us in. We waited in line at wardrobe to be handed our costumes. We were both extras on *San Francisco,* starring Clark Gable and Jeannette MacDonald. The first day on the set I'd nearly cried, so faithful was the studio's replication of my beloved old streets, of the grand old opera house, where I'd made my debut so many years before. Even the clothes brought back memories. The long, high-collared dresses we used to wear, the lace-up shoes, the ruffled bonnets. One wardrobe assistant, who I'm sure was really a pansy, quipped to Molly, "Sure is a shame you've gotta cover up those gams."

She winked at him.

"Molly, if you'd only been able to see the real thing," I gushed to her as we strode out onto the set. "San Francisco before the earthquake was a wonder to see. A shining city on the hill, as people like to say."

But Molly only had eyes for Gable's dressing room. It was quite the elaborate structure, a bungalow decorated by the studio's art director Cedric Gibbons. The extras would gather around every morning, waiting to catch a glimpse of the King as he came outside to take in his breakfast tray.

"Look, Flo," Molly pointed suddenly. "There he *is.*"

There he was at that. Standing on the steps, barking some order at some sniveling prop boy, was Gable, the biggest star at MGM, the biggest star in the world. And he was standing in nothing more than a sleeveless T-shirt and his checkered skivvies, his strong hairy legs bared for all the world to see.

"Gable in his BVDs!" I cried out.

Molly dissolved into laughter. He heard us and looked over, realizing he'd been spied. He gave us a hale and hearty salute. "Ladies," he called, bowing.

"Oh, dear!" Molly laughed, covering her face.

Gable was now sauntering toward us. Molly's pale skin blushed a bright pink. I couldn't help but smile.

I never really could understand the fuss the ladies made over him. Now John Compson, who played Mr. Jones to my Mrs., or the Great God Kerrigan, or my dear Matt Moore—now, *they* were my idea of matinee idols. But Gable? With those ungainly appendages flapping at the side of his head? I couldn't help but think of Harry. Later, I used to laugh that Gable had "the best ears of our lives."

But he was all chivalry and gallantry as he bowed before us. "I see from your costumes you two lovely ladies are playing in our film," he said.

Molly could barely nod.

"That we are, Mr. Gable," I said. "We play ladies in the saloon."

But he wasn't looking at me. He cupped Molly's embarrassed cheeks in his hands. "And what is your name, O mirthful one?"

"Molly," she said. "Molly Butz."

He raised those famous eyebrows. "My dear, you'll have to do something about *that* or you'll never get your name up on a marquee." He turned his gaze on me. "And you, madam? What's your name?"

There was my usual pause. "Florence Lawrence," I told him.

That crooked smile of his. It crept across his face, his brow creasing. "Do I know you? The name seems—"

"Oh, Flo was a *gigantic* star," Molly offered helpfully. "I'm *sure* you remember her."

Did he? Did the name mean anything to him? He would've been a *boy* in those days, a boy who ran to the nickelodeon every week to see the new selection of one-reel pictures. John Bunny. William S. Hart. Broncho Billy Anderson. I watched his face closely to see if I could spot anything there, any flicker at all—but Molly's voice distracted him, bringing him back to his real interest.

He dropped his big arm around her slight shoulders. "Have you ever seen the inside of a star's dressing room, my dear?" he asked roguishly. "They're pretty fancy. May I give you a tour?"

She giggled, covering her face again. He turned back to me and gave me that jaunty salute. "Wonderful to have met you, madam," he said as they headed back toward the bungalow.

I smiled dryly. "And you, Mr. Gable."

I watched them until they'd climbed the steps and Gable had shut the door with a kick of his foot. I assumed Carole Lombard wasn't coming around anytime soon.

He certainly did have nice legs.

Even despite the ears.

"Bob, leave her alone," I commanded.

He was trying to get Molly to sit on his lap. It was some party at my little cottage on Westbourne Drive. I can't remember the occasion. Sometimes there weren't any occasions. Sometimes we just threw a party to throw a party. Bob and his friends. Marian, the slightly dotty old lady from next door. Molly and me.

Bob was one of those Hollywood gadabouts who knew just about everyone well enough to say hello, from Thalberg down to the janitors. He'd been in the navy and had the tattoos to prove it, and he liked nothing better than to break into a rendition of "What Do You Do With a Drunken Sailor?" with his buddies. He'd grown up in L.A., his parents having been in the industry, and might've become an actor himself— even a star—if he'd ever been able to keep his mind on one thing longer than it took to mow the lawn. A good man, just one who prized good times over anything else. Drinking, singing, making love to pretty women—these were his goals. I imagine he ended his life a satisfied man.

Marian was an L.A. native, too, but from a family who had been appalled by the movies' invasion. They'd been staunch old Baptist stock, fairly affluent orange growers at the turn of the century. But I got the impression that Marian's father had been something of a gambler. We always suspected she had a stash of money hidden under her mattress— she said she never would trust a bank again after the crash of '29—but she lived quite frugally, even meagerly. Now, approaching seventy, she was an eccentric old maid who loved to sit and listen to the scandalous stories we brought home from the studio. "Oh, Papa must be turning over in his grave to see such goings-on in his beloved Hollywood," Marian would lament, but she found nothing but vicarious excitement in our stories. She was slightly daft, easily drunk, and quite nearsighted. A dear woman—but really, a three-way lightbulb set permanently on dim.

I always invited Marian to my parties—better to have her here than complaining we were too loud. You see, we sometimes got a bit boisterous in that little cottage on Westbourne Drive. I tended to enjoy my Scotch at our parties—especially since Bolton, since the divorce, and the recurrence of my pain. Headaches, dizzy spells, arthritis. I had them all. It seemed lately that my pain was only getting worse. Sometimes they'd call from the studio with a walk-on part and I'd have to tell them I was just too sick. I hadn't yet seen a doctor, despite Molly's—and Bob's and Marian's—urgings. I'd *seen* doctors. What could they do that Scotch couldn't?

At this particular party, Bob's friends had brought their guitars, and they were strumming discordantly. Bob himself was busy pursuing Molly all night. They'd been sleeping together on and off for the last few months—as if I hadn't been able to predict that. This night, she'd finally consented to sit on his lap, and he promptly began nuzzling her ear with his nose.

"No," she said, dissolving into those damn giggles. "Never heard of it. Oh, *Bob!* Stop that! It tickles!"

"Have a drink, Molly," I told her. "Bob, give her some of your beer."

"You know I don't drink, Flo," she said to me.

"Hmmph." I put my own whiskey to my lips. I didn't trust women who didn't drink. Mother didn't drink. "Women who don't drink," I said, "are afraid of revealing themselves."

Someone was banging on the door. I opened it and let in the dark night. Standing there was the sour-faced old man who lived across the street. His feet were bare and he wore his flannel robe. "If you don't lower this racket," he threatened, "I'll call the police!"

"Oh, come on, fella," I said. "Lighten up." I thrust my whiskey at him. "Have a pop?"

He just blew himself up with hot air and stormed off. We all laughed.

"All right, everyone," Molly said as I shut the door, standing up from Bob's lap. "I have an announcement to make."

"Well, you've got *me* standing at attention," Bob said, elbowing his buddy next to him, pointing down at his crotch. They laughed. Men can be such *boors*.

"*Listen.*" Molly stood there, arms akimbo. Everyone but she was a little tipsy, even Marian. The music stopped—just as well, too, or else the cops probably *would* have shown up.

"Listen, everyone. I have good news." Molly beamed. "I was offered a *real* part today."

"A real part?" Marian asked. "Not extra work?"

"Nope." Molly grinned. "A *real* part. I actually have two lines. I say, 'Thank you, sir,' and 'Somebody get a doctor!'"

I knocked back the last of my whiskey. She was looking over at me. Nobody else. Such big doe eyes. The little fool.

"Well," I said to her, "the Academy better get busy engraving your name on their goddamn statuette."

Molly's eyes flickered away. The boys laughed, but Bob just looked at me sternly. I poured myself another drink.

"What's the picture, honey?" Marian asked.

"*Cain and Mabel* with Marion Davies and Clark Gable." Molly paused a moment, then burst out into those ludicrous giggles again. "Hey, that rhymes."

"You're a poet, an' you don' even know it," said one of the boys.

Bob stood up and planted a kiss full on her lips. "Good for *you,* sweet cakes," he said. "Ain't she a star?" Everyone applauded.

Molly blushed. "Well, it's the first step," she said. Bob extended his kiss down to her neck. "One of these days," she said, oblivious to him, "I'll be Mr. Gable's leading lady. *Everybody's* gonna know my name then!"

There was merriment all around.

But I didn't feel so merry.

"*Well.*" There was something about my voice—the whiskey, maybe, *something*—that made everyone turn to look at me.

I smiled tightly. "I'm glad that roll in the hay with him got you *some-thing,* Molly."

She just flushed a deeper shade of red.

"'Cuz rumor has it Lombard says he's a lousy lay." I laughed derisively.

Bob looked up from Molly's neck and glared at me. The boys on the couch just nudged each other, snickering. I heard Marian say softly, "Oh, Flo."

Molly's eyes instantly welled with tears, as if I'd slapped her. What a ridiculous child she was being.

"Well, it's *true,*" I said. I felt something twist and snap inside me. I suddenly tossed my whiskey across the room. The glass shattered against the wall, leaving a wet trail all the way down to the floor. The boys on the couch yelped and ducked.

"Well, it's *true,*" I shouted. "*Isn't* it?"

She just kept staring at me, looking as if she might cry, but no tears actually came.

"Oh, cut the sweetheart routine, Molly," I spit, walking over to the window and throwing it open. I breathed in the cool night air. "Just give it a *rest.* You're not gonna be *anybody's* leading lady, except maybe some Friday night at Gable's bachelor party." I was on a roll now. "All of you girls who come out here thinking you're gonna make it big—I could *puke.* I could *puke* over every last one of you."

And I felt like it, too—felt like heaving my guts out the window. But I turned back to face them and went on. My voice was calmer now, but just as hard. "Did you ever hear of Peg Entwistle, Molly?" I asked.

"Flo, don't," Bob said, taking a few steps toward me.

"Well, *did* you, Molly?"

"No," she said finally.

I smiled. "She came out here thinking *she* was gonna be a big star, too. She had high dreams and hopes, just like you. Just like all of you silly foolish little girls. And do you know what happened to Peg Entwistle, Molly? Do you know what she *did*? After she played a couple of bits and *nobody cared?*"

Marian was crying. Bob turned to Molly. "It's the whiskey talking," he told her.

"I'll tell you what she did, Molly," I continued. "Peg Entwistle climbed up on top of the thirteenth letter in the Hollywoodland sign and *she jumped off.*" I looked around at everyone in the room. "*That's* what she did. Took a swan dive right down into the Hollywood Hills."

Nobody said a word. I walked up to Molly, whose eyes were now cast down to the floor. "Everyone knows *her* name, Molly," I told her sweetly. "Nobody will *ever* forget *her.*"

I walked out of the house and into the quiet indigo night. The orange blossoms were ripe in the air. I walked all the way down Westbourne to Santa Monica Boulevard, then up the steep hill to the Sunset Strip, where even then there were prostitutes, some as old as I was. I walked all along Sunset to Crescent Heights, then back down to Santa Monica. When I finally got back to the house, the sun was turning the horizon pink. The house was a wreck. Whiskey bottles and cigarette stubs everywhere. Everyone was gone, including Molly. She had taken all her clothes. Her closet was empty, the bare wire hangers tinkling softly together in the early morning breeze from the open window.

Ah, what did I care?

After all, she was just a girl.

"How long have you had these headaches, Miss Lawrence?"

The doctor sitting across from me, his hands folded on his high-polished, clutter-free desk, was young. Oh, not really young, not like Molly and Bob and their friends. But young for a doctor. I was used to doctors being older than I was, gray-haired and craggy with whiskers growing out of their ears. But this doctor had freckles and red hair. A cowlick even. He'd seemed terribly anxious when he'd shaken my hand.

"Oh, the headaches have been around for *years*," I told him. "They come and they go. Sometimes I feel so weak I can't get out of bed."

He looked down at my chart. He seemed so slight sitting there behind that big mahogany desk. His credentials hung in frames on the wall. All very impressive looking—but *he* looked like a child sitting there in his tweed sport coat and blue tie. The papers fluttered in his hands as he read.

"Have you had a blood test?" he asked, looking up at me. "You might be anemic."

"Oh, dozens, I'm sure. I've been back and forth to doctors for years. You know, I was never sick as a girl. But ever since—"

"The fire, Miss Lawrence?"

I looked at him. How did he know about the fire?

He gave me a little smile. "I'm wondering if all your health problems date back to that studio fire—the one where you saved Matt Moore by carrying him down the stairs."

He knew me. He—he knew who I was.

"I'm surprised you know that," I said finally. "I don't think it's in my charts."

He blushed—and when redheads blush, their whole body turns pink. It was quite the sight to see.

"I must confess, Miss Lawrence," he said, laughing, "when you walked in today, I was somewhat startled. You see, I was—you were—"

I couldn't help but smile back at his embarrassment. "Yes, Doctor?"

He took a deep breath. "You were my *heroine* when I was a boy."

He *remembered* me. He remembered *The Biograph Girl*.

"I saw *all* your pictures," he said. "Every single one. My parents began to despair of me, said all I could talk about was The Biograph

Girl. I even wrote you fan letters. You were so kind to send me back your photograph a number of times." He smiled almost guiltily. "I still have them," he admitted.

I felt terribly wistful in that moment. For Harry. For Mother. For the girl I once was. I couldn't respond for several seconds. "It's nice to know not everyone has forgotten," I said finally.

"Oh, but of *course* not, Miss Lawrence. I'm sure there are *thousands* who remember. You were the biggest star in the *world.*"

"A long, long time ago."

"Not so long." He leaned across his enormous desk. He seemed quite serious about this. "Not so very long at all."

"Twenty years," I said. "A generation. A *lifetime* in cinema years. So much has changed."

He sighed. "Oh, how I remember when the news was reported that you were retiring from the screen because of that fire. I was devastated. Simply *devastated.*"

"Well," I said, "it's true I've never been the same. I've tended toward being—well, rather *high-strung* ever since."

"Yes." He cleared his throat, trying to shift back into his professional role. "Yes. High-strung. It says here you were hospitalized a few times for nervous collapse?"

I nodded.

"We should do a blood test," he said. "And maybe I can prescribe something for the headaches."

I stood. "Anything you can do will be a great help." I smiled weakly. "There are times—times when I'm just not myself. I do things, say things—the pain, you know."

He stood as well. "I'll write something up and give it to the nurse. In the meantime, you should probably take a rest from—what is it that you do now?"

I hesitated. "I've been doing some work at Metro," I told him.

His face brightened. "Oh, how *marvelous!* What's the picture?"

I couldn't bear to disappoint him. "A small part—a featured part—in the new Gable picture." I paused. "With Marion Davies."

"Grand! I'll look for it! Oh, Miss Lawrence, I can't *tell* you how thrilling it's been to meet you."

I shook his hand. "Thank you very much, Dr. Slocum."

"*Please,*" he said, clasping my hand with both of his. "Call me Lester."

The Present

Richard sits at his laptop, staring at the screen. From downstairs the *bang, bang, bang* of the decorators in the kitchen can be heard. They're ripping out a wall. They don't disturb him. Normally they would, but not today. Today, he's too far gone to pay much attention to them.

He's reading—and then *rereading*, over and over—the last paragraph he's written. It's based on the research he did yesterday at the library, looking at microfilm of the Buffalo city directories and telephone books.

"Hon," Rex calls from the hallway. "Are we going to want the ceiling repainted?"

Charlotte Dunn . . . West Eagle Street . . . Ann Dunn . . . The names check out.

"Hon?"

Hadn't Flo said . . . ?

"Richard!"

"Huh?" He turns around in his chair. Rex is in the doorway, hands on hips. "What *is* it, Nooker?"

"Now don't get snappy with me, mister." Rex folds his arms across his chest. "I asked if we wanted them to repaint the ceiling after they're done."

"How much extra will that cost?"

"Richard, it looks *awful!* It's all rusty and scarred and I really want that textured look we saw in *Architectural Digest.*"

"Okay, okay. Have them repaint it." He'll figure out how to pay for it later. He reaches down and picks up his tape recorder from the floor. "Hey, Nooker, come here."

Rex approaches. Richard hits PLAY on his tape recorder. "Listen to this."

Flo's voice: "My mother was an actress, you see, and we were on the road a great deal. She was one of the best of her time."

Richard's voice: "What was her name?"

Flo's voice: "Charlotte . . . Dunn."

Richard's voice: "Was that her stage name?"

Flo's voice: "No, that was her real—you know, back in those days."

He hits STOP. He looks up at Rex. *"Dunn.* How would you imagine that's spelled?"

"D-U-N-N," Rex says. "Or D-U-N-N-E, as in Irene."

Richard holds up some photocopies from the 1900 City Directory for Buffalo. "Look at these. I checked both Bridgewood and Dunn. In 1900, a Charlotte Bridgewood lived at 115 West Eagle Street. Flo said her mother's name was Charlotte."

"Yeah, and that poster above her bed. Charlotte Lawrence."

"Wait, there's more." Richard holds up another photocopy. "That same year, I looked up *Dunn.* There's a Mrs. Ann Dunn also living at 115 West Eagle Street."

"Flo's grandmother, you think?"

"Quite likely. Because"—he produces the pièce de résistance, handing it up to Rex—"much later, looking through the phone books, look what I found. From 1968."

"Florence Bridgewood," Rex reads. "At 115 West Eagle Street."

"She must have come back and lived in the family house," Richard surmises.

Rex's eyes dance. "So that *proves* it. That proves Flo Bridgewood and Florence Lawrence are the same person."

Richard shakes his head. "Not completely. I need to establish the familial relationships. You know, that Charlotte was indeed Flo's mother, that Ann Dunn was the grandmother. I'm going up to Buffalo to check the property deeds. There must be *some* record of the relationship when the house was deeded over to Flo. I'm going to check the census records, too."

"Well, I think it's all pretty convincing even without that."

"I do, too, Nooker, but I want to do it right." He studies the paragraph on his computer screen again. "I suppose I *could* write a speculative story, emphasizing the mystery, but I want to cover *all* my bases here. I want to state *conclusively* that the two Flos are one and the same."

"So no one else will beat you to it, right?" Rex stoops down so that his face is even with Richard's. "I can see it in your eyes, sweetheart. The drive. You're going full throttle on this one."

Richard grins. "Once this gets out, there will be a rush of stories on Flo. But I'll be the only one who's spoken with her. I can't imagine Sister Jean allowing any more interviews."

Rex nods. "Because of the *girl*," he says significantly.

Richard sighs. "The biggest unanswered question is who's buried in Hollywood Memorial Cemetery." He stands up, rifling through a stack of papers on his desk. "And you know what's so ironic? There had been nothing to mark her grave until a few years ago. But then an anonymous donor felt it wasn't right that the world's first movie star lay in an unmarked grave, so he paid to have a little plaque placed for her."

"Who could it have been?" Rex asks.

"Rumor says Roddy McDowall."

"I *love* Roddy McDowall," Rex says.

"And he's known for his love of old movies and movie stars."

Richard produces a photocopy of an article with a photograph of the grave. He hands it over to Rex. The inscription reads:

FLORENCE LAWRENCE
"THE BIOGRAPH GIRL"
THE FIRST MOVIE STAR
1890–1938

The phone rings shrilly, causing them both to jump.

"Hello?" Rex answers, picking up the cordless from the floor. "Yes, just a minute," he says, handing the phone to Richard. "The Beverly Hills Hospital."

"Oh, good," Richard says, snatching his notepad and pen. "I called them earlier." He takes the phone. "Hi, yes, this is Richard Sheehan."

"Hello, Mr. Sheehan," a woman's efficient, slightly nasal voice crackles over the phone. "I *did* check our records as you requested. But I'm afraid I find no mention of a Florence Lawrence, a Florence Bridgewood, or a Florence Bolton."

"*None?*"

"None. I'm not really surprised. You said she died in 1938. Our records don't really go back that far. And especially not for emergency room cases, as this appears to have been."

"I see. But is the scenario I suggested possible?"

The woman pauses. "I spoke with a doctor here. Of course, this was so long ago, we can't possibly begin to speculate. But he *did* say that it was at least theoretically possible that someone could be misidentified, even after an autopsy—*if,* of course, the body had already been identified before the procedure. If the autopsy was simply a routine matter, then there'd be no questioning of the doctor's identification."

Richard's nodding. "And the doctor? Is there anything on the doctor?"

"Not much. Certainly nothing uncomplimentary. Let me see here. Dr. Lester Slocum. Yes, he practiced here at the hospital from 1933 to 1940. After that we have no record."

"All right. Well, thank you."

"Good luck with your story."

There'd be no questioning of the doctor's identification.

It's the *doctor.* He's who's key here.

Rex has gone back downstairs to check on the work crew. The banging has stopped; Richard can hear a buzz saw now screech into life and whine through a sheet of wood. The sweet fragrance of sawdust reaches his nostrils.

Dr. Lester Slocum. Richard writes the name on his list of things to do. *Check L.A. city directories. Census. AMA records.*

If only he could get back in to see Flo.

He hears the doorbell. Rex's voice. Anita.

"Hey, honey," Rex calls, coming back up the stairs. "Our favorite soap opera star is here."

Anita's gotten a small, two-week part on a new soap being shot here in New York for cable television. She plays the illegitimate daughter of the new husband of the show's wealthy society matriarch. She's hoping it'll turn into a regular gig. Richard's optimistic for her; even if Ben has little confidence in her abilities, Richard thinks Anita's a terrific actress.

"Hey, Neet," Richard says as she comes into the room. She bends down and gives him a kiss.

"Looks good down there," she tells him. "I *love* the glass tiles."

"I'll have to take your word for it," Richard says. "I haven't been down all day. Buried in this story." He smiles. "How's the job?"

She tosses her hair in that way he loves. She's *glowing.* Her eyes shine; her skin looks fresh and scrubbed. It's wonderful to see her so happy.

"Oh, it's *amazing,*" she tells him. "I can't tell you how invigorating it is to have *lines* to memorize. I mean, *real lines.* Like more than just, 'Thank you, sir' or 'May I help you, sir.' I have *real* dialogue."

"I can't wait to see it," Rex says, leaning against Richard's desk.

She beams. "The premiere airs in a few weeks. I'll keep you posted."

"How's Ben treating you?" Richard asks. "Like a star, I hope?"

Her glow fades, just a little. "Oh, he's very happy for me."

"Yeah? Has he done anything special? Like taken you out to celebrate?"

She shrugs. "We'll do that. He's just busy right now."

"Marge What's-Her-Name?" Rex asks.

Anita looks at him, then back at Richard. "No. He's given up that idea."

"And there's surprise in that?" Richard laughs, shaking his head. "Well, give my dear brother a few weeks. He'll come up with yet another fruity idea only to discard it yet again—"

"He's already come up with a new project."

Something about Anita's voice. Richard looks at her. She's biting her bottom lip.

"Dare I ask what it is?" he ventures.

"Oh." Anita sighs, walks across the room, puts her head against a bookcase and closes her eyes. "That's why I came over. I had to talk to you guys. I felt it was only fair."

"What? What's only fair?"

She opens her eyes. "He's gone up to see Flo."

Richard blinks. "He's gone up to see . . ."

"Flo," Anita repeats.

Richard just sits there. He doesn't move, doesn't say a word.

"Honey?" Rex tries.

"*Goddamn Ben,*" Richard finally says, looking from Anita to Rex to his computer screen. "Goddamn *Ben.* And Sister Jean will be only too glad to let *him* in."

Anita's nodding. "After meeting Flo, he finally agreed that it was a good idea. He spoke with Sister Jean yesterday. He assured her that he'd respect Flo's privacy, that she should just be videotaped for posterity—and that any future deals would only come with Sister Jean's approval. So he and Xerxes went up this morning—"

"*Xerxes?*" Richard barks. "He took his *agent?* Oh, right—like Flo's privacy is something *Xerxes* will care about!"

"Oh, Richard, I told Ben that it was your idea—that he couldn't just shut you out, that *you* should write the screenplay—and he may in fact agree to that."

"*He may agree?*" Richard snaps. "What? I have to ask my *brother* for permission to write about a story *I* found? *I discovered?* I don't *think* so."

"Easy there, sweetheart," Rex whispers, his hand on Richard's shoulder.

"No fucking way. *I'm* writing this story. It's going to appear *next week* under *my* byline. Ben can go ahead and make his goddamn movie, but I'm going to be there *first*. You just watch. *I* can get an agent, too."

"But sweetheart," Rex says, squatting down next to him now. "I thought you wanted to wait until you had all the facts."

"There could be a book deal in this, Nooker," he tells him plainly.

Anita's near tears. "Oh, God, I hope this doesn't turn nasty," she says.

But Richard knows it's been nasty for a very long time.

Not forever, but for a long time.

When they were very little, the twins had been inseparable. Catching pollywogs, sledding down the snowy banks of Chicopee, eating bags and bags of popcorn at each successive *Planet of the Apes* movie. But there came a point when all that changed. Richard's always felt it somehow coincided with Dad sleeping in the den instead of with Mom. When Mom and Dad stopped being close, so had Richard and Ben.

There was never any evidence of problems between his parents, except for Dad sleeping in the den. They never fought, at least not so that their children heard, and Mom's never once intimated there was any disconnection in all the years since Dad's death. But Richard can't remember any intimacy between them either: no kiss hello, no laughter, barely any conversation at all. Mom kept as far away from Dad's deathbed as she could, and at his funeral she stood stoically between her two boys.

Except—and Richard has to admit this—it was his own hand she clung to, not Ben's. He knew he was his mother's favorite, just as Ben had been his dad's.

We were pawns, he thinks. Or maybe simply substitutes, partners by proxy in the face of whatever estrangement existed between husband and wife.

Yet the origin of the brothers' hostility does little to temper it, so deep and lasting are the memories of their embattled youth.

"Fuck you, Richard!"

"No, fuck *you*, Ben!"

They're pushing each other back and forth in their room. It's 1979, and they're each sixteen. The famous poster of Farrah Fawcett in the red bathing suit hangs over Ben's bed. Over Richard's is a lobby poster of Olivia Newton-John and John Travolta in *Grease*.

"She's not interested in you," Richard spits. "She likes *me*."

"Oh, yeah?" Ben levels his eyes at his brother, ready for the kill. "Well, you don't even *like* girls."

Richard jumps him. They each land a few punches before Mom is between them, pulling them apart.

"Benjamin! Richard!" Mom shouts. "Holy Mother of Jesus, you boys are like wildcats." She's huffing from her run down the hall, even though she's only about a hundred and eighty pounds at this point. "What is going *on* here?"

"Ben is a fucking asshole," Richard sneers.

"What did you say to him, Benjamin?"

"Nothing that isn't true." He stands, retreats to his side of the room.

Richard sits on his bed, nursing his upper arm, where Ben had landed a good one. "He's just pissed off because Mary Kay Silenski is going to the prom with me."

"You're just *using* her," Ben yells.

"You're just jealous."

Mom sniffs. "Benjamin, Mary Kay is *Richard's* girlfriend. Everyone knows that. You're just going to have to ask someone else."

"She's *not* his girlfriend. They never even kiss." He smirks. "She's told me. I bet he's a homo!"

"Fuck you, Ben."

"Fuck *you*, Richard."

"Boys! Now, Benjamin, you just think of someone else to ask. And no more fighting. I'm trying to watch Phil Donahue."

Mom leaves. They sit and stare at each other for several minutes. "Well," Ben says finally. "Then I get to use the car that night."

"No way!"

Ben stands up, ready to go again. "You don't get to take Mary Kay *and* the car. You guys can walk."

"You're crazy. You don't even have a date."

"What? Do you think I can't get one?"

"I think it'll be mighty hard."

Ben grimaces. "You shouldn't even be drivin' Dad's car. He told me I could have it."

"I never heard him say that."

"That's because you were never around!" Ben leaps across the room at him. Richard pulls back on his bed. "You weren't *there!* You never were! I took care of him all by myself with no help from you! So how could you hear *anything* he said?"

Richard maneuvers off his bed past his snarling brother. "I'm sick of your crap," he cries. "I'm sick of you going on about how I wasn't there to take care of Dad. You think just because you used to go off and play hoops together every night after dinner that you were his special little boy or something. Well, Dad's *dead*, Ben. That car belongs to *Mom,* and *she* said I could take it to the prom."

Richard leaves the room. Ben just sits there for a long time.

Richard always got what he wanted.
Ben's staring down at his knuckles.
Even Mary Kay Silenski.

Mary Kay was chubby and pimply, the kind of girl Ben might've at least had a chance with back in those horrible high school days. She liked him. They'd go for long walks together while she waited for Richard to get home from play practice or his goddamn National Honor Society meetings. They'd talk about life and acne creams and Ben's father's death and the soundtrack of *Saturday Night Fever*—lots of stuff, and then Richard would be home and Mary Kay would scamper back to him. She could've been *Ben's* girlfriend if his fucking homo brother hadn't already claimed her as his fag hag.

Ben never did go to the prom that year. He asked two other girls but they turned him down. Ben was an outsider, not in the clique. He knew it was mostly his own choice: It was better to go off, by himself, delivering newspapers or working in the garage, than to risk being compared to Richard.

It didn't matter, in the end, about the prom. Richard got to drive Mary Kay in Dad's old green Buick, and they sat real close together as if they really *were* dating. Richard wore a bright blue tux with a ton of ruffles and Mary Kay wore a low-cut red silk gown that showed all the pimples on her tits. Mom kept their goddamn picture up on the television set for *years*.

"Hey," Xerxes whispers, "do you think I ought to tell this nun I'm Catholic?"

"What?"

Ben blinks back to the present. Mary Kay's pimply tits dissipate as he looks over at his agent.

"Well, Greek Orthodox isn't *that* much different," Xerxes is saying. "I could pull it off—if you think it'd get us in better with her."

They've been waiting so long he'd forgotten where he was, allowing him to get lost in his memories. As usual, when he did that, they weren't pleasant.

They're waiting for Sister Jean in her office, seated in two chairs in front of her desk. The clock on the mantel clicks the seconds. Its echo fills the room.

"No," Ben says finally. "Don't try anything with her. She's sharp."

They hear the door open behind them and Sister Jean comes in. They stand to greet her. She shakes their hands with little enthusiasm.

She says, "Ben, you know I'm talking with you against my better judgment." She takes her seat behind the desk. The men sit back down as well.

"I know that, Sister, and I'll be frank." Ben levels his eyes with her. "I don't trust reporters either. Not even Richard." He makes a tight smile. "But the good news is, we're not reporters. We're filmmakers."

"Well, actually," Xerxes says, smiling, "I'm an agent who *represents* filmmakers." He winks. "But I don't trust reporters either."

Sister Jean looks at him for a second, then moves her eyes back to Ben. She clasps her hands together as if in prayer on her desk. Its surface is covered with a piece of shiny clear glass. Ben can see her face—and his—reflected there as he stands.

"We'll keep this very quiet," he says, presenting his case. "We'll get Flo's story on video the way *she* wants to tell it. We won't pursue any avenue she doesn't want to take."

"If Flo wants to do this at all," Sister Jean reminds him.

"Of course. This is *completely* contingent on her willingness. I'll certainly respect whatever she decides."

Ben tries to look as sincere as possible. Not that he *isn't* being sincere, he tells himself. He just wants to make sure Sister Jean *believes* his sincerity. "Maybe if I could talk with her," he says.

"No." Sister Jean holds his gaze. For the first time, Ben notices her eyes. Really *notices* them. How green they are. *Pretty,* like a girl's—not a nun's. "*I'll* talk with Flo," she tells him. "And I'll let you know if she's interested."

"Fine." Ben sits back down. He'd wanted a chance to try to persuade Flo himself. He had a feeling Sister Jean would be urging her against it. He thinks up another game plan quick. "But, Sister, I'll tell you something," he says. "Richard's going to go ahead with his article. That means you'll get some inquiries. You know, film historians and people like that. All coming around here asking questions. We could keep them at bay by saying Flo was giving an oral history and all their questions would be answered by that."

She seems to appreciate the point. "Well, I'm not giving anyone else permission to speak to Flo. If anyone approaches us, they'll be turned down."

"I think that's a very wise decision," Xerxes says. Sister Jean looks over at him. It's not a pleasant look. Xerxes smiles awkwardly. Ben wonders if it was a mistake to bring him. Xerxes can be grating at times.

But he could also be charming. Especially if the person he was trying to charm was narcissistic, self-absorbed, ambitious, and greedy—like most of the Hollywood producers he dealt with. People who could be coddled, flattered, aggrandized.

People, in other words, exactly the opposite of Sister Jean Levesque.

She doesn't like this agent. She doesn't trust him. Not in the least. Why did Ben bring him?

"I think that's a very wise decision," Xerxes says.

Jean looks at him. *Of course, you do,* she thinks. *Because then* you'll *have exclusive rights to Flo's story.*

She looks over at Ben. Still, if *it's Ben* doing the interviewing, making the film . . .

She'd found the video of *One Chance, One World* last night, stashed among her papers in some cardboard boxes she'd brought from St. Vincent's. She watched it again, remembering how moved she'd been the first time. It took her right back to that day, when the fears of Armageddon were so palpable, with Reagan in the Oval Office and all the tough talk about the "evil empire." Anne Drew was sitting at her side in a little college theater in Hartford. They'd cried together when the film was done. "Whoever made this picture," Jean had said, "surely practices peace as a way of life."

Did he? She looks over at Ben now, sitting on the edge of his chair in front of her. How eager he was to talk with Flo. Why?

"What's in this for you, Ben?" she asks. "Why this interest?"

He smiles. "Sister, I can't begin to tell you how affected I was by Flo's story the other day. Hearing about her long life—how she figured in the history of motion pictures. But more than that, really—indeed, *much* more than that. What *really* inspired me was her story of starting over. Beginning a new life. About how we can be so much more than just what we seem. Personally, unlike my brother, I find Flo Bridgewood far more fascinating than Florence Lawrence."

He couldn't have given a better answer if Jean had scripted his response herself. She settles back in her chair and smiles. "You truly believe that, Ben? Those are your true feelings?"

He doesn't miss a beat. "Absolutely, Sister."

"Well, I'll talk with Flo. See how she feels about it." She unclasps her hands, runs them over her face. "It's no secret she got tired pretty quickly the other day. That some of the questions Richard was asking made her a little unsettled."

"That's not the part I'm interested in," Ben assured her.

Sister Jean turns suddenly to Xerxes. "Then why are *you* here? What's in this for you?"

He clears his throat, sits up straight in his chair. "Well, Sister, to be honest, I'm not sure. Except that I represent *all* of Ben's films. He's a brilliant filmmaker. I handled *One Chance, One World*." He looks at her significantly. Jean imagines Ben's told him she's a fan. When she doesn't respond, Xerxes continues. "I imagine that perhaps, at some point, when you and Flo deem it appropriate, we might consider releasing an edited version of Flo's story commercially. I mean, it *does* have the power to inspire."

"Flo's legacy is larger than just film history," Ben says.

Jean sighs. A week ago, she'd have been far more receptive to the idea. Flo *would* make an inspiring film. A hundred and six and still sharp, still teaching the world lessons. But now . . .

She was just a girl.

Her name was Molly.

What had happened on that day in December back in 1938? What Pandora's Box were they opening up? Even if it was nothing—Jean hated to even think the word—*illegal,* it still caused considerable distress for Flo to remember it. She *had* to protect her. Jean wouldn't let any harm come to Flo.

She's all I have left.

"I'll talk with her." Jean looks up at both men. "That's all I can promise."

"Of course, Sister," Ben says.

"Ben." She leans toward him ever so slightly. "Other than making the film, were you involved in the peace movement at all?"

"Oh, Ben's an old diehard liberal, a real peacenik," Xerxes answers for him.

Jean doesn't even turn her eyes to him. She keeps looking at Ben.

He looks surprised. "Well," he says, "I—well, Sister, you know, I felt my contribution could best be made by making the film. We all have our talents, you know."

"Of course." That disappoints her, but he has a point. How many were *inspired* by his film to get involved? Surely that was enough.

She stands. "All right, gentlemen. I'll get back to you."

They stand as well. "Sister," Xerxes says, grinning widely. "You know, I was at the Lincoln Memorial when Dr. King gave his 'I Have a Dream' speech."

She looks at him. "Oh? Were you there looking for the rights to market it?"

He laughs awkwardly.

No, she really does *not* trust this man. She manages a small smile. They shake hands. They all bid each other good-bye. The men leave. Jean sits back at her desk and covers her face with her hands.

"Well, what do you think?" Richard asks.

Mady Crenshaw, his editor, is sitting with her back to her computer. Her hair is pulled back severely in a gray knot. Tiny octagonal wire-rimmed glasses perch at the end of her nose. She's just read Richard's story, which is up on her screen behind her. He can't tell what she thinks. One never could tell simply from looking at Mady's face: an un-lined, inexpressive countenance that masks one of the sharpest minds Richard knows.

She swivels around on her chair and looks back at the story. "It's good, Richard. Quite good."

He can feel his face flush with relief. "I know it's not what I was orig-inally assigned, but—"

"You've done some good research," she says. "I wish we had a little more concrete proof, however."

"I didn't write it as a conclusive story. I wrote about some old woman's claim, and how the evidence *seems*—I repeat, *seems*—to sup-port her."

"An acceptable angle." Mady gives him a rare dry smile. "Now that Anna Anderson has been proven a hoax, maybe we *need* a new Ana-stasia."

"Speaking of which, I'm hunting around for a biological relative of Florence Lawrence," Richard tells her. "For DNA testing."

"As if this Big Nun would ever allow it."

Richard admits, "Sister Jean could well prove an obstacle to any fur-ther attempts to solve the mystery."

"We don't need her." Mady taps the computer screen with her finger-nail, making a little clicking sound. "We can do it without her. The only problem with the piece is how little we know about the woman who was apparently misidentified as Lawrence and buried in her place."

"Well, if we could identify *her,* then we'd know Flo was telling the truth." Richard sits down on a chair opposite his editor. "I've talked with the L.A.P.D. They told me, if they suspect foul play, there may be a request for a court order to exhume the body."

"Why didn't you put that in the story? That's *important,* Richard." She swivels around again on her chair to stare up at him. *"That's* what's missing. The sense of ongoing investigation. That this sweet old lady might, in fact, be a—"

"No." Richard shifts uncomfortably. "I mean, I understand your point. I just thought it made the piece too dark. This is more romantic mystery than unsolved crime."

She's shaking her head. "Richard, you need to include your conversation with the L.A.P.D. It sets the stage for a follow-up article if they *do* dig up the grave. This story could take all sorts of interesting twists over the next several weeks."

He sighs. He knew, even as he wrote the piece, that it was missing something. He knew Mady was right. But it made him feel like a real shit to include that part, to even make the vague implication that Flo could be . . . *involved* in something. *Guilty* of something. He thought of Sister Jean, how angry she'd be.

But he was a *reporter,* damn it. He *had* to tell the story.

All of it.

It just made him feel pretty lousy.

This morning Rex had pleaded with him. "Just think about it one more time," he said, "before you E-mail Mady the story."

Richard had frowned. "Nooker, this could be *big.* I could write a *book* about this. A book that maybe gets turned into a miniseries for TNT."

"Yeah, maybe." Rex had folded his arms across his chest, the way Mady was doing now. "But *think* about it, okay? Just one more time before you go ahead and send it. Think about that old lady up in Buffalo and the life she has there. How her biggest worry right now is selling enough Girl Scout cookies."

He *had* thought about it. For nearly an hour. Just sitting there in front of his computer, staring at what he had written.

Then he took his mouse and clicked the SEND NOW button on his screen.

"All right," he tells Mady. "I'll add a graph or two about the L.A.P.D."

"Good." She drops her arms from her chest, pulls a clipboard from her desk, and makes a notation on it. "Let's run it in Monday's Arts." Then, to herself more than Richard, she says, "This is going to get a lot of attention."

Monday's Arts.

It was Friday.

Richard doesn't like the feeling in his gut. It's the feeling he got when Dad came home from the doctor that first time and said they wanted to do some more tests. He'd felt then as if all of their worlds were about to change, and he'd been right.

He has that feeling again now.

He gets busy writing the new graphs.

* * *

"On *World News Tonight,* we look at the amazing story of Florence Lawrence—or at least, of the woman who *claims* she's the very first movie star of them all."

The camera moves closer in on Peter Jennings. A photo of The Biograph Girl, circa 1909, materializes behind him.

"Not sure who this mellifluously named lady is? Well, you're not alone.

"Few remember her today, but Florence Lawrence was the world's *first* movie star, internationally famous as The Biograph Girl *eighty* years ago. She's long been believed to be dead, but according to news reports, she's been discovered alive and well—living in a rest home in Buffalo, New York, at the age of one hundred and six.

"In an article in today's *New York Times,* a spry, witty lady named Florence Bridgewood—the original name of Miss Lawrence—makes the claim that she actually *is* the pioneer movie actress. She explains that in 1938, the Beverly Hills Hospital misidentified a suicide victim as her. Disillusioned and weary with the movie industry, Miss Bridgewood—or Miss Lawrence—says she saw an opportunity to head out and start a new life for herself.

"A fantastic story. But possible. Hospital officials concede it *could* have happened, and there are no records to authoritatively dispute her claim.

"If what Miss Bridgewood says is true, this is a significant find for film historians, and around the world today, they have been reacting with barely contained excitement. Florence Lawrence was perhaps the most popular actress of her generation and the *first* to be named as a moving picture star back in 1910. She was one of the first actresses to work with a then-inexperienced director, D.W. Griffith—who, of course, went on to be recognized as the father of motion picture art. One historian has likened discovering Miss Lawrence to finding an assistant to Mozart still alive or a student of Manet.

"For more on this astounding story, we go to Catherine Colby in Buffalo."

"Thank you, Peter. This is *indeed* an astounding story, if true, and journalists and television crews from around the world have descended on the quiet, tree-shaded grounds of St. Mary's Roman Catholic rest home here. No one has been allowed in to talk with Miss Lawrence, but Sister Jean Levesque, administrator of St. Mary's Home, has confirmed that The Biograph Girl does indeed live here, and that she's been going by her original name, Florence Bridgewood. Sister Jean has adamantly refused to comment beyond that or to allow any access inside the rest home."

"Catherine, has Miss Lawrence herself issued any statement beyond what we've read in the newspaper?"

"Not yet, Peter. I have the sense from talking with some of the nuns here at St. Mary's that they're simply as stunned as we are and a little unprepared for the media assault that continues to descend on this tranquil estate."

"All right. Thank you, Catherine Colby, coming to us from Buffalo. Well, we've put together what we know about the life of Florence Lawrence, who up until today has been a rather obscure figure in the history of film. With me is Jameson Collins, a noted film historian and author of *D. W. Griffith and the Rise of Film as Art*. Tell us, Dr. Collins, who *is* Florence Lawrence, what do we know about her, and why is this potentially so important?"

"Well, I cannot stress enough that, if what Miss Bridgewood alleges is true, this is a major historical find—akin to discovering someone who'd worked with the masters in other art forms, like music, painting, literature—like discovering Mark Twain's copyeditor still alive. Of course, *film*—being a collaborative medium—means that not only was Miss Lawrence a *student* of Griffith's, but that *her* contributions are important as well. She brought a certain vibrancy of her own to motion pictures, creating the entire star system as we know it by the *sheer force* of her personality—communicated, we must remember, without the sound of her voice or the use of color. Everyone from Mary Pickford to Meryl Streep owes a debt to her."

"And quite a debt that is. What do you think, Dr. Collins? Do you think this is really The Biograph Girl?"

"I can't yet say, Peter. I'd like to have the chance to meet with her, ask her several questions that only the real Florence Lawrence would know. But so far, she's not granting any interviews."

"All right. Thank you, Dr. Collins.

"Efforts to determine the veracity of the story are ongoing. According to the Los Angeles Police Department, Florence Lawrence's remains in Hollywood Memorial Cemetery may be exhumed. DNA tests could be conducted on the remains to see if an identification can refute Miss Bridgewood's claim. Born in Canada in 1890, the same year as Miss Lawrence, she has no known living relatives.

"Florence Lawrence had a brother, but he is believed to be dead with no survivors.

"A fascinating and compelling story—and one we're sure isn't over yet. We'll keep you up-to-date on all the latest developments concerning The Biograph Girl."

March 1910

"Dear God, *look* at all of them!"

I peered from the window of the train as it pulled into Union Station in St. Louis. Hundreds of people lined the platform, jostling each other, angling for a better view. Photographers perched on stepladders, balancing their cameras on tripods. Most were well-dressed folk—men in waistcoats and women in wide-brimmed hats. Some held small children by the hand. All were eagerly trying to catch a glimpse of the train as it pulled into the station.

But their faces were frenzied. They appeared angry and overwrought. Their children were crying. Young men scrambled up the ladders, only to be kicked back by the photographers. I saw one woman slap a man across his face for daring to move in front of her.

"It's worked better than I ever *imagined,*" Mr. Cochrane was saying to Harry.

I turned back to watch them shake each other's hands, faces beaming. Harry clapped Mr. Cochrane on the back. Mother was behind them, her smile as big as her hat.

But I wasn't smiling.

"I don't want to go out there," I told them simply as the train puffed to its final stop. We lurched a bit; I grabbed hold of a seat to steady myself.

"But you *have* to, Florrie," Harry said, gripping me by my shoulders. "They've all come to see you."

"They *love* you, Florence," Mother assured me.

I looked back out the window. There were *hundreds* of them standing there. *Hundreds.* I could hear their excited voices, their anticipatory shouts.

"Florence," Mr. Cochrane said, putting his arm around my shoulders. "Don't you see? This is what we've been planning for. This is the fruit of all our labors. It's worked even better than we planned." He put his face very close to mine. "Now's the time to tell the world that you aren't dead—and in so doing, make you the biggest star the world's ever known."

The porter was suddenly beside me, smiling widely, his shiny black face eager to assist. "It's been a great honor, ma'am," he said. I thanked him. He opened the door for me. I looked back at Harry. He gestured for me to go.

I took a deep breath and stepped out of the train.

Now's the time to tell the world that you aren't dead.

That's what the papers had reported. That I was dead. Strange, isn't it? How it's happened *twice* in my life? The first time was that cold February morning back in St. Louis. The second time was that cold December morning nearly thirty years later, when I glanced down at the newspaper in Doris's diner to see that I'd died by drinking ant poison. So many years and a world away from each other. But both times I died, I made the front page.

MOVING PICTURE ACTRESS MEETS TRAGIC END BENEATH THE WHEELS OF A SPEEDING MOTOR CAR

"Brilliant, *just* brilliant," cheered Mr. Laemmle, the headline blaring up at him from his desk.

Mr. Cochrane, his able, conniving partner, had stuck his thumbs behind his lapels and crowed. "Just as I told you, Carl. Just as I told you."

I was no longer The Biograph Girl. I was now an Imp. Mr. Laemmle had hired me for his Independent Motion Picture company. Oh, I thought I was just the *bee's knees* then—and I *was*. I really was. So what if Mr. Griffith had canned me? *He'd* live to regret it. I was the most popular star in the world. Who did he think he could replace me with? That silly Pickford girl?

"Miss Lawrence, meet Miss Pickford," Mr. Griffith had said.

So she was the one they'd threaten me with. "It's an honor, Miss Lawrence," the little waif said, looking up at me with big saucer eyes.

That's right: looking *up* at me. Although I was small, Mary Pickford was even smaller. Smaller and younger and far daintier, with all those damn curls. The kind of girl-woman Mr. Griffith preferred. Oh, I've heard the stories of Little Mary being a tiger, and I don't doubt them—but that day at Number 11, she was sweet and angelic, and I loathed her.

"Oh, my!" she gasped later on the roof when I lit up a cigarette and knocked back a whiskey, nearly in one movement. Mr. Griffith was gone for the day; a few of us had hightailed it to the roof to unwind.

"What's the matter, Mary?" I asked. "Do you not smoke or drink?"

She just shook her pretty little head at me, those damn curls bouncing.

"I don't trust a woman who doesn't drink," I said, blowing smoke nearly into her face.

Oh, wasn't I terrible? Poor little Mary. Of course, later on, she became *quite* fond of her whiskey. But back then she was just an anxious pretender to my throne, a fact that made me angry and defensive. And bitter, too, for how Mr. Griffith—and his wife—nurtured her.

So could anyone blame Harry and me for inquiring at other studios? If they were grooming Little Mary to take over my spot, we needed to, as they say, cover our arses.

"I can't believe you'd *do* such a thing, Flo," Linda had shrilled my last day at the Biograph studio. "Going over to inquire at Essanay. David had no *choice* but to let you go."

Harry stepped between us. "She's worth far more than Biograph is paying her," he charged. "You just back off now, Linda."

"After *all* David has done for you," Linda seethed. "For *both* of you."

I chose not to meet her gaze. "Well, Linda," I said, "I'm sure you'll be *very* happy to get all the parts I would have played." I was gathering my belongings from the wardrobe closet. "Or is Little Mary going to be the beneficiary? Don't go thinking she can be The Biograph Girl now. Even *I* have a hard time being her sometime."

"Flo, what has *changed* you?" Linda pushed past Harry and stood close to me. I nearly choked on her heavy perfume. "You're not the girl I once knew."

"Oh, no?" I turned and faced her. "And what of the girl *I* knew—the one who wrote me every week, promising me we'd be friends forever?"

"We would have been, but for your duplicity."

Harry was between us again. "We had every right to inquire elsewhere. Flo's the most popular star in the *world.*"

Linda reached over and grasped my hand. I let her hold it. For a moment, I saw myself in the translucence of her blue eyes, and we were back on that hill in San Francisco, and the sun was shining.

"It's still the applause, isn't it, Flo?" Linda asked, her voice softer now. "The letters. The crowds in the street."

I pulled my hand away and snapped my case shut. "I'm ready to go, Harry," I announced and quickly moved away.

"David's transforming the medium," Linda called after us as we moved away. "No other studio can match him! No one else has his vision! If you had only trusted that, how far you could have gone."

"She'll go *plenty* far," Harry shot back. "You just watch."

I didn't turn back. We left the building. I walked down the brownstone steps of Number 11 for the last time.

When I returned, fifty years later, I fought traffic congestion and smog driving down Fifth Avenue. When I turned on to East Fourteenth, my mouth went dry. I could scarcely believe what I saw. Nothing was left. The studio. The building. The entire block.

Nothing left, but my dreams.

"All right, so here's the plan," Mr. Cochrane told Mr. Laemmle, my new boss, who'd been thrilled to grab The Biograph Girl. "We'll come up with a story that she was killed. Then we'll *resurrect* her!"

"And reveal her name," Laemmle added.

"I like it," Harry said, his eyes lighting up. "Do *you* like it, Flo?"

"I imagine it'll stir up some interest," I admitted.

We were sitting around Mr. Laemmle's desk. He was a kind-faced old gentleman with a heavy East European accent and perpetually moving hands. They were clapping now in front of him as the idea took shape in his mind.

"*We'll* show that damned Biograph," he gloated. "This'll put the IMP on the map."

"Of course, since it will be Flo's name that will now be your chief asset," Harry said, assuming an air of authority that somehow worked, even with his droopy eyes and elephantine ears, "we'll expect a *considerable* raise from what she was getting at Biograph." Oh, dear Harry. Always fighting my battles.

Mr. Cochrane lifted an eyebrow. "How considerable is considerable?"

"Oh, can't we settle the money later?" Mr. Laemmle asked, standing up, his hands molding an invisible structure in the air. Maybe a new studio. Maybe an entire *city*. "Believe me, Miss Lawrence, you'll be well taken care of. We'll build our studio with you. Together we'll dismantle the trust of the existing studios and make our pictures known around the country—around the *universe!*"

"So I'll receive billing then?" I asked. "On all my pictures? Just like on the stage?"

Mr. Laemmle nodded. "I imagine we might even start a trend."

"All right," Mr. Cochrane said, leaning over to us. "Here's the story.

We're going to say the streetcar accident happened in St. Louis. I'll leak the story to the New York press that you got run down on a visit. They'd be able to check it out too quickly if I said it happened here. Then, Carl, *you* denounce the story, saying it must have been *Biograph* that planted it because you'd stolen their top star from them. You reveal her name and say she'll make a public appearance in St. Louis to prove she's not dead. I'll drum up support for a reception. I've got connections there."

"Such shenanigans." I laughed. "What is the world of entertainment coming to?"

Mr. Laemmle was moving his hands in front of Mr. Cochrane's face. "Do you really think we can get a crowd? Maybe a couple dozen people to turn out to greet her train?"

"I'll do what I can," Mr. Cochrane promised.

That would show Mr. and Mrs. Griffith, I thought. Harry reached over and took my hand. He winked at me.

We were going to St. Louis to tell the world I wasn't dead.

"Harry! Harry!" I screamed. "Please, Harry, help me!"

The mob had closed in around me. A woman took hold of my shoulders. "Thank God you're alive!" she cried, but other hands tore her away suddenly. She was pushed down under the wave, and I heard her terrible shouts as she was trampled underfoot.

Mother screamed from somewhere behind me.

"Harry!" I called. "Dear God, Harry!"

The crowd surged in again. Faces, faces—all crazed, all with wild eyes seared onto my memory. "It's *her!*" they cried. "It's *The Biograph Girl!*"

Camera flashes exploded in my face. The stink of magnesium.

I caught sight of Mr. Cochrane trying to get to me, the utter terror on his face.

It's all worked even better than we planned.

But dear God, what had we done? What kind of monster had we set free?

The shrill sound of a policeman's whistle pierced through the rabble. Then more of them, all around me. *Tweet! Tweet! Tweeeeeeeet!*

Hands, hands, *hands* groping at me, tearing my clothes.

"Harry! *Haaaaarrrry!*"

The cameras flashed.

I felt my legs give out.

I lost consciousness.

* * *

The sharp snap of smelling salts under my nose. Mother's face hovering above me. Blue-suited policemen around me in a ring.

"Save . . . me," I cried weakly.

Harry's arms, lifting me. "Come on, Florrie," he was saying. "There's a car waiting."

The cheer of the crowd as I stood. Later, the local paper would write:

> When a way was cleared for her, a tiny woman with the face of a wildflower nervously passed through the narrow aisle.

A few in the mob were chanting, "We want The Biograph Girl." But even more were now calling, "Miss Lawrence! Miss Lawrence! We love you!"

I have never forgotten it. I have dreamed of it for eighty years, waking each time with clammy skin on damp sheets.

"It was *horrible!*" I screamed at Mr. Cochrane from my bed back at the hotel. "I won't do it! Not ever again!"

Mother pressed a warm wet facecloth on my brow. I sat up abruptly and shook her aside. "Do you hear me? *Never!*"

Harry sat down on the edge of the bed beside me, taking my hand in his. "Oh, but you *must* go back out there, Florrie," he insisted. "It's the only way!"

"Florence," Mother said, "these are your *fans!* They *love* you! You *owe* it to them!"

"I've never *heard* of such a thing." I lay back down, shivering under the blanket. "If they love me, why did they try to *hurt* me?"

Mr. Cochrane tried to steady my nerves. He gave me a glass of whiskey, which I accepted gladly. "They just got a little carried away—that's all," he said.

"I've never heard of Sarah Bernhardt's fans pushing *her* to the ground. What *is* it about the movies? Why do they cause people to react so?"

"Not sure," Mr. Cochrane said. "But I know more folks turned out to see you today than were on hand to meet President Taft's train a week ago. Same station, same platform—half the people."

"More than the *President!*" Mother gushed.

I closed my eyes. Once, a decade before, I'd seen William McKinley. I remembered the crowds pressing around him—how he was trotted out on the stage at the Pan-American Exposition in Buffalo like Jumbo the Elephant and forced to perform.

That was how I felt. I couldn't bear to go through it again. But I did. Of course I did. Harry, Mother, Mr. Cochrane—they wouldn't have *let* me stop. Everywhere I went that week I drew enormous crowds. The police protected me better now, with five of them surrounding me at all times. But they couldn't prevent the cameras from flashing, keep the hands from reaching out, trying to touch an article of my clothing. Someone snagged my scarf at one stop, pulling it into the crowd. The cameras burst, blinding me.

Mr. Cochrane was speechless. None of his machinations had been needed to bring out the public. They came anyway, even without his bidding. I traveled with my new IMP costar, King Baggott, a tall, stolid man, dear and sweet but just a little bit dull, the way most handsome actors were in those days. For two days and two nights, we went around the city of St. Louis making appearances: "clever little speeches," the newspapers said.

We had *names* now. I was now Florence Lawrence, Motion Picture Star. Mother was treated like Queen Mother Alexandra at our hotel. For all her previous reticence about pictures, she was clearly adoring the attention. She took to calling me "Queenie," in fact. She even condescended to be civil to Harry. After all, his nurturing of my career seemed to have been on the mark.

But after every stop, after every crush of screaming crowds, I'd come back to the hotel and puke my lunch into the toilet. All the crab cakes and sweetmeats and champagne that were always being pushed on me. Mother was quite embarrassed by my purging. Harry kept wanting to send for the hotel doctor—but I said that it was just nerves.

Just nerves. Of *course* it was nerves, but it was hardly "just." Those nerves *wrecked* me. They plagued me *every day* from then on—until the day Lester pronounced me dead and I walked out of that hospital a free woman.

That's not to say I didn't want it—the fame, the celebrity, the applause. Linda was right. It still *was* the applause. Standing there with King, waving to the crowds, hearing their cheers, I was Baby Flo again, back on the stage, the men in the tall silk hats applauding me. So full of myself was I that I told one reporter: "The American public, when it loves its heroes and heroines, can love them with a better spirit than any people I know."

And *forget* them, I might have added later, with precisely as much spirit.

* * *

It had all been timed so perfectly. My new film—costarring King Baggott—came out just days after the St. Louis triumph. *The Miser's Wife,* it was called. I can't even remember now what it was about. But I was the star. Right up there with my name above the title. It had never been done onscreen before. Can you imagine such a time? It's so standard now. But the concept of *movie star* didn't exist until 1910, and then it was the product of one publicist's imagination and one actress's ambition.

Within months, dozens of other names were revealed. Gene Gauntier at Kalem. Broncho Billy Anderson at Essanay. My old friend Flossie Turner and John Bunny at Vitagraph.

But over at Number 11 East Fourteenth Street, Mr. Griffith stubbornly kept his players' names locked in his safe. Pickford was still just "Little Mary" to her rapidly growing public. "The star isn't what matters, David," I could hear Linda telling him, her perky little nose in the air. "It's merely a *fad*. What's important is what *you're* doing—it's the *art* that you're creating."

I had to smile when I imagined Linda's reaction to the explosion that greeted my appearance in St. Louis. The fan magazines with my picture on the cover. The trading cards with my face on them. The deluge of reporters surrounding the little apartment Harry and I shared in New York. It got so bad that within a few months I bought us a secluded house on a farm out in quiet Westwood, New Jersey. Oh, how I loved that house. With the money I was suddenly making, I could afford to make it the home I'd always wanted but never had. An apartment for Mother. Another for Ducks and his latest beau, an Italian immigrant named Alfonso. A stable of horses. Acres of beautiful rosebushes.

But I rarely had time enough to spend there. The rosebushes quickly grew wild. If not for Ducks, the horses would have gone untended. I was forever in New York at the studio, churning out two reels a week. The public demanded to see Florence Lawrence, in just about anything.

There was no one bigger than I was. Except . . .

"This one," Mr. Laemmle said, slapping a page in *Moving Picture Weekly.* A photograph of a girl with curls. *Pickford.* "And I'll be damned if I'll let Biograph keep her."

"The public doesn't even know her name," I protested.

Mr. Laemmle nodded. "This one doesn't seem to need a name. You didn't either, Florence, and they still discovered you. The public's calling her The New Biograph Girl. The fan magazines say she inherited your old dressing table."

How old was I then? Twenty? Twenty-one? Maybe a bit older. Who can remember now? But Mary Pickford was younger than I, by a number of years. I know that much. Such things *mattered*. And the fact that Mr. Griffith's pictures—which now starred *her*—were still the most popular on the market was distinctly unnerving to me. And to Mr. Laemmle.

I decided the only thing that could console me was horseback riding. It had been so long since I'd been on a horse. I'd been so busy. Out to Westwood I drove, snatching Harry's automobile without his permission. He'd have to follow on the train. I got to the stables and found Ducks brushing the amber coat of my favorite horse.

"Ah, Florrie," he said.

"I need to ride, Ducks. It's all so crazy. I just need to feel the wind in my hair."

He nodded. "Ride like you did when we were out west. Remember how you'd ride ahead of the company, getting to the next town hours before we came lumbering in?"

I did remember. "Ducks, it's not what I thought," I said as he helped me mount the horse.

"No, it never is." He looked up at me with his old eyes. When had he gotten so old? "You've been working too hard, Florrie." He reached up and took my hand in his. "Promise me. You've got to stop. You can't let it take over."

I felt like crying. "But you always said I'd be a great star," I told him.

"You can be anything you want to be, Florrie."

He truly believed that. Ducks, more than anyone, believed in me. More than I believed in myself at that point.

"Ride with me, Ducks," I said.

He laughed. "Wish I could. But the lumbago, Florrie. Keeps me from doing a lot of things I used to do."

I understood. Sometimes I'd get a headache or a dizzy spell, and I couldn't bear to get behind the wheel of my car. Driving could usually make me feel better, especially when I could escape from New York, but not on days when I couldn't even drag myself behind the steering wheel.

Ducks gave me a little salute. But I made him no promises. I took the reins in my hands and smacked the horse. She began to trot. Then faster and faster still. The wind in my hair, filling my nostrils. I wanted so much to clear my head, to stop thinking of the crowds, of Pickford, of Mr. Laemmle. . . . Out into the fields I galloped. Where the only sounds were red birds and—

"That's her!"

Off to my left, a group of three horsemen. I pulled on my horse's reins, steering her toward them, intending to tell them that they were trespassing and to please—

That's when I noticed they had cameras slung around their shoulders. "Miss Lawrence!" one of them called. "May we take your picture?"

"Who are you? How did you get here?"

I heard the fast gallop of another horse behind me. It was Harry, breathless and red. "Ducks told me you'd come out here," he said, huffing. Poor Harry wasn't used to riding. "You left the city so quickly I hadn't a chance to tell you. These gentlemen are from *Photoplay*. They're doing a feature on our life here on the farm."

"But Harry, I just want to—I can't bear—"

Harry smiled awkwardly. "Just a moment, gentlemen, while I talk to my wife."

He brought his horse close to mine. "Darling," he whispered, "*Photoplay* has just done a poll of the most popular moving picture actresses in the world. Do you know where you ranked?"

I dared not say.

"Number one. By an *enormous* margin. No one else comes close." He grinned. "Not even Pickford."

I put my hand to my head. Was that a red bird off in the trees?

"You are so loved, Florrie. So admired. The world over. Feel that love. Let it strengthen you."

I sighed, looking back over at him from the trees. "All right, Harry," I said. "Let them take their pictures."

He brightened, sitting up straight on his horse. "Very well, my good men," he called. "Come and get a photograph of the Queen of the Movies atop her noble steed."

I bore the flashes of their cameras. I answered their questions as we escorted them around the farm. Harry was bursting with pride, calling me the greatest screen artist in the universe, the most beloved figure in all of dramatic history.

"But no one," he whispered in my ear, "loves you as much as I."

Dear Harry. He was always there. Urging me on, reassuring me, consoling me. Telling me how much the world loved me.

But all I really wanted to do that day was ride my horse.

He directed most of my pictures at IMP. If I'd complain of a headache or a case of high-strung nerves—which was more and more often the case these days—he'd always call a break in the shooting. I'd lie down on a daybed, the wardrobe girls swarming around me, offering me a drink of lemonade, fanning me with Chinese fans.

Poor, dear Harry. At home, I often made him sleep on the couch. I'd be too distraught to sleep easily, too worked up from the day at the studio. I needed the bed to myself. When he would try to climb on top of me, I'd cry I couldn't bear it. *Florence Lawrence* couldn't bear it anyway.

That's when I became fully aware of the split. Somewhere between the time her name was revealed to the world and the time she left Mr. Laemmle for what she considered to be even greener pastures, I'd stopped thinking Florence Lawrence and I were one and the same.

The Present

"My, what a stir I seem to have made," Flo says, wide-eyed, as Jean walks into her room.

"There's a media crew from Channel 7 on the front lawn," Jean tells her. "I'm going to have to call the authorities. This is private property."

Flo just stands there in front of her, swaying a little. The *New York Times* article written by Richard is open on her bed.

Sister Kate is suddenly in the doorway. She looks stunned. "Jean," she says, "*Barbara Walters* is on the phone."

Flo says, "Oh, my," and puts her hands to her mouth.

Jean turns quickly. "I don't care if it's *Saint* Barbara, the Virgin Martyr—*no one* is going to see Flo!" She feels the anger rise up like perspiration on the back of her neck. She turns back, eyes blazing, to glare at Flo.

"Oh, but I *do* so like Barbara Walters," Flo says, tilting her head. *She finds this all amusing,* Jean thinks. *She's actually enjoying this.*

"Flo," she says, "we need to talk."

"What should I tell Barbara Walters?" Sister Kate asks.

"Tell her—" Jean looks over at Flo, who smiles weakly. "Oh, dear God, Katie. Tell her to call back tomorrow." Sister Kate nods quickly and moves off.

Flo raises her eyebrows like an ingenue. "It's happening all over again," she says dreamily. "I never would have imagined." She pauses, smiling. "I thought the photograph they used in the *Times* was a very nice one, didn't you? It was from one of the Jones pictures I made with Mr. Griffith."

"Flo, there are *people* outside—*reporters*—with microphones and cameras," Jean says.

Flo sits down in the chair in front of her mirror. "How very strange that people would still *care*."

"Flo, they care about anything they can turn into a sensation. Your story has been *all over* the news shows. We're getting calls from *everyone.* Flo, I need to know some things from you before it goes much farther."

"There she is."

In the doorway is Henrietta, Flo's plump friend from the dayroom. She seems quite pleased with herself, as if she's just done a good deed—like selling all of the Girl Scout cookies Flo had given her. But what she's actually done is quite another story. Behind her is a man, a tall, gangly fellow with dark glasses and bright yellow hair—and a *camera* hanging around his neck.

"That's her," Henrietta is pointing and saying. "That's Flo."

"Thanks, doll," the man says and snaps two photographs, rapid-fire, of Jean and Flo before they have a chance to respond. For a second, Jean feels like the proverbial deer caught in the glare of . . . not headlights, but a camera flash, and she watches in mute horror as the man bolts from the doorway and back down the hall.

She recovers. "Stop him!" she screams, rushing out into the hallway, nearly knocking over Henrietta. "Stop him!" But she can already see him bounding down the stairs.

She spins on Henrietta. "Why did you bring him up here? I said *no one* was to have access to Flo!"

"Oh, dear," says Henrietta, her plump cheeks reddening and her squinty little eyes misting with tears. "He seemed like such a nice man. He told me he was Flo's nephew."

Jean turns to Flo. She's standing there as if frozen by the flash. She seems lost in time somewhere, her eyes looking through Jean, her ears cocked to the sounds of a crowd no one else can hear.

"*Flo,*" Jean says. The old woman's eyes return to her. "He said he was your nephew."

"I don't have a nephew," Flo says, approaching them slowly. She's grown very pale. Jean worries she might faint right there in front of them.

"Henrietta," Jean orders, "*no one* is to see Flo. *No one.* Do you *hear* me?"

Henrietta starts to cry. Flo puts her arm around her. Some of the color has returned to her wrinkled cheeks. "There, there, dear," she says to her plump little friend, but she's looking instead over at Jean. "Don't you fret. Everything is going to be all right."

Flo draws in a long drag on her cigarette. She lets out the smoke slowly, watching it as if transfixed. Jean sits opposite her. The door to Flo's room is closed now; Sister Kate stands sentinel outside in the hall.

"Once, such attention made me physically sick," Flo's telling Jean. "But I'm much stronger now. There's no need to worry, Jeannie. Really."

"Flo, you're *a hundred and six years old.* Yes, you're active. Yes, you're a wonder of energy and agility for your age. But you get tired very quickly. I've seen you. You have no idea what it would be like out there."

Flo stubs out her cigarette in the ashtray beside her. "And the questions they'd ask. Is that what worries you?"

"Precisely." Jean reaches over and takes her hands. How cold they are. Her knuckles are big like acorns, the backs of her hands spotted and dry. "Flo, are you prepared for the kinds of questions they'd ask?"

Flo sighs. "I've thought about this ever since Richard first interviewed me," she tells her. "Of course, I never expected such attention. I never expected people to remember or to care. But I think I *am* prepared, Jeannie. It was such a long time ago, after all."

"Flo." Jean feels a tight warmth constrict her chest, a signal she's about to cry. She's *got* to learn the truth, even if it's painful for both of them. "Flo," she says again, leaning in toward her friend. "Who was Molly? And don't tell me just a girl."

Flo smiles kindly. She doesn't seem troubled by the question. "But that's what she *was,* Jeannie. They mistook her for me. Surely I can't be blamed for that."

"No?" Jean hears the hopefulness in her own voice, the desperation to believe whatever Flo tells her, without looking too deeply beneath her words. "Then why, Flo? *Why* did they mistake her for you?"

Flo hesitates. Her eyes go back to that place Jean can't see. She seems to be searching for something—perhaps asking herself the same question. She closes her eyes, folding and unfolding her hands in her lap. Finally she returns her gaze to Jean. "She lived with me for a time," she says. "I suppose—I suppose when the ambulance came for her, neighbors told them it was my house. And so they assumed—"

"Is that it then? An honest mistake?" Jean can hear the hopefulness rise again. "Tell me that plainly, Flo. That it was an honest mistake and you had nothing to do with her death. Tell me and I'll believe you."

Flo just sighs. "Oh, Jeannie," she says quietly.

She won't say it plainly, Jean thinks.

Because Flo never lies.

"It was so long ago, Jeannie," Flo says. "It was *sixty years* ago. More than twenty years before you were even *born.* Do you have *any* understanding of how much has happened in my life since then? How much has come after? How much has *mattered?* I knew Molly for only a few years—people I met after that, after I started my new life, I knew for *decades*. Ask me about them, and I'll tell you. But Molly—how can I tell you about her? I can't even remember all the details myself. I just know they made a mistake. I saw my chance, and I left."

"What if some reporter presses for details? What if they think . . . ?"

Flo smiles weakly. "Remember Clare Blake?" she asks.

"All too well," Jean says.

"Remember how I handled myself then? I'll be fine now, too, Jeannie."

"But these people aren't pushovers like Clare Blake. They're *reporters*."

"Oh, I handled any number of reporters in my day," Flo assures her.

"They're *different* now, Flo. You don't understand. It's a completely different world out there. In 1910, you didn't have Jerry Springer and Geraldo and *Hard Copy*."

Flo reaches over to her pack of cigarettes on the table with her scarlet-tipped hand. Jean lights one for her, placing it in her own mouth first and taking the first drag. Flo accepts it shakily, bringing it to her hot pink lips.

"*Why*, Flo? Why do you want to do it?" Jean looks at her hard, trying to find something in her eyes. "Why after all this time?"

Flo makes a little shrug. "I'd forgotten her," she says simply.

Jean assumes she means Molly. "You'd forgotten who, Flo?"

"Florence Lawrence." She exhales, holding the cigarette between two fingers down at her lap. It burns awhile there, growing a long, precarious ash. "I'd forgotten what she was like," Flo says, after some thought. "There's much I don't care to recall, of course, but maybe I *should* remember at that. Maybe I should finally make some peace with her."

"Then you have some regrets?"

Flo considers this. "The only thing I regret about my past is the length of it." She laughs. Jean can't help but do so as well. "If I had to start over," Flo continues, "I'd make all the same mistakes—just sooner."

The ash on her cigarette shivers free, leaving a dull gray powder on Flo's blue silk dress.

She grins suddenly. "And there's an awful lot of *fun* I'd forgotten about her, too." Her voice drops into that devilish, tough-old-broad tone Jean knows so well. "She used to *love* the applause, you know. It's strange to think some of it might still be out there."

"The applause?"

"Yes." Flo smiles more to herself than Jean. There's a glint in her eye, a tilt to her smile that Jean hasn't seen before. "I *was* the biggest star in the world, you know—and the *first*."

Jean observes her for a moment, sees Flo's eyes move off to the place only she can see. She stands and walks over to Flo's bed, looking up at the poster hanging there of Baby Flo, the Child Wonder Whistler.

"Flo," she asks, "do you not feel loved enough here?"

Flo laughs. "Oh, don't go getting melodramatic on me, Jeannie." She stubs out her cigarette, stands with some difficulty, and moves over behind Jean. "I *treasure* your friendship," she tells her. "Living at St. Mary's these past fifteen years has given me a *home*. I've *loved* playing bingo and putting together the talent show and selling Gertie's Girl Scout cookies every year. But, Jean—"

Flo looks up at the poster as well.

"We can be many things." She takes Jean's hand and pinches the skin on the back. "Not just this."

"Flo, this is my agent, Xerxes Stavropoulous," Ben tells her.

Flo is seated on her purple leather throne in the day room. She extends her hand out to Xerxes, who takes it gallantly and presses it to his lips. "I am most charmed and honored, my good lady," he says.

"Your name—Greek?" she asks.

"Yes, ma'am. My parents were born on the island of Paros."

She smiles. "Ah, yes. A lovely island. We stayed in a little pension where we slept on the roof under the stars. But, of course, my favorite island was Santorini."

"Just a ferry ride away," Xerxes says.

"There's a volcano there—do you know it?" Flo looks at Xerxes with crystal-clear blue eyes. He nods. "It's off the coast in the Aegean Sea," she continues, looking at the group assembled around her. Ben thinks she looks like some ancient schoolteacher reciting a geography lesson—like Mrs. Maxwell, his fifth grade teacher, proper and regal but a little bit crazy, too.

"Some say the volcano is the tip of the lost continent of Atlantis," Flo's saying. "When it exploded all those centuries ago, it took Atlantis down with it into the sea. The waters are *black* around it—black as night. And *hot*, very hot, from volcanic hot springs." She smiles. "You know, I don't think I was ever happier than I was swimming in the hot black waters off Santorini."

Ben notices the smile Sister Jean gives to Carla Ortiz, the diocesan lawyer she's asked to sit in on their meeting. Carla Ortiz doesn't smile back. She's a severe-looking woman, with a long neck and shiny black hair swirled around on the top of her head in a bun. She keeps eying Ben and Xerxes, not saying anything, writing in a small spiral-bound notebook.

"I was convinced the volcano was going to explode once again while I was there," Flo's saying, a little sadly. "Every day I expected a terrific blast. What a grand finish that would be. What a way to go. But it never did."

"Well, I'm glad for that," Xerxes says. "Otherwise you wouldn't be here."

She just smiles wistfully. "You remind me of a young man I met there," she tells Xerxes softly. He grins. "But, no," she says, taking a closer look. "Not really."

Ben clears his throat. "Well, I understand you've been getting a lot of media interest," he says, looking back and forth between Sister Jean and Flo.

"*Yes,*" Flo tells them. "Do you know *Barbara Walters* called?"

"It's getting a bit out of hand," Sister Jean says, looking over at Carla Ortiz, who nods. "A photographer snuck inside and snapped Flo's photo. That will *not* happen again. I've gotten the police to keep the reporters off the property."

"The press," Xerxes sniffs, shuddering. "Dreadful."

"Maybe that's what we could start with, Flo," Ben suggests. "About how the press has changed. You could tell us what it was like dealing with reporters back in 1910—"

"We haven't agreed to talk with you yet," Carla Ortiz chimes in finally. She has a sharp, lovely Latina accent but the dry, matter-of-fact tone of a lawyer. Ben looks over at her. Her deep brown eyes are like mirrors: He can see himself but nothing behind.

"Of course," Xerxes says. "We want to do this right, Ben. Now, what we were thinking was videotaping Flo here, in her element, talking about her story . . . and then moving out and filming her at various sites that have historical relevance, like the old Biograph studios and the MGM lot."

"Biograph's gone," Flo tells them.

"Well, the site of the old studio then," Xerxes says. "We could find all sorts of places."

"Just a moment," Sister Jean says. "I can't see Flo traipsing all around the country."

"It might be fun, Jeannie," Flo says.

Ben sees the look Jean gives her. *So,* he thinks. *That's the ticket. Get Flo excited about all this. It's* her *decision, after all. If she wants to do it, there's little the Big Nun can do to stop her.*

"Oh, you'd travel in *style,* Flo." Ben sees Flo's eyes sparkle as she turns to look at him. "Believe me. We could get a sponsor—"

"A sponsor?" asks Carla Ortiz.

"Sure," Xerxes says, picking up from Ben's point. "Look, let's face it. In the past few days, we've seen an outpouring of interest in Flo's life. Why not ride the wave?"

"I thought we were taping her story simply for posterity," Jean says.

Ben feels he's at the precipice. He can either jump and make a calculated, fabulous landing, to the applause of all those down below—or he could slip and tumble all the way down, the laughingstock of the crowd. He gives it his best shot and leaps.

"We have a unique opportunity here, Sister," he says. "*Somebody's* going to do Flo's life story. It's out there now—it's public domain. They'll do it without *any* input from Flo since you're not going to grant them access. For which I don't blame you, of course. But they'll do it anyway. You need to understand that. They'll do it and get it *wrong.*"

He looks hard at Sister Jean, then over at Flo, then back to Sister Jean. The nun glances at Carla Ortiz, who shrugs, as if to say: *He's got a point.*

"They'll get it *wrong,*" Ben repeats. "If *we* do it—with your input, of course, and with Flo herself telling her story—then no matter what else anyone does, *this* will be the version that's noticed. This will be the one that *counts.*"

Flo's eyes are glistening. "Oh, Jeannie, it would be a *lark* to go back." She giggles like a girl and looks around the day room. "I never thought I'd leave here. I thought this was it. That these walls would be the extent of it, that I was through seeing the world. But if Ben is right . . ."

She turns to him, suddenly aflame with an idea. "San Francisco," she gushes. "Could I go back there? I'd *love* to see San Francisco one more time."

"Of *course,* Flo," he tells her.

"Carla?" Sister Jean asks.

The lawyer crosses her legs. She's wearing a tight gray pin-striped suit and skirt with black silk stockings. Ben notices the fine shape to her calf, the delicate ankle, the long spiked heel on her black pump. "There would need to be certain parameters," she says officially. "Certain areas Miss Bridgewood would *not* be asked about. No inferences made about them anywhere in the film."

"Of course," Ben says. Xerxes is nodding, too. They've already talked about this.

"I suppose you see this as a commercial enterprise," Carla Ortiz says.

"Well," Xerxes says, "I would think the public will want to see—"

"Then you need to make us an offer," Carla says plainly.

Xerxes seems taken aback briefly; then he smiles. "Ah, so you're acting as Flo's agent?"

"I am." Carla smiles, finally. "I've worked as an agent before. Writers. A couple of Christian rock bands. In San Juan, I even represented a few filmmakers." She bats her eyes in a way that says she has no need to prove herself further than that. "Of course, none of my clients have been as high profile as your roster, Mr. Stavropoulous, but I think I can manage Flo's affairs competently."

Ben was quite sure she could at that. There was an efficiency, a confidence about her that Ben found lacking in his own agent. He couldn't help himself—he was *turned on* by this woman.

There you go again, Benjamin. Mom's voice. *A pretty girl and you forget everything else.*

Flo's grinning like a little imp. "You know, I never had an agent before. Back in the old days, you just let your mother or your husband handle things."

"So make us an offer," Carla repeats.

"Okay, okay," Ben says. He hadn't thought they'd want money. He's got about three hundred dollars in his savings account. Anita has about four. Maybe he could borrow some money from Richard or Mom. No, he didn't think that was likely.

"All right," Xerxes says, shifting uncomfortably. "We'll get back to you with a figure."

"Look," Jean says. "I know you don't have a lot of money to offer. I've explained that to Flo and Carla. And we're not in this for money. I think you know that. But I agree with Ben: *Someone* will do Flo's story, and it might as well be him."

She turns to look at him directly. "I trust you, Ben. I think we share some common values. I know your work. *One Chance, One World* had a great impact on me." She pauses. "But we'd be foolish if we didn't look out for ourselves."

"I imagine," Carla says, wiggling her foot in the air, "you'll try to sell the idea to a producer once you have our cooperation."

Xerxes nods.

"And I imagine," she continues, taking in a deep breath, revealing the firm outline of her breasts beneath her tight gray suit, "that should be relatively easy to do, now that the media is hot on Flo's trail."

Ben shifts in his chair, worried his boner might show through his pants. "I think . . . I think, yes, that should make our job easier," he admits.

"Then let's agree on a percentage," Carla says.

Ben feels prepared to be generous. "We'll split it," he offers. He can sense Xerxes looking at him disapprovingly.

"Not good enough," Carla says.

"Not good en—" Xerxes barks.

Carla shakes her head. "It's *Flo's* story. It's *Flo* who's going to have to traipse around to these places, and she's one hundred and six years old." She pauses. "Sixty–forty, and that's it."

Flo puts her hand over her mouth to cover a smile.

"Fine," Ben says. "Fine. Sixty–forty."

Xerxes lets out a long sigh. "I'll draw up the agreement," he says resignedly.

"But," Ben says, looking over at Flo, "you *are* aware that we may need to have you do some—well, prepublicity work."

Flo raises her eyebrows. She doesn't comprehend.

"That's right," says Xerxes. "If we're going to be partners, you'll have to do some legwork."

"What are you talking about?" Jean asks.

"Well," Ben says, "we need to make Flo a household name again. If we're going to get the best deal we can, we have to make her a sought-after commodity."

"This kind of talk makes me very uncomfortable," Jean says. "Flo isn't a *commodity.* She's a human being."

"Jean," Carla says, "let me handle this." She levels her black eyes at Ben. "Go on, Mr. Sheehan. What's your point?"

God, he thinks. *Catholic attorneys in tight executive suits*—now *there's* a fantasy he hasn't had before.

"Well," he says, a bit huskily, "I hate talking this way, too, and I think you know that, Sister, but one *has* to when talking business. Our feeling is that, if we can get Flo on a few of the talk shows, then our chances for securing the best possible offer are heightened."

"*Talk shows?*" Jean looks over at Carla. "What do you think of that?"

The lawyer's still got her eyes on Ben. "He has a point," she concedes.

"Don't worry," Ben says appealingly. He widens his eyes as he looks over at Jean. "You trust me, don't you? I won't let anything happen to Flo. It'll all be tightly controlled."

Xerxes is nodding. "That's right. We're not talking the trash shows here. No Springer, no Jenny Jones, not even Leeza. We might have to do Ricki Lake to get the Gen-Xers, but we've been talking with Rosie O'Donnell. She's the Queen of Nice. She won't go anywhere Flo doesn't want to go."

"Rosie O'Donnell!" Flo says, clapping her hands the way she'd once clapped them remembering The Great McGinty. "I *love* Rosie O'Donnell! We watch her every morning here in the dayroom!"

"And then maybe Regis and Kathie Lee, and of course, Oprah."

"*Oprah!*" Flo gushes, turning to Sister Jean.

Ben thinks she's the exact image of a little girl—the same spirit, the same expression on her face. It didn't matter that her hair was white or that her face was creased in hundreds of folds or that the skin on her arms was spotted and flaky and sagged. She was a little girl turning to her mother for permission to go out and play.

"I don't know," Jean says, clearly troubled.

"Well, *I* do," Flo says. Her voice grows quiet and severe. "When does one cease being an adult, Jeannie? At eighty? Ninety?" She's no longer a little girl. She looks like Mrs. Maxwell again—with the same air of prerogative Ben remembers his old teacher having, telling the children it was time to put away their crayons and take out their math books, and that was simply *that*. No further questions.

"I *want* to do it," Flo says simply, turning to look at Ben. "I had forgotten her, you see. Florence Lawrence. I'd put her far out of my mind and forgotten all about those days, those places. Who I was. But who I *was* is still a part of who I *am*, no matter how far I go or how much I try to separate it. I used to think that God had forgotten to call me home, just left me down here without a plan. But maybe I'm still around for a reason. Maybe I have to go back to being Florence Lawrence one more time."

They're all quiet for a moment. Finally Jean says, looking at Flo, "All right. But if you're going back to being Florence Lawrence, just make sure you bring our lawyer along."

It breaks the tension. They all laugh, even Carla Ortiz. Whether or not that had been Sister Jean's intention isn't clear, but it has the effect anyway. Later that day, Xerxes produces an agreement, and Carla comes up with a set of guidelines. They all sign both documents, and then it's done.

Richard and Rex have made the trip up to Chicopee on this chilly gray November day because they know they'll be in California for Thanksgiving—and possibly Christmas—and Richard wants to make sure he sees his mother before the holidays. Rex has gotten a great gig to perform *Broadway Royals* at Highways Performance Space in Santa Monica. It's great exposure, and they could be out there a month. So Richard has promised Mom a special preholiday brunch.

Yet convincing her to leave the house hadn't been easy. "Oh, but I've got a headache," she'd protested. "I've nothing to wear." But after Richard announced neither he nor Rex would move from the living room floor until she agreed, she finally wrapped an old white cardigan sweater around her enormous form, letting it drape down the front. She didn't even attempt to button it.

Now she settles into the front passenger seat of Richard's Saab. The car creaks and sags under her weight. Rex squeezes in back.

"This is a nice car," Mom's saying. "Ben's got that *little* car. What's it called?"

Richard snorts. "It was a *rental,* Mom. Ben's never owned a car."

"Poor Benjamin." Mom sighs, looking around the street as they back down the driveway and head down the road. "Oh, look. The Piatrowskis have new siding. Horrible color, though. Gosh, I haven't been out of the house in ages."

"I thought it would be good for you, Mom," Richard tells her.

She grins, her cheeks pushing her eyes shut. She reaches over and grabs Richard's chin. "That's my boy." She chuckles. "Always looking out for his mother."

A military aircraft booms overhead. Its shadow passes over the car.

Downtown Chicopee doesn't offer much in the way of Sunday brunch, Richard discovers. There are a few boarded-up old shops, a couple of video stores, a Spanish market, and several bars. Looming over the street are the rusty spires of the abandoned factory where Richard's father once worked, where Richard once feared he himself was destined.

Even if Dad hadn't left the money to escape this place, I'd still have had to go elsewhere to find work, Richard thinks. The factory is all bricked over now, rotting away on the edge of the river.

Richard is very grateful that he'd made it out of here. He'd left Chicopee and its decaying brownstones far behind. He thought of his old friends from high school. Last he heard, Teddy Gluck was working as a cashier at Wal-Mart. Gio Bonelli was in jail. And Mary Kay Silenski—who once had dreamed of marrying Richard—had been a two-time divorcée with a couple of kids when she'd stuck a pistol in her mouth and sent a bullet down her throat.

Oh, yes. He was extremely fortunate to have made it out, driving back now in his turbo Saab to survey the damage.

So what if he was up to his cranium in debt? So what if he lived with a pesty little nag at the back of his mind at all times, a frantic little voice that told him it could all come crashing down at any minute? Sure, he had bills up the butt, but he hadn't gone *completely* under yet. And maybe he never would. Although with Rex's increasingly grand plans for the redesign of their house, he was beginning to think it was inevitable.

No, he promises himself, *I'll get through it. I always have. Even in the dark days right after I went freelance, I managed to find a way. I was able to buy this car. I bought a gold membership at the gym. I kept my monthly tickets to the Met. I took Rex to Spain to celebrate our five-year anniversary.*

Credit cards were wonderful things, weren't they? And the cash advances they gave even better. So what if they charged outrageous finance fees and interest? He's always gotten what he *wanted,* hasn't he? And now he was making better money, writing for places that paid five grand or more per story. No more nine cents a word. He could get out of debt—slowly, maybe, but he could eventually pay it all off.

Sometime in the mid-twenty-first century.

Unless, of course, things took a turn for the better.

"Mom," he says, "this Florence Lawrence story could mean *paydirt* for me." He maneuvers the Saab into a parking space on Main Street. "My ship may be coming in."

"That's what Benny said, too," she tells him. "Are you boys going to work together on this?"

Richard turns off the ignition. "Ben's a weasel, Mom."

She sighs. "Oh, Richard. You've got to make allowances for Benjamin. I always told you that you'd have to take care of him."

"He's trying to steal this idea from under me, and I'm not going to let him." He hops out of the car. Rex joins him as they each take one of Mom's hands and pull her out. She struggles to get steady on her feet, but she's out of breath from the effort.

"Richard," she manages to say, "maybe you can find *something* for him. Maybe he can be the cameraman or something if you sell your screenplay."

He ignores her. "I think there's a diner around the corner," he says. "We used to eat there with Dad."

"Oh, that's long gone," Mom says. "It burned down about six years ago and nobody's ever bothered to rebuild."

"There's a Chinese place across the street," Rex points out.

Another plane booms overhead. They wait for it to be gone before they continue.

"We could get some General Tsou's chicken," Mom says. "That's my favorite. I haven't had that in ages."

Richard thinks it's too high in fat for himself, but doesn't say so. "All right," he says, settling. Chinese food wasn't how he imagined brunch. He wanted to take Mom out to a classy place, buy her a fabulous brunch with mimosas and eggs Benedict and Belgian waffles. It wasn't often she got a chance to eat out.

They cross the street. A couple of teenaged boys are leaning against a closed, iron-gated pharmacy. One's tall with sharp features, wearing a backward baseball cap. The other looks younger, maybe twelve or thirteen, with acne-riddled skin and baggy jeans, the waistband down around his thighs, his Tommy Hilfiger underwear showing.

The taller kid eyes Mom as she waddles past. "She be breakin' the sidewalk," he says in a low voice.

Rex stops in his stride and jumps back at him. "What did you say?"

The younger boy pops a knife seemingly from the palm of his hand. "He said she was *fat,*" he tells him calmly. "Disgusting. Gross."

Richard comes up behind his boyfriend. "Hey, chill," he says, taking Rex by the shoulders. Rex's ears are bright red—a sure sign he's angry. Richard eases him away, raising his hand to the youths in a conciliatory gesture. "Hey, we don't want any trouble," he tells them. "We're just going in the restaurant to eat."

The knife disappears back into the boy's hand. The two of them just stare steely eyed at Richard.

"You see what happens when I go out of the house?" Mom says. She doesn't appear frightened or offended or hurt, just resigned to the wisdom of reclusivity. They move off toward the Chinese restaurant.

There would have been a fight if I hadn't stopped it, Richard thinks. *Rex is so impulsive—like Ben. Ben would've jumped them, too. Ben would've gone after them for insulting our mother.*

Well, Richard tells himself, *that's because he's the hot-tempered one. He would've gotten us stabbed in the street. I'm the levelheaded one. I'm the one to provide the protection, the guidance. It's always been that way. That's why I've gotten ahead and Ben hasn't.*

But he slips his arm around his mother's broad waist anyway. He looks down at her tiny little eyes, puffed up by overfed cheeks. His heart breaks. He leans in and gives her a kiss on the forehead.

Sixteen years ago he'd felt the same way toward her. His heart had splintered in half. She was standing in front of him in the kitchen, a few weeks before his last day of high school. And she'd said to him, "I don't imagine you'll be wanting to have a graduation party." It was the saddest thing he'd ever heard her say.

In just a year she'd ballooned—from a hundred and sixty to two hundred and twenty to a walloping *two hundred and eighty* pounds. The house was a mess. She rarely vacuumed anymore, never washed the kitchen floor. So much had changed since Dad died. Once, Richard had enjoyed having his friends over. They'd play *Dark Shadows* in the basement, with Richard scrunching himself up to fit in Mom's old hope chest, then sitting up and raising the lid like the vampire Barnabas

Collins emerging from his coffin. But Mom was right: Now, neither he nor Ben wanted a graduation party. They didn't want their friends in the house, in that dump, seeing the monstrosity that once had been their mother.

Ben had readily admitted not wanting a party. But Richard hesitated, seeing the look on Mom's face. She knew why they'd probably defer. She saw the shame they bore in their eyes. "Well," Richard said, "maybe just a couple of friends." She looked surprised. "I'll bring a couple of friends by and we'll have some cake," Richard promised.

How Mom had brightened. For the next few weeks, she got up early, even began fixing her hair. She cleaned the kitchen as best she could and baked a cake from scratch. On graduation day, a headache kept her from the ceremony. Richard knew she was just too embarrassed to be seen by all her old friends. But she'd been busy while they were all pomping and circumstancing in the school auditorium. When Richard got back to the house, he discovered she'd strung crepe paper across the living room, securing it with thumb tacks in the plywood. Mom stood there glowing, wearing lipstick and a dress actually buttoned down the front, her hair done up in an Ogilvie home perm.

Ben was nowhere to be found, of course. Later, he'd claim Mom had thrown the party just for Richard. But that wasn't the case. CONGRATU- LATIONS RICHARD AND BENJAMIN was scrawled on a large piece of con- struction paper taped to the front door. Inside, her peach cobbler awaited alongside a pitcher of fresh-squeezed lemonade and a pile of paper plates.

Mary Kay had been the only one of his friends to see Mom since Dad died. She tried to brace the others for Mom's appearance, but Richard could still see the looks of shock and revulsion on their faces. Mrs. Sheehan had always been a little chunky, but she'd never looked like this. Only Mary Kay had a slice of cake with her in the kitchen; the oth- ers stood in the living room and giggled to themselves. After a half hour, everyone was gone, but Mom seemed pleased.

"I'm glad your friends could come, Richard," she told him, reaching up and kissing him on his cheek, her chubby hand pressed against the other side of his face. "I'm glad we could celebrate this special day."

"You do *like* Chinese food, don't you, Mom?" he asks her now. They're almost to the restaurant. "I mean, we *could* drive up to North- ampton."

"Oh, no, I don't want to go that far," she says.

"Mom, it's just fifteen minutes."

"This is *fine*, Richard. None of those fancy-shmancy places with sprout sandwiches for me."

They're about to enter the restaurant when Rex stops in front of the tobacco shop next door. "Oh, no," he groans, looking down.

Newspapers are displayed in a rack out on the sidewalk. *The Springfield Union-News*. *The Boston Globe*. *The New York Daily News*. And *The National Exposé*.

"Look," Rex says, snatching the tabloid up in his hands. "It's Flo."

And sure enough, there she is, with Sister Jean, on the front page under the headline:

FIRST PHOTOS OF THE BIOGRAPH GIRL

Flo's in a paisley caftan, her long white hair loose and down to her shoulders. Sister Jean's eyes are wide and outraged. Her mouth is open.

"Holy shit," Richard says. "Someone got *in*. Sister Jean looks *pissed*."

"Yeah, but Flo looks pretty amused by it all," Rex observes. It's not a bad picture of her really, not for one so obviously taken by surprise.

"She looks *ancient*," Mom says, peering up at the paper.

"Mom, she's a hundred and six," Richard tells her. "She's *supposed* to look that way."

"Oh, God, listen to this," Rex says, briefly scanning the article. He reads: "'Could this sweet old lady be a murderess? That's what some investigators are beginning to wonder. Her answers to a reporter's questions on the subject have been tantalizingly vague.'" He looks up at Richard. "Oh, poor Flo."

"Do you think she *is*, Richard?" Mom asks. "A murderess? Do you think she killed that girl just so she could get away? I heard Regis and Kathie Lee talking about it after your article came out. It was also on *Good Morning, America*. Some people suspect she might have had something to do with it."

Richard makes a sound of exasperation. "Mom, we don't even know for sure yet that she's telling the truth. She might not even *be* Florence Lawrence." But he's not convincing, least of all to himself. He sighs. "We'll know soon enough anyway," he says.

"Why? What's happening?" Rex asks.

Richard closes his eyes. "I was going to wait and tell you later after brunch. I got a call last night. They're going ahead with the exhumation. The L.A.P.D. pressed the court to act quickly, given Flo's age, in case they need to question her. I'm going to cover it while we're out there."

Mom gasps, her eyebrows high on her face. "They're digging her *up?* There'll be nothing *left* of her!"

Rex locks eyes with Richard. "I guess there's no turning back now, huh?"

No, none. And Richard wouldn't, he supposes, even if he could. This past week, he hired an agent himself, and on the basis of his *Times* article, he's already received book offers from two publishing houses. Meanwhile, he's cleared his desk of everything but this story; he's prepared to spend the next year researching it if necessary. He's going to try to talk with Sister Jean again, convince her to give him access to Flo. He'll even negotiate with *Ben* if he has to.

Because in the course of just a couple weeks, Flo has become *big.* A hot property all over again—eighty years after the fact. He's had calls from every major film historian and archive in North America and Europe. *Everyone* wants to know what he knows. While in L.A., he'll appear on *Entertainment Tonight.* He's agreed to be part of a special being put together on the life of Florence Lawrence for A & E's *Biography* series. A month ago, they would never have been interested in profiling her. Now, nearly every time Richard has turned on the television, he's seen reports on the Flo Bridgewood story, with grainy old clips of Florence Lawrence acting with Mary Pickford or Mack Sennett. The Biograph Girl is *big* again.

And he's found his ticket to ride.

But he feels tremendously sad. He looks down at his fat mother. The kids in the neighborhood used to call her Tyrannosaurus Rose. He feels as if he might start bawling right there on the street.

"Come on, Mom," he says huskily. "Let's go get you some General Tsou."

April 1912

The sounds of the ship in the harbor: the great scrape of iron, the angry hisses of steam, the long sad horn. Once again, it's sound that comes first to my mind. The shouts of the crowd, the laughter of children. The beating of my own heart, high in my ears.

And smell, too: everywhere the scent of sea salt and burning coal. The heavy fragrance of oil, the great ship's perfume.

The vessel berthed at Pier 59 was as tall as an eleven-story building. I looked up, my chin raised to the sky. I kept my hands in my muff and pretended not to be awed.

It was a new Gilded Age. What a perfect epithet, don't you think? For everything *was* gilded in those years. Our ships, our cars, our homes. Our ambitions. Of course, that was *my* experience. I imagine others weren't as fortunate. But when my name was announced at the pier, the crowd parted and Harry and I made our way through. "Bon voyage, Miss Lawrence," someone called from the throng. I paused, waving a lace handkerchief from my gloved hand. A dozen cameras flashed.

I was working then for "Pop" Lubin, one of the film industry's earliest pioneers, and a shrewd, crafty man. He'd promised us more money than Mr. Laemmle, so of course, we'd left, just as we'd left Biograph. Now, after six months of uninterrupted filmmaking, Pop had wangled first-class tickets for himself, his wife, Harry and me aboard the *Olympic,* the jewel of the White Star Line.

"Florrie needs to get away, take a rest cure," Pop had said. He and Harry deemed it the best thing for me. I wasn't consulted. They just secured the tickets.

Six months doesn't even begin to count it. Between my work at IMP for Mr. Laemmle and now with Pop Lubin, it had been *two years* of moviemaking without a single break. *Two years* of appearances, of mobs, of hands everywhere, of reporters and cameras and interviews. It got to the point where I'd receive them in my dressing room, still in bed. One wrote:

Florence Lawrence languished on her settee, arm draped over her head. She has a frail constitution. Her nerves are easily rattled.

Mother just called me "moody." Pop Lubin seemed inclined to indulge my moods. "Actresses have busy minds," he told the press. "They're always changing them."

Moody. I'd never thought of myself as moody before. I had to laugh when I read the words "frail constitution." Tell that to the grooms who taught me how to break a horse. To Mr. Griffith, who said I had the soul of a boy. To Linda or Harry or Ducks, after I'd given them their first ride in an automobile. Tell it to my brother Norman, who'd get socked on his nose when he teased me just a moment too long.

But that wasn't me. That was Florence Bridgewood, a girl I might have read about or played on the screen. In front of the camera, I still rode horses. I still popped boys in the nose. I still drove cars dangerously across railroad tracks, just missing the onrushing train. But once Harry would call "Cut!" I retreated to my bed. Wardrobe girls fluttered close behind with pitchers of water and cold cloths for my brow.

Lincoln had freed the slaves, but he couldn't have anticipated me or my kind. In truth, Florence Lawrence did indeed have a "frail constitution." She was forever feeling faint, forever being gripped by mysterious headaches and phantom pain. Harry would take me out to our farm in New Jersey, but still I couldn't relax. Even petals falling from my rosebushes kept me awake.

The press didn't know what to make of me. I wasn't like the other girls—Norma Talmadge, Lillian Gish—who greeted them with polite chatter, with ethereal glances. Mary Pickford was their greatest darling, posed and petted and puckered prettily. I told one reporter, "Say anything you want about me, but don't say I like to work. That sounds too much like Mary Pickford, that prissy bitch." The line appeared in print, albeit without the last three words.

One morning all I could do was cry. Heavy, wracking sobs that shook my bed. The drapes were still drawn and the maid cowered in the doorway. Harry rushed in from the couch, sitting on the edge of the bed, helpless to comfort me.

Pop Lubin suggested a trip to calm my nerves. "We sail next week," Harry told me, showing me our tickets. I managed a smile. I'd never been to Europe. He handed me brochures on all the places we'd visit. Rome. Athens. Cairo.

Of course, Mother was opposed to the idea. Mostly, I'm sure, because Harry hadn't included her.

"Florence," she scolded, over the telephone, "this trip is too *long*. Is Lubin out of his head? *Months* will go by before you have a new picture in the theaters."

"Pop says there's a backlog, Mother," I told her. "In any event, Harry says I need a rest."

"Harry! What does *he* know? It was his bungling that led you astray from Griffith and then from Laemmle! And now look! Pickford has risen steadily in the *Photoplay* poll from five to four and now to two! Florence, Harry will *ruin* your career!"

"Mother, I have to go." She was out in New Jersey; I was in our New York apartment. "I have to get back to the studio."

"At least come out tonight and see Ducks," Mother said, knowing how to drive the knife. "He'd like that. It's been so long."

"I can't *possibly* get out to Westwood tonight, Mother," I told her. "The ship departs tomorrow, and I have to finish shooting some scenes here."

"It's just that he's been *asking* about you, Florence." Mother's pause over the phone was deliberate. "And he hasn't been well, you know."

I let out a very melodramatic sigh. Harry took the receiver from me and pressed it up to his ear. "Now, listen, Lotta. Don't go upsetting Florrie," he growled. "She's worked up enough as it is."

I don't know what she said back to him, but Harry's voice got louder and angrier, and finally he just slammed the receiver back onto its cradle. "Damn woman," he spit.

"Oh, Harry, sometimes I think I'm going *mad*," I cried.

"Don't you worry, sweetheart." He wrapped me in his big arms. He smelled sweet, a man's perfume that seemed so incongruous to his bullish frame. "That's why we're heading to Europe. They call it a European rest cure. Lots of them big society matrons take 'em." He kissed me on the cheek. "Your mother's just jealous she's not coming. She wants to make you feel guilty about Ducks. But he'll be fine. He'll be here when we get back. And you'll be a new woman, rested and happy and ready to go."

But I wasn't so sure. Pop Lubin was bringing a couple of the studio's cameramen. They were planning to take pictures of me in Rome and Athens and on a barge sailing down the Nile. "Just for stock footage," Pop assured me in his heavy Germanic accent. "You won't have to do any acting. But who knows when you'll be making an Egyptian picture and we'll need it?"

I eased myself out of Harry's embrace. I was tired. I hadn't even begun to pack for the trip. I wished I was getting in my convertible Oldsmobile Autocrat with the tiger-print interior and heading out to New Jersey. The wind would be in my hair, the sun on my face.

I picked up the telephone. Harry glowered at me.

"Ducks?" I said when he answered.

His voice sounded tinny. A bad connection. "That you, Florrie?"

"Ducks, how are you?"

"Oh, they can't seem to figure it," he said. "These aches. But I took a walk out in the rose garden today and felt better."

"I'm glad, Ducks. How are the roses coming?"

I heard him snort. "Just beautiful, Florrie. I'm keepin' them trimmed for you. They're halfway over the trellises now. Come next month, they'll start blooming some beauties."

"I can't wait," I told him. "How's Alfonso?"

"Oh, didn't your mother tell you? He's gone and run off, like all of 'em have done eventually."

I smiled sadly. "You'll find another soon enough, Ducks."

"I don't know anymore, Florrie. I'm an old man."

We were quiet for several seconds.

"Well, you come out as soon as you're back," he said to me.

"I will, Ducks." I paused. "Ducks, do you have your harmonica on you?"

"Sure, I do, Florrie. Always right here in my pocket."

"Just play it a minute. Play 'Annie Laurie.' Over the phone."

He chuckled. I heard him set the receiver down. There was a quick zip of music as he tested the harmonica. I imagined his lips running along its shiny metal as he leaned in close to the mouthpiece on the stem of the phone. I could see him so clearly, just as he was in those days when he'd accompany me on the stage or lull me to sleep. Dear old Ducks, who once shielded me from the world. The whine of the music filtered through the phone, and for just a moment, I closed my eyes and forgot my pain.

The music ended. He got back on the phone. "Haven't played that old tune in years."

I smiled. "It was lovely, Ducks."

"You'll say hello to the Sphinx for me now, won't you?"

"I will, Ducks."

"Good-bye, Florrie."

The phone crackled.

"Good-bye, Ducks."

*   *   *

The First Officer welcomed us on board. "It is a distinct honor to have you with us, Miss Lawrence," he said.

I smiled demurely as way of reply. The truth was, I could barely speak. The ship's magnificence was overwhelming, and to my state of mind, *overpowering*—so vast and gargantuan that I felt puny, even *threatened,* by its grandiosity. While Harry conferred with the purser, I stood off to the side, clutching the railing, my body trembling.

"We've got a parlor suite done up in Louis XVI," Harry whispered to me when he'd finished, taking me by the arm and leading me across the deck. "One of the best on board."

The accommodations *were* spectacular, to be sure. Our sitting room was edged in gold, with an elaborately woven Oriental rug. We had our own bath and lavatory. Instead of the traditional portholes, our full-size windows afforded us gorgeous views of the ocean. We even had our own private promenade deck.

We set sail to the cheers and streamers of the tumultuous crowd on the pier. Mother hadn't come down to see us off. I stood on the deck and waved to the people anyway. A Lubin cameraman cranked away, recording the event.

In the first-class lounge, we enjoyed cigarettes and brandy with British millionaires and Greek shipping tycoons. It was a magnificent room. A frisky blaze danced in the fireplace under a statue of Artemis. A chandelier of Irish crystal hung over us, so carefully aligned that I never once saw it shiver as the ship crossed the seas.

Harry regaled our ascotted friends with stories of the movies. Pop Lubin even arranged for a screen to be set up and to show some of my pictures. Afterward, the millionaires' wives all flocked around me, asking for my autograph.

I never saw any of the third-class passengers. They weren't allowed up on our decks. But I *felt* their presence nonetheless, so far below. There, but for a few years, was I. Now, instead, I made pleasantries with ladies wearing tiaras and carrying little dogs with ribbons tied in their pipe-curled fur. I spoke very little, fearful that my underschooled language would embarrass me. I just smiled prettily and docilely—playing the coquette in ways Florence Bridgewood would have found laughable.

One woman—I think she was a countess or something equally outrageous—was trying very hard to convince herself that the theater was a noble profession, that acting was a true art. I suspected she'd always looked down on the stage and was probably horrified by the flickers. Yet here I was, the toast of the ship, so she had to rationalize why she would be talking with me.

"Bernhardt, Duse," she was saying, rambling on, and I nodded my head, barely alive it seemed. I gripped a chair behind me to steady myself.

"Don't you agree, Mrs. Solter?"

"What?"

She smiled. Her face was powdery white. A great knot of pearls dangled from her turkey-wattle throat.

"Your endeavors with the films are an attempt to create a literature for the photoplay, are they not?"

I could no longer abide her pretensions. "*Life's* what's important," I told her. "Tending roses and driving automobiles. Eating fresh oranges and getting the juice all over your chin. Birth and death and hunger and pain. Acting's just waiting for a custard pie. That's all."

And I excused myself, much to Harry's consternation.

Our second night at sea, we dined with the First Officer in the elegant Palm Court, surrounded by high-arched stained glass windows and trellises covered with ivy. We sat on delicate wicker furniture and were served by authentic French chefs and waiters. The menu promised a superb feast, but I only picked at my lamb in mint sauce.

"Miss Lawrence," a messenger said, appearing behind me at the table. "I have a message for you that's come through on the wireless."

He handed me a slip of paper folded in half. I looked down at it, then up at Harry, who sat across from me, looking awkwardly pompous in his white tie and tails.

"Well," the First Officer said politely, "I should hope it's nothing *upsetting.*"

"Do you want to step outside to read it, Flo?" Harry asked.

I smiled around at the table. The ladies in their glittering emeralds and pomaded hair smiled sympathetically at me. "No, that's all right," I said. "I'm sure it's just a well-wisher."

I opened the message. At the top of the paper was the insignia of the *Olympic* and the White Star Line. Below, in the scrawled handwriting of the wireless operator, was the message:

Ducks died this morning. Asked for you. Funeral tomorrow.

I folded the message back in half. "Just as I thought," I said, smiling. "Mother just wanted to wish us Godspeed."

Everyone smiled. The first officer went back to telling us how powerful the *Olympic* was, how great were the possibilities for the future of oceangoing travel.

I stared down at my dessert of Waldorf pudding. I scooped a bit on my silver spoon, kissing it for taste. Then I set it back down on the table and covered my face with my hands.

"Are you all right, Miss Lawrence?" the first officer asked.

"Florrie?"

I stood up abruptly, knocking over my glass, spilling water onto an industrialist's lap. He jumped up, startled, upsetting a tray of eclairs. I didn't apologize for the commotion. I just ran off through the dining room.

Harry found me on the deck, staring into the roiling black sea. "What is it, Florence?" he demanded. "What did the message really say?"

I had thrown it into the ocean. It floated there awhile, caught by the moonlight, before vanishing under the waves.

I turned to look up at Harry. I tried to speak, but found my throat tight and filled with tears. "He was the only father I ever knew," I cried at last. "My earliest memories are all of him. The smoke from his cigars. His . . . harmonica." I felt as if my gut would tear open. "He'd hoist me up on his shoulders, carry me up into the flats where we lived between shows. When the children came around, he was there to protect me from them. Ducks always there to protect me."

Harry just stood there. He didn't attempt to comfort me. His face clouded; his lips grew white.

"Damn the bitch," he finally seethed. "Why did she have to send the message now? Go to all the trouble of wiring a message to the ship?"

"Because she knew I'd want to know," I said weakly.

"Because she knew it would interfere with *us!*" Harry shouted. "You need *rest,* Florence, and she's upset you again!"

He tried to grip me by my shoulders, but I yanked myself away.

There was some commotion then, a flurry of crew rushing past. The ship lurched a bit in the water. Harry and I steadied ourselves on the railing. He took off his coat and wrapped me in it, leading me downstairs, past the Turkish bath and the smoking room, where the men had gathered, puffing on their cigars with looks of consternation on their faces. The ship had changed directions, they told us, and was heading north. I could not have cared less at that point *where* we were headed, but Harry found great camaraderie with the men and their cigars, huffing over their umbrage in not being kept informed.

Finally the First Officer came down to explain. "One of our sister ships is in trouble," he said. "We need to alter our course and go to her assistance."

I sat on the deck all that night alone, watching the moon dance along the waves. It was a cold night, and my teeth chattered, but I couldn't bear being down with Harry and Pop Lubin, keeping vigil with the men, smoking hundreds of cigars, reveling in their own sense of inclusion in the rich boys' club. I watched the sun edge the far horizon, the water gradually reflecting shards of pink.

In the distance, I finally spotted a vessel, but there seemed to be nothing wrong with it. As we got closer, I could see smaller boats being hauled on board.

Mrs. Lubin was behind me, wrapped in a shawl. "That's the *Carpathia,* rescuing the ones who survived," she told me. "They say *hundreds* went down with the ship."

I watched passively. My mind could not embrace the tragedy of others. The morning sun now revealed debris littering the waves, wooden planks and deck chairs. To our left came the excited cries of a group of women looking over the side of the ship. Mrs. Lubin took my hand and urged me to follow. We found a spot for ourselves along the railing.

"There!" cried one of the women. "There it is again!"

A body came bobbing in the water near our ship. Its face was as black as the man I'd once found hanging from the tree. There were screams from the women. Mrs. Lubin fainted.

I sat back down on a bench. I began to cry. I think I must have sat there for hours, just crying, for I remember eventually becoming very warm. The sun was high, full on my face. Finally Harry found me. He said nothing, just helped me to stand. Then he escorted me back to our room.

The ship's doctors pronounced me a complete nervous breakdown. Oh, who knows what that means? All I know is, I couldn't stop crying, and I *hated* Harry for taking me to Europe. I was convinced I was going to die. "It's God punishing me—don't you see?" I cried, pounding Harry's chest again and again with my fists. "For lying to the world that I was killed in St. Louis! Now I'm *really* going to die!"

I passed through the stately dining rooms of the ship like a ghost. Harry would find me wandering down the majestic central staircase, eyes lost, in bare feet and only a flimsy white nightdress, my hand lightly gliding along the banister. Or else I'd be up on the deck, the moonlight in my hair, the wind catching my dress, exposing my calves. He'd wrap his coat around me, gently chastising me for walking off, guiding me back to our suite of rooms and easing me into bed.

"Oh, my poor beautiful little daughter," Pop Lubin clucked over me, then straightened up to glare at Harry. "But she'll be all right to film when we get there, won't she?"

"She'll be all right," I heard Harry reply.

He tried to engage me with stories of the places we'd visit. We'd disembark from the *Olympic* at Cherbourg and board another ship to Gibraltar. From there, we'd take a series of cruises that would take us through the Mediterranean and bring us to Corsica, Rome, Egypt, Cyprus, Turkey, and finally, the Greek islands.

Of all of them, only Santorini produced a glimmer of interest. I read the guidebook from cover to cover, sitting on a chaise on our private promenade deck, wrapped in a blanket. "It says here that someday the volcano off Fira will explode again," I said to Harry. "That in ancient times it took Atlantis down into the sea."

He just smiled indulgently. I closed my eyes and imagined the great shudder of the earth, the rumbling sound as the lava pushed its way to the surface. I saw the first spit of fire from the volcano's mouth, then the great mass of molten rock spilling down the sides, turning the black waters red, claiming everyone on the island for the sovereignity of the sea.

Miss Lawrence is a globe-trotter, some reporter would write a year or two later. I kept the clipping in my scrapbook for many years. It yellowed and faded and finally crumbled into dust. But I can remember its breathless prose to this day. It read:

> *She can tell you how the moon looks rising on the Sphinx in the Egyptian desert, or how the dawn comes up like thunder, out of China, across the bay.*

Breathless indeed. They were my exact words. I remember telling the woman about the trip, as I reclined on my velvet remarpé, dressed only in my pink negligee. Wide-eyed and far too young to be out on her own, she was eagerly taking everything down in her notebook.

"Why did you go to Europe?" she asked. "You were there so long."

I sighed as only a star can sigh. "My work had been very arduous and trying," I told her. "I was extremely nervous, so much so that I couldn't work to my own satisfaction. I wanted to get away from motion pictures and motion picture studios for a while. But it was a great mistake going to Europe. I found no rest there."

All those wonderful places—I barely noticed them. Harry propped me up against the rail of the barge steaming up the Nile. I was dressed in some absurd tunic. The other tourists looked quizzically at me and at the cameramen frantically cranking their cameras, perched precariously on tripods that slid around the deck each time the boat lurched. Yes, I can tell you how the moon looks rising on the Sphinx, but I felt no passion, no romance. Only weariness and an aching, unnameable sorrow.

Mother arrived while we were in Turkey. I'd written her, begged her to join us. Harry was vehemently opposed to the idea, and he sulked about it for weeks. He slept out on the little balcony of our hotel like a pouty child.

Once Mother had joined us, they had terrible quarrels. "Why don't you get her a fitting picture, like the kind she was making with Mr. Griffith before you spirited her away?"

He folded his big arms across his chest. "Flo's more popular than ever!"

"And how long might *that* last with her here idling away precious weeks?" She hurried over to me where I lay stretched out lethargically on my bed. She cupped my chin in her palm. "Oh, Queenie, you are capable of so much more than what you've been doing with Lubin. You just don't have the *vehicle*. Come back with me and we'll find a director who knows what makes you so special."

"I know very well," Harry shouted.

Mother ignored him, her eyes fixated on me. "We'll get something with an elaborate setting," she said. "Shakespeare or Bulwer-Lytton— what d'you think? I played in *The Lady of Lyons* on the stage to *great* acclaim! It was one of the *biggest* hits of our company. Do you remember, Florence? Or maybe a good riding picture. You were always so *good* in them. I want something *thrilling* to bring the audience to its feet—not that ordinary trash *he* keeps putting you in."

Harry stalked off, slamming the door behind him.

I looked up at Mother. "You just don't want to go back to being poor," I managed to say to her.

"I've never *been* poor, only broke," she sniffed. "Being poor is a way of life. Being broke is just a temporary situation."

I closed my eyes and turned my face to the wall.

"The industry is changing so fast, Florence," Mother warned, her voice lower now. She sat down beside me on the bed. "There are all *sorts* of new things on the screen now. Pictures are getting longer. New stars are appearing all the time." She gave me a small smile. "Did you know Pickford was just voted Number One in the *Photoplay* poll?"

My eyes flickered up to her.

"It was only a matter of time, Flo, especially with you gone so long."

"What about me? What number?"

"Number Two," Mother said with a great clucking of her tongue. I went back to silence for the rest of the day.

* * *

Yet I couldn't think about going home. I had to get to Santorini. I was convinced there lay my destiny. The volcano would explode and take all of us with it.

MOVING PICTURE STAR PERISHES
IN VOLCANIC ERUPTION

Yes, yes—that would be the way. A wonderful, magnificent, fitting way to go.

"There it is!" I cried. "There it is!"

Santorini loomed ahead of us. The ferry carrying us from Paros would dock within the hour. Mother stood with me on the deck, a kerchief wrapped around her head. The sun was full and bright above us, the sky a vivid, sharp blue.

"The volcano," I asked, turning to our Greek guide. "Is that it? There?"

The guide was on the deck of the ferry slicing open a squid. His knife caught hold of the jellylike flesh and slid down its length. A white ooze flowed forth. He lifted his eyes to look in the direction I pointed. His face was a deep bronze, lined and cracked. He was missing several teeth but his eyes were clear and large. "Yes," he grunted and spoke the name of the volcano in Greek.

Great rocks stood black against the dark, smooth waters. The bay is the volcano's collapsed crater, the largest caldera on earth, you know. We sailed past sheer cliffs of volcanic layers that rose a thousand feet in the air. Far above our heads sat the gleaming white structures of the capital city of Fira, edged along the rim of the cliff.

"You'll need to take a mule up to the town from the dock," our guide explained. "There's no way you can walk."

"A mule?" Mother grimaced. "Florence, are you sure you can?"

"I'll be fine, Mother," I told her. And I was quite sure I would be. All at once the idea of a mule ride up the side of the sheerest cliffs I'd ever seen seemed exhilarating. It made the whole trip suddenly worthwhile.

How I laughed watching Mother and Harry grapple with their mules. Mine was pliant and obedient, dutifully plodding up the nearly six hundred stone-ramped steps that zigzagged up the side of the island. I kept turning around, the sight of the black volcanic water filling my sight. The wind whipped under my bonnet, roguishly untying its drawstrings. Halfway up the cliff, my hat lifted free of my head and sailed out madcap over the sea.

My laughter echoed against the volcanic cliffs as my mule trudged onward.

"Three thousand years ago," our guide told us as we sat on a deck built into the side of the cliff, "Santorini was called Stronghyle, or the Round One. Even then it was the most beautiful of all the Cyclades. But then the volcano erupted, the most colossal explosion the world has ever known. It created these high cliffs, and many say the lost civilization of Stronghyle is really the Kingdom of Atlantis. They say Plato simply mistook the symbol for 100 for 1,000 in his calculations. That would put the sinking of Atlantis squarely at the time the round Stronghyle became the crescent-shaped Santorini."

I sipped my wine and breathed in the cool night air. A small fire had been lit to keep us warm on the terrace of our pension, and I spotted other blazes on the many similar terraces along the cliff. Across from us the "burned isles" of Palia and Nea Kameni stood as testimonials to the volcano's wrath. "There are still some sparks over there," our guide told us. "Just to keep us guessing."

I didn't need to guess. The caldera was quiet and smooth, but it didn't fool me. I knew at any moment we might feel the rumbling beneath our feet. The first wisps of smoke would rise up from the sea.

"Do you remember the papier-mâché volcano Ducks made?" Mother asked suddenly. "For *The Winds of Pompeii*? How we had to cart that thing around with us? It took more space in our wagon than our costumes."

Mentioning Ducks made me sad again. I turned to our guide. "Is it too cold to swim? Have the waters warmed up enough yet?" I asked.

He grinned, exposing his gapped teeth. "Here they don't need warming. There are hot springs from the volcano. I'll take you tomorrow."

"No," I insisted. "Tonight."

"Oh, Florence!" Mother scolded.

"I forbid it!" Harry said, all bluff and swagger.

I disregarded him, which had become easy to do. "Please," I said again to the guide.

"It means going back down by the donkey," he told me.

"I'll do it!"

So we did. Harry insisted he accompany us, but I barely noticed him. All I could think of was swimming in those black waters, the waters that would claim me, take me home. Our guide took us out in a little boat toward the burned isles and had us disrobe. I stripped completely to Harry's horror. Oh, how *warm* the waters were. How glorious. At one point, I completely submerged myself, holding my breath and opening my eyes, staring only into the murky blackness that enveloped me. I burst to the surface in a spray of water and laughter.

"No more, Florrie," Harry pleaded. "It's too dark out here."

But I kicked and splashed like a girl—like the girl I'd been—for over an hour, as naked as the day I was born. I don't think I've ever been happier, before or since.

At the end of our first week on the island, Harry departed with Pop Lubin and the camera crew. I stayed behind with Mother. Harry, sour and belligerent, told Pop I needed time to "come to my senses."

Of course, that was exactly what I was doing.

I was glad to see them go. Harry and Mother had taken to quarreling incessantly, which only added to my stress.

"She's a nasty, antagonistic witch!" Harry shouted at me, his face moist with sweat and his big ears bright red. "She's an old sow and you're her stubborn calf! She'll destroy your career if you let her!"

"How dare you speak of my mother that way!" I threw a tomato at him. It hit the wall, leaving a smudge of red flesh.

Harry packed his suitcases and stormed off. I watched from the deck as he flopped around on his mule, heading back down the cliff, desperately trying to hold on to what little dignity he still had left.

That's really the last image I have of him. Oh, certainly there was much more to come. Harry's story doesn't end there, but in many ways, the image of the man being jostled about on the back of his mule was the last of the husband I loved. I can't bear to go into what eventually became of Harry, what became of our marriage. That's for another time, when I feel stronger. For now, suffice to say that I've chosen to remember the shy, awkward bear with the bouquet of slightly wilted chrysanthemums, the one in whose embrace I found solace, albeit fleetingly. This is the man who loved me, whom I continue to love in return. Not the desperate, unstrung man who saw me only as Florence Lawrence, the movie star, and not his wife.

Mother and I spent a month on Santorini. I felt the yawning distance, the great protective stretch of sea between the island and New York. Every morning I'd rise with the sun, breathe in the warm, salty air, and stare down into the roiling caldera. I set out on daily excursions around the island, finding the simple joys of life returning as I waited for the end to come. Wandering through the narrow, twisting streets of Fira, I bought fresh fish at Plateia Theotokopoulou, the central square. I picked baskets and baskets of the wild tomatoes that grew from the rich, dark soil in the cracks of the pumice. I'd sit on a black rock under the brilliant blue sky and watch pelicans dive into the sea at perfect right angles. At any turn between the white stone buildings, I would come to the edge of the caldera and gaze down at the multicolored cliffs and black water below.

Everywhere I felt the *magic* of the island. On Santorini, where rocks float and crumble in your hand when grasped, I came to *believe* in magic.

"We are built of air," our guide explained to me. "Air and water and fire."

Elemental things. Magical things. The same, really.

I took long walks outside the village. Here, no one knew me. Here, there were no cinemas, no cameras, no reporters.

It was a warm, glorious day when I hitched a ride on a cart up the rocky headland of Mesa Vouna to see the ruins of ancient Thira. The driver was a boy, probably not much older than eighteen, a black-eyed, black-haired youth with olive skin and dirty fingernails.

"Do you go to see the temple?" he asked.

I was surprised he spoke English, even haltingly.

"Our priest, he teach me," the boy said. "We have visitors like you who speak only the English and I bring them to the temple."

"What temple?" I asked.

"Dionysus," he told me. "The god of wine."

Later, I'd read all I could find on Dionysus. Yes, he was the god of wine, but also of the fertility of nature. In his honor, countless orgies had been celebrated in the ancient world. Bacchanalias, they were called, since Dionysus was also known as Bacchus.

"What is your name?" I asked the boy as he pulled on the reins to direct his mule up the crumbling hills of pumice.

"Demetrius," he told me. "Demi."

His eyes were so black. So black that I could see nothing, not even myself, reflected there. His hair was a tangle of ebony curls, his back a taut outline of sharp bone and sinew. He was shirtless and smelled of boy sweat and sweet wine. He turned to me and smiled, a dazzling flash of white against his dark skin.

"Your name? And your name?"

"Florence," I told him. After a moment, I added, "Florence Bridgewood."

"It is an honor, Florence Bridgewood." He smiled.

I felt my face flush. I was suddenly filled with energy. "Demi," I asked, "may I take the reins? May I drive the cart?"

He looked at me quizzically. "But you do not know . . . ?"

"You can direct us, but let me drive the horses. I can do it. Trust me."
I looked at him eagerly.

I don't know what possessed me or why it suddenly mattered so, but I wanted so much to take that wagon up the hill to the temple. Something in my eyes must have convinced Demi, for he slid over on his seat and handed the reins to me.

"Take this road," he said, pointing. "It takes us to the top."

It was dry, dusty, scratchy terrain. We spoke little on the way. After about forty minutes of rattling over pumice, we reached the ruins of the temple. Demi pointed without speaking, and I climbed down from the cart to wander among the ancient marble. He watched me; I could feel his eyes as I stepped over the broken columns, the cracked altars. He seemed intrigued by me, by this woman who drove her own cart.

I sensed his intrigue, but was too overcome by the place to dwell upon it. I sat down on a mosaic of tiny green and blue tiles, sensing the energy, still vibrating, of those who had worshiped here two millennia before.

I sat in silence for a long time, listening to the wind whistle among the old stone. I wasn't even aware at first that I had begun to cry. I made no sound, just shed tears that felt warm on my face. Tears for Ducks. For Harry. For Florence Bridgewood and the dreams she'd once had. Tears for how imprisoned I now felt, how empty.

But there was more to my tears. In retrospect, I can see that. I cried for passion's sake, for the yearning I felt deep down inside. I cried for what I had yet to discover, and feared I never would. I could not have articulated that then, the meaning of my tears, but I can see it now quite plainly. I was twenty-two, twenty-three, twenty-four. I felt terribly old. As if I had seen and done all I was meant to see and do in this life.

The boy's shadow suddenly fell across me. I looked up, and there he was: this young Greek godlet, this black-eyed fisherboy who knew nothing of my world but a few snippets of phrases, who had never been inside a cinema or read *Photoplay* or penned a heartsick letter to Mary Pickford. His lips were full and red, like a woman's, like mine, and I don't honestly know who kissed who first after he stooped down to look into my eyes. But kiss we did, deep and wet and passionate, there in the Temple of Dionysus, the god of wine and fertility and nature, under the sharp blue of the Aegean sky. I felt his strong small hands on my face, my breasts, and I let my own hands explore his body as well—something I'd never considered doing with Harry or any other man. I felt the tautness of his chest, the indentations of his ribs, the hardness of his back, and the roundness of his buttocks.

He made love to me. Rather, we made love together—the first time in my life that was true. It was an awakening, all right. Finally I understood in some place deep within me that this—*this*—was what it was meant to be. This was what it was all about. We made love twice, then three times, as the sun rose higher and higher and then began to set. As darkness began to fall, we made love yet again.

"Demi," I breathed.

It had gotten chilly. He lifted his mouth from my neck, where he was busy planting a thousand tiny kisses. Our eyes found each other in the last of the sunlight.

"You should go back?" he asked.

"No, no, I never want to go back," I told him.

He smiled. He stood, unblushingly naked, his plump little uncircumsized member bouncing as he walked back to his wagon. He returned with a blanket, a canteen of water, and some grapes.

"For you," he said.

He draped the blanket over me, unscrewed the cap on the canteen. "To drink?" he asked.

I accepted his offer. The water tasted cool, sweet, refreshing. He touched my face tenderly as I handed the canteen back to him. He set it down, then tucked the blanket more securely around my bare feet.

I have found passion with other men in my life. I have come to know what sex is, understand its power and its depth. But Demi was the first. Had he not handed me the reins when I asked, I doubt any of what came after would have happened.

"Do you believe in this god?" I asked him, his head next to mine. "Dionysus?"

"I believe in all gods," he told me.

So did I, suddenly. I'd never much thought of God before then. Mother had insisted we were Catholics—appeasing my old Irish grandmother, I imagined—but I never thought much about religion. Yet that night, finding a glint of moonlight reflected off Demi's eyes in the dark, I knew I was seeing the divine.

Am I getting too maudlin? Stop me if I am. But I imagine most women, the first time they are really made love to, tend to go on a bit. You'll have to indulge me. There aren't many such unblemished episodes in my life.

In the morning, we ate the last of the grapes and kissed one last time in the ruins.

"I can't go back," I said to him as he returned the blanket and canteen to the wagon. "I can't go back—to all that."

He didn't understand. He had no idea about my life. About things like cameras and arc lamps and publicity men.

238 / William J. Mann

"It is all too difficult," I told him as best as I could. "Too hard."

He offered me a small smile. He took my hands in his. "Perhaps you go back to get through it," he said. "Perhaps that is why you came here. Perhaps you go through it and you find there is another side."

He smiled innocently. "My English," he said. "Does it make sensible?"

I just smiled. Finally I sighed and let him help me up into the wagon.

I turned for one last look at the Temple of Dionysus. I have never forgotten it. The way the rising sun reflected against the tipped and cracked old marble, the pinkish glow it cast and the purple shadows it brought into relief. The sight of the temple on the top of the hill as we descended, getting smaller and smaller until it was obliterated by the glare of the sun.

When we returned to Fira, Demi helped me down off the wagon and kissed my hand. The tenderness in his eyes was so awful that I couldn't speak. I just took his dark little hand and pressed it to my lips.

Then he rattled off in his wagon into the startlingly yellow day.

I never saw him after that day.

Tenderness is greater proof of love than the most passionate of vows or exquisite of jewels. Demi taught me that. Even in the most fleeting of encounters.

A letter awaited at the pension from Harry, sent from aboard the steamer *Wilhelm* and mailed from the vessel's first stop in Athens.

Florence, my darling,
I swear my love is eternal, and each day until the end I will write you of my love.

"What does he mean, the end?" Mother asked. I had passed over the letter to her once I had finished with it.

"Read on," I told her.

I don't want to cause you any pain, and I will spare you all the harrowing details. Everything will appear accidental. No one need ever know, so fear not that it will interfere with your career.

"He's planning to kill himself," Mother said, supremely indifferent. She was lying beside me on the terrace of our pension. Our chaises were positioned to watch the setting sun. "Do you think he means it?"

"We'll have to keep reading what he sends, I suppose."

The next letter came from Rome:

Dear heart,
The sea is so calm and looks so peaceful. I began work upon the
railing today. I have a bottle of mureatic and nitric acid, which will
gently but surely eat away at the rail. Soon I shall lean upon that
rail. But I promised to spare you all the details, and my words to
you must only be of love.

Love. Poor, deluded Harry. I passed on this latest letter to Mother as
well.

She looked up from behind her dark glasses. "Should you write back
to him?" she asked. "Perhaps have a cable waiting for him when the
ship docks at Gibraltar?"

"I think not," I said after considering it. What would be the point? I
was confident the volcano would have erupted by then. It would all be
moot.

A week later, another missive:

Oh, darling,
All the cruel things I ever spoke were all lies. I would overturn
hell itself if those thoughts were put into my brain by the devil
himself. And those mean, nasty things I said about your mother—
when she is part of you, your own flesh and blood. If it had not
been for her, I would never have met my Florence.

Once again, I handed over this latest installment to Mother. "Well, is
he going to do it or *not?*" she asked, sending the letter fluttering in the
air when she was done.

Finally, this one, from Gibraltar, just as the ship set out for the long
voyage across the Atlantic to New York:

Oh, sweet Florence,
I want to live *and live by your side. This morning I threw away*
the bottle of acid, and when I went upon the deck the sun was
smiling and the world looked so beautiful. Darling Florence, come
to me. We will build a home together on some beautiful lake. We
will have music—we will have flowers—we will have laughter—
and each day we will grow younger and younger. We shall be
young lovers dancing in the sun for all time to come.

* * *

The volcano never exploded, and it wasn't going to, at least not this time.

For several days, as I came to this realization, I didn't speak. I just got up in the morning and walked for miles. I'd sit in the ashy soil that slopes away from the cliffs. I found a grapevine one day, picked a dozen grapes idly and ate them, watching the sun reach midday overhead and then begin its slow descent toward the horizon. When I returned at dusk, I looked once more into the caldera, at the craggy peaks of the burned isles.

I can't go back.

Perhaps you go back to get through it. Perhaps that is why you came here.

Mother was waiting for me on the terrace when I returned to the pension.

"Let's go home," I said quietly to her.

She just nodded.

The innkeeper brought us a letter from Harry. He wrote that he'd broken with Pop Lubin, gone back to Mr. Laemmle, promising him we'd never leave again. He'd secured me my own production company under Mr. Laemmle's new firm, Universal. "The public is clamoring for you, Florence," he wrote. "You mustn't let them forget you."

Perhaps you go through it and you find there is another side.

My English. Does it make sensible?

"Yes, it makes sensible," I answered him from the deck of the ferry, watching as Santorini disappeared from view. From the ferry, we switched to a barge and finally to a great ocean liner at Gibraltar. Mother insisted I have my hair dressed in pearls and arranged for me to pose for photographs with a group of British tourists.

When the ship steamed into New York harbor, a cheering crowd greeted us at the pier, courtesy of Mr. Laemmle.

I expected nothing less.

The Present

"Oh, my Gawd, I am *so* excited today," says Rosie O'Donnell, talking to her musical director, but keeping her eyes on the camera. "Do you know who's *here?*"

"Yes, I *do,*" he tells her.

"Flahrence Lahrence," she says in her thick Long Island accent. "Don't you just *love* that name? Flahrence Lahrence. I could just say it all day. *Flahrence Lahrence.* Just kinda rolls off your tongue, ya know?"

The audience titters.

"It's just *so* amazing, isn't it, John?" The musical director starts to respond, but Rosie talks over him. "She was the very first star of them *all.* Before *anybody.* And she's still *with* us! Everybody thought she was dead, but she wasn't. She had *them* fooled. I admit that I, like most people, hadn't heard of her, but she was *big* in her day, John."

"I know," he replies.

"Big like Madonna kind of big." She mock shivers. "I cannot even *stand* it. *The Biograph Girl* herself is here with us today—her first public appearance in nearly *seventy years!*"

The audience applauds.

"*If* it's her," John interjects quickly.

"Oh, come on, John. *If it's her.* I met her backstage. This is one sharp lady. What she says *goes.*"

The audience cheers.

"Also today," Rosie says, looking out into the crowd, "we have Dennis Rodman, just as bad as he wants to be, and—John, hold on to your seat—the *Spice Girls,* and they'll be wigglin' through a number just for us!" Rosie sings, "*If you wanta be mah lovah. . . .*"

Hoots, hollers from the audience.

"We'll be right back with The Biograph Girl!" Rosie shouts.

The music picks up as the show cuts for a commercial.

* * *

Ben clears his throat nervously. He's sitting in the front row of the audience next to Jameson Collins, the film historian. On Collins's other side is Anita; Xerxes and Sister Jean are behind them.

"This whole thing is just too surreal," Collins whispers to Ben.

Ben knows what he means. The preshow announcement had blared: "Coming up on *Rosie* today—The Spice Girls, Dennis Rodman, and . . . *Florence Lawrence!*"

"The mind boggles," Collins says.

"Flo can hold her own with all of them," Anita pipes in.

Ben watches Collins smile over at her. His small eyes glow behind his thick glasses. "She certainly is fascinating, isn't she?" he gushes.

After meeting with her backstage, the historian had been convinced Flo was telling the truth. Meeting Ben first, he'd admitted to some skepticism, but came away a believer. "There's no way she could know all of what she does," he pronounced to Rosie's producers. "She's the real McCoy." He promised he'd reaffirm that conviction on camera from the audience later in the show.

"What's especially significant," he added to Ben, "is the fact that all of her contemporaries are gone. We've finally gotten to a point where all the silent stars had passed on: Pickford, Swanson, Gish. And now she turns up alive. It's terribly ironic that the first star is turning out to be the *last*, as well."

What a couple of days it had been. Flo had been giddy about the thought of seeing the world from which she'd been absent for so long. She hadn't left St. Mary's since she'd moved there fifteen years ago, and she hadn't been out of Buffalo in nearly two *decades*. Xerxes hired a special van to pick her up to make the trip into the city easier. An electric ramp moved down to allow her to walk on board, and plush, comfortable seats gave her plenty of room inside. Ben and Sister Jean accompanied her, with a chauffeur driving them into New York.

Traffic had snarled on the Palisades Parkway as they approached the George Washington Bridge. "So many motor cars," Flo said in amazement, peering out the tinted windows of the van. "I used to *love* to drive. But it was so easy then. Just hop in your auto and fly down the road, with the wind in your hair."

She said very little as they entered Manhattan, her eyes growing wide as she looked out—and up—at a city she hadn't seen in decades.

"Still the same grimy old place, eh, Flo?" Ben asked her.

"No," she said, seeming a little cowed. "No, not the same at all."

At the Helmsley Park Plaza, she found a royal reception. The hotel clerks and bellhops had all been instructed by Xerxes to treat her like a star. "Welcome, Miss Lawrence," they gushed, holding open doors for her. "Right this way, Miss Lawrence."

In the lobby they passed a tourist couple. The man wore sweatpants and sported a New York Yankees baseball cap on his head. Around his neck dangled a 35-millimeter camera. His wife wore a sweatshirt and very tight blue jeans, despite a very large butt.

"Excuse me," the woman asked in a broad Midwestern accent, "but aren't you The Biograph Girl we've heard about on TV?"

Flo smiled shyly. "Yes, I suppose I am."

The woman's eyes sparkled. "Would you pose with us for a photograph?"

Flo looked up at Ben. "Sure," he said. "I'll take the picture."

The woman nudged her husband, who awkwardly removed the camera from around his neck and handed it over to Ben. The couple then hurried to stand on either side of Flo, putting their faces in next to hers. Ben snapped the shot.

"Where are you from?" Flo asked.

"Indianapolis," the man told her.

"Oh! I played there at the Majestic Theater when I was just a girl," she told them, clearly delighted. But they didn't seem to hear her or care. They just rushed off, chatting frantically to each other.

Flo's room was on the twenty-ninth floor. Her eyes grew wider and wider on the elevator as she watched the light hop like a little flame from floor to floor. She was given a whole suite of rooms, with a separate adjoining bedroom for Sister Jean. She looked out over the city just as the sun was setting, the tall spires of silver and aluminum and red brick bathed in a golden glow. "I never thought I'd see it again," Flo said quietly, staring out the window. "It's changed so much."

"When was the last time you were in New York?" Ben asked.

"Shortly after the war," she said.

Which war she didn't say. For Flo, it could've been just about any war this century.

She slept in luxury. Early the next morning, Ben knocked on her door. "We'll be right out," Sister Jean called to him. "Just as soon as Flo finishes with her bubble bath."

"I thought she could only tolerate sponge baths," Ben said through the door.

Jean opened it just a peek. He caught a glimpse of her in a green silk nightgown, so unlike what he imagined a nun might wear. It was unlaced in the front, revealing just a hint of cleavage. "Funny thing," she said, smiling. "She asked me to help her into the sunken tub, and she's loving it."

When Flo finally emerged, she looked magnificent. Magnificent, but somehow posed—as if she'd been art directed rather than dressed up. And in fact, she had been: Xerxes had arranged for a makeup artist and hairdresser to meet her at the hotel. Her hair was swept up under a pure white wig, woven through with a strand of tiny pearls. Her naturally thick eyelashes were plumped even further, her signature pink lipstick outlined and sharpened. A dress of blue satin was found for her, and around her shoulders, she wore a delicate lace shawl. She looked less the image of a silent film actress and more that of a visiting queen dowager.

"She's what the Queen Mum would look like if she had *style*." Xerxes laughed.

"I've always liked the Queen Mother," Flo said, just a hint of protest in her voice. "I always thought she was lovely. Of course, I remember when she was just a princess."

"Now, Flo," Ben said as they walked off the elevator and into the lobby, "we've gone over everything that we talked about with Rosie and her producers." Flo was seated in a wheelchair and was being pushed by a bellhop. "Do you have any questions?"

"Just one," she said, grinning up at them. "Where are we goin' for lunch?"

They laughed.

"Because I remember a place we used to go to when I was working on East Fourteenth," she said. "They made the most wonderful steamed cheese sandwiches. Oh, but I don't suppose it's still around."

"No," Jean said. "Probably not, Flo."

At the front of the hotel, they were met by a pack of photographers, crowding around the revolving doors. "Dear God," Ben groaned. "We should've known. The paparazzi."

"The what?" Flo asked.

"Here, Flo," Ben said, giving Flo his hand. "Let's have you walk out."

"It'll be easier if she's in the chair," Sister Jean objected.

Ben looked at her sternly. "I want to send the message that she's strong, that she isn't feeble."

"It's all right, Jeannie," Flo said. "I can walk."

Ben and Xerxes helped her to her feet. She was a little shaky at first, but she found her balance. "This way," the bellhop said, holding open the door for her.

"Just smile and wave, Flo," Xerxes said. "The car's waiting right over there."

They stepped outside. Immediately the cameras began popping. Flo stiffened, halted in her stride.

"Hey, Miss Lawrence!" cried one photographer.

"Look! It's The Biograph Girl!"

She stood there frozen in place on the sidewalk, holding on to Sister Jean's arm for support. The cameras kept flashing in her face.

"Come along, Flo," Ben said.

"Flo, are you all right?" Sister Jean asked.

She still just stood there, staring into the mob of photographers.

"Miss Lawrence, over here," came a cry.

She turned. A camera flashed.

"Flo?" Sister Jean asked again.

Flo blinked. A small smile crept back onto her face, and she seemed to emerge from whatever paralysis had momentarily gripped her. "I'm fine, Jeannie," she said, summoning a reserve of strength and resuming her walk. But the photographers kept snapping away, capturing each precarious step until she was safely inside the car.

Jameson Collins leans over to Ben. "If you're doing a film on Florence, you'll want to see *Her First Biscuits,*" he whispers. "Come up to my house in Connecticut. I've got a print. A short little comic masterpiece. Mary Pickford's first film, by the way."

He turns to Anita. "You must come, too, Miss Murawski."

She smiles.

"You have a lovely fiancée, Mr. Sheehan," Collins tells him, turning back to Ben. "Simply lovely."

Ben begins to tell him that they aren't engaged, but decides against it. He wonders briefly why Collins assumes they are, but then discards the thought as he pulls out his notepad from his inside jacket pocket and jots down: *Her First Biscuits.* He doesn't want to forget it.

His mind these days feels pulled in a dozen different directions like taffy. There are the ongoing videotaped interviews with Flo, in which he gets her to reminisce and tell stories. Then there are the negotiations with Xerxes, the discussions about financing, weighing the offers that were beginning to come in. Not to mention the writing of the script—or maybe *two* scripts. Ben's thinking a documentary first, culled from the videotaped interviews, and then maybe a feature biopic, with actors.

That made him think of Anita. Of course, she'd expect a part. But he wasn't making any guarantees—not even to her.

He hears her giggle. Jameson Collins is leaning over, saying something to Anita. They're both grinning like schoolkids. *Dear God,* Ben thinks. *They can't be* flirting.

"Here she is, ladies and gentlemen," Rosie calls out as the cameras begin rolling again. *"The Biograph Girl!"*

Ben's stunned by the thunderous roar of the audience around him. He sees Flo appear in the wings. She's a tiny figure glittering in blue satin, a flicker of light and terror. Sister Jean grabs his shoulder from behind. Rosie makes her way across the stage and escorts Flo out, walking slowly and speaking some words of reassurance into her ear.

The audience goes crazy. Whooping and hollering, standing up and whistling. Flo stops in the middle of the stage and looks out in wonder. She reaches out with her hands, as if imploring them to continue. Rosie backs away, allowing Flo to bask in the applause.

"Who'd have ever *thought?*" Jameson Collins says as they all get to their feet.

"So, Flo—I can call you Flo, can't I?"

"You can call me anything you like except late for dinner."

Rosie looks a little taken aback by Flo's wit. "Well, that's a good one, Flo. I'll have to remember it."

The audience chuckles.

Rosie grins. "So what a welcome, huh? How does it feel to be found?"

"I wasn't aware I was lost," Flo says. She lets the audience—and Rosie—laugh before continuing. "But seriously, I'm delighted to be here. I'm delighted to be *anywhere* at my age!"

Ben can feel the buzz going through the crowd. *This old lady is a revelation,* people are thinking. A revelation and an inspiration. So old, and yet so . . . *alive.*

It's clear Rosie, too, is both surprised and delighted by the old dame. "Well, I must admit, Flo," she says, "I *love* old movies. When we went to Arlene Dahl's house, I was like, 'Oh, my Gawd, that's *Arlene Dahl'* all day long. But you know, you were around a while before Arlene Dahl even."

"Who's Arlene Dahl?" Flo asks innocently.

The audience erupts in laughter. Rosie reaches over and touches Flo's shoulder. "Spoken like the first true star of them all," she pronounces, and the audience roars in appreciation.

Flo puts her hand over her heart and bats her eyes like a young girl. *She's loving this,* Ben observes.

Rosie eyes Flo admiringly. "You played a very important role in the history of moving pictures, Miss Flahrence Lahrence."

"Ah," Flo says, fluffing off the praise. "I've always said movies aren't so important in the scheme of things. *Plumbing*—now that's important. I've known plumbers who were far more important than I was."

More appreciative sounds from the audience.

"I get your drift, Flo. I hear ya." Rosie smiles. "But you were a big star nonetheless. You *started* all this." Rosie gestures with her hands around at the studio, the crowd, the cameras now rolling in for a close-up of Flo. "And you're going to be a hundred and seven in a couple of months!"

The audience applauds madly.

Flo just shrugs as the applause dies down, although she's clearly loving it. "Ah, anyone can get old. All you have to do is live long enough."

Rosie cracks up, shrugging her shoulders at the camera. "*What?* Do you have a joke writer back there?" She laughs, pointing with her thumb over her shoulder backstage. "If so, I want him!"

Flo smiles. "No, no, it's just me."

Rosie contains herself. "Okay, Flo. So tell me. Did you enjoy it? Hollywood, I mean, in the early days."

She shrugs. "Hollywood. You have to remember I did most of my work here in New York. When I went out to Hollywood it seemed everyone was a little bit crazy. I remember Fred Allen saying Hollywood was a place where people from Ohio mistook each other for stars."

More hoots, cheers from the crowd.

Flo's continuing, "It was a strange place, Hollywood. Especially for a woman of my years. In Hollywood, a woman having a mind was all right—so long as she hid it with a low-cut dress."

Rosie shakes her head. "Ain't it the truth, Flo. Ain't it the truth."

"Well," Flo says, seeming to reconsider, "in some ways, women had an unfair advantage in Hollywood. If we couldn't get what we wanted by being smart, we'd get it by being dumb."

"I can see *you* never let the male species sway you," Rosie tells her.

"Well, I had my moments," Flo confesses with a grin.

"I'll *bet* you did, Miss Flo," Rosie goads her.

The audience titters.

"But my best affairs were always matters of the mind and soul as much as anything else." She leans over Rosie's desk as if to tell her a secret. "A love affair with a stupid man," she says, mocking conspiratorially, "is like drinking a cold cup of coffee."

Rosie cracks up again. This isn't just the standard polite-host chuckle. It's an honest-to-God belly laugh.

Ben can't get over it. The rapport between Flo and Rosie. Flo's ease in front of the cameras. How readily the audience is eating her up.

"A star is *re*born," he whispers over to Collins.

Then he spots Sister Jean's face, unbroken by any smile, looming over his shoulder. He settles back into his seat.

On the stage, Rosie's saying, "Now, Flo, I can't say I grew up with your pictures like I grew up with Doris Day or anything like that, but my producer got a whole bunch of 'em here for me to see before the show—and you were *good*. You were ta-rific!"

"Thank you," Flo says.

"And guess what we got here?" Rosie asks with a wink. The audience giggles. Flo looks wide-eyed. "A clip from *Resurrection.*"

"Oh," Flo says, clapping her hands in that way of hers. "With Arthur Johnson!"

"Just watch," Rosie says, and the lights dim. On the monitors, a jerky black-and-white image pops up. Flo, in a long, old-fashioned dress, hair piled up on her head, discovers Johnson in the arms of another woman. She twirls around, nearly fainting. The audience, already tittering, dissolves into uproarious laughter.

"It's a drama, damn it," Jameson Collins grumbles under his breath to Ben. "A *drama.*"

The lights come back up. The audience applauds. But Flo's leaning over to Rosie. "Why did they laugh?" she's asking, unaware her microphone has picked up her question.

"Because you were so *wonderful!*" Rosie tells her, and the audience cheers again. This seems to satisfy Flo, who smiles and nods.

It's the first moment that Flo hasn't seemed in total control of the situation. Ben can feel little beads of sweat suddenly pop out on his forehead. He peeks around at Sister Jean, who sits unblinking as she stares at the stage.

"Now, let's see," Rosie's saying, "you worked with D.W. Griffith and Mary Pickford."

"And so many others," Flo tells her. "There was John Compson and King Baggott and Matt Moore."

Rosie shakes her head. "It's amazing, your memory."

"Oh, that's all right," Flo says with a smile. "Sometimes I can't remember what I had for breakfast."

"Who can? Now, Flo, I have to ask you. Some people are still doubtful that you are who you say you are. Now, I believe you, and we have an expert here who believes you, but everybody's wonderin' how—and why—you pulled it off. 'Cause let me tell you, that was *sure* some trick you pulled—you know that?"

The audience cheers. Flo smiles.

Ben licks his lips.

"Well, the hospital just made a mistake, and when I heard—" Flo shrugs. "You know, I just wanted to find a place where there wasn't any trouble, a place far away."

Rosie squints at her. "You're not goin' to break into 'Somewhere Over the Rainbow,' are you, Flo?"

Laughter from the audience.

"What I don't understand," Flo says, and Ben once again marvels at her dexterity in getting around topics she doesn't want to discuss, "is why no one ever asks what my life was like *after* that point. That's when I got back to being *me*. I made a lot of friends and had some good times. It was *sixty years*, you know—longer than what came before."

"You know, I think you may be on to something, Miss Flahrence Lahrence," Rosie tells her. "You are one very wise lady, I think. All this fame stuff—it's not what it's cracked up to be, huh? It's not the *real* part. Am I right?"

Flo just smiles.

"You are one fascinating lady," Rosie says. "And this isn't the first time you came back from the dead, huh?"

Ben keeps his eyes on Flo. They've practiced this part. "As a matter of fact, no," Flo explains. "Once before, the papers said I'd been killed in a streetcar accident. That was in St. Louis, back in 1910."

"1910!" Rosie gushes. "And she's sitting next to me today! Can you *stand* it? Now that episode was a publicity stunt, eh, Flo? In fact, the *very first* studio public relations ploy—the grandmommy of a long, long tradition of publicity tricks in Hollywood."

Flo just sits there with an enigmatic grin.

"Okay, Mona Lisa," Rosie says as the audience laughs and applauds. "Still keepin' those trade secrets, I see! You're not gonna admit to it even after all these years. Fine, fine. Have it your way."

The audience hoots.

"Tell me, Flo," Rosie says. "What's the most different thing about show business today? How has it changed?"

Flo looks off toward the cameras. "I don't think it really *has* much changed," she says simply. "Of course, I don't know because I've just arrived back in New York last night, and I haven't been back to Hollywood since I left in 1938. But from what I see—not much. Not much has changed." She smiles. "There's just a lot *more* of it."

"Like television and videos and all that?"

"Yes," Flo says. "That's the only thing that's different."

"Because, let's see, you left pictures in . . . what year?" Rosie looks down at her notes. "Wow. 1915. There was a fire, right, Flo?"

Ben sits forward in his seat. He hadn't given Rosie that information. It must have been Collins. He watches to see how Flo will answer.

"Oh, yes, there was a fire," Flo tells her without any apparent unease. "It was just *terrible*. We were filming a Western picture, and my costar was Matt Moore. Matt was almost *two hundred pounds,* a big, strapping man, a big, big cowboy star—and he was supposed to be saving me from a burning building. Well, the fire simply got *out of control,* Matt *passed out* from the smoke, and I had to *carry him down* the stairs to safety."

"Wooow," Rosie gushes. "And you so little. How did you ever manage?"

"It was either that or let him die," Flo says.

She sounds exactly the same as she had when she'd recounted that story for Ben on video. There's a quality to it that Ben thinks sounds *phony* somehow—a little too self-serving, too polished. It was so out of keeping with the spontaneous, unself-conscious banter with which she'd engaged Rosie earlier on. It was as if this particular story had been repeated many times, told to countless scribes down over the years. Her other stories are warm, rambling. This one is just too—too *precise.*

"And you suffered some burns and injuries in the course of it," Rosie's saying.

Flo nods. "That's what forced me off the screen. I had to recover. There was no way anyone could have forced me back in front of the camera after that."

Ben feels Sister Jean's fingers lightly touch the back of his neck. *So she's not comfortable with the story either,* he thinks.

"Well," Rosie says, grinning. "Guess what, Flo? Here you are, back in front of the cameras again!"

The audience applauds wildly. Flo gazes out at them with effusive astonishment, as if each time they applaud she needs to be reconvinced that it's real.

Rosie stands suddenly. "All right, now, Flo. Are you ready for what we practiced?"

She laughs. "I suppose so."

"What is this?" Jameson Collins whispers to Ben. "What are they doing?"

"Just watch," Ben tells him.

Rosie's telling the audience, "Flo was once known as Baby Flo, the Child Wonder Whistler. She's also a big fan of the Spice Girls. So, in honor of the fact that they're both on my show today, Flo and I will do our rendition of 'Wannabe'—you know: 'Tell me what you want, what you really really want' and all that."

Collins mutters in disbelief, "This has now left the realm of possibility."

Rosie helps Flo stand and they take a few steps toward the center of the stage. "Ready, Flo?" she asks.

"Ready," the old woman tells her.

And they're off. Flo pulls her old lips together and begins whistling the tune to the Spice Girls' Top 40 hit. Rosie whistles along with her, but Flo's just as loud, just as forceful and vibrant as the much younger woman. Their microphones pick up the sound clearly, sending it all through the studio. The audience goes crazy. By the end of the tune, the whistling is drowned out by a raucous standing ovation.

"You are one amazing lady, Flahrence Lahrence," Rosie shouts over the thundering applause. "I want to thank you very, very much for the honor of your being here today. You are my inspiration! If I'm half as good as you are when I'm *fifty*, I'll be happy!"

The audience stamps its feet, cheering for Flo.

"Okay," Rosie's calling, "stick around. We'll be back with Dennis Rodman, bein' bad, and the Spice Girls, bein' . . . well, spicy!"

She hands Flo one of her trademark koosh toys and Flo slingshots it into the audience.

The music comes up. Fade to a commercial.

"Hey," Jameson Collins says, a mite ruffled, "she never called on me."

The audience stays on its feet cheering as Flo is helped off the stage. Ben turns around to Sister Jean.

"That wasn't so bad, huh?" he says to her. "They really loved her!"

"One more condition," she says softly to him. "No more questions about the fire."

But Ben doesn't make any more promises.

He knows that, sooner or later, he may have to start breaking them.

"That's it. Easy now," says the foreman.

Richard watches as the coffin is gingerly lifted from the earth. It's in pretty bad shape, a grayish-blue oblong rotted through at one end. From the sides of the hole, tree roots dangle like lifeless limbs. A smell like old fruit rises from the moist soil.

"Easy, easy," the foreman commands again. "We don't want nothin' breakin' apart here." Five men ease the muddy, stinking thing into the waiting van. They'll carry it off through the streets of Los Angeles to their lab, to discover . . . what?

Richard's watched the whole process without speaking. Rex is with him. A couple of times Rex has had to go off by himself, wandering through the pretty, daisy-dotted, tree-shaded cemetery. "Richard," he's cajoled. "It's just too creepy to stand here and watch." But Richard hasn't moved from his spot.

The gravesite is covered by a large olive-colored tent, the cemetery having closed its gates for the morning. The gravediggers have done their work quickly and efficiently. A line of curious spectators has gathered out on the street, their faces pressed through the rungs of the iron fence. They'll be let in now, to gawk at the wound left in the earth where a body buried as Florence Lawrence once lay.

Rex crosses his arms across his chest and shivers. "This is just totally freaky," he says.

They'd arrived in L.A. the day before. Flying into LAX, they'd both noticed the heavy blanket of smog that had settled over the sprawling city. They picked up their rental car and headed up La Cienega Boulevard. "You know," Rex quipped, "they used to say God felt sorry for actors, so he created Hollywood to give them a place in the sun and a swimming pool." He looks out the window into the gray air. "Well, at least they've still got their pools."

They had reservations to stay in the cleaner air of West Hollywood, at the lush and leafy San Vicente Inn. But first they decided to take a detour through Hollywood proper, down Hollywood Boulevard past Mann's Chinese Theater. Rex shuddered at the kitsch, the fast food joints, and the drug addicts loitering along the Walk of Fame.

"Mary Pickford once observed," he said, "on one of her last drives along this strip, 'What a tawdry monument we've left behind.'" He looked over at Richard behind the wheel. "I wonder what it was like before all this—back in the days when the orange groves were still a part of the scene, when Gloria Swanson and Mabel Normand and the Keystone bathing beauties rode the trolley down to the beach."

"We can only imagine," Richard said.

They drove up to Sunset. "You know," Rex said, continuing his sad tour, "the Norma Desmond house wasn't really on this street. It was on the corner of Wilshire and Irving. Belonged to J. Paul Getty."

"Really?" Richard asked. He loved *Sunset Boulevard,* both film and play. "Let's go see the house."

"Can't," Rex said. "Torn down to make way for an office building."

Richard sighed. "Isn't there *anything* left to see?"

"There." Rex pointed to a nondescript storefront, just down from the giant Tower Records. "The Viper Room. River Phoenix died right there on the sidewalk."

Tawdry monument, indeed, Richard thought.

Richard has sensed his lover's melancholia ever since they arrived. "Can we leave yet?" Rex asks now, still clearly disturbed by the exhumation. The workers are still securing the coffin in the van. "I want to get out to Highways to go over logistics for the show."

"Just wait until they're gone, okay, Nooker?"

He keeps his eye on the van, now being locked shut. He feels some kind of strange responsibility for the corpse—whoever it is. Or was. *Just a girl.*

"Look," Rex says, pulling Richard's sleeve to distract him from the van's progress out of the cemetery. "Over there's Marion Davies's crypt. You want to go see? Next to it is Tyrone Power's really foofy grave. He was a closeted queen, you know."

Richard nods, but he keeps his eyes on the van as it drives through the gate and turns right onto Santa Monica Boulevard.

The cemetery is a quiet, tranquil place. Not as large as the more famous Forest Lawn, but most of Hollywood's pioneers are here. Davies. The Talmadge sisters. Cecil B. DeMille. Douglas Fairbanks, in the middle of a lotus-dotted lake. Rudolph Valentino, in a locked crypt to keep out his more fanatic followers. And Florence Lawrence, off to the side, near the far wall.

"Mr. Sheehan?"

They look up. A man has approached them, Chinese, about sixty, a little plump. He smiles at them.

"I'm Detective Philip Lee," he says, extending his hand.

"Richard Sheehan," Richard says, shaking with him. "This is Rex Rousseau."

Detective Lee grasps Rex's hand. "Come for the show, huh?"

Rex shudders. "It's not something I'll soon forget."

Lee smiles. "When you've seen as many exhumations as I have, they all look alike. Except, of course, when the coffin breaks in two and they bring the guy up a piece at a time."

"Oh, *dear,*" Rex says, and he sits down on the grass.

Lee turns his gaze back to Richard. "They told me you were the writer of the original article. That you actually talked with this old lady who's all over the news. Did you see her on *Rosie?*"

"Yes," Richard tells him. "She's pretty amazing, isn't she?"

Her appearance had caused a sensation. She had been funny, sharp, and wise—even if she hadn't looked anything like herself. *Where was the caftan?* Richard thought. *Where were the cigarettes?* But America had fallen in love with The Biograph Girl all over again.

Detective Lee scratches the top of his head. "Well, you know, my mother's ninety-nine herself," he tells Richard. "She still walks to the market every day. Does all her own cooking."

"Guess the average life expectancy is going up right before our eyes, huh?"

Lee shrugs. "Me, I'll probably drop dead tomorrow. Too many hamburgers and ice cream floats. Tell me, do you think she's a murderer?"

Richard blinks. "You mean, Flo?"

"Sure didn't mean my mother," the detective says, laughing.

"No, sir," Richard says. "I do not."

"But you've been talking with these *L.A. Times* reporters. You've spoken with my department at the L.A.P.D."

Richard nods. "That doesn't mean I think she's guilty of murder." He narrows his eyes at the detective. "But I guess you must have enough suspicions yourself that the department pressed to have the grave opened."

Lee sighs. "We know *somebody* was buried there. It's not like they found just soil and earthworms this morning." He stretches. "Me, I want to be cremated. Can't stand the thought of maggots eating through my cheekbones."

Rex makes a little sound from the grass behind them.

"Anyway," Lee continues. "So the question is, whose body is it? We need to try and make some sort of identification. I don't know if the old lady had anything to do with it or not. But *some* kind of hoax was pulled over on the coroner's office, if what this old dame says is true." He smiles. "And there's no statute of limitations on murder."

"You have no reason to think a murder was committed," Richard says.

Lee's smile fades. "We have reason to think a woman died who's not been identified—who was, in fact, actually *misidentified* as somebody else. And that somebody else admits it was just what she wanted, because she wanted the hell out of town."

"So what are you hoping from the exhumation?" Richard asks.

"The same thing you are. Hoping it'll prove whether or not the old lady is who she says she is."

Richard laughs. "But we have no DNA sample of Florence Lawrence to compare the remains to," Richard says. "I've tried to hunt down a blood relative. I can't find any. She had a brother, but he doesn't appear to have had any children. If there *were* some relatives, you'd think they would have come forward by now, given all the publicity."

"Well," Lee says, "at the very least we'll learn if the body in that casket was a woman, if it was white, and if it was about fifty years old at time of death. And if it doesn't fit all those things—"

"Then it's not Florence Lawrence," Richard finishes.

"Bingo." Lee closes his eyes and lifts his face toward the midmorning sun. "Gonna be a scorcher, I think. Can feel it in the air already." He looks back at Richard. "I've gone over what our records have on missing persons reported for 1938 and 1939. Granted, it's pretty sketchy, but there are a number of girls their families never saw again. None for that particular month, December, but a bunch in the spring. Could have been it took that long for the families to notice. Hollywood was in its heyday then, you know."

Richard feels the tingle at the top of his head, the pulse of a story heating up. "Maybe I can get that list from you?" he asks. "Maybe I can help you in your investigation."

"Here's my card." Lee hands Richard a small rectangle with his name, division, and phone extension. "Give me a call. In the meantime," he adds, looking around at Rex on the grass, "enjoy the rest of your stay. No graverobbing, you hear?"

He moves off. They watch him without saying anything. The tent is now being taken down, the yawning hole in the earth covered with tarp.

"Richard," Rex says softly, "I don't feel so good."

Richard looks down at his lover. He's pale and his lips are a little blue. "What's wrong, Nooker?" he asks, sitting down next to him on the grass.

"Maybe just jet lag. I need to rest." Rex smiles. "It'll pass."

Richard stares at him. He doesn't like it when Rex feels sick. It happens far less frequently than in the old days, but Richard still gets freaked out every time it happens. He can't help but always fear it's something worse than what Rex says it is—worse than jet lag or a cold or too much hot sauce on his tofu pup.

Richard runs his fingers down the side of his lover's face. Rex closes his eyes and turns up to the sun. Richard watches him carefully. He looks strong. Healthy. There's color in his cheeks. He looks fit.

Doesn't he?

Rex opens his eyes. "Hey," he says quietly. "Over there. Do you see who that is?"

Richard looks. He *does* see who it is. Roddy McDowall himself. He's dressed in a natty tweed sport coat and bow tie, a floppy hat on his head.

"Well, that cinches it," Richard says. "He's got to be the one who placed the marker on Florence Lawrence's grave."

"Go over and talk with him, Richard," Rex urges.

"Don't you want to come? You *love* him."

"No," Rex defers. "You go. I'll just wait here."

Richard touches his face again. "You really *don't* feel well, Nooker, if you'd pass up a chance to meet *him*."

"I'm fine," Rex insists. "Just tired. Go *over* there, Richard. Before he leaves."

"You sure?"

"*Go.*" Rex smiles. "And get his autograph."

Richard hesitates for a second more, then stands, brushing off his khakis. He heads off across the lawn.

The actor looks up, sees him approach. He extends his hand.

"Ah, the reporter," he says in his British—or was it Welsh?—accent.

"Yes, sir," Richard tells him, shaking his hand soundly. "It's an honor to meet you."

"Well, I had to come see what they've done to poor Flo," Roddy says with a smile.

"Did you know her?"

The actor gives him a little smirk. "Oh, come now, my young friend. I'm not *that* old."

Richard blushes. "I'm sorry. I didn't mean—"

"Of course you didn't," the actor says. There's a sparkle in his eyes that does indeed belie his years, making him seem ageless. "You see, I'm just an old movie buff myself. Tell me, do you think that's really *her* up in Buffalo?"

"I *do* think so, yes," Richard says.

"Hmm," the actor says. "Fascinating." He strokes his chin as if considering something. "But not anymore, even if so. Do you understand my drift?"

"I'm not sure I do," Richard admits.

The actor sighs. His face is elfin, a sharp little nose with round, clever eyes. "Let me tell you a story," he says. "I went to see Mary Pickford once. Oh, maybe ten years before she died. She was famously reclusive, you know. *No one* got in to see her. But I'd run in to her husband, Buddy Rogers, and told him I'd just *love* to tell Mary how marvelous I'd always thought she was. So one day, out of the blue, I got an invitation to come up to Pickfair. Well, it was like getting an audience with the Queen in Buckingham Palace. I dressed up as spiffily as I could, and I arrived with a whole *spray* of cala lilies and orchids for her. The maid greeted me at the door, took the flowers, and asked me to sit at a little table in the foyer. So I did. I sat there and waited and waited. A half hour went by. Forty-five minutes. Nothing. Finally the telephone on the table in front of me rang. Very shrill. Startled me out of my wits. The maid came in and told me to answer it. I thought, 'How very strange.' But I did anyway."

He pauses. "And it was *Mary.*"

"Where *was* she?"

"She was *upstairs!*" Roddy laughs. "She thanked me for the flowers, told me how kind it was for me to come visit her, and told me she would remember me in her prayers. Then she said good-bye and hung up!"

"That was it?"

"That was it! That was my visit with Little Mary at eighty." He smiles at Richard. "Do you understand my drift now?"

"I think so," he said. "But Flo isn't like that. She's very accessible. She's very down-to-earth. She doesn't care about the image."

"You know, it's never a good idea to take soft lights off tinsel. Ever see a Christmas tree during the day? How sad it seems? How lifeless?" Roddy sighs dramatically. "Even the *Sphinx* loses its mystery in the noonday sun."

"But Flo is more intriguing now than she was back then," Richard tells him.

"Maybe so. But if dear old Flo is still alive," the actor tells him sagely, "she can hardly be The Biograph Girl anymore, can she?"

Richard nods. "That's what she said," he says. "That once, a long time ago, she used to be Florence Lawrence."

Roddy grins. "Precisely. Because Florence Lawrence is . . . *here.*" He gestures around him.

"You put the marker on her grave, didn't you?" Richard asks.

The actor chuckles, his hand held faintly over his heart. "You must understand, through *all* of this," he says. "We live in a world of make-believe and illusion, but to Hollywood—to *old* Hollywood, that is, and to those of us who keep the candle lit in its memory—make-believe is the *truth*. For us, the truth is often quite different from what it is in the rest of the world. Our creatures live by different rules of logic and physics. They are ethereal, made of wisps of light and smoke and memory."

"But Flo's hardly ethereal," Richard tells him.

"Of course she's not," he says. "But Florence Lawrence was—*is*."

He laughs. "Oh. You must think me mad. And perhaps I am, a little. We all are. *Have* to be, you know. But look around you. Can't you feel it? There's *enchantment* in places like this. In Rudy's tomb. Out on the lake with Doug Fairbanks. Here one learns very quickly that ghosts are as real as you or me."

They take a few steps toward the lake where the great swashbuckler slumbers peacefully in his crypt. A blue heron descends gracefully, its long legs unfolding and taking root in the still water.

"There aren't many places like this left out here anymore." Roddy sighs, lifting his eyebrows, looking over at Richard. "Hollywood the *civic* has been dreadful in enshrining Hollywood the mythic. That's why I put the marker on poor Flo's grave. Now they've gone and dug it up. And to prove . . . ?"

His voice drops into a whisper. "*That's* the danger, you see. Proving too much destroys our truth." He smiles kindly over at Richard. "Just remember that as you go through all of this."

Suddenly a flock of birds takes off from the trees overhead, startling Richard, their wings flapping furiously through the air in the glorious sunlight. Richard's eyes can't help but be drawn to them, and he watches until they're gone, vanished into the blue of the sky.

When he turns back, he discovers Roddy is gone, too. Although Richard looks around several times and scans the horizon for as far as he can see, the actor is nowhere to be found—vanished, as if by the magic he preached, into the illusion of the day.

May 1921

The train hissed a sudden breath of steam and came to a jarring halt at the platform.

"Hold on, hold on," the porter grumbled, pushing past me.

I thought of that porter in St. Louis, all those years ago, on a very different train ride. His eager, shiny face had lit up as he held the door for me. "It's been a great honor, ma'am," he'd said.

This one merely unhitched the door and swung it open, never glancing up at me.

I stepped out onto the top step leading down to the platform. It was my first time in Hollywood. I looked out across the crowd into the bluest skies I'd ever seen—even bluer than the treasured skies of old San Francisco. In the air I could smell the perfume-sweet fragrance of orchids and oranges. *Hollywood.* Even the name was pretty.

On the platform below, wives and children and sweethearts were greeting passengers departing the train. I scanned their faces eagerly.

"Come on along, ma'am," the porter said sharply behind me. "Step lively down the stairs."

"I'm looking for my entourage," I told him.

He clearly didn't know who I was. I'd been away from pictures five years—but five years in the early days was much longer than it is today. Mr. Kerns had promised to meet me at the station with a band. He'd even asked Mary Pickford, Lionel Barrymore, and Lillian Gish to accompany him—three of the stars of the old Biograph to welcome The Biograph Girl back to the screen. "It'll be great press," he told me. "The fan magazines will eat it up like peanut butter!"

But I looked down into the jumble of people and saw no one I knew. Surely they were here *somewhere*. I narrowed my eyes into the throng, now rapidly diminishing.

Yet if Mary Pickford was here—why, there would be a good *deal* of commotion. And where was the band? Why hadn't Mr. Kerns given the command to strike up a tune? Hadn't he *seen* me standing up here?

"*Please,* lady," the porter growled. "Go down the stairs."

I gave him a foul look and made my way down. At the bottom I looked around hopefully, but saw no one. I walked alongside the still smoking train, the taste of soot bitter on my tongue. I clutched my suitcase in my right hand. Around me lovers were reuniting; fathers were embracing their excited little children. I stopped at one scene: a little girl being hoisted in the air by a proud, ebullient papa. "Annie!" the father crowed, kissing her plump little cheeks. "My little Annie!"

Annie.

Annie Laurie.

I forced myself to look away. Why did I *do* such things to myself? *Because the girl—she's the same age—*

As—

Stop it, Florence. Why waste time gazing at them when Mr. Kerns was surely in this crowd looking for me? I was *back*—I had returned—I had become Florence Lawrence again and now I had to live with that.

I pushed onward. A woman ahead of me glanced up and saw me approach. I'm sure she recognized me. I saw the familiar flicker in her eyes, the wonder on her face.

But then she looked away.

So I found a bench off by myself and waited, my suitcase at my feet. Very well then. Let Mr. Kerns find *me.*

I waited on that platform for nearly thirty minutes until all of the people had departed and I was alone.

Panic only gradually began to settle in. *What do I do now? What did this mean?*

Oh, take hold of yourself, Flo. You know *what to do. Pull yourself together. Don't let it overtake you this time. You've spent five years recuperating. You're stronger now. You take a cab to your hotel and call Mr. Kerns from there. There's obviously been a miscommunication. Perhaps he expects you tomorrow.*

I laughed to myself. *Perhaps we can restage it—get Pickford down here and I'll pretend to step off the train, cameras flashing.*

"Florence?"

I looked up. A woman.

"*Florence Lawrence?*"

"Adela," I said, the gratitude and relief clear in my voice.

"My dear, *look* at you," she said, taking my hands. "Still as lovely as ever."

Adela Rogers St. Johns was the Mother Confessor of Hollywood. I'd known her before, when she was one of Hearst's reporters. Now she was head writer for *Photoplay*. I'd sent her a letter before I departed, telling her of my return to the movies. I suggested she come down to Union Station to see the welcome Mr. Kerns had planned for me.

"There must have been a mix-up," I told her, trying to laugh. "Mr. Kerns will be *so* amused by it."

Her brow creased sympathetically. She was a tall, aristocratic lady—thin, arch, beautiful in her day. She wore upswept auburn hair and a choker of pearls around a long, long neck. Today she boasted bright red lipstick and one of those newly popular short skirts, riding up above her knees. Her legs were quite shapely, encased in the sheerest black silk.

"Of *course* there was a mix-up, darling," she said, looking down at my one suitcase. "Here, let me take that for you. I suppose you'll be needing a ride to your hotel then?"

"We'll come back and stage it tomorrow, Adela," I said. "You'll come back, won't you? Well, of *course*, you will. Pickford will be here."

"Mary's in New York meeting the Prince of Wales," Adela told me plainly, lifting my suitcase. "Come on, Flo. My car's in the lot. You staying at the Hollywood Hotel?"

I gave her a little smile. "No. The—the Rose."

She looked at me queerly. "The *Rose*? I'm afraid I don't know—"

I handed her a piece of paper with the address Mr. Kerns had sent to me. She glanced down at it and sighed. "All right, Flo," she said quietly. "Let's go." She smiled over at me. "Welcome to Hollywood."

"Well," I said, once we were safely in her car and I began to peel off my gloves, making light, "it certainly wasn't the welcome I got at the pier when I returned home from Europe. Do you remember that, Adela?"

"Oh, I do, Flo," she said.

"Or St. Louis," I said, shivering. "That's when we met, wasn't it, Adela? In St. Louis?"

"It was," she said. "That was the trip that started everything."

I smiled. Yes, it did. *Start everything.* All of this. Hollywood was once a sleepy little farming community, with orange groves stretching as far as the eye could see, tumbleweeds somersaulting down dusty dirt roads. But *now*—I looked out around me from Adela's Cadillac Torpedo convertible. The chauffeur was up front, and we sat on plush leather seats, the wind catching my hair despite my wide-brimmed hat. We drove down the most enchanting streets. Adela had decided to give me a little tour. Los Angeles was a revelation. Instead of the narrow lanes crowded by brownstone tenements that I knew from New York, I looked out onto wide avenues edged with tall, swaying palm trees and pastel-colored Spanish haciendas.

On Hollywood Boulevard, I thought I spotted Gloria Swanson whiz by in her famous leopard-print car. I didn't dare betray my excitement to Adela. For hadn't I been a star longer than Swanson?

But that was a ruse difficult to perpetrate when we pulled up in front of the Rose. It was a small, shabby inn on a side street close to downtown Los Angeles. A great brown water stain marred the white stucco of the front. A potted palm on the sidewalk drooped lifelessly. We said nothing, just stepped out of the car.

"I'm awfully tired, Adela," I told her. "There's no need to see me up. I'll be fine. Thanks ever so much for the ride."

"Are you sure, Florence? Do you need anything?"

"No, no bother, dear. But do come by tomorrow, will you? Perhaps we can all go down to the station—if Pickford's not here, why then I'll just *insist* that Barrymore and Gish turn out. Oh, won't it be such a *hoot?*"

She just looked at me. Then she embraced me roundly and said nothing else before turning and heading off in her car.

I *had* to come west to Hollywood. The movies had moved there while I was away. There was nothing left in New York anymore. "If you want to get back on top, Florence," Mr. Kerns had insisted, "you *have* to come out to Hollywood."

Mother, of course, had been adamantly against the move. "*Vaudeville* is what's exciting now, Florence," she begged. "Vaudeville! We can return to the stage—*together* — a mother-and-daughter act! What do you say?"

"Don't be absurd," I snapped at her. "I'm going to Hollywood. Mr. Kerns has promised me a picture."

"At a studio tied together by a *shoestring!*" Mother's hard, careworn face tightened into a network of a hundred creases. "Florence, you have *no idea* what you're blundering into."

I spun on her. "You talk to me as if I were still ten years old and didn't know anything about the business I happen to be in." I stared at her until she blinked, backing down, a defeated old woman. "I am tired of having everyone butt into my affairs."

But the truth was, there was no one left to do any butting except Mother. Not since Harry—and thinking of Harry always made me sad.

So I left the next morning on a westbound train. It took three days.

Somewhere near Iowa I caught cold, and the alkali dust irritated my lungs. I lay in my berth, rarely venturing out to the rest of the train. All my meals were brought in. I convinced myself it might cause a ruckus if word got out that Florence Lawrence was on the train, that she had emerged from retirement. I was doing the porters a favor by lying low, I told myself.

I had forgotten much of what she was like, Florence Lawrence. For five years, I'd gone back to being just Flo Bridgewood, tending my roses at my house in New Jersey, taking long walks in fields of goldenrod and Queen Anne's lace. I'd even started riding again, taking my horse across the acres of clover and crabgrass, feeling the old intoxicating rush of wind in my nostrils. But Florence Lawrence had been needed: Bills weren't getting paid. All that money we had made—gone. Someone once told me that movie money isn't hard cash. It's just so much congealed *snow;* it melts in your hand. Then, of course, the Great War came, and everything became more expensive.

Still, there was more to it than that. If truth be told, I was missing her a bit, Florence Lawrence. Missing the glare of the arc lamps, the clamor of the crowds.

Queer, isn't it? That I should so despise it when I'm there and miss it when I'm gone? But much was happening in pictures. It was all so much bigger now, more exciting, more glamorous. Hollywood was being colonized. And there were so many new stars. When I came back from Europe, I'd still been in the Top Ten, but dead last. Among actresses, nine new faces—nine new names—preceded mine, women no one had heard of just a year or two before. Mabel Normand. Margarita Fischer. Kathlyn Williams. Vivian Rich. Mary Fuller. Florence La Badie. Marguerite Snow. Beverly Bayne. And, of course, always on top, Mary Pickford.

Now only a select few of them remained. Pickford still, of course, and Normand. But the others? Who remembered Margarita Fischer in 1921—let alone today? Mother had tried to dissuade me from giving movies another shot, but I was determined to prove her wrong. Sure, there were dozens of new faces crowding the fan magazines now, but if Pickford could still be on top, then there was no reason I couldn't come back.

The picture Mr. Kerns had found for me was called *The Unfoldment.* I played a reporter, of all things, who wins the heart of a gruff city editor. Mother was right on one count: It was indeed made at a studio held together by a shoestring. My director was barely known, and Mr. Kerns wasn't exactly a mover or shaker in the new industry. But it was the only thing offered to me in those five years, and I was determined it would be

264 / William J. Mann

a success. Sure, Barbara Bedford may have played the ingenue, winning the handsome young man in the final reel—but I was the *star.* That was important. It was *my* name up there above the title, where it belonged.

That first night in Hollywood, I sat in my hotel room and watched the sun set. It looked as if the sharp blue sky had been cut, rent by a gigantic blade, the firmament bleeding in vibrant pink and red. I bought a crate of oranges from a vendor out on the street, and they served as my first meal. Their fragrance filled my room and made me think of happier days.

Mr. Kerns was not in his office when I called. I left a message for him to ring me at the hotel, but I didn't hear from him that night. Instead I watched the sunset and held a little piece of pink satin ribbon in my hand. I'd taken it from atop an evergreen at my farm in New Jersey, where I was certain Harry had tied it. I ran it between my fingers over and over. Without it, I don't think I would ever have been able to get through my first night in Hollywood.

In the morning, I determined I needed a car. I couldn't just sit and wait in my room, hoping for Mr. Kerns to arrive. In New York, I could travel easily around the city on the subway; Los Angeles offered no such convenience. And I certainly couldn't take cabs all the time—I'd quickly deplete my small savings, all of which I'd withdrawn from the bank the day before my departure.

I walked the thirteen blocks to the motor car dealership out on La Brea Avenue. I'd seen an advertisement and decided on the spot what car I wanted to flash around the palmy streets of Hollywood. A "Big Six" Studebaker—fast as anything yet made, with six cylinders. It was a dash of Flo Bridgewood coming through—the love of driving fast, of speeding up to the top of a hill and then flying down the other side.

"A big car for such a little lady," the salesman said.

He was handsome. Younger than I was. No recognition in his eyes. We struck a deal. "Say," he said to me. "You're going to pay in cash?"

"Yes," I told him, handing over my four hundred dollars. "Isn't that the fashion anymore?"

He grinned. Yes, he was *very* handsome, I thought. Slicked-back dark hair, a pencil-thin mustache. Looked a little like John Gilbert. He put his thumbs behind his lapels, where he sported a bright orange carnation.

"Actually, ma'am," he said, "I'm finding most folks out here pay that way, if they're in the films."

I blinked my eyelashes several times at him. "I'm an actress," I said.

"You are? What's your name again?"

I repeated it.

"Ah, of course," he said, lying through his gorgeous straight white teeth. "Of course, of course. Well. Aren't I honored to have you buying a car from me?"

The fool. Was he so busy polishing cars that he hadn't been to the movies? He was young, but not *that* young. And it had only been five years, after all. Just *five years.*

"I was in the war," he told me, as if reading my mind. So that was it. I excused him his ignorance. "I was awarded the Croix de Guerre."

"A hero," I purred.

He flashed those white teeth. "If you say so, ma'am."

I puffed myself up, held my bosom high. "My new picture is called *The Unfoldment*," I told him, enjoying the flirtation. "It'll be finished in a few weeks. We hope to have it out by summer."

"Well," he said, counting my cash, all twenties, "I'll look for it."

"You do that," I told him.

Something about this handsome young car salesman compelled me. Fascinated me, fixated me. I felt the need to *convince* him, to *prove* to him that I was, indeed, a famous star—that I was the *first*. That if not for me, none of this would be here. Not even his damn car dealership— what need did orange pickers have of Studebakers?

"Here," I said, withdrawing a card from my purse. "It's my producer's card. Won't you call? Come by the studio—see us put the picture together. You can be my guest."

His lovely dark eyes twinkled. Maybe they conjured up thoughts of my dark-eyed island boy. I don't remember.

He took the card, glanced down at it, then up at me again. "I will," he said. He gave me a dazzling smile. "I will do that, Miss Lawrence."

"Good," I said, folding the title to the car and pressing it into my purse. "And your name again?"

"Charles," he said, extending his hand. I shook it. "Charles Woodring."

"Very well then, Mr. Woodring," I said. "Pleasant doing business with you."

He escorted me to my car, opening the door for me as I slipped in along the seat. It didn't have the tiger print of my old car, but what mattered was that it was *mine*. I now had wheels under my feet. Florence Lawrence wasn't going to stay shut up in a shabby little sidestreet hotel.

"I'll take you up on your offer to visit," Charles Woodring called after me.

I tooted the horn at him. In moments I was out on the road, and I felt better than I had in weeks.

* * *

Adela Rogers St. Johns lifted my chin with cold, efficient fingers.

"Where's the scar, Florence? You said the fire left scarring. I don't see a scar."

She pulled the shade off the table lamp at our side and brought the glowing bulb close to my throat. She narrowed her eyes, leaning in to see.

"It's there," I told her. "It took *weeks* to heal."

After several seconds, she drew back, replacing the shade. I swallowed, folding my hands in my lap.

"It's not so bad," Adela said, sitting back down across from me in a rocking chair. She opened her notebook and wrote something. "No deeper than the one Nazimova carries on her cheek."

"Will you say that?"

She looked up from her notebook and smiled. "Of course, my dear," she promised. "Makeup can hide *anything* these days."

I smiled at her in gratitude.

"And how old are you now, Florence?" She looked down at the papers she'd brought with her. "Let's see. I have in my notes you were born—"

"I'm twenty-nine," I told her.

She looked up at me. A smile slowly crept across her face as she marked down the age in her notebook. "All right," she said. "'She is just twenty-nine,'" she read as she wrote. "'Not really an old lady. In fact, even a bit younger than some of our highest-paid luminaries.'" She laughed and told me, "It's true, you know. Clara Kimball Young just turned thirty-two, and Nazimova's *forty* if she's a day."

"Thank you, Adela."

She sighed. She set down her notebook on the table beside her and looked over at me kindly. "Oh, Florence. Are you sufficiently prepared for all this?"

"I think so."

She shook her head. "Oh, I don't know if you are. I mean, *look* at this place."

The room cried of poverty. Paint peeled away from the walls; the floor was covered in a layer of grime. The windows looked out over gray city roofs. I'd tried to spruce it up, arranging some cala lilies in a pitcher of water on the table. I opened a large box of chocolates. I was glad for the sweet fragrance from the box of oranges on the floor; it rid the room of its mustiness.

But I couldn't disguise how meager were my circumstances.

"Look, Florence. Level with me," Adela said. "When you're washed up in pictures, it's like starving to death outside a banquet hall with the smell of the filet mignon driving you slowly mad."

I just dropped my eyes to the floor.

"It's been, what?" Adela asked. "Five years, Florence? Five years you've been off the screen?"

I looked up at her.

Her eyes were big. They didn't seem to blink. They just grew larger and larger as they stared at me. I felt as if I'd drown if I looked into them too long.

"We need to explain that to the readers," she said. "Five years is such a long time. Especially in pictures. It's a *lifetime*." She looked at me directly. "What were you doing all that time, Florence?"

I slid the soft satin of the pink ribbon between my fingers.

"I was . . . recuperating from the fire," I said in a small voice, looking away.

"Ah!" Adela said, as if something just struck her. She reached over, grabbed back her notepad, and scribbled something down. "It's a good angle. Trust me. I haven't been a scribe for ten years for nothing. Let's see—how long were you paralyzed?"

"It wasn't paralysis, Adela. My nerves—"

"But you have the scar!" She looked up at me quickly, then back down at her pad. She continued scribbling. "That would prove it!"

I instinctively reached up and touched my neck. The fire had occurred on the set of *Pawns of Destiny,* one of my last pictures, made for my own production company at Universal and directed by Harry. Matt Moore had been my costar. He was supposed to be rescuing me from a burning building, and the fire had gotten a little out of control. A piece of the floor fell in, and I tripped. Cut my throat.

"But it was my *nerves,* Adela."

She looked at my fiercely. "Your nerves and . . . what else?"

There was no way I could tell her. It was all still so raw. All I could do was tell her the least of it. "The fire left me unnerved."

She sighed. "Oh, we *all* have nerves. But they don't last five years, Florence. No one would buy that."

"There was just—" I paused. "There were a number of things, Adela. I just needed some time away."

"The last interview you gave me was right before you left." Adela held up an old copy of *Photoplay.* Pickford was on the cover, of course. "In it, and I paraphrase, you said you were taking some time off to motorcar around the country with your mother. Well, did you get *lost* somewhere, Florence? It was an awfully long drive!"

"I just needed some time away," I said again.

Adela sighed. "I'm trying to *help* you, Flo. Do you realize that?"

"Yes," I said. "Mr. Kerns was very happy I was talking with you, very pleased you'd write up the film big in *Photoplay*. He's having trouble finding a distributor."

Adela sniffed. "All the more reason to come up with a good angle. And if you're not going to tell me what happened in those five years, I'll need to *invent* something. Tell me about the fire. *Pawns of Destiny,* right?"

"Yes. There was a fire—"

"Yes, yes," she said, writing furiously. "And your former husband was the director—"

"I never divorced Harry."

She looked up at me in surprise. "I thought you did."

"We just separated," I told her. I suddenly felt so alone, sitting there without Harry at my side, negotiating for me, wheeling and dealing. "We never divorced."

"Were you with him when he died?"

I felt the tears, but held them back. "No," I admitted. "I wasn't there."

"But you didn't divorce." She wrote something else. "All right. Good then. No one needs to know about the separation. We can say you were in mourning."

That much wouldn't be a lie. I *did* mourn for Harry. I mourned for everything we'd had—or rather, everything we might have had. For five years, I wrestled with all the what ifs and if onlys. The time passed without my even knowing it was passing. Long days and nights in my bed, just crying, Mother despairing of me. Day after day, I'd lay there, my rosebushes growing tangled and sparse. It was only with enormous effort that I pulled myself to my feet, wandering outside into the sun-drenched fields one spring. It was then that I'd found the pink ribbon tied to the crown of a blue spruce. Harry had tied it there the night he'd learned about Annie Laurie. It had to have been him. Who else was that tall?

"Now, the fire," Adela's saying. "You said you fell through a floor."

"No, no. Nothing so dramatic. The fire was supposed to be under control. Harry had me walking too close to the flames, but I tripped, trying to help Matt Moore. That's how I cut myself. Here." I touched my chin again. "Harry kept filming. I was calling for him to stop, but Matt Moore came rushing up as the hero and picked me up in his arms. It made for quite the realistic scene. The critics said so."

"I imagine there must have been a lot of smoke," Adela said, not looking up as she continued to write in her notebook. "So you saved

Matt Moore. You risked your life to save him and were burned yourself. You carried him to safety the way he was supposed to carry you."

"But I didn't carry him, Adela. He's a huge man, two hundred pounds, and me so little."

"It was either that or let him die."

The simplicity of her words struck me. I repeated them. "Either that or let him die," I said, as if trying the words out, as if seeing how they felt on my tongue.

"So you took the time to recuperate from your injuries and the death of your husband, and now you've come back to start again," Adela was summarizing.

I blinked, looking into her eyes. "Yes," I said quietly. "Yes, that's the case."

She shrugged. "I'll give it my best shot, Florence. But things have changed. You've never made a feature-length picture, have you? Just those old one reelers, right?"

"I did one feature," I protested, but she didn't hear me. She just kept writing in her pad. It didn't matter, really. The picture had been made in New York, and nothing made in New York mattered anymore.

"They say I grew up with the industry," I mused out loud as Adela wrote. "Well, it's true. I did. And coming back now—well, it's like coming back to your old home and finding it changed, all your friends and neighbors moved away. I know the studios today are nothing like they were in the beginning. But I'm confident acting is like riding a horse. Once you learn, you never forget."

Adela had looked up at me with tears in her eyes. Dear, kind Adela. I think she really wanted to help me. I think she really tried to do her best, tried to do the impossible and turn back time. "It's coming together in my head," she told me. "I know *just* the angle to take." She wrote something else down in her pad. "Poor Florence Lawrence," she said as she wrote. "Such a trial your life has been." She looked up again and smiled. "I think it'll work splendidly."

* * *

THE RETURN OF FLORENCE LAWRENCE
THE AMAZING STORY OF A GREAT "COMEBACK"
BY ADELA ROGERS ST. JOHNS

Florence Lawrence is coming back to the screen.
Florence Lawrence, the first screen star, the first movie queen.

"The Biograph Girl."

Do you remember her? After five years, she is going to walk again the path she pioneered.

And now that I have talked to her, I cannot help wondering whether her return is to be a triumph or a tragedy.

I cannot tell you why she struck me instantly as being such a sad little figure. But when I first saw her, I felt my heart stop and sink a little—as it did when I first saw the vacant places in the ranks of the returned marching regiments of Yankees from the Great War.

She has in her blue eyes the same look I saw in Sarah Bernhardt's the last time she came to America—that look of brave, spiritual struggle against overwhelming odds, the look of a woman who knows what it is to fight a losing fight.

Yet she is quite gay, fluffy, blond, and given to sweet and rather easy laughter. In no wise a gloomy person. She talks cheerfully, entertainingly, and you must read between the lines to patch together the story of her sorrows. But over and over again, I felt a lump in my throat.

I found her in her room at a small hotel on a side street in Los Angeles. There were flowers in a white pitcher, a huge box of chocolates, and a sweet, pungent smell of oranges from a big basket on the floor beside a small couch-bed. On a chair was a cardboard box that frothed with pink silk and lace and ribbons. So it managed to be quite cheerful and feminine in spite of the drab wallpaper and ugly furniture.

But it was the last place where you would expect to find a motion picture star.

I know—as part of the short but crowded history of motion pictures—the story of Florence Lawrence. I know that she was the first motion picture star, the idol of the thousands who first answered the lure of the screen. I know that only the brief span of ten or twelve years ago she was "The Biograph Girl," photographed, sought after, marveled over, adored.

But I had not counted upon the long, harrowing months of illness—brought about by a fall through a burning building while she was making her last picture, when she saved her costar from certain death while risking her own—nor upon the sad death of her husband, nor the deep wound that was to cut her on finding how short, how very short, is the memory of not only the public but of fair-weather friends.

"Sometimes," she said, smiling, "I think it is harder to 'come back' than it is to 'arrive.'"

She did not tell me why she had chosen to come back now. But as she talked of her mother, her husband's death, the years of terrific expense of doctors, nurses, travel, I suspected that the little fortune she had accumulated when she took America by storm had dwindled until it no longer seemed an adequate barrier for two women alone in the world.

Then, too, I believe she has a deep, sincere love of her work, that drew her back when she found herself physically able to go on with it.

"No one is ever happy unless they have their work to do," she said with quiet conviction. "I do not think I have forgotten much. They used to say I 'grew up with the industry.' But it seems to have outgrown me now."

She has returned to a land where once she ruled supreme, where her name was a magic word, to find herself an outsider, her place usurped, her very name forgotten by gatemen at the studios. A famous producer who was once an extra in her company was "out" when she called. Girls who today have their names in electric lights, but who used to borrow her makeup and her gowns, have overlooked her return.

She is not bitter. But she is hurt.

For—it makes me smile to think it—she is only 29. Not really an old lady, you see. In fact, even now a bit younger than some of our highest paid luminaries. She is frail, easily tired, but she is still lovely. She has a scar under her chin from her fall, which adds to the strange pathos around her, but it is no deeper than the one Nazimova carries on her cheek, which the makeup hides so perfectly even from the all-seeing eye of the camera.

"It's a big citadel I'm attacking," she said. "And today there are thousands besieging it. Every technical handicap has been overcome since the old days when I helped Mr. Griffith make those old two reelers. But I would not take anything for my experience in working against every handicap.

"Somehow I feel sure that I am going to succeed. I—I must!"

Her first picture is called The Unfoldment *by George Kerns, head of the Producers Pictures Corporation. Never heard of them? She says to watch and see.*

I heard an old stage carpenter say the other day, "Florence Lawrence was the best of 'em all. I ain't seen anybody yet can touch what she used to be, and I seen most of 'em work. She could make folks love her, she could."

They used to call her "the girl with a thousand faces." If she had a thousand faces then at 16—17—20—, she ought to have 10,000 now. If she does "come back," if she can win back her place in the hearts of the people—what a triumph it will be!

So how about it? Will you rally around her? Will you rescue our little Biograph Girl from oblivion?

Her sweet, sad little face is counting on you.

* * *

"Sweet, sad little face?"

Charles threw the magazine down on the table in overplayed disgust. "Sweet and little, I'll give you," he said. "But sad?" He took my cheeks between his cold hands. "I hardly think so."

He kissed me. A little too hard. Our teeth clinked like champagne glasses.

We certainly had enough of those around. Prohibition might have been the order of the day, with all the legal taverns closed down, but Charles was pals with the top bootleggers in L.A. He kept a well-equipped bar at his house. He also had a maid and a butler and a fabulous sunken bathtub. His house shone of marble floors; his walls were draped in velvet. Charles hadn't had money for most of his life, but now that he did, he was making a show of it. Auto sales were hot. After all, it *was* Hollywood on the cusp of the Roaring Twenties.

He'd taken me up on my offer to visit the set. I was gracious and polite, escorting him around, securing permission for him to sit in the wings and watch me emote. The next day he arrived again, this time with a bouquet of red roses. We used them in a scene. He came every day after that, and I found myself looking forward to his visits. Every day he brought me flowers, and sometimes he'd bring a box of pastries for the entire crew. He became friendly with Mr. Kerns, promising to get him a car. When he flirted too long with perky young Barbara Bedford, I found myself absurdly jealous.

Now he was escorting me to the premiere. He was drinking his whiskey straight. "So who will be there tonight? You got Mack Sennett?"

"We sent him an invitation," I said.

"You worked with him, right? He's an old friend, you said."

"Sennett was just an extra at Biograph," I told him. "He was nobody then."

But now he was. And he hadn't returned any of my calls.

I'd tried calling my old costar King Baggott, too, who was now a big-time director. He'd been polite, but couldn't promise he'd make it to the premiere. Late-night shooting, he said. He was sure I'd understand.

"What about Pickford? She coming?"

"Really, Charles," I said, smiling. "I would think you'd only be interested in *one* star." I batted my eyelashes. "Me."

He kissed me again. His tongue tasted of whiskey. He was really far too young for me. I should've known that. Mother would have prevented it had she been there.

But she wasn't. There was only Charles. He was handsome, to be sure—none of the cragginess that had so characterized Harry, no droopy ears or puppy-love eyes. He was tall and dark, with that flashy smile, that cleft in his chin. His hands, in contrast to Harry's, were petite and cultured, and his nails were always clean. Charles never sweat. Never that I saw.

Oh, he was smooth. He provided an enormous leopard-lined limousine for the premiere. We rode over as giddy as jaybirds, passing a bottle of champagne back and forth between ourselves. I was dressed to the nines, in clothes paid for by Charles.

"I've got to try to appear casual," I told him. "I want people to think I'm *used* to mink."

He laughed, leaning across the limo seat to kiss me again. "The triumphant return of Florence Lawrence!" he crowed.

I smiled, pushing him gently away. "Careful you don't spill the bottle."

But when we arrived at the theater, the sidewalks were barren. Just a couple of ushers and a few reporters, and the long blue shadows cast by the street lamps. Mr. Kerns had promised us a crowd.

"I can't get out," I whispered to Charles. "There are *photographers* out there. And no people!"

"They must all be inside already," Charles said, peering over my shoulder onto the empty sidewalk.

"Drive around the block," I commanded the driver. "We can go in through the back."

"Like *hell* we will!" Charles shouted. "I didn't rent this monkey suit I'm wearin' and spring for this here limousine to go in through the *back*. No, sirree, Florence. I'm gettin' my picture in *Photoplay*."

"But, Charles, there are *no people* out there. The reporters—they'll write about it—make me sound so—so pathetic!"

"Hey," he said, shrugging. "We're used to that."

I looked at him, hurt.

"Go *on*," he insisted. "Get out of the car."

"No," I told him.

I didn't see him strike me, just felt the sharp sting of the back of his hand across my face. I was more startled than hurt. I stared at him in silence.

"No woman says no when I give an order," he told me. "I won't tolerate that. I paid for all of this—this car, that corsage you're wearing, that goddamn mink stole. I'm going to get my *money's worth,* Florence."

"Please, Charles," I said, beginning to cry.

He grabbed my wrist. "*Open the door,* Florence. Get out of the car."

His eyes were yellow in the dark. My face still stung and now he was hurting my wrist. I knew then there was no escape. That Florence Lawrence wasn't strong enough to fight him off. I was stunned by how quickly—and how completely—I'd become her again.

I did as I was told. I stepped out into an ugly silence, marred only by the short crash of flashbulbs popping. I smiled up at them as best I could.

Adela was there. "Darling," she said quietly as I passed. "Your face."

I placed my hand over my cheek where Charles had struck me. "It's nothing," I assured her.

"Keep yourself turned to the left for the photographers." She smiled sadly. "You have a lovely profile."

My name was up on the marquee, the last time it was ever there.

FLORENCE LAWRENCE
STARRING IN
THE UNFOLDMENT

I looked up at it for a moment. Charles took me by the arm. "Come on," he hissed into my ear. "You don't want to be late for your own show."

Mr. Kerns and my costars greeted me in the lobby. Barbara Bedford was unable to make it; she'd started a new film with Douglas Fairbanks and was too busy. I posed in profile with Charles for a picture taken by a *Photoplay* photographer. It never made it into print.

Inside the cavernous theater, thirty—maybe forty—people sat staring at a magnificent red velvet curtain. An usher announced, "Ladies and gentlemen, Florence Lawrence," and the people turned in their seats to look at me. A scattering of applause. Oh, I'm sure it was enthusiastic. Adela later wrote that it was. But in that enormous, echoing space, it seemed impassive and uninterested. I took my seat down near the front. I wasn't even aware of the picture as it unfolded.

The Unfoldment. What an unfortunate name. What a dreadful film.

What a horrible memory. The picture went nowhere. It didn't even get panned. It was just ignored. It was as if I'd never even made it—as if I'd never come back. I don't imagine it still exists. Surely long ago it deteriorated back into its original nitrate stock, crumbling into dust and blowing away with the breeze. I hear the cries of film preservationists today and I laugh.

I'm *glad* that film is gone.

Two days after its premiere, I married Charles Woodring. Of course I did. It was just what Florence Lawrence would do. She needed someone to fight her battles, to keep her going. Charles promised to restart my career, to triumph over the disaster of *The Unfoldment*. He could do it, he insisted. And maybe he could at that, I tried to reason to myself. He had the money to invest, after all, and the ambition to succeed—both qualities I was lacking at that point.

So I married him. At least I could pay the bills that were threatening to send Mother and me to the almshouse.

But I was no longer strong enough to force my husband to sleep on the couch as I had with Harry. For the next decade, the image of Charles's yellow eyes in the dark was a nightmare that was all too real.

The Present

"I was married to Charles for nearly ten years," Flo tells Ben, her eyes off in that place she goes whenever she tells stories of the past. "We separated after eight, however, when I found him with another woman in our bed."

"That must have been hard for you," Ben suggests.

She sighs. "Oh, I can't say it was easy. But it wasn't a surprise—let me put it that way."

"He'd been unfaithful before?"

"It was a *difficult* marriage. Charles expected to have his way. In *everything*." Her lips tighten and she folds her hands in her lap before she continues. "He used to tell me that Hollywood was no place for a woman to find a husband—particularly her own."

Ben's not sure if he's meant to smile at that. He doesn't want to appear disrespectful. But then Flo laughs, and it's clear she's made a joke. Ben smiles in return.

"You see," she continues, "when I went back to being Florence Lawrence, I took what I could get. Florence Lawrence couldn't be expected to manage her own affairs. There had always been Mother or Harry. And I suppose, for all his shortcomings, Charles *did* help me out financially. He always insisted on living the high life. 'There are only two classes,' he'd insist. 'First class and no class.' He set me up in a business of my own after movie offers faded away. A cosmetics company: Florence Lawrence's Hollywood Cosmetics. My face was on every tin of talcum powder and rouge. But the crash of '29 wiped us out. Charles lost a *fortune*."

She lets out a long sigh and says nothing further. Ben's got the videocam positioned in front of her. It's been rolling for nearly two hours as Flo has talked, taking Ben back with her to San Francisco in 1904, before the great earthquake—and then to Los Angeles in 1921, the time of her failed comeback. In none of their sessions—almost fifty hours of interviews so far—has she spoken in a precise chronology. It's been a rambling daisy chain of consciousness—a slow, wandering stroll through her long, long life. Occasionally she's mentioned a name Ben has jotted down, meaning to ask her about later. Sometimes she gets around to explaining who they are—or *were*. And sometimes she doesn't.

Ben looks down at his list. *Bolton. Doris. Marian. Winnie Pichel. Annie Laurie.* Names she's dropped in passing, but details of whom he still has no clue.

This session, however, she's done a pretty good job filling him in on Charles Woodring and Adela Rogers St. Johns. He wants to press on, to take advantage of the fact that for once Sister Jean isn't here. He's free to push Flo toward topics she's been reluctant to explain in any detail: the fire, the death of her first husband, and most of all, just what happened with "that girl" who was misidentified as her at the hospital.

But now she's wound to a halt, it seems—as if her batteries were wearing down.

"Are you getting tired, Flo?" Ben asks.

She blinks. "Oh, a little." She looks over at him. "I guess because I was up so early this morning."

Ben nods. He'd gotten up with her, at three-thirty A.M., to make a seven o'clock appearance on the *Today* show. Both Katie Couric *and* Matt Lauer had interviewed her, confirming Flo's sudden megastar status. Ever since the *Rosie* show, Flo had been in hot demand. "She's sassy, saucy, and just what everyone hopes to be—if they live that long," Xerxes has said. Like Clara Peller—the "Where's the Beef?" crone of the 80s—and Mother Jefferson from the old *Jeffersons* TV show, Flo engaged people because she defied their notions of what "old" meant. Offers had come pouring into Xerxes's office for Flo to appear on television and in print interviews.

Xerxes and Ben, with input from Sister Jean, had determined the *Today* show to be the best follow-up to the *Rosie* appearance. Both Katie and Matt had been extremely gracious, allowing Flo to reminisce about the early days of moviemaking without pushing her too hard on the mystery of her supposed death. But Flo, while getting off a few one liners, had seemed a little groggy, considerably less sharp and witty than she had been on *Rosie*. Maybe it was the early hour—but Flo was often up that early. Maybe it was the one reference Katie made to the hospital mystery: *how* the erroneous identification had been made in the first place. Flo had just shrugged. "Maybe she just looked like me," she said.

But as Flo's fame grew, the questions came faster and harder. An article in the *Los Angeles Times* this week had reported on the exhumation of the grave marked as Florence Lawrence's in Hollywood Memorial Cemetery. No conclusions had yet been drawn by the coroner's office, but the *Times* raised some intriguing questions about Flo's story. It explored in some detail the accounts of the poisoning as described in the newspapers of the day. As Ben knew, Flo was reported then as having banged on the doors of neighbors, telling them she'd poisoned herself, asking them to call for help. She had even left a note, which the *Times* published:

> *Good-bye, my darlings. This is the only way. You've all been swell guys. Everything is yours.*
>
> > *Lovingly,*
> > *Florence*

If Flo was to be believed today, she never left that note, and if someone had gone banging on her neighbors' doors, it wasn't she.

But how could that be possible? The *Times* concluded that it was not:

> *Miss Bridgewood's story is shot through with holes. She may truly be The Biograph Girl, as film experts are convinced. But she's not telling the full account of what happened that day in 1938— nor, possibly, about various other episodes in her long and eventful life.*

Ben was the only person allowed full access to Flo. Outside of the controlled public appearances he and Xerxes were orchestrating, only *he* had the chance to ask the questions and get the answers. He wanted so desperately to just ask her forthrightly to tell the truth. *Quit this ruse,* he wanted to snap. *Just quit it right now and—*

Fine one you are to be talking about a ruse, Ben Sheehan.

Whose voice? Mom's? Anita's?

Pretending to Flo and Sister Jean that you care only about their welfare, that you're only in this for the sake of posterity. Oh, Ben Sheehan, don't you go giving lectures about being truthful. If you've got to be a liar, don't add on hypocrite, too.

It might be Mom. But it sure sounded like Anita, too.

Anita had been sleeping on the couch for the past week. Ben didn't even try to persuade her against it. She just started doing it one night. There had been no fight, no harsh words. Just a tension that hung over them like the hot, damp mugginess of August in New York, even though the first snowfall of the winter had come last night, a dusting like confectionery sugar that melted as the sun rose.

But no such thaw occurred for Ben and Anita. They spoke very little, except to ask if the coffee was brewing or if one or the other of them was finished in the shower. Partly it was because both were so busy, Ben told himself: he with Flo and Anita rushing off to tape the soap opera. Her role had been extended for another three weeks, and if she wasn't caught up learning the script, she was dashing off for rehearsals. Ben overheard her running lines sometimes late at night; she was pretty atrocious, he thought, and couldn't imagine *how* she'd landed the part. Still, he had promised to take her to dinner to celebrate her good fortune, but their plans had not yet materialized.

If I'd taken her, he scolds himself, *maybe she wouldn't be on the couch. Maybe this tension might have evaporated.*

But Anita was as much to blame, he thought to himself. She rarely asked how things were going with the interviews or if Xerxes had sold the film rights yet. She would just say, "I hope you're being straight with Flo."

"Of course," he'd tell her. "What do you think I am?"

A liar, for one.

And a hypocrite, too, Ben Sheehan?

Ah, jeez. Go ahead and call me names then. But Ben knows he'll have no film unless he resolves these nagging questions—unless Flo responds to them in her own words. Already Xerxes has gotten major interest from both Universal and DreamWorks for a film—or *films*—based on Flo's life. He was promising them "the true, inside, completely revealed untold story"—straight from Flo's lips.

But with Sister Jean always lurking in the background . . .

"Flo," Ben says, "maybe we can talk about just one more thing before we call it a day."

She looks at him. "All right, Ben. What is it?"

"What about that *girl*? The one whose body was just—"

"Exhumed?" It's Sister Jean, coming into the hotel room behind him.

Ben jumps. *Shit. What perfect fucking timing.* "Jean, I didn't hear you come in."

She's carrying three shopping bags loaded with boxes. "Apparently," she says. "I thought we agreed that subject was off limits, Ben."

He sighs. "Look. We can't avoid it anymore. It's just that, with the exhumation, I thought—well, people are asking questions. You heard Katie Couric. We need to get a story that we can all stick to."

Jean sets the bags down. From one, she withdraws a box, crinkling the paper as she does so. She hands it to Flo. "Go ahead," she says. "Open it."

Ben keeps filming. This is good stuff. Flo's face brightens with excitement, like a teenage girl on her birthday. Delicately, her old fingers lift the lid of the white cardboard box. She pushes aside the paper and gazes down. She makes a little sound of delight, then lifts a rainbow-striped scarf out of the box.

"Oh, Jeannie," she says, wrapping it around her neck. "Whatever for?"

"For all your television appearances," Jean tells her. "A little dash of color."

"Oh, thank you, dear," the old woman says. Jean moves in for a quick kiss.

"You look fabulous, Flo," Ben tells her.

"Okay," Jean says, looking back at him. "Now shut that thing off."

"But—"

"I *am* getting tired, Ben," Flo admits.

He reluctantly complies. Jean helps Flo up from her chair and walks with her into the bedroom. Ben watches them go. Jean's wearing Capri pants and sneakers. She's got a pretty good shape on her, he thinks—before scolding himself and shaking his head. *Keep it in your pants, Sheehan. She's a nun. You can't have this one.* He pops out the video from the camera, labels it with the date, and files it away with all the rest of them.

Jean barely manages to get Flo's shoes off before the old woman is sprawled back on her pillows and snoring. A nap will do her good, Jean thinks, as she quietly closes the door to her room.

All these appearances. This was exactly what the board at St. Mary's had been worried about. "She'll be *exhausted*," chided Sister William. "Is this really *wise?*" intoned Father Horrigan.

Jean had told them it was Flo's choice. "You know her as well as I do. She can make her own decisions, after all. When does one cease being an adult? Eighty? Ninety?"

Flo's words. She was doing this because *Flo* had wanted to, because she wanted to respect her friend's wishes.

Yet Jean has to admit she's enjoying it herself. She can't deny that the freedom from the bureaucracy of St. Mary's has been exhilarating. To walk once again along city streets, to escape from the stultifying grandeur of marble staircases and heavy oaken doors . . .

"Hey," Ben's asking her, his voice low, conscious of Flo being asleep. "What else did you buy?"

Jean smiles. "Oh, I went a little crazy on Canal Street."

She lifts a box out of one bag. She holds it against her chest, blushing. "Do you know I haven't bought myself any new clothes in *years?*"

"Show me," Ben says.

She laughs.

"Come *on,*" he urges, a great smile taking over his face.

"Oh, all right." She opens the box. It's a black-and-white-striped cotton tank top. "It's a little stretchy," she admits.

"You mean, like *spandex?*"

She can feel her face burn. "Oh, God," she says, laughing. "Where am I *ever* going to wear this?" She holds it up in front of her. "I just bought it. A complete whim."

"I think it'll look great on you," Ben tells her.

"Oh, I don't know what I was thinking. I bought this and a pair of jeans and a couple of sweatshirts."

"Well, you need more than the old plaid skirt nun uniform," Ben says, grinning.

"I imagine once I'm back at St. Mary's I'll donate them all to Goodwill." Jean holds up the striped tank top in front of her again, looking at herself in the mirror.

"It's perfect for L.A.," Ben says, coming up behind her, looking at her through the mirror. "Make sure you bring it when we head out there next week."

Their eyes hold in the mirror. "You know, I'd forgotten what it was like to be called 'ma'am' by store clerks," Jean tells him. "At St. Mary's, it's always 'Sister.' When I was at St. Vincent's, I could escape for a while. You know, head into town and go shopping or stop for lunch. I'd be just another woman, maybe somebody's wife or mother." She smiles. "Or a high-powered, kick-ass corporate exec."

They both laugh.

Ben looks at her, growing serious. He places his hands on her shoulders. The warmth of his hands sends a shiver down her back.

"Jean," he asks, "aren't you happy in religious life?"

She smiles. She's come to trust Ben. She feels she can admit certain things to him. "Oh, there's no question I feel a calling to do God's work," she says. "Always have, and that's never changed." She pauses, letting her hands with her new purchase fall to her side. "But sometimes I wonder just what that work *is,* what form it's supposed to take."

"And running St. Mary's seems a little . . . too cushy perhaps?"

Jean turns around to face him. They're standing awfully close, but she doesn't back away. "How'd you figure *that* out, Ben Sheehan?"

He shrugs. "Well, you talk with such passion about your years at St. Vincent's, working with the poor, with drug addicts, all of that. But St. Mary's seems to be—well, maybe a little too *bourgeois* for you."

He's been listening, Jean thinks. *He pays attention.*

"Don't get me wrong," she tells him. "I love the residents there. Many of them have taught me a good deal. Especially Flo. But I can't deny that I'm grateful the board granted me this leave. Maybe it's just what I needed."

Ben smiles down at her. They're standing so close that suddenly there's a moment of awkwardness. Jean laughs, backing away. She drops the tank top to the floor. Both she and Ben stoop down to pick it up, their hands touching as they grasp its silky material.

They look up into each other's face.

Then the phone shrieks from across the room.

"Oh, sweet Jesus," Jean gasps, clutching her chest, standing up straight.

Ben lunges for the phone. "Yeah? Hello?" He listens. "Oh, Christ. Yeah, fine. Send her up."

He hangs up the phone. He looks over at Jean. "It's just Anita," he tells her.

"Oh."

Jean hurriedly replaces the tank top in the box. Her heart is thudding loudly in her ears. *The phone just startled you—that's all,* she tells herself. *There's nothing more to it. Nothing.*

But she peers around at Ben, now taking down his tripod.

He *does* remind her of Victor. No one else would probably see the resemblance, but she can. The shoulders, maybe. The way he stands. And the *eyes.* Definitely the eyes—despite the fact that Ben's eyes are blue, and Victor's eyes were chocolate brown.

She resolves then and there to return the tank top tomorrow. What was she ever thinking when she bought it?

Jean notices Ben and Anita don't kiss when she enters.

"Hi, Anita," Jean says. She feels crazily guilty, as if she'd done something wrong by her. But how ridiculous is *that?* "I haven't seen you in a while," she says awkwardly, offering the young woman her hand.

Anita shakes it and gives her a small smile. "Hi, Sister."

"Finished taping for today?" Ben asks.

Anita nods. "I came to see Flo. Is she here?"

"She's sleeping," Jean tells her.

"Well, I just wondered if she heard."

Ben creases his brow. "Heard what?"

"I just talked with Richard out in L.A." Anita looks up at him and then over at Jean. "The coroner's issued his report on the body."

"And . . . ?" Ben asks.

Anita shakes her head. "It's not Florence Lawrence," she says.

Jean makes the Sign of the Cross.

"Well, we could've told you *that*," Ben exclaims. "Florence Lawrence is in the other room sleeping. So who *is* it?"

"That they don't know," Anita tells him. "How could they? They just know it's *not* a middle-aged woman. They've determined the body buried in that grave was female, white, and aged between sixteen and twenty-five."

"Poor young thing," Jean says softly.

"Yeah," Ben says, looking off in the direction of the room where Flo slumbers peacefully. "That's what Flo said, isn't it? She was just a girl."

Anita looks at him. "There was one other part of the report I thought you'd find interesting," she says.

Ben and Jean both raise their eyebrows in anticipation.

"The coroner determined that, whoever she was, she died—from arsenic poisoning."

"Well, it looks as if Florence Bridgewood may well be telling the truth," Regis tells Kathie Lee. "The coroner's finding is that the woman they buried is actually a *teenager.*"

Kathie Lee shivers dramatically. "I find the whole story just a little creepy, don't you?"

"Creepy? You think everything that's not sunshine and daffodils is creepy. This is a mystery—exciting—romantic."

"You just want to get her on the show."

"Well, you know, she's *very* particular about her appearances, but we've been talking with her agent, and it looks as if she might be sitting right here very soon."

"Gosh, Reej, how old *is* she?"

"One hundred and six."

"Right in your ballpark, huh?"

The audience guffaws. Regis shoots her a look. Kathie Lee moves out of profile to give a rare full-face wink at the camera. The audience laughs some more.

*　　*　　*

"They always laugh whenever my age is mentioned," Flo observes.

"Who does?" Ben asks.

"Audiences."

Xerxes is on the phone, motioning for them to turn the volume on the television down. Ben mutes it with the remote control, cutting Regis off in midcomeback.

"Yeah, yeah, all right," Xerxes is saying into the phone. He slams the receiver down.

"We've got to get Flo an Equity card," he says to no one in particular.

"Why?" Jean queries.

"Flo, were you ever in SAG?"

"What's that?" she asks.

"What's going *on?*" Ben insists, standing up now and approaching his agent.

"Flo baby," Xerxes says, "how'd you like to *act* again?"

"Act?" Jean asks.

"Yeah. *Act.*" He looks at Ben, his eyes big and his grin shit eating wide. "Do you know who that was on the phone? John *Waters.*"

"John Waters?" Ben repeats.

"Yessiree. Himself. *Pink Flamingos* and *Hairspray* and all the rest." He lets out a loony laugh. "Do you know who he is, Flo?"

She shakes her head.

"A very important director," Xerxes tells her. "Like Griffith."

Flo smiles. "Oh, I doubt he's like Griffith."

"Your doubts are on target," Jean tells her, clearly troubled. She stands from where she'd been sitting with Flo in front of the TV and approaches Ben and Xerxes.

"Waters wants Flo for a *film?*" Ben is gushing.

Xerxes nods. "He's doing another one of his pictures loaded with cameos. Wants Flo to play—what else—a screen legend." The agent's eyes are wide and his hands are wringing. "What do you say, Flo? Can you imagine your name back up there on the screen?"

"Oh, dear," is all she says.

"Excuse me," Jean interrupts, "but last I remember, Flo had her own agent. Why hasn't Carla been informed of this?"

"Oh, we'll call her, of course." Xerxes grins. "But come *on,* Sister. John Waters is a personal friend of mine. Trust me here."

"Who else is in the picture?" Ben asks.

"Edward Furlong, Christina Ricci, Patty Hearst, of course, and—get this—Jeff Stryker!"

"Jeff Stryker—the porn star?" Ben says.

"The very same." Xerxes seems as if he might pop his shirt buttons with excitement.

"I'm not sure I like the idea of Flo becoming *camp*," Jean says. "And I think the Board would go apoplectic at the idea of her appearing in a John Waters film."

"Sister, Sister," Xerxes reassures her. "Don't worry. Waters is past the dog-turd stage. He's gone mainstream."

"As far mainstream as Waters can go," Ben adds.

"*Besides*," Xerxes says, arching a bushy black eyebrow, "if we do this, there's a good chance we can get her in the new Altman film."

"*Altman?*" Ben chokes. "As in *Robert* Altman?"

"Look what he did for Gish in *A Wedding*. Reignited her whole career."

"*Robert Altman*," Ben just breathes to himself.

"And this is just the start," Xerxes is saying, pacing the room. "I understand Cameron's kicking himself because he would've *loved* to have had Flo for *Titanic*. Gloria Stuart's only eighty-something playing a hundred plus. Can you *imagine* the publicity Flo would've gotten him? I mean, she was actually *on* the damn ship."

"No," Ben says, pacing now with sudden excitement himself. "She just saw it go down."

"No, no, that's not true either," Flo tells them, but neither one of them are listening to her. They've begun chattering between themselves about what Flo's "going rate" for acting should be.

"Waters is offering a quarter of a million for two days' work," Xerxes says.

"We can get more," Ben urges.

"Easy now," Xerxes says. "Remember this is just a start."

"I really think this is more appropriate for Carla to handle," Jean protests. She sighs, going back to sit next to Flo on the couch.

"It *would* be rather exciting to act again," Flo whispers to her. "I never would have imagined that I'd make another picture." She grins. "Do you think they'd put my name above the title?"

Jean just gives Flo a small, tired smile and reaches over to take both of the older woman's hands in her own.

Rex is in their hotel room in West Hollywood, sitting shirtless in front of the mirror, applying theatrical glue to his left eyebrow. His right eyebrow is already done, covered over by long antennae-like white hairs. It's his Lionel Barrymore guise, and he's making himself up to show the artistic director at Highways. The show starts in a couple of days.

Richard watches him. The sunlight casts a warm golden glow across Rex's body as a ceiling fan drones in rhythmic circling overhead. Richard feels somewhat mesmerized by the sound, by the sun, by the lush greenery that surrounds their guest house. It's wonderful to be out of New York in December, even if they will miss having a white Christmas.

Rex stands. The sunlight hits his face, and Richard is jogged out of his trance. On Rex's back, he spies a lump—distended skin and muscle between his shoulder blades, like the beginnings of a small hunchback. How had he not noticed it before? He *had* observed that Rex was getting a little fleshier, but not this.

Rex has sat back down in front of the mirror to fix an eyebrow. Richard stands and goes over to his chair, beginning to gently massage Rex's shoulders.

Rex smiles up at him through the mirror. "What do you think, sweetheart? Do I look like grouchy old Mr. Potter from *It's a Wonderful Life?*"

Richard smiles. "I still think your Ethel's the best." He pauses, running his hands across the lump on Rex's back. "Nooker, what's this? Have you noticed?"

"Oh, that. Don't worry about it. It's just a side effect of the new drugs. The doctor said it'll probably go away."

Richard tries to catch his eyes in the mirror but Rex evades him. "Side effect? No one told us about side effects."

"They didn't know." Rex holds the left eyebrow up in front of him. It looks like a mangy caterpillar. As if it has a life all its own.

"Why didn't you tell me? How long . . . ?"

"Just a couple weeks. It's gotten larger, but the doctor said not to worry. And I didn't tell you right away because I know how worried you get, and then I get worried, and the whole thing becomes too much."

"This isn't supposed to happen. Not anymore."

"Everything's still so new, sweetheart. It's still trial and error."

"Yeah, but the virus is eradicated, so how can—"

Rex pastes the eyebrow in place. "Richard, I've *told* you. Don't use words like 'eradicated.' It only charges us up. The drugs have simply brought the amount of virus in my body down to undetectable levels." He frowns into the mirror. He *does* look like Mr. Potter, Lionel Barrymore's most famous role. "And if it means living with a bit of a lump and some love handles, I can deal with it. My porno days are over, after all."

Richard runs his hand over the distended skin on Rex's back. "That's right," he says, more to himself than Rex. "We can live with lumps if we need to."

But there's another thought that he can't quite suppress, try as hard as he might: *They were wrong. The drugs won't last. You're going to get sick again and then you're going to die, and I can't go through it again. I won't.*

The sudden fear is too much for him. He drops his hands from Rex's back and turns away. He looks up at the ceiling fan. *I love him, and I'll be here for him. No matter what, no matter how sick, even if he . . .*

Oh, yeah? Maybe the time to split is now, before he gets sick.

Richard runs his hand down in front of his face. It's almost like a cartoon, with the Good Richard in a halo and the Bad Richard in horns sitting on his shoulders, trying to persuade him to their side. *This is crazy. I can't think about it.*

"Get me my shirt, will you?" Rex asks suddenly, breaking through.

"Yeah, yeah. Sure."

Richard moves off to fetch the shirt from the closet. *I just won't think about it. I just won't . . . not now . . .*

There's a knock on the door, and Richard's grateful for whoever it is. He welcomes a distraction, *any* distraction, from the lump on Rex's back. He opens the door, revealing a bellboy holding a large manila envelope.

"This just arrived for you, Mr. Sheehan," the bellboy says.

"Oh, thank you." Richard takes it, closes the door. "Look, Nooker," he says. "From the AMA." He'd been anxious to get this, but he is even happier that it came just when it did. *Think about Flo. I need to concentrate on Flo.*

Rex eyes him suspiciously. "What are you getting from the American Medical Association?"

"It's about *Dr. Slocum*," Richard tells him. "I had them send the documents here."

They sit down together on the edge of the bed as Richard rips open the envelope. He'd requested any information they had on Dr. Lester Slocum of Los Angeles, California. He'd learned the AMA keeps files on all licensed U.S. physicians this century.

There are two documents, both of which are photocopies of information cards. "Let's see," Richard says, scanning across the first one. "Lester Horace Slocum. Graduated Grand Rapids, Michigan, Medical College, 1928. Practiced Mount Clemens Hospital, Michigan, and Beverly Hills Hospital, Los Angeles."

"What does the note at the bottom say?" Rex asks.

Richard peers down at it. The handwriting is small and crowded and badly faded. But he makes it out slowly. "'The license of Dr. Lester Slocum was . . . suspended . . . for a period of two years . . . at the June 1939 meeting of the Board.'" He looks up at Rex, then back down at the paper. He continues reading. "'This suspension will be automatically lifted June 1941.'"

"I wonder why," Rex says.

"It doesn't say." Richard turns to the next page. Another information card, containing information from Dr. Slocum's obituary in the *Journal of the American Medical Association*. "'Lester Horace Slocum,'" he reads. "'Beverly Hills, California. Grand Rapids Medical College, 1928. Died January 2, 1941, aged 39.'" Richard pauses. "A suicide."

"A *suicide*," Rex whispers. "Maybe because of the suspension?"

Richard shrugs. "He killed himself six months before his reinstatement."

"Well, those are tantalizing clues," Rex says, grinning. "Just enough information to keep us guessing. But do you think it has anything to do with Flo?"

"I can't imagine what, but still . . ." Richard sighs. "I've *got* to get in to talk with her again."

Rex smirks. "You'll have to go through Ben."

Richard stands. "Fine. I'll *go* through Ben if I have to. I'm going to assemble this goddamn puzzle one way or another."

"Sweetheart?"

Richard doesn't respond. He's still studying the documents on Dr. Slocum.

"*Richard?*" Rex asks, louder this time.

Richard finally looks over at him.

Rex gives him a wry smile. "I know there's a book in this," he says, "and that you've had some terrific offers and that you fall asleep at night dreaming of Pulitzer Prizes and movie deals and *whatever*. But I have to ask you, even with all that: *Why are you doing this?*"

Richard laughs. "You just answered that question."

"Is there any chance you're just pissed that Ben is making the film on Flo's life?"

Richard makes a face. "Sure, that pisses me off, but come *on*, Nooker. This is big stuff. Flo's all over the television. *Biography* did her life. *Mysteries and Scandals* is doing something. I even saw an item yesterday in Liz Smith—or Army Archerd—one of them—that said John Waters wants her for a cameo in his new film." He paces back and forth, the papers in his hand fluttering. "A dozen other guys are now onto the story. Any one of them could do a book—and *I'm* the one who discovered her."

"I just worry about you—that's all."

Richard stops. "You worry about *me?*" He hurries over to the bed to sit back down next to Rex. "Oh, baby. I don't want you worrying about me. *I'm* the worrier in the family, remember?"

"You mean, this here li'l ol' lump on my back?" Rex grins. "Just call me Quasi, for short."

Richard puts his arms around him. He pulls him in close, embracing Rex's slight body. He can feel the swollen muscle on his back. He can feel Rex's heart, too, chirping between them like a bird. He presses his lips against Rex's neck. His skin tastes warm and salty.

"Hey, Romeo," Rex says. "Watch the eyebrows."

"Promise me it's all going to be okay," Richard says suddenly to him.

Rex smiles gently. "I can't promise you that."

Richard makes a face. "Just always know I love you, Nooker," he says, suddenly awash with emotion. He can't say anything else.

"I will always know that, Richard." He strokes his lover's hair. "No matter what."

They hold each other until Rex has to go—Rex in an old man's whiskers and Richard near tears, Lester Slocum's suicide report forgotten for the moment on the floor beside them.

"Why *can't* I go to L.A.? I can go if I want. It's a fucking free country, in case you've forgotten, Ben Sheehan!"

Anita's in a fit. Her face is red, blotchy. She stands in front of Ben with her fists clenched and her lips drawn back to reveal her teeth. It's not a pretty sight.

"Anita, I didn't mean I didn't *want* you to go," Ben says. "I said you *can't* go because you're working on the soap."

She doesn't move out of her fighting stance. She doesn't say anything either.

"Anita?"

"I'm *going* to L.A.," she seethes. "As soon as we have a break in the shooting. I'm flying out. Even for just a couple days."

"Okay, okay." He swallows. "That'll be great."

She sidles up close in front of him. It's a slinky move, but not at all sexy, not at all seductive. Instead, it's threatening. Ben stiffens.

"For *years* now," she says, in a short, brittle voice, "I've been wanting to go to L.A. Even just temporarily. Get my resumé out there again, talk to some agents. But I *didn't*. And do you know *why* I didn't go?"

He doesn't answer, just looks down at her.

"Because *you* weren't ready, Ben—*that's* why. I wanted to wait and do it *together.*" She smiles. A cruel smile. Her eyes glint. "Now *you're* going. You're going and you'll be meeting with producers who wouldn't have given us the time of day before. And you didn't even *check* with me to see what *my* schedule looked like."

"Sweetheart—"

"Don't *sweetheart* me, Ben. Just tell me. Will it be *Spielberg* you'll meet with from DreamWorks? Or Geffen?"

"Honey, I'm sure neither—"

"It *might* be! Xerxes walks around here with a fucking *hard-on* all the time waiting for it!"

Ben tries to place his hands on her shoulders, but she shrugs them away. "Anita," he says, "you know I'll do what I can for you. I'm sure there will be a part—"

She grins. "Oh, there had *better* be a part, Ben. And not just for me. Have you talked with your *brother?*"

Ben sighs.

"He should be in on the meetings, don't you think? He *found* her, Ben. Why not at least *try* collaborating on a screenplay? He's out there already. They're staying at the San Vicente Inn. Do you want the number? Have you even *called* to tell him when you're arriving?"

"I wasn't sure how long he'd be out there."

Anita laughs. "That's bullshit, Ben. Rex is doing a show. Isn't this the show you said you wouldn't miss, no matter where it was?" She stares at him for several seconds. He doesn't meet her gaze. "And what about Flo? What are your plans for *her?* How many pieces of silver will you take for her life?"

"Aw, jeez, Anita—"

"I'll be out there, Ben," she promises. "I'm not sure when, but I'll be out there. You can count on that."

She turns on her heel and storms out, slamming the door behind her. *God,* Ben thinks. *What an overwrought* actress *she can be.*

Richard's walking down the steep incline of San Vicente Boulevard from their guest house to his rental car. The sun is strong overhead, the scent of lilies in the air.

"Yo, Sheehan," comes a voice.

He looks up. Across the street is Detective Lee, getting out of his car, which he's parked illegally.

"Hey," Richard calls. "Wrong side for today. Street cleaning."

Lee dismisses the warning with a wave of his hand. He hurries across the street. He and Richard shake hands.

"You heard about the body then?" Lee asks.

Richard nods. "Just a girl, huh?"

"Pretty young, near as we can tell." He belches a little, covering his mouth. "Sorry. Had a steak-and-pepper sub for lunch. But it was arsenic that killed her."

Richard smiles. "Arsenic, as found in ant paste."

Lee shrugs. "You draw the conclusions."

"That's the problem. I can't yet. But I'm trying."

Lee looks down the street. "She lived near here, right? The Lawrence dame."

"Want me to show you?"

Lee grins. "Lead on, Sherlock."

Richard walks with him the rest of the way down San Vicente, crossing at Santa Monica. The boys are out in full force today, in their Daisy Buchanan cutoffs and sleeveless flannel muscle shirts. A couple of them check out Richard, who's wearing shorts himself—although khakis— and a white-ribbed tank top. He catches a glimpse of himself in the window of A Different Light bookstore. *I look as good as any of these WeHo movie star wannabes,* he tells himself.

He notices one guy in particular looking at him. He realizes who it is too late to duck.

"Richard? Richard *Sheehan?*"

It's Scott—the one boyfriend to ever dump him. The only one Richard had ever wanted to keep, before Rex, and the only one who hadn't wanted him in return.

"You know this guy?" Lee asks as Scott rushes up from the street.

"Yeah, he's an . . . ex," Richard says before Scott bounds at him like a panther, wrapping his arms around him.

"Richard! Oh, my God! What are you doing in L.A.?"

"Visiting—I—"

"Oh, my God, it's *so* good to see you. You look fabulous! Really!"

And, Richard hated to admit, so did Scott. Still blond and chiseled. Still broad shouldered and small waisted. Still . . . so goddamn *perfect.* He's wearing bike shorts and a tight white-ribbed tank, exposing every cut and every definition.

He's completely ignoring Lee, moving up close into Richard's face. "I saw your article. About the old lady movie star." He shudders dramatically. "Oh, Richard, *everybody's* talking about it out here. I mean, she was the *first.* The one who started all this. How exciting it must have been for you." He pauses. "I live here now, you know. I'm acting. Living in New York was holding me back—you know what I mean?"

Richard manages a smile. "Films? Television?"

"Commercials mostly. But I was on *Party of Five*. Played Mitchell Anderson's date. Did you see it?"

"I haven't had much of a chance lately to watch TV."

"I understand, with all the exciting work you're doing." He smiles again. God, what a smile. "Though I told my agent I don't want to only do gay parts. That's how you get typed—you know what I mean?"

"I guess so."

Scott laughs. "So are you here about The Biograph Girl? You know, they just dug her up."

"Yes, I'm here covering the story."

"Well, keep me in mind when they make the movie—and you know they will. Everybody here is *sure* of it." He winks. "You know, it really *is* good to see you again, Richard. I *mean* that. I've thought about you often."

Richard eyes him. "Hey, buddy, *you're* the one—"

"We all make mistakes."

He sounds sincere. Richard looks at him. He's *gorgeous*. Richard can't deny he still finds Scott very, very attractive. He stands there in front of him so perfect—so *available*. And, last Richard knew, HIV negative.

"So what are you doing this week?" Scott asks, moving in even closer. "Maybe we could—"

No. This is not good.

"Scott," Richard says abruptly. "I'm with—" He looks over at Lee, who's backed off and stands looking at his nails while Scott slobbers over Richard.

"*Him*. I'm with *him*," Richard says.

Lee looks up. He looks startled, to say the very least.

"*Him?*" Scott asks.

"Yeah." Richard swallows. "*Yeah*. Scott, this is—this is Philip." Richard reaches over, pulling the sixty-year-old detective closer to them.

"You're with *him?*" Scott asks again, looking back and forth between Lee and Richard.

"Yes," Richard answers. "Philip. Scott. Scott. Philip."

Lee looks up at Richard cagily. He smirks. "Well, that's what they call me, but the girls all call me Phyllis," he says, shaking Scott's hand.

Richard smiles uncomfortably.

"Well," Scott says, pulling back now, "I didn't mean to intrude."

"No. No problem," Richard says. "Good to run into you."

Scott gives a little wave as he moves off down the street. He keeps looking back at Richard and Lee, as if to convince himself. Richard pushes Lee along in the opposite direction.

"And what, may I ask, was *that* about?" the detective snarls.

"Forget it. Sorry to drag you into it. I just needed to get away from him. But thanks."

Lee shrugs. "Don't mention it. Wait'll I tell the wife. She'll get a kick."

"Scott can just be a little—you know, aggressive."

"And your defenses are down."

Richard sighs. "Something like that."

Lee shakes his head. "Don't know how you gay guys do it. Keep on in the face of AIDS. Me, I'd have given up long ago and never hit on another soul."

Richard says nothing.

"It's a terrible thing. Cutting kids down in their prime."

"Well, there are new drugs," Richard says, a little too defensively. "People aren't dying like they were. The virus gets eradicated." He pauses. "Well, it becomes undetectable."

Lee shrugs. "So they say. I just have a hard time believin' in miracle cures." He pauses at the curb. "Westbourne's over here, no?"

Richard looks across the street. "Yeah," he says. "That's Westbourne."

They cross over to a twisting avenue lined with palms. The gardens are lush here, leafy ferns and sharp yuccas, orange birds-of-paradise poking out of the greens with their pointy little faces. The cypress trees are tall and ragged. The houses are small, more like cottages, with red-tiled roofs and white stucco exteriors. It's so unlike New York. The side streets of West Hollywood are leafy and cool and green. Just off the main drag, the world suddenly goes lush with green palms and white cala lilies.

Richard stops halfway down the block past Melrose. "This is it," he says, pointing up at one house. "This was where Florence Lawrence lived."

Lee laughs. "I was going to say, 'And died,' but caught myself." He squints up at the cottage. There's a line of knotted blue cactus dividing the property, and a small garage out back. Yellow roses grow wild over a trellis out front. "Well, *somebody* died here anyway."

Richard stares at the place. He's been here a number of times since coming to L.A. Each time he stands on the cracked sidewalk looking up at the peaceful, tidy little cottage, he gets the same sensation. Sadness. Loneliness. Dreams dying long, drawn-out deaths—despite the pretty roses and thriving ficus trees.

"Here." Lee's handing him a slip of paper. "You asked for 'em. The names of the missing."

Richard takes it. He looks at what's typed there. A list of names. Girls' names.

"Maybe you can help me find out something about them," Lee says. "We've already been able to eliminate several, because their ages didn't match the corpse. These are what's left. Don't go publicizing them yet though. I'm giving it to you only on account I need your help."

"I'll do what I can," Richard promises.

"There's more. I want you to help me get in to talk with the old lady. I understand she'll be out here in a few days for a whole round of TV appearances."

Richard lets out a long sigh. "I didn't know that. Ben doesn't do a very good job of keeping me informed. Detective, I'm not even sure *I'll* be able to get in to see her."

"Do what you can," Lee tells him. "I can't force her to talk yet. But the exhumation raised a whole lot of questions, and we feel she might have some answers."

"I'll give it a shot," Richard promises him. "But I still don't believe Flo did anything wrong."

"And what makes you able to state that so categorically?"

He shrugs. "Call it a reporter's instinct. It's never failed me before."

"Maybe you're right. But the question is: How does she define *wrong?*"

Richard just sighs. They shake hands. Lee heads back up the street. Richard takes one more look at the cottage: the last house Florence Lawrence lived in during her time in Hollywood—the place from which she walked away when that girl's death gave her the chance.

He glances down at the list of names. Six in all.

Ann Kiely. Norma Cooney. Heloise Harker. Jean Ott. Teresa Sabatini. And Margaret Butz.

He folds the list in half and slips it into the back pocket of his shorts.

Spring 1937

I put in the roses. I wonder if they're still there, if they could have survived all these years. Yellow roses, as I recall. Just a few bushes, out in front, to remind me of my old farm in New Jersey, where I had *hundreds* of roses. Molly loved tending to them. Watering, powdering, dead heading them in June so they'd bloom through the summer.

I close my eyes and see it still, that little cottage where we lived. The softly swaying palm trees on the street, the white stucco of the walls. Molly sitting on the picnic table out back, eating a slice of watermelon and spitting the seeds out into the grass. "Hey!" Bob would shout. "You want to grow a watermelon bush?"

How you'd laugh, Molly. And when you swallowed a seed that time, Bob joshed that it might take root in your stomach. You looked over at me with those big innocent eyes of yours with a momentary flush of fear—until my expression reassured you that such a thing was impossible. *Lunacy.* And then you laughed. Laughed and laughed and laughed.

I can still hear you. Like the wind chimes outside my window. Your laughter—tinkling, brittle in the breeze.

"Flo, you are such a card!"

I was dancing a hula. Buzzy with rum and cigarette smoke. What were we celebrating? May Day? Decoration Day? Who remembers? It didn't matter then—it doesn't matter now. It was just one of our parties: Molly and Bob and Marian and Lester and the boys.

And me.

"Oh, Flo," Molly called, "let's make you a grass skirt!"

She and Lester began gathering palm leaves, tying them together with a long twine. It looked crazy, but I tied it around my waist, continuing to hula to the music Bob's friends were strumming on their guitars. A snapping bonfire was blazing and Marian was cutting wedges of pineapple for all of us. The moon was overhead and the sweet smell of marmalade chicken on the grill was in the air.

Yes, we did have some happy times together. There *was* laughter in that little cottage. It wasn't always gloom and misery. There was lightness and gaiety, music and merriment.

I won't let the sorrow crowd out the rest.

And yet . . .

Molly standing over me, her eyes wide and bloodshot.

"Flo, don't cry."

The pain had returned. Lester stood at the foot of the bed, shaking aspirin into his hand. "Take these, Flo," he said, handing the powdery white pills over to Molly, who cupped them to my mouth. She followed with a glass of water, and I swallowed the pills down with a sip.

Oh, how Lester wanted so much to cure me. To find the trick that worked. But I'd come to accept the fact that a cure was impossible for what ailed me. Some people think doctors can put scrambled eggs back into the shell. I knew no doctor held the power to fix me.

"What's wrong with her, Lester?" Molly asked, as if I weren't even in the room. "Yesterday she was dancing around the yard."

He came up beside her to stare down at me. "I don't know," he said. "The pain just comes over her and she can't seem to even get out of bed."

I just watched them. Said nothing.

Lester had become my friend as well as my doctor. There was no one else in his life: no parents, no wife, no children, no nieces or nephews. I suspected that there had never been very many in his life, that he'd never really had friends before. At least not like us. Lester always seemed a little bewildered by Bob and his boys from the sound department, how boisterous they were. He'd blush at their racy jokes, recoil just a little from the language they used. Bob would tease him about girls. "Aw, come on, Les—a big manly hunk o'doc like you? You must have to fight 'em off."

Lester would just smile meekly and that all-encompassing red blush would take over his face and arms. "No, no," he'd protest, as if Bob weren't joshing him. "Really. No girls. I've never had any girls."

"Leave Lester alone," I'd tell Bob. "I'm all the woman he needs."

And he'd beam up at me. I mean, really *beam*. Lester was *devoted* to me. The way Harry had been—no, more the way Ducks had been. He wanted so much to make me happy—to make me well.

"Will you stay with her?" Lester asked Molly, snapping his black medical bag shut.

"Of course," she said, sitting down on the edge of the bed and look-ing into my eyes. "I'll never leave her."

"Good." He smiled sadly down at me. "I'll be back tomorrow, Flo."

I didn't respond.

He let himself out through the kitchen. Molly took my hands in hers. "How do you feel now, Flo?"

I just closed my eyes.

"Give the pills time," Molly said. "Lester is certain they'll help." She looked down at me. "He's in love with you, Flo," she said.

I just turned my face on the pillow.

"Really," she continued. "I think he is. The way he's always coming by. Always so concerned about your health." She lifted a damp com-press from the side table and replaced it across my forehead. I opened my eyes to look up into her face. She smiled.

"Molly," I managed to say.

"What is it, Flo?"

"You don't need to sit here with me," I said hoarsely.

"I told you. I'm not leaving. Not until you feel better."

She took my hand. What a sweet child. Even after my cruelty to her, she'd come back. She came back and told me she'd never leave again. And she didn't. No matter that I was sometimes cross or often sad or frequently sick. Molly never left again. She stayed right there, right by my side, making me laugh, urging me to dance, pressing cold cloths on my head.

Movie Mirror came out a few days later, after I'd managed to get back on my feet. I think Bob had brought it over while I was sick to give me something to read. I remember the issue so distinctly. A picture of Bette Davis was on the cover.

"Look, Flo," Molly said. "Here's a photo of *you* inside."

"Me?"

I looked up from the stove, where I was stirring a pot of beans. I low-ered the blue flame and wiped my hands on my apron, going around the table to peer at the magazine over Molly's shoulder. Lester was sitting to her right. I was making both of them dinner to thank them for their care.

"Yes, it's you. See there?"

I did see. Me, from twenty years earlier. And there, next to mine, was a picture of Flossie Turner, also from the old days. Below the photos was a headline:

UNWEPT AND UNHONORED

"Let me see that," I said.

Molly handed the magazine up to me.

"Is it a good story?" Lester asked.

I read it in silence.

"Well?" Lester asked again.

I tossed the magazine down on the table. "I've never taken charity," is all I said. I went back to stirring the beans.

Molly picked up the magazine and began to read out loud.

"'Included among the nearly 500 bit players and extras in MGM's *The Great Ziegfeld* are two pioneering movie queens, Florence Lawrence and Florence Turner. So unimportant to the story are the characters they enact that the two are denied any billing.'"

She stopped reading and looked over at me. "Extras are *too* important," she said, all pouty. "We give a film its veri—veris—"

"Verisimilitude," I finished for her, the heat rising from the stove to my face. That's the line the studio gave us.

"Yeah, we make pictures *real*," Molly said.

"Molly," Lester said gently, "put the article down."

"No, go on," I told her. "Read the rest of it. Read every last *bit* of it."

Lester sighed. Molly picked up the magazine, searched for her place, and resumed her recitation.

"'Neither do you find the names of Florence Lawrence or Florence Turner in the press sheet thoughtfully prepared and provided by the MGM publicity department—although ample attention is paid to "Hollywood's shapeliest atmospheric players," the young girls recruited for the chorus.

"'What must have Miss Lawrence and Miss Turner been thinking as they found themselves relegated to the nameless "potter's field," while the publicity staff's manpower concentrated upon the "shapeliest eleven"—whose assorted blondes, brunettes, and redheads were as yet unborn when our two Florences were queens of the box office?

"'Once great stars. Today, extra women accepting charity in exchange for character roles. Theirs is the tragedy of Hollywood.'"

Molly put down the magazine. Lester gave her a look.

I served the beans. Molly put one forkful to her mouth and then began to cry. Just sat there in her place and cried loudly, like a baby in a high chair, clutching her fork still in the air. I finally reached over and took the fork from her hand, setting it down on her plate. I found the napkin on her lap and held it to her nose. She was beginning to slobber.

"Go on," I said. "Go to your room."

She pushed herself away from the table and ran across the kitchen to her little room. Lester and I could hear her muffled sobs into her pillow.

"The most important thing in this business is apparently growing old gracefully," I said, holding up the magazine and looking at the fresh, un-lined face of Bette Davis. "You can't do that on the cover of a fan magazine."

"Flo, don't let such things wear you down," Lester said. "You were the greatest of them all. The very first. All the rest live in your shadow."

"Molly didn't read everything," I said, avoiding his words. "They quoted Pickford. She was the first to take my place, you know."

"She never had what you had," Lester insisted.

"Listen. She tells the reporter, 'I made up my mind to step into the wings while the audience was still applauding.'" I put down the magazine. "Now she lives in splendor at Pickfair, Hollywood's royal dowager." I looked around my tiny cottage. "And we're here eating beans."

Oh, I wasn't feeling sorry for myself. I really wasn't. Whenever the pain didn't have me by the throat, I counted my blessings. Who I felt sorry for was Molly, whose sobs we had to listen to all through dinner.

"I suppose she thinks it could be her," Lester said as we cleared away our plates.

I didn't respond. How many years had Molly been in Hollywood by now? Two? Almost three? She hadn't yet landed a single speaking part in a film. The one she thought she had landed ended up on the cutting room floor, as so many of them do. I suppose she *did* see herself in my situation, twenty, thirty years from now. But the difference was, I had tasted it. I had been there. I had been on the cover of those damn fan magazines. She never had.

And never would.

That night I sat up with *her* for a change. She lay in her bed unable to sleep, plagued by fits of tears.

I was telling her about my marriages. I'm not sure how we'd gotten onto the subject, but my tales seemed to distract her from her crying jags.

"When I discovered Charles with that woman," I explained, "I had two choices: I could close my eyes to it, or I could kick him out."

"So you kicked him out," she said.

"No. I closed my eyes for as long as I could." I laughed. "I kept them *squeezed* shut, in fact—so tight that I barely saw the sun rise and set." I took her cold, soft, tiny hands in my own. "You see, I was Florence *Woodring*. At least, being *her*, I didn't have to face who I'd be otherwise."

"I don't understand," she said softly.

I sighed. "It was the same later, when I married Bolton. Oh, boy, what was I thinking *then*? If I'd thought *Charles* was a mistake, Bolton exceeded all my worst expectations."

"Why did you marry him?"

"Who knows? Maybe it was just my ego. Someone wanted me again. Charles had finally left me—I didn't leave him. He left me because the other woman wasn't content. *She* wanted to be Mrs. Woodring. So what could I do? I divorced him and found somebody else. *Bolton*." I spit the name as if there were fuzz on my tongue.

"Who was he?" Molly asked.

"Nobody. An unemployed actor. So he said. A boy. A spoiled little boy. I never really knew him. It was all over so quickly."

"He hit you, too," Molly said. "That's what you've said."

I nodded. "Right from the start. We rushed out to Arizona, so we wouldn't have to wait. Got hitched up by a justice of the peace in the middle of the night. Oh, we were *tempestuous*. That's the word. I was so happy, so thrilled that a man was paying me attention again, after Charles's betrayal. Bolton was young, handsome. Younger than me anyway and handsome by my standards, which had fallen pretty low by then."

I laughed at myself. Molly reached over and took my hand.

"And that night, our wedding night, in our hotel, he slapped me so hard my teeth cut my cheek. There was blood all over the wall. I wasn't very happy performing my conjugal duty after that, as you can well imagine. I tried to run off. But he wouldn't let me."

Molly's hands tightened their grip on mine. "You mean—he raped you?"

"If you believe husbands can be rapists, as I do." I smiled down at her. "I thought that it would be better when we got back to Los Angeles, that I could just settle into being Mrs. Henry Bolton. *Anything* not to be Florence Lawrence again. But it went on that same way for a month and a half, and finally I ran away, filed for divorce. Three months it lasted, from start to finish."

"Oh, Flo."

I shrugged. "There was nothing left for me to do but petition the court to go back to my maiden name." I looked off toward the window, where a full moon seemed to fill the sky. "Which, on the record, at least, was Lawrence. Once more, I had to go back to being Florence Lawrence. It was the only way to survive." I paused. "And I've been her ever since."

"That's when Mr. Mayer hired you?"

I nodded. "Florence Lawrence wasn't worth much by then, but I found I could still trade on her name with people like Mr. Mayer, who had long memories and enough guilt."

Molly sat up, her own pain forgotten for the moment. "But what about *Harry*, Flo? Wasn't *Harry* good to you?"

"That's enough talk for tonight, missy." I ran my hand over her brow. "Try to sleep. Just remember: Margaret Butz can be whoever she wants to be. Don't wait until it's too late, when you can't go back."

I kissed her gently on the lips. She reached up with her frail little arms to encircle my neck. I held her for a second, then let her go.

They wonder if I could really have taken that poison. If I could really have gone that far, been that depressed, that miserable, and tried to take my own life.

Of *course* I could have. It's actually quite easy to imagine. I thought about it often. Pills, bullets, gas. Whatever might work. Hadn't my father killed himself? Maybe it ran in the family.

The thought was a constant presence in those months, when the pain would suddenly arrive in the middle of the night, like a drunken husband, angry and insistent on having his way. I had no way of fighting it off. It would simply pin me down, its hot horrible breath on my cheeks, its wet, burning tongue slithering down my neck, between my breasts. I was helpless before it. Death seemed a sweet alternative.

Florence Bridgewood, in her short time on earth, had never known such pain. But I had none of her resources, none of her means. She wasn't even someone I *remembered* anymore. So I just lay there in my bed, letting the pain have its way with me.

"Sometimes I think about taking a gun to my head," I admitted to Marian, my dotty old neighbor.

Her old face had lifted in animated shock. She was the daughter of Baptists, after all. Such things were sinful even to speak of—even if she secretly delighted in hearing about them.

"Florence!" she scolded me. "How *can* you say such things? Suicides are the same as murderers—left to dwell among the unsaved."

She sounded like my grandmother. Looked a little like her, too, with her knotted white hair and burlap skin. Marian was a dear old lady, one who could knock back her gin with as much ease as Bob and his young bucks, but who, to all outside appearances, was a very prim and proper old maid.

"Oh, come now, Marian," I chided. "When you've seen as much death as I have, staring you in the face, none of it seems so shocking anymore."

"You sound like a cold-blooded killer," she snapped. "I won't hear any more of this. You're just down in the dumps—that's all."

It was Sunday morning. Marian and I sat at my kitchen table sipping coffee. The birds were busy chattering in the ficus trees. I'd spent a fitful night, tossing and writhing, the headaches taunting me, one moment wracking my body with pain, the next disappearing into the darkness.

There was a knock. I spied Lester through the checkered curtains on the door.

Marian gave me a sly wink. "Your *beau*," she whispered.

"Please, Marian," I said. "Lester's my doctor."

"Who's always making house calls."

I frowned at her, then stood, with some sharp difficulty, to answer the door.

"Hello, Lester," I said.

In his hands, he held a glass-covered plate with a chocolate cake inside. "I can't stay," he said. "I'm on my way to church. But I wanted to check in with you and Molly."

"She's still sleeping," I told him. "But the headaches kept me up most of the night."

He just shook his head sadly. Poor Lester. How badly he wanted to rescue me, to find a way out of the maze for me. But all he could do was stand there in front of me, impotently, shaking his head back and forth.

"Here, take this," he said. "I thought maybe it would cheer you up. I bought it at the church bake sale."

I smiled, accepting the cake. How kind he was.

"Helloooo, Lester," Marian sang, waving her hand from the table.

"Good morning, Marian," he said in reply.

I looked down at the dish. I could see through the glass how carefully the baker had swirled the frosting. I reached up and kissed Lester on his pink cheek. He blushed, of course.

"You're still my heroine, Flo," he said huskily.

His heroine. In his eyes, I wasn't a pathetic old woman eking out a life in pictures, drinking and smoking too much, plagued by suspicious headaches and spells of weariness. No, I was still The Biograph Girl, whom he loved most in the world—even more than Jesus, he'd written all those years ago.

"Take care of yourself now, Flo," he told me. "And Molly, too. I'll be back tomorrow to check on the both of you."

"Thank you, Lester." I smiled up at him. "And thanks for the cake."

"Good-bye, Marian," he called.

"Toodle-loo, Lester." She waved her handkerchief after him.

She was standing behind me now. I felt as if I might cry, watching him walk back down past the dewy roses and gnarled cacti to his car. I turned and handed the cake to Marian. "Put this on the table, will you?" I asked.

She took it. I watched her—and it was good that I did, because she misjudged the distance of the table and almost dropped the cake on the floor.

"Marian!" I shouted, and despite my pain, I lunged over in time to catch the cake and set it safely on the table myself. "My goodness, Marian. When will you get your eyes checked? You need glasses! You're practically *blind!* I keep telling you."

She lifted her old chin haughtily. She'd never admit to being near-sighted. Dear, vain old thing. Sometimes, in the yard, she'd call over, "Yoo-hoo, Molly!" when it would be me hanging out the clothes. *Me.*

And it wasn't easy to mistake *me* for Molly.

Another bad night. At five A.M. I rose. Somehow the nights were the worse, and I often cut them as short as I could.

Even in the hazy light of dawn, I could see Molly had been up during the night. The top of Lester's cake dish had been removed and still sat at the far side of the table. I could see a slice had been cut, crumbs trailing across the table to an empty plate. I smiled to myself. *She must be feeling better if she was eating cake in the middle of the night.*

I sat down at the table myself. Outside the sun was rising higher in the sky. The light behind the drawn shades was growing stronger.

Cake for breakfast? *Oh, why not, Flo?* I told myself. *Live a little.*

I found the knife Molly had left on the table and cut into the cake.

I can still remember how perfect it was. How rich, like devil's food is supposed to be. *Sinful.* I sliced just a small wedge, and I rested it in my hand before transferring it onto Molly's crumb-strewn plate. I decided to go full speed ahead—dispense with a fork, eat it with my hands.

I broke off a hunk and brought it to my mouth. So delicious. So rich, so fudgy—

But something else.

Crunchy—on my tongue—

I looked down at the table.

The crumbs littered there were *moving*.

I snapped up the shade behind me. The sun streamed in. The shade rattled around and around, sending a terrible noise and shudder throughout the room.

Ants.

The cake—the table—my hands—were covered with *ants*.

I spit what was left in my mouth back onto the plate, standing up frantically, knocking over the chair.

"Oh! Oh! Dear God!"

Ants. Everywhere. Big, fat, round-bellied black ants. Crawling out of the cake, down the legs of the table, across the floor.

I screamed. My fingers were in my mouth, madly scraping at my tongue. I screamed again and again until Molly finally came running out of her room and threw her arms around me. We both collapsed to the floor and cried there together until there was no more air left in our lungs to cry.

The Present

Oprah Winfrey stands in front of her studio audience with her arms spread wide. "Today, more and more people are living to be 100 or older," she says. "In fact, they are the fastest-growing segment of the U.S. population. Today, there are 61,000 people past the century mark—imagine that. *61,000*. And by 2020, that number will more than *triple*."

The camera pans the audience. Mostly women in their thirties and forties, a good mix of white and black.

"The very concept of 'old' is being redefined," the talk show hostess continues. "Listen to what one geriatrician from Boston's Beth Israel Hospital says: 'Eighty-five is nothing. Eighty-five is young. Eighty-five is fifteen years away from 100.'"

She laughs. So does her audience. "Living to 100 is no longer a quirk of nature," she says. "But rather, it is a possibility to strive for. A *goal*. Obviously, the rate of disability is high among this segment of the population, but even that is changing. In talking about increasing the average life span, doctors aren't looking to simply prolong dependency. They're talking about people living full, active, rich lives to age 100—and beyond.

"Today we are honored to have with us a number of centenarians, all of whom are *thriving*—enjoying life and continuing to contribute to society. We are pleased to be joining forces with a nationwide campaign led by the National Institutes of Health, designed to encourage healthy lifestyles and push the average life expectancy higher in the twenty-first century.

"And to help us kick off the 'Dare to be 100' campaign, I am thrilled to have with us perhaps the nation's most famous centenarian—the first star of them all, The Biograph Girl—Miss Florence Lawrence!"

The audience cheers. The theme music swells. The camera pulls in for a closer shot of Oprah. Seated now beside her is Flo. Her entrance wasn't shown on camera; her walk today was deemed a bit too shaky by the producers. The cheers rise in volume as Flo acknowledges the audience with a little wave of her hand.

"Her lipstick is too subtle," Richard says. "What's wrong with scarlet?"

Rex brings him a bagel with cream cheese and they settle down on the floor in front of the TV in their hotel room. "And that wig," he grimaces. "She looks like a cross between Jennifer Aniston and Margot Kidder in the Superman movies."

"Yeah," Richard agrees. "What's wrong with her *real* hair?"

"She looks tired," Rex says. "Poor Flo."

Richard just nods.

"Dare to be 107!" Oprah is saying as a stagehand wheels out an enormous birthday cake, one hundred and seven candles flickering.

The audience sings "Happy Birthday" to Flo. She laughs. "Careful you don't burn the damn place down," she quips.

But there's no suggestion that she attempt to blow out the candles.

"Flo, you beat the odds, girl," Oprah's telling her after they've settled down. "Because according to statistics, a newborn girl born at the turn of the century in the United States or Canada had a life expectancy of 51 years. So you *rule.*"

Flo seems unsure how to respond. Her eyes seem a little bloodshot. Gone is the witty banter she'd displayed on *Rosie.*

"Well, I think it's just about perseverance," she finally says, and Richard suspects she's trying to remember what Ben—or the "Dare to be 100" people—have been coaching her to say. "I can't say I always ate the best foods, but I always preferred the outdoors and I got a lot of exercise."

"What's Ben *doing* to her?" Richard asks, more to himself than to Rex.

"You're amazing," Oprah's gushing. "*Really.* At 107, you're traveling the country, making a documentary on your life, being interviewed everywhere, and I understand preparing a return to acting in John Waters's new film."

Flo shrugs. "Well, if someone was crazy enough to offer me a quarter of a million dollars to make a picture, I certainly wasn't crazy enough to turn 'em down."

The audience hoots, claps.

"*There* she is," Rex says. "There's a flash of the Flo we love."

"You realize you're an inspiration," Oprah tells her. "I mean, the image the world always had of older actresses was Norma Desmond or Baby Jane Hudson. You've changed that stereotype, Flo. Hopefully forever."

Flo just smiles. Richard waits for a sassy retort but it doesn't come.

Oprah cuts to a commercial. The camera fades out on Flo's face; Richard thinks she looks a little slumped over in her chair.

"Flo's got a hump on *her* back, too," Rex says, winking at Richard as he picks up their plates, careful not to spill bagel crumbs on the floor.

"Yeah, but you never knew it on *Rosie*," Richard muses. "They're wearing her out. They've got her doing too much. *The Today Show.* Yesterday *Regis and Kathie Lee*. Today *Oprah*."

"And tomorrow *Good Morning, America*," Rex tells him.

"They're taking some pretty big risks," Richard says as the show returns after the commercial break. "One of these days, someone's gonna ask Flo a question she doesn't want to answer."

Now Oprah's introducing six other guests who've passed the 100 mark. Two men, four women. Both men are black, and among the women two are white, one is black, and one is Asian. All are dressed in their Sunday best, the men's ties loosely knotted at their flabby throats, the women wearing corsages.

One of the two men still plays the church organ. He gives a demonstration, but plays only a few chords before he seems to get confused. The black woman still quilts, and a stagehand displays her handiwork to the oohs and ahhs of the crowd. One of the white ladies claims to have been a Ziegfeld dancer and performs a little soft shoe.

But they speak in halting phrases and seem unable to hear or fully understand Oprah's questions.

"They're *nothing* like Flo," Richard tells the TV, "and she's the oldest of the bunch."

"Okay. Easy, sweetheart," Rex cautions.

When the camera pans the group, Flo has joined the ranks of her fellow centenarians. She sits there seemingly as lifeless as the rest of them, not looking at the camera, hands in her lap. It's hard to distinguish her at first glance.

Richard shivers. He stands up, snaps off the TV.

Rex stays sitting on the floor. "Excuse me," he says, "but I was watching that."

"So go ahead and watch it. I'm going out to the gym anyway."

"Richard," Rex begins, then stops. "No, forget it. I'm not going to get into it with you. Been there before, and it does no good."

"Fine. Good idea." Richard ties on his sneakers.

Rex sighs. "I thought you were going to call Ben," he says anyway. "You wanted to try to talk with Flo."

Richard glares at him. "I *tried*. But he hasn't returned my calls. I called Anita back in New York and she hasn't heard from him since he got out here either."

Rex sighs again.

"It's *Sister Jean* who I don't understand," Richard says. "How Ben's managed to hoodwink her. I thought she was sharper than that. He's exploiting Flo in the very ways she was against."

"And you aren't?"

Richard's eyes bug out at his partner. "Me?"

"Richard, I just worry that you're getting into this without thinking through all the implications, for you, for Flo."

"I have nothing to do with it anymore," Richard insists. "Ben's calling the shots."

"You're still investigating. You have offers."

"And so I should stop? Just give up? Let *Ben* have it?"

Rex runs his hand down in front of his face. "That's what this is about," he says quietly.

Richard's steaming. "Can we just drop it?"

"Fine."

"Thank you." Richard stands and looks at himself in the mirror. At the gym yesterday, he ran into Scott again. They said hello, exchanged a few pleasantries, then cruised each other from across the pec deck for the rest of the hour.

It's crazy, Richard tells himself. *I don't know why this guy is in my head. I love Rex. I want to spend the rest of my life with him.*

Maybe that was it. Maybe it's that rest-of-life thing riling Richard up, because how much of life was really left? Ever since he'd spied that lump on Rex's back, ever since the efficacy of the drugs was called into question, Richard has found himself short with Rex. Resentful. Like now, finding himself instantly annoyed by Rex's mother-hen scolding. Richard wonders if he's somehow angry way deep down—or maybe not so deep—with Rex, angry that there's still the chance he might get sick again when Richard had thought that fear was gone for good.

Or maybe it's simply that Scott looks so good in his gym shorts, he says to himself.

Rex stands and stretches, and immediately Richard feels guilty. "Nooker," he says. "I'm sorry."

"For what?" Rex smiles. "By the way, I forgot to show you something I bought."

"What?"

Rex walks around the bed and unfolds a plastic bag sitting there. From inside he withdraws a small paperback book. "Did you see this?" he asks, handing the book to Richard, who takes one look and groans.

The title on the cheap, glossy cardboard cover reads:

RISEN FROM THE DEAD:
THE STRANGE LIFE OF FLORENCE LAWRENCE,
THE FIRST MOVIE STAR

Two photos of Flo stare up at him, divided by a zigzag line. One photo dates from the Biograph days, with an angelic glow hovering around Flo's head; the other is the startled look caught by the trespassing photographer from the *National Exposé*.

"Some fleabag publishing house," Rex tells him. "This leach of an author concludes Flo *could* have killed the girl they found in the grave to cover up her own botched suicide attempt."

Richard just stares down at the cover. In his head, his *own* book is still taking shape. What title would *he* use? What questions would *he* pose? What conclusions would *he* draw?

And how different would he be from the leach who wrote this bullshit?

"I'm going to the gym," he tells Rex. "I'll be back in a while."

"Sweetheart," Rex says.

Richard looks back at him.

"My point before was I think you need to try Ben again. I think we need to check in with Flo."

The flight attendant wheeling Flo onto the plane had seen her on *Oprah*. He's quite awestruck.

"My grandma is ninety-seven," he tells Flo in a heavy Southern accent. "And because of you, she's been inspired to take a ceramics class at her church."

Flo manages a small smile. "How nice for her."

Ben picks up on Flo's sarcasm, but says nothing, just lets the young man bask in his good feeling.

But once they're all settled into their first-class seats, Flo sniffs, "*Ceramics?* I *hated* ceramics when they'd try to lure me into it at St. Mary's. All they do is paint funny little figures. If I'm going to make a vase, for God's sake, I want my *hands* in the damn clay. I want to fire up the kiln."

"Now, now, Flo," Jean gently reprimands her, a small smile playing with her lips. "Not everyone is as vital as you are."

"*None* of them were. They gave me the chills, those old codgers on *Oprah*. Did you see that woman try to soft shoe? They'd have pelted her with tomatoes if she'd done that on stage. They'd have brought out the *hook!* Ziegfeld Girl, hah!"

"Flo, give her a break—she's 103," Ben reminds her. He's seated across the aisle from her.

"A chick," Flo snaps.

"Look, Flo. *You're* the exception here," Xerxes tells her, turning around in his seat in front of her. "Those other old folks on *Oprah* are what most folks your age are like." He gestures to the flight attendant. "A gin and tonic," he whispers, then turns back to Flo. "That's why we've got doctors calling you a medical phenomenon. That's why the 'Dare to be 100' campaign is paying us *big bucks* for you to endorse it."

"It's a good campaign," Jean says, seemingly trying to convince herself—yet again—about the wisdom of doing it. "Isn't it, Carla?"

The attorney is seated in front with Xerxes. "It is, so long as we're all comfortable pretending Flo doesn't smoke."

Carla smiles over her shoulder. Her eyes catch Ben's. He thinks maybe they sparkle, and he tries to lock on to them, but she's quickly back to looking down at her lap and reading the contracts Xerxes has drawn up. *Damn her,* Ben thinks. *Frigid, that's what she is. Never anything in her eyes when I look at her.* He notices she's kicked off her black pumps. God, he'd love to massage her silk stockinged feet. . . .

"What's good," she says, not looking up, "is that St. Mary's will benefit."

That was their deal. The bulk of the money from the "Dare to be 100" campaign goes to a new physical therapy wing at St. Mary's—minus a commission for Xerxes, of course, since he did manage to land the deal.

"Flo's involvement is a good thing," Ben says, transferring his gaze from Carla's feet to Sister Jean. She gives him a look of gratitude for the affirmation, her eyes clear and honest and lively. He relaxes looking into them and smiles at her reflexively. How different were Jean's eyes from Carla's icy mirrors.

"Yes, it's a good thing for Flo to do," Jean is saying, convincing herself. "I just need to make sure she doesn't get tired out. She wasn't really herself on *Oprah.*"

"Oh, she was marvelous," Ben assures her. He's still scared Jean will try to put the brakes on the whole enterprise. The campaign means more appearances for Flo, more work—but also terrific publicity. She'll be a household name by the time he's ready with the film.

"Well, if you want my opinion," Flo interjects, "I'm not too crazy about the no smoking in public part." She looks up at the flight attendant handing Xerxes his drink. "I can smoke during the flight though?"

"I'm sorry, Miss Lawrence," the flight attendant tells her. "All domestic air travel is now smoke free."

Flo sighs. "Just like me, I guess. This campaign wants me to say that I owe my long years to good nutrition, exercise, and an avoidance of alcohol. Hoo boy."

Jean shakes her head. "I don't like lying any more than you do, Flo, but it's a good message. You've lived as long as you have *despite* your bad habits, not because of them."

"You sure of that, Jeannie?" Flo asks, just as the flight attendants commence their safety instructions.

Jean smirks. "With you, Flo, I'm never sure of anything."

The last time Flo had been on an airplane—or aeroplane, as she persists in calling it—had been in 1954. She's quite struck by the changes in air travel in the ensuing four decades. "It's so *enormous,*" Flo says to Jean as they take off down the runway. "How can it *possibly* stay in the air?"

Jean makes a little Sign of the Cross.

"I remember reading about Kitty Hawk," Flo tells her. "Ducks was fascinated that they could actually get that contraption to fly. I remember my brother Norman had little model airplanes at my grandmother's house in Buffalo." She peers out the window into the bright blue sky above the clouds as the plane reaches its cruising altitude. "Who'd have thought I'd ever see *this?*"

Jean watches her. *Am I doing the right thing, agreeing to this trip to California?* Oh, there was no question that Flo was excited about it, but all the questions people are asking disturbs Jean. That, and how weary Flo seems. Yesterday she complained of a mild headache. Flo *never* had headaches.

And the *look* Xerxes had found for her. Those horrible modern wigs and all that powder. The overblown Versace dresses and Todd Oldham suits. The jewels that made her look like some dowdy grand duchess of a Benelux country.

"Did you mail in those passport forms, Sister?" Xerxes asks, turning around again as he snaps his fingers at the attendant for a refill of his drink. "The Altman film will be shooting in London."

"Yes," Jean tells him. "I mailed them yesterday."

Flo had seemed excited about the prospect of going back to Europe. "They used to call me a globe-trotter in the press," she'd said.

Carla reaches over the seat to hand Jean the contracts. "These look all right," she says. "You and Flo look them over and see if you have any questions."

Jean nods. But Flo's asleep already. She sleeps almost the entire flight, and Jean gazes over at her, worried that it's already too much.

As the plane begins its descent into LAX, Flo wakes, and Jean points out the byzantine highways of the city below. "My *God*," Flo says. "Where are all the orange groves? How can there possibly be so many *cars?*"

They're staying at Xerxes's house in Malibu, on Carbon Beach. Xerxes bragged that it was called "Deal Beach" because so many deals are made by show biz execs at their weekend homes here. "Katzenberg's just down the street from me," Xerxes bragged, furthering Jean's dislike of him. "Geffen's been over for barbeques. Aaron Spelling and I walk our dogs together."

A limo meets them at the airport and whisks them off to the beach house. Jean feels a little overwhelmed and *very* out of place.

Ben smiles over at her. "Not bad for a coupla kids from Putnam and Chicopee, huh?" he asks.

So he feels it, too. The displacement. She laughs, takes his arm.

She was very grateful for Ben. He remained as steady, as unspoiled, as grounded as he was that day at St. Mary's when he'd first asked her to trust him. Without him, Jean doesn't think she could get through all this—this—Hollywood glitz.

Xerxes's "weekend house" is three levels, made of brick and spun glass. Huge windows look out over the beach. There are rooms for each of them and private terraces. There's a housekeeper, a middle-aged Mexican woman named Graciela. Below, the coast highway threads along the rocky cliffs. From anywhere in the house, one can hear the waves crashing up on shore.

Flo stands on the deck, looking down.

"I passed this way," she says softly.

"What's that?" Jean asks her, not sure she heard her correctly.

"I passed this way. When I left."

Jean places her hand on Flo's shoulder. "You mean, when you walked away from the hospital?"

Flo nods. "I walked along the coast road. None of this was here then—except the surf and the sand."

Jean smiles warmly, then leaves Flo to her reveries. If what she told them is any indication, the last time Flo passed this way she was forgotten, destitute, and hungry, eating out of trash cans and drinking from garden hoses. Now here she was, ensconced in the lap of Hollywood luxury, very much alive again, as big a star as she ever was.

How life sometimes twists so ironically back on itself.

The next day begins a flurry of activity. Ben's got his videocam on his shoulder as the limo takes Flo to various Hollywood landmarks—or what's left of them. "Just talk to me," he instructs as Jean helps Flo out of the car and escorts her across the old MGM lot. "Just say what you feel, what you remember when you see the old soundstages."

There's not much of them left to see. Ted Turner, who'd bought MGM/UA, had sold what remained of the old Culver City lot to Lorimar, which in turn was bought by Warner Brothers, which eventually was swallowed up by Time, Inc. Now Columbia—owned by Sony—was in control of what remained of the old soundstages.

Flo can't even find her way around and seems a little dazed. She makes no pithy remarks, reacts with none of the pathos Ben was hoping for.

Next he takes her down Hollywood Boulevard and shoots some tape of her talking about the stars' footprints outside the Chinese theater. He's asked Xerxes to explore the possibility of getting Flo's feet so immortalized. It would make for great publicity. At the very least, she should get a star on the Walk of Fame.

Finally, she stops. She looks up at the Hollywood sign, then back into Ben's camera.

"It used to say Hollywoodland," she tells him. "Peg Entwistle jumped off the thirteenth letter."

Ben keeps his camera rolling.

"You know, I can't help but think about Egypt and the pyramids," she says.

"Yes?" Ben asks. "Go on."

"Hollywood is like that. Our pyramids are crumbling, and they'll just keep crumbling until the wind blows the last prop across the freeway."

"Brilliant, Flo!" Ben exclaims. At last, some good footage. "Brilliant!"

He's noticed how tired she's been getting, how easily she seems to fade. But there are still moments where she shines through.

He instructs the limo driver to drive past Flo's old home on Westbourne Drive. Flo looks up at the little cottage through the tinted window, then looks away.

"That's all right," she tells Ben. "I don't need to get outside."

They travel back to Malibu in silence. Finally Flo says very quietly, "They're still there."

"What is, Flo?" Ben asks.

"My roses."

Despite his urge to turn on his camera, Ben respects the silence.

The next day Flo attends the dedication of a statue to herself at the Universal Studios theme park at Universal City. "We are pleased to welcome Universal's very first star back to the lot," says Charlton Heston, who was tapped to do the honors. A cord is pulled, and a bronze statue of Flo is revealed. She looks sweet and demure in her 1910–era clothing, her long curls cascading around her shoulders. At the base is the legend:

FLORENCE LAWRENCE, THE FIRST UNIVERSAL STAR

"Thank you very much," she says haltingly into the microphone. "I accept this honor not only on behalf of myself, but also for my husband, Harry Solter, who got me the position with Mr. Laemmle at the original Universal studio, way back when it was just a little IMP."

Afterward, she's too tired to do anything else but go back to Malibu and sleep.

"I freely admit to being a hypochondriac," the Hollywood producer is saying. "Even as a kid, I'd eat my M&Ms one at a time with a glass of water."

His name is Sam Glick, and he's a development exec at Universal/ MCA. He's sitting at his desk, unscrewing a jar of vitamins and shaking several into his wide pink palm. He reminds Ben of Sidney Greenstreet in *The Maltese Falcon*. He's a big man—not fat, but *big*, like those elephants in *Fantasia*. Wide, but somehow graceful, too.

He's *comfortable* in his bigness, Ben thinks. That's what sets him apart from other big men. He's comfortable with being big in a small world.

Now Glick is raising his hand, the vitamins still aloft in his palm. He pops them into his mouth in one swift move, washing them down with a swig from a can of Diet Coke, pinky upraised.

"I'm constantly complaining about headaches or ingrown toenails or some such thing," he says. "So don't take it personally when I tell you that after reading your script, Mr. Sheehan, I felt as if I needed some Pepto-Bismol."

Ben swallows uncomfortably. Xerxes lets out a rollicking laugh, slapping his leg.

"You crack me up, Sammy," he says. "Always have. Remember that time at Bruce and Demi's? You had me nearly peeing in the punch. Isn't he wild, Benny? I told you he was a card."

Ben smiles awkwardly.

Glick replaces the vitamins in his top drawer. He has Ben's script sitting in front of him. It's not much more than a treatment really, but Ben has put a lot of work into it, typing it up on his laptop in the wee hours of the morning after Jean and Flo are asleep. As each new tale has spilled from Flo's lips, Ben has incorporated it into the script.

A number of studios, watching Flo's fame skyrocket, had expressed interest to Xerxes in a biopic. All have wanted *dramatic* treatments, not documentaries, so Ben has increasingly focused on the former at the expense of his original idea.

The most enthusiastic, according to Xerxes, was Glick—although today you'd never know it. All he's done since they've arrived at his office is fret about the flu, which he's convinced he's getting. He barely acknowledged Ben when he came in, despite the fact that Ben went to a lot of trouble to make a good appearance.

Oh, if only Mom and Anita and Richard could see him now. His hair's buzzed close, like Richard's. He's wearing an unlined waist-length black leather jacket, a black shirt, and black jeans. Xerxes said it was the look of a cool, collected, *confident* indie filmmaker.

But Glick barely notices. He and Xerxes exchange some industry gossip—something about a pair of twentysomething wunderkinds named Affleck and Damon who've apparently written some hotshot screenplay that's set to take the industry by storm. Ben hates them already. *I always wanted to be a wunderkind,* he tells himself. *Now, even if I achieve my goal of getting a film by the time I'm forty, I'll still never have been a boy wonder.*

"Anyway, I liked it," Glick says. "I liked it very much."

It takes a moment for Ben to realize Glick is talking to him about his treatment. He blinks a few times at the producer. He can't seem to process the words. *I liked it. I liked it very much.*

"But I thought—the Pepto-Bismol—"

Glick makes a face. "Anything I read sends me to the Pepto-Bismol. I drink it like Coke." He produces a jar of the bright pink stuff from his desk as evidence, shaking it a few times. "If I *hadn't* reached for it, that would've been a problem. No, I liked it. I liked it very much."

How many years? How many years has it been since *One Chance,*

One World, since someone's spoken words like these to him? *I liked it. I liked it very much.*

Ben is suddenly ensnared by a net of disbelief, feeling all at once like a tremendous fraud, sitting there in front of this big-time Hollywood producer, in his big-time Hollywood studio office. He shifts uncomfortably in his chair.

"I *told* you it was good," Xerxes says to Glick, filling up the space of Ben's silence.

Ben forces a grin. He can't let them see his incredulity.

"Of course," Glick says, leaning back in his chair now, "it's still speculation. She hasn't confirmed the part about the murder."

"Oh, but we feel confident she had a hand in it," Xerxes says, sitting forward. "Whether *she* did it or someone else, I'm not sure. But there's definitely a connection. That girl's death is going to make the story of Florence Lawrence even more explosive."

Ben tries to speak, but finds the words are sticking. As if he doesn't want to say them.

But if he wants this deal, he tells himself, he had better say *something.*

"Whether they charge her with anything or not," he says, his throat suddenly tight, "any investigation is bound to turn up *something.*" He pauses, a picture of Flo all at once coming to his mind.

She trusts you, Ben. She's beginning to trust you.

Mom's voice?

Glick blows his nose noisily. "Well," he says, wiping his face with a white monogrammed handkerchief, "to be honest, I wouldn't be interested in a script that turns her into a monster. Look. Part of the reason I'm hoping this will fly with the uppity-ups upstairs is the fact that she was Universal's first star—back when it was run by old Uncle Carl."

Xerxes beams. "You know they just dedicated a statue to her."

"I *know* about the statue, Stavropoulous," Glick says. "*Who* do you think *pushed* the idea to the powers that be?"

Ben sits forward in his chair. "Mr. Glick, I can assure you I have no intention of turning Flo into a monster. Because she's *not.* She's a sharp, honest, forthright lady. A real survivor. Any script I write will reflect the complexity of who she is, and yes, what she's done."

Glick flutters a hand dismissively at him. It's a pudgy pink hand, adorned with too many gold rings.

"Now, not *too* complex, Mr. Sheehan," he says. "I'm not interested in a deep psychological character study either." He pauses. "Flo must be heroic, and yet a little scandal wouldn't be bad either."

She trusts you, Ben.

Goddamn it. Whose voice *was* that?

Ben swallows. "As she provides more information, I'll adjust the script. What you have there is just to give you an idea."

Glick sighs. He pats the front of his jacket, then produces a tin of Sucrets. He pops one into his mouth. In seconds, Ben can smell cherry eucalyptus permeating the room.

"Tell me," Glick says, the lozenge making a little clicking sound against his teeth. "Who do you see in the lead? If you could get anyone, anyone at all."

Ben's taken by surprise. "You mean, to play Flo?"

"Well, I don't mean to play *me*."

Ben's not sure. He hasn't thought about this. In fact, he's never dared think beyond getting the treatment written. To actually imagine *Universal* giving him a contract to write a screenplay is incomprehensible. Might they even allow him to *direct*? It was too much to process.

Too much.

"I don't know," Ben stammers. "Um . . . Meryl Streep?"

Glick makes a face. "Are you off your stump?" He looks over at Xerxes, who makes a face now, too, in imitation of Glick's. "*Streep?*" Glick repeats. "Flo doesn't have an accent, last I knew."

Ben feels like an idiot. He can sense the sweat beading out on his forehead. Suddenly he feels like a big old *dunce* sitting there in his goddamn leather jacket. How ridiculous. Why not take the stupid thing off? He was *inside,* for God's sake.

Glick laughs. "I guess that's why *I'm* the producer." He leans across his desk at Ben. "What I need for *you* to do is write me some good dialogue between Flo and whoever this girl was that she killed. We need to get a handle on what their relationship was all about. Pump her for as much information as you can get, and then give me a fleshed-out script. Do that, and I've got a pretty good chance of convincing those upstairs to give us the green light."

Ben feels a drop of sweat fall from his chin.

Maybe next time Richard can help you with the dialogue.

It had to be Mom's voice.

He's the writer, after all.

"We'll get her to talk. Don't worry about that," Xerxes is saying. "I'm confident that Ben can."

But his agent's voice sounds very faraway to Ben, drowned out by another. . . .

What makes you think you can write a dramatic film?

Mom?

No. Maybe Anita.

"You do feel *some* connection with this girl's death *will* eventually come out?" Glick is asking.

Ben tries to answer, but his throat feels dry. He simply nods.

How many pieces of silver will you take for her life?

That's Anita. He's sure it's Anita's voice. . . .

"Well, then we may have a deal," Glick says, blowing his nose again.

Just remember to always do your best, never cheat, and work your hardest.

Ben shivers.

It's not Mom *or* Anita.

It's *Dad.*

"Excuse me," he says, standing. "Is there a men's room?"

Glick looks at him quizzically, then nods to a door at the far end of the office. Ben hurries over to it. Once safely inside, he doesn't unzip his pants. He just sits down on the toilet and covers his face.

Ben, Dad's saying. *There's so much . . . so much I still want to do.*

He can see his father, stretched out on the bed, his hair wild, his eyes big and unblinking. He rambles on like this a lot. Nothing ever too specific. Just scraps of melancholy, regret. Ben's fastening the diaper back around Dad's emaciated waist. His stomach is sunken in, his pelvic bones sharp and protruding.

"Try to rest, Dad," Ben tells him.

"So many things," he says, drifting off. He catches himself and moves his eyes almost desperately back to his son. "Do your best, Ben. Promise me?"

"I'll try, Dad." Ben sits down on the edge of the bed. "One way or another."

"No, not one way or another. Do your *best.*" Dad closes his eyes. "Never cheat. Work your hardest. That's the only way."

The only way.

"You finished in there, you nimrod?" Xerxes whispers urgently, rapping on the door.

Ben's startled back to the present. "Almost," he says.

"Glick's just been called in on a conference. Come *on.* What's going on with you? Hurry *up.* Get out here before he gets back."

"Yeah, okay."

Ben stands. The voices are gone.

He looks at himself in the mirror. He *likes* his new haircut, the leather jacket, the golden tan he's gotten from a bottle. He looks good. Damn good.

"I *am* doing my best," he tells himself.

He takes a deep breath, opens the door, and strides back to his place.

Flo completes her work on the Waters film in just one day instead of two. Xerxes assures her she'll still get the full quarter mil. "It's not like Biograph, sweetheart, where they paid you by the day," he tells her.

No, not like Biograph. Not at all, as it turns out.

She has just one scene in the picture. Most of it's being shot in Baltimore, of course, that being Waters's habit, but he and some of his stars and crew have come out to Hollywood to get Flo's scene. She plays a social dowager who's secretly a motorcycle mama. Jean had squawked a little after reading the script and had insisted on one line of Flo's dialogue being cut. It's where she tells Edward Furlong that she's "got *ants* in the parlor."

The film is being shot at a fabulous old house high in the Hollywood Hills. Flo seems to think it once belonged to somebody famous in the '20s. Pola Negri? Ramon Novarro? She can't recall. But while she had seemed excited about her "comeback" in the week leading up to it, on the day of the shoot she seems distracted, even a bit confused.

"Are you sure you want to go through with this?" Jean asks.

Flo frets. "I'm afraid I won't remember the lines. I never had to learn lines. Pictures were silent then, you know."

But she only has a few. Furlong knocks on her door, asks if he can use the phone. He then notices the leather jacket and Harley Davidson memorabilia lying around her house. In seconds, she reappears in full leather and riding cap—a touch that appealed mightily to Flo, who said it reminded her of the gear she used to wear in the early days of automobiling. Later, she lets Furlong borrow her "chopper"—setting the plot in motion.

On the set, she's received like visiting royalty, with costars Furlong and Jeff Stryker clamoring to get their pictures taken with her. She smiles and shakes their hands, but Ben thinks she seems a little dazed by the whole thing—as if she were wandering in her sleep.

"Over here, Miss Lawrence," an assistant director calls.

She turns.

"Your makeup, Miss Lawrence," someone else chirps.

She turns again.

Then Waters arrives. He gallantly kisses her hand. "The first star of them all, back from the dead," he says reverently.

They dress Flo up in a long blond wig and heavy mascara for her first scene. "Stand here," someone tells her. "You open the door, see Edward, and say, 'Whaddya want?'"

She nods.

"Okay!" an assistant calls. "Quiet on the set."

The crew settles down. Flo puts her hand on the doorknob.

"We have speed," a technician shouts.

"And—action," Waters commands.

Flo opens the door. Edward Furlong salutes her.

"Whaddya want?" Flo asks.

"Cut," Waters barks. "That was great, Flo."

"That was it?" she asks.

"For that take, yup. We'll edit everything together."

The other scenes go similarly. She delivers her line, and Waters calls, "Cut." Flo looks perplexed, so Ben hurries over to her between shots.

"How can you get *mood* when all the takes are so short?" she asks him. "Mr. Griffith used to have violins playing for us while we acted. He didn't keep stopping and starting the camera every few minutes."

Now she's dolled up in her black leather jacket and chaps. It took a long time for the wardrobe people to get her into *that*. But she looks adorable, Ben thinks, and he can't help but smile. He wonders for a second if he should write this scene into his script for Glick. But then he pushes the idea away. He doesn't want to think about that right now.

Flo says her last line to Furlong—"Go ahead. Take my chopper there."—with perfection. Her costar bends over and gives her a quick peck on the cheek. Ben can't help but imagine how differently she once was kissed by her leading men—King Baggott or Matt Moore.

"Cut! Beautiful!" Waters calls. "Print it!"

A flurry of technicians mob Flo, removing the microphone hidden in her leather blouse. One snatches the motorcycle cap right off her head and walks away.

"That's it?" Flo asks.

"That's it, Miss Lawrence, and *thank you*," Waters says. "You were *brilliant*."

She looks over at Ben, hovering off to the side. "Quarter of a million dollars," she says to him, shaking her head. "Things certainly *have* changed."

The library has that huge quiet all libraries have: a deep, dull, echoing hush that Richard finds magnificently soothing. Enveloping. Like being back in the womb.

He sits there at a long oak table, volumes of musty-smelling Los Angeles city directories spread out in front of him. This is when he's happiest: researching a story, lost in a world of facts and figures that he can gradually piece together, slowly but surely, to make a sensible whole.

That's what he's trying to do with Flo. Find a way to make sense of it all.

But he'll be damned if the sense doesn't keep eluding him every time he thinks he's gotten a grasp on it, like mercury from a broken thermometer running through his eager fingers.

The 1938 directory is open in front of him to the Ls. Florence Lawrence was still at MGM for most of that year, doing extra work. He runs his finger down the list of names. Lawlor. Lawn. Lawper. Lawrence.

There she is: *Florence Lawrence, actress, 532 Westbourne Drive.*

Okay. Richard jots down the entry in his notebook. He flips ahead a few pages. Sligo. Slip. Slocum.

Lester H. Slocum, M.D. General practice. Beverly Hills.

Not much data. Except by omission. Usually a wife is listed in parentheses. Looks like old Lester was a bachelor. Richard makes a notation of it.

He takes out the list Detective Lee gave him from his inside jacket pocket. He unfolds the piece of paper and looks down at the list of names. Girls who disappeared.

Ann Kiely. Richard flips back through the pages of the directory. No listing for her. Next name. *Norma Cooney.* He turns back a few more pages. There she is: *Norma Cooney, clerk, 3819 Sawtelle.* Richard writes the address down in his notebook.

Heloise Harker. No occupation given. Address, Santa Monica.

Jean Ott, teacher's aide, 1575a Ingraham.

Richard records all the data.

No Teresa Sabatini.

The last name on the list. *Margaret Butz.*

Richard lifts a whole chunk of pages to get back to the front of the book. He finds the Bs. Bumpers. Butterworth. Butz.

There. Margaret Butz.

He picks up his pencil to write the information.

Margaret Butz, actress, 532 Westbourne Drive.

His hand freezes. He actually hears his breath catch in his throat. He looks up a few lines to where he'd written Florence's name. The same address. 532 Westbourne Drive.

"God*damn*," he says out loud into the silence of the library. A few heads lift to glare over at him, but he doesn't notice.

He just keeps staring down at Margaret Butz at 532 Westbourne Drive.

"How the *hell* did the cops miss that?" Rex is asking.

Richard's pacing on the deck of their guest house. "Remember, these are the same folks who couldn't get enough evidence to convict O.J."

Rex grins. "So now we know that a woman living with Flo was reported missing shortly after Flo's supposed death." He crosses his arms in front of his chest. "She was 'just a girl.'"

Richard picked up the phone. He dials nine for an outside line, waits for the dial tone, then punches in the number of the house where Anita said Ben and Flo and Sister Jean are staying. "I'm calling again," he says. "But this time . . ."

"Hello?" It's a woman's voice. Mexican, Richard thinks—the same voice that's answered each time he's called.

"I'm calling for Sister Jean Levesque," Richard tells her.

"Just a moment, sir."

"Think she'll talk to you?" Rex asks.

"I can only try. I've left ten messages. I'll leave anoth—"

"Hello?"

Richard's caught by surprise that she's actually taken the phone. "Sister Jean? Richard Sheehan."

"Hello, Richard."

"I take it you've gotten my messages?"

He hears her sigh. "I have. We've been rather busy, as you can imagine."

"Yeah. Keeping Flo's life peaceful and free of intrusion, I'm sure."

He can't help the sarcasm. Throwing Jean's words back at her was just too irresistible. She'd been so adamant, so sanctimonious that day at St. Mary's, dismissing him as if she were his grade school teacher. *Flo's a very old woman who enjoys her life here tremendously and I don't want anything to affect that.* Yeah, except for movie deals and appearances on *Oprah.*

Sister Jean doesn't respond right away. Finally she asks, "Did you call for a reason, Richard, or just to scold me?"

"I need to see Flo, Sister."

She laughs. "Oh, I see. Censure *me* for letting Flo make this tour—but then press your own agenda to pump more information out of her. Tell me, Richard. Have you sold your book proposal yet?"

"Not yet, but I'm close." He stands his ground. "But that's not why I want to see Flo, Sister."

"Then why?"

"Because I want to help her. Because I don't trust my brother." He hears Jean start to object, but he talks over her. "And I've found some information that I think Flo should know, because it's not information that will remain a secret long."

"Are you making a threat?"

"No. Not at all. Look, Sister. I'm trying to *help* Flo. Believe me."

She's quiet. Richard begins to think she may have disconnected the phone. He's about to say something when she finally responds. "All right, Richard. Come by today. Ben and Flo are out, taping a segment for the 'Dare to be 100' television campaign. Come by and we can talk on our own."

"Thank you, Sister. I'll come right now."

She's already hung up.

"She's gonna talk with you?" Rex asks.

"Yeah." Richard starts to pull on his sneakers. "Hey, Nooker."

"What?"

"How long does your run at Highways last?"

"Two weeks."

"Good."

"Why good?"

"Because I don't want to head back to New York for at least that long. Things are going to start *happening* here. You know Lee is going to stumble upon the connection between this Margaret Butz and Flo. People are already saying her story doesn't jibe. And Ben's going to exploit the headlines for all they're worth."

"You think you can make a difference?"

"I don't know. But I'm gonna try." He gives Rex a quick peck on the lips. "When do our free digs courtesy of Highways kick in?"

"In just a couple days."

"You know, subletting our place back home was a great idea, especially with us going rent free here. Maybe we can even save enough moola to finish paying for all your redecoration."

Rex just smiles. "Say hello to Flo for me."

"*If* I see her." He winks at him; then he's out the door.

I don't trust my brother.

Richard's words still hang in the air after Jean has replaced the phone. They seem suspended in front of her, written as if in smoke, or lipstick on a mirror.

Ben has said the exact same thing: *He* doesn't trust Richard. What *was* it with these brothers—these *twins?* Jean had always heard of twins having a special bond, a special kinship of love and trust—or at least, a distinctive understanding of each other, a perspicacity unique to themselves.

And maybe they did. Maybe that's why they didn't trust each other.

"Ben," she'd asked a few days ago. "What has Flo said about the fire? The one that ended her career?"

He laughed. "You told me that was off limits."

"But you have a video labeled 'Fire Discussion.' I saw it in the pile."

He'd flushed a little. That had made Jean uncomfortable. Was he hiding something from her? She had relied on her instincts—her heart—about him. There was no reason to doubt him, was there?

I don't trust my brother.

"Don't worry," Ben assured her. "As soon as I saw Flo getting anxious, I changed the topic. All she did was repeat her standard line: that the fire got out of control, that she got badly burned saving her costar, and the recuperation took so long she was off the screen for five years."

"Do you think there's more to it than that? She gets so anxious."

He shrugged. "Hey, there are a *lot* of things she gets anxious talking about. That *girl,* for instance."

"All right." Jean sighed. She didn't want to get into *that* again. "I *do* appreciate your respecting the limits, Ben."

He *was* respecting them. She had to believe that. Richard was wrong not to trust his brother.

Jean walks over to the French doors leading out to the deck overlooking the ocean. It's an overcast day. Gray and gloomy. The sea is dark brown with pesky little whitecaps. Poor Flo's bones had been *aching* this morning. They always did in damp weather. But Ben had insisted the "Dare to be 100" taping was too important to cancel.

She didn't like the way things were going. The way Flo was on every TV talk show. The way Xerxes found—every week—yet another new offer that they just couldn't refuse. Carla had gone back east for a week—there *was* other business in her life—and Jean felt just a little outdrawn by Xerxes's big guns.

Oh, she could see the weariness in Flo's eyes, hear it in her voice. She'd try to insist that Flo rest, but the old woman persisted every night, walking out onto whatever stage they'd found for her, moving as if she were some brittle mannequin operated by strings. The cameras were always flashing, and Flo always waving to the adoring crowd. But increasingly she was confused and inarticulate when confronted with any questions. Where was her old sense of humor? Where were her *wits?*

So why was Jean acquiescing to all this? Why did she let it go on?

"Hi," the man had said to her.

Jean had been startled. She was in the supermarket, buying some fruit to keep in their room, when the man had casually moved beside her, squeezing the tangerines, and said hello.

"Hi," she managed to respond.

"They've got a wonderful selection here," he said. "Don't you think?"

It was his eyes. His damn eyes. The eyes were her weakness. She nodded quickly, then hurried away.

That was all. Just that. An innocent, fleeting encounter in the grocery store. But *that* was why she stayed. *That* was why she let it go on. *He was flirting with me,* Jean realized. Or trying to anyway. She had rushed off so promptly that she couldn't even recall his face now—whether he was handsome or homely, tall or short, black or white. She just remembered the greeting—how wonderful it had sounded, how fearfully passionate it had been.

That's why you let it go on, she scolds herself. *Because you don't want to go back.*

Outside the air takes on the deep gray green of a thunder sky. Inside it feels thick and heavy. Jean stands as if transfixed, her eyes cast over the ocean, waiting for the rain.

"Couldn't you put in for a transfer?" Ben had asked her just last night. "Couldn't you say you'd rather be working with the poor?"

She smiled over at him. "It doesn't work that way, Ben." They were eating takeout Chinese from little white cardboard boxes, sitting crosslegged on the floor. Both were tired of dining out, of endless meetings with endless producers and reporters. Flo was exhausted, too, and fell sound asleep in her bed at six-thirty. Ben and Jean decided to eat in, to make a picnic on the elegantly carpeted floor: sweet-and-sour chicken and egg rolls and a bottle of cheap red wine. Xerxes had flown back to New York that morning; with both him and Carla gone for a while, they could afford to just be normal human beings again.

"But if you're not happy," Ben persisted.

"It's not that I'm not happy," Jean said, bewildered by her double negative. She frowned, trying to make sense of what she'd just said. The wine made her mind floaty and giddy. She just laughed.

"From what you've told me," Ben continued, "it sounds as if you did some real good work at St. Vincent's. You'd think they'd want you to do what you do best."

She looked at him. Part of her wanted to tell him what had happened. But she'd never spoken of it to anyone, except to the Board, when she'd assured them nothing like that would ever happen again. They were trusting her now, she told herself, allowing her to take this trip with Flo.

They were putting a great deal of faith in her. Jean wore that faith—that trust—like a bulletproof vest. They were trusting her, but also *testing* her.

"What I do *best*," she said, raising her glass of wine to him, "is not necessarily what they want."

"That's the church for you, I guess."

"You're a lapsed Catholic, aren't you, Ben?"

He shrugged. "I prayed and prayed to God to save my father, but He wasn't listening."

"Oh, He was listening, Ben. I'm sure of that."

"Well, He ignored me then. Don't get me wrong. I don't bear any grudge against God if He's up there. I just figured that life was pretty hopeless and let it go at that."

Jean set her glass down on the floor and looked over at Ben. "Do you still feel that way?"

"I don't know." He met Jean's eyes.

Oh, there's no question about it, she thought. He *did* have the same clear vision she'd recognized in Victor, the same window directly onto the soul.

"This is the first time in a long while that I've begun to have any hope again," he told her. "First time since *One Chance* really. But I learned from that experience not to believe *anything's* going to last."

"But that was such a *hopeful* film, Ben. It was *filled* with hope."

He shrugged. "And look what happened. The Cold War ended."

She blinked. "Which was a good thing, Ben."

He hesitated, then laughed. "Of course. Of course, of course."

She reached over, placed her hand on top of his. "I remember the scene in *One Chance* where you had a little African-American girl meet a little white boy, and they sat together holding hands in a bombed-out doorframe. Ben, that single image spoke *volumes* about your soul. About the things you *believe* in—the fundamental goodness of humankind, the intrinsic connection between all of us and our world. Try to remember that scene, the hope behind it. You are a *brilliant* artist, Ben Sheehan, and the best kind—an artist who uses his talents for the good of others."

He looked at her strangely then—queerly, even sadly. His look unsettled her. She withdrew her hand. Maybe it was her touch—unexpected, perhaps inappropriate. That must have been why he had looked at her with such unease in his eyes.

But they were beautiful eyes. Jean couldn't deny that—how lovely she found Ben's eyes. How in the mornings, when she'd first awake, she was filled with a strange, intoxicating abundance inspired by vaguely remembered dreams. She'd lie there for close to an hour, basking in the afterglow of her forgotten reveries. Try as she might, she could never salvage them with any precision—except to remember that they were filled with rapture.

And the spirit and form of Ben Sheehan.

She opens the door and Richard finds himself a little taken aback.

"Sister," he says. "I almost didn't recognize you."

She smiles a little bashfully. Richard can detect the blush spreading up from her neck to her cheeks.

"Come in, Richard," she says, standing aside to let him in.

Richard is overwhelmed by the affluence. The house is perched at the edge of the ocean, and the floor-through plan affords majestic views of the sea from any angle. He looks up into a cathedral ceiling and chandelier. On the table near the door is a pile of newspapers and magazines with Flo on the covers. Off to the side is a pile of videotapes and one of Ben's camcorders.

"You're looking good," Richard tells Sister Jean as they move into the living room.

He's being sincere. Dressed in khakis and a cotton blouse, she looks like some preppy college girl out of the J Crew catalog, all tanned and strawberry blond.

"Thank you, Richard," she manages to say.

"How's Flo doing?" Richard asks. "I saw her on *Oprah*. And *Regis*. And *The View*."

Jean manages a small smile. "She seems to have rediscovered her love affair with applause," Jean tells him.

"But you know what, Sister?" Richard looks at her intently. "She doesn't seem like *herself* on TV. Do you know what I mean?"

She takes in a long breath and looks away. "How does she seem to you?" she asks.

"Well, it was different on *Rosie*. She seemed like herself then. But it's all been downhill from there." He pauses. "She seems like some shy, fragile, *genteel* old lady. The way they've got her decked out, in those pearls and wigs. I miss her caftans and bloodred fingernails. And her cigarettes."

Jean smiles. "The 'Dare to be 100' campaign doesn't want Flo seen smoking. It goes against the message."

There's a crack of thunder in the distance. Richard hears the sudden *tappity-tap* of raindrops on the skylights above.

"So what is it you've found out, Richard?" asks Sister Jean, suddenly all business. "What is it I need to know?"

She hasn't even asked me to sit down, Richard thinks. "Well," he says. "A couple of things. First of all, a Detective Lee will be contacting Flo. He wants to ask her questions about the body that was buried under her name."

Jean walks over to the couch and sits. Richard follows, sitting opposite her in a chair. She looks over at him.

"I knew someone would, at some point," she says.

"He's not a bad guy. A little eccentric. I've told him I'm sure Flo did nothing wrong."

"You did?" Jean seems brightened by this, as if she had expected differently. "Do you really believe that, Richard?"

"You might not like reporters, Sister, but we've got something pretty special. And that's instinct. Good reporters always trust their instincts. And mine tells me Flo did nothing more than take advantage of a situation."

"I have a healthy respect for instinct," Jean says. "My own has served me well." She smiles. "All right. What else?"

"Well, I've found out the girl's name."

"The girl who died," Jean says simply.

Richard nods.

Another rumble of thunder, followed by a crackle of lightning that slices through the gray sky outside the window. From the glass doors overlooking the water, they can see the ocean roiling, crashing against the rocks. The rain comes fast and frantic now, the drops exploding in a torrent on the deck.

"At least, I *think* it's her," Richard says. "In February 1939—just a little over a month after Florence Lawrence apparently 'died'—Margaret Butz was reported missing to the police."

"I'm sure any number of girls were reported missing at any given time."

"Margaret Butz lived with Florence Lawrence on Westbourne Drive for three years."

Jean sighs. "Her name was Molly," she says, very quietly.

"What?" Richard asks.

"Her name was Molly. The girl. Flo's told me that, at least."

"Molly." Richard considers it. "Which could be a nickname for Margaret, no?"

Jean nods.

"Look, Sister. We've got to get Flo to start telling the truth. At least to us." He pauses. "Or to you anyway. We've got to know the full story of her past if we're to help her. Like I said, I don't believe she did anything wrong—but people are asking all kinds of questions, and I just don't want any negative publicity to hurt her."

"You're right, Richard. It's time she told me everything."

Jean stands, pressing her hands against the glass door leading out to the deck. The rain is dying down. There are snatches of blue along the far western horizon.

"Such a quick storm," she muses. "So much bluster, and then it's gone. Guess that's the way out here."

Richard stands up and walks over behind her. "And, Sister," he says. "Just be careful of how much you share with my brother."

She doesn't say anything. Richard watches her for a while, and then she finally turns. "Thank you," she says. "I'm sorry if I've misjudged you."

He's surprised how good that makes him feel. He doesn't quite know what to say in response. He just smiles and shifts his feet like a kid in front of his teacher.

She promises to talk with Flo. She doesn't make any promises about Ben.

"Are you very tired tonight, Flo?" Jean asks.

"Not so," Flo tells her, enjoying a puff on her cigarette in the privacy of her room. Jean helps her steady it and rest it in the ashtray.

She's seated in a large plush armchair, wrapped in just her flannel nightdress. Jean had helped her shed her fashionable street clothes, designed exclusively by Donna Karan for her promotional spots in the "Dare to be 100" campaign. Now her feet are barefoot, and Flo's flexing her toes. "Those heels were tight," she complained when Jean helped her out of them.

Jean gently rubs Flo's feet. "Do you feel up for talking a bit?" she asks.

Flo moves her eyes down at her. "All right, missy," she says. "I know that tone. What do you got cookin'?"

Jean smiles. It makes her happy to hear flashes of the old Flo. The fiery, ornery Flo. Not the lady on TV.

She sits up on the small footrest at Flo's knee. "Richard Sheehan came by today," she tells her.

"*Richard.* How *is* he? Why has he been such a bad boy and not come to see me? Was Rex with him? Anita?"

"No, he was alone." Jean looks sincerely into Flo's eyes. "You trust him, don't you, Flo?"

Flo nods.

"He told me a police detective wants to ask you some questions."

Flo shrugs. "*Everyone's* been asking me questions for weeks!"

"But this one we can't control," Jean tells her, reaching up and placing her hand on Flo's knee.

Flo shakily lifts her cigarette, which had been burning unattended in the ashtray. Jean watches as she slowly moves it to her lips and takes a short drag. "What does he want to ask me about?"

"Molly," Jean says.

Flo sets the cigarette back down in the ashtray, then leans her head back and closes her eyes.

"Flo," Jean says. "You trust me, too, don't you?"

"Of course I do, Jeannie," she tells her without opening her eyes.

"Then you need to start giving me all the answers. We're in too far to go back now. Tell me everything that anyone could possibly ask you about. If we need to come up with a story that will satisfy people's curiosity, we will—but until you tell *me* the truth, I can't help you."

"In other words, we'd lie?"

"If necessary," Jean tells her. "If it means . . . protecting you."

"Protecting me from what?"

"From . . . whatever."

Flo opens her eyes. "Are you afraid they'll put an old lady like me in jail, Jean?"

"I'm only afraid of you being made uncomfortable." She reaches up and stubs out Flo's cigarette in the ashtray. "Let's start with the fire."

"The fire?"

"Yes. The one that ended your career in pictures."

"But I've told you about that. The fire got out of con—"

"No, Flo. Don't tell me what appeared in the fan magazines. Tell me what happened. What *really* happened."

Flo lifts her head and looks down at Jean. There's a strange little smile playing with her lips. "Why, Jeannie," she says. "You're not accusing me of *lying,* are you?"

"No. Just of being clever with the truth."

Flo laughs.

"You've spoken about Charles Woodring and Henry Bolton, Flo. But what happened to *Harry?* You spoke so much about him, then just stopped. There's a whole long blank in the recollections you've given to Ben, and it starts with the fire. What happened, Flo?"

The old woman once again closes her eyes.

"All right, Jeannie," Flo says. "But light me another cigarette first."

Jean obeys. Flo accepts it gratefully, takes a long drag.

"All right," she says, exhaling smoke. "I'll tell you what happened.

I've never spoken of it, not in eighty years. It's funny—how when you don't speak of a thing for a long time, you think you'll forget it. That it will go away somehow, become what you want it to be. But that doesn't happen. It stays with you, Jeannie, stays right with you, always there."

She pauses. "Always there . . ."

Jean watches as Flo's eyes move off to that place far away.

"There *was* a fire, Jeannie," she says. "There really was a fire. . . ."

Spring–Summer 1915

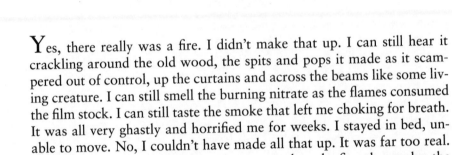

Yes, there really was a fire. I didn't make that up. I can still hear it crackling around the old wood, the spits and pops it made as it scampered out of control, up the curtains and across the beams like some living creature. I can still smell the burning nitrate as the flames consumed the film stock. I can still taste the smoke that left me choking for breath. It was all very ghastly and horrified me for weeks. I stayed in bed, unable to move. No, I couldn't have made all that up. It was far too real.

Oh, but you see, there's far more—more than the fire, the smoke, the terror in my bed—those things will forever remind me of what else—*what else* happened in those months. . . .

Harry. Dear, loyal Harry. Dear, dear, *desperate* Harry. Ever since I'd come back from Santorini, he'd been terrified of losing me. I could see it in his eyes, in the way he fluttered his hands, in his eagerness to accommodate me in all things. He tried to love me, in his way, but I had changed. If I'd ever sought love in my marriage with Harry, it had ended that day in the ruins of the temple, in the thin brown arms of a Greek fisherboy.

How I *despised* being back in the studio. It all seemed to bear down around me: the whir of the camera, the sputtering of the blazing lamps. We had a quota to fill for Universal: two films per month. And always, *always*, there was the pressure to work my way back to the top.

"Number *ten*, Florence," Mother would chide. "You don't want to languish at number *ten*."

But the latest *Photoplay* poll didn't even *include* me in the Top Ten. Harry tried to hide the magazine from me, but I found it. "It's just a temporary lull, sweetheart," he said. "Wait till you see the new picture I've got in mind. Real flames and an exciting rescue! That'll do it!"

Oh, Harry. I carried his picture in my purse for years. I still have it, you know, in my drawer. I'll take it out sometimes, look down at him, and wonder if he ever really existed. He's been dead more than seventy years now. I doubt there's anyone alive who remembers him. Except me.

I'll trace the line of his face in the photograph with my finger. *Harry loved me*, I'll tell myself. It was love for a fragile, high-strung girl: a girl he could drive around in a borrowed car, a girl he could impress, a girl he could comfort and cajole, a girl whose career could ensure his own. I can't say he didn't love Florence Bridgewood. He just never *knew* her. Florence Lawrence was the only girl he knew, and for her, he would do anything.

And so it was that I hit upon my solution.

My way out.

Perhaps you go through it and you find there is another side. Does it make sensible?

Oh, very much so.

I let Harry in my bed for the first time in over a year. Since coming back from the Greek islands, I was frequently too distraught to permit what we used to so delicately call "marital relations." But this night, I turned back my satin covers and gestured for him to enter. His face flushed a deep purple, his big Adam's apple lunging up and down in his neck.

I can still recall that night so clearly. It was around Christmastime. We were all out at the farm in New Jersey. How I loved that place. I wish you could have seen it. I wish I still had my pictures of it. I planted rosebushes everywhere. We raised asparagus—oh, what feasts we had in season! There were *three thousand* trees: fruit trees of all kinds, apple and pear and cherry. The land reached back into the woods for a full mile.

I remember Christmas there especially. The tall white pines that would reach the ceiling, the circle of pillows we'd place around the tree. Ducks would play his harmonica and I'd whistle to my own accompaniment on the piano. We'd play such games—you know, hiding a prize in a stocking and then hunting the entire farm for it. You should have seen us, climbing up on the haymow and in and out of the stalls of the horses and cows and up in the attic!

But this Christmas was different. Ducks was gone, of course, and I was still too fragile, too high-strung to be climbing around in haymows. It was a quiet Christmas, but we still had our tree, and Harry bought me lovely gifts. A pair of shoes, a fur coat, a new motor car. There were even gifts from my brother, I think—but Mother chose not to invite poor Norman down from Buffalo for the holiday.

Thinking about it now, I'm quite certain it was Christmas Eve *itself* that I invited Harry into my bed. It would have been fitting, after all: I had a gift to give him as well. It was a cold night, cold and snowy, I remember that much. The wind was wailing outside our windows and the snow fell six inches in an hour. We kept a fire going all night long in the hearth.

I let Harry penetrate me, his big, wet, sloppy tongue all over my face. I cringed, tightened my fists at my side. There was no passion, no tenderness. I closed my eyes, tried to imagine the Aegean sky, and said a little prayer that Harry's efforts would take.

A week later, I discovered my prayers had been answered.

I didn't tell him. Not right away. That was part of my plan. I just kept going into the studio, following his directions, churning out our quota of celluloid.

We began work on a film called *Pawns of Destiny*. Harry showed me the plans for the fire.

"You'll come down here, Flo," he said, pointing on his blueprint. "And, Matt, you'll come in from here and save her."

All very simple. Matt Moore was a big tree of a man, broad shouldered, gorgeous. He looked terrific that day in his brown leather chaps and ten-gallon hat. He winked at me and took his place. I gathered my skirts and walked up the short flight of stairs. Harry moved off behind the camera. "Roll 'em," he commanded the photographer.

Somewhere behind us a prop man lit a trail of gasoline. I heard the *whoof* as the fire ignited, and I spotted it quickly rising behind a stack of crates. I threw my hands in front of my face for the camera. "That's it, Flo," Harry called. "You see the fire and think you're trapped!"

I ran down the stairs. By now the flames were higher; the smoke filled the room. "No, no," Harry barked. "Go back and come down again."

We had to do the scene three times. I was coughing, wheezing. Matt came rushing in, spitting black soot. I was supposed to faint on the second landing. Harry kept calling for me to do it again. The flames were edging closer to me. I could feel their intense heat on my face and hands. My foot broke through some floorboards and I saw flames there. "Do it again, Flo!" Harry shouted, heedless of any danger. "One more time!"

Matt came rushing in again. By now I couldn't hear Harry's directions anymore. The only sound was the roar of the flames. *Damn him,* I was thinking. *Why doesn't he call "Cut?"*

Matt tripped, sprawling like a great fallen oak in front of me. I saw a pesky little flame jump from the wall and land on his back. I threw myself at him, smothering the flame, pulling at his chaps to get him out of harm's way. I cut my neck on a splintered doorframe as I did so. I felt warm blood on my throat.

"No more, Harry!" I screamed, standing up suddenly. I was surrounded by a wall of bright yellow flame. "No more!"

I felt panic grip me. Matt was up, out of sight now, but I felt as if I'd faint right there, facedown into the flames. I heard the spray of waterhoses, the frantic shouts of prop men. I began to scream. I stood there like some crazy Joan of Arc, my hands in my hair, howling.

It made for great footage, Harry later told me.

"You *bastard!*" I screamed at him when the flames were finally out. "You bastard!"

That Florence Lawrence could find such a voice startled not only him but myself as well. It convinced me that I was on the right path, that my plan would take me back to who I wanted to be.

"Florrie," Harry said, trying to calm me down. "Sweetheart, you were never in any real danger! I was watching all the time."

The makeshift building on the Universal–Victor lot was in ruins. Charred black wooden beams still smoked, with prop men spraying them with hoses.

"I could have been killed," I seethed at him. *"Killed!"*

"No, Florrie, I was—"

"And you would've been my *murderer!*" I shrieked. The crew looked over at us awkwardly.

Then I began to laugh. Crazy-like-a-loon laugh. I sat down hard in my star's chair. I covered my face with my hands. Blood seeped through my fingers from the wound on my throat.

"Florrie," Harry said, trying to soothe me, stooping down beside me.

"And not just me, Harry," I said all at once, looking up to meet him eye to eye. My laughter ceased. "But your *baby,* too. You would've killed your *baby.*"

He didn't say anything. He just continued to stare back at me for a long, long time.

"She's in no fit condition to have a baby," Mother sniffed.

"I'll not hear of any butchers, Lotta," Harry insisted. "I won't do it."

I was in bed. I had a bad case of the shakes, brought on by the aftermath of the fire. I shivered under a mound of blankets, my teeth chattering so loud they could hear me down the hall.

I could hear them, too.

"How far along *is* she?" Mother was asking.

"Maybe about four months," Harry told her.

"She *can't* have this child," Mother snarled. "It won't do to have America's ingenue a *mother.*"

"Maybe it's time for a new image."

Mother's laugh was hard. "She's not even in *Photoplay*'s Top Ten at all anymore. To take time off now would be disastrous!"

"I'll not hear of it, Lotta! I mean that!"

"You are a selfish, stubborn man!"

"And you are a pigheaded, greedy sow!"

I just continued to shake under my blankets, unable to get warm.

"My mother and I are going on a long road trip," I told the reporter. I had greeted her in my pink negligee. Now I lay stretched out on the daybed. "I've been very tired, you see, working so much. I just feel the need to get away."

Mother stood behind me, beaming like a fool, her hand on my shoulder. Harry lurked off to the side, staring out the window.

That's what they reported. The fan magazines. One reporter wrote:

> *Poor Florence Lawrence. One expects to find a stately lady whose charm of mature development would compensate for her lack of the first beauty of youth. Instead, one finds a delicate, brittle flower of a girl. It is hoped the trip will do her some good.*

I sniffed. "Mature development? The lack of the first beauty of youth?" I threw down the magazine. "Don't they know I'm only twenty-five?"

"That's what you were *last* year, Florence," Mother scolded. She was reading the *Dramatic Mirror*. Probably still dreaming of a comeback. Hers, mine, ours. "You can't stay twenty-five forever. Reporters *remember*. They have minds for such things."

I walked over to the French doors that looked out onto my rose gardens. "Suppose they come back? Suppose they come out here and see we haven't really gone anywhere?"

"They won't, Florence."

And they didn't. I guess things *were* different then. You could tell a story to the press and they'd accept it. Maybe not believe it, but they'd accept it. They wouldn't go around trying to prove you wrong, let me put it that way. We told them we were leaving. They ran with it and didn't bother us again.

Of course, Florence Lawrence's name wasn't exactly selling their magazines anymore.

I stood in front of the full-length mirror, my hands on my belly. "It will be a girl," I told Mother, running my fingers along its shape.

"I should hope so," she said, turning a page in the *Dramatic Mirror*. "I wouldn't want a boy who would grow up looking like *him*."

"I'm going to name her Annie Laurie," I said. "Remember, Mother? How I'd sing the song when I was a girl?"

She remembered. I began humming it, watching myself in the mirror, the way my belly moved when I turned, imagining the child within.

I sent the maid out to buy clothes for the baby: pink suits lined with lace, adorable little white booties, a frilly bonnet with satin ribbon dangling from its sides. I set the bonnet on the post of my bed and would lie awake at night, the ribbon in my hand.

I admit that I'd conceived the child as a way out of pictures. A way to throw off the yoke, an excuse for retirement solid enough that neither Harry nor Mother could force me back. But something changed as I watched my belly grow. Something deepened.

It's clichéd to say motherhood changed me. I don't know what it was exactly. But *something* shifted inside me. I felt strong again, confident. I rose early, worked the earth, picked flowers and ripe fruit. I found a book of poems and essays that had been Ducks's. He'd underlined one passage that I read over and over to myself, practically memorized. It was Emerson:

> *When I go into my garden with a spade and dig a bed, I feel such an exhilaration and health that I discover I have been defrauding myself all this time letting others do for me what I should have done with my own hands.*

I was close, very close, to my goal—of going back to *me*. Maybe it was the rosebushes that thrived under my care. Maybe it was the quiet of my farm, the low mooing of the cows as I milked them at dawn. Maybe it was the gentle swish of the trees late at night, with all the windows open, an early summer breeze tickling the curtains. Maybe it was being away from the studio and the cameras and the reporters' demands. Maybe it was the fact that I'd asked Harry to leave, and I could forget the temperamental actress who once was his wife.

"But it's my baby, too!" he'd cried.

He said I was being irrational, delusional: reading Emerson out loud to myself in the garden, getting up before the sun to milk the cows when we had hired hands to do such dirty work. He didn't recognize me, and neither did Mother, who fretted about the "crazy look" in my eyes—my father's madness, she feared, visiting itself upon me.

I ignored her melodramatics. I promised Harry I'd contact him when the child was born. But in the meantime, his presence distressed me. I played upon his guilt over the fire, told him the sight of him reminded me of that horrible day. He left grudgingly, and I breathed a long sigh of relief.

"When the baby is born, Mother, I'm not leaving her side," I insisted.

"Florence! You will *have* to go back to making pictures. How do you think you'll pay our bills?"

"Harry will pay them," I told her. It all seemed so simple.

"*Well*," Mother said, arching her shoulders, "he'll make demands of you if you have expectations of him. I say divorce him now, Florence, and ask Mr. Laemmle to give you a new contract with a new director. Better yet, we could approach *Mr. Griffith* again, with our sincerest apologies. Why, if you'd stayed with him, you could've been in *The Birth of a Nation*."

I stopped listening to her. She would prattle on for *hours* if she had the chance. I just smiled to myself, staring at my swelling stomach in the full-length mirror.

Annie Laurie.

That would be her name. Just that. No last name necessary.

Just Annie Laurie.

It was all the name we'd need.

Looking back, I suspect Mother must have colluded with Harry. There was a doctor she brought in who asked me a number of peculiar questions and declared, "Any woman who keeps a loving husband from her side while expecting his child cannot be fully sane."

I responded that any doctor dispensing such lunacy would not be fully paid.

He left in a huff.

I imagine some papers were signed before he left. I imagine now that Mother and Harry had called an uneasy truce to combat a common threat to their ambitions: *me*. They called that doctor in to declare me unfit, unstable. Insane, perhaps.

And maybe I was, at that. Maybe my plans *were* preposterous. But they were *my* plans. The first I'd ever made completely on my own.

Harry was there the day the baby came. I have never known such pain. I remember once, as a very young girl, licking the block of ice under the icebox. My tongue had frozen hard; I screamed as best I could, flailing my arms until Ducks had come running in to see what was wrong. "There, there," he tried to comfort me as he warmed up a poker in the fire. "Don't move, Florrie. Don't move."

But the idea of the poker terrified me even more than the pain on my tongue. I know now he meant just to melt the ice a little, but I panicked as he approached. I pulled away, ripping my tongue off the ice, leaving chunks of flesh and blood there. The pain was excruciating. I was lucky I didn't lose my sense of taste completely.

That's all I can compare childbirth to, except that childbirth was far, far worse. I felt my body twist and contort, split in half. The midwife was gruff and unsympathetic, telling me to push harder and to stop my crying. My labor went on for *sixteen hours*—sixteen hours of sheer, wrenching, burning pain. Mother would say later that my shrieks echoed throughout the house. The maid put on earmuffs to go about her work.

Finally I felt something rip, like the flesh from my tongue, and then a final rive of pain. It was over. I was left with a shuddering sense of nothingness, of the pain being spent.

Then I heard the slap, and the baby's shrill, tiny cry.

I *know* I heard her cry. I had fallen back, my head deep into my drenched pillows. I couldn't see anything but the wooden beams of the ceiling. "Let me see her," I cried. The midwife said nothing.

I was breathing heavily, trying to catch my breath. "Let me see her!" I cried again, raising my arms, but too weak to sit up.

Suddenly Mother's face, and Harry's, hovered over me, looking down with big round eyes.

"Let me see her!" I shouted, my voice so hoarse I barely recognized it as my own.

"The baby's dead, Florence," Mother told me.

"No! I heard her cry!"

"The baby's dead," Harry said solemnly. He turned away, disappearing from my view.

"She is *not* dead!" I cried. "Give her to me!"

Mother didn't try to console me. She just kept looking down at me, hard, not saying a word.

I managed to get up on my elbow. My hair fell into my face. I saw the midwife bundling something in a blanket. She was covered in blood. She handed the bundle to Harry.

"*Let me see her!*" I cried.

Mother tried to force me to lie back down.

"Let me see her! Annie Laurie! *Annie Laurie!*"
But Harry just turned with the bundle and left the room.

The months that followed are the only ones in my life that I can't remember. There are snatches, but only snatches: walking through the rose garden, being caught by a sudden rainstorm; waking up at night with my sheets and pillows drenched in sweat, as if I were in childbirth all over again; rocking in a chair in front of the fire, Mother staring at me from across the room.

I never believed them. When I began to find my way out of the haze, I told Mother plainly and simply that I knew my baby was alive. She told me I spoke nonsense, that often mothers of stillborn children refused to accept the truth. When Harry tried to visit, I locked myself in my room, covering my ears with my hands when he would bang upon the door.

Harry died about a year later. I don't know from what. Heart attack, maybe. That's what Mother thought. Or else he killed himself. That's what I always secretly believed. No one would hire him without me. I remember the trades didn't even carry an obituary when he died.

Without me, he had often said, life was just not worth living.

One afternoon, a few years before we were forced to sell the farm, I was walking along a row of white pines, the ones Harry would cut down for Christmas and drag into the house. There, on a branch higher than my head, was tied a pink ribbon, flapping in the wind. The same pink satin ribbon that once had hung from my baby's bonnet.

I reached up and, with some difficulty, managed to untie it. I slipped it through my fingers. It was indeed the same ribbon.

I knew somehow that Harry had tied it there the night she was born.

His own private little ceremony? His solitary expression of grief?

She was his daughter, too.

Somehow I just couldn't bring myself to hate him for what he had done. There was just a tremendous, overarching sadness.

A few weeks before she died, Mother—delirious and feverish, an old, old woman by then confined to her bed—admitted the truth. She spoke of the child, the baby, the adoption agency, the cash that had changed hands. "You were so *nervous,* Florence," she kept repeating, over and over. "So *nervous.*" There were no specifics, no names—just the terrible, trembling relief of a deathbed confession.

She was eaten up with cancer, a shrunken apple of a woman, her big eyes protruding from her skull, making her look like some oversize insect. Just as with Harry, I couldn't bring myself to be angry with her. I bore her no hate, no rage, no blame as she lay dying. For I suppose there was some truth to her diagnosis: Florence Lawrence had indeed been too nervous to raise a child.

And besides, it's not as if Mother told me anything I didn't already know.

I had heard her cry.

My baby.

Annie Laurie.

The Present

"So that's the story of how I retired from pictures," Flo is telling them. "The fire, as you can see, was just one small part of it."

She takes a breath and gives them a weak smile. They're mesmerized by her tale. "When I tried to come back," she continues, "the pictures had moved on. Off to the West Coast, off to bigger and better things. Not too many folks remembered me anymore."

"Oh, Flo." Jean moves over to embrace her. "I'm sorry you had to go through that all over again, but I thought Ben should hear it."

Flo's old blue eyes are clear. No sign of tears. They look over Jean's shoulder and seek out Ben. He sits across from her, shifting awkwardly in his chair.

"She might still be alive, you know," he says softly. "Have you ever thought of that? She'd be, what? Early eighties. She might have even had children. You might have grandchildren out there, *great*-grandchildren. Did you ever think about trying to find her?"

"I thought I had, once," Flo tells him. She sighs. "But that's another story for another time." Her hands fold around Jean's arms. "I'm pretty tired now, Jeannie."

"Of course, Flo," Jean says.

"Flo." Ben stands, approaches her. "Just one more thing. How in the world did the story ever evolve into you saving Matt Moore's life? Lifting his two-hundred-pound frame?"

She shrugs. "You know how people love to say things, especially movie people. Each story just built on the last. I was trying for a comeback, so I was happy for whatever they said about me."

"I'm going to help Flo into bed, Ben," Jean tells him. "I'll be out in a minute."

He nods. "Thanks, Flo," he says. "For . . . for sharing all that."

She smiles up at him.

* * *

Beautiful. Just beautiful.

In his head, he's already rewriting a part of his script. The way Flo had described it was just perfect. Her baby torn from her body and whisked away, Flo barely able to sit up, pleading for them to come back. Fantastic. Unbelievable. So . . . so . . . *cinematic.*

Glick will eat it up.

Now, if he can only get her to talk about the murder . . . or whatever it was that happened to that girl.

He picks up the remote control and clicks on the television.

Frasier Crane is making some wry remark to his brother, Niles, who flips back with an even wryer retort of his own.

Ben sits down on the couch. Laugh track crescendo—Niles wins the sparring match for this round—and then the show fades to a commercial.

"Hello, I'm Florence Lawrence."

Ben sits up. It's the first of the spots she taped for the "Dare to be 100" campaign.

"Oprah Winfrey and I want to make you a dare. Don't settle for the old average life expectancy." She smiles sweetly into the camera. Her eyes seem a little glassy. "Instead, we *dare* you to live to 100. I'm 107. I still read the newspaper every day, take walks around the block, and co-ordinate talent shows."

"And smoke," Ben says to the television.

"And oh, yes," Flo adds with a wink. "My new picture comes out in the fall."

Close-up. She smiles. Hair's perfect. Kevyn Aucoin did her makeup. Very tasteful.

"Learn the facts," she's saying. "Live right. *Dare* to be 100."

An 800 number appears on the screen.

"Hey, Jean, you missed her!" Ben calls as Jean comes out of Flo's room.

"Was that one of the commercials?"

"She was ta-*rif*-ic," Ben gloats. "She's lost none of the sparkle that made her a star."

Jean folds her arms across her chest. "Richard said she didn't seem like herself on TV," she says. "I have to agree."

"You spoke with my brother?"

"He was here today." Jean sits down next to Ben on the couch. "He's spoken with a police detective who wants to interview Flo."

"Flo doesn't have to talk to anyone," Ben says defensively.

Jean nods. "I know she doesn't. But it's better if she does, Ben. It's better if she tells the truth. Especially to us. That's what tonight was about. I talked to her. I told her she had to start telling us the whole story because too many people were asking too many questions."

"So nothing's off limits anymore?"

"So long as the camera isn't rolling." Jean rests her head against the back of the couch. "If we know the truth, we can make the best decisions about who she talks to, and when—as well as what she says."

"You mean, we'd keep some stuff to ourselves?"

Jean closes her eyes. "Possibly. You were right, Ben. She might indeed have grandchildren out there. What if Annie Laurie *is* still alive? What might *that* do to Flo if a truckload of descendants suddenly turns up in her life? Suddenly Flo's worth something again. The money from the Waters film, the 'Dare to be 100' campaign, possibly the Altman film if that comes through. And who knows what else, Ben—*your* film, for example. Who knows where that will go?"

He shifts uncomfortably on the couch.

"Money brings out the worst in people. I don't trust anyone, Ben."

But she trusts me, Ben thinks. *She trusts that I won't tell what I know.*

But the film, he tells himself. *I owe it to the film.*

The film *needs* the story of the baby, he rationalizes. It's too fabulous for words. Not only does it answer the question of why she bowed out of the movies, but it's *great* drama. *And if we could sponsor a nationwide hunt to find Annie Laurie,* he suddenly thinks, *what publicity it would make.*

"There's more, Ben," Jean says.

He blinks back to her. "What?"

"Richard also discovered the name of the girl. At least we think it's her. She lived with Flo for three years before the supposed suicide. Then she was reported missing. Her name was Margaret Butz. Flo called her Molly to me."

"Well, my brother is sure the ace reporter, huh? There's no fact he can't dig up."

Jean looks over at him and the exasperation shows on her face. "What *is* it between the two of you? You're *brothers,* for God's sake. *Twins* even. The same flesh and blood, the same genetic material. Why is there such competition?"

"Ahh," Ben says, trying to dismiss it.

"No," Jean says, sitting up, leaning in close to Ben. "What is it? Something from your childhood?"

"Jean, leave it alone. Really. It's dumb. I shouldn't have made the remark. It's really *Richard* who's always had the problem with *me,* not the other way around."

"Why?"

"I don't know. He's always felt he had to prove himself, I guess. Prove himself better than me." Now it's Ben's turn to lean back into the cushions of the couch. "Nothing's ever been enough for him. He's always pushing himself farther and harder for more, more, more. He writes for the *New York* fucking *Times.* He makes a good living. He drives a nice car. He's got an amazing body that he worked really, really hard for, and he wears only the very best clothes. He's gone to Europe a couple times. And he just bought the most fabulous town house in Chelsea that he and Sexy Rexy are turning into the Taj Mahal."

"So?" Jean frowns. "How does any of that make him better than you?"

"Money and a great body can't guarantee happiness—is that what you're trying to say?" Ben laughs bitterly. "Try telling that to Richard. He seems happy enough. And I can't say I wouldn't mind having his dough and his pecs to see if the old adage is true or not."

"Ben, pursuing one's art means a struggle."

"Tell me about it," he agrees. "I know from struggle. Until two months ago, I nickel and dimed my days away at Penn's Advertising. Look at where I live, for Christ's sake. A Hell's Kitchen hellhole. My body's flabby around my waist and skinny through my shoulders, and until Xerxes bought me these new threads, I got all my clothes at the Salvation Army." He shrugs. "And, oh yeah, I've never been to Europe."

He turns and looks Jean square in the eye. "On top of all that, my girlfriend's dumped me. So tell me again that Richard's life isn't better than mine."

Jean can't seem to help a small smile as she leans back with him into the couch. "Anita hasn't dumped you," she says. "The two of you are just . . . adapting." She winks. "And just to keep things in perspective, I've never been to Europe either."

"You went to Central America," he reminds her.

She ignores him. "And I happen to *like* the clothes you can get at the Salvation Army."

He turns to face her. They're practically nose to nose. "Flo can change all that for me," he tells her.

"She doesn't need to, Ben." He feels Jean's hands take his in her lap. "You've already accomplished more than many people. You made a film—an award-winning film. Richard can't claim that. You made a film that touched people's lives."

"Yeah, yeah," he says, suddenly sitting up, pulling away from her. She doesn't get it. "We've been over this before."

"You don't allow yourself to celebrate your own accomplishments," she tells him.

"*What* accomplishments, Jean? Sure, you liked *One Chance, One World.* But you know what? I never made a goddamn *dime* from it. It's never helped me do anything else in my career. People have very short memories, Jean. I was a star for about nine months after taking *second place* in that contest. Then it was over. And I came back to New York with nothing. Oh, sure, sure, *One Chance, One World* was a very high and noble thing—but it never helped me pay the bills. Or open any doors."

He looks back at her. "Maybe you can't understand that, with the church as your own private sugar daddy."

He stands up. He faces the TV. He's suddenly afraid to turn around and look at her.

And with good reason.

Jean rises from the couch. She can feel the anger constricting her throat. "Just one minute, Ben Sheehan," she says slowly. "I have always *worked* for my pay. If you add up all the hours I work and then divide that into what the diocese provides for me, I think you'll find I come out on the definite short end of the stick."

He turns and faces her. She stiffens.

"I'm sorry," he says. "I don't know where that came from."

He gives her a schoolboy smile. *Dear God, does he ever look like Victor.*

"Forgive me?" he asks.

Jean senses the warmth in her cheeks. "Ben, I *do* know where it came from," she tells him. "If only I could convince you of how talented you are."

"There won't be any need of convincing anybody of that fact once my film of Flo's life comes out," he tells her, suddenly animated again. "I *know* it's going to be something special. I just know it."

"I know it's going to be special, too, Ben," she says. "With Flo telling all her stories combined with your talent, you're in like gold."

"It's not just the documentary, Jean," he says, approaching her, taking her hands.

She looks up into his eyes. "What do you mean?"

"I'm working on a script for a dramatic film," he tells her, the passion in his eyes evident.

"A dramatic film?"

"Yes. Of course, when I'm done, I'll let you read it."

She blinks a few times. "Ben, I didn't think that was your area of expertise. I thought that *Richard* was the writer, that it was *Richard* who's written screenplays."

He tenses. "Do you think I can't because my brother can?"

She squeezes his hands and lifts them to her mouth. Without even thinking she kisses his cold fingertips. "Of course not, Ben. Of *course* you can do it." She pauses. "I'm just . . . curious . . . how you'll portray Flo."

"I'll show you a draft when I'm finished," he says. "Okay?"

She nods.

He kisses her cheek quickly. "Good night, Jean," he says.

"Good night, Ben."

He winks once, then goes through the door to his own room.

Jean sits back down on the couch.

Just be careful of how much you share with my brother.

"Oh, Ben," she says in a small voice as the sea crashes below her in the still night.

"Hey, didja hear Florence Lawrence is making an appearance over at McDonald's?" the radio shock jock asks his cohort.

"No, I didn't," she responds.

"Yep. They're launching a new special sauce for the Big Mac. Tartar sauce with ant paste!"

"Damn fool," Richard says, switching off the radio.

"She's become the butt of all his jokes lately," Rex gripes. "*Everybody* seems to be doing her. Letterman, Leno, Conan O'Brien. You fell asleep last night, but I stayed up to watch *Saturday Night Live.* They did a whole skit, with Cheri Oteri playing Flo, forcing ant poison on all the residents of a nursing home so she could escape."

"Oh, *that's* funny," Richard says sarcastically.

"Actually, it *was,* kind of," Rex admits, shamefacedly.

Richard sighs. "She's all over the Internet. There's a ton of Web sites devoted to her. Xerxes even set up her own home page."

"Well, no doubt about it now," Rex says. "Flo's *back.* Having a Web page is a sure sign of '90s fame."

"This is even more," Richard says, handing over a newspaper to Rex. It's a supermarket tabloid, *The Weekly World Report.*

"Oh, Jesus," Rex says, scrunching up his face.

The headline:

FLO LAWRENCE REALLY DID DIE IN 1938;
CURRENT INCARNATION IS CLONE, SCIENTISTS REPORT

* * *

"Pleased to make your acquaintance, Miss Bridgewood," says Detective Lee, nodding his head, "or should I say, Miss Lawrence?"

Flo just smiles.

Go ahead, Flo, Jean thinks. *Say it. Say what you always say.*

"You can call me anything you want, except late for dinner."

But she doesn't, of course. She just sits there, worn-out. Detective Lee takes the seat opposite her. Jean watches him carefully. This time, her instincts aren't helping. She can't read anything about this man. He seemed friendly enough when he called yesterday morning, requesting a meeting. At first Jean hesitated. She hadn't been able to get Flo to talk about Molly yet. Flo had been stubborn, sticking to her line that there was nothing to tell, that the hospital just made a mistake. When Jean persisted, Flo grew agitated and flustered; Jean backed down reluctantly.

So she told the detective that they were leaving for San Francisco in a matter of days, that they really didn't have time to talk with him right now. He countered by saying he'd come to San Francisco and interview her there. Jean didn't want to give the impression they were trying to avoid him—even if they were—so she consented to a visit today, for just a half hour. "Flo gets awfully tired," she told Lee. "I'm sure you can appreciate that. She's *one hundred and seven*, after all."

Immediately after she hung up with Lee, Jean called the diocesan office back in Buffalo. "Get Carla out here right away," she insisted. The lawyer flew out on the red-eye last night and now sat primly at Flo's side, her knees sharply held together, her hands folded in her lap, watching Detective Lee as closely as Jean was watching him.

He seems to sense the eyes on him. "Don't worry," he assures them, first Carla and then Jean. "I'm not gonna bite her."

"She'd bite ya right back," Jean tells him.

At least, the old Flo would have.

"May I videotape the interview?" Ben asks.

"I don't mind," Lee says.

"Absolutely not," Carla says, quickly and efficiently. She glances over at Ben. He just swallows, shrugs, and sulks a little over by his tripod.

"I just want to ask a few questions, Miss Lawrence," Lee begins. "Just a routine matter."

Flo nods. She spreads her floral-print caftan over her knees and laces her fingers together when she's finished. Her big blue eyes look straight at Lee.

He gets right to the point. "Any idea how this girl they dug up was misidentified as you back in '38?"

"I don't know how the hospital did things," she says.

"How'd you hear about it?"

"Hear about what?"

"That she'd been identified as you and that you were declared dead."

"Flo," Carla says, "remember what I told you. You don't have to answer any question you don't want to."

She smiles. It's a weak smile. Tired. "It's all right, dear. Let's see. I believe I read about it in the newspaper. A few days later. I was in a diner. Yes, a diner on the coast highway. I was traveling, you see."

"Traveling to where?"

"San Francisco," she tells him, and she breaks out into a broad grin.

"Why were you going to San Francisco?" Detective Lee asks.

"To start a new life. Have you ever wanted to do that, Detective?"

There it is, Jean thinks giddily. *A flash of the Flo I love, challenging her inquisitors, turning the tables.*

Lee smirks. "I'm asking the questions here, ma'am." He pauses. "But yes, actually."

"Well, that's what I was doing. And then I picked up the newspaper to see I'd been declared dead. Well, you can see how that just pushed me along."

He nods his head. "So you had no prior knowledge that this was going to happen? None at all?"

"No prior knowledge," she says.

She's telling the truth, Jean thinks. She'd know if Flo were lying about something. Everything she's told him has been truthful. Truthful without revealing the full truth. Jean marvels at how canny Flo can be.

"Do you know the name Margaret Butz?" Lee asks suddenly.

Jean sees Flo's face change. No one else could have noticed it. Only Jean. It was as if Flo were an electric sign and someone had just unplugged its cord. The power just went off behind her eyes. She continues to look directly at the detective but there's no life in them. They're dead.

"Miss Bridgewood," Detective Lee says. "Margaret Butz? Any recognition?"

"I didn't know Margaret Butz," Flo says finally, her voice tight.

Of course not, Jean thinks.

She knew Molly.

"You sure? I've checked the city directories. They say she lived with you on Westbourne Drive."

"It was a very, very long time ago," she says, her voice softer now. Her head drops forward just a little.

"I think Flo's getting tired," Jean says. "Will there be anything else, Detective?"

He looks long and hard at Flo. "No. Not for now." He stands. "It's been a great honor, Miss Bridgewood. I thank you most kindly."

She manages a small smile as he shakes her hand.

Ben sees him out.

Carla looks up at Jean. "Who's Margaret Butz?"

"Do you want to tell us, Flo?" Jean asks.

She seems so weary. Her sparkle fades in and out so quickly these days.

"Why do they always ask about her?" Flo asks, in a low, tremulous voice. "Why do they always want to know about my life *before*, not after?"

She lifts her old eyes to meet Jean's. Jean can see such sorrow there, such longing. Such truth, too. "What do you mean, *after*?" Jean asks. "After what?"

"After I left. After I became *me* again."

"Tell us about that then, Flo," Jean says kindly. "I want to hear about what came after."

But Flo just closes her eyes. She doesn't open them or speak again for the rest of the day.

Richard sits on the deck, staring up at the moon. He can feel the *boom-boom-boom* vibration from the clubs down on Santa Monica Boulevard. The whole night seems to pulsate with energy: the reddish glow over the palm trees in the indigo sky, the slightly electric edge to the chirping of the crickets. Richard keeps his eyes on the moon, a burning white hole in the dark celestial ceiling.

He feels guilty about his decision. The disappointment had been clear on Rex's face.

"Nooker," Richard had cajoled, "I've seen your show in New York."

"But I've added stuff," Rex replied. "It's not the same. You're always there for opening night. You're my good-luck charm."

"Sweetheart, things are breaking wide open with the Flo story. I've got to be there if I'm going to write a book." His eyes had pleaded with Rex for understanding, but Rex had only looked away.

Why did he have to be so goddamn sanctimonious? Richard could see it in Rex's eyes: the disapproval he felt for how involved Richard was getting. *He thinks it's just the competition with Ben,* Richard tells himself. *He just can't understand what a reporter's duty is. How the story gets in your blood, in your dreams—how you've just got to ride it like a wild pony until it's tamed. He just can't understand that because ultimately he doesn't understand* me.

Even as the angry thoughts rush past his brain, Richard's begrudgingly aware of another voice telling him he's being absurd: *Of course Rex understands you. He understands you better than anyone else. That's why you love him. And why, at this moment, he's pissing you off more than you can express.*

Maybe he just needs to get away for a bit, Richard thinks. Maybe all this time together, twenty-four by seven since coming to L.A., has left him a bit weary from Rex's unspoken accusations.

And what might Rex's accusations *be* if he spoke them? Richard feared not just obsessiveness about Flo and Ben's involvement—but maybe something *else,* too.

Now that *is really absurd,* Richard tells himself. This stupid flirtation he was having with Scott—it's nothing. Nothing at all. Most of it's just been in his mind anyway, just a stupid diversion from everything else.

Okay, sure, maybe I'm still getting used to the fact that the new drugs might not be the miracle cure, free of complications, that we'd originally hoped for. That didn't mean—

An image of Scott at the gym, lying on his back, grunting and sweating as he presses two hundred pounds, passes through Richard's mind.

—that I have any desire for some silly blond ex-boyfriend....

"Jesus," he groans, running his hand over his face.

All right. So maybe he *did* have some desire. Maybe he *did* think about what life might be without pills and medications, without the ever present fear of relapse and the looming promise of death. *I need to get away,* he tells himself, for the hundredth time that night. *I need to be away for a while.*

Hey, I'm doing this for him as much as for me, Richard thinks. *How does he think I can continue to afford our standard of living? If he wants goddamn skylights put in that town house, then he'd just better hope I write a good enough book that's going to bring in an advance worth* something.

And the story was breaking wide open. Lee had announced this morning—first on an interview on the *Today* show and later in an Associated Press story—that he had a lead on the identity of the body exhumed from Florence Lawrence's grave. He had done the research, found her name in the directories, just as Richard had.

"Her name might be Margaret Butz," he told Matt Lauer. "She was reported missing in February 1939 by a guy she lived with. He said she came from Iowa. That's all the information we have." He was hoping that Margaret's family might come forward.

Oh, someone will come forward, Richard thinks. *There are a lot of gold diggers and wackos out there.*

And Flo will be in San Francisco as of tomorrow. Richard *had* to be there for her reaction. Sister Jean had promised he could talk to her again.

Rex would just have to understand.

Below him, a gaggle of West Hollywood clones has arrived to sit around the pool. Their arms are draped across each other's shoulders. Some are shirtless, some wear white tank tops, all have amazing bodies, tight cutoff shorts, and boots. They're swaying drunkenly, singing some Cole Porter tune. Richard can practically smell the testosterone in the air.

But there's something else he smells, too. He sniffs, looks around him. Behind him, the room is dark, a tiny red orb glowing faintly over the kitchenette counter as a night-light. Rex had gone to bed about a couple of hours before. Richard wonders if he left the coffeepot on.

But it's not coffee he smells. It's something more acidic, heavier. He stands, walks back into the room. He looks around among the dark blue shadows, but sees nothing. The moonlight cuts a slice through the darkness, glinting off the metallic stools at the kitchen island and the clock on the wall. It's five after midnight.

Richard checks the burners on the stove and the coffeepot. All off. He sniffs. He smells it again.

Sweat.

Like a locker room.

Then he senses the movement on the couch.

"Nooker?" he whispers.

From the shadows, he hears Rex clear his throat. Richard hurries over to the couch. Rex is lying there naked, his arm over his head. He's drenched.

"Rex," he says. "What is it? What's wrong?"

"Nothing. I just got really hot in bed. I came out here."

"You're all wet," Richard says, touching his clammy torso.

He feels the old familiar cold terror raise the flesh on his arms. "This can't be night sweats," he breathes. "Not again. Not *anymore*."

The panic speeds through his body. He can almost visualize it, like a diagram of his veins and arteries suddenly going from red to blue, terror replacing blood.

Rex sits up. "Calm down. It *happens,* Richard. Sometimes it still happens."

"Jesus Christ, let me get you a cold cloth," he says.

He jumps up, finds a dishtowel, wets it under the tap. He brings it back to the couch and begins applying it to Rex's face and wrists.

It's just like before, he thinks. *Those nights. Those terrible nights when I thought Rex was going to leave me. It can't be happening again. It can't. But the lump on his back . . .*

"This is impossible," he says out loud. "You don't have any more virus in your system! It's *gone!*"

"It's *not* gone, Richard," Rex says, a little exasperated. "Why do you keep insisting it's gone even when you know it's not?"

"Okay, so I mean it's undetectable," Richard corrects himself.

Rex sighs. "Not even that anymore, sweetheart. I got my latest viral-load test results in the mail. It's about 300."

Richard stops patting Rex's wrists with the cloth. "How can that *be*? How can you be loaded again?"

"I'm *not* loaded. It's just that the old tests couldn't detect levels below 400. Now they can. You've got to have less than forty copies of the virus to be undetectable now."

"Jesus," Richard says. He feels his whole body stiffen. He has to force the words out with his tongue. "So what the fuck does that mean?"

Rex smiles. He reaches up and places a hot hand on Richard's cheek. Richard grabs it, holds it there. "Sweetheart, nothing's changed," he tells him. "Stop worrying. Just because they can detect the virus doesn't mean the drugs are failing. Treatment failure is indicated by a viral load that continues to rise. There's no need to think it's going to rise beyond this. It's probably been 300 all along."

"But these sweats . . ."

Rex shrugs. "Maybe just nerves. People *do* get sweats, you know. Especially actors the night before a show." He rests his head against Richard's chest. "But you can be sure I'm going to tell the doctor about it."

"Oh, baby," Richard says, stroking his hair. "What's it all mean?"

"It means the same thing this fucking virus has been teaching us all along," Rex tells him. "That life is a goddamn crap shoot. I know guys who take their meds religiously and still get sick. Others who screw up all the time are healthy as hogs."

He's cooling down, Richard tells himself. *His skin is cooler now than it was just a few minutes ago. I'm sure of it.*

"Nooker, I'll stay for opening night," he tells him.

Rex looks up at him and laughs. "Oh, knock it off, Richard," he says.

"No, I mean it. I don't know where my head was at. I can go to San Francisco the next day. Things will hold till then."

Rex pulls away from him, leans into the back of the couch. A spill of moonlight highlights his face and body. *Still so beautiful,* Richard thinks. *Still so perfect, even with the softness to his waist and lump hidden on his back.*

"Richard," Rex says, "I don't want you to stay unless you've really thought about it. I don't want you staying just because you freaked out finding me here on the couch. I'm not going to die, Richard. Don't stay because you feel sorry for me."

"No, that's not it, really."

"Oh, no? Then why, Richard? Is it because you've realized your pursuit of this story has become an obsession? Because you've realized you've lost all sense of perspective around it? That you've become a one-man Florence Lawrence brigade?"

Okay. Here it comes. Richard girds for it.

"Look. You need to hear this. That old lady *trusted* you, Richard. She told you a secret she'd kept for sixty years. Okay, you're not to blame for all the media excess that's happened. Maybe you're right to pin that on Ben. But the fact is, Richard, *you're* not doing anything to stop it. You're actually *part* of it. You're following them around like a dog after a circus, hoping the clowns will toss you a bone."

Rex stands up, taking the wet cloth from Richard and dabbing it under his armpits. He lets out a long breath. "You know," he says, looking down at his lover, "this rivalry between you and your brother is getting very tired. It's so stupid. What's it *about* anyway? Your daddy didn't love you as much as he loved Ben?" Rex clucks a sound of disgust. "Ever since I've known you, you've had this need to prove yourself against Ben. You put him down all the time, but the truth is, you don't *want* Ben to succeed. You *like* him being a loser. It's as if somehow Ben being a loser makes you a winner. Well, it's *bullshit,* Richard."

"All right, all right," Richard says, standing now. "Don't get worked up. You need to be cooling down."

"I'm fine. Really." He looks up at him. "I love you, Richard. But I don't like you very much when you get all competitive with Ben. That's what's driving this whole obsession with Flo. You're pissed that Ben stole your girl."

He shakes his head before continuing. "It's like how you'd tell me back in high school you'd get so upset finding him hanging out with Mary Kay what's-her-name."

Richard just looks at Rex. He finds his eyes, hangs on.

Of course Rex understands you. He understands you better than anyone else.

That's why you love him.

Rex reaches up to touch Richard's face. Richard covers it with his own. *He has cooled down, thank God.*

"You go to San Francisco, sweetheart," Rex says, gently now. "But promise me one thing."

"What's that?"

"If you go, promise me you're not just *following* the circus. You're going to San Francisco so you can put an *end* to it."

Richard doesn't say anything. He just takes Rex's naked form into his arms. They stand there in the moonlight like that for a long time.

November 1963

So you want to know about *after*. Oh, dear, there's so much. Where to begin? Well, I *did* make it to San Francisco that day with Winnie Pichel, the man I met at Doris's diner. I lived in San Francisco for nearly twenty-four years. Longer than I was ever in Hollywood. You see what I mean? How everyone wants to know about just a few years, not about the entirety of my life?

I'll never forget the day I returned at last to my golden city on the hill. It was the second day of 1939. Winnie took me up to the Golden Gate. Oh, it was so beautiful, so magnificent, so—

But, come to think of it, before I get into all that, I think I should tell you first not about the day I *arrived* in San Francisco, but about the day I *left*, some twenty-four years later.

You see, I'd gone to San Francisco to find Florence Bridgewood again. But after more than two decades, there was still a piece of her that was missing.

I knew I had to go back. Back east. Back to Buffalo, where I'd lived such a short time with Mother, Grandmama, and Norman.

I bought a car, a '57 Bel-Air convertible. Oh, it was such a beautiful car. Aquamarine with white leather interior. It had a rearview mirror that kept falling off, but boy, did that baby have power. All the way across the country, I'd just *sail* across the highways. They were new then, you know, just built as part of the whole interstate system. Quite a change from the old dusty roads I'd known when automobillies first came out. The wind in my hair, the radio on. I drove all the way down to Barstow because I wanted to go out on Route 66. *I get my kicks on Route 66 . . .* Oh, how did that old song go? *San Bernadino, Kingman, Flagstaff, Arizona . . . Oklahoma City sure is pretty . . .* Oh, dear, such fun.

You know, I still have that old car. Haven't driven it lately, but I've still got it. Parked there, waiting for me.

How old was I then? Seventy-three, seventy-four. Somewhere around there, I guess. I didn't feel like an old lady, but I guess I looked like one. When I'd stop for gas, my kerchief snapping in the wind, the sky so big and blue behind me, some young man in dungaree overalls would always insist on helping me.

"You know where you're headin', ma'am?" I remember one asking, taking the pump from me and sliding it into the tank.

Such delicious accents down along that route. He pronounced "ma'am" with two syllables. Such a polite young man.

"I sure do," I told him, opening up my container of rouge and inspecting my cheeks in the mirror. "I'm headin' home."

That's when the damn mirror fell off for the last time. The nice young man offered to glue it back on for me, but instead I just tossed it out the window.

"What's behind me isn't what matters anymore," I told him as I revved up the engine. "Let the rest of 'em look out for *me*."

Oh, I know. I wasn't really heading "home." I was born in Hamilton. I was a Canadian by birth—and proud of it. But Hamilton was never home. The only memory I have of Hamilton is that wrinkled old codger they called my father, hulking silently over his whittling knife, until one day he snuffed himself out with his coal stove. No, it wasn't Hamilton I was heading for.

It was *Buffalo*.

Buffalo—where for a few years at the turn of the century, I'd gone to school, living in my grandmother's house. I hadn't been happy there. I don't mean to imply by calling it "home" that I was or that my memories were nostalgic and carefree. Far from it. During our whole time in Buffalo, I badgered Mother to get us back on the stage. My brother was cruel, taunting me until I'd pop him in the snout. That usually worked to shut him up for a few days at least.

But, you see, Buffalo was where the last bit of Florence Bridgewood still eluded me. Here, in the place where Mother had grown up. Where she had left my father and brother behind to devote herself to me and my career. Where, for a few years out of seventy plus, I'd been just an ordinary girl, going to school, going to church, going to the magnificent world's fair that ripped a hole right through my innocence . . .

All together, I was on the road from San Francisco to Buffalo for about a week and a half. I stayed in little motels along the way with names like the Vista or the Weary Traveler. Usually the proprietor's wife made me breakfast—hot cakes and scrambled eggs and big, fat sausages.

It made me think of all those years, crisscrossing the country with Mother and Ducks and the Lawrence Dramatic Company. Back then, we'd lumber along in horse-pulled wagons, covering in a month the distance I traveled in my Bel-Air in a week. Then, it was Ducks's harmonica that accompanied us on our journey. Now, I'd turn on the radio with just a flick of my hand and whistle my way with Johnny Cash. When I turned northward, heading up through Missouri and Indiana and Pennsylvania, I was snapping my fingers to Bobby Darin and "Mack the Knife."

I pulled over briefly just outside Buffalo to check my map. Who knew if my grandmother's house was even still standing? I had no idea where I'd sleep that night, nor even what I'd come to see. What might I find there? What bit of Florence Bridgewood still remained that I might recognize?

On the radio Frank Sinatra was crooning. Suddenly there was a stutter, followed by a crackle of static. I looked up from my map. A man's somber voice announced that the young president of the United States had been shot in Dallas.

I turned off the radio and drove the rest of the way in silence.

Grandmama's neighborhood looked much the same as it had sixty years before. Except now the trees were taller and the houses smaller than I remembered, and a crosshatch of telephone wires interrupted the sky.

I parked the car on the corner of West Eagle Street. Everything was eerily quiet. Like one of those sci-fi movies where the hero's been off in space and comes back to earth only to find all the people gone. The echo of my shoes clacking on the pavement seemed to ricochet off the houses as I looked for number 115.

There, ahead of me. That was it. The two-story brown Victorian, with the wraparound porch and overgrown lawn. Hedges were spiky and unkempt; the grass was long and starting to seed. A maple tree that once had been small enough to leap over as I eluded my brother now towered above me, its great bare limbs seeming to implore the sun. But the sun had gone behind a cloud. I felt a deep and penetrating chill.

As I approached the house, the tinny sound of a radio wafted in the air. A man's voice—the same, perhaps, who had preempted Sinatra earlier. Up on Grandmama's porch sat an old man, just a shriveled white figure wrapped in a faded blue afghan, listening to the radio. The announcer's words filtered down to me on the sidewalk through the quiet of the neighborhood.

I repeat: President Kennedy has died at Parkland Memorial Hospital, due to a gunshot wound to the head. . . .

I walked slowly up the steps of the front porch.

"It's not the first time," I said, disturbing the stillness.

The radio announcer went on about how Lyndon Johnson would be sworn in as president.

"Over at the fair," I said. "Do you remember?"

The old man didn't stir. He was hunched down in his chair, the afghan around his shoulders. His face was wizened and spotted. He was almost completely bald.

"You remember, don't you, Norman?" I asked. "It's not something we could easily forget. Strange, isn't it? Live as long as we have, and the world starts coming back around."

I stood beside him, looking down.

"Who are you?" he croaked.

"It's your sister, Norman."

"I don't have a sister."

"No, I suppose you don't." I sat down in an old wicker chair beside him, its seat frayed and coming apart. I reached over and touched his gnarled old hands, curled like dead bird claws in his lap. "But I've come back around, too, Norman." I sighed. "I've come back around, too."

Norman was blind. Had been for about six years. A nurse came in twice a week to look after him, but the house was a mess. Dishes piled everywhere. Broken glass on the floor. Poor Norman's feet were all scarred and cut. He'd learned to feel his way around the house, but he was eighty years old, after all. A weak, frail man. Sometimes he'd trip and fall, and instead of trying to get up, he'd just sit there and wait for the nurse. Even if that meant three days.

He'd steadfastly resisted being put in a nursing home. He'd worked hard all his life as an electrician and built up quite a sizable nest egg. It paid for the nurse and his food. Grandmother had long ago paid for the house, and when she died, it was left to Mother, who in turn left it to Norman and me. I remember when I read Mother's will and realized I partly owned my grandmother's house. "I'll never go back *there*," I'd sniffed at the time.

I found the deed to the house, filed away in Norman's desk. My name was still on it. *Florence Bridgewood*. Well, Florence Bridgewood had come home.

In the parlor stood the old clock I remembered so well, with its deep, heavy chimes in the middle of the night. In the glass cupboard the Irish crystal—brought to this country by my grandfather—was covered by a layer of dust a half inch thick.

"What are you doing?" Norman demanded, coming in from the porch, his hands held out in front of him, the screen door banging shut.

"I'm cleaning up this mess," I told him, pushing the broom across the floor, sweeping shards of glass, coffee grounds, and egg shells in my path.

"Who *are* you?"

"Your sister, Norman."

He was quiet. He stood there staring at me with his sightless eyes. Finally he felt for the kitchen table and eased himself down into a chair. "Florence," he said softly.

"Have you eaten anything today, Norman?"

He shook his head no.

"What have you got here in the refrigerator?"

"Whatever they bring me."

I opened the door of the old Frigidaire. A glass jar of milk. Some apples. Two eggs. A plate of spaghetti covered in tin foil.

"How much do you pay for groceries a week, Norman?"

"Twenty dollars."

I made a face. "They've been ripping you off," I told him. "From now on, I'll do your grocery shopping."

"Flo?"

"Yes, Norman?"

"How'd you manage it?"

I laughed. "They just made a mistake, Norman. So I decided to run with it."

Of course, it wasn't long before we spoke of Mother.

"You were all she cared about, Flo. You were her whole life. She never cared a whit about me."

It was late. Getting close to midnight. I'd built a fire, wondering when the chimney had last been cleaned. Oh, well, I figured. If the house was going to burn down, so be it.

We were sitting in Grandmama's parlor. Her old rolltop desk was still in the corner, exactly where I last remembered it. The rest of the furniture was new—or rather, new to me. It looked as if it dated from the

'40s. Dusty and worn, covered in old moldy blankets and afghans. There was no television in the house, just a big radio with gigantic knobs. We had it turned down low. They were still rambling on about Kennedy.

"Mother sacrificed a lot," I admitted.

"It was always you she cared about," Norman said.

There was no bitterness in his voice. Not anymore. Even though she had left him with our silent, surly father as a very little boy, never to return. Even though she always promised she'd send for him, but never did. We sent him money, of course, after our father was dead and Norman had gone to live with Grandmama. We could afford it then: I was making a fortune. But when the well ran dry for us, we forgot about Norman. By then, of course, he had his own life. A job. A house. Friends. In so many ways, his life had turned out far more fortunate than mine.

"To be honest," I told him, "I never knew Mother much more than you did. She kept herself hidden from me, and so I did the same with her. Oh, she was *with* me—can't say she wasn't. She *did* sacrifice a lot for me. She was always there, pushing me onward."

I paused. "But in truth, she only *really* knew me as Baby Flo, the Child Wonder Whistler—who later was turned into Florence Lawrence." I smiled sadly. "Now, Florence *Bridgewood*—well, Mother never could quite figure *her* out."

Norman was quiet, rocking in his chair, staring over at me with his sightless eyes. "How did she die?" he finally asked.

"It was cancer," I told him.

"Yes. I remember your letter. I remember you writing to tell me that Mother had died, that she wanted to be buried out there in Hollywood." He paused. "But how, Flo? *How* did she die?"

I closed my eyes. The older one gets, the more details one wants about death.

"It was hard at the end," I told him. "We had a small apartment in the garment district of Los Angeles, above a tailor and a shoemaker. I can't imagine how we paid our bills at that point. But we managed somehow. I did a few parts in the movies here and there. Mother took in laundry—like she used to do in our early days in New York." I smiled to myself. "You see, Norman? What I mean about those full circles everyone's always talking about?"

"Did she suffer long?"

"Not too long. Maybe a couple of months. The cancer started in her stomach, and it just ate her alive. Bit by bit she'd go every day. It seemed as if she just shrunk in front of my eyes. Finally she was in her bed all the time, a tiny little creature with enormous eyes."

I stopped, remembering Mother. "And then she died," I said. "I'd gone out for licorice. She asked for some, just to suck on. I bought her a gigantic bag, red and black. But when I got back, she was gone."

He just sighed.

"What about you, Norman?" I asked. "Did you ever marry? Any children?"

"No," he said. "It was just me. Old Man Bridgewood."

"It's a good name," I told him.

He made a sound.

"What was he like?" I asked. "Our father?"

Norman shrugged. "I was still a child when he died."

"Yes, but you lived with him. I never knew him. I just remember him glaring down at me as if he despised me."

Norman laughed. "Despised you? Hah. He had every clipping ever written about Baby Flo. He had 'em all pasted up on his wall at the shop. 'That's me gul,' he'd say to people. 'Me gul.'"

I had nothing to say in reply. I just sat there, trying to fit this new image of my father into my mind. It was difficult after so many years.

We sat in silence for several minutes. "I wish I could see you," Norman finally said. "I can't remember what you looked like."

I laughed. "Well, even if you could, I'm quite changed from when you last saw me."

"I didn't like you much," he said.

"I didn't like you much either."

He made a snort. It was the closest thing to a laugh Norman ever did. "And what about you, Flo?" he asked. "Did you ever marry? Have children?"

"Yes, I was married," I told him. "I had a little girl. Her name was Annie Laurie."

"What happened to her?"

"I'm not sure. I like to think she died young and beautiful." I sighed. "I'm pretty sure she did."

History is nothing more than a series of small yesterdays. I have crossed the country in both a horse-drawn wagon and an aquamarine Chevy Bel-Air. In San Francisco, I had signed petitions protesting the military buildup in Southeast Asia. In my grandmother's house, I found my grandfather's discharge papers from the War of 1812. My father's father. He, too, had been an old man when his child was born. He fought on the British side, of course. *1812.* I sat reading his papers as the radio spoke of Kennedy. Yes, just small yesterdays. Very small.

History hung heavy in that house. That night, I couldn't sleep.

Norman had nodded off right in his chair, and I decided to leave him there. I explored the house, remembering not only the unhappiness, the loneliness, and the longing for the stage, but also the occasional fleeting moment of joy: spying a robin's nest in the trellis outside my window, watching fireworks from the roof, playing dress up with the strange, outdated fashions I found in a chest in Grandmama's attic.

Tiptoeing quietly past Norman, I discovered a small box in the old rolltop desk. I opened the lid and found a gold band. Under the lid was inscribed, in handwriting I still recognized as my mother's:

Charles and Lotta, August 6, 1881

I slipped on what was clearly my mother's wedding band, which I never remember her wearing, which she must have kept here in this box. Out of sight, a reminder of a painful episode in her life? As a treasured memento, one that brought heartbreak and regret?

"Who's to say I didn't marry for love?" she once said to me.

There was so much I didn't know.

From his chair, Norman was snoring like a buzz saw. I tiptoed past him and stopped at the door to the basement. I pulled it open with some difficulty, yanking the string that dangled from the ceiling to illuminate the bulb overhead. I carefully made my way down the broken steps to the earthen floor. The cellar smelled dank and musty, but sugary sweet, too—like rotting apples or the decaying carcasses of squirrels and mice.

I don't know what I was looking for, if anything. But it didn't take me long to find them. There, behind Grandmother's old trunks, at the base of her ancient dressmaker's dummy, leaning in three stacks against the old stone wall, were our posters. Mother's and mine.

THE LAWRENCE DRAMATIC COMPANY PRESENTS
"MEDEA"
WITH CHARLOTTE LAWRENCE

THE MAJESTIC THEATER PRESENTS
THE GREAT McGINTY

GABY DUBOIS, THE FRENCH SENSATION

And finally, there, at the very back:

BABY FLO, THE CHILD WONDER WHISTLER

* * *

Norman had lived in that house nearly all his life. The farthest he'd ever traveled from Buffalo were two brief trips into New York City in the 1930s. Eighty-three years he lived, and that was as far as he went. Me, I'd crisscrossed the country with Mother and our troupe, lived in New York and Hollywood and San Francisco, floated up the Nile on a barge, and found tranquility on a Greek island. But Norman—Norman didn't need to go so far. Down to his electrician shop in the center of town and to the corner market for food. That was all.

I never counted family by blood. Blood has no particular claim, no rank. Maybe that's why I could come back to my grandmother's house and have it be all right. I'd never expected anything of Norman, and he never expected anything of me. The money Mother and I sent in our heyday must have been welcome, but when it dried up there were no squawks for more. I never knew my brother. I never thought about him all those years. I didn't even come back to find him. I just knew I had to come back.

Norman lived another two-and-a-half years. I like to think I made his life better. The few acquaintances he had were surprised to learn he had a sister. The visiting nurse eyed me at first with some suspicion, but in the end, I think she was relieved when I let her go. I was all the nurse Norman needed. I kept a clean house, cooked him some good meals, even took him for drives in my Bel-Air through the town. We came to enjoy our routine and even each other's company, though we spoke very little. Occasionally something on the radio would catch our spirits, and we'd laugh. And that—I think, *that*, more than the meals and the clean house—was what Norman appreciated most.

I found him one morning out on the porch, sitting in the old rocking chair, the radio on at his side, as always. "Hard Day's Night" by the Beatles was playing. His head was down on his chest. I placed the palm of my hand on his forehead. He was cold.

There are worse things than to die on one's own front porch in the spring, just as the forsythia is bursting into life. I turned off the radio, folded his hands in his lap, and sat opposite him for nearly three quarters of an hour, just looking at him.

When Norman died, the house became my own. People in town knew me as Miss Bridgewood, the old lady with the fancy car. I'd show up at the market or the library, cigarette in hand, my nails painted scarlet, a flowing scarf around my neck. I'd drive through town, beeping at the children, waving from my open-top car. "Hello, Miss Bridgewood!" they'd call. "Sure is one fine car, Miss Bridgewood!"

Miss Bridgewood. That's who I was. There was no connection, none at all, to anyone else I'd ever been, any other life I'd ever lived. And that was just fine with me.

I lived there in my grandmother's house until climbing the stairs proved too difficult, until I could no longer get in and out of the tub with ease, until driving my beloved aquamarine Bel-Air became impossible. That's when I sold the house, deposited the cash, and moved to St. Mary's.

I hear they've torn the house down now. Put up high rises all along Eagle Street.

Guess I made it back there just in time.

The Present

"We just want some answers," the woman with the bleached-blond hair and broad Midwestern accent is saying. "We just want to know what happened to our aunt."

She pronounces "aunt" as "ant." She's one of three women on *20/20* tonight, sitting opposite Barbara Walters. All three have similar hair teased very high up on their heads. They look to be in their mid- to late forties, all wearing tight black jeans and red satin Western shirts. Earlier there was a clip of them singing together in a nightclub. They're known throughout the Midwest as the Cherry Sisters.

Now the scene shifts to show them clustered around an older woman with bright orange hair, her face a mass of creases, a beauty mark in the shape of a star to the left of her mouth. She's crying. Her tears cut shiny trails down her powdered face, taking her mascara along with them.

"Our mother has been heartbroken for *sixty years*," another of the Cherry Sisters tells Barbara Walters. "All she wants to know is what happened to her sister."

"Do you think," Barbara asks slowly, "that Flowence Lawwence . . . knows more . . . than she is saying?"

The redheaded woman looks up. The camera moves in to frame her mascara-streaked face. She speaks for the first time. "That woman may have killed my sister," she croaks. "I don't care *how* old she is. My darling sister. Lovely Maggie."

Flo just watches from bed. She's propped up with several pillows. Her face is drawn; she wears no lipstick. To look at her, one wouldn't think she even understood what the Cherry Sisters and their mother were saying. But finally she turns her face on her pillows—seemingly with great effort—and says softly, "Her name was *Molly*."

Jean sits on the edge of her bed. "Do you want more aspirin, Flo? How's the headache?"

Flo just closes her eyes.

"Flo," Jean says, taking her hand, "I know all this is upsetting to you. But it's time. You need to tell me about Molly."

"I'm . . . too ill," the old woman says.

Flo. *Ill.* It seems so incongruous. Flo has never complained about pain before in the entire time Jean has known her. Even when her joints must surely have been aching, she never uttered a word. Now for the last several days, she's seemed as weak and lifeless as . . . as the other old folks who'd appeared with her on *Oprah.*

Jean turns her eyes back to the program. Now there's a clip of the exhumation. Barbara Walters is saying how DNA tests seem to link the remains of the corpse with the redheaded woman, Myrtle Butz Pickles, suggesting the girl buried as Florence Lawrence may indeed have been her "lovely Maggie."

Ben appears in the doorway. He's been watching in the other room.

"That's it," Jean tells him sharply. "No more interviews."

"Jean," he says, obviously weary of this argument. "We've just arrived here in San Francisco. We have *a lot* of media set up."

"*No more interviews,*" she states unequivocally. "Not until we can find out what exactly happened to old lady Pickles's sister."

She turns back to Flo. She's just staring at the set. Jean can see nothing in her eyes.

Richard thanks the flight attendants and heads down the walkway into the terminal. He hasn't been in San Francisco for a number of years. He's looking forward to being in the city again. It's a town that knows how to have a good time, but without all the mess and craze of New York. San Francisco always does things with a touch of class. He saw a bit on the news last night, a clip of a banner draped across Castro Street:

SAN FRANCISCO WELCOMES THE BIOGRAPH GIRL

The Castro Theater was all set with its special program of one-reel films, all starring Flo. She's scheduled to make an appearance later this week.

Leave it to the queens, Richard thinks, smiling.

Then, of course, had come the *20/20* interview with the Cherry Sisters and their mother, the dollar signs nearly popping up in their tear-filled eyes the way they do in cartoons. But whatever trailer trash they might be, Richard knows they're legit. The day before, he'd gone over to the library and checked the index to the 1920 Census for Iowa. Lee had said the missing person report had identified Iowa as Margaret Butz's home state. Sure enough, he found them, on a farm in Red Oak: Glenn Butz, age 37; his wife Vera Butz, age 35; and their four daughters, Madeline, age 10; Miranda, age 7; Margaret, age 5; and Myrtle, age 1.

"She doesn't look too bad for her age," Rex had said, watching Myrtle call Flo a murderess on national TV.

"Oh, I'm sure that's her *real* hair color," Richard had said.

Rex just shivered next to him on the couch. "I guess now is when the vultures begin to circle."

Richard put his arm around him and drew him in close.

Opening night of *The Royal Family of Broadway* had gone remarkably well. A packed house, an enthusiastic crowd, and great reviews in the next day's papers. "Brilliantly hysterical!" said Kevin Thomas of the *Times*.

Richard's favorite part of the show had been when Rex did a dialogue back and forth between Ethel and Drew. This was new stuff; he hadn't seen it in New York. Ethel's just come out of a theater, a little dazed after watching Drew's grisly performance in *Scream*. "Simply regal, my dear, simply regal," Ethel intones, trying to find something to say. "Only a Barrymore could drip blue blood as elegantly as that."

His heart had nearly sprung a rib watching Rex take his bows. How handsome he looked up there. How vibrant. How *alive*. The sweats had disappeared. Rex was fit, trim, and ready for anything up on that stage.

And I'm ready for anything, too, Richard thinks. *I hope*.

Some of Rex's fans from his porno days mobbed him after the show, slobbering over him for his autograph—and possibly, they hoped, more. Why did people think once a porn star, always a porn star—and that their idol must surely be willing and ready to hop into bed with them? Richard stood proprietarily beside his partner, who was still dressed as Lionel, caterpillar eyebrows and all. The fans were telling him how *hot* he was, how his videos were *still* the hottest on the market. Rex handled them all with such aplomb, winking occasionally over at Richard. They made their way to Richard's waiting rental car and then laughed like kids all the way back to their room.

"Okay now. Get a move on," Rex urged Richard this morning. "Hop on your white horse and charge up the coast to save milady."

"You'll call me after you've seen the doctor?"

"Yes, yes."

"He's good?"

"My doc back home recommended him. He'll be fine."

Richard takes him in his arms. "I don't know what I'd do without you."

"You won't have to find out." He kisses him quickly on the lips. "Now, *go*. The fair damsel is in need of rescuing."

Richard laughs.

The fair damsel.

He's stopped now by the face staring out at him from the airport kiosk. Flo, of course, on the cover of *People* magazine. The headline reads:

ONCE MORE, A STAR

He decides not to buy it. He's here to stop it, not subsidize it. He hurries outside and hails a cab.

The real Flo's waiting for him at the Warwick Regis.

"Oh, yes," Jean says into the telephone. "Send him up."

"Who's that?" Ben asks.

"Richard," she tells him.

Ben just makes a face.

"Ben, it's only right. Richard's been helpful. He says he has more information that might encourage Flo to tell us about Molly."

Ben smirks. "He's really working hard on that book of his, isn't he?"

Jean just frowns.

Sure, Ben's thinking. *Just as I get close . . . just as I begin to get to the heart of my interviews with Flo, Richard turns up with "more information." Why can't he just leave it* alone? *Why can't he accept the fact that this has turned into* my *show now?*

He watches as Jean opens the door and Richard walks in, dressed in his L.L. Bean sweater and khakis. He's brought Flo a single white rose—how classy. Richard's *always* so goddamn classy.

But wait—he has another one. Behind his back. This one is for Jean. She's touched. Hand over heart. And now she's hugging him. They say nice things to each other. She hugs him again.

"Ben," Jean says. "Richard's here."

Richard approaches him, extending his hand. "Hello, brother," he says. "Well, *you* got a new look."

Ben shakes his hand, running his free hand over his close-cropped head. "Xerxes's idea," he tells him.

Richard nods. *That's it*, Ben thinks. *He won't say,* Looks good *or anything like that. That's all he'll do. Just nod.*

"Looks good," Richard says.

Ben blinks a couple of times in surprise. "Uh . . . well, thanks." He shifts awkwardly. "Where's Sexy Rexy?" he asks finally.

"Still in L.A.," Richard says. "Sorry you couldn't make it to his opening night."

Ben's sorry, too. He feels a little pang of guilt. "Well, we had to get up here," he explains.

Richard nods. He looks around the room. It's another suite, with connecting rooms for the three of them. A big canopied bed in this one, with a bar, a sitting area, and a terrace overlooking Geary Street.

"Where's Flo?" Richard asks.

"She's sleeping," Jean tells him. "Here. Let me take her rose and I'll put them both in water." She smiles at them, accepts the second flower, then disappears into her own room.

"So," Richard says.

"*So*," Ben repeats.

"How are the interviews with Flo coming?"

"Good. Good." He pauses, clumsily. "Very good."

"That's good."

Richard walks around the room. He presses down on the bed. "Good mattress," he says.

"Oh, yeah," Ben agrees. "Very good."

Another pause.

"Did you see *20/20?*" Richard asks.

"Oh, yeah. Yeah, we saw it."

"What did Flo think?"

"Um, well, she didn't say much. She just kept shaking her head."

"But it's clear she knows who this girl was," Richard says, folding his arms now across his chest.

"Uh, well, yeah, I think so." Ben scratches his head, desperate to change the subject. "So have you talked with Mom lately?"

"Yesterday." He keeps looking at Ben. *Damn him. Is he* trying *to make me uncomfortable?* "How's Anita?"

Yep. He's trying, all right.

"She's—" Ben pauses. "Well, you know, she's still on that soap—"

"Yes, I *do* know," Richard says. "I talked with *her* yesterday, too."

"Oh." Ben turns, walks over to the window, looks down at the traffic on the street. *Enough games,* he thinks.

"Okay, Richard," he says, still looking down at the street. "So why are you here?"

"To protect Flo from you," Richard says plainly.

Ben spins back around to look at him. "*What?* Are you out of your mind?"

"I don't think so. Are you?"

"Look. This wasn't my idea to have you come by. It was Jean's."

"Oh, it's just *Jean* now, huh?"

"I don't have to take this, Richard. All my life you've been trying to lord it over me. Trying to tell me what to do. Not anymore."

"Lord it over you? Is that what you think I've tried to do?"

"Yes. Absolutely. You and Mom both. Taking sides against me. You just can't believe I can accomplish anything on my own."

"Ben, you can't deny you've sidestepped taking responsibility—"

"Don't talk responsibility, Richard. It was me who took care of Dad."

"You're always throwing that at me, Ben! It doesn't change the fact that you have no ambition, that you've always—"

"This is what I'm talking about! Back off, Richard! You have nothing to say to me anymore!"

Richard narrows his gaze at his brother. "Oh, but I do. Just one thing." He takes a step closer to Ben, who takes a step backward. "You've put Flo in a very awkward position. Something's going to come out about what happened back in 1938 and it's likely not going to be good news for her."

"Hey, it's not my fault."

Richard moves closer to him. "It's just what you want, isn't it?" His voice is soft, and the look in his eyes changes from anger to revulsion. "You *want* something to come out. It'll make a better *movie*." He stops not six inches from Ben. "*Jean* told me that you were writing a script. For a *dramatic* film. Not just a documentary anymore."

"So?"

Richard keeps staring at him. "I'm just curious, Ben. About what you're going to do."

Ben smiles hard. "Of *course* you're curious. I'm sure you'll be trying to get a film option on *your* book." His grin tightens further. "And we wouldn't want to find ourselves in competition now, would we?"

Richard just stares at him for several seconds. Finally, very low, he says, "I'm not going to let you hurt that old lady."

Ben feels his smile fade off his lips.

"Richard."

They turn around.

It's Jean, standing in the doorway across the room.

"Flo's up," she's telling him. "She can see you now."

Flo sits propped in an armchair, the white rose in her hands. Right away Richard can see something's different. Horribly different. She looks washed out. There's no color to her. Her cheeks are pale, her lips are dry and cracked. She's not even wearing that damn subtle pink lipstick.

She's a hundred and seven, he reminds himself. But Flo was never like other old folks. She *defied* age. Now she seems withered, wilted—nothing like how he remembers her, in her big red bow and bright eyes, sitting in the colorful day room of St. Mary's, surrounded by her courtiers, clapping her hands and whistling a tune. She sits there with her head slunk slightly forward, as if it's become too heavy a burden for her to hold up.

"What have you *done* to her?" he says to Ben and Sister Jean.

"She's just a little tired," Ben says.

"Flo," Sister Jean is saying. "It's Richard. Richard Sheehan."

Flo's eyes flicker up to him. "Hello, Richard," she says, her voice no more than a whisper.

He sits down in the chair opposite her. Jean stands behind Flo. Ben hovers in the background.

"Flo," Richard says. "Are you all right?"

She gives him a small smile. "Oh, I guess the miles are just catching up with me."

"How are you feeling?"

She closes her eyes. "I had a headache earlier. It's passed."

"I've asked Carla Ortiz to come by," Jean tells him. "Our attorney. I hope you don't mind."

"No," Richard says, his eyes still held on Flo. "I'd like to meet her. See what she thinks."

"Thinks about what?" Ben asks from across the room.

Richard turns to face him. "About all of the questions being asked out there," he says. "About Detective Lee."

Flo opens her eyes, yet nothing Richard says seems to register with her. She just keeps watching him, not responding, as if he were speaking a language she doesn't understand.

"Flo," Richard says, trying to break through. "I heard you spoke with Detective Lee. How did that go?"

She just blinks at him a few times. Finally she says, "Oh, it was fine."

"Did he ask you some difficult questions?"

She seems to consider this. "No," she says. "Not so difficult."

"About Molly, Flo? Did he ask you about Molly?"

Ben steps up quickly. "What's he doing?" he asks Jean. "Is he doing another interview?"

Richard turns to look over at him again. "I'm just trying to gather how Flo is feeling."

"You said you had some more information for us?" Jean asks, deflecting Ben's objection.

Richard sits back in his chair. "Yes," he says. "Flo, are you aware that there have been articles in newspapers and magazines—this week it was *Time*—that publicly accuse you of not telling the whole story about Molly's death, that by implication accuse you of murder?"

"Richard, please. Let's wait until Carla is here," Jean interjects.

Something seems to pop behind Flo's eyes, as if she just suddenly woke up. "No, Jeannie, it's all right," she says, taking in a long breath. Her pupils dilate, her chin rises a little. "I'm aware of the speculation out there, Richard. Yes."

"So don't you think it would be wise to put it to rest?" He leans in closer to her. "If you could tell us what happened, then we could help you."

"Look," Ben says, now striding up almost between Richard and Flo. "Jean and I have been over this with her. Did you think we weren't even *talking* to her about it? We've got a *lawyer* here counseling her, for God's sake. Did you think we needed you to come waltzing in here and set things straight for us? We're doing *fine* here, Richard."

"He just wants to help," Jean tells Ben.

"He just wants the last chapter of his book!" Ben snaps.

Richard lets out a very long sigh. "Ben, put it aside for now, huh? I'll get out of here in just a minute and you don't have to worry about my coming back. I just wanted to say my piece to you and to let Flo know one thing." His eyes turn back to her. "I'm truly sorry if my article unleashed any pain for you."

"Oh, Richard," is all Flo says.

"There's one other thing," he says both to Flo and to Jean. He avoids looking at Ben. "If Lee was able to do the research on Margaret Butz and put two and two together about her, chances are he'll soon discover something interesting about Dr. Lester Slocum."

"Lester?" Flo says suddenly.

"Who's he?" Jean asks.

"The doctor who signed the death certificate, who pronounced Flo dead. Or rather, who pronounced Molly dead and identified her as Flo."

"What about him?" Jean moves in around Flo's chair. "What might Lee find?"

Flo just stares at Richard.

"Do you know, Flo?" he asks. "Do you know what happened to Lester?"

Her eyes are wide. She just shakes her head, very slowly. Richard believes her. He reaches over, takes one of her cold, dry hands in his.

"He took his own life," he tells her. "He killed himself in 1941."

"Oh!" Flo shakes in reaction, as if she'd been struck. Richard can feel the vibration shudder through her frail body. Her hands become warm and moist in a sudden, single rush.

Jean puts her arms around the old woman. "Flo," she comforts her. "Flo."

And then something very strange and unsettling occurs. Flo *cries*. None of them has ever seen her cry like this before. Oh, sure, she's gotten misty-eyed, and Jean's seen some silent tears. But she's never really *cried* in front of them, not to the point of making noise. Not when she recalled the death of Ducks, not when she spoke of her pain, not even when she told them the sad tale of Annie Laurie. Only now: tears for this man named Lester. It surprises them all.

"He was more than just your doctor, wasn't he, Flo?" Richard asks.

Her ancient blue eyes, wet and red, peer over Jean's arm. "He was my friend," she tells him.

"I'm sorry, Flo," Richard says. He feels like such a shit heel. *How much pain am I going to bring this old woman?*

"How did he do it?" she asks.

Richard takes a deep breath before responding. "He hanged himself," he tells her reluctantly.

Flo closes her eyes. Jean's gently rocking her in their embrace. Flo struggles to speak. "I saw a man hanging once," she says. "His face was all blue, his neck all black." She's quiet for several seconds. "Oh, poor Lester. Poor, poor Lester." She begins to cry again, terrible wracking sounds.

By the time Carla Ortiz arrives, Flo's in no condition to talk further. Jean's helped her back to bed. Richard turns to say something to Ben, but his brother seems to have slipped out when no one was looking.

"I appreciate the warning," Jean says to Richard when she comes back out of Flo's room. "Carla and I will discuss a strategy to put the stories to rest."

No one sees him to the door. He just lets himself out, and figures that's the last he'll see of any of them.

Including Flo.

Ben and Xerxes are striding quickly down Castro Street under the banner welcoming The Biograph Girl to San Francisco. They walk quickly so they aren't late to their appointment. Sam Glick is in town to see the films at the Castro and to meet Flo in person. He likes the revised script Ben sent him, although there are a few points he still wants to discuss. They're all having lunch today at the Patio Restaurant. "Nothing very fancy—used to be a favorite of mine," Glick told Xerxes on the phone. "I used to spend a lot of time in the Castro in my youth."

Xerxes takes a last drag on his cigarette and tosses it onto the sidewalk. "Did you see *Crossfire?*" he asks Ben.

"*Crossfire?*" Ben replies. "No. Why?"

"They were going on and on about getting tough on crime," Xerxes tells him. "Buchanan brought Flo's name up, using her as an example of a no-excuses policy, saying just because she's a hundred and seven shouldn't qualify her for special treatment if she's found guilty."

"Jesus," Ben says. "*What,* has he already tried and convicted her? Like, just throw her in prison and that's it? Maybe *electrocute* her? Goddamn right-wingers."

Ben feels sick to his stomach. Maybe it was Flo's tears. Maybe it was his brother's fucking superior attitude, asking what they had *done* to her. Maybe it was the sausage he had for breakfast—it *had* seemed a little pink. He should've sent it back.

"Buchanan's off the wall," Ben says. "Of *course* Flo should be treated differently if she's guilty of anything. It's been sixty years and she can barely walk on her own."

"*If* she's guilty?" Xerxes lights another cigarette. "Don't say that to Glick. He's banking on a good murder mystery."

"Well, Flo doesn't have to be the villain."

"Glick doesn't want her to be. He just wants a little *scandal.*"

Ben stops walking. "Xerxes, you should have seen her just now. She was crying. I mean, really crying. She's a wreck. All of this is turning out to be too much for her. She's tired."

"Hey. She's been very adequately compensated."

"She's *a hundred and seven,*" Ben protests. "Look. I'm not sure it's a good idea for Glick to meet her right now. She's . . . not herself."

"Quit worrying." Xerxes urges him along and they resume walking. "All Glick cares about is keeping her name in the headlines until the film comes out."

Ben sighs. "You know, I'm all for hype, but I don't want to make trash."

Xerxes again tosses his cigarette to the ground. "You want to make something that makes money," he snaps. "Art very rarely turns a profit." He drapes an arm around Ben's shoulders as they cross the street. "Remember, Benny, no less a personage than Pauline Kael said, 'Movies are so rarely great art that if we cannot appreciate great trash we have very little reason to be interested in them.'" He laughs. "I've got that pasted on my bathroom mirror."

Ben makes a little snort of disgust.

The agent stops in his tracks, looking up at the sign over their heads. "Hey," he says. "This is it."

They enter the restaurant. Xerxes tells the host that they're meeting someone. "Right this way," they're told, and they're escorted outside into a sunny courtyard surrounded by lush green plants. In a far corner, at a table by himself sipping an extraordinarily large glass of Diet Coke, sits Glick in a white suit.

"Sammy," Xerxes bellows warmly, extending his hand. "How are you?"

The large man shakes it. "Coming down with a case of the shingles," he says.

Ben shakes Glick's sweaty hand as well. *This is the man,* he tells himself. *This is the one who unlocks the door for me.*

He just wishes he didn't feel so miserable. Goddamn sausage.

"Sit down, Ben," Glick says, gesturing to an empty chair. "Here, next to me." He winks.

There's no chair for Xerxes. The agent looks around awkwardly for a second; then he drags a chair over from the next table.

Ben can clearly detect a change in Glick's attitude. In L.A., he had seemed distinctly uninterested in Ben as a person. Now he seems almost—well, *flirtatious.*

A waiter hovers over them. "Would you gentlemen like to order?"

"A turkey burger for me, rare, please," Glick says. "And another Diet Coke."

"And for you?" the waiter asks Ben.

"Oh, just a—just a Diet Coke for me, too."

"You're not eating lunch?" Glick asks, eyebrows raised. "I flew all the way up to San Francisco and you're not even going to eat lunch with me?"

"Of course he's eating lunch," Xerxes says, laughing. "He was just saying how hungry he was."

Ben's stomach threatens to somersault up his throat. "Um. Yeah. I'll have—" He opens the menu on the table in front of him. "I'll have a grilled cheese, please."

"Fries?" the waiter asks.

"Sure," Ben says.

"I'll have a turkey burger like our friend here," Xerxes says. "And make it a round of Diet Cokes."

The waiter notes it down and moves off.

"So did you see *Crossfire?*" Xerxes asks Glick.

"No, but I got your fax telling me all about it." He looks over at Ben, dropping his eyes from his face to his lap and then back up again. "Buchanan wants to send the poor old girl off to the penitentiary. And the boys in the Castro want to make her queen." He gives Ben a small smile. "Will you be at the theater this week to see her films?"

"Yes," Ben says. "It should be quite the show."

"I'll say." Glick sips the last of his soda through his straw, making a slurping sound. "Coming up here gave me the opportunity to see her in person. I want to actually meet this woman you've been writing about in your script." He narrows his eyes at Ben. "You're positive there's going to be a juicy ending to all of this? A suitable resolution to the Margaret Butz mystery?"

Ben nods. "I'll be the first to know when Flo finally tells."

Xerxes's eyes are twinkling. "In fact, just today Ben learned another fascinating little nugget." He looks over at Ben. "Go ahead. Tell him."

Ben feels the room begin to spin. The sun is bright overhead but it's as if a gray mist has dropped into the courtyard. His cheeks and palms bead suddenly with sweat. Damn it. Why does this always happen when he's talking with Glick? He grips the sides of his chair to anchor himself against the nausea.

"Well," he begins, "it seems that . . ."

Glick's face fades in and out of focus. *Oh, Christ—I'm going to puke all over his white suit.*

"Are you all right?" he hears Glick asking.

The sun seems to burn through the mist enough for him to respond. "Yes," he manages to say. "I just felt a bit dizzy there."

"Told you he was hungry!" Xerxes laughs.

"What is this new discovery?" Glick asks.

"Flo's doctor," Ben says thickly. "The one who identified Molly Butz as Florence Lawrence. He killed himself a few years later."

He was more than just your doctor, wasn't he, Flo?

He was my friend.

"They were . . . friends," Ben says.

"A—*ha*," Glick says, his eyebrows rising up on his enormous forehead. "Perhaps out of some ethical guilt for contriving the fake death certificate?"

"I—I don't know."

"All along, Ben's suspected some sort of collusion," Xerxes tells Glick.

Ben looks off across the restaurant. He can't get the sounds of Flo's sobs out of his head. He'd never heard her cry before—hadn't even imagined it was still possible. Hadn't all her tear ducts dried up or something?

"Of course," Xerxes is explaining, "the final act will depend on how the current situation turns out, whether Flo gets charged with anything."

"But you're quite confident that we'll have *some* resolution within the next few weeks?" Glick asks Ben.

He nods. "I am," he says. "I am."

The waiter brings them their Diet Cokes. Ben quickly takes a sip. It seems to settle his stomach for the moment.

"Well, I'm prepared to make you an offer," Glick says. "On one condition. The script has everything—mystery, intrigue, scandal—but it is missing one very important element."

"What's that?" Ben asks.

"A love story at its center. Look. With *Titanic* making such waves— pardon the pun—that's all anybody wants. The trappings of a story can—and perhaps *should* be—monumental. Luxury liners sinking. Asteroids heading toward the earth. Old-time movie stars thought dead turning up alive—and implicated in murder. But at the heart, we need a love story that will transcend all that."

He burps, just a little, covering his mouth with his fingertips. "Ask yourself," he challenges Ben. "What role could DiCaprio play in your script? Or Brad Pitt?"

"*Harry,*" Xerxes interjects from across the table. "*Harry* was the great love of Flo's life."

Glick scoffs. "But Harry's such a shit heel in the script. There's nothing worse than a shit heel." He looks over at Ben, who quickly drops his eyes and takes a sip of his soda. "We *cannot* make a hero out of someone who steals the heroine's baby. Can you imagine DiCaprio doing that to Kate Winslet?"

"Then the Greek kid—the kid on the island," Xerxes offers.

"I thought of that," Glick says. He turns to look at Ben. "Do you think we could beef up his part in the story more? Maybe he and Harry get into a slugfest over Flo. And they have to meet cute. Maybe Flo falls off the hay wagon or something."

"I don't think it was a hay—"

"Let's see. What else?" Glick glances down at Ben's script in front of him. "Yes, there's a good sex scene on the Greek island, but we need more. A movie without sex is like an Almond Joy without the nuts. Which is a Mounds. Which is not a good movie."

"Right," Xerxes agrees. "More sex. Absolutely. It's a romance, after all."

Ben swallows. "I thought it was more of a mystery."

"It's a romance," Glick says, "with some mystery and true crime thrown in."

Ben steels himself. "With all due respect, Mr. Glick, just because herring tastes good and ice cream tastes good doesn't mean they taste good together."

Glick raises an eyebrow. "Oh? And how many screenplays have you written, Mr. Sheehan?"

Xerxes is eager to smooth over Ben's impudence. "He's just being wry, Sammy. We get your point."

The producer takes a sip of his Diet Coke and looks back down at the script, dripping soda on the pages as he does so. "Oh, and the *girls*," he says. "Linda and Molly. We can't have there be any suggestion of lesbian tendencies toward them on Flo's part. We're not doing *Fried Green Tomatoes* here."

"I'm sure Ben didn't mean to imply any such thing," Xerxes says.

"Your lunch, gentlemen," the waiter says, appearing behind them with their sandwiches.

The smell of the rare turkey nauseates Ben. "Would you all excuse me one minute?" he asks, standing up. "I just need to use the—the men's room."

Glick looks up at him with one eye. "You seem to have stomach troubles," he says. "Whatever you need, I've probably got in my bag."

Ben just smiles.

In the men's room, he retches over and over—but nothing comes up. He sits there on the floor, out of breath, cradling the cold ceramic of the toilet, his face inches above a public shit hole.

Shit hole. Shit heel.

What's the difference?

Finally he rouses himself. He brushes the dust off his pants. When he gets back to the table, Xerxes has gotten him the deal. They shake on it all around, and Glick winks at him just a little too familiarly.

Then they all eat their lunch.

He sees Jean from a distance first, standing on the little wooden bridge that crosses the stream in the Japanese tea garden. The sky is pink and the shadows in the garden are long and blue. He just watches her for a minute before he enters, as she closes her eyes and turns her face to the setting sun.

She's beautiful, he thinks. *I've never allowed myself to really see before.*

Damn, he abruptly scolds himself. *Don't even go there, Ben.*

Her eyes open and she spots him. She waves.

He begins to enter the gardens when a Japanese woman stops him. Ben can't tell whether she works here or is a visitor. "No, sir," she says. "First."

She hands him a bamboo dipper. "Here," she instructs, pointing to a stone trough filled with water near the gate. "Your hands."

She seems insistent. He's not sure what to do, but reaches over with the dipper, ladles up some water from the trough. She nods. He rinses his hands with the water. She smiles and takes back the dipper.

He proceeds inside.

Jean's smiling as he meets up with her on the bridge. "She had me do that, too," she tells him. "It's like dipping your fingers in the holy water when you enter a church. A ritual cleansing." Her smile fades as she looks out over the lush green garden. "You leave the debris of your outside life behind upon entering another realm."

The pink glow of the sky reflects across her cheeks. Her strawberry-blond hair takes on a pinkness, too, making her look like a faded color photograph from the '50s in which everything eventually turns pink.

But Ben thinks it only makes her look prettier.

"What's going on?" he asks. "Your message said to meet you here."

"Oh, Ben," she says, looking back up at him. She seems near tears.

"Is it Flo? Is she all right?"

"She's fine. At least, for now. She's still resting. The news about that doctor upset her." Jean looks off across the garden. "But that's not why I asked you to meet me."

"Come on," he says, putting his arm around her. "Let's walk."

The evening's getting a little chilly. They walk across the bridge through a row of pines, across a carpet of deep velvety green moss. Conical junipers and round-shaped spruces greet them as they turn, facing the teahouse. "Do you want some tea?" Ben asks.

Jean nods.

The teahouse, made of bamboo and looking out over a small, placid, lotus-dotted lake, is empty. A kind-faced old man bows gracefully as they enter. Ben gestures to Jean to sit at the bench overlooking the lake.

"They want me to come back," she tells him after they're settled.

"Who does? Come back where?"

"The Board." The old man silently brings them their tea in a steaming copper pot. He places two tiny porcelain cups in front of them. Ben pours them each some tea as Jean continues. "They called this afternoon. They said they weren't comfortable with how things were going for Flo, all the media attention and speculation. We should return to St. Mary's immediately."

"But we have an agreement," he says.

Jean sighs. "I don't know what to do. You've seen her, Ben. She hasn't been herself since we got here. She'd been so anxious to see San Francisco again, but she doesn't have the strength to leave the hotel room. She just sits for hours without saying a word."

"She needs a good rest," Ben agrees. "We should just let her be for a while. Let her get her strength back. She'll be fine."

Jean runs a hand through her hair. "The Board said if Flo chooses not to return, that's up to her. She'll have to sign some papers saying she absolves St. Mary's of all responsibility, and she can remain with you and whoever else she chooses."

She takes a small sip of tea. "But I'm to return. As soon as possible."

Ben looks over at her. "What are you going to do?"

She looks to be near tears. "I don't want to go back, Ben. I don't want to go back to that life, living in those cold, sterile rooms, surrounded by all that grandeur that masks the misery. I want to go back to doing the work that I entered religious life to *do*: working with the poor and the disenfranchised and the sick in the inner cities. I've decided if the church won't let me do it under their auspices, I'll do it on my own."

"You'll resign from St. Mary's?" Ben asks.

"I'll resign whatever I need to."

Ben's not quite sure what to say. All he knows is he wants to say *something*. He wants to find *something* to say that will make it easier for her.

"This must be really hard," he finally offers, feeling lame and inadequate.

She nods.

He lifts his hand to place it on her back, then reconsiders. He lets it fall back into his lap.

"When I decided I had the calling," she tells him, "I never questioned it." Her face is set calmly as she stares out over the unmoving lake, its surface reflecting the pink and gold shards of the setting sun. "I met this woman. She was a Sister of Mercy, and she had devoted her life to helping others. I wanted to be like her."

"But you *do* help others, Jean. You're like a mother hen to Flo. All the residents of St. Mary's love you."

She shakes her head. "No, you don't understand," she tells him. "They've helped *me*. Especially Flo. She's the only family I have. What she's given me is incalculable. I just help her in and out of bed. I just tie her shoes."

Ben's quiet for several seconds. "What if Flo decides to go back? What will you do?"

"Go back with her." She smiles. "You see, Ben, for however much longer God intends to have Flo stay on this earth, I will be with her. Wherever she goes, I will go."

"Ruth and Naomi, I think," Ben says with a smile.

"Right." Jean smiles, too. "But after that point, after Flo goes home to God—"

"You're going back to the work you feel called to do."

Ben sees a tear collect in the corner of her eye and then drop slowly down her cheek. "Some nuns talk about their calling as a need to serve God," she says. "They see it as being in the convent, cloistered in prayer, or teaching in Catholic schools. Not me. I've never seen it that way." She makes a small laugh. "Anne Drew, my mentor, used to call us heretics. She was just kidding, of course, but we never bought the idea of God being up on a cloud somewhere, an old white man with a beard."

"I bet you believe God's a woman," Ben says.

"Sometimes God *is* a woman. Sometimes God's a man." She looks off into the garden. "God's that tree over there, those giant goldfish in the lake. God isn't *separate* from us, Ben. Heaven isn't just for those who follow the rules. It's already here, available to *anyone*."

Ben chuckles. "You *are* a heretic," he says.

She smiles back. "Only the heretics ever made a difference."

He can see the wisdom in her eyes. The stunning sense of *self*. He's bewildered by it actually. It makes him feel like a kid again at the Chicopee Public Pool, when he'd wade too far into the deep end. That's how he feels now: He's in too deep and everyone will learn that he can't swim. Richard, of course, had already mastered the breast stroke, so he'd be swimming laps across the entire pool—but Mom would always be standing up there on the cement in her too tight bathing suit, shrieking at Ben to get back to the kiddy side before he drowned.

"You're—you're pretty special," is all he manages to say to Jean.

She takes his hands. He can feel her warmth. It feels good on this chilly night. "So are you, Ben," she says. "So are you."

Anita never said that to him. He imagines she must have thought so, once upon a time, but not anymore. Now she just gripes that he's wasting his time, spinning his wheels, letting the world pass him by.

Yet it's not *Anita* he sees when he looks across at Jean. It's Mary Kay Silenski, the first girl he ever really fell hard for, and they're sitting on his bed, in his room, back in Chicopee. They're sixteen.

"You're all right, Ben," Mary Kay said. "You know that?"

He blushed.

"I mean, here I am, going on and *on* about Richard, and here *you* are, his brother. I don't mean to lay all my shit on you."

"He should treat you better," Ben told her. "He's an asshole."

Mary Kay shrugged. "He's just not as . . . sensitive . . . as you are."

She reached over and kissed him. Right on the mouth. Ben felt his body tense, his dick swell.

Why hadn't he kissed her back? The thought plagued him for weeks. *Years.* Here she was, spilling out her guts to him about how horny she was, how Richard hardly even *kissed* her, and Ben freezes up. He just sat there, let her plant her big red lips on his, and did nothing. Just swallowed and blinked his eyes a few times.

If I'd kissed her back, maybe I could've made her my *girlfriend. Stolen her right away from Richard.*

Maybe even gone to the prom.

Jean's looking over at him now with eyes so round and filled with pink light that Ben thinks he might cry. Or laugh. He's not sure. She's still holding his hands.

"I think you're *very* special," Jean tells him again.

He kisses her. Just reaches over and puts his lips against hers and kisses her. He feels no resistance, no surprise.

She kisses him back.

Jean gently breaks the kiss. The server passes, smiling indulgently down upon them.

He thinks we're lovers, Jean thinks. *Maybe even engaged to be married.*

"I'm . . . sorry," Ben tells her.

"Don't be," she says.

"I just—it just—felt right."

"More tea?" the server asks.

"No, thank you," Jean says. She's still holding Ben's hands. She releases them, looks out over the lake.

"It won't happen again," Ben is telling her.

Victor had said the same thing the first time he'd kissed her. *It won't happen again.* But it had. Once, twice, three times—and then Anne had discovered him in Jean's bed.

"Will I go to hell for kissing a nun?" Victor had asked her right at the start.

Jean laughed. "I think God makes certain allowances," she reassured him.

Such a child, Victor was, in so many ways. Like Ben. He sits there now next to her, overcome by his impulse, surprised and shocked and angry at himself.

That's because he hasn't a counterfeit bone in his body, Jean thinks. The sincerity in his eyes is almost too awful for Jean to look upon. In the past few weeks, she's come to rely on Ben more than she could have imagined. In New York, faced with the first crush of reporters, he'd been there to guide her—and Flo—through it all. In Hollywood, as the stories and questions mounted about the girl, Ben had been Jean's rock, her sounding board, her guarantor that they'd make it through.

He'd been something else, too: her admirer. Her solicitor. Not since Victor had she seen such tenderness, such affection, in a man's eyes when he looked at her. He'd caught her one afternoon, the day she dared to try on that absurd purchase, that stretchy tank top with the stripes. "Lookin' good," he'd said, and she'd felt her blush spread from her face and neck down her goosefleshy exposed arms.

"Ben," she says. "I *wanted* you to kiss me. I think lying is a far worse offense than lust, and I'd be lying if I didn't admit I wanted it."

He seems uncomfortable with her honesty. "But it won't happen again," he repeats.

She nods. "No, I don't imagine it will." She smiles at him. "That doesn't mean I won't *want* it again."

He blinks, as if uncomprehending.

"Oh, Ben." She laughs. "Do you think just because I took a vow to a religious order means I stop being human? That I've lost the capacity to love? To *fall* in love?"

He doesn't respond.

"There was a man once, Ben. A man I loved very dearly. And still do. I have no problem telling you that. Love comes from the soul, and it gets expressed through all our human conditions. Through our hearts, our minds, and yes, our bodies. I have no shame for how I loved him." She pauses as Victor's face fills her thoughts. "I broke my vow of celibacy to be with him. It was a conscious, deliberate, and terribly difficult decision—one that for many reasons I'm not apt to make again. But it doesn't change how I feel, how I respond."

Ben seems touched by her words. "Where is this man now?" he asks softly.

She wants to say, *Here with us. In the lake. In the trees. In the air. In you, Ben.*

But instead she tells him that Victor died.

"I'm sorry," Ben says.

"Stop apologizing, Ben, as if everything is your fault." She finishes the last of her tea. "Let's walk some more."

They stand. They pause for a moment, looking at each other. Jean reaches up and kisses him lightly on the lips.

"But if Flo doesn't go back," she tells him firmly, "I'm staying here."

"What if they kick you out because of it?"

She doesn't answer. She just takes his hand and leads him down the hill, past the statue of the Buddha, and back through the park.

It's late when Jean gets back to the suite she shares with Flo. She thanks the hired nurse for sitting with her. "She's awake," the nurse tells her. "She's watching television."

Jean opens the door a crack to the bedroom. "I'm back, Flo."

She steps inside. Flo's propped up in bed with pillows, and she's wearing her blue glasses. None of the lights are on; Flo is bathed in the blue-and-silver glow of the TV set. The remote control is in her hand.

"What are you watching?" Jean asks, sitting down beside her on the bed.

"They were showing *Camille*," Flo tells her.

"Isn't that with Garbo?"

Flo nods. "And Robert Taylor. I tried to spot myself. Molly and I were extras in the opera scene."

"Were you successful?"

She shakes her head.

"Flo," Jean says, stroking the old woman's thin, wispy hair, "we can stop now, you know."

"What do you mean?" she asks.

"Flo, you're tired. You've had aches and pains you've never had before."

"Oh, I've had them before," she tells her. "Just not in a very long time."

"Do you want to go back? To St. Mary's?"

Flo just looks at her.

"We can, you know. We can pack our bags and go back tomorrow. I'm sure Henrietta will be happy to see you. And maybe Gertie's kid has more cookies she needs to sell."

Flo grins, as if Jean's being foolish. "They only run the cookie drive once a year," she tells her.

"Do you want to go back?"

"I'd hate to disappoint them," she says weakly.

"Disappoint who, Flo?"

She looks up at Jean as if she's being silly. "The fans," she says.

"The *fans?*" Jean laughs. "Oh, Flo, you talk as if you were a movie star again."

Flo seems not to comprehend Jean's point. "I have to keep working. It's the only way."

Jean leans in toward her. Her eyes are distant. "Flo. The only way for what?"

"To get back to number one," she says.

"Flo," Jean says, getting a little alarmed now. "I don't think you know fully what you're saying."

Flo looks back at the television. She says nothing further.

"Flo, I think we ought to go back."

"No." Flo turns her eyes back to Jean. "I can't. Not yet."

"Why not?"

"I'm supposed to appear at the theater this week, aren't I?"

"They can show the films without you."

Flo manages a small smile. Just seeing it makes Jean feel a little better. "Do *you* want to go back, Jeannie?"

"The decision is yours, Flo."

She flicks the channel with the remote control. A *Seinfeld* rerun. A shopping channel. A Pepsi commercial. *The Tonight Show* with Jay Leno.

"You know, it's not just Bill Clinton who's suspected of having affairs," Leno's saying in his monologue. "Heard they caught *Bob Dole* with a dame the other day." A beat. "Florence Lawrence."

The crowd hoots, whistles.

"They're laughing at me," Flo says in a terribly small voice.

"Flo, we can get on a plane tomorrow and fly back east." Jean takes her hands in hers but Flo's eyes are off in that place all their own. "Or we can fly anywhere we want. Just you and me." She rests her head on Flo's shoulder.

"No," Flo says, her eyes still faraway. Her old hand with all its veins and creases reaches up to caress Jean's face. "Not yet, Jeannie. Not yet."

"She wants to go on then," Ben says.

Jean nods. She seems as if she might cry, so Ben draws her to him for an embrace. "I'm worried," she says. "She's just so . . . incoherent at times."

"There's nothing on the schedule at all this week until the screenings at the Castro," Ben tells her. "She'll perk up."

Jean appreciates the hug. She likes the feeling of being held. She's torn between allowing Flo to make the decision to stay or just ordering her back on the plane.

"We still don't know any more about Molly," Ben adds.

"That's why I'm so worried about the theater appearance," Jean says. "That no one asks anything too hard."

"We've got that Jameson Collins doing the brief talk with her on stage," Ben assures her. "It'll go smoothly. There are no questions from the audience or the press."

"And then that's *it*, right, Ben? No more appearances?"

"Well, we're still contracted to do a couple more 'Dare to be 100' spots."

"No," Jean says. "No more. Let them sue us."

"I'll talk with Xerxes," Ben promises.

"Maybe if I tell the Board that we just have the theater appearance, they'll be okay." She looks up at Ben. "We could be back in a week, right?"

He nods. She settles back against his chest, closing her eyes. She can hear his heartbeat. How good it feels to be held like this. If things were different, she could imagine looking up at Ben now and finding his eyes, safe in his embrace, and kissing him.

"Jean," he says.

She makes a sound.

"You know I'm working on that . . . dramatic script."

She nods.

"Well, you know, the stuff about Molly," he says. "Well, some of it has to be conjecture because Flo isn't telling us what really happened."

She looks up at him. "Why do it at all, Ben? I thought you wanted to portray Flo as she is today: a survivor, a woman who's embraced life so fully."

"Well, I'll have to at least *reference* Molly."

"No, I don't think you have to." Jean's gotten stiffer in his arms.

He laughs awkwardly. "Jean, you can't just ask me not to do something in my own script."

"Yes," she says. "Yes, I believe I can."

They hold each other's gaze for several seconds. Then Jean rests her head back against Ben's chest. She hears him take a deep breath and then heave a long, long sigh.

The line to the theater stretches all the way up Castro Street and snakes around the corner down Seventeenth Street. It's mostly gay men, chatting animatedly among themselves, laughing and carrying on, waving to friends farther back in line. There's a local news crew in front of the theater, and Ted Casablancas from E! Entertainment Television is interviewing people in line, trailed by a cameraman. The crowd hoots when Mary Hart strolls by and waves to them like the Queen of England.

Richard stands in the lobby. Sister Jean made sure he got a free ticket, but there was no backstage pass for him as there was for Ben. He'll just have to watch the show by himself from the audience.

He sure missed Rex. Rex would *love* this. All the hype, the old movie posters, the films themselves. But Rex was still doing the Barrymore show in L.A. Tonight was actually the closing; he was flying up to San Francisco tomorrow. Richard could hardly wait. He was struck by how much he missed him. After feeling so troubled those last few days in L.A., now all Richard could do was miss him. He even missed Rex scolding him about Ben. *He'll be glad I said what I did,* Richard thinks. *He'll be proud of how I handled myself with—*

"Ben!" comes a voice.

Richard turns.

It's a large man in a wrinkled pink suit, with a face as broad as a prairie and a wicked little smile playing around with his lips. He reminds Richard of that guy in *The Maltese Falcon*—what was his name? Rex would know—Sidney Something . . .

"No," Richard says, finding it amusing at long last to be mistaken for his brother. "I'm not—"

The large man sidles up to him, ignoring his words. "You look *magnificent,*" he purrs in that way only large gay men can purr. "Had no idea you had such a *body.* Guess because you've always worn that unflattering leather jacket."

Richard grins. "I'm *Richard* Sheehan," he says. "Ben's brother."

"Oh." The man steps back, looks him up and down. "*Twin* brother, I take it."

"Yup."

"Well. I see." The smile gradually returns to his face. "I'm Sam Glick. Are you alone?"

"For the evening," Richard tells him.

"Good enough for me," Glick says.

They shake hands. "How do you know my brother?" Richard asks.

Glick seems taken aback. "He hasn't *told* you?"

"Um, no."

"I just bought his script."

Richard tries not to react. "His script? You mean his documentary about Flo?"

"Oh, sweetheart, I wasn't interested in any old documentary. Let him make that if he wants—but this is going to be a blockbuster mini-series! It'll revive the genre!"

Richard nods his head slowly, turning around to look into the auditorium at the drawn curtain. "Oh," he says. "I see."

Glick snorts. "I hope I haven't spoiled his surprise."

Richard smiles. "I don't think that's possible."

Their eye contact is broken all at once by a voice. "Oh, my God! Richard!"

He turns. It's Scott. Of all people. Scott, rushing up to him.

"Richard! I've been looking for you! I figured you'd be here."

He stops in front of Richard and Glick. He's wearing a tight blue T-shirt and tan velvet pants. Richard notices Glick's eyes open wide, his lips part slightly as he sizes Scott up and down.

"What are you doing here?" Richard asks.

"Well, you know how much I love Flo. I had to come." He smiles seductively. "Plus, I figured I might catch you alone."

Richard suddenly feels like laughing. To think he was ever attracted to this empty-headed narcissist. He can just hear Rex's catty appraisal of the velvet pants.

"Oh, but Scott, I'm not alone," Richard says, barely able to suppress his laughter. He turns to Glick. "Let me introduce Sammy."

Scott looks up into the enormous face of Sam Glick. Glick, for his part, falls easily into the role, much easier than Detective Lee.

"Yes," he purrs, slipping an arm around Richard. "Aren't we the pair?"

Scott sniffs. "You're a pair all right," he mutters. To Richard: "Your tastes have certainly changed."

Richard just grins. Scott slinks off into the crowd. All Richard can feel is amusement, even when Glick suggests they sit together "just to keep up the charade."

"Although," he says with a leer, "why you'd want to give such a specimen as *that* the brush-off, I can't imagine."

"I'll introduce you to Rex someday," Richard tells him. "Then you'll understand perfectly."

The lights dim.

"Oh, come on," Glick urges. "The show's starting."

They take their seats halfway up the orchestra section. Glick asks for the aisle. "To stretch my legs, you know," he says. Richard marvels at the dexterity with which the man folds his large frame into the tiny seat.

Jameson Collins walks out onto the stage to a scattering of applause. "Ladies and gentlemen, we are here tonight for an historic evening. A lost treasure has been found: the very first star of them all. The woman who jump-started the star system. Ladies and gentlemen, I present to you . . . Florence . . . Lawrence!"

The crowd thunders to its feet. Cameras roll down the aisles. But instead of Flo appearing on stage, the curtains open to the movie screen. An image flickers to life there. A jumpy image at first, but then it steadies itself, revealing an enormous iris of a woman's face.

It's Flo, Richard thinks. *Even eighty years later, I can see it's her. Her eyes are the same. The way she smiles.*

It's a Griffith close-up. Her face is simple, sanguine. In her eyes dance the incandescence of the master's lighting. In her eyes, Richard can easily discern the magic of the medium—as well as the dreams of a young girl. This was before the pain, the disillusionment, the terror, before the enchantment she first created nearly ninety years ago turned into the excess and tawdry sensationalism they knew today. This was before the dream got out of hand.

The crowd stays on its feet, applauding. She bears down on them with grace and light, the first goddess of them all.

And suddenly Richard gets it. Why they loved her. How she captivated a generation, the first generation ever to stare up in wonder and awe at the silver screen.

This—*this*—was The Biograph Girl.

Three short films are screened, each about eight minutes long. A live piano accompanist creates a lovely musical bridge between the scenes. The prints are pristine, projected at the correct speed to avoid the fast, jerky motion associated with silent films. "Not *everyone* walked like Charlie Chaplin," Rex has told Richard many times.

Next comes a clip of Flo on a barge up the Nile River in Egypt, part of a longer Lubin film. She looks distracted, weary, even sick. Following this, there are more clips, sometimes just seconds long, of Flo's walk-ons at MGM. There she is, behind Myrna Loy's shoulder. There she is, glaring at Gable. There she is, with opera glasses seated next to a pretty blond girl in *Camille.*

The montage ends with a scene of Flo trapped in a burning building. Matt Moore rushes in to rescue her. Her hands are in her hair and she's terrified—almost as if the flames were real.

The crowd whoops as the lights come up. They begin chanting: *"Florence! Flor-rence!"* They stand and applaud over their heads.

"Ladies and gentlemen," Jameson Collins announces once more, shouting to be heard above the din. "I present to you—Miss Florence Lawrence!"

Richard has to stand on his toes to get an unobstructed view. Flo is helped out on stage by Sister Jean. She can barely walk, all hunched over in a sparkling blue dress, an absurd tiara on her head. She seems dazed by the applause—not dazzled, as she had been that first day on the *Rosie* show. She doesn't acknowledge the whistles and the cheers. She just passes from Sister Jean to Jameson Collins, who eases her down into a chair a stagehand has just provided.

The applause goes on for at least five more minutes. Finally she manages to lift her chin and cast her eyes out into the lights. She smiles weakly.

"Thank you, thank you," Collins says for her.

The cheering dies out into scattered pockets. Somebody yells, "We love you, Flo!" from the balcony.

"And she loves you, I'm sure," Collins says.

He sits down in a chair opposite her. The last of the applause fades away. "Now, Miss Lawrence," Collins says, "we have just seen some wonderful clips. What did you think of them?"

The cameras at the foot of the stage bear in on her.

She blinks into the lights and doesn't respond right away.

It's the same glassy stare from the other day, Richard says to himself.

"Miss Lawrence?" Collins asks again.

"It was quite exciting to see them," Flo says, her voice barely above a whisper, sounding coached by Ben.

Glick turns to Richard. "She's hardly as robust as your brother portrayed her."

"She's not herself," Richard tells him, his eyes steady on Flo.

"Yes, so many wonderful scenes from the dawn of moviemaking," Collins is saying. "You can't rent these from Blockbuster!"

The audience laughs. Flo just sits there.

"Now, that last scene, Miss Lawrence," Collins says, clearly a bit unnerved by her vagueness. "That was you and Matt Moore, in *Pawns of Destiny*. We saw him rescuing you from a wall of flames. *But,* in fact, as you would point out later, it was *you* who had to rescue *him*—isn't that right?"

She doesn't respond. She just blinks a few times.

Collins smiles in embarrassment. "I guess it was *after* the cameras were turned off? Is that right? The fire got out of control and—"

"No," Flo says.

"No?"

Flo's shaking her head slowly. "It wasn't." She stops as if she's forgotten what she was going to say. "The fire got out of control. So I had to rescue him."

She just reverted to her old well-rehearsed line, Richard thinks. *What the hell have they done to her?* Flo just stares off at nothing from the stage.

"Well, yes, that's what I'd read." Collins clears his throat. "Let's see what else here. Ah, yes. The first film we saw tonight was *Her First Biscuits.* You looked so lovely in that."

"Thank you," she manages to say.

"And that was Mary Pickford, wasn't it? The small girl who does the spin after she's eaten the bad-tasting biscuits?"

"Is she here?"

Collins looks surprised. "Pickford?"

Flo nods.

"No, no," he says, terribly uncomfortable now. "I'm afraid Miss Pickford—Miss Pickford passed on a few years ago."

There's a ruffle of programs from the audience.

Glick says, "Is she *daft?*"

Richard just shakes his head. "She's . . . confused."

Collins clears his throat. "The last clips we showed," he says, more to the audience than Flo, "were compiled after much diligent research, viewing hundreds of films over and over, to locate Miss Lawrence in the cameo parts she did at MGM."

"The scene from *Camille,*" Flo says.

Collins brightens. "*Yes,* Miss Lawrence. You're *right.* That was indeed the opera scene from *Camille.* Do you remember making that?"

"Oh, yes, yes. I saw it. I saw myself up there."

Collins is evidently delighted to be getting something out of her. *Anything.* "That was directed by George Cukor," he says helpfully.

"Yes. Mr. Cukor."

She seems to notice the audience in front of her for the first time, almost as if she'd just woken up. She squints into the crowd. Richard thinks he sees her sit up straighter in her chair.

"It was made by Mr. Cukor," Flo says, smiling. "He was very kind to me when he learned who I was. A good man."

"Yes. And an excellent director, too. What else do you remember, Miss Lawrence?"

"I—I—" She seems to want to say something, but can't frame the words. "I—up there—"

"Hey, Flo!" someone calls from the audience. "Will you whistle for us?"

The crowd hoots, laughs. Flo stops in midreverie and smiles.

"They want me to whistle," she says to Collins. The audience cheers. Collins seems flummoxed. "But—are you sure?"

"Oh, I can whistle." Flo beams. "I can whistle."

Richard's on the edge of his seat. *Sure you can, Flo. Sure. You can do it.*

Collins glances backstage. It appears he gets the go-ahead from someone back there. Ben? Sister Jean? He rises and then helps Flo stand shakily. He escorts her to the center of the stage as a prop boy sets up a mike. The audience cheers again.

"Here, Miss Lawrence," Collins says. "Into here."

He taps the microphone. It makes a thudding sound that ricochets through the audience. "All right," he says with a little resigned smile. "Ladies and gentlemen, Baby Flo, the Child Wonder Whistler!"

The crowd goes berserk. Baseball caps are tossed into the air. Flo smiles, looking out at them in wonder. She waits until they quiet down, then pulls her lips together, her face creasing into a thousand folds—

—but nothing comes out.

There's a collective intake of breath from the audience.

She tries again. A tiny little whistle emerges this time, a short, dissonant sound. Then another. Richard thinks she's trying to whistle "Daisy, Daisy" as she did for him back at St. Mary's. But it might easily be "Tell me what you want" by the Spice Girls.

It's clear she can't do it. A few more twists of air into the mike and the audience, in sympathy, begins to applaud. Still she stands there, straining to make a sound. Collins comes up behind her, takes her by the shoulders, and gently leads her back to her chair. The applause grows louder.

"Enough," Richard says, struggling in his seat. "Enough, *enough.*" Where the hell were Ben and Sister Jean?

Flo seems to shrivel in her chair. The cameras draw in for a close-up. Collins looks up befuddled and glances off toward the wings.

"I saw her," Flo says, her tiny voice picked up by her clip-on microphone. "I saw her . . . Molly . . . up there."

"That's it. *That's it!*" Richard says, standing up and pushing past Glick's legs out into the aisle.

His first inclination is to head backstage and tell his fucking brother and that irresponsible nun guardian to get her the hell off the stage. But then he hears Flo start to cry. He hasn't been able to get that sound out of his ears since he'd told her about Lester, and here it is all over again. He stops in the aisle, turning to look back up at the stage.

Flo's covered her face and she's crying.

"What are you *doing?*" Glick shouts as Richard makes a dash for the stage. The audience, showing its support for Flo, is now on its feet, in a standing ovation. Collins stands behind Flo, gesturing wildly to someone.

Richard hoists himself up on the stage. A security guard attempts to follow, but stumbles backward. Richard reaches Flo as the applause becomes a roll of echoing thunder. He falls down on his knees in front of her just as Ben and Sister Jean rush out onto the stage.

"*Where the hell were you?*" Richard shouts at them. "How could you let this happen to her?"

He takes her hands in his. "Flo. Come on, sweetheart," he says. "Come with me."

Her eyes find him. "Richard," she says.

"Sure, Flo. You know me. Come along."

"I saw her," she whispers. "Up there. On the screen."

"Flo," Sister Jean says, stooping down next to her now as well. "Let's go, Flo."

"I saw Molly," she says.

"It's going to be all right, Flo," Richard assures her.

But she's shaking her head, more animated now than she was moments before. "*This is why I left,*" she's crying, and suddenly ripe terror replaces the vacancy in her eyes. "*This is what I was like before.*"

She squeezes Richard's hands, her eyes now sharp and wide in his. Her voice is strong, commanding. "You've got to *help* me, Richard," she tells him. "It's happening just like before. I've *become* her again. *Florence Lawrence.*"

He feels his heart break. "I'll help you, Flo," he promises.

Their eyes hold for several seconds.

He assists her as she stands. The applause rises. Whooping, whistling, calling her name. Sister Jean stands back, saying nothing. Ben is behind her, his lips tight.

Jameson Collins shouts over the din, "Ladies and gentlemen, The Biograph Girl!" as Richard walks Flo slowly off the stage.

December 28, 1938

Just like before.

Florence Lawrence was always *so* weak. So easily rattled. Sometimes her mind would wander, and she couldn't find the answer to the simplest question, so cloaked was she in fog and pain. She was a poor pathetic little creature, a brittle bundle of nerves.

Florence Lawrence.

What more can I tell you? Oh, yes, yes. The girl. It always comes back to her, doesn't it? Seeing her again, up there on the screen, sitting next to me in *Camille* . . . No, I can't talk about it. I promised I never would. She'd be too horrified, too shamed. I can't do that to her.

And yet . . .

I suppose I can't avoid it. I suppose it was inevitable. But how—how can I go back there? How can I even *begin* to tell you—tell you what you need to know?

It's Lester I keep seeing. Dear God, it's *Lester*, and he's blue, all blue, and it's my fault—my fault he's hanging there.

Why was his license suspended? Can you tell me that? No, you can't, can you? What was his life like after I left him? What did I bring upon him? Who found him? I wonder. Who cut him down? He had no friends, no family, none except Molly and me. Who cried over his body? Was there *anyone*?

I haven't been able to stop thinking about him. And then, tonight, I saw Molly. I saw her again, so large that she filled the theater—Molly, there, in all of her wide-eyed hopes and preposterous dreams.

For Molly. For Lester.

All right.

I'll tell you what you need to know.

*   *   *

It began at midnight, the night before. Lester had brought over a bottle of champagne, as he had every year for the past three, marking the anniversary of my first day in pictures.

"To the return of The Biograph Girl," he intoned, raising a toast, and Bob and Marian chimed in with a chorus of "Hear, hear."

It was a dim and dreary celebration, despite their best efforts. I was depressed, reclusive—had been for weeks. The pain kept me to my bed, and the last time Metro called with a walk-on assignment, I'd turned surly and mean. "I'm far too ill to come all the way down there just to walk across a soundstage," I'd snapped. Who knew if I'd ever be called back now?

Molly raised her glass of champagne and smiled over at me. It had been some time since she'd frowned on alcohol, turned down offers of beer or wine. Or Scotch. The bubbles were sparkling out of her glass. We all clinked.

I remember how sweet it tasted on my tongue.

Cheap stuff.

But then, we were a cheap group, weren't we? Marian with too much rouge, her vanity too overbearing to allow eyeglasses to sit against her beady little eyes. Bob with his dirty T-shirts and tattoos on his hairy forearms: *Singapore Sue* and a fire-spitting dragon. Molly with streaks of platinum still in her hair, the remnants of one night's giddy attempt to emulate Harlow. She'd dyed my hair, too, but now Harlow was dead and the platinum irrelevant. Neither of us had fully dyed all of it out.

I was so weak I could barely lift my glass to acknowledge Lester's toast. I was a sick, tired old woman. How old then? Forty-eight? Forty-nine? Around there. Years older really.

And my birthday just days away. I was dreading it. Dreading it so much that I refused to let any of them speak of it. "I can't face another year," I told Molly. "I can't go through another one."

She no longer tried to persuade me otherwise. She was no longer the innocent. The lines around her eyes were deep and dark, the corners of her mouth folded into a permanent frown. She was just a girl, but how old she looked. Too much booze, too much heartache, too many broken dreams. She looked old and tired, nearly as old as I was. We weren't that different, Molly and I.

My depression had spread like a cancer. My darkness had shadowed all of us. I looked over at Molly and saw she hadn't slept in weeks. She'd get up at midnight and pace our little cottage, smoking cigarette after cigarette. A new flock of doves had descended upon the studios, and the bloom was off the rose. Molly had begun to wilt, and no amount of platinum could disguise that.

She wasn't much different from me, not then—except that she didn't have the pain, of course, or the memories. She had never known fan letters or crowds or the thrill of seeing her name on a marquee. She had only known the dream, the crushing promise, the pluck and ambition that brought too many girls west and left them stranded in the sun.

"I can't go on another year," I repeated to her, and I saw in her eyes not only compassion but a horrible empathy, a terrible recognition of self. She said nothing then, didn't try to dissuade me. She just sat back in her chair, her eyes cast down to her lap.

She wasn't much different from me.

I *can't*. I can't go back there. Oh, dear God, was this what I came back to find? Was this what I came three thousand miles to relive? Why I became *her* again?

I just walked away. That's all. The hospital just made a mistake and I—

No. No, that's not it. Oh, please. Just let me sit here a bit. Just let me collect my thoughts.

She wasn't much different from me. That was the rub. She even looked like me. Don't think I didn't fantasize about it—especially when Molly said she'd always felt she'd been adopted, left on the doorstep of her hard, cruel family in Iowa—a changeling child, as they called her. Don't think that I didn't look over at her and imagine she was my own.

Annie Laurie—grown to the full flower of womanhood. They were the same age. She had my build, my coloring.

She wasn't much different from me.

Oh, but she *was*. She was *young*. She wasn't sick. Yes, she had been awakened to the realities in that land of dreams, but she could have *escaped*. She could have found a life somewhere else, found love.

Of *course* she could have. The girl who had survived her father's fists, her mother's indifference—the girl who had run off and learned to dance, learned to hustle, learned to make love far earlier than I ever had. *She* could have gotten out. She and Flo Bridgewood, together. Oh, why couldn't it have happened that way? We came so close. . . .

But the morning after the toast—thirty-two years to the day after Mother and I first ventured out to Bronx Park to play in *Daniel Boone* and I found a body hanging in a tree—that morning I told Molly it was hopeless.

"Look at me, Molly," I said to her.

She did as she was told.

"This is what the truth is." I had pulled myself from my bed, tired and in pain. My joints ached. My skin was sallow and dry. "Nothing lasts. Nothing but the pain."

She began to cry. "Oh, Flo."

I had little patience for her tears. "You and Bob should just get married," I told her. "Run off to Arizona and get hitched, raise a few kids."

"That's not the answer, Flo," she told me. "You tried that. It didn't work."

You see? She was no longer the innocent.

"Besides," she said, "Bob has a new girl. She's younger, prettier than I am."

She took my hands in hers. Gently, because she knew how much they hurt. "Flo," she told me. "I've been thinking. There's *got* to be a way. There's got to be."

Oh, why didn't I encourage her? Why didn't I *see?*

Her eyes pleaded with me to understand. "You're right that the only future here is pain and misery. That's why I'm going home. Back to Iowa."

I laughed at her. "Iowa? You're crazy."

"My father's dead," she told me. "I called last week—out of the blue, in a fit of curiosity. And the operator said, 'I'm sorry, ma'am. That party is deceased.'"

She looked at me as if expecting me to respond. But I sat still.

She tried to feign brightness in her eyes. "Don't you see, Flo? Maybe if we went back there. You and me. You could raise roses again, Flo. And we have *horses* on the farm."

"I can't go to *Iowa*, Molly," I told her. "Are you mad? I can barely walk down the street. *Horses!* I can't ride a horse anymore."

It would have been so easy for her just to acquiesce, to slump back down in her seat, to give up this last crazy, impossible dream. But something kept her going, even if barely.

"There's nothing else, Flo," she said. "I can't go through another year either. I came out here with such *plans,* Flo. Such *plans.* And none of them—none of them came true."

I said nothing.

She stood up, summoning strength from some hidden reserve I didn't know she had. "All this place holds is bad, spoiled dreams," she pronounced in a loud voice. "Out there we can be free of them. *Out there,* Flo—out there you'll be well."

"You talk nonsense," I said to her.

"You can teach me how to ride. I was petrified of horses when I was a girl. But you could teach me. I wouldn't be afraid with *you* there, Flo."

I tried walking away from her. From her absurd plan. She moved in front of me, refusing to let me pass. "If we go, Flo," she said, very softly, "we'll be all right."

"Don't you think it'd just follow us wherever we went?" I asked her. "I can't get away from what I've become as easily as that, Molly."

Still she defied me. "I'm going down to the corner to call my sister," she said. "I'll tell her we're coming."

Our phone had been disconnected for lack of payment. When we needed to make a call, we had to walk down the block to the drugstore on the corner of Melrose. I leaned on the back of a chair for balance and watched Molly pull on her sweater. "Don't go looking for pain," I told her. "We got plenty right here."

She couldn't be dissuaded. For a brief, flickering moment, I saw *light* around her again—the same light I'd seen three years before when I'd first met her in the wardrobe closet, imagining herself to be Garbo. All the hopes and aspirations she had carried with her across the country had still been alive then. She was a creature *filled* with light, until finally the wick went dry and the flame was snuffed out. Yet for a moment— one tiny, quivering moment on the last day of her life—I saw again that same light, glowing around her, from *within* her.

She left to make the call. I watched her walk down the path and out onto the street. I stood at the side of the kitchen table, looking out the window through the frayed, dusty curtains. The day was a clear one. Filled with sunshine. There was a chill to the air, but nothing like the Decembers I remembered from back east. I watched until she was out of sight, and then I watched some more. Just watched whatever I could see: a squirrel in the grass, a child on a tricycle, a flock of birds drop down onto the utility wires.

That's when it happened.

There are moments in our lives we can't explain. Moments of crystal clarity, unheralded and unexpected. They happen despite ourselves, despite any defenses we've constructed. Such moments awaken the spirit, animate the body. And their catalyst is usually surprisingly simple: a glance, a smile, a break in the clouds.

For me, it was the palm trees outside my window. Standing there, it was as if I were watching one of those very earliest motion pictures, the kind the Vitascope had thrown upon the makeshift screen. Just movement, simple repetitive movement. The window was tightly shut, so there was no sound, just the movement of the swaying palms. Hypnotic.

Green. Restorative. I must have watched those palms for several minutes. Maybe longer. It could've been weeks for all I knew then.

"You think they only know Florence Lawrence."

A voice. A man's voice. I knew it, but couldn't place it. I didn't react, didn't turn around. I kept staring at the swaying trees.

"But she saw through her. How many people could do that? How many, Florrie?"

Slowly I turned my head. Ducks stood by the door, just as I would always remember him: in his slouch hat and bow tie, his shotgun at his waist, his eyes twinkling above his round nose and walrus moustache.

"Ducks," I breathed.

"She believes in you, Florrie. Like I do. Florence Bridgewood is still there. Down deep, she's there, just waiting to be let out. Molly can see that. She's always been able to see that."

I was too overcome to speak.

"Go ahead, Florrie," he said. "Close your eyes. Close your eyes, and when you open them, everything will be different."

Oh, I know what you must be thinking. That I was delusional. Hallucinating. Maybe I was, and if I was, it doesn't matter. Because I did as Ducks said, and Ducks was always right. He always knew how to take care of me.

I took in a long breath and closed my eyes, placing my hands down on the table. I steadied myself there, breathing in and out. I felt lightheaded and faint. I opened my eyes again and watched the soundless breeze move the palms outside my window again.

Then I straightened up.

The pain was gone.

If we go, Flo, we'll be all right.

"If we go," I said aloud.

I turned around. The pain was still gone. I approached the mirror. And the woman I saw there wasn't the one I'd seen when I awoke this morning. Something had happened. She was gone.

It was *Flo Bridgewood* staring back at me.

"Did you know I used to whistle for the audience when I was very young?"

"Whistle!" Linda exclaims.

I hear the laughter of young girls.

"How alive do you feel now?" I'm asking. Our automobile skids to a stop in a cloud of dust at the foot of the hill.

She kisses me.

I look back at the palms.

"We aren't only this," Linda is saying, pulling at the pink skin on the back of her hand. *"We can be so much more."*

I was filled all at once with a rush of energy, a spate of passion. My blood seemed to pump faster through my limbs. My skin felt warm and flushed. My breath came in short, quick gasps.

Get out, Flo. Get out now.

Florence Bridgewood is still there. Down deep, she's there, just waiting to be let out. Molly can see that. She's always been able to see that.

Ducks was right, and so was Molly. We had to leave. Get out as quickly as we could. I'd go with her. I'd ride her horses. I'd teach her to ride. We'd go to Iowa—we'd go to so *many* places. Yes, yes—it was the way.

We could be so much more than this.

I found a pad of paper on the table. Yes, yes—I would leave Bob a note. We couldn't wait for him to get home. By then, I was sure, it would be too late. The pain would have returned. I'd be *her* again. We needed to go now—as soon as Molly got back.

"Good-bye, my darlings," I wrote, reading aloud as I committed the words to paper. It was for Bob, but for Marian, too, and Lester. "This is the only way. You've all been swell guys. Everything is yours."

I looked down at the note.

"Lovingly, Florence," I signed it.

Then I folded it in half and wrote Bob's name across the front.

I hurried into my room, threw open my drawers. I began pulling out slips and brassieres and stockings. I flung open my closet door, pushing aside hills of old shoes trying to find my suitcase.

"I can ride better than any boy," I'm bragging to my brother.

"Look at Florrie go," Ducks crows. *"Go, Florrie, go!"*

I laughed out loud. I felt as giddy as a ten-year-old.

That's when I heard the kitchen door open and Molly come back inside.

"Molly?" I called out.

I walked out into the kitchen. She was crying.

"Molly? What's wrong?"

Her face was red and blotchy from tears. "She didn't want to hear from me," she managed to say.

"Your sister, Molly?"

"A *man* answered the phone, Flo. Her *husband.*" Her eyes couldn't seem to focus on me. They wandered the room. "I told him who I was, and he went off to tell my sister. But then he came back to the phone and said Myrtle told him she didn't *have* a sister named Molly." She pauses for a second. "Then he hung up the phone."

"Oh, Molly."

Her eyes still wouldn't focus. "I was so sure, Flo, so sure that if we went back there . . ."

I took her hands. "We can still go, Molly. We can still pack our bags and go. It's still the way. You were *right*, Molly."

But she didn't answer me. She just moved away from me, walking languidly to her room.

"Molly," I called after her. "We don't need her. We don't need anyone."

She turned and looked at me. Her eyes were steadier now. "Don't you see, Flo? I wanted to go *home*. But home doesn't exist anymore. I went away, and so I lost it."

"Molly, Molly," I chided. "We wouldn't have been happy there. You go in and pack your bags. You'll see. We can go anywhere we want to."

I was still so passionate that Molly's torpor failed to reverberate for me. It failed to penetrate very deeply, and if I sinned, that's it. That's where I'm guilty. I didn't recognize the truth her eyes were telling me.

I returned to my own room to finish packing. There were stockings and sweaters scattered all across the floor. What to take? What to leave behind? Few items actually made it into my suitcase. Most were simply strewn around the room in my haste. Later they'd say my messy room attested to my disturbed state of mind. I suppose in many ways it did.

That's when I heard a sound. A small sound, like a bird. Like the bird that had once flown inside our cottage through an open window and become panicked. It flew madly, crazily, hitting the walls. We tried so hard to catch it but it was just too frantic, too terrified—until, stunned, it fell behind the armoire and fluttered helplessly. We found it by the little sound it made: a hiccup of defeated terror.

I listened again for the sound from Molly's room. It was quiet. I stood, walking out into the corridor. "Molly," I called. "Are you packing?"

She was sitting on the edge of her bed, just staring ahead of her, her hands dangling between her legs.

"Molly," I told her. "It will be all right once we get out of here."

She just shook her head.

"Molly, look at me," I insisted. "It will be *all right*."

"You said it, Flo," she said, her eyes rising to meet mine. "This is the truth. There's nothing more than this."

"I was *wrong*, Molly," I said, grabbing her by the shoulders. "God knows how wrong. I can finally see that. We can be so much more—"

She made a face, clenching her teeth.

"The pain is gone, Molly," I told her. "Look at me. The pain is gone!"

But it had merely leapfrogged. From me to her.

Molly took my pain.

She groaned suddenly, doubling over in front of me.

"Molly!"

I stooped down to embrace her. And then I saw it. On a stand beside the bed.

A glass. With the remnants of some liquid.

Behind it, two bottles.

Cough syrup. And the other . . .

I picked it up.

The skull and crossbones made me gasp out loud.

Ant paste.

"Dear *God,*" I breathed. "Dear *God,* Molly. You mixed them! You—you—poisoned yourself!"

She stood with some difficulty, made it halfway into the hall, then crumbled in a heap to the floor.

"Molly!"

I bent over her. Her eyes were still open. "Dear God," I kept repeating over and over. "Dear God, dear God!"

I lunged suddenly for the phone on the kitchen table, but the phone was dead. Of course.

I ran outside. Now terror—blind, hysterical terror—propelled me. I ran to Marian's house, banging on her door. "Marian! Marian! Come quickly! Oh, Marian! Dear God, call a doctor! She's poisoned herself!"

I saw Marian peer out from behind her curtains, squinting her beady little eyes at me. Her windows were closed tightly. Had she heard? Had she heard *correctly?*

I couldn't wait for her. I ran back to my cottage. Molly had tried to crawl. She lay now on her side, stretched out in the corridor.

"Flo," she said weakly.

"I've got to get a doctor, Molly," I cried.

"No, Flo, no, please." She lifted her hand toward me.

I bent down next to her. "Why did you do it, Molly? We were going to *leave.*"

Her eyes found mine. "There was nowhere for me to go, Flo. This was the only home I ever knew." I took her hand. "With *you,* Flo."

"Molly, let me call a doctor."

"*Go,* Flo. Your pain is gone."

"Molly!"

"Go before it comes back."

She closed her eyes.

I squatted there next to her. She was right. The pain *was* gone. It was *still* gone. Just this morning I would never have been able to run about as I had, never been able to stoop down beside her, never been able to encircle her in my arms.

She began to vomit against my blouse. It didn't matter. Once, long ago, they had taken her away before I'd ever had the chance to hold her. Now I made sure to hold her close, once, before she was gone.

The pain *would* return. I knew that. *She* knew that. I had no plan then, just instinct. I was still fired by the conviction to leave, and I couldn't remain there, not even to wait for the ambulance. I set Molly gently back down on the floor. I ran outside, grabbing only my purse. I hid among the rosebushes and cacti and watched as Marian finally emerged from her house and discovered Molly on the floor. Her scream ripped through the quiet neighborhood. Soon others had gathered, others I barely knew, peering in through my door at Molly's body.

"Who is it?" the ambulance driver asked when he arrived.

"Florence Lawrence," Marian cried, dabbing her pitiful old near-sighted eyes. "She came over and banged on my door, saying she'd poisoned herself. She was in such a state—just the other day she said she could imagine taking a gun to her head—oh, *dear!*"

"Get her up on the stretcher," his partner said. "Is there still a pulse?"

"Yup, but faint."

"Look," another of the ambulance crew said, coming out of the house. "There's a note."

I watched as they carried Molly down the steps on a stretcher to the waiting ambulance. I had even come out from the bushes, clutching my purse to my chest. I stood just a little apart from the gathered crowd of neighbors. No one knew me. No one recognized me. So it had come to this. I stood there, nearly among them, and they didn't know me.

But of course not.

Florence Lawrence was the woman being carried away.

I was someone else.

Of course, it took Lester to make it real.

"Lester," I whispered.

He looked up at me, his face white. "Flo," he said.

I had taken a cab to the hospital and walked in without any notice. I found no sense of urgency within those walls; everything proceeded as I imagined it always had. Nurses strode calmly down corridors, clipboards in hand. Over the intercom, doctors were paged with apparent composure. In one room, a woman lay peacefully on a table, smiling up at the ceiling. In another, a man in a wheelchair sat twiddling his thumbs.

Only at the far end of the unit was there any commotion. A nurse hurried out of the last room, her white smock flapping. A red light over the door blinked on and off. I paused, pulling back, my purse nearly up under my chin.

Lester was inside the room. I saw him standing over a white-sheeted body on a metal slab, just gazing down at it. He was alone.

He looked up at me with little surprise, just terrible sadness and a haggard, lost expression in his eyes.

"I couldn't save her," he said.

I nodded. "They think she's me," I said softly, stepping inside.

Lester put one arm around me and closed the door with the other. "She was asking for you, Flo, at the end," he said.

I looked up at him. "What did she say?"

"She said for you to *go*," he told me. "Go *where,* Flo? She kept repeating, 'Tell Flo to go.'"

I nodded, looking down at her body. The sheet had been draped up over her face. A stain of vomit had seeped through the sheet near her mouth.

"She was right," I said. "It's the only way."

"The only way for what, Flo?"

"They think she's *me,*" I said again, looking up at Lester.

He looked up at me peculiarly. "But it isn't you, Flo. It's Molly."

"Did you tell them that?"

"I've been too busy trying to save her. All I said was that she was a friend."

I gripped his hands. "You mustn't say anything, Lester. You must let them *go on* believing it was me."

He looked at me strangely. "Flo, you're not making any sense."

"Oh, yes, I am. Don't you see? For the first time in many years, I'm *finally* making sense. Florence Lawrence needs to *die,* Lester. It's the only way."

"The only way for what?"

"For me to get away. I've tried everything else. I've tried getting married. I've tried changing my name. I've tried all the medicines you've given me. I've even tried new careers, but Florence Lawrence kept coming back. She was always *there*. Ready with the pain, the sadness, the memories—worst of all, Lester, with her incessant need for applause. I can't let her live again. I've got to let her die."

"But this is *Molly*, Flo. Not you."

"No one knows who it is. She has no family. *We* were her family, Lester. We'll be the only ones to grieve her."

"You're asking me to falsify a death record? To identify Molly as you?"

I squeezed his hand as tightly as I could. Still no pain.

"I'm more than asking you, Lester," I said to him. "I'm *begging* you. If you ever loved me, ever cared about me, please, *please*, do this for me."

He seemed staggered by my request. "Flo, it's not ethical."

I shook his hands in agitation. "Oh, Lester. It's what she wanted. She doesn't deserve to be remembered with such a shabby end. Don't make her another Peg Entwistle. She can live on in our hearts as she always was, young and lovely and full of hope. Let me take this death from her. Let Florence Lawrence be remembered for eating ant paste—if she's remembered at all!"

I had to laugh then. I let go of Lester's hands and turned around and looked at Molly. I carefully pulled back the sheet to reveal her face. None of the pain that had been there before remained. I touched her cheeks. Still warm.

"You see, Lester? We're both without pain now. Don't let it come back."

He seemed to realize for the first time how agile my movements were, how easily I walked around the room. "Flo, how . . . ?" he asked.

"Let me go, Lester, please," I said.

He just kept staring at me, as if mesmerized by this person in front of him. As if he didn't recognize me.

"Did you plan this with her? Did she do this for you?"

"There was no plan, Lester. But yes, she did it for me. I truly believe that. Molly's given me a chance. A chance to live."

He ran his hand through his thinning red hair. "You'd just leave us all?" he asked. "Where would you go?"

"I don't know," I said. "When I was a girl, we just blew from place to place. The road's an old friend of mine, Lester. I'm sure I'll go someplace."

He seemed near tears. "Flo, I can't," he said. "The nurse will be back in just a moment with all the forms. I can't do what you ask."

"You *must*, Lester. *Please.* I know I'm asking an enormous favor. I know I'm putting you at terrible risk. But I wouldn't do so unless I truly believed it to be the only way. You've tried so hard to cure me now for so many years. And look at me: I have *no pain,* Lester. None."

"Life's sharpest rapture is surcease of pain," he said quietly, almost to himself as a way of comprehending me. "Emma Lazarus," he added.

I nodded. "Yes. Oh, yes. You have the power at last to cure me, once and for all." I looked at him as hard as I could. "*Please,* Lester."

His face was white. His eyes looked lost and old, as if there were so many truths behind them, so many hidden stories he'd never revealed. Oh, poor Lester. I know the pain I caused him, the moral dilemma I thrust upon his life.

But he loved me. He did it because he loved me. He gave his life for me as surely as Molly had.

"When I was a boy," he said to me, "the other children would taunt me on the playground. I had no friends as a child—only you, Flo. Only you up there on the glorious screen. I'd come home and read your letters to me. Touch the photographs you had sent. Everything would be all right in the world when I did that." His voice cracked. "I've never loved a woman. Only you, Flo."

"Oh, Lester," I said.

"You've been the only pure love I've ever known," he said.

"Then *do* this for me, Lester."

His eyes bore into me. "I'll never see you again," he said, his voice no longer a doctor's, or even a man's—but a boy's, standing forlorn in the play yard, my photograph in his hands.

"You wouldn't *want* to see me, Lester," I told him as gently as I could. "Because I'd be *dead.* Florence Lawrence would *have* to be truly dead and buried—because *you* signed that document. *You* swore it was so."

He said nothing.

I turned and looked down once more at Molly. Lester came up beside me and looked down at her as well. How beautiful she was. So slight, so young, with the same pale skin that I had, the same platinum-streaked hair.

"Go on," Lester finally said, his voice thick and somehow very different. "Get out before anyone sees you."

That's when I walked away. I just walked out the hospital doors into a whole new life and—well, you know the rest.

The Present

"Then you didn't kill her?" Ben asks as if surprised.

Or disappointed.

Richard glares up at him. They're back in Flo's hotel room. They'd whisked her away from the theater in a waiting car and brought her here, where she seemed to revive somewhat.

And she finally told them what they'd been wanting to know.

"Poor, poor Molly," Flo says.

"I find it incredible that Lester could pull off the deception," Richard says. "That you could just walk out of there."

"But I *did*," Flo tells him. "I'm telling you the *truth*. All of it. I walked right out under the reporters' noses. Marian had been convinced it was me, and I'd even left a note. So why would there be any suspicion? It was hardly surprising that Florence Lawrence ended her life after so many years of humiliation."

"But didn't anyone notice Molly was gone?" Ben asks.

"I imagine Bob did. I suspect it was he who eventually reported her missing." She sighs. "Oh, my poor little Molly. They had to go and dig her up. Because of me."

"Flo," Sister Jean says, "you need to tell this to Detective Lee. It will end his questions, clear your name."

"Well, hold on," Richard interjects. "Not so fast. We should talk with your lawyer. Flo still might not be free and clear."

"Why not?" Jean asks.

Richard bends down next to Flo. He looks up into her eyes. They're sharp and clever again. "I just don't want to see an argument made that you somehow *encouraged* Molly to do it—or made her depressed enough —or ignored the warning signs—and then walked off and left her."

"Richard!" Jean stands over him. "That's absurd."

Ben sniffs. "Really, brother. You're thinking like a pulp-fiction writer instead of a journalist. Besides, it's ancient history what happened that day."

"Not to Myrtle Pickles and the Cherry Sisters."

Flo reaches over and takes Richard's hand. She hasn't appeared to be listening to anyone other than him. "You promised you'd help me," she reminds him.

"And I intend to keep my promise," he reassures her.

Jean places her hands on Flo's shoulders. "This is the end of the road. We're ending our tour *tonight*." She looks down at the old woman in her care. "Shall we go back to St. Mary's, Flo?"

Flo doesn't say anything. She just keeps looking at Richard.

"Hold on, Jean," Ben says. "We can't just leave. What about the campaign with Oprah? We're still contracted to do a couple more spots."

"We're *done*," Jean says definitively. "Aren't we, Flo?"

She sighs. "Yes," she finally admits. "We're done."

Ben starts to speak, then turns away.

"Ben," Flo says. "Don't you see? I can't do any more. You saw me on the stage tonight. That's how I *was*. That's how *she* was—Florence Lawrence—just a bundle of nerves moving from spotlight to spotlight. I can't become that again. Oh, I fell for the lure all over again. I can see that now. The clamor, the attention. The *applause*. But I walked away from all that, Ben. Molly died and I lived. I know it sounds hokey, and maybe it is. But I can't go back to being Florence Lawrence. She's dead and buried—and *reburied*!"

She looks back at Richard.

"Don't forget," she says softly so that only he hears her. "You promised you'd help me."

He makes a small, tight smile.

"Come on," Jean says to Flo. "Let's get you to bed."

"I met Mr. Sam Glick tonight," Richard tells his brother after Jean and Flo are gone.

Ben looks over at him. "Oh?"

"He mistook me for you. Guess it's your new hair."

Ben seems uncomfortable, anxious for Richard to leave.

"So you've written a script," Richard says.

"And if I have?"

"I only care how you treat Flo in it."

Ben laughs. "Like *hell* that's all you care about. What you're in a huff about is that I've just squashed any chance for *your* book to get optioned."

"I'm not writing a book," Richard tells him.

Ben makes a face. "Of course you are," he says.

Richard shakes his head. "Not about Flo. Not about any of this. I think we've both exploited her enough as it is."

"I don't believe you."

"Believe whatever you want," Richard tells him. "But I've let all of that go. Ben, the Hollywood dream is fucked up. Haven't you learned *anything* from listening to Flo?" He lets out a long breath. "Look. If it happens for me, it happens. But what's important to me is what I've already *got*."

"I'm not giving up," Ben states plainly. His lips are tight with conviction.

Richard runs a hand across his face. "Even if it means hurting Flo?"

"I've worked *too* hard, waited *too* long—" Ben stops. "Flo's a tough lady," he says, "no matter how much Jean coddles her."

Richard approaches him. He can see Ben tense as he gets closer. It's the old instinctive response Richard remembers from when they were kids. They approach, draw nearer; then one of them throws the first punch.

But Richard just stands there. And what he says is the last thing in the world Ben would ever have imagined he'd say.

"Ben," Richard tells him, "I'm sorry that I've been such a shit for a brother at times."

Ben just stares at him.

"Maybe I *have* tried to lord it over you. I'm sorry, Ben. I'm sorry we were caught up in whatever shit was going on between Mom and Dad. Mom took me and Dad took you and they left us nothing between us. I'm sorry for that, Ben. There's a lot about you I admire. Your talent. Your wit. Your convictions. Don't forget them, Ben."

He reaches over and touches his brother's shoulder.

"Do right by Flo," Richard says. Then he turns and leaves.

What the fuck was that about? Ben can't take his eyes off the door for several seconds after Richard has left. *What the fuck is he* up *to?*

I'm sorry that I've been such a shit for a brother at times.

There's a lot about you I admire.

Ben feels suddenly adrift, as if nothing makes sense, as if everything he's ever known or believed in has all at once been disproven. Mom, Dad—what was Richard talking about? *They left us nothing between ourselves.*

It's true that Ben has to go way, way back to remember being close to

Richard, back to kindergarten, first, second grade—way back before the comparisons and the competitions began, when life was simple and they were just two little identically dressed boys, catching pollywogs, eating Mars bars, laughing as Bunny Rabbit dropped the Ping-Pong balls (yet again) on *Captain Kangaroo.*

Maybe I haven't always been the greatest brother either, Ben thinks. *And wouldn't it be nice if—*

He snorts. Who the hell is he kidding? That goddamn Richard has got *some* plan—some plan that surely involves screwing Ben. That's the way it's always been, and there was no reason to think it was going to change.

He punches in Xerxes's number back in New York. It's close to three A.M. there. He doesn't care. He gets Xerxes's machine. "Pick up!" Ben shouts. "Wake up and pick up the phone!"

"Wha . . . ?" comes Xerxes's groggy voice, cutting off the machine.

"You're gonna see Flo crack on the news tomorrow," he tells him. "The Castro Theater was a fiasco."

"What? What?"

"She just broke down. Then my fucking brother jumps up on the stage like some goddamn Harrison Ford or something. But we got the story out of her. The full story about the girl."

"Richard jumped up on the stage?"

"Are you *listening* to me? We got the story. She didn't kill her. At least, not directly. But I think a fair case can be made to say she manipulated the situation. It's ambiguous, but I *like* ambiguous screenplays. Let the audience decide."

"I'm not following," Xerxes tells him.

"Look. Glick was in the audience. He saw her fall apart. You need to call him first thing in the morning. Tell him that we've got the full story, that I'll do a rewrite as soon as I can. Jean's taking Flo off the tour. It's done, kaput."

"What about 'Dare to be 100?'"

"Screw them. The point is to get the film into production as soon as possible. We've got to work fast while all this is still news. Before people stop giving a shit about Florence Lawrence, after she's back in Buffalo hidden away."

"So how did she do it?" Xerxes asks. "How'd she get them to think the girl was her?"

"It's so simple you won't believe it. It's not too far from what she's always been saying. They made a mistake, and she took advantage of it. But this Molly—she was unstable. A flake. And Flo encouraged her depression, and then didn't call an—"

He turns.

Jean is sitting in a chair behind him, watching him. Her face is white. He swallows, staring at her.

"Ben? Are you there?" Xerxes's voice crackles over the phone.

"I'll talk to you later." Ben finds his throat terribly dry.

"What is it? What's—"

Ben hangs up the phone.

"How long have you been there?" he asks Jean.

"From the time you were screaming into Xerxes's machine to pick up the phone," she says.

He feels his neck tighten. The sides of his torso suddenly become damp. He can't say anything else. He fights the feeling that he's back in grade school and Sister Mary Bernardine has discovered him in the boy's lav, smoking cigarettes, and there's no use trying to squirm out of it, because the evidence is hanging in the air.

This is not *like that,* he tells himself. *I'm not a sixth-grade kid anymore. This isn't Sister Mary Bernardine. It's* Jean, *and I've* kissed *her, even though she's a nun. I've kissed her and I might even be starting to like her—like her a lot—even if she* is *a nun.*

"How could you, Ben?" she asks.

He's unnerved by how calm she is. She's just sitting there, her hands folded in her lap. Her face is white and her lips are drawn tight, but otherwise she seems a model of poise and composure. She repeats her question when he doesn't answer, showing only mild pique. "How *could* you, Ben?"

"How could I what?" He tries to smile. "Look. Don't get worked up about how I sounded with Xerxes. That's just agent talk. Tough Hollywood trade talk." He laughs uneasily. "Macho games. Silly, really. I'm still committed to—"

"To what, Ben?" Jean stands, approaches him.

He tenses. *Goddamn,* he thinks. *It's just like Richard earlier.* He recoils a bit, instinctively afraid she's going to haul off and sock him.

"I'm—I'm committed to writing a script that will be fair—and honest."

"Let me read it, Ben."

"Well, I'm not really comf—"

"*Let me read it!*" she screams, causing him to jump back.

Now her fury catches up with her. "I don't give a—how would you say it, Ben?—a good, long *shit* if you're comfortable or not. You get that script *right* now and let me read it." She folds her arms across her chest.

He starts to protest again, but stops. He walks over to his briefcase, pops it open, withdraws a bound photocopy of the screenplay and hands it to Jean.

"It's still a draft," he says weakly.

"I gathered that from your conversation. There's still a case to be made that Flo manipulated the situation, that she killed Molly indirectly." She looks down at the title page.

SILENT SHADOWS:
THE TRUE STORY OF FLORENCE LAWRENCE
BY BENJAMIN CARTWRIGHT SHEEHAN

She settles down into a chair and begins to read. Ben paces anxiously behind her. She doesn't get through many pages before she puts it down.

"Flo never agreed to let you talk about the baby," she says, looking back at him.

"I *had* to, Jean. I *had* to include that."

"But this is too painful. You can't do this to her. She's held on to that secret for eighty years. What right do you have to expose it?"

He makes a sound in disbelief. "What *right* do I have? What right does any filmmaker—any biographer of any public figure—have to expose *anything*? That's just the way it's *done*, Jean."

She stands, approaching him again. "Well, I don't like it, Ben. I don't *like* the way it's done." She puts her face close next to Ben's. "It's not *my* way—or Flo's either. We *all* carry around secrets, Ben. We *all* have parts of our lives we keep inside ourselves. That we treasure or grieve or fear. You want to take those parts of Flo's life that she's kept so close to her all these decades and throw them out there to the public—like scraps of flesh to a pack of ferocious dogs."

They just stare at each other.

"Well, I say *no*, Ben. Our contract gives Flo and I script approval. And I'm afraid I'll have to call this one in."

"Actually," Ben says, his face hard, "you only have the right to be consulted. And Flo's a public figure again. There's nothing to stop me from writing another script about her outside of any contractual arrangement with you."

She seems taken aback by his rigidity. "You would *do* that, Ben?"

His icy demeanor cracks. "I don't *want* to, Jean. I don't want to do anything to hurt Flo. Or you. You've just *got* to trust me, Jean. Please. I—I don't want to lose you."

"Then tear up the script," she says.

"I can't," he says.

"Why not?"

"Because it's already sold."

It seems to take a moment for the words to penetrate. Then Jean asks, "It's already sold?"

Ben nods.

"Don't say any more to me," she tells him, dropping the script to the floor as if she was suddenly afraid of being infected by it. "You'll be hearing from our lawyer."

She turns to leave the room, then stops. She looks back at Ben. Her face is red now and her eyes filled with fire and gleaming with tears. "I *did* trust you, Ben," she tells him, and he knows she's not crying for Flo now. "More than that. I *believed* in you. Believed you to be a man of honor. A man of compassion. An *artist*, Ben. I believed you to be an artist. I even" —Her voice cracks, and she can't finish. She looks down at the floor, then back up at him. "And it was even more than that, too, Ben."

She leaves him standing in the middle of the room. A breeze from the open window catches the pages of his script on the floor and blows them gently, one by one, as if an invisible hand were turning them.

"Hey, Nooker! Anita!"

Richard encircles both of them for a three-way hug. He's just come outside the hotel, where Jean and Flo are waiting for him in a limo. Rex and Anita have just stepped out of a cab.

"I saw what happened to Flo on the news," Anita tells him.

Rex nods. "We both did. We were watching it in L.A. last night after my show."

"Is she all right?" Anita asks.

"She's fine now," Richard tells them.

"Are you sure?" Rex asks. "She seemed so distraught."

Anita's face clouds with anger. "What have they *done* to her?"

"Well, whatever it was, we got to her in time," Richard says. He looks over at Rex. God, it was good to see him. "Hey, how was closing night?"

"Terrific," Anita answers for him. "Ovation after ovation. I flew in just so I could see it."

"Isn't she fab?" Rex winks over at Anita.

"More fab than ever," Richard says, giving her a kiss. "Hey, come on with us to dinner. It's Flo's last night before she heads back east."

"Where's Ben?" Anita asks, a little apprehensive.

Richard shrugs. "Persona non grata, I'm afraid. Come on. Get in the car."

It's a limo that Richard's paying for. Okay, so he had to put in on credit, but it was Flo's last night, after all. Might as well live it up.

Flo is delighted to see Rex and Anita. They reach over and each hug her in turn, telling her how lovely she's looking. "In this old dress?" she says. "Who gave this one to me, Jeannie?"

"That's Calvin Klein," Jean tells her.

Flo winks. "You should see the Bob Mackie number back in the hotel," she tells them. "That one I like. All *sorts* of sequins."

"How about your hat?"

Flo smiles. She's wearing a black sequined cloche. "Oh, this was mine. Bought it right here in San Francisco in 1939. Thought it would be appropriate to wear."

"Well, you look *magnificent*," Rex tells her.

They all concur. Flo eats it up.

"It's good to have you back, sweetheart," Richard whispers to Rex, slipping his arm around him as the limo driver starts the engine.

"Were you a good boy without me?" Rex asks, nuzzling his boyfriend's neck with his nose.

"Nooker," Richard says, "I'm only good *with* you."

Jean watches them. How much in love they are. Even after six years. How lovely. How *rare*.

She has tried very hard not to think of Ben. Not to think of how vulnerable she made herself with him. Not to think of how wrong were her instincts. *He conned me. He used me. He* lied *to me.*

Her instincts have never been so wrong. That's what threw her for the farthest loop. Not even the heartbreak was as terrible as that. Worse than anything was the fear that her instincts had failed her, that she could no longer trust her own heart. "It's the one thing that never fails you," Anne Drew had always told her. "Your heart is the one thing that's *always* reliable."

But hadn't Anne's heart deceived *her* as well? Hadn't Anne believed Jean's love for Victor had somehow crowded her out of Jean's soul?

"How have you been, Sister?"

Jean looks up. Anita Murawski's pretty, pleasant face—too much mascara, perhaps, but pleasant nonetheless—smiles over at her.

How could Jean tell her? That she had fallen in love with the man Anita once loved—and likely still did? That he had turned out to be a deceitful louse? That he had caused her to doubt the one thing in this world she had never doubted before?

"It's been—well, it's been a bit of a bumpy ride," she tells Anita.

"I guess so," Anita agrees. "But you're going home now."

Jean looks over at Flo. *Yes, I'm going home. We're going home together. Maybe St. Mary's isn't where I want to be, but for now, home is wherever Flo is. For however much longer she has left, no matter what comes out, no matter how many movies people make about her or books they write.*

"Yes," Jean agrees. "We're going home."

She takes Flo's hand in her own.

They cross the Golden Gate Bridge, resplendent in its span across the bay in the late afternoon sunshine. There's no fog for miles around. The orange-gold spires of the bridge streak upward into the blue sky, and Flo strains to look up at them.

"It's so beautiful, isn't it?" she says. "I remember the first time I saw this bridge. I was *awestruck*. It hadn't been built when I first came out, you know, back before the earthquake. But when I returned, I thought the bridge was so lovely that in some ways it made up for all of what was lost."

She sighs, looking back inside the car around at all of them. "There's only one place in the world more beautiful than San Francisco, you know."

Richard grins. "Santorini—right, Flo?"

"You've been *listening*," she says to him.

"To *everything*," he tells her.

Their eyes hold.

They enjoy a lovely dinner in a quiet, secluded restaurant up the side of Mount Tamalpais. The soft fir trees cloak them as they eat, shielding their laughter from the outside world. Anita regales them with stories of her last days on the soap opera, in which her character contracts a rare South Seas malady and dies just as she is about to reveal the identity of her real mother. She reenacts the scene, leaning back melodramatically in her chair. Flo laughs and laughs, smoking practically a hundred cigarettes.

"You're the only person I tolerate cigarette smoke from, Flo," Rex tells her.

"Actually, I've considered giving them up," Flo says. They all look startled. "They say every month you don't smoke adds a month onto your life. I figure if I stop now, I might just break even."

They laugh.

"Well, I have some news," Anita says.

"Tell us," Flo instructs.

"You'll never guess who took me to dinner right before I left New York."

"Who? Who?" they all ask.

"Jameson Collins."

"The film guy?" Richard asks, incredulous.

"The very same." Anita grins.

"Well, he didn't waste any time, did he?" Rex laughs.

Flo twinkles. "You never know about those bookish types."

"And isn't it a coincidence you're both here in San Francisco?" Richard observes.

"Well, he *has* asked me to a little function for the Academy," Anita says, batting her eyelashes.

"That would be the Academy of Motion Picture Arts and Sciences," Rex says.

Anita winks. "Which reminds me. He told me that the Academy wants to give you an honorary Oscar, Flo."

Flo grins. "Well, isn't that something? I remember when Mr. Griffith got his. They quoted him in the papers as saying, 'What art? What science?'"

They all laugh.

"You seem like your old self again, Flo," Rex tells her.

"Do I?" She seems pleased by this. "If only I could stay this way."

"You can," Jean tells her.

Flo just sighs. She looks back over at Rex. "What about you?" she asks. "You've been sick. Don't lie to me."

He shrugs. "Not really sick. Just adjusting to some new meds."

She narrows her eyes at him. "I remember the influenza epidemic of 1918," Flo says. "I thought it was the most horrible thing that could ever happen." She pauses. "I never could have imagined AIDS."

Rex raises his eyebrows in surprise. "How did you know I have AIDS, Flo?" he asks.

"Oh, *please*," she tells him. "I've lived a long time. There's not much I can't figure, can't deduce from the clues available."

Jean looks over at Rex. Flo might have known, but it's clear *she* hadn't guessed. "Are you . . . doing all right?" she asks.

Rex grins. "To be honest, Sister, things change so fast it's hard to say. These new drugs have done wonders but they've also added on some rather unexpected fatty deposits. Now, if it were just a case of vanity, I'd say I could live with it. Even with this little old hump on my back. But it does things to your cholesterol—and that in turn increases the risk of heart disease."

He sighs. "I figure there's always going to be *something* in life, so there's no use getting too worked up about it." He laughs. "So to answer your question: Yes, I think I'm doing all right."

Richard takes his hand under the table.

"Well, listen, Sexy Rexy," Flo says. "I've had a hump on my back for twenty years and it hasn't slowed me down a whit." She smiles wistfully. "All right. Maybe just a whit."

"You're my inspiration, Flo," Rex tells her and blows her a kiss.

"*Hold on to life,*" Flo says, more to herself than any of them there. "As I used to hear Johnny Weissmuller say, swinging over the Tarzan river, 'The main thing is not to let go of the vine.'"

They all laugh yet again.

Flo's still looking at Rex. "When it's time," she says softly, "you'll know when to let go."

They fall quiet for a moment. Then Flo lifts her eyes from the table and laughs. "Do your act for us, Rex," she commands. "Give us the Barrymores."

He laughs in return, feigning modesty. The others urge him on. "Okay, okay," he says. "All right. First John."

He stands, clears his throat, and waves a glass of water in his hand. "Method acting?" he growls, slurring his words. "There are quite a few methods. Mine involves a lot of talent, a glass, and some cracked ice."

"Hear, hear," Richard says.

Rex's eyes dance. He straightens his back, assumes an air of regality—Ethel as the Empress Alexandra. "Oh, holy Rasputin," Rex cries to the giggles of the table.

Finally he hunches down, pulls in his lips, narrows his eyes. "George Bailey, I *own* this town," he cackles—Lionel as old Mr. Potter in *It's a Wonderful Life.*

Flo claps her hands together. "Oh, yes! Yes, you have them down! Oh, how wonderful it is to laugh again. It sounds just *like* them, Rex. You've got it. I was there! I should know!"

What she doesn't know—what none of them know—is their waiter, realizing the old chain-smoking lady at his table is actually The Biograph Girl, has called a photographer friend. Who in turn let the information slip to someone else. And someone else.

By the time they leave the restaurant, six photographers ring their limousine.

"Aw, Jesus," Richard grouses.

"Miss Lawrence!" the photographers shout. "Over here, Flo!"

The cameras snap like turtles. Flo recoils from the flash. Rex puts his arm around her, and Jean walks ahead of her, trying to shield her from the glare.

"Why can't you guys let up?" Richard shouts. "She's just an old lady."

"Hey, Flo," calls an overweight guy in a smiley-face T-shirt and backward baseball cap. "Did you hear Margaret Butz's family is thinking of a civil suit against you? Wrongful death, they're claiming. They want half of what you got from Waters. Any comment?"

"*No* comment," barks Richard.

"What happened onstage at the Castro?" another photographer shouts. "Myrtle Pickles says it's guilt taking over!"

"Get out of our way," Rex yells.

The photographers push in. Anita gets up between them and Flo. She scuffles with them a bit, trying to get by. One of the photographers gives her a shove.

"Hey!" Rex shrills suddenly. "Don't touch her!" He jumps the guy who pushed Anita. They fall down into the pine needles and begin throwing punches.

"Oh, *dear!*" Flo shouts.

A couple of photographers are all at once upon her, cameras not three inches from her face, a steady lightning storm of flashes. She falls back up against the limo. Sister Jean lashes out, smashing one camera to the ground, as if it were some prehistoric predator.

"If that's broke, you're payin' for it, lady!" the photographer shouts.

Flo is trembling, her hands clenched in front of her in tight white fists. The limo driver has opened the car door and Jean is easing her inside.

"She's a hundred and seven years old!" Anita is shrieking. "How can you be so goddamn *barbaric?* You're hounding Flo to death like you did Princess Diana!"

"Hey, people want to know if she did it," the overweight guy in the baseball cap lashes back. "If she killed that girl."

Richard is separating Rex from the brawling photographer. "Get in the car, Nooker," he commands. He pushes the other guy back into the bushes. "You're lucky we don't file an assault suit against you."

"Ah, fuck you!"

They all manage to get back into the car and drive off.

"Are you okay, Flo?" Richard asks.

Jean has her arm around her. She's shaking quite visibly.

"Dear God," she says. "Look at me."

Anita reaches over and takes Flo's hands in her own to steady them.

"Oh, this can't go on," Flo says. "My head—"

"Is it a headache again, Flo?" Richard asks.

She nods. "I don't know why I should be surprised by all the fuss. Florence Lawrence created it, didn't she? That day on the track in St. Louis. Now it just won't go away. For anyone."

"Well, we're getting *you* away," Jean promises.

"It won't be that easy," Flo says softly.

Her eyes meet Richard's.

"This can't go on," she tells him.

He nods.

"You won't forget your promise to help me?" she asks.

He assures her he won't.

"I just wish there were another way—another way to—" Richard says back at their hotel. His voice cracks. He runs his hands across his hair. He can't finish his thought.

It's quiet now. Jean and Anita and Rex are asleep. Flo and Richard sit alone, opposite each other, in her room. He leans forward in his chair, wringing his hands between his legs.

"There's *no* other way," Flo assures him. She brings a cigarette, back in its old holder now, to her mouth. "God's forgotten I'm down here. A hundred-plus years and still He hasn't called me. I have to take matters into my own hands. It's time." She pauses, exhaling smoke. "Don't you see I've got to do it before it happens again?"

"Yes, but, Flo, maybe we could do something—something less—"

"*Dramatic?*" She exhales smoke. "Come now, Richard. You know Florence Lawrence always enjoyed her theatrics." She laughs. "No, this is the only way. I can't think of any other way I'd rather do it." She looks at him with a wicked little gleam in her eyes. "*Indulge* me."

"But maybe you could just—go away . . .'"

"What? And end up like Mae Murray, crazy as a loon? Or *Pickford?* Oh, she thought she was so smart, stepping out while the audience 'was still applauding,' or so she said. So much bull *that* was. She *craved* the spotlight. Always did. I know how she ended up, hiding out in her room, boozy and terrified. The press writing mysterious little blurbs about her. Not me, Richard. Not me."

"I don't want to lose you."

She smiles kindly. "Oh, Richard. You remind me so much of Lester." She stubs out her cigarette. "But you know, it's just going to keep getting worse, what with Ben's film and who knows what else."

"I know."

"So you'll help me?"

He can't speak for several seconds. He just looks over at her. It's almost as if she isn't real, sitting there opposite him. It's as if she were nothing more than smoke and mirrors, a figment of his imagination—of the collective imagination of the world. It was like Roddy McDowall said, that day in the cemetery: They were all part of the magic, the illusion.

He asks, "This is what you really want?"

She nods. She's got all her senses back, all her power. At least, for now. "It *is*, Richard," she says. "It's what I want."

"All right then," he says hoarsely. "I'll help you. I gave you my word."

"Thank you, Richard."

They're quiet for several seconds. They just sit there, feeling the enormity of the weight that has settled between them.

Finally Richard says, "Flo, I need to ask you one more thing. In case, I don't get a chance later."

"Go ahead."

"I was never able to find a birth certificate for you. The Hamilton records weren't complete."

"My birthday is January 1."

"I know." He smiles. "But what year, Flo?"

She smiles back at him. "I'm one hundred and seven. Do the math."

"I did. But, Flo"—he takes out a document from his inside jacket pocket—"this suggests something else."

"You're always taking *something* out of your pocket, Richard." She leans back in her chair. "What do you have for me this time?"

"The 1900 Census, Flo. For Buffalo, New York. I found a listing for your grandmother's house. You and your brother and your mother were living with her."

She nods. "That's right. For about three years around the turn of the century."

"The census lists you as fourteen in 1900, Flo. So if I do *that* math . . ."

She grins. Like the proverbial cat with feathers in its whiskers. "Oh, dear," she says, not surprised, not in any way defensive or confused. "I guess that would make me—what? A hundred and eleven? Twelve? Somewhere around there." She winks over at Richard. "A lady can still be coy about her age, can't she?"

He just gazes at her. "How do you do it?" he asks finally in obvious awe. "*How?* There really is something *magic* about you, Flo."

"*Magic*," she says, relishing the word. "Do you believe in magic, Richard?"

"I've come to. Since meeting you."

"Magic is for the audience—or the readers, in your case—to discover," Flo tells him. "It is no concern of ours."

"Maybe not, but your life has been—"

"Magical? Yes, Richard. For it's *life* that matters. You see, that's why I must do what I need to do. I fought long and hard to find my way back to my life. What I realized—and what Florence Lawrence never could—was that life doesn't start when Hollywood—or Lady Luck or whoever—starts paying attention to you. Nor does it end when they stop. Life is all the rest of it, all the crazy lot rest of it."

She sighs. "I brought her back to life. She was still there, down deep, all this time. And she hadn't changed."

Richard shakes his head.

"No, she hadn't," Flo continues. "Hadn't changed one little bit. I should have known, of course. She always was a foolhardy girl. Weak and easily seduced by flattery. Vainglorious. Like a swan. She forgot all about Jumbo and—but I haven't told you, have I?"

She looks over at Richard with some mild surprise on her face. "I've *never told* you about the fair. I've told you all *so much*—but never about that. About the year the great Pan-American Exposition took over the town."

"No," he says. "You've only just mentioned it in passing."

"Well, it deserves far more than that." She smiles. "All right, Richard. Then I have one story left. Let me tell you about the fair."

September 1901

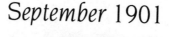

There are times when I close my eyes, even to this day, and I see the radiant outline of the Electric Tower and all the buildings surrounding it, the brilliant white of two million lightbulbs configuring the fair against the purple night sky.

The Pan-American Exposition left a big impact on a little girl. How old was I then? Does it matter? Twelve, thirteen, fourteen—somewhere in there. Take your pick. I was young and impressionable. Oh, I liked to think of myself as worldly and sophisticated—after all, I had been the Child Wonder of the stage—but in Buffalo, I was merely a schoolgirl, a fact that my brother Norman delighted in reminding me.

"You think you're so high and mighty, Miss Florence," he had taunted as we walked home from school down the shady expanse of Delaware Avenue, past all the fine, stately homes that would never be ours. "Well, nobody cares anymore, Flo, because you're growin' titties." He was eminently pleased with himself for having said such a nasty thing. "Baby Flo ain't s'posed to have no titties."

I ignored him. I had gotten quite proficient in doing so ever since Mother and I had returned here to live in my grandmother's house. My brother had been living here in Buffalo since my father died, and we barely knew each other. Even Mother looked at this tall, leggy boy with his wild hair and pockmarked face and drew in her breath. She had no idea how to deal with boys. None.

Who could have predicted that Norman would end his days rocking next to me on the porch, riding around in my aquamarine Bel-Air? Surely not me. I despised Norman then and wanted nothing more than to find the courage to punch him square in the snout.

But the summer of the fair gave us all a little truce. A dash of excitement dropped down in the middle of our humdrum lives. At night, from my window in Grandmama's house on West Eagle Street, I would peer out over the angled roofs and red brick chimneys to catch a glimpse of the line of white light through the trees. On still nights, I could hear the music wafting over the roofs: the tinny carnival melodies of the carousel, the Negroes singing and clapping to their rollicking tunes. I could smell the pretzels being baked, too, and the pungent scent of burning oil from all the machines.

We'd been to the fair several times already that summer. The old man at the front gate reminded me of Ducks, with his heavy mustache and broad face. He came to recognize us as local children and would wave us on inside. It was as if an entire city had sprung up in the center of Buffalo: roads, street signs, fireplugs, shops, and offices were all part of the expo, in a spiral of color and modern design. And the heart of it all was the Electric Tower—rising up from the splendor of the fair like a gigantic illuminated flower. "It shines as if it were made of *diamonds,*" I gushed to Mother after seeing it for the first time.

But my favorite attraction was the Midway, where Colonel Bostock put on his animal show every day at noon. We'd sit wide-eyed on the wooden bleachers, sawdust at our feet, the smell of horse and lion dung in the air. Out would come the Colonel from the massive marble house followed by a white tiger or a ten-foot grizzly bear. I remember how all of us—even the strongest men in the audience—would pull back a little, stiffen our backs, clutch the hand of the person seated next to us. Once I took Norman's hand—it was always clammy and damp—and he wouldn't let it go until I bit him.

But the biggest attraction was Jumbo. Nine tons of clamoring elephant. The ground shook—it really did—when Jumbo came out of the animal house.

"Ladies and gentlemen!" Colonel Bostock barked, a whip in his hand. "I present to you—Jumbo! Decorated by Queen Victoria herself for meritorious service and unsurpassed bravery in the wars in Afghanistan!"

Jumbo lifted his trunk as he had been trained to do. His ears flapped a little, and those in the front row laughed from a spray of water on their faces. The elephant's saggy gray skin was even more wrinkled than Grandmama's, hanging from his enormous body in great folds.

"He looks sad to me," I told my brother.

"Sad? He's not sad," Norman said. "Why should he be sad?"

"Because he's kept in that smelly old house all day," I said, "and then trooped out here so we can gawk at him."

We watched as Jumbo obediently walked back and forth on the runway, lifting his front leg when commanded, his tiny sad eyes seeming lost in a world he couldn't understand. Of course, this day, people cheered with even more vigor than usual, because today was a great day at the fair: The President was here. The President of the United States.

How people loved President McKinley. I wasn't sure why, but they did. Nobody much remembers him today, I suspect, what with Kennedy and all—but a hundred years ago, they *adored* him as if he were some god—as if he were Harry Houdini—as if he were Eddie Foy, my favorite from my days on the stage. Buffalo was bedecked in red, white, and blue ribbons in honor of his visit. From every storefront flapped a flag. His portrait—I thought he looked like a rather somber old man—hung from all the street lamps and nearly every window.

We took the trolley home from the fair. It was packed, with people hanging from the steps. Thousands of nickels must have been collected that day. Everyone was hurrying about, jostling each other, men in tall hats and frock coats, women in their Sunday bonnets and gloves—all because of the President. He was coming to speak at the fair tonight.

There were fireworks in his honor. That night I climbed up on top of Grandmama's roof to watch them explode in the night sky. Such a thing was a marvel to behold. You must understand that. Everything in life seemed to be breaking open, bursting with possibilities. Electric street-cars. Magnificent fairs with amazing rides that were lit up by night. And these—these pyrotechnics that discharged comets through the air. At four thousand feet, red, white, and blue shells exploded into an outline of the United States. The popping and booming and whirring of the bombs set a dozen dogs barking along the street. Rivulets of color streamed across the dark sky, falling back down to earth in burning spirals. Finally an image of the man himself—President McKinley—sparkled momentarily before shattering into a thousand tiny fireballs.

The wonders of the new century, it seemed to me, knew no bounds.

At school, the next morning, I sat beside the window. I could see the buildings of the fair at the end of Delaware Avenue, the Electric Tower shimmering even in the daylight. Miss Thornton went on with our lessons, scratching her chalk against the slate.

But I allowed my mind to drift, to wander out along the avenue. I hated school, thoroughly *despised* being there. I couldn't wait to be back on the stage with Mother. I didn't belong in Buffalo. I belonged in the footlights somewhere, curtsying left and right and center.

Out on the sidewalk I spied a man, a gentle-looking old fellow in a black frock coat and tall silk hat. He seemed to be in no hurry as he walked, as if he had not a care in the world. He passed by the school, and to this day, I can still recall his deep, kind eyes, the soft white hair at his temples. He seemed to catch my gaze; he nodded discreetly at me. Then he passed by the school and was gone.

I tell you this because I saw him again that day. Mother met me after school. She was done up in her largest hat and wore the most elegant dress she owned—the one that made her look like Lillian Russell. Or so I thought at least.

"Come along, Florence," she whispered. "Before your brother comes out."

"What is it, Mother?"

"We're going to go see the President," she said. "The line is forming now. Come! Don't tarry!"

I imagine taking Norman might have slowed us down. Or he may have caused too much of a stir. It wouldn't do to have to apologize to the President of the United States for an unruly, bad-mannered son. We hurried down Delaware Avenue, just the two of us, past all the elegant homes with their fine manicured lawns. It was a scorching-hot day; Mother's cheeks were beaded with perspiration despite the shadow cast across her face by her large hat. At the gate, the friendly man who looked like Ducks winked and waved us through. But there was already a tremendous crowd.

Mother set her jaw and was determined not to give up. Taking my hand she elbowed her way through the crush of people. "Excuse me, excuse me," she cried. "My little girl needs to get to the fountain. She's near to fainting."

That was Mother. How many crowds would she part for me in her life? People stepped aside, allowed us to pass. I couldn't help but admire Mother's pluck, even if the looks from some in the crowd embarrassed me. I kept my eyes on the Electric Tower, so tall and central it was never fully hidden from view. We approached the door to the Temple of Music. Here the crowd was thicker and more unyielding. We finagled ourselves a place in line and waited.

The doors were finally opened and we all began moving inside. I was impressed by the orderliness of the crowd, the fortitude with which the people waited, despite the heat. The line moved slowly. There were maybe one hundred people ahead of us. "Hope they don't close up shop 'fore we get there," said the tall black man ahead of us.

Mother had withdrawn a fan from her sleeve and was batting away at the air in front of her face. It was terribly hot.

We were nearly inside the auditorium. I watched the tall black man in front of me, his big arms straining within the confines of his too tight coat. The sleeves were frayed a little, but I imagined it was his best suit, not worn very often, only on special occasions such as this.

"Step lively, folks," said a man in a bright blue uniform—one of the expo's security guards, ushering us into the Temple of Music. "No time to stop and talk with the President. Just shake his hand and move along in line."

Ladies in front of us were now wiping their brows and necks with handkerchiefs. Gentlemen were loosening their collars. I spotted the President far down in the front of the auditorium, flanked by men in dark suits, receiving each passing visitor in the single-file procession.

"It must be ninety degrees in here," Mother said, flustered. "How does he *stand* it?"

The line continued to move closer to the President. He was bending over, shaking hands with an old woman. Then he straightened up, turning to kiss a baby proffered to him by a proud father.

And I recognized his face.

"Mother!" I whispered, tugging on her sleeve. "I saw him today! This morning! Walking past my school!"

"Oh, hush, Flo. It couldn't have been him."

"Oh, but it was. I recognize him. He was all by himself. Just out for a walk, early this morning."

"Flo, they wouldn't let the President of the United States go out for a walk all by himself."

No, I supposed they wouldn't. Still, it had looked so much like him— the same coat, the same gray trousers, the same white waistcoat. As we got closer, I saw his eyes: How deep they were, how gentle. Yes, it was him. It had to be him.

And suddenly I was struck by the sight of him, standing there, with all these people filing by, barely speaking, just looking, just pointing, all of them craving a single, simple touch from him. As if he were Jesus, healing the sick. As if he were one of Colonel Bostock's animals, paraded around on display for everyone to look upon in awe.

I suddenly felt very sorry for President McKinley. To have to stand there. To have to shake all these hands. Not to be able to walk outside under the brilliant sun without the crowd surging in. *They wouldn't let the President of the United States go out for a walk all by himself.*

No, they wouldn't.

I couldn't fathom the attraction. He was just a man, a kindly old man with warm eyes. I thought about the applause—how proud I had felt as the little children crushed around the stage door to get a glimpse of me. "Look at her!" Ducks had called, holding me up so the crowd could see. "Doesn't she have lovely hair?"

But Ducks's arms were encircling me. Ducks protected me from the crowd. When we made our way through the throng of little girls crying out to touch my hair, Ducks had shielded me. What if he hadn't been there? What would that crowd have been like then?

"Poor President," I whispered, just as we reached him.

I think he recognized me, too. There was a glance in my direction, the small shading of a smile. Then he turned to greet the man in front of him—a slender man with a handkerchief draped over his hand. In those seconds—seared onto my memory—I remember the tall black man ahead of us standing even taller, straightening his tie as he prepared to meet McKinley. I remember the President noticing the slender fellow's outstretched hand, wrapped in his handkerchief. He must have thought him injured, for he reached out to shake his left hand.

And then he was shot.

I remember Mother's scream in my ear. I remember blood splattering suddenly on the front of my dress. I remember the tall black man lunging at the slender fellow who had shot the President, smashing him to the floor. I remember thinking—strange how one can think so much in so short a time—how quickly gentleness can be turned to rage.

"Don't hurt him," the President said, his face white, his hands clutching his gut as blood seeped between his fingers. He was kept from falling to the floor by two guards on either side of him. "He must be some poor, misguided fellow," the President managed to say.

And yet the crowd descended upon the assassin. I saw the tall black man's enormous fist rise up and down several times; I heard the thud of the man's head against the wooden floor. I saw other men—some in waistcoats and ties, others in security uniforms—fall in on top of him, adding their own fists to the job. I couldn't tear my eyes from the horror.

Mr. Griffith once asked me if I'd ever really been terrified. If I'd ever been confronted with a horror so profound that my own reaction surprised me. I told him yes. I told him I *laughed*. I told him I was so terrified that I stood there like some mad little creature escaped from the asylum, laughing with a sound that was alien to my ears.

Around me the crowd had erupted into cries and panic. Mother grabbed my hand and pulled me. We ran toward the door. Somewhere an alarm had gone off, a horrible whine. I would hear that sound in my dreams for months.

The President died about a week later. All of the colorful trappings came down from the stores, replaced by drapes of solemn black. Mother and Grandmama and Norman stood on the side of the road to watch the hearse carry the body from the hospital to the train, where it would be borne back to Washington.

I didn't watch the funeral procession. Instead, I went horseback riding. I didn't cry for my country. It was my adopted country, after all. We were still Canadian citizens by law. Instead, I cried for the man with the gentle eyes, who, I was convinced, had eluded his guards the morning of his death for one last walk by himself—breathing in the crisp clear air along Delaware Avenue and taking the time to smile at a little schoolgirl through a window.

Just a few weeks later, they electrocuted the slender fellow who'd killed him. Norman took delight in reading the account from the paper to me. With a sadistic grin, he read:

> Electrician Davis turned the switch that threw twenty-seven hundred volts of electricity into the living body. The rush of immense current threw the body so hard against the straps that they creaked perceptibly. The hands clinched up suddenly. For forty-five seconds the full current was kept on and then slowly the electrician threw the switch back. The body, which had collapsed as the current reduced, stiffened up again against the straps. When it was turned off, Dr. McCauley stepped up to the chair and put his hand over the heart. He said he felt no pulsation, but suggested that the current be turned on for a few seconds again.

Norman looked up at me and widened his grin. "Just to be safe," he added in his own words.

"You don't scare me, Norman," I told him.

That day we got word of another electrocution to take place. Jumbo the elephant had turned savagely on Colonel Bostock, prompting his owner to decide to execute the animal. Many people complained that it was simply a gimmick, sacrificing Jumbo to bring back attendance to the fair, which had declined sharply following the President's death. Norman called me chicken for not wanting to go see Jumbo electrocuted, and for some reason, I gave in to his taunts. I went along, taking my seat next to him with a heavy heart.

The crowd, which days earlier had thrilled to Jumbo's exploits and applauded his tricks, now called for his blood. I couldn't understand their fury. Bostock made a short speech extolling Jumbo's military career. He asked the crowd to remember Jumbo for who he had been, not the mad creature he'd become. He told us about Jumbo's long voyage from Africa to England and then here to Buffalo, how it had been too hard for the tired old elephant to adjust, how the ordeal had stripped him of his sanity. "He has become a killer," Bostock intoned. "Death by electrocution is the only way."

"Throw the switch!" cried one man down near the front.

Poor Jumbo was led out—seeming quite tame and serene—and chained between two large wooden blocks. His eyes looked as sad as before. His great trunk hung lifelessly, awaiting his owner's command. He probably thought they were just setting up another trick. I began to cry.

Bostock gave a signal to throw the lever and a loud humming sound was heard. Eleven thousand volts of electricity pulsed through the animal. I stood suddenly, hardly aware of what I was doing. "Don't kill him!" I shrieked. "Let him live!"

But the crowd's shouts of outrage drowned out my voice. Their taunts turned to laughter, however, as Jumbo barely moved, hardly seemed to even notice the electricity. The humming stopped and the animal simply raised his trunk—as he'd done so many times before for approval of the audience. The crowd gasped, some laughing out loud, some demanding a refund.

Jumbo had *survived*.

Of course he had. His thick hide had acted like rubber, proving impossible for the electricity to penetrate. A few of us mustered cheers. But most roared their disapproval, saying they'd been gypped. Colonel Bostock tried to calm them, assuring them they'd get their money back.

The mob had its revenge. People began smashing electric signs, tearing bulbs from their posts. Tables and walls were crushed under the fury of the crowd as if they were so much pasteboard. Windows were shattered; statues overturned; doors knocked down. Cleopatra's Needle was uprooted. I turned and ran before the crowd had a chance to move on to the Electric Tower.

Norman stopped me.

"There's something I never told you," he said, and I could smell foul beer on his breath. He gripped my upper arm hard with his hand. "Something you oughta know."

"Let me go," I spit at him.

"He *killed himself,* Flo. Our father."

"Let me go," I snarled. All around me came the sounds of destruction: glass breaking, wood snapping, electricity zapping out. I struggled but couldn't break free from Norman's grip.

"They said it was an accident, Flo. But he *killed himself,* I tell you. They held an inquest and everything, but I knew the truth. *He killed himself.* He fired up that old coal stove and closed all the windows and sat right in front of it. He killed himself because his wife was a whore and his daughter a tramp on the stage!"

I broke free and hit him. Curled up my fist and pulled it way back, the way I'd seen the tall black man do. Some sixty years before our uneasy peace, before I cooked him his meals and made him laugh riding in my car, I smashed my fist into Norman's face and saw blood spurt from his nose. His hands flew up to cover his face; his eyes just held me in a startled gaze. As if he were suddenly terrified of me.

"Don't ever try to scare me again, Norman," I told him. "Because I won't be scared!"

I ran all the way home.

Mother was sitting on the front porch. She was rocking in Grandmama's chair, and she looked terribly old to me in the moonlight. Behind me the lights of the fair went off in random patterns. I huffed up the steps and sat at Mother's feet.

"Florence," she said, continuing to rock. "What on earth has gotten into you?"

"Let's leave, Mother," I said, catching my breath. "Let's go. We don't belong here."

She didn't say anything for quite some time. She just continued to rock. Then she reached down and began to stroke my hair. It's the only time in my life that I can ever remember my mother touching me.

"All right, Florence," she said softly. "Maybe it's time to go at that."

We sat there until all the lights had gone out at the fair.

The Present

Ben stands looking down the sheer side of the cliff into the Pacific Ocean. It's three thousand feet to the white surf below, which roils the rocky coast in a brilliant spray.

He takes in a deep gulp of air. So clean, so crisp. It nearly causes him to lose his balance. He steps back away from the cliff.

Ben feels *engulfed* by his surroundings: the vast turquoise sky, the iridescent sea, the majesty of the cliffs. This is *hero's* country, he thinks. Not for the faint of heart.

So what are you doing here, Ben?

He closes his eyes, then opens them again. As far as he can see, the shaky, sinuous line of Route 1 is cut into the side of the cliff, following nature's random and precarious path. Driving up the coast yesterday, he'd gripped the wheel of his rented Mercedes with sweaty, tight fists. He'd needed to get away, to put some distance between him and all that had happened. He just got behind the wheel and drove. He had no idea where he was going, just that he needed to go, and the coast highway north of the city seemed as good a route as any. He'd been unprepared for the deep valleys Route 1 descended into, for the sharp, breathless, hairpin turns, the crumbling pavement at the very rim of sun-cracked crags thousands of feet in the air.

But he'd made it through. He spent the night in a little town called Stinson Beach, tucked within a fertile green triangle between two mountains. The only restaurant in town was closed when he pulled into the village, the generic gas station also dark for the night. The sun hadn't even fully set, but already the deep purple shadows of the mountains had nearly obliterated the center of town. He knocked on the door of a run-down guest house of redwood and slate, only to be peered at by an old Indian woman with missing teeth through the lace curtains of the door. With great coaxing he finally convinced her to let him inside, and then it cost $79.95 on Xerxes's Visa card for one night's stay.

He hadn't been able to sleep. The room smelled musty and old, and even the sound of the surf a half mile away couldn't lull him. His stomach rumbled from hunger, and he sat up at one A.M. to dig through his backpack for a bag of M&M's. He'd opened the bag earlier on his drive up the coast, and now he discovered the candies had spilled deep into the linty and cluttered bottom of his pack. Annoyed, he threw the whole thing across the room.

I believed in you, Ben.

He rubs his temples now standing in the dust of the pull-off area, looking over the side of the cliff. Out a hundred yards, he thinks he sees a whale, but he can't be sure.

Florence Lawrence—107-year-old motion picture star riding the crest back to an unorthodox new fame—collapsed last night at the Castro Theater in San Francisco. . . .

The newshounds had jumped all over it. Flo's vacant blue eyes, her slumped stance were all shown repeatedly on the nightly news, the morning shows, and *Inside Edition.* Xerxes called him to say *60 Minutes* wanted to talk with Flo. Ed Bradley had already interviewed the Cherry Sisters and their mother.

"Hey, mister, is that the Pacific Ocean?"

He looks around. It's a little Japanese girl with a heavy accent, her parents standing behind her with cameras and eager looks on their faces.

"Of course it is," he says with some annoyance. The girl scampers back to her family, talking in Japanese, everybody nodding their heads a million times.

"Of course it is," he says again, looking back out onto the sea.

He finds an easy-listening station on the radio as he starts the drive again. He expects he'll be back in the city in about an hour. And then what?

There was nothing to keep him here anymore. He had talked with Glick yesterday; things were rolling. "What do you think about Julia Roberts as Flo?" Glick asked. "I'm going to approach her people. Then again, she may be too old. How about Kate Winslet?"

Ben didn't even quibble that Flo was a blonde. Hey, that's what wigs and dye jobs were for.

A VW Beetle gets on his ass and then passes him out. "Christ," Ben says. "What an idiot." These roads are *treacherous*. What an asshole.

Ben looks out over the shiny blue sea, reflecting a thousand shards of sunlight. How easy it would be for someone to drive off this cliff. To just keep going instead of turning and drive right off, plunging nearly a mile to the rocks below. That would be it. End of story.

How many people have done just that, chosen to end their lives here, in that way?

He laughs at himself. His life wasn't going to end here. His life was just *beginning*. He'd make it back to San Francisco, and tomorrow he'd fly back to New York.

What he'd find *there*, of course, he couldn't be sure. Anita had left a message for him on his voice mail saying she'd moved out of their apartment. His social life was in tatters. Richard and Rex had been his most frequent dinner and movie companions, and he couldn't very well expect to see them now. And of course, his job at the advertising agency was kaput.

He supposed he could live off the money he was getting for the screenplay—for a while. Xerxes was still negotiating the terms—whether he'd get it all in one lump sum, how much a royalty cut he'd get, all the stuff that seemed to addle Ben's brains when he thought about it too long. He'd given up any hope of directing the film himself; Glick wanted some hotshot, not an unknown. "Lots of directors start as screenwriters," he said. "You'll get your chance."

Ben would have to come up with another idea. The old search for inspiration would have to begin anew. The thought terrified him.

But, hey, this time he was *in*—this time it would be *different*. He'd sold a script to fucking *Universal*, for God's sake. He was moving into a whole new world now. He'd make new friends, hang out with a whole new crowd. Xerxes would certainly invite him to his fabulous parties now, finally introduce Ben to his other, more prestigious clients. Ben imagined his little apartment in Hell's Kitchen would no longer suffice. Even without Anita there, it was too small. And he was tired of living like a penniless student—milk crates for bookshelves and a futon on the floor.

But it had been home for an awfully long time.

"Well," Anita had chirped, their first day moving in, "aren't you going to carry me over the threshold?"

He had, of course, and they'd made love right there on the bare hardwood floor, afterward consuming a jug of cheap red wine and eating cold pizza and staying up until four A.M., unpacking boxes and laughing over the stupidest things.

He wasn't sure he could stand going back inside and seeing Anita's closet empty, her slippers gone from under the bed, just one toothbrush left in the holder.

On the radio, Crystal Gayle's singing about making brown eyes blue. Ben snaps off the radio in a hurry.

"I *did* love you, Anita," he says out loud as Route 1 snakes around a sharp bend, going down into a valley before rising up again along the edge of the cliff.

He *did* love her—that was undeniable—but his own inertia had eventually taken the edge off that love. He saw what it was doing to her. Once a bright-eyed kid filled with dreams, she'd exchanged ambition for security, chance for refuge. The known, despite its dreary complacency, became preferable to unexplored opportunity. He had observed for some time how his lack of faith in himself had translated into the same for her. Their fears fed off each other's. They were mired in the quicksand—and so long as they kept holding each other's hands, they could never climb out.

Jean had been different. She had *believed* in him right from the start. The first one ever to fully and truly *believe*. Anita had been swept up by the glamour of dating a "filmmaker"—at just the time she was losing her father. Jean, however, had come to Ben grounded in her own place in the world, her own mission, firmly set in her own convictions.

And she had *believed* in him.

I believed you to be a man of honor. A man of compassion. An artist, *Ben. I believed you to be an artist.*

"Oh, God," Ben says out loud, the pain a physical thing in his gut.

But it wasn't just that.

It was even more, Ben.

"For me, too, Jean," he says softly. "Goddamn it. For me, too, it was even more."

But he could never tell her. Not now. Not at the moment Julia Roberts's people were reading his script. Not at the moment he had everything within his reach.

And what chance did he and Jean have anyway? She was a goddamn *nun!*

I'll resign whatever I have to.

You see, Benny, he hears his mother saying, *Jean won't live a life that's not true to herself. You could learn a lesson.*

"Ma, *please*," he says, shutting her up.

The road moves away from the coast, heading back through the thick, murky woods of Marin. Redwoods tower over the winding road. There's a morning mist rising from the earth, thickly carpeted with needles and moss.

"You'll see, Ma," he says suddenly. "Your Benny's gonna turn out to be something. One way or another."

What's important to me is what I've already got.

Richard's voice. God, they're ganging up on him. Richard and Mom, as always.

But there's more. . . .

Just do your best.

It's Dad's voice. *Jesus.* Dad, too.

Just do your best. That's the only way.

"Shit," Ben says.

Up ahead, the traffic on 101 slows down on the approach to the Golden Gate Bridge. Ben doesn't understand what could be causing the backup. Rush hour isn't for another several hours. But even before he can spot the golden spires, he's forced to a total stop. "Aw, come *on,*" he gripes.

He flicks the radio back on and turns the knob in hopes of finding a traffic report. A snatch of Billy Idol. A squeal of the Bee Gees. A puff of hot air from Rush Limbaugh. "*Eeew,*" Ben says. "Get off of my radio."

"—backed up at least into Sausalito at this hour. . . ."

Here it is.

"Any confirmation yet on whether it was really her?" a female announcer is asking the traffic reporter.

"Not yet. But people are stopping their cars as the word spreads and gathering on the city side of the bridge. That's what's causing the backup."

Directly in front of Ben is a bright yellow school bus. Two little fat boys stick their heads out the back window and pull open their mouths with their fingers.

Ben makes a face back, scrunching up his eyes and sticking out his tongue. One of the boys laughs and flashes him the thumbs-up sign.

"Let me repeat," the radio announcer is saying. "We have an unconfirmed report that *Florence Lawrence* has *jumped* from the Golden Gate Bridge."

"*What?*" Ben asks.

"Police are arriving on the scene now."

"*Jesus!*" Ben slams the car into neutral. "No way! No fucking *way!*"

"Apparently, forty minutes ago, Miss Lawrence either jumped or fell from the bridge. Eyewitnesses say it seemed a deliberate act. . . ."

"No!" Ben cries. "*No way!*"

"As we get more details, we'll—"

He turns off the ignition and jumps out of the car. He looks ahead of him at the line of traffic leading up to the bridge. He finds that he can't get a breath, that he's gulping air—almost as if he'd been punched in the stomach.

"Goddamn it," he manages to say and starts to run.

"Hey, buddy," shouts a truck driver. "You can't just leave your car in the middle of the road!"

But he barely hears him. He just keeps running, darting in and out between cars, running with no thoughts in his head, just the blue sky in his eyes and the wind in his ears—until he rounds the bend and sees the gold of the bridge glinting in the sun.

They've closed all but one of the lanes going into San Francisco and traffic is inching along again. There's no traffic at all coming from the opposite direction. They must have closed all the lanes on the other side of the bridge.

At the entrance, big digital caution signs flash. Up on the bridge itself, near the apex, Ben can see several police cars and a crowd of people all gathered at the side. He hops over a line of orange cones and begins running up the ramp.

This is crazy, he keeps repeating to himself. *This is crazy. Crazy.*

He reaches the crowd. A black woman is crying hysterically. Beside her, two young white guys are eating licorice and giggling. Ben pushes through them. He sees a line of cops. And a phalanx of photographers.

But of course.

Then he sees Anita. She's standing in the glare of the camera, and a TV reporter has thrust a microphone in front of her face. She's crying, her face bright red with the blotches of blue he remembers so well from her father's funeral, the big heaving sobs that seem to threaten to snap her fragile little rib cage. Her mascara runs in heavy black streaks down her face.

No, Ben thinks. *This can't be happening.*

"She—she was here," Anita's telling the reporter. "And then—I—I—turned around—and she was—"

The reporter finishes for her. "She had jumped?"

Anita covers her face with her hands. *"Please, no more!"* she screams.

Ben moves up to her, pulls her away from the camera. She doesn't even seem to register him.

The reporter continues speaking into the camera. "That was an eyewitness to the tragedy, a friend of Miss Lawrence's." She moves over to thrust the microphone into the face of the black woman Ben saw crying. "You, too, ma'am. You saw her jump?"

"I did," the woman says, bawling again. "Little old lady. I saw her fall all the way down there." She points over the side of the bridge.

The reporter moves her microphone to a white man in shirtsleeves and tie standing to her other side. His eyes grow wide as he recounts his tale. "I was walking my dog like I do every day across the bridge and I saw something fall," he says, staring into the camera. *"My God,* I realized. *That was a woman!"*

"Thank you, sir," the reporter says. "And will you spell your name for me?"

He does, eagerly. "Will this be on the six o'clock news? I've got to call my wife and tell her to watch."

Ben grips Anita by the shoulders. She still doesn't seem to grasp the fact that it's him. "Anita," he says, shaking her a little.

He moves her long hair away from her eyes. She looks up at him, a frail, flickering gaze. "Ben," she says, as if even now not fully comprehending.

"Why? *How?"* he asks.

"Oh, Ben," Anita cries. She reaches up and embraces him, her arms encircling his neck. He holds her, pulling her close to him. "Oh, Ben. We were supposed to leave tonight. We were all set to go. She said she wanted to see the city one more time. She wanted to see it from out here, on the bridge. You know how she loved San Francisco. She just said she wanted—to—see it."

Sobs rack her body again. "Easy, babe, easy," Ben says.

She pulls back and looks up at him. "Richard and I brought her up in her wheelchair, and then she wanted to stand, to look out—and before I knew it. . . ."

"Could she have fallen?"

"No, Ben! Oh, dear God, she *jumped!"*

A policeman has approached them. "Miss Murawski, we're going to have to ask you to come down to the station and make a statement," he says.

She nods.

"We need to get traffic moving again," he says loudly to the gathered crowd. "We need to clear this area."

Ben doesn't want to let Anita go. He clings to her arms, but she gently extricates herself from his grip and moves away with the officer. He stands there mute, watching her leave.

And that's it, he thinks. *Just a few months ago we would have clung to each other, but now....* He watches Anita walk away from him alone, her head down.

Ben looks over toward the spot where Flo jumped. Her wheelchair sits at an odd angle. Richard's standing there, just looking over the side of the bridge as if in shock.

Ben walks over to his brother. He says nothing, just stands next to him and looks over the side.

"This can't be real," he finally manages to say.

Richard doesn't reply. He just keeps staring down. The water is a deep dark blue below them. It moves fast under the bridge. Every once in a while it curls into a frothy ribbon of white.

Flo's down there—in there—

"This can't *be*," Ben says again, louder now. *"This isn't the way it was supposed to end!"*

"What did you expect?" his brother says to him—but it's sixteen years earlier, and it's Thanksgiving morning. Richard had just gotten up, rubbing his eyes. Mom was still in bed. Ben was sitting at the kitchen table. He looked up at his brother and told him their father had died an hour earlier.

Richard didn't respond then, just as he isn't responding now. They had remained there in the kitchen, in a kind of mystical silence for several seconds. Finally Ben spoke again. "This isn't the way it's supposed to be," he said, the hot tears streaming down his cheeks.

Still Richard had said nothing. His face twisted in an emotion Ben couldn't identify. Grief, surely, but more than that. Anger, perhaps, that he hadn't been there. Resentment, very likely, because Ben had. He stood there in the kitchen, unable to speak, and when he finally found his voice, he said simply, in a cold, hard tone Ben would never forget, "What did you expect? That you could keep him alive forever?"

Ben looks at his brother now leaning on the rail of the bridge. "Please, Richard," he says. "Please say something."

"She said she had to go," he tells Ben simply, not taking his eyes away from the water. "She said—just last night—that she never should have brought Florence Lawrence back. 'I've got to let her go,' she said."

Ben feels a sudden flood of anger—more welcome, more familiar, than the grief. "That should have been a clue!" he shouts at his brother. "You should have known that's what she meant to do!" He shakes Flo's wheelchair. Her black cloche hat is lying in the seat. "How did it happen, Richard? *How?*"

"We were all just looking over at the city," Richard says numbly. "The sunlight was sparkling off the buildings. Flo said she wanted to see the hill where she and Linda had first met, where they picked daisies and daffodils together. She wanted to stand, so I helped her out of her chair."

"You helped her stand," Ben snaps.

"Yes. And I moved off to the side and Flo stood there, the wind in her hair. She was quite beautiful. I remember thinking how beautiful she looked in the sun and the wind—and then I followed her gaze off toward the city." He closes his eyes. "When I looked back, she was gone. For a second, I thought she had just walked up a ways. But then Anita was screaming. A man ran up to us, said he saw her jump."

"You said you would *protect* her!" Ben charges.

Richard looks over at Ben. He doesn't respond. For once, he doesn't mirror his brother. He doesn't copy his rage.

"You don't understand, Ben," he says. "This is what she wanted." His words are calm but forceful. "This was the only way."

"So you *accept* this? You accept that this was *destined* to happen?"

"I accept Flo's choice."

"You should have *known* what that choice was," Ben says bitterly. He looks over at his brother, a thought taking root in his mind. "Maybe you did. Maybe you *did* know."

Richard says nothing further. He just keeps staring down at the water.

Ben feels the anger dissipate as quickly as it arrived. "Jesus Christ," he says, and the tears come—as hot as they were sixteen years ago. "Jesus Christ, Richard. This isn't the way it should have ended."

Richard places his arm around his brother's shoulder. "Maybe it is," he says. "Maybe it is, Ben."

"Maybe she's still alive," Ben says desperately, his head turning to Richard, his eyes wide. "Has anyone gone down?"

"Ben. We have several eyewitnesses who saw her hit the water. There's no way she could have survived that." He smiles weakly. "She's a hundred and seven years old, remember." He pauses. "Or somewhere around there."

"This can't be real," Ben says. "This can't be happening." Something suddenly strikes him. "Where's Jean?" he asks.

"Oh, dear God," Richard says as if the thought had just hit him too. "*Jean*. She and Rex left this morning on a flight back to New York. We were going to follow later tonight—oh, good God—I've got to call her before she hears it on the news."

"Mr. Sheehan?" It's the same police officer who'd spoken with Anita. "We need your statement. Including what Miss Lawrence told you last night."

"Of course, of course." He turns, looks at his brother. "I've got to go, Ben."

"Richard, I—"

Richard looks at him.

But Ben doesn't know what he was planning to say. He just stops, stands there with his mouth open.

"Good-bye, Ben," Richard says and moves off with the policeman.

Behind them, an old man is saying, "I seen her go." Ben turns in the direction of his voice. He has wild white hair and unruly eyebrows that seem to have a life of their own. The reporter is thrusting the microphone in front of the old man's face.

"I was drivin' my van over there," he rasps, "and I seen her get ready to do it. I pulled over and yelled, 'Hey!' But it was too late. There she went, her dress flyin', her arms flailing all the way down. You know, the city keeps votin' down guardrails. It's lunacy. It's the third suicide this month!"

"Come on, Grandpa," a cop is saying. "Move along."

"Ahh," the old codger snarls at him. "You ever hear of freedom of assembly?"

"You, too," the officer tells the news crew.

"How about freedom of the press?" the old man shouts. The reporter smiles at him, thanking him again for his story.

Ben just stands there, at the spot where Flo jumped, and watches the old man limp his way back to his van.

The news is full of it. Ben sits in his hotel room with all the lights off, watching it over and over.

"A tragedy today in San Francisco," says Dan Rather. "Florence Lawrence—the world's first movie star, rediscovered earlier this year and the center of a mystery nearly sixty years old—ended her life by jumping off the Golden Gate Bridge...."

"Police tonight are calling the death of Florence Lawrence a suicide," Peter Jennings reports. "Eyewitness accounts are numerous, and no criminal negligence charges will be brought against her companions, Richard Sheehan and Anita Murawski. Police are calling this simply an unfortunate incident...."

"Sadly," says Dr. Joyce Brothers, speaking on *Entertainment Tonight,* "no one apparently seemed to realize just how *depressed* Miss Lawrence was. Not even those closest to her. But it was quite apparent in her appearance at the Castro Theater. The stress of the publicity, the accusations surrounding Margaret Butz's death—these things seem to have weighed heavily on her."

"Of course, the *irony* of it all," says Deborah Norville, in an exclusive interview with Jameson Collins on *Inside Edition*, "is that *this time* she really *did* take her life when in 1938 it had, in fact, been someone else. . . ."

"Actually, Deborah, this is the *third* reported death for Florence Lawrence," Collins tells her. "Remember, in 1910, she was reported killed in a streetcar accident in St. Louis. Of course, both then *and* in 1938, she eventually turned up alive."

Deborah shudders. "Well, I can't imagine she'd survive that plunge into the frigid bay," she says. "Divers tonight are still searching for her body, but suicides are often never recovered after jumping from the Golden Gate."

The phone keeps ringing. Ben doesn't answer, just lets all the messages pile up in his voice mail. Xerxes. Glick. Mom.

He had tried to call Jean earlier, but Sister Augustine at St. Mary's told him she had departed without leaving them any clues to where she was going. "She came in and gave her resignation this morning," she confided to him. "We were all stunned. She seemed so—so *filled* with life. So *excited*. She was going to go back to doing the work she wanted to do—you know, with the poor. Then came the news about Flo. She didn't say anything. Her face just got very stoic, and she took Flo's keys and before any of us knew what she was doing, she was gunning out the driveway in Flo's old Bel-Air. No one knows *where* she is. . . ."

He just sits in the dark and watches television. David Letterman cracks a joke about Flo and gets booed by the audience. "Okay, okay," he says. "Guess she's becoming a national folk hero now."

E! Entertainment runs a special report on her life. On *Larry King Live*, the Cherry Sisters insist that the suicide just proves Flo killed their "ant." One says, "We still might sue her estate, if she's left one."

Yet on the eleven o'clock news, Detective Philip Lee of the Los Angeles Police Department says he's convinced Flo was innocent of murder. "My guess is her story wasn't too far off the mark," he says. "She'd left, gone on to start a new life, she told me. Meanwhile, the hospital made a mistake. Her neighbors mistook the dead woman for her, and she wasn't around to prove 'em wrong. No one at the hospital thought to question the woman's identification. So that was it. No big mystery. No scandal. I'd just chalk it all up to a bizarre set of circumstances, and let both of 'em rest in peace."

Ben just sits there deep in the cushions of the couch, watching the news reports over and over again on CNN and MSNBC, flicking back and forth with the remote.

The images repeat themselves: Anita's hysterical tears. "She—she was here—and then—I—I—turned around—" The caption under her face gets her name wrong: *Anita Murinsky.*

The black woman. "Little old lady."
The white man in the tie with the dog. "I saw something fall."
The old man. "It's the third suicide this month!"
They become like family to him.
Especially the old man and his crazy eyebrows that seem to move across his forehead.
"I seen her go. Dress flyin', arms flailing all the way down."

Finally he stands. He has to see her again. He has to see her face. He forages in his crate of videos and pulls one out. One of the last video-taped interviews he did with Flo.
He pops it into the VCR and hits PLAY.
She's smiling into the camera. Smoking. Her long red nails catch a glint of light. She's wearing the scarf Jean bought her, a rainbow of color swathed around her shoulders.
He hears his own voice off camera. "So, Flo," he's saying, "you keep saying I never ask about what came *after.*"
She nods grandly. "No one does. It's as if those second fifty years don't count. All anyone's interested in is *drama.* But what is drama except life with the dull parts cut out?"
"Yet I take it those second fifty years were far from dull?"
"They were the most satisfying of my life."
"So *tell me* about them," he says to her.
The camera moves in for a tight close-up. Her eyes are so blue, so clear. She takes a long drag on her cigarette, letting out the smoke dramatically. For a moment, it obscures the entire screen. When it dissipates, she's smiling again.
"All right, Ben. I'll tell you. Let's see. January 1. My birthday. 1939. The first day of the first year of my new life. . . ."

January 1, 1939

Each of my stories is a season of my life. And my life was given a second chance that New Year's Day in Doris's diner.

Winston Pichel drove me the rest of the way up the coast, all the way up through Lompoc and Monterey and Santa Cruz. It was a dangerous road, up and down those cliffs, so close to the edge—but it was thrilling for me. Invigorating. Winnie had a sporty car. Red, real flashy. I forget what kind. A convertible though. I've always been partial to the wind in my hair.

"Well, Miss Florence," he said, looking over at me with that sly grin of his. "What awaits you in the golden city by the bay?"

"The rest of my life," I told him.

He laughed.

Oh, how I had him snared.

We became very good friends, Winnie and I. He was a tub of a man—but still, you remind me of him, Ben. Not in looks, surely. You're far more handsome and certainly more trim. And of course, Winnie was a pansy. A *flamer*. That's what he would've called himself. But nonetheless, the two of you have similar spirits. The same kind of entrepreneurial dreams. You're both *dreamers*. That's what it is.

I suppose that's why I like you. *Trust* you. I'm a dreamer, too. Always have been. It was *Florence Lawrence* who couldn't dream. Me—well, I think once you've stopped dreaming, you've stopped living. I'm a hundred and seven—or somewhere around there anyway—and I haven't stopped dreaming yet. When I do, then it's over. Only then.

Oh, how I remember driving into the city that bright and chilly January day. We had to put the top up as we got farther north because it got cold, and I pulled on a sweater Doris had given me. But there it was: my city on a hill. I hadn't seen it since my days with Linda, so long ago. In the interim, the earthquake had destroyed it all—but there it still was, nonetheless. Rebuilt, risen from its ashes. Nearly as beautiful as before. Still with the same vistas of land and sky and sea. I felt a kinship with the city. We were both phoenixes, after all. Both had died and come back.

Winnie drove me for a tour. Down past Mission Dolores and through Fisherman's Wharf and past the Presidio. And then—up ahead of us—a wonder to see: the Golden Gate Bridge, one of the true marvels of this century. I remember it sparkling in the sun. I had Winnie stop the car, and I walked up its side. Once, long before, Ducks and I had walked across the Brooklyn Bridge. Now I stared out into San Francisco Bay. They were building an island out there for yet another world's fair.

"Life keeps finding its way back," I told Winnie. "It keeps doubling back on itself."

I'm sure he didn't catch my drift. But when you've lived as long as I have, Ben, you begin to see things. Like watching a garden grow. I remember when I was confined to my bed at my farm in New Jersey, in those long, sad months after I lost Annie Laurie. I'd just lie there in my bed, looking out the window into the gardens, into the woods. Every morning, it was the same thing. The birds arrived on schedule, went about their business. The flowers opened when the sun was high enough, then closed when it went behind the trees. There was a stray cat that came by at the same time every day—the same time, to the *minute*—to drink water from the birdbath.

I watched as if my window were a movie screen. I saw the seasons change, then change again. I saw the frost, and I saw the bloom of the spring. Life keeps coming back. You watch it long enough, as long as I have, and you'll see.

Oh, but I'm sounding like a sentimental old fool, aren't I? And I hate sentimental old fools. Still, when I think of those first few days in San Francisco with Winnie—oh, I was so full of celebration. I used the money Winnie had given me for the pocketwatch to buy a new hat. The first purchase of my new life. A black beaded cloche—I still have it. Maybe I'll wear it for you sometime.

He got me a room with a friend of his. Her name was Ginger. She was a dancer and singer, performing in some of the city's clubs. She was getting up there in years, but my *goodness*—what *legs* she still had. What a *voice*. Gentlemen were always tucking tens and twenties in her stockings.

Ginger and I were friends and roommates for *seventeen years*. Jeannie reminds me of her. Oh, they're nothing alike really—Jeannie's a damn *nun*, for heaven's sake. But it's their *spirit*—again, it's the *spirit* that's similar.

Ginger was fiercely loyal. Like Jean. Like a tiger sometimes—until the day she died. I took care of her at the end. Cancer, like my mother. Funny. No one's asked me about Ginger. I was closer to her than almost anyone we've talked about. Knew her *years* longer than I knew Molly or Lester or Linda, but no one's asked me about Ginger. Winnie either— and he and I were friends up until 1959, when a heart attack took him. We were always after him to take better care of himself—Ginger and I, and Hank and Jose and Myra and all the rest of the gang. How we missed him. His fidgety manner. His fluttery ways.

How I miss them all.

And isn't it peculiar? All these interviews, and I haven't told you about any of them. You know, no one part of a long life matters more than another, Ben. Wherever we are, that's where we're supposed to be. Oh, there are times you've got to be somewhere else—and you've got to have the sense to get up and *go* there. But you start from somewhere, and wherever that somewhere is, that's the place you're supposed to be at the time.

Do you understand, Ben? I had good, *good* friends in San Francisco. No, not just friends—*family*. I've never counted family by blood, you know. My *family* brought Florence Bridgewood back to life. They allowed her to *be*.

It was through Winnie that I met most of them. He got me my first job. I was a waitress at a nightclub in the bohemian North Beach neighborhood. It was across the street from the old Hall of Justice, which was a little bit of irony, because the place was often getting raided. After a while, I became something like the *hostess*, who greeted the customers and made sure they were happy. I remember serving John Steinbeck once and Allen Ginsberg many times. It was a place where no one asked anyone too many questions—me included—which was good. Especially in the beginning. The place was called The Black Cat. I used to wear my cloche hat and black fishnet stockings. Oh, what a hoot we all were! There was Hazel the piano player and Jose—darling Jose, he reminds me so much of Rex—in his sequined gowns and red pumps singing, "God save us queens!"

We went through the war together, rationing our gasoline and batteries and hosting fund-raisers. So many of the fine young men who used to come to our bar never returned. I'd been through a world war before; I knew what to expect. It's so futile, war. I don't know if it's ever done much good. When it was over, we all danced in the streets and I stood out on the Golden Gate Bridge, singing the national anthem with a thousand others. Oh, it was a glorious day.

And do you know? All those years of being sick? Weak? Fragile and high-strung? Never again. The pain never *did* come back. Molly was right. Ginger and I often went scuba diving off Big Sur. I rode horses until I was seventy-eight. I even jumped out of an aeroplane with a parachute once—for my sixtieth birthday! I landed amid the hoots and hollers of my family. "You *do* it, girl!" Jose shrilled. "Flo, you are the *queen!*" Myra shouted. Winnie just trembled and handed me a shot of brandy, pinky extended as always. Ginger stood there with her arms folded across her chest. "Woman, you get down and kiss this here earth," she told me.

I did as I was told.

It makes me smile just to think of it all. Oh, they tried to close down The Black Cat more than once. Paddy wagons would roll up to the doors and any man dressed as a woman was carted away. How silly. The bar owner was a good family man. He had a wife and children, and he'd bring the kids by. We'd all eat spaghetti dinners that I'd make out in the kitchen in back. There was nothing unsavory about the place. *Nothing.* But finally, he had to close it down. After some twenty years, The Black Cat ceased to be. It just got to be too much. All the raids. All the publicity. Halloween, 1963. That was the end.

Well, for me, too. Ginger and Winnie were gone. I visited their graves every day, placed freshly picked daisies and daffodils on the spot. But I decided it was time. I needed to *go.* As much as I loved them all, as much as I loved San Francisco, there was still one thing more I needed to do for Flo Bridgewood. I had to go back to Buffalo.

So I bought the Bel-Air, packed up my belongings, and headed east. *I get my kicks . . . on Route 66. . . .*

So that's all. That's all I have to say.

The Present

A skinny blonde in a microminiskirt—no more than ninety pounds and most of that hair—is having a supremely difficult time maneuvering across the icy main street of Park City, Utah. She wobbles on her spiked heels, her long legs threatening to slide out in opposite directions. She clutches on to her companion, an older man with slicked-back gray hair and wearing a long black leather jacket. They don't speak as they try desperately to appear confident and aloof.

"Don't worry," says the maitre d', who's watching them through the large plate-glass window. "Before the week's over, she'll fall flat on her ass."

Ben can't help but laugh. The little street with its quaint shops and trendy cafes is packed with cars, mostly Beemers and Jags and the occasional Porsche. People are crossing back and forth in both directions, causing the traffic to back up even more. The locals are dressed in parkas and down vests, the movie people in miniskirts and unlined leather jackets.

"It's getting crazier and crazier," the maitre d' tells Ben. "Every year it gets bigger. They're estimating sixty thousand this time. The rest of the year, we barely break six."

"Hey, it's an honor to be showing at Sundance," Ben says, buttoning up his coat and wrapping his scarf around his neck.

Carla Ortiz is pulling on her suede gloves. "You do realize you're looking at the next winner for Best Documentary," she tells the maitre d'.

"I've looked at a lot of 'em," he says, supremely unimpressed.

Ben puts his arm around Carla. "Did *you* know this was the very restaurant that Harvey Weinstein infamously shouted down a sales rep over the rights to *Shine* a few years ago?"

Carla gives him an eyebrow. Hollywood lore holds no fascination for her. "Oh, I have chills," she says dryly.

"I assume your lunch was satisfactory?" the maitre d' asks.

"Very good," Ben assures him.

"Well, then, I hope to see you again," he says.

"You'll be seeing *a lot* of him," Carla promises.

They step out onto the sidewalk. It's begun to snow lightly. Ben sticks out his tongue, catches a few snowflakes and licks his lips. "Can't do that in New York," he tells Carla. "By the time they get down to our level they're pretty nasty."

She pays no attention to him. "Remember, you have an interview with Kevin Thomas from the *L.A. Times* at five. You *are* going to shave, aren't you? And wear the blue shirt with the blue tie. It's a good look."

He grins. "I wasn't aware when I hired you as my agent I was getting a fashion consultant as well."

"A good agent provides many services. Too bad your last one didn't understand that." They share a quick kiss as her cell phone chirps. She extracts it from her coat pocket and answers it. "Ah," she says. "All right, I'll be right there."

She snaps the phone shut. "Sam Glick has finally agreed to have a drink with me. I'm going to meet him at the Riverhorse."

"So maybe he's not pissed at me anymore?" Ben ventures.

"We'll see. I'm sure he'll act the wounded diva. After all, you *did* break a contract with him."

"Yeah," Ben says, "but now I've got the indie documentary of the *year.*"

She smiles at him. A good smile. "Yes, Ben," she says. "You do."

He watches her head off down the sidewalk. The snow is coming down harder now, collecting on top of people's moussed-up hair the way it caps the peaks of the mountains around him. It's a beautiful snow, light and airy and just cold enough—not icy or sticky, just soft and cool. Refreshing.

He walks through it, his hands pushed deep down into the pockets of his old corduroy jacket, nodding to harried passersby as if he hadn't a care in the world. His hair's grown back in, and he's tied it back in his old ponytail with an elastic band. The profile in *Entertainment Weekly* had called him "unassuming." He liked that.

He stops in front of the Eccles Theater. It's an enormous venue, seating capacity 1,300. He stands in front of the poster for his film.

LIVING PICTURES:
A FILM BY
BENJAMIN CARTWRIGHT SHEEHAN

The buzz around town was that it stood a good chance of winning the Best Documentary prize. He had some tough competition, but a couple of reviewers had already made the prediction. And if he won at Sundance . . .

Hey, just being here was achievement enough. He'd had no connections, no clout—just a good film, and the judges saw that. Sure, the name Florence Lawrence helped, and the fact that even now, nine months after her death, the public was still curious about the mystery of her life.

"I don't attempt to explain it," Ben told the interviewer from *EW*. "I don't think you can explain magic. This isn't really about The Biograph Girl anyway. It's about an extraordinary woman who lived a long, long life—a walk through the twentieth century by someone who lived through all of it. It's about friendship and commitments. It's about family. It's about being where you're supposed to be. I think we can all learn a lot from Flo Bridgewood."

He traces his finger around the photo of Flo on the poster. She's got a big red bow in her hair and a cigarette in her hand. The "Dare to Be 100" people didn't like that very much. But that's *her* there, not Florence Lawrence.

That's the way she would have wanted it.

So *Silent Shadows* became *Living Pictures*. The first was about one woman; the second was about another.

On the elevator going back up to his room, Ben closes his eyes. And as often happens in those moments, when he blocks out the world even for just a few scattered seconds, the face he sees is Jean's.

Has she read the interviews? Would she see the film?

Ben hopes so: It was for *her*, after all. Her even more than him.

He'd tried finding her, but no one knew where she had gone. St. Mary's had no clue, and with the proceeds from Flo's contracts going all to them, they didn't much feel compelled to track her down. He called St. Vincent's, but they hadn't heard from her either. He read a piece that Richard had written about Flo for the *New York Times Magazine*. It was similar to Ben's film in spirit—a tribute to the woman they'd met in the dayroom, a woman he said now becomes a myth for the ages. In the article, Richard quoted Jean as saying she needed some time alone to grieve for Flo. Richard apparently knew where Jean was, but Ben hadn't spoken with Richard since the day on the bridge.

The elevator doors open. He steps out onto his floor, fumbles in his pocket for his room key, swipes it through the electronic slot, and enters.

"Well, I was starting to get worried."

He looks up. There, in a chair with her hair dolled up on her head, is his mother.

"Mom?"

"I'm *starving*," she tells him. "And don't tell me about any fancy place that serves sprouts and sun-dried tomatoes. Is there a place we can maybe get some good sweet-and-sour chicken?"

"Mom," he says, standing in place, shaking his head in disbelief, "how did you *get* here . . . ?"

"I brought her."

Ben turns. Richard comes out of the bathroom. He looks at Ben with an expression that's one part apprehension and two parts puckish mischief.

"I hope it's okay," Richard continues, approaching Ben and extending his hand. "The clerk let us in when I said she was your mother. All she's been able to talk about for weeks is *Benny's film* this, *Benny's film* that. I thought she might like to see the premiere."

Ben meets his brother's eyes. After a few seconds' hesitation, he shakes his hand.

"Of course it's all right," he says finally, turning to his mother. "Mom, if you had asked, I'd have been happy to bring you out."

She smiles tightly. "Oh, you know how I hate to be a bother."

Ben approaches her, looking at her oddly. "Mom, you *love* to be a bother."

"Well, you're always saying I don't get out of the house much."

Richard joins them. "That's right. She doesn't. So what does she do yesterday? She gets on a plane to *Utah*. Just a short little trip down the block."

She shrugs. "It's not every day your son has a hit movie."

"It's not a hit yet, Mom," he tells her. "It's just getting great advance press."

"We traveled first-class, you know," she tells him. "I wouldn't have fit so good in those little coach seats."

"Thank God for credit cards," Richard says, smiling at Ben. "Guess I've just accepted that God made them for a reason."

"For first-class, I didn't think the food was any good," Mom says, scrunching up her face. "Those little cucumber-and-sprout sandwiches. I'm *still* hungry."

Ben smiles. "I'll take you out for a great lunch, Mom. And I'll have Carla get you both tickets for tonight."

"She's good, huh, that agent?" Mom asks. "Better than that last one. She's getting you some good things. I saw you on *Rosie* yesterday. You looked very handsome, Benny. I like that blue tie."

"What did you think of the film clip they showed, Ma?"

"Well, it was just that old woman talking." She pauses. "But it was *good*, Benny. I liked what she said. About appreciating what you've got."

"She was a very wise lady," Ben says.

"Now how about lunch?" she asks, attempting to stand. Her sons help her. "Let me go freshen up and you two think of a good place. Nothing fancy-shmancy. Are there any Big Boys around here?"

"I'll check with the concierge," Ben says, laughing.

She waddles off slowly toward the bathroom. The brothers watch her until she's closed the door behind her. For several seconds they remain quiet, until Ben turns to Richard and says, his voice husky, "Thanks for bringing her."

"Hey," Richard tells him. "She *wanted* to come. I'm serious. All she's been talking about is you."

Ben sits down. He feels a little light-headed.

"It sounds as if it's a pretty terrific film," Richard says. "That was a pretty gutsy move on your part, Ben. Backing out of the deal with Glick to do this instead. How'd you manage to get financing?"

He shrugs. "Carla helped. It wasn't easy, but we found enough people who believed in the message."

"Which is?"

"Everything that Flo was always telling us. That life is worth living, I guess, is the bottom line."

Richard nods. "I can't wait to see it."

They smile at each other.

"I've been thinking about what you said," Ben tells him. "About Mom and Dad and us."

Richard waits for him to continue.

"And, well, I don't claim to understand, but I do know we've been at each other for so long, and it sure would be nice to let all that go. Maybe we could . . . I don't know . . . maybe we could try to change things . . . somehow."

Richard smiles. "I think we've just started."

They laugh awkwardly. For a second, both thinks a hug might be coming, but instead they just laugh some more.

"So," Ben asks, "how's Sexy Rexy?"

"He's terrific. He just sold the film rights to his Barrymore show. Looks as if he'll be able to pay off the rest of our renovations himself. He's *ecstatic*. He walks around in his Lionel Barrymore makeup all day, snorting and snarling like old Mr. Potter."

Ben can see him—white haired, wrinkled.

But that's odd, he thinks. He's never seen Rex do his show.

There's a knock at the door. Ben walks across the room to answer it. It's a bellhop with a large vase of daisies and sunflowers.

"Who are they from?" Richard asks.

"I don't know," Ben says, setting the flowers down on the side table. They're beautiful: fresh and filled with sunlight, a burst of spring on a winter's day. He removes the card and reads it.

Thanks for restoring my faith that the heart is never wrong.
                                                                    Jean

Ben stares down at the signature. He can't lift his eyes to look at his brother. He can't even yet put his lips around the word to say her name. Even when the phone rings he doesn't look up.

"Ah," Richard says. "The timing is impeccable."

Ben finally raises his eyes. "What?" he asks.

Richard answers the phone. "Yes, yes, he's here," he says, a broad grin stretching across his face. He looks over at his brother. "It's for you."

"What's going on?" Ben asks. Then, all at once: "You *knew* about the flowers, didn't you? You set this up."

"Just take the phone," Richard tells him.

"It's Jean, isn't it?" he asks. His heart is suddenly up in his throat and flapping like a bird in his ears.

Richard thrusts the phone at him.

"Jean?" Ben asks into the receiver.

But the laugh isn't Jean's.

"Oh, Ben, it's just as beautiful as ever," a woman tells him.

"Who is this. . . ?"

"Of course, there are more tourists now. But we've found a nice little pension where we have a lovely view of the caldera."

Ben feels his body go numb from the neck down. His cheeks flush hot. He looks over at Richard, who's grinning.

"We even took a ride up to the Temple of Dionysus. *That* hasn't changed much."

"This can't be real," Ben breathes, barely audible.

Richard levels his eyes at him. "That's what you kept saying that day on the bridge," he says. "You were *right.*"

"Ben," comes the voice over the telephone, "are you there?"

"*Flo?*"

She laughs. "Last night, our guide took us out on a boat to the warm black waters of the volcano. I didn't swim—I guess there are a *few* concessions I have to make to age—but I *did* manage to put my feet in." She pauses. Ben can tell she's inhaling on her cigarette. "Just as wonderful as I remembered."

"How . . . ?" Ben stammers. "How did you . . . *do* it?"

"I just took my shoes off and lifted my leg over the boat."

"No, no," Ben says, breathless now. "How did you pull it *off*? How did you get everyone to think you had . . . *killed* yourself?"

He hears her chuckle. "Oh, that's an old question, isn't it, Ben? Haven't I had *tons* of practice?"

He looks over at Richard. "You *knew*," he says. "You were *part* of it."

He shrugs. "She asked me to help her. Hey, if Lester could do what he did, I had to at least try."

"But *how*?" Ben demands. "How?"

"It was pretty simple, really," Flo tells him. "I just got out of my chair and Rex helped me into his van."

"His van! The old man! The one with the crazy eyebrows! I *knew* I recognized him! It was *Rex!*"

"As Lionel Barrymore," Richard says.

"Then Anita began screaming," Flo says. "What an *actress*, don't you think?"

"She was *acting*," Ben says, thunderstruck. "Anita was *acting*."

"And pretty damn well, too," Richard says. "She convinced *you*, didn't she, Ben? The best part is that being all over the news like that got the soap to hire her back, as her character's evil twin sister. Now she's getting offers left and right."

"But the *others*," Ben asks. "How could the *others* say they saw you fall?"

Flo laughs. "Richard's very shrewd. He was right on the money that people will say and do anything to get their faces on camera these days. Once Anita and Rex said I'd jumped, there were any number of other folks only too willing to corroborate their story if it meant appearing on the evening news."

"We counted on their reaction," Richard tells him. "And we were right."

"And no one saw you? No one saw you get in the van?"

"Apparently not. It was all quite swift. I don't think Anita went into her act until I was safely inside. Jeannie was waiting for me in the back, and Rex whisked us off to the Oakland airport once the traffic got moving again. Before you knew it, we were back in New York in just enough time for Jeannie to pack a couple of bags."

"But the airline clerks," Ben says, almost desperate to punch a hole in the story to prove this must be a gag. "Surely *they* must have recognized you . . . and your passport—"

"Says *Florence Bridgewood*. Luckily it didn't set off any bells. Because that's not how people knew me. It never was. They knew me as Florence Lawrence, with the jewels and the wigs and the subtle pink lipstick. They didn't know Flo Bridgewood in her paisley caftan and scarlet red nails."

"You went back to being you," Ben says quietly.

"And it's been *delightful*," she tells him. "You should see us now, Ben, sitting here on the terrace. The sun's going down; the sky's a brilliant wash of color. Reds and blues and golds."

He feels his eyes well with moisture picturing it. "The most beautiful place in the world," he says to her.

"Don't you ever doubt it." She's quiet a minute. "Never thought I'd see it again. But here I am. Who'd have known? Life keeps surprising me."

She laughs. "The volcano still hasn't exploded," she whispers almost conspiratorially to Ben. "But I figure this time I can stick around and wait. I've got all the time in the world."

All the time in the world.

"Ben?"

Jean's taken the phone.

"Jean," he says.

"Did you get my flowers?"

"They're beautiful."

"Good." She pauses. "I'm sorry about our last encounter."

"No, Jean. Don't be. I'm the one who should be."

"It's a good film, Ben. I *know* it. Richard described it for me. It sounds even better than *One Chance*."

"I dedicated it to you," he tells her.

She's quiet. Touched. "Thank you," she says softly. "You're an *artist*, Ben. Simply and truly."

He can't speak.

"You'll keep our secret?" she asks.

"Of course." He swallows. "Jean?"

"Yes?"

"When will you—I mean—how long. . . ?"

"I'm here with Flo for the duration. Ruth and Naomi, remember? She's my family. I won't leave her. Not until she leaves me first."

Ben manages a laugh. "Which could be *years*," he says.

"*Decades!*" She laughs in return. "She's getting ready to welcome in her *third* century!"

There's a pause.

"Good-bye, Jean," Ben finally has the courage to say.

"Good-bye, Ben," she says in return.

"She's *alive*," Ben breathes after hanging up the phone.

"Yep," Richard says. "Yet again."

Ben just shakes his head. "She's *never* going to die, is she?"

"I don't think it's likely."

Ben runs his hands over his face. "I just can't believe you pulled it *off*."

Richard nods, seeming to understand his brother's incredulity. It's as if, despite having played his part, there's a part of him that can't quite fully accept it either.

"I've come to understand that you have to suspend your disbelief when it comes to Hollywood's stories," Richard says. "That's the only way any of them make sense—the only way we can grasp their truth. These people—they don't operate according to the same rules of logic we do. Things just happen. Wonderful coincidences and amazing leaps of faith." He shrugs. "It has something to do with wisps of light and smoke—and *magic*."

Ben nods. He thinks he understands. "Life just has that way of coming back around," he says, and Richard smiles in agreement.

Mom has come out of the bathroom. "Who was on the phone?" she asks.

"Just another fan of Ben's, Mom," Richard tells her.

"You know, you've got to watch out for them, Benny. I've read the stories. They can go a little loco on you."

He puts his arm around her. "I'll be careful, Mom."

He looks up and meets his brother's gaze. "You'd better be," Richard's telling him. "You never know who'll be watching you."

They smile at each other. For the first time, Ben can see something of himself in his twin brother. Maybe it's the little twitch of the eyebrow or the curl of the smile. Maybe it's the shape of their ears or maybe—just maybe—it's something in their eyes.

He turns to look down at his mother.

"What about some General Tsou, Mom?" he asks. "Isn't that your favorite?"

"I believe it is," Richard agrees.

"I saw a little Chinese place a few blocks from downtown," Ben says.

"Nothing fancy," she reminds him.

"Nothing fancy," he assures her.

Both brothers put their arms around their mother, their hands meeting behind her back, and head out into the rest of the day.

AUTHOR'S NOTE

Florence Lawrence was a real person, flesh and blood. I didn't make her up. She really *was* the world's first movie star, entering films in 1906, becoming the world-famous Biograph Girl by 1908, and finally being identified by name by Carl Laemmle in 1910 after faking her death in a publicity stunt. I've tried to be as accurate as possible in recreating her life and times; most of the details presented here are real. She was born Florence Bridgewood in Hamilton, Ontario. She began in vaudeville as Baby Flo, the Child Wonder Whistler. On her first day shooting a film in the Bronx, she found a man hanging from a tree. She caused a riot in St. Louis in 1910, the first in a long line of movie-star riots. She blamed the end of her career on a fire that was never reported in the press. She married three times; details of those unions were gleaned from her divorce records. Along with other forgotten stars, she played extras and bits at MGM in the 1930s. And in 1938, she killed herself by drinking ant poison.

I've had to take some liberties, of course, in recreating her. I've stuck as close as possible to the actual details of that tragic day in 1938, imagining *around* them rather than rewriting them. The suicide note, the newspaper accounts, the hospital report are all accurate. What becomes my author's flight of fancy are the relationships with Bob, Marian, and Lester (all shades of real people), and of course, Molly, a fictional character. I've also imagined the early friendship with Linda Arvidson. That Florence Lawrence may have been pregnant in 1915-16 has been speculated about by her biographer, Kelly Brown.

Despite the fiction, I hope I've done justice to a truly fascinating and complex woman. The personality of Flo in these pages developed after I read dozens of interviews with her, as well as letters between she, her mother, and her husband Harry Solter, archived at the Museum of Natural History in Los Angeles. While there were many places where I had to fill in the gaps, the portrait of a fiercely independent, ambitious, free-thinking, *modern* woman is authentic. Reading her stories, I was struck by how much like a phoenix she was: triumphing over odds, the faked death in 1910, recreating herself over and over. Even though that ant poison did its job all too well in 1938, I hope I've enabled the phoenix to rise once more.

As ever, I thank my agent, Malaga Baldi; my enthusiastic editor John Scognamiglio; my friends Victor, John B., Brendan, Michael, Susan, Wendy, Cherie, Laura, John U., Nereida, Surina, Suzanne, Jack, John F., Tom, John H., and Matthew; my sister Kathie and niece Dayna; my parents; and my partner, Tim Huber, my first and best critic and forever my inspiration.